# THE DELIVERYMEN

## Alan Cooper

MINERVA PRESS

LONDON
ATLANTA  MONTREUX  SYDNEY

THE DELIVERYMEN
Copyright © Alan Cooper 1998

ISBN  0  75410  050  2

First Published 1998 by
MINERVA PRESS
195 Knightsbridge
London SW7 1RE

Printed in Great Britain for Minerva Press

# THE DELIVERYMEN

*I dedicate this book to my brother, Ken.*
*As a child I used to make up stories for Ken, none of which were ever committed to print. Ever since, he has been urging me to put my creativity into writing. It was his encouragement that caused me to commence writing the book in the first place.*

# *Acknowledgements*

Firstly, I must thank my long-suffering wife, Francy, who put up with the disruption that my writing caused in most rooms of our home, and never stopped believing in my dream throughout the three years it took to write this book. If she hadn't supported my objective so strongly I would have probably never completed the task.

I also wish to acknowledge the help of my friends: Lydia Krnjic, who dedicated so much time and effort to deciphering my notes and putting them on to the computer; and Helmut Winzler and Georgia Prattis who read my manuscript and gave their honest opinions about my work. Without their input the book would not have ended up the way that it did.

## About the Author

Alan Cooper left England in 1973 having served in the Metropolitan Police for fifteen years.

He has lived in both New Zealand and Australia, where he has held executive positions in national and state training development organisations. He is currently living in Melbourne, Australia, where he is the Executive Director of the Victorian Industry Training Board which is responsible for the public sector and community safety bodies including the Victoria Police.

He is married with adult children and has now completed his next book titled *Paid in Full*, also a murder mystery novel.

In a world where violence can only be overcome
by even greater violence, there are no heroes.

Alan Cooper

# Contents

*Part One*    Somewhere in Vietnam
February 1972        11

*Part Two*    Ajax Bay, San Carlos Water,
Falkland Islands
June 1982        129

*Part Three*    The Coral Sea, off the Coast of East
Queensland, Australia, Southward
Bound – January 8th,1997        237

*Part Four*    Manly, New South Wales
March 1997        407

*Part Five*    Sydney, New South Wales
Late April 1997        529

*Part One*
# Somewhere in Vietnam

February 1972

# Chapter One

*Somewhere in Vietnam! What a joke!* he thought as he strained his eyes to see through the torrential rain into the pitch black of the Gulf of Tonkin.

The storm had commenced almost as soon as they had put to sea, and now ten hours and countless course changes later it was raging at typhoon ferocity, and causing many a hapless sailor to wonder why he had not joined the Army instead of the Navy.

Already there had been several accidents on board as the result of men being thrown around by the outrageous gyrations of the ship as it was tossed about like a flimsy toy. The most recent incident, and the worst so far, involved a stoker who had fallen ten feet between decks in the engine room and had broken both legs; and a lot of other minor parts that would be given greater attention at a more appropriate time. Meanwhile he was strapped down and heavily sedated in the sickbay.

David Brandon, Commander, US Navy, commanding officer of the USS *James Cunningham*, was forced to hang on tight to the hand rail at the forward screen of the bridge. The ship was corkscrewing and pitching deeply into the troughs of the enormous waves that it was battling through on its passage north into what could prove to be an arduous, and perhaps dangerous night for the entire crew.

This was real 'Indian Country'; one of the major killing grounds for the navies of both sides in the Vietnamese conflict.

The ship was deep in enemy waters in a part of the Gulf of Tonkin where North Vietnamese naval vessels, mostly of the non-traditional variety, were in great abundance and very aggressive towards trespassers.

The war was not going well for the United States, and that was reflected in the increased daring of the enemy at sea, and from the point of view of the good guys, for that was what Brandon truly believed they were, the almost reckless abandon with which US missions behind enemy lines were being planned and executed.

Even on the best of days the Gulf of Tonkin was no place to be unless you really meant business. However, Brandon and his highly trained crew of professionals had no say in the matter. They were heading north to participate in a special small war, a discreet military action with discreet military objectives, within the bigger, greater war.

Brandon and his crew meant business all right, and woe betide anyone who got in their way. They were extraordinarily well equipped, and trained to deal with anything that could possibly happen to them.

That is Plan A, anyway. Brandon smiled to himself as this thought flashed through his mind. How many Plan As had he seen turn into Plan Zs during the course of a brief mission like this one?

To command a US Navy man-of-war in a conflict such as this put great strains on the powers of creativity of each captain. Regardless of how good the Navy Department's Plan A appeared to be, each captain had to devise a series of creative alternative plans, and even then be prepared and able to make new decisions on the run, at a moment's notice, if and when all the other plans went wrong, as they often did.

Murphy's Law? If things can go wrong, they will! He smiled to himself as he looked back on all the occasions that the Navy's Plan-bloody-As had gone hellishly wrong for him and his ship.

For this mission to be successful he had to keep to a very tight schedule, which was being strained to the limit by the extreme weather conditions. The whole thing could go horribly *off* schedule if the *James Cunningham* was to meet an enemy vessel, any sort of enemy vessel, and become engaged in battle. Keeping to the timetable and making the rendezvous was the whole object of the exercise.

Because of the atrocious weather conditions, however, it was hoped and considered most unlikely that they would be seen by any North Vietnamese ships and thus be forced to engage, but then you could never rely on things going as per expectations during a war. You sure as hell could never rely on the North Vietnamese military to do what you expected them to do. Brandon could never quite figure out whether this was due to their superior strategies, or whether they were just big in the luck stakes.

★

On a night like this, and on a mission of the sort that they were engaged in, discretion, as stated in that old cliché, was the better part of valour. Long gone were the days when gung-ho behaviour was considered the norm on front line warships.

This certainly appeared to be the attitude of most of the enlisted men onboard, who tended to have two major ambitions in life. First, and the most realistic, was to get back to land and their next sexual encounter, which seemed to be the major preoccupation of sailors when ashore. Secondly, but by far the most urgent and pressing ambition was to complete their tour of war duty at the earliest possible time and to get the hell out of Vietnam, back to civilisation and the security and luxury of the peacetime Navy: you know, the one that existed everywhere else.

Wasn't it only last week back in the States that a group of navy wives and families demonstrated against their loved ones having to go to war, stating that that was not what they joined the Navy for? Shit! What is the Navy – my Navy, coming to? thought David Brandon as he braced himself for the next massive wave which appeared to be suspended over the port side of the ship, just waiting to crash on to its decks and engulf it.

One of the disturbing characteristics of this particular storm was that the weather seemed to be coming from everywhere at once. This was playing havoc with the ship's control and navigation, and making the life of the crew on the bridge in particular most unpleasant.

If only visibility would clear just a little bit, he thought to himself. He didn't mind the roughness of the sea, both he and his crew could and would be able to handle that, but if he couldn't see what was out there, either visually or electronically, God only knows what he could run into.

Already the radar and sonar equipment were being affected by the foul weather conditions, both atmospheric and wave-bound. It was also playing tricks on their much suffering operators who were having to use the full range of their skills as well as their gymnastic ability to decipher and make judgements on what the display panels and equipment were indicating, whilst at the same time hanging on for grim death.

Brandon was constantly aware that his greatest problems could arise from stumbling upon one of the many small fleets of fishing junks that carried out their trade in the Gulf of Tonkin.

They belonged there and the *James Cunningham* didn't. Sure, they were all potential enemies. They were citizens of North Vietnam and in that respect should be treated as hostiles. However, it was not the policy of the US Navy to attack unarmed civilian vessels on the high seas, or elsewhere if it came to that.

Not that it could be guaranteed that all or any of those innocent civilian fishing junks were truly innocent – or even civilian.

Firstly, in most cases, at least one of the junks in each fishing fleet, regardless of its size, would be likely to have a radio, and perhaps even be crewed by naval or army personnel. These vessels were a wonderful source of intelligence information for the North Vietnamese High Command.

It would be a hopeless task to try to search all of them from top to bottom. This would not only be very time consuming in a stretch of water as large and as unpredictable as the Gulf of Tonkin, but extremely dangerous.

Several US sailors had met with untimely and violent ends during such searches, and several US patrol ships had been sunk or badly damaged by a suicidal North Vietnamese bomber when alongside such a vessel; so great was the fanaticism of the enemy in this unbelievably frightening war.

Then there was the real possibility that the seemingly harmless fishing fleet was likely to be a naval task force, armed to the teeth with all sorts of destructive hardware. Both the North Vietnamese Navy and Army often used armed fishing boats for a variety of military missions, particularly for commando raids.

Even the United States own special forces units used nondescript civilian boats, fishing or otherwise, for their commando raids and special missions. Once such a force was at sea it became a highly dangerous and versatile adversary, even for a modern and well-equipped war machine like the USS *James Cunningham*.

Endless difficulties and dangers could be encountered if even seen by fishing vessels or cargo-carrying junks whilst operating in this region. So a ship on a mission of the sort that Brandon was on would often change course and get the hell out of it rather than become involved in a confrontation that could hinder progress or offer valuable intelligence to the enemy.

Nevertheless, on a mission such as this it could also be militarily unwise to do so. Some naval tacticians, playing their war games in their safe berths ashore would argue that the most sensible thing to do would be to engage and sink all the vessels involved so that the mission would not be prejudiced.

However attractive such action might appear on paper during a hypothetical exercise, it would only be a worthwhile military option if it could be done fast enough to prevent a radio message being transmitted. In view of the technological advancement of radio transmitting equipment, the chances of achieving that objective fast enough would in reality be very unlikely.

In other words, he thought, I'm damned if I do and I'm damned if I don't. They've got me by the short and curlies.

The 'they' in this instance being the Navy top brass.

First and foremost though, Brandon was constantly aware that commanding officers of US naval vessels had to remember that they were currently viewed by the American people at large as mere public servants participating in a war in which the public demanded their service and servitude. The media had TV cameras hung from anywhere and everywhere to ensure that they got it. Orwell's *1984* had nothing on the real world of the Vietnam War during 1972.

Owing to this very real restriction on military options it would be most reckless to sink mere fishing boats or cargo junks, even if they were military ones in disguise. This would be viewed by the outside world in general, and the

US public in particular, as a crime against humanity. Wasn't that what he read in a newspaper from home just recently?

The war in Vietnam was a war that was so closely viewed, worldwide, by the general public of virtually every country, that it was becoming increasingly difficult to confront the enemy military on an equal basis. For the first time ever in history a war was being presented as a prime-time TV show, together with much of the razzmatazz that normal prime-time TV shows would be offering.

A more worrying factor was that with the fantastic innovations of new technology, the war, allegedly being filmed as it happened, was being edited just like any other prime-time show, in ways that would create the greatest impact and sensationalism.

Who was it who said that the first casualty of war was truth? he mused.

Like most combat commanders in Vietnam he constantly felt, and often complained to his superiors, perhaps unwisely, that it was like going into a fight with one's hands tied.

He knew full well the public's views on this war, and the penalties that were meted out to those whose conduct brought the Navy to the notice of the people with the ability to cause the most harm. The Navy's instructions were generally, as one of Brandon's junior officers had once put it, 'concisely vague'.

The commander of a US naval vessel in any critical situation was to take whatever action was deemed essential to successfully conclude the mission in hand.

Back to the Plan A to Plan Z scenario. What is it the Aussies and Kiwis call it, a High Command Cop-Out? He smiled to himself.

It was well known that the Aussies and their Kiwi counterparts were often quite irreverent about their officers, particularly those in the upper echelons of the services. They tended to call a spade a spade. Generally their publicly spoken views on the powers that be were so accurate that they caused considerable discomfort to those who had the dubious honour of being the target for their attack.

Brandon liked that aspect of the Australian and New Zealand military. It was so different to the approach taken by many of his own colleagues who, in order to keep on the right side of the top brass, kissed far too much arse for his liking.

★

Brandon was shaken out of his brooding thoughts by a giant wave that was roaring towards the ship and looking as if it would run straight over her. He quickly glanced at the Executive Officer and the yeoman at the wheel but saw that everything was under control. The Executive Officer appeared completely unfazed and the yeoman, Bridgewater, was the most experienced enlisted man on the ship. Both he and the EO were ready and waiting for the impact of that mighty, massive, terrifying wall of water.

The gigantic wave ploughed into the bow of the *James Cunningham* and lifted it clean out of the water; so high that all control was momentarily lost and Brandon feared for the safety of his ship. Bodies were flying around the bridge like rag dolls. Suddenly they were in the relative calm of the trough of the wave, and the ship was for a brief moment sufficiently stable for some semblance of order to be restored. Taking professional advantage of this moment the yeoman brought her back on to her designated course.

Over the thunderous roar of the sea he could hear the Executive Officer calling for damage and injury reports from the ship's many stations.

He knew that throughout his ship off-duty men were being ordered out of the relative safety of their bunks to replace other crewmen injured during the battle with the storm. From the reports that he could hear over the noise of the storm Brandon calculated that there were upwards of fifteen seamen injured so far, fortunately most of them still fit for duty. He decided to discuss the injury rate with the Executive Officer at the first opportunity. On a warship the size of the USS *James Cunningham* every man had a vital role to play, but more so if and when it came to a battle situation. There were no passengers on a warship, particularly one the size of the *James Cunningham*. Everyone was essential!

That immediate crisis over, the screws were biting hard into the tormented water and the ship was making way once again. The atmosphere was electric on the bridge with every man's nerves strung tight as a bow. Everyone was ready and waiting for the next big wave and wondering where it would come from, all dreading that it would hit them broadside on.

If a wave the size of the one that they had just encountered hit the ship broadside on it could easily turn it over. It almost certainly would.

Then suddenly, when the ferocity of the storm and the fear of that next big wave appeared to have plummeted morale to the lowest possible level, a moment of light humour was injected into the situation with a signaller calling out loud, 'Why don't we go down to periscope depth for a while, sir, just to ride out this fucking storm?'

Everyone laughed, even Brandon, who quickly turned away to hide his amusement as the Executive Officer reprimanded the man sternly for his flippancy and his failure to comply with bridge procedure. Nonetheless, it was just what was needed to lift the sagging morale of the bridge crew. The Executive Officer knew this. He also knew that it was critical to retain one hundred per cent plus discipline and concentration on the bridge at all times.

As the officer responsible for the control of the ship he must never allow that to waver, especially at times such as this. Brandon was impressed with the way the Executive Officer was handling the situation, and would later note it in the officer's file.

He recognised the offending sailor as O'Malley, a tough New Yorker who regularly fell foul of the authorities when ashore. He made a mental note to look favourably on that man when next he appeared before him on discipline charges. O'Malley didn't know it, but he had earned himself a couple of bonus points which would be called in at some later date to his advantage.

The storm continued wildly for many more hours, creating ongoing difficulties for the officers conning the ship, and the crew members manning the many important ship's stations. As well as fighting the storm and the sea the officers in charge were required to carry out regular course changes, and zigs or zags, in order to confuse any enemy who may be at large in the Bay of Tonkin.

On active service the crew of a ship of war had to carry out their duties under the most trying conditions. Usually as individuals they did so with great confidence and competence, but almost always in complete ignorance of what was going on with regard to the general condition or disposition of the ship at large.

However, despite the difficulties under which everyone worked because of the storm, and the problems they had to overcome merely to perform the most basic of tasks, the ship was, give or take a few broken limbs, on course, on time and ready for action at a moment's notice.

Commander Brandon noted this and was extremely pleased.

## Chapter Two

Brandon had retired to his tiny, almost broom cupboard size sea cabin just aft of the bridge where he ploughed through the reams of paperwork that a ship's captain was required to deal with on a daily basis. Running a ship was just like running any other sort of business, and whilst he hated this aspect of his work he accepted that it was essential and that it went with the territory.

The paperwork, his pet hate, was not made any easier by the constant and violent movements of the ship.

David Brandon was not a happy man. Whether it was just the fact that he was physically tired, and after months of hazardous missions he had every right to be, or whether there was some deeply buried psychological reason he wasn't sure. What he did know was that things that he used to be able to take in his stride now affected him, often quite badly.

The war was not only going badly for his country and its allies, but it was also going badly for him. He resented the American public who had turned so viciously against the war and everyone who was involved in it: people like him and his crew, doing their duty for their country. God! It was hardly as if he and his crew had started the damn war.

He was bitter about what he saw as the gutless attitude of some of his superior officers right up the chain of command to the Navy Department. He felt sure that their failure to stand up against the politicians, who after all were only pushing for votes, was getting in the way of the war effort. He resented their seeming lack of interest in supporting their people; the guys in the front line, the ones who were fighting the war for them.

He particularly hated the media, both printed and electronic, for what he considered to be their total lack of care or understanding regarding what this was all about. He often wondered whose side they were all on.

These bad feelings that he harboured were wearing him down, for it was a well-known fact that hate can be a self-destructive emotion. He also felt sure that his publicly displayed emotions were not doing his career prospects any good. Nobody in authority liked a whinger, and Brandon knew this was how some of his superior officers viewed him.

★

Over the past few hectic months he had grown into a loner, preferring his own company to that of fellow officers, many of whom, it seemed, merely wanted to drink and screw themselves into oblivion. Few of them had his respect any longer. They didn't seem to care what happened to the Navy, or to the entire goddamn war.

This was a war conditions mission, yet as part of the administrative work of a ship's captain he had just spent half an hour examining outgoing mail. This was to ensure that there were no give-away details written in his men's letters that could be of benefit to the enemy if they came into their hands.

Censorship was one of his least enjoyable duties. To him it was a sick joke. Firstly it made him feel like a peeping Tom, reading these often most intimate letters from his crew to their loved ones back home.

Mainly though, it angered him intensely, because he knew that there was nothing that he or his men could write that could in any way match the daily information and misinformation about the war, both printed and electronic, that was disseminated worldwide by the media.

Just before setting sail he had been told by a fellow skipper about a news report in a New York daily that gave the troop dispositions of virtually every unit in the Saigon region. It apparently included the numbers of personnel, details of weaponry and names of their commanding officers.

Brandon didn't see the report personally, and he didn't know whether the information was true, and if it was, whether the details given in the daily were correct or not. He had a damn good idea that it probably would be pretty near the mark. Even if not accurate enough to be of great use to the enemy, it could be unnervingly accurate enough to dismay and even frighten a great number of the allied troops in the Vietnam theatre of action; many of whom, like Brandon, already felt that the American media were almost as much an enemy as the Vietcong and the North Vietnamese Army.

*

It reminded him of a time when he was a teenager. His father, also a full Commander in the US Navy, had been posted as a naval adviser to the United States Embassy in Grosvenor Square, London, England. It was in late 1956 and the British and the French were making threatening noises towards Egypt which had just nationalised the Suez Canal. It looked like the British, and the French, their most unlikely allies from across the British Channel, were about to jointly invade Egypt. There were also rumours that the Israelis were in on the act.

He remembered his father being dropped off very late one night having attended an emergency briefing at the US

Embassy. He was very drunk, which was most unusual for him, and very angry about something. He was talking very loudly to Brandon's mother and was swearing profusely: something his son had never heard him do before.

'For Christ's sake, Maureen, it could only happen in this godforsaken country. The crazy bastards have allowed the newspapers to draw a map for the fucking Gippos. The Limey idiots have shown the arseholes where every British military base is in the Middle-fucking-East. Every fucking base, and the numbers of soldiers in every shit-arsed regiment is listed. Christ, this is too fucking crazy for words. What's worse is that the information is so accurate it could only have come from a military source.'

His mother had eventually quietened and coaxed her drunken husband into bed. Next morning he looked very unwell and Brandon and his younger sister, Rae, had been warned by their mother to keep quiet, and to keep out of the way until their father left for work.

Shortly afterwards his staff car had arrived and he left.

Even though they only lived just south of London in a lovely rural area called Esher, his father had not been able to return home for several days after that, during which time the invasion of Suez by the armies of Britain and France had taken place.

Brandon remembered telling a friend about the incident whilst at school the following morning, though not about his father's drunkenness and bad language. During the morning break the boy had shown him the offending newspaper article, and sure enough it was exactly how his father had described. His friend had a brother serving in the Middle East as an officer in a British regiment called the King's Royal Rifle Corps, so he and his family were very concerned about the newspaper article. As the result of this incident David Brandon had grown up thinking that the

British must all be pretty stupid to have allowed that to happen.

That was long before he learned about the freedom of the press.

★

Here he was, fifteen years later, in a much more significant war, and things were even worse. The dispositions and numbers of troops and their locations were being shown on a daily basis to everyone who could be bothered to turn on their television set.

It was a standing joke in the ward room that the VC and NVA were fighting the war with commercial breaks, just like the TV programmes which many cynics claimed formed the basis of their planning.

Brandon felt angry that every action taken by the US Forces was immediately reported back, often as it happened. It came to the dinner table of the United States public in a graphic and horrifying fashion that more often than not tended to be very selective in what was reported.

In the opinion of most of the military personnel involved in this horrible war, many of the war correspondents tended to treat the truth as a downright hindrance to good copy.

★

Then of course, there was the anti-war movement. These groups were well organised and funded, highly motivated and greatly encouraged by the daily media presentations. They, the anti-war movement and the media, seemed to Brandon to feed off each other. It had become quite fashionable back home in the good old US of A to treat military personnel, particularly those who had served in Vietnam, quite badly in public.

About nine months previously two of his men had got into strife with both the civil and military authorities whilst on an R and R in Honolulu. They had ended up in a fight with a group of so-called students who had apparently hounded them for nearly two hours carrying banners emblazoned with the words 'Murderers', 'Child Killers' and 'Rapists' and chanting similar slogans. His men had been badly beaten in the ensuing confrontation with the civil police. It seemed from all of the Navy Department discipline reports, and from the personal descriptions of the incident given to him by his men, that in their handling of the incident the police were very much prejudiced against the military.

Ironically, contrary to the alleged military image that the students were demonstrating against, the two sailors in question had been awarded their R and R by Brandon as the result of their bravery in rescuing a group of women and children from a burning building that had received a direct hit from a mortar bomb in a VC attack in Saigon.

The sailors probably would have been formally decorated for their bravery but for one critical factor; critical from the point of view of the military, that is. They were in an area strictly out of bounds to US military personnel where they had been enjoying the questionable delights of a rather sordid and very low-class brothel, and they were also under the influence of alcohol.

The alleged low level of the brothel was later confirmed by the medical officer's report on the particular strain of STD that one of the men had contracted. It was almost a joke. By the manner in which the Navy hierarchy had treated these sailors, they must have believed that bravery was the sole domain of the pure in body and mind.

Some months later, however, Brandon was able to pull strings and call in a few favours from friends in positions of power in order to arrange leave and travel authority for these men who had become local heroes, not only on the ship, but also among the Vietnamese community.

Sadly, the facts about the bravery of the men had not even been considered by either civil or naval authorities when punishing them. It seemed to Brandon that those desk jockeys back in Honolulu had forgotten that they were in the Navy, and they had become glorified bureaucrats working to satisfy the whims of the media-guzzling general public. Both men were demoted for conduct prejudicial to naval order and discipline, and had been expected to be further punished with extra duties on return to the ship, as was the normal naval practice. David Brandon made sure that this did not happen.

As the result of this terrible injustice he had a very bitter crew on his hands, and he feared that unless he was able to break down that anger some form of organised retaliation could take place when next the USS *James Cunningham* shipped into Honolulu.

Sailors tend to have long memories. There is a saying in the Navy that sailors don't always get pissed off, but they always get even. Brandon had discussed the issue with his officers and senior petty officers and instructed them to be constantly alert for problems in this area.

*

This public animosity toward the military was not confined to confrontations with enlisted men. Brandon recalled only too well how, on a leave to the United States about a year before, he himself had been hassled by a group of long-haired young men in a railway station, and taunted about killing children.

He had intended to ignore them but unfortunately, before he could get into his taxi, he had been approached by a group of burly, young uniformed infantrymen who had appeared from a bar in the main concourse. They had apparently seen the plight that Brandon appeared to be in and had decided, against his best wishes, to come to his aid. On their arrival the long-haired demonstrators withdrew slightly but continued their taunts from a safer distance. Brandon thought that the arrival of the young soldiers would give him the opportunity to slip away in his taxi and leave the trouble behind him. This was not to be.

Whilst smart and clean, the soldiers had obviously had far too much to drink. They were all wearing Vietnam ribbons, and were apparently on leave after completion of a tour of duty in the war zone. From the manner in which they responded to the demonstrators Brandon formed the view that they had probably been through this sort of thing before. They certainly didn't appear to be unduly fazed by the taunts, however they did seem less inclined than Brandon to turn the other cheek.

Their leader, a tall young black corporal, smartly saluted him. 'Leave this to us, sir. These long-haired motherfuckers don't know any respect. Me and my buddies are real sorry that you have been bothered by this trash.'

Brandon's first thought was to order the corporal and his men to back off, but for some reason, probably because they were all vets like himself, he decided to play it cool and get away from the scene as quickly as possible. He felt completely out of his depth and wasn't sure how to handle such a situation. This was not something they had prepared him for at Quantico.

'Thank you, Corporal, but I really don't need any help. I would be more pleased if you and your men didn't get into any trouble over something that isn't worth shit. Perhaps with a bit of luck we'll meet them all again over there in

Vietnam in the not-too-distant future. Then we'll see if they have the same opinions as they have now.'

'That would suit us real fine, sir. But me and my buddies have a problem there. You see, sir, how in the fuck would we recognise those mo'fos with their hair cut and their noses clean? You just leave it to us, sir,' the corporal said as he opened the taxi door for Brandon.

'Me and the boys don't like the idea of any shitheads like this being rude to one of our officers.'

The reference to him being one of their officers made Brandon go cold. The Army did not consider naval officers to be anything to do with them. In fact, as a general rule they did not consider the Navy to be worth anything at all. In reality sailors and soldiers were virtual arch-enemies ashore, as a matter of historical tradition. He realised, therefore, that these soldiers were merely using him as an excuse to have a go at the demonstrators. He also realised that there was nothing he could do to stop this happening.

''Specially not when that officer is a Nam-Man,' continued the corporal, still rigidly at attention. 'We are proud to have made your acquaintance, sir,' he said as he closed the taxi door behind the confused and angry naval officer. The other soldiers all then jumped to attention, and the corporal, swaying slightly, and with a big smile on his face snapped up a fine parade ground salute. This action brought loud jeers from the demonstrators who, whilst realising that Brandon, the softer target, was leaving, had stupidly become more daring and had moved in closer with their banners raised high.

Brandon knew he was out of his league. If the soldiers had been naval personnel he probably would have acted differently. He knew that he should have done something to try to stop the inevitable fight. Yet he somehow knew the situation had gone beyond that point and that if he did intervene he might only end up becoming involved in a way that he could regret. He could just imagine what the media would make of that.

*Naval officer leads army thugs against peaceful protesters.*

That he did not need.

He was abandoning the situation, and in doing so he knew he was abandoning his responsibilities as an officer. He could not recall ever being so confused and feeling so helpless, and even ashamed of himself. Then, as his taxi turned out of the railway station forecourt, he saw something that made up his mind for him.

A small truck loaded with military police passed his taxi heading into the station yard. Someone had probably put in an emergency call to prevent the problem getting any further out of hand.

Why, he didn't know, but for some reason he was suddenly apprehensive about what was going to happen to the drunken young soldiers. Misguided though they were, he did not see why they should have to put up with any further provocation. And after all, their only crime was having had too much to drink and, more to the point, having served their country in Vietnam.

'How dare they treat us like this?' he shouted out loud, startling the taxi driver who appeared to be glad to be getting away from the situation developing at the railway station. Brandon ordered the protesting driver to turn around and head back to where they had started from.

What he saw there shocked and astonished him. The protesters were standing back laughing whilst the military police were attacking the soldiers with large night sticks, beating them to the ground. No mercy was being shown, particularly not to the young black corporal who was on the ground, bleeding profusely from numerous wounds and apparently unconscious.

The taxi was still moving when Brandon leapt out on to the roadway and placed himself between the prostrate corporal and two burly MPs. They had been kicking him about the body and head and to Brandon's outrage they were, amongst other things calling him 'nigger bastard!' out loud. They were screaming the words, their apparent hatred towards their helpless victim plainly apparent.

Brandon's arrival confused the MPs completely and caused them to stop their assaults on the young soldiers instantly. His fury was far greater than the military police expected or were used to. The sergeant in charge was a big, arrogant man with a face that looked as if it had been on the losing side in too many fights. Brandon immediately noticed that none of the very few medal ribbons he wore were for active service. He also quickly noted that none of the other MPs wore any ribbons at all. Later he was to ask himself why this was so significant, but at the time it was all important.

The incident resulted in four of the soldiers being transported to the local hospital, two of them with quite serious injuries. The black corporal, who it was later revealed was only twenty years old but already a veteran of some of the bloodiest battles in the Vietnam War and the recipient of a Purple Heart, had a fractured skull and numerous other injuries, including several broken ribs.

The military police sergeant, a man named Mason, insisted that the soldiers had attacked him and his men as soon as they had got out of the truck, and that all they were doing when Brandon arrived was protecting themselves. As he had not been present when the MPs had arrived he could not prove whether Mason was telling the truth. He was, nonetheless, convinced that the MP sergeant was lying in an attempt to justify the extreme violence that he and his men had used on the soldiers.

★

The die was cast. Brandon was involved in this thing up to his neck whether he liked it or not. He was, however, determined to discover what had really happened and bring the facts before whatever hearing resulted from this sick and sordid business.

Peterson, the Military Police Captain in charge of the MP Depot, left no doubt regarding his resentment of Brandon's intrusion and was extremely uncooperative, rude and abrupt, which angered him considerably and only made him more determined to put the facts right.

Leaving the Military Police Depot Brandon called a taxi and returned to the railway station. Within a few hours he had rounded up no less than six witnesses to the fact that the soldiers were attacked by the MPs, without any provocation.

Ironically, one of the most forthright and determined witnesses was one of the demonstrators, who was more incensed by the apparent racist overtones of the attack on the black corporal than the viciousness of the assaults by Sergeant Mason and his men. He was, however, fully prepared to give evidence on both counts.

By the time Brandon was finished the investigation was out of the hands of Captain Peterson and was being dealt with by a young lieutenant colonel who had a chest full of ribbons and was a veteran of two tours in Vietnam. Again, quite irrationally, this was a comforting factor for Brandon, who was starting to feel most satisfied about how things were proceeding.

The Colonel, whilst most efficient and correct in his behaviour to Brandon made a point of stating that, like Captain Peterson, he was not overly pleased with his intervention. There were some very clearly defined borders between the different branches of the armed services over which one was normally not expected or encouraged to stray, but at least the Colonel appeared determined to investigate the matter efficiently, and above all honestly.

As the result of his investigations Sergeant Mason and three other MPs were arrested and placed in custody awaiting the commencement of court martial proceedings for a series of serious assault charges and various other specifically military offences.

Captain Peterson had also caused serious problems for himself through the manner in which he had conducted the initial investigation, and his obviously blatant attempts to mask the behaviour of his men. This cover-up included a falsified report which the Colonel assured Brandon would hurt Peterson badly at the eventual court martial.

The MP Captain had obviously not anticipated Brandon's determination to act on behalf of the soldiers. He had thought that once the situation had been brought under control the navy Commander would go on his way, like a good sailor boy.

'After all, isn't this interfering bastard supposed to be on leave?' he complained to his less than sympathetic senior officer.

Just as Brandon was leaving the Military Police Depot at the conclusion of the investigations, the young Lieutenant Colonel took him aside.

'I don't like what you did, Commander. We military police do not appreciate interference in our business, especially when it means we end up washing our dirty linen in public. We particularly don't like inter-service interference. Do you hear me Navy?'

'I hear you, Colonel. Perhaps if your people hadn't behaved like undisciplined and uncontrolled fucking savages I wouldn't have felt obliged to get so involved,' replied Brandon, not quite managing to control his anger at the man's rude rebuke.

His point had hit home. The Lieutenant Colonel's face dropped and he turned away.

⋆

Later, as his leave progressed, Brandon began to develop a nagging premonition that his own superiors would probably be as annoyed about his involvement in this unseemly incident as the military police.

He was right in that respect. Over the next few months he was to learn just how unpleasant, unforgiving and downright nasty the military bureaucracy, the navy in particular, could be, even to the captain of a US Navy warship.

Over that trying period he began to feel that he was being victimised by his own hierarchy, the very people he believed should be supporting him. He became introverted and sullen owing to the attitudes that confronted him as the result of the actions he had taken on behalf of the arrested soldiers.

During the subsequent court martial proceedings these had been distorted by the military police as being some sort of vendetta by Brandon against them. In the event, the young soldiers who were attacked by the MPs were all returned to their units with minimal punishment.

As for the MPs, Sergeant Mason was reduced to the rank of private and he and two of his fellow MPs received short terms of imprisonment in a military jail, followed by a posting to Vietnam as infantrymen. This latter action gave Brandon the greatest satisfaction of all.

The MP officer, Captain Peterson, was severely reprimanded and punished with loss of seniority. Brandon was satisfied that, if nothing else, justice had been seen to be done.

As the direct result of the publicity caused by the court martial he had gradually found himself left with few friends outside his own ship. He felt quite justified in thinking that the brass hats were all against him.

Yes! They are all against me, the Navy, the Army, the media and the American public at large, and not forgetting the Vietnam fucking War, he thought as he completed his paperwork.

# Chapter Three

The initial business with the military police had occupied two whole days of David Brandon's long-awaited home leave but he did not care. He was determined to see the matter put right.

'That'll show those soft-billeted, home-based feather merchants that they can't treat Vietnam veterans that way,' he said as he related the story to his sister Rae when he finally arrived at her home a day or so late.

She hadn't seemed too sympathetic, or even interested in his story. She was merely put out by the fact that he had upset some of her plans for him by arriving so late. He found himself wondering who she thought she was, treating him like a recalcitrant child late home from school. He let it pass over his head though, and felt much better after a good night's sleep.

His anger had barely abated when it all came surging back in a sudden rush. The cause? A cocktail party organised by Rae and her husband Geoff to welcome him home from the war.

He needed this sort of shit like he needed a hole in the head. Why the hell hadn't they asked him? It wasn't actually the cocktail party that caused his anger, it was what happened to him, and what he did in retaliation at that stupid party, that triggered it off.

Rae and Geoff were both lawyers and it seemed quite normal, to them anyway, that virtually all of their guests were also lawyers. Brandon should have been more astute and somehow stopped Rae from proceeding with the party, or alternatively made up an excuse that he had to return to base early because of the railway station fracas.

He wasn't, and she didn't, which led to what was probably the most exciting party that had ever occurred in that godforsaken neighbourhood; depending, of course, on your definition of the word exciting.

The excitement was brought about when Commander David Brandon, US Navy, stopped the party with a bang. The bang was the noise that was made when Adrian Lang, one of Rae's academic law senior colleagues, and obviously more the guest of honour than he was, collided with a table full of hors d'oeuvres and wine glasses – on his way to the floor.

★

The party started off well enough, although almost from the start Brandon had realised that this was not going to be his idea of a fun night.

The function was two hours off when Rae sprung on him the fact that it had been planned to be semi-formal – suit and tie. His leave period was intended to be totally relaxed and casual, and because of this he had not packed any formal civilian clothes. In fact, just about the only formal clothes he owned were his naval uniforms. He certainly didn't have anything vaguely resembling formal civilian clothing this side of Saigon. This caused a minor panic while Brandon tried on several of Geoff's suits without any luck. Geoff was far shorter and dumpier than he was. He considered going out to buy some clothes, but the nearest men's clothing store for this style of man's attire was over thirty miles away, and it was far too late for that anyway.

He would have to wear his uniform. That didn't worry him, but from the look on Rae's face it caused her great concern. Later he was to regret that he had not read her body language and the worry that it expressed far better than he did.

Several times between then and the start of the function he had seen her in earnest and confidential discussion with Geoff. It was obvious that they were very worried about something. Brandon should have been astute enough to realise that it was his uniform that was the cause of their concern.

★

This particular welcome home party was doomed to be a disaster from the very beginning. For a start Brandon wasn't a great drinker and this party was obviously intended to be a real boozy event. If he had been half alert during the previous three evenings he would have noticed that Rae and Geoff drank an extraordinary amount of red wine, in fact, two or three bottles each night. It would almost naturally follow that two such heavy drinkers would be most likely to invite other heavy drinkers to join them; which was exactly what happened.

They, Rae and Geoff, had also assumed for some reason of their own that Brandon, being a sailor, would enjoy a drink or two. This was their view, in Brandon's case a misguided view, of what sailors were all about, and they made no attempt at disguising their surprise when they discovered that this was far from the case. In fact, Brandon rarely drank more than one glass of wine, if any at all, but because of their drinking excesses they had not picked this up over the preceding evenings.

★

It had been some years since Brandon had visited his sister. This was whilst she was still at college, and in those days whenever they ate out they had both enjoyed soft drinks. She had probably forgotten this or more likely, if she had remembered it all, put it down to him being polite to his kid sister, who at that stage had not discovered the thrill that the grape had now injected into her life. The trouble was that both she and Geoff experienced that thrill far too often, and too quickly became drunk and often unpleasant to each other, and sometimes to anyone else who just happened to be around.

By the time the night of the party arrived Brandon had already made up his mind to leave the next day. He had had enough of trying to fit into Rae's little plans for him, and he needed a change. This wasn't his thing. He came from a background where he made the decisions about what was to happen, and here he was having those decisions taken out of his hands by his sister, for reasons that she obviously was determined not to share with him in advance.

He had decided that he would catch the first train out in the morning, and that he might head for San Francisco for a few days before flying back to Hawaii to rejoin his ship which was undergoing a weapons refit.

From the minute he arrived downstairs in his uniform he realised his bad feelings about the whole affair were completely justified. In fact they were more than just bad feelings. He had a worrying premonition that something pretty awful was going to happen. Murphy's Law!

His premonition came true within a very short time after the arrival of most of the guests. Adrian Lang was the first to arrive. He had already been drinking, as had his wife Amanda. She was a beautiful woman with the sort of body that belonged on the front cover of fashion magazines. She wore a close-fitting dress that emphasised that very image. Amanda Lang was really quite gorgeous. She was aware of that fact and played on it from the very moment she arrived. That was probably what started off the whole unpleasant chain of events.

During his earlier days, while still a lieutenant junior grade, a senior officer, noticing that Brandon did not drink much, had suggested to him that this could lead to his downfall.

'If you do not drink at parties you will soon get bored, and boredom inevitably leads to young officers getting into trouble,' was the solemn advice of the officer.

He was suddenly reminded of this event, and he smiled to himself at the prospect of getting into trouble with Amanda, if only to put her pompous arsehole of a husband in his place. The prospect became more likely to become a reality as the party progressed. Amanda attached herself to him during the early stages and was obviously hoping that he would return the attention she was giving to him.

Seeing that his wife was openly making a play for Brandon, Adrian Lang decided to make it clear that he was a person of great power and influence, and not someone to be taken lightly. It was his own childishly pompous way of trying to frighten people off, and it probably worked on people within his law firm, where he was the senior partner. It was, however, totally wasted on Brandon, who quite frankly began to enjoy the attentions of Amanda, probably more so because they were obviously annoying her husband.

The cocktail party was about an hour old when Lang, who was by now very drunk, stormed up to Brandon and loudly warned him about his behaviour towards Amanda. Brandon got the distinct impression that the Adrian Langs of this world did everything loudly.

In fact, Brandon's behaviour towards Amanda had been quite good considering the advances that she had made towards him. In reality, she had only spoken to him for fifteen minutes or so earlier on in the evening before moving on to more receptive male drinking companions. However, the fact that he was in uniform tended to highlight the occasion more than it warranted.

More recently she had rubbed her beautiful drunken body up against him in a most sensuous manner on her way to the bathroom but he had not in any way responded to her advances, so naturally resented Lang's attack.

He was used to handling the drink-induced bad behaviour of fellow officers, so he decided to let it go, promising himself that he would definitely slip away at the earliest opportunity.

Adrian Lang was not the sort of person to be put off by gentlemanly behaviour, and thus he continued his verbal attack, only this time it was quite specifically targeted at Brandon. Not at Brandon the person, but at Commander Brandon the naval officer, and Vietnam veteran.

'Bit boring being so far away from the rape and pillage in Vietnam, old buddy?'

Brandon tried to ignore him and turned away, heading through the crowds of people towards the door.

'Not so fast, kid killer,' slurred Lang, determined to continue his confrontation. 'I want to know how it feels to be a murderer of innocent people in an unwarranted invasion of the sovereign territory of another country.'

'Go away and cool off,' replied Brandon, trying very hard to maintain his temper and continuing towards the door.

Determined not to be ignored, and equally determined to persist with his anti-war point, Lang hurled himself between Brandon and the door and turned to face him with an angry sneer on his face.

'I suppose you're only used to facing your critics with a gun in your hand, buddy boy.'

Just at that moment Rae and Geoff appeared out of the kitchen area and both rushed to intercede and quieten things down. Rae, herself the worse for wear after too many wines, was obviously concerned about remaining on the right side of her boss. Consequently she immediately got the wrong impression of what was happening, or more likely made the most appropriate political decision, and decided that her brother must be at fault.

'Don't ruin our evening, David. After all the trouble I have gone to in order to make your welcome home a special occasion; how could you do this to me?' she slurred in a sobbing voice.

By now Brandon had really had it up to the neck. He decided that the only thing he could do was to get the hell out of it as quickly as possible.

He turned on his heel and, pushing his way through the drunken revellers, was almost in the hallway on his way to the front door when Lang, with spit dribbling from the corner of his mouth, bellowed at the top of his voice, 'Don't you dare ignore your fucking sister in front of me, you child murdering, rapist bastard.'

Brandon instantly paused and turned, at the same time swinging a right uppercut that seemed to come from his boots all the way to Lang's jaw. Lang was lifted completely off his feet almost in slow motion, and appeared to levitate on his back over the coffee table. A loud shriek came from his bleeding mouth before he crashed, unceremoniously and unconscious, on to the table.

The glass-topped table, which was laden with an assortment of hors d'oeuvres and several glasses, smashed into numerous pieces and together with its contents, which now included Adrian Lang, scattered itself across the entire room.

Brandon was suddenly aware of a dozen gaping mouths beneath shocked, staring eyes. More noticeable, however, was the absolute stunned silence, broken only by Lang's heavy snoring which was causing bubbles of blood to blow out from both his mouth and his nostrils.

★

It didn't take more than a minute or two for him to pack his holdall, and within five minutes he was in a taxi on his way to a downtown motel, near the railway station.

He booked into a room on the top floor and ordered coffee and sandwiches from room service, asking for them to be delivered in half an hour. He then undressed and took a long hot shower.

He was still towelling himself down when there was a knock on the door. Slipping into his dressing gown he opened the door, expecting it to be room service.

It wasn't. Or at least, it wasn't the room service he had expected. It was Amanda Lang, looking as beautiful as before, and surprisingly sober considering the amount of alcohol he had seen her consume earlier. She wore a stunning, black sequinned jacket over her cocktail dress and, as when he first saw her earlier in the evening, her beauty momentarily took his breath away.

Still angry and uptight about the evening's events Brandon looked out into the corridor, expecting her to be accompanied, but she was alone.

'Can I come in, sailor?'

## Chapter Four

'What the hell are you doing here?' he asked, more out of astonishment than anger. 'What on earth do you want, Amanda?'

'I would have thought that was painfully obvious, David. So can I please come in?'

Brandon stepped back into the room and allowed her inside, wondering what the hell this was all about.

'I suppose your bastard of a husband has called the police and laid charges against me.'

'He was going to, but I told him and everyone present that if he did I would make it quite clear that he started the fight, and that you only acted in self-defence. He's a pompous prick and has had this coming to him for such a long time. You wouldn't believe how many times I have had to stand and listen to him abusing the shit out of people who were intimidated by him. It was so good to see him get his just desserts after so long. You will never know how pleased I was, and how grateful I am to you for doing what you did this evening.'

'But he's a lawyer, surely he is bound to go for my jugular at the first opportunity.'

'I can see you don't know much about the law business, David. Adrian is a property lawyer and a pretty useless one at that. He is only the senior partner because my father bought a share of the company to ensure that the useless bastard retains a profile that matches the level of my social standing. Most people in the business are aware of that.

That's why they all took notice of me when I threatened to support you if the police were called. Without my father's money they will all be out of a job, and they're all as nervous as hell. Your sister is about the only one left who is still totally overawed by my ever-loathing husband.' She smiled at her own clever play on words. 'Still, I suppose he is her boss, regardless of how super dumb he is.'

At that moment the food arrived from room service and Amanda, who had by now removed her coat and shoes, made herself useful by pouring the coffee and passing Brandon the plate of sandwiches.

'This is really crazy, you know. I beat the shit out of your drunken husband, and less than an hour later here you are sharing my supper in my motel room.'

'Yes! You are right. It is crazy,' she replied. 'We should forget the supper and move straight into the bedroom. What I have in mind is far more satisfying than a sandwich. According to the neon sign outside the beds are king-size,' she said with a soft sexy chuckle, leaning over to dim the lights.

She stood up and moved slightly away from him, slowly reaching behind her back to release the catch at the neck of her beautiful dress. It came apart and began to slide slowly down over her shoulders, revealing her large wonderfully shaped breasts clad in a silky low-cut bra. Even in the half light he could see the nipples hard and taut pointing at him through the thin and partly transparent material. The dress was so tightly fitting from the breasts down that Amanda virtually had to peel it down her shapely body. Once past her hips it slithered to the floor, the sequins shimmering in the dimmed glow of the side lamps. She wore an extraordinarily brief pair of black silken panties and, to Brandon's utter delight, black stockings with feathery black suspenders. She looked amazing and he felt an urgent need surging inside him as her watched her slowly walk towards his chair.

As she reached him he attempted to stand, but she pushed him back into the wide-armed chair.

'Stay there, lover boy, I have work to do.'

And work she did. Within seconds she had undressed him completely, and she fell on her knees between his outstretched legs and began to make love to him with her mouth. Slowly and deliberately she caressed him and kissed him in places and in ways that he had never experienced before.

He lowered his hands to her breasts and tried to remove her bra but fumbled and couldn't find the catch. To his surprise, without interrupting or even pausing in her oral caresses Amanda suddenly placed both of her hands on the centre of her bra and ripped it violently from her body in one pull. She then returned her hands quickly to the task of fondling his penis and testicles. Brandon's hands moved to her beautiful breasts. He was amazed at the size and firmness of the nipples, the mere touch of which increased his excitement and sent a pleasant tingle through his body. Amanda continued with her ministrations, quietly moaning and humming to herself – completely in control.

This control that she exerted was both electrifying and unnerving; so much so that at one stage he tried to release himself from her exciting touches and kisses and take control of the situation himself. He felt strangely embarrassed and even threatened by Amanda's dominant manner of lovemaking.

Until now he had always felt that he had had a full and satisfying sex life, and that in this regard he was a worldly and experienced man. Suddenly, Amanda's control and her wild sexual abandon made him feel uncertain and at a disadvantage.

As a naval officer and the master of a warship he was the sort of person who had previously felt totally in control of his life in every way. Yet during something as natural as a sexual act, which in his past experiences had always been dominated by him, he found himself to be the dominated one, totally at her command. Regardless of his concerns, however, he was experiencing sexual pleasure unlike any he had ever experienced before.

After what seemed like an eternity she moved away from him and, holding his hand, led him into the bedroom, pushing him backwards on to the bed.

She removed her panties and stockings in a most erotic manner, yet with a haste that really astonished him. In fact, he was just thinking how most things she had done so far had been unexpected when she gave him the biggest surprise of all. She leapt on to the bed, her legs stretched wide, and plunged her body on to his, engulfing his manhood inside her.

'Hole in one!' she screamed, laughing.

She appeared to go into a frenzy for several minutes, lifting her body up from his then violently plunging it down, each thrust accompanied by a loud scream which he felt sure would attract the attention of the hotel staff.

Then almost as suddenly as she started she stopped dead. She quietly sat astride his body, his penis deep inside her. With a strange, faraway look on her face she started slowly and tenderly rocking back and forward on him. It was almost as if she was in a trance. She began humming gently to herself, the tempo of the humming gradually increasing as her movements started to speed up until he came to a shuddering, raging climax, such as he had never known before. At the same time Amanda screamed out loud and appeared to experience a violent climax that she later described as a 7.5 on the Richter scale.

During the course of that night they made love time and time again, and in many ways. Brandon became far more relaxed and felt less threatened by her sexual dominance. As the night wore on he found himself overcome with desire for this beautiful and amazing woman. He was thrilled and pleased to discover that Amanda was highly skilled in her manner of sexual expression. She had an extraordinary capacity for lovemaking, as well as an extensive and varied repertoire of positions and styles.

She seemed to have an almost insatiable thirst for sex, and had no inhibitions regarding variations to the theme. Brandon had never experienced anything so wonderful and exciting in his life. He felt something more than a mere sexual relationship with this woman. He felt emotionally bonded to her, and thanked his lucky stars that she had come into his life. He wanted this night to go on for ever. Such was his feeling for this beautiful woman that he found himself telling her again and again that he loved her.

To his utter delight she whispered that she loved him also. To his joy she continued to prove her absolute love for him throughout the entire, wonderful, sexually satisfying night.

*

However, nights always had to come to an end, and the light of day often tended to put a totally different complexion on events; even nights as beautiful as the one that Brandon had just spent with the lovely Amanda.

He was woken by the sun glaring into his eyes. He turned over to where Amanda had been lying when he fell asleep, but she was not there. He leapt out of bed and went to look for her while fumbling for his watch. It was 10 a.m. and she was gone.

He showered and dressed, then caught the lift down to the reception desk where the clerk handed him a sealed envelope. Selecting a seat near the window, out of sight of the clerk, he opened the envelope and found it contained a letter from Amanda.

It was written in a beautiful style, and he could vaguely smell Amanda's perfume on the paper.

*Dear David,*

*Nothing personal, sailor. It was a reasonable way to spend a night, even with an average lover like you. Sorry I faked it and lied to you about your lovemaking skills but I had to keep you on the boil in order to get to stay with you until morning to achieve what I set out to do.*

*I am leaving my husband, Adrian, and I intend doing it in the most dramatic and embarrassing way possible for him. Not only am I going to withdraw my family's funding of the company and ruin him financially, but I am going to kick the shit out of that fat ego of his by letting as many people as possible know that I slept with you.*

*You of all people. Part of the US military machine that he despises so much. He has spent so much time publicly attacking the military and the war that once this story gets out, as I intend to make sure it does, he will never be able to show his face in this town again.*

*I have been planning to do this for some time, but I had intended to use someone else as my sexual playmate. When you suddenly appeared on the scene at just the right moment it was just too good to be true. Knowing how he feels about the military and the war I couldn't let the opportunity pass me by. All I had to do was make a play for you, then sit back and let him dig his own grave by challenging you in public, and in front of the people whose respect and subservience he most needs. Your response was beyond my wildest expectations. I couldn't have planned it better if I had tried.*

*Adrian is such a hopeless egotist that by doing things this way I will cause him the most damage possible, and that is all I ever wanted to do. I want to punish that bastard for the years I have wasted, and the terrible way he has treated me.*

*Sorry that you have to suffer in order for me to achieve this end. Still, I know that you did get to have a bit of fun. At least you can go back to your cosy little war and forget it all. The world is a big place to get lost in.*

*You got your rocks off in a big way last night, David. I gave you that, and in return I am using you to get rid of my husband. I know you are not attached, so there is no need for self-righteous indignation regarding what I am doing.*

*By the way, David, that sister of yours is a stupid social-climbing bitch so you shouldn't lose too much sleep over what she will think of you.*

*By the time you read this letter the story will be out. I hope that you are able to get out of town before the shit hits the fan. As for me, I will be on my way back home to New York to tell my father the sort of story that will convince him that I am merely the unfortunate victim.*

*Sorry, David! The reason I am writing this letter is because I believe that you are probably a nice guy and don't deserve to have someone shit on you like this. You were just in the wrong place at the wrong time. Convenient for me. Tough luck for you.*

*Amanda*

His first impulse was to go after Amanda and confront both her and her husband in order to try to put things straight, but he soon began to realise how futile that would be. After all, he had slept with her, and judging from the tone of her letter and the obvious premeditation of her actions she had probably made sure that some of the hotel staff, and probably others, had been aware that she was visiting his room. Then there was the room service guy who saw them together the night before. It was all so stupid, but also so hopeless.

He had been taken for a fool and had acted the part very well. He was so angry and hurt that it would have only made matters worse if he had chased after her. After all, the rotten bitch had used him badly, and had achieved her objectives so effectively that he had only one thing left to do. Cut his losses and get the hell out of it.

He returned to his room and quickly packed his gear. After settling his bill he sat in the foyer and waited for a taxi to arrive. He was toying with the idea of calling Rae and Geoff in an attempt to explain things to them, when he became aware of someone standing in front of him. He looked up and was quite shocked to see it was his sister, and that she was in a very distressed state.

She angrily informed him that Amanda had contacted her and told her the sick story, and also where he was staying. The scene that followed was extremely unpleasant, and Rae's voice was so loud and hysterical that a small crowd gathered to watch and listen. He couldn't recall all of the detail of that confrontation, other than that it was very loud, nasty and embarrassing, and that it was obviously orchestrated by Amanda to be just that. She must have known Rae well enough to guess how she would react to her sordid and well-planned story. What stuck in his mind the most was the shame and disgust that he felt as he hurried to the waiting taxi followed by his screaming sister and the highly amused crowd of heckling onlookers who had gathered to enjoy the event.

★

Since returning to his ship he had written to Rae twice in an endeavour to let her know the truth of what had really happened on that ill-fated night. He had received a brief and curt reply just before sailing on this present mission. It was obvious that his letters of explanation had not been well received. All that her reply said was:

*David*

*You have cost me my job and my friends thanks to your obscene behaviour. Why Amanda? She is a whore and everybody knows it now. You have destroyed the life of that wonderful man, Adrian. I never wish to see or hear from you again. I hope that you feel satisfied with what you have done.*

*Rae*

## Chapter Five

Brandon returned to the bridge to check the progress of his ship. During his absence the storm had eased slightly and, if nothing else, was now constantly hitting them head-on, which made it easier from the point of view of handling the ship.

The weather was not his only concern. Whilst he was generally unhappy regarding the way his life was going, at this particular time he was hopping mad about this mission which in his opinion did not warrant risking a ship of the type of the USS *James Cunningham*. These pick-up type jobs were ideal for smaller craft, especially the various classes of motor torpedo boats which had top speeds in excess of fifty knots and could run right up into the shore.

During the previous few months his ship had carried out many uncharacteristic missions for a man-of-war of its size. She had delivered supplies to both US and Allied Forces, often to the most obscure places and in the most dangerous circumstances. His ship was often required to drop off and pick up special forces groups involved in top secret missions behind enemy lines. Not that too many people in Vietnam could clearly indicate on a map where the enemy lines began or ended, as both the Vietcong and the North Vietnamese Army operated, often in large units, way south of the recognised battle lines.

On all of those previous assignments he had felt convinced that his ship was appropriate, even essential, for the job in hand. He did not feel that way on this occasion. In his opinion the entire mission sucked.

Firstly, it was to pick up just a handful of men. This in itself was not the reason why he felt so concerned, for those handful of men were possibly extremely important to the war effort. The high command must have thought them valuable enough to risk the lives of two hundred sailors and a multi-million dollar warship.

His real anger stemmed from the fact that normally on these missions his ship was accompanied by a number of high-speed, motor torpedo boat escorts. These small and deadly warships were specifically designed for such work, and it was generally they that carried out the specific drop-off or pick-up work whilst the *James Cunningham* provided the comforting support of its awesome firepower.

These smaller boats were also able to conduct wide sweeping patrols, sometimes at great distances from the *James Cunningham* to ensure that she was not surprised by the ever-vigilant torpedo patrol boats of the North Vietnamese Navy or by the multitude of converted junks and fishing boats used as attack vessels by the enemy.

The combination of the well-armed destroyer and its accompanying motor torpedo boat escorts had proved invaluable on past missions. On each of those occasions the *James Cunningham* and her high-speed playmates had proved more than a match for the enemy's naval challenges, and between them they had destroyed and damaged numerous enemy vessels.

There was also a matter of honour and credibility to be considered. The Tonkin Gulf was renowned for its very volatile weather and fierce thunder and lightning storms which often caused havoc with the detection gear on warships. Over the past years many a ship had reported the apparent presence of enemy craft that probably wasn't there. In a few cases the curious nature of the weather resulted in the most embarrassing incidents occurring where ships moved into action against these electronic apparitions created by the peculiar weather conditions in that violent area of ocean.

Like all of his fellow captains, David Brandon was well educated in the history of naval warfare, both ancient and modern. His daily role was to keep himself briefed on all recent actions that could have some bearing on decisions he would need to take if confronted with a similar situation.

He was, therefore, well aware of the incident back in August 1965 in the Tonkin Gulf, when the destroyers USS *Maddox* and USS *Turner Joy* were on a patrol off the North Vietnamese coast. Herrick, the captain of the *Maddox* became aware of a South Vietnamese commando raid that was taking place in the region and sought authority to move out of the area. The authority was denied him and *Maddox* and *Turner Joy* continued their patrol, and by doing so probably put themselves in the situation where they were considered by the enemy to be part of the South Vietnamese military action.

The USS *Maddox* had sonar problems and both ships experienced problems with radar signals. This, together with the information from some intercepted and probably misunderstood enemy radio messages had caused Herrick to believe that both *Maddox* and *Turner Joy* were in imminent danger of attack.

They then began firing at the enemy that they believed they had encountered. During the ensuing battle they counted more than twenty sonar reports of enemy torpedoes, none of which hit either *Maddox* or *Turner Joy*. The engagement continued for over four hours during which time the US ships even reported sinking some enemy craft.

During this hectic battle, however, at Herrick's request the aircraft carrier USS *Ticonderoga* had provided air cover which circled the scene of the battle for its duration without sighting a single enemy ship. In fact, neither the USS *Maddox* nor the USS *Turner Joy* had made any visual sightings of the enemy. Afterwards Captain Herrick had suggested that perhaps the radar sightings of the enemy had been the result of freak weather conditions and requested that an evaluation of the incident be conducted.

Back in the USA, however, the politicians had their own agendas and the political decision was made that no evaluation was necessary. For their own reasons the politicians had determined that regardless of the reservations of Captain Herrick and the Navy, the US ships had been in battle. To justify their decision the Government ordered reprisal raids to be made on North Vietnamese bases to punish them for daring to engage US warships.

The Navy remained sceptical about the event, and even now, some seven years later, regardless of the dramatic technical advances made in the period since that fateful day, all ship's commanders, especially those operating in Vietnamese waters were acutely conscious of the effects that a repeat of such an incident could have on their future careers.

The presence of accompanying motor torpedo boats on missions such as this present one made such incidents much less probable. Owing to the mobility and speed of these craft they were able to physically search for and identify an enemy under such weather conditions, but on this mission the motor torpedo escorts had been denied to Brandon. He was not told why, and was angry when he discovered from a most reliable source that several of these smaller craft were in port and none scheduled to go to sea. He challenged the decision with his flotilla commander and was told that the impending weather conditions were such as to make it impracticable to use the escorts.

'Bullshit!' was Brandon's one word reply as he left his superior's office.

## Chapter Six

David Brandon was a quiet and studious man who, even though he was a highly proficient naval officer and ship's captain liked by his officers and crew, had lately acquired the reputation of being something of a loner. Loners generally are not well regarded in military circles where teamwork is considered to be essential.

He would always go to extreme lengths to support his crew members and to maintain the good name of the USS *James Cunningham*. In this regard he had even been known to send out scouts to bring in wayward crew members discreetly, rather than have them publicly mishandled by shore patrols who, like the military police, tended to be overzealous with their summary punishments.

It was a known fact that whenever sailors were apprehended by shore patrols the discipline sheets were prepared in large numbers, and duplicates had the unfortunate habit of ending up on the desks of people who could make or break the careers of naval officers like Brandon.

Not that he was lenient with his crew. On the contrary, crew members brought back on board by Brandon's scouts could expect to be punished in the most severe manner. Such punishments had less chance of appearing on sailor's record sheets, however, and therefore were seen by all to be more fair and appropriate, regardless of their severity.

Brandon was rarely ever seen to indulge in the usual high jinks that officers tended to get up to when ashore. He was not known as a drinker, and very rarely joined his fellow senior officers on their visits to the 'special hotels' which provided high class and guaranteed clean young women for the honoured officers of the United States military.

On the few occasions that he did accompany other officers to such establishments he usually stayed only long enough for a drink or two at the bar during which time he indulged in light-hearted social, rather than sexual, inter-course with one or more of the usually attractive and sexually enthusiastic hostesses.

Probably because of his unwillingness to indulge in this type of behaviour, even though he was a bachelor, some talk had developed amongst a small group of fellow officers and inevitably reached certain important people in the higher echelons of the Navy, that he was possibly a homo-sexual. Nobody could have had any evidence to support such an assumption as David Brandon was definitely not a homosexual and had never behaved in any way which could have given rise to such speculation. It was obvious to him that somebody was gunning for him.

In fact, Brandon was very much heterosexual. However, since his brief and disastrous intimate encounter with Amanda Lang he had become bitter about sex, and his only sexual encounter since returning to Vietnam had resulted in him inflicting considerable pain on the young Vietnamese hostess who was his unfortunate partner.

It happened during a night out at a hostess club. The club was not in the best part of town, situated very close to the Ben Nghe Canal, near where it joined the Saigon River, but it had a good reputation for better than average clean girls and nicely appointed bedrooms.

He had only had three drinks but by his fairly sober standards that was at least one drink too many. He was feeling tired and pretty tense, having just completed a long drawn-out two-day negotiation process with stores officers in an attempt to get his ship's equipment upgraded. He really couldn't believe these guys. It was almost as if they did not know that there was a war on.

His head was still full of their demands for some form or other, in quadruplet.

God! To do everything that they demanded I would need an extra ten clerks, and even then my ship would be lucky to get to sea on time, he thought as he tried hard to wipe the frustrations and stupidity of the last two days out of his mind.

The girl was very pretty and nicely dressed in normal clothes rather than the usual bar girl get-up. He had played the game and bought her the required two or three drinks to appease the proprietor of the establishment, even though he knew they were not what he had paid for, and at best were probably only mineral water. They had danced for a while and it felt good to have her warm body close to his. Even though he had not started the night off with the intention of doing any more than having a few quiet drinks to drown his sorrows, he found himself being led up the stairs and along the hallway to a room at the far end of the building.

He was struck by the quietness of the room and decided that it must be situated above the storeroom of the premises rather than the bar areas. This was later to be his salvation. The room was very clean and tidy, and the bed which was already drawn back had spotless white sheets and pillows: so different from the shabby bedrooms that he had been taken to on those rare occasions in the past. He peeled a few notes from his wallet and laid them on the dressing table. The girl smiled, seeming most satisfied with the financial arrangements.

She wasted no time and quickly undressed herself and then began to remove his clothing. He felt detached from what was happening, almost as if he were a spectator watching from the sidelines. It wasn't long before she had aroused him and he was on top of her and thrusting himself into her small body.

It was then, for the first time during the evening, that he took a close look at the person that he was making love to. The girl was just lying there. She wasn't even trying to pretend to be enjoying herself. This really infuriated him. After all, wasn't this what he was paying her for? She owed it to him to at least pretend that she was having a good time. It was at that moment that he realised that he had gone limp and had lost the desire that was so urgent a moment before.

Suddenly he was no longer with this nameless bar girl. He was back in bed with Amanda Lang; only this time he knew that she was pretending and was intending to do him harm. He looked down at Amanda's face, and she was laughing at him.

'How dare you laugh at me,' he screamed, 'You bitch! I'll fix you.'

Then he started to pummel Amanda's face. He punched it again and again until through the mist of his anger he realised that his hands and arms were covered in blood. The sight of the blood suddenly brought him back to reality and he found himself sitting astride the girl from the bar.

She was unconscious. Her face was covered in blood and her eyes were both swollen and closed. Her nose was obviously broken. He stepped back off the bed in horror, noticing that the spotless white sheets were speckled in blood. He sat down on a chair near the bed, staggered at what he had done. He was aware that he had a lot of blood on him and he picked up a towel and began to clean himself up. He looked at his reflection in the mirror and noticed for the first time that once again he had a rigid erection. He stepped back in horror and then realised that his body was heaving with excitement.

My God! he thought as he considered what he had done. I actually enjoyed doing what I just did to that poor girl. What on earth has happened to me?

He finished cleaning himself up and then dressed. He was now feeling more rational and thought to himself that it very fortunate he had dressed in civilian clothes. It might help him get out of the situation easier if nobody knew he was an officer. He then gently cleaned all the blood from the face and shoulders of the girl and propped her up in the bed.

By now he had calmed down considerably and his major concern was for the poor kid whom he had just beaten up. He had not really stopped to consider what might happen to him and his career if the police were called.

The girl came round gradually. When she saw Brandon she sunk back into the bloodstained bedding in fear, recalling what he had done to her. She started to scream and he quickly but gently placed his hand over her mouth, silencing her with an authoritative and reassuring, 'Shush! You are okay now, I am so sorry.'

She was obviously terrified and expecting him to do her more harm. Eventually he calmed her down and convinced her that she would not be hurt any more. She just lay back in the bed sobbing and carefully feeling the swellings on her nose and face with her tiny hands.

It had taken most of the night, a lot of gentle persuasion, his Rolex watch and nearly two hundred dollars, together with the fact that much of the girl's pain and fear had begun to subside. The money alone was something of a small fortune to this girl but luckily for Brandon it appeared that she may have been in some sort of trouble with the police, and did not dare go to them, even with clear evidence of such a savage beating. The result was that he was able to slip out of the back door of the club with a promise that she would not report him, provided he never returned.

This incident plagued him for months; not simply because he dreaded that she would report the attack and have him arrested, but more because he had been so violent, and because he got a strange sort of sexual satisfaction out of it. That he was so physically and sexually aroused by inflicting pain on that poor girl appalled him, and that what he did to the girl was really aimed at Amanda Lang disturbed him even more.

The rumours and innuendo concerning Brandon's sexuality continued to prevail. It appeared that there was nothing he could do about it without causing himself even more embarrassment and pain. Thankfully his popularity with his own men and with a few fairly high-ranking officers was such that nobody within his anonymous group of enemies dared attempt to take any overt action or enquire deeper into his private affairs.

*

Throughout his military career David Brandon had impressed some very important people. As long as those people continued to be impressed he had nothing to fear from the few malcontents who were probably only attacking his reputation because theirs would stand up to very little scrutiny.

Outwardly he was the perfect officer in every regard. However, although in many ways he was greatly admired by some of his commissioned colleagues, he was seen by others to be too perfect. Squeaky-clean to the point that worried and intimidated certain senior officers who worked with him. He tended to make them nervous. Whilst he did not know it, it was this feeling of nervousness that had caused a few less scrupulous officers, particularly among the married group who frequented the clubs and massage parlours of Saigon, to endeavour to explain away his different behaviour by speculating on his sexuality.

Two of that group of people who had taken a dislike to Brandon were officers who could cause him real problems if they put their minds to it, as they both worked in the headquarters of the Admiral. They were senior staff officers, Captain Andrew and Commander Neville.

Eventually Brandon had become aware of these rumours and felt sure that he knew who was spreading them. They caused him a great deal of concern and anger. In the US Forces homosexuality was not permitted. It was a crime and merely to be accused of being homosexual, however wrongly, would have jeopardised his career.

During his service Brandon had known of several officers and other ranks who had been dismissed from the armed services, or had been required to resign because of their sexual preferences. In some instances it was generally believed that the persons concerned were not homosexual, but merely the victims of allegations by people who for some reason wanted them out of the way. Such allegations, therefore, were potent weapons to use against one's enemies. Nevertheless Brandon could not understand how he could possibly have made such enemies. He certainly felt that he didn't deserve any.

There had been some occasions, however, when he was almost grateful for the dubious reputation they gave him. It relieved him of the necessity to justify not wishing to involve himself with certain of his fellow officers in their sordid sexual pursuits. Sordid, because he had reason to believe that they sometimes involved small children.

However, he often questioned himself how he could think their activities sordid, when he had so recently behaved in such a strange and violent sexual manner.

These ongoing rumours about homosexuality caused him to develop a general dislike for a few of his fellow officers, and a deep hatred toward the two who he felt sure were the ringleaders of what he considered was an evil campaign against him, Andrew and Neville.

Those deep felt feelings indirectly influenced certain dramatic decisions that he was soon to make regarding his future career.

Brandon was a very mixed-up person at this time. If he had been presented with a case history of one of his own officers which indicated the emotional condition that he was currently experiencing and displaying he would have probably relieved the man from duty.

However, he did not even consider that he had problems of that dimension; not currently anyway.

# Chapter Seven

The USS *James Cunningham* was as quiet as the grave as she proceeded slowly, so slowly forward to her rendezvous point. She had moved out of the storm-tossed seas into the still and calm waters of the wide estuary of the river in which the pick-up was to be made.

The estuary was sheltered from the open sea by a high, densely forested headland. It was very calm and would remain so as long as the storm continued to come from the north. The Met officer had indicated that the storm was on the move and could shift around to come from the east at some stage during the next hour or so, but for the time being the ship and its crew were relieved from the pounding that they had endured for over twelve hours.

The eyes of every man on deck were on the dark, evil-looking shoreline. Every man on watch had been instructed to look out for a flashing signal from the shore to the starboard of the ship. The signal would read one word only, the password of the land mission; Senator.

Besides knowing that they were some considerable distance behind what were currently considered to be enemy lines, and that they were to attempt to pick up the remains of a special forces group that, according to the intelligence reports, had been beaten up badly, none of the crew except the Captain and the Executive Officer knew exactly where they were. It was doubtful whether too many of them would have cared to know. Their main concern, and for many of them their only concern, was survival.

Nevertheless, such was the eerie silence and the intensity of the darkness along this most inhospitable shore, that survival and all that it meant seemed most unlikely to some of these apprehensive sailors.

The ship was low and sleek with the lines of a speedboat and could probably not be seen from the shore in the intense darkness. Yet under the present circumstances many of the crew could have been forgiven for feeling that she was probably standing out like a battleship.

Theirs was probably the first such naval mission so far north up the coast of North Vietnam for quite a long time. Few military strategists would have given such an operation the slightest possible chance of success.

The pick-up point had no name, only a set of map co-ordinates, and was in the estuary of a river, which as far as they were concerned, also had no name.

The intelligence report stated quite clearly that there may be few survivors, if any, from the ill-fated special forces mission. Brandon and his Executive Officer, Lieutenant John Tincey, had discussed the pick-up zone at some length whilst poring over their charts.

'Why the hell would anyone want to go there in the first place, skipper? There are no battles taking place in that area and I can't imagine what could be of any strategic importance in such a location.' Then he smiled broadly and said, 'But quite frankly I don't give a fuck anyway.'

'Ours not to reason why, John. I guess there must be something of great importance in that area. They don't send out special forces units and risk ships for nothing.' He chuckled to himself. 'Ignore that last remark. They seem to spend a lot of time and energy thinking up little stunts that put this particular ship at risk.'

Having thus made light of the situation, Brandon was very uneasy about this mission and couldn't stop worrying about why it was considered so important to risk one of the

Navy's latest warships with its highly specialist crew to pick up just a few survivors of a small military mission. There were plenty of ships in the region that were far better equipped to get in and out of such a small location speedily and without much fuss.

Thirty minutes later this was still the question that James Brandon, Commander US Navy, was asking himself as he personally conned his ship closer to the coastline and to its rendezvous with the unit code-named 'Senator'; or the remains of that unit. He didn't buy the bullshit about the weather conditions being unsuitable for the motor torpedo ships. Those ships and their crews revelled in such weather. He had seen them handle storms that left bigger ships in a state of chaos.

Although the pick-up point was in a river estuary the charts showed that there was very deep water until fifty metres off shore where it shelved up steeply on to the beach. Brandon was relieved about this, because the last thing he needed right now was to run ashore or collide with any underwater obstacles. To his further relief radar and depth sounding reports confirmed the details on the chart so far.

The Met officer's weather prediction was proving to be correct, for as they neared the pick-up point the wind was noticeably increasing from the east and even in the pitch black, white caps could be seen on the crest of the dark waves.

For a brief moment he thought back to his early childhood and to his naval officer father. His father used to tell him that the white caps on the waves were really King Neptune's horses rushing into the shore to meet their king. Even now he sometimes forgot himself and referred to them as white horses, which caused many a raised eyebrow or smile on the bridge.

He was very pleased with his ship, particularly on occasions like this when stealth was the password. The *James Cunningham* was one of the latest models, with superbly quiet engines. As she slowly glided towards the pick-up point the only sound from the engines was a very low, soft throbbing and humming noise which Brandon doubted could be heard from very far away. In fact, so quiet were the engines that he was conscious of the sound of the waves that were beginning to smash against the port side of the ship. He made a mental note to report this positive factor in his next fitness report on the ship.

At the same time that he was thanking his lucky stars for the silence of the engines, many of the more anxious crew members were forming the opinion that the noise was so loud that it could probably be heard back in Saigon.

Brandon was also pleased with the performance of his crew. Mostly experienced sailors, they had settled down into the running of their new ship with great ease and considerable expertise. His crew, including the officers, were predominantly young men, young enough for him, at the age of thirty-one, to be the old man, not just in terms of the Navy nickname for the captain, but also with regard to his age.

On this current mission they had performed exceptionally well, particularly since the time that the ship had gone into total blackout and silence routine pending its approach to the land.

'We are approaching the rendezvous point, John,' he whispered to his Executive Officer. 'Look out for a signal off the starboard bow.'

'Aye aye, sir. Look out for a signal off the starboard bow,' repeated the Executive Officer.

A few minutes later, 'Flashing light three o'clock, sir,' called a lookout forward of the bridge.

All heads turned to starboard as a dim white light began to flash from low down on the shoreline.

'Signal reads, "Senator", sir.'

'Make "We're coming to get you. How many passengers?" signaller.'

Within two minutes the signaller reported again. 'Reply reads, "Six passengers, two wounded", sir.'

'Acknowledge,' said Brandon, and the signal lamp clattered briefly.

As the signal was being sent he ordered the lowering of a motor launch and instructed the Executive Officer to proceed ashore with six men. Since he had bad feelings about this mission he decided to send his most experienced officer. Under normal circumstances the shore party would have been led by a less senior lieutenant.

'Everyone is to be armed, John. Take a medical kit and make it sharp. I want out of here within forty-five minutes. And by the way, minimum lights during the pick-up please, I feel like we're a sitting target out here,' he lowered his voice before continuing, 'and I have an uncomfortable feeling about this mission.'

'Aye, aye, sir.' For the first time the EO understood why he was being given this task.

The motor launch was lowered on the port side of the ship away from any prying eyes on the shore. Once fully manned it moved away from the ship and circled around the bows and started towards the shore.

At that moment fate took a hand in James Brandon's future. Just as the launch moved away from the cover of the ship there was a flash of light from the hillside, followed by a loud 'crump'.

'Sounds like a mortar, sir,' a lookout shouted.

'Incoming fire, all guns stand by,' called Brandon to the deck officer, and was immediately aware of the ship's guns moving, their barrels being trained towards the area where the flash had occurred. A split second later there was a loud 'whoosh' sound followed by an explosion to the starboard side of the ship which sprayed water over its bows. Brandon immediately looked towards where the launch had been and was relieved to see it still in one piece, but it was turning back towards the ship.

The hillside to the right then erupted in sound as several mortars began firing in the general direction of the USS *James Cunningham*.

'Captain to gunnery officer, try to lock on to those bastards on the hills and keep their heads down if you can. Fire when ready.'

'Aye aye, sir, we have already pinpointed two of them,' came the reply.

The USS *James Cunningham*'s guns came into life and began their systematic search and destroy fire plan into the darkness of the hills. They must have had some success, because the mortars ceased firing almost immediately. The gunnery officer, although young, was an experienced veteran of several such engagements. Like many of his gunnery colleagues he was a graduate mathematician. His selective fire tactics were most effective and did not allow for wastage of ammunition or time.

Brandon had left the bridge in charge of the officer of the watch and was at the port side as the launch drew near. A scrambling net was thrown over the side and without even thinking Brandon clambered down into the launch. The Executive Officer and two seamen were wounded, having been caught in the blast of the mortar explosion. The EO appeared to be the worst injured. He was covered in blood and was unconscious.

Within seconds two seamen had scrambled down beside Brandon and the EO and had tied a looped rope under the armpits of the injured officer, whilst other willing hands gently lifted him up on to the deck. Meanwhile the two wounded seamen had also been helped back on to the ship.

Brandon climbed up hurriedly and as he scrambled on to the deck the EO and the other wounded men were already being hurried to the sickbay where the doctor was busy preparing for the wounded special forces men. Normally the ship never carried a doctor, but because of the specific nature of the mission and the likelihood of wounded amongst the special forces group, a surgeon lieutenant had joined the ship in Ka Son just prior to their departure.

How fortuitous for John Tincey, thought Brandon. I hope that he is not too badly injured.

At that moment the sound of mortar fire was again heard coming from the hills above the point where Senator had signalled from. Brandon yelled out to the officer of the watch, a young lieutenant junior grade.

'Best. You are in command. If we are not back in forty-five minutes get the hell out of here and stand out to sea to await our signals. If you still don't hear from us an hour after that, you head straight back home pronto. Meanwhile, continue with selective fire and make sure those enemy gunners keep their heads down. Do you understand?'

'Aye aye, sir,' came the somewhat surprised and shaken reply. Lieutenant junior grade officers were not normally left in charge of a warship of this type.

## Chapter Eight

With two armed seamen to replace the wounded men, and himself armed with a pistol, Brandon once more clambered over the side and into the launch. He hit the deck and looked around at his men. They were all wearing standard issue flak jackets and steel helmets. Each man held an M16 rifle and carried several extra magazines in the long ammunition pockets of their combat fatigues.

It suddenly occurred to him that he was terribly under armed. Hell! He wasn't going over the top at the Somme. He was going into what could amount to a real fire fight, armed only with a bloody pistol. He shouted to the coxswain to 'wait one' and clambered back up the netting, calling for an M16 and some spare mags as he did so. On reaching the top of the net he was handed a rifle and a small duffel.

'There are plenty of fresh magazines and some grenades in there, sir,' shouted the anonymous sailor from the darkness of the ship's deck.

As Brandon climbed back down he was already shouting the order to cast off and head as fast as possible towards the shore.

'Make for where the signal light is flashing, coxswain.'

'Aye, aye, sir,' came the reply. He recognised the voice as that of Petty Officer Smallman. A second tour man with lots of common sense. He felt very glad that Smallman was in charge of the launch. He had the nagging feeling that skill was going to be more important than luck on this little operation. He hoped, however, for his fair share of luck as well.

Brandon suddenly felt very cold and, for the first time since the mortar incident, realised that he was shivering violently and hoped that none of the seamen could see him in the dark, just in case they thought he was shivering because of fear. Come to think of it, he wasn't all that sure whether it wasn't fear.

The mortar – what a twist of fate. That was either one hell of a good shot, or more likely a one-off God almighty fluke, he thought.

In any event, it seemed likely that the ship's guns had again hit their targets as no further fire had been seen coming from those locations.

Brandon looked back towards where the ship was, and although only a hundred yards away was relieved that he couldn't see her. If he couldn't see her from this close and low down it was hardly likely that the enemy would be able to see her from their positions in the hills. He wondered how it was that the enemy had spotted his ship in the first place. He also wondered how John Tincey, the wounded executive officer, was. He recalled the excessive amount of blood and wished he could know right now what his condition was. It seemed like it had happened ages ago, but on looking at the fluorescent face of his watch he realised that it was less than ten minutes since the EO and his men had been wounded.

Returning to the more immediate matter of the pick-up, he remembered the bag given to him at the ship. Opening it he felt inside and counted sufficient grenades to give three to each of his men. Taking three himself, together with three fresh magazines for his M16, he passed the bag around with instructions for each man to take three grenades and as many extra mags as they wished to carry.

As they neared the shore Brandon recognised the sound of mortars with their most distinctive crumping noise and hoped like hell that the first enemy shot had really been a fluke and that they had not worked out the location and range of the ship. As if to satisfy him that they hadn't, two mortar bombs landed in the water some fifty metres away to starboard of the launch and everyone in it was soaked with spray.

Rather them trying to hit us, he thought, at least we are a smaller target than the ship.

Just then the sailor in front of him leaned backwards and whispered something. Brandon was about to ask him what he had said when he noticed that the sailor was falling over towards him. He made a grab for the man and gripped hold of his shoulders to prevent him slipping.

He felt something hard and sharp in the palm of his right hand. At that moment a star shell lit up the sky above them and he saw to his horror that the sailor he was holding was obviously dead. Half of his face was missing and his right arm and part of his shoulder had been blown off. Brandon then realised that he was gripping what was left of the man's shoulder bone in his right hand and he was covered in the man's blood. He let go of the sailor in shock and disgust and the body fell on to the deck of the launch. Brandon tried to reach the water over the side of the launch in an attempt to wash off the blood and gore, but was unable to do so. Instead he was violently sick.

As he was hanging over the side he heard the sound of loud gunfire. He looked back out from the shore and realised to his dread that his ship was under heavy and continuous fire from the shore and had obviously been hit. There was a deep crimson flame burning on the after deck. He was, however, encouraged to see that she was firing back furiously and was heartened to see the violent eruptions of flame as the shells hit their targets on the hillside overlooking the pick-up beach.

'That'll keep the bastards heads down,' he shouted aloud.

He urged the coxswain to make more speed and to zig-zag in order to put the enemy mortar men off their mark. They were fast nearing the land and he could see the white spume of waves hitting the beach. The launch was moving parallel to the shore while Brandon and the other men on board looked for a further signal or signs of life. He was suddenly aware of the whine of small arms fire flying over their heads, and then thuds as several of the bullets hit the boat.

The coxswain suddenly called out and grabbed his left side. Brandon quickly moved forward, carefully stepping over the dead seaman. He took the controls of the launch from the coxswain who was obviously wounded. The man turned towards his captain and smiled.

'Sorry, sir, I nearly lost her for a moment. I'll be all right now. We are just coming into the shore. If you could go up forward and see us in I'll manage the rest. I don't think I'll be able to come ashore with you though.'

'Good man, Smallman! You'll be fine. Just wait in the launch for us and don't get any parking tickets or I'll have your balls,' said Brandon with a forced chuckle. Then he hurried forward to the bows of the launch where the remaining four seamen were crouching with their weapons at the ready.

As the launch lifted on to the last wave Smallman cut the engine. A figure came running out of the undergrowth of the jungle and shouted, 'Senator! Over here you guys.'

Bullets were hitting the water all around the boat as it neared the shore.

'Tell that guy that someone is firing real fucking bullets at us,' said the leading seaman on Brandon's right. He was a black man from Kansas who was well known and liked for his ready wit, only this time there was a touch of fear in his humour.

Brandon grabbed him by the arm and shouted, 'We'll soon give the bastards a taste of their own medicine, Peters. Follow me, men.'

It suddenly occurred to him that he had just said something that must have sounded pretty John Wayne-ish and probably very stupid under the present circumstances. He didn't get much time to give the matter any further thought, for at that moment the launch hit the beach hard. Brandon and his sailors were half thrown out, half leapt out, and fell on their faces on to the wet sand. They quickly got up and ran like maniacs for the tree line and towards their welcoming party.

The man who met them was a small, thin black man dressed in filthy combat fatigues and armed to the teeth with a range of weapons. He had a pistol in a holster strapped around his hips. He also carried an M60 machine-gun over his shoulder, which is no mean feat for the largest and fittest of men, for together with its 25 lbs of weight one always had to carry sufficient ammunition for the weapon. This guy had several heavy bandoliers of M60 bullets strung over his shoulders.

He seemed to ignore Brandon, but rushed to welcome Peters with the hand shake of the 'brothers'. Then he appeared, for the first time, to recognise Brandon's rank.

Almost with a snarl he asked, 'What the fuck are you doing here, Commander Bro? Who you got looking after the ship?' His question appeared to Brandon to contain an accusation. 'If anything happens to your war canoe we's in real deep shit. I hope you left it in good hands, man.'

'Cut the crap and tell me who's in charge of this mission, soldier?' demanded Brandon. Although realising he must have sounded pompous, if not stupid, he was acutely conscious of the urgency of their situation. Their only method of escape, the launch, was exposed out there on the beach under fire with a dead man on board and a wounded sailor in charge, who could be dead by now for all that he knew.

Brandon's danger awareness was greatly enhanced by the constant rifle and mortar fire that was coming with increasing ferocity from the jungle all around them.

Then he was suddenly aware of a tall, broad-shouldered man standing alongside him, having appeared as if by magic.

'I'm in charge of this team, mate, so let's get the hell out of here,' said the tall man in a pronounced Australian accent. 'Oh, and by the way, we have now got four wounded thanks to you bastards taking so long to get here. What do you think we're doing on this fucking beach, having a sodding picnic?'

Brandon started to respond, but was violently interrupted by a mortar shell that landed close by, to their left. Much as he wanted to put this arrogant bastard right, he decided it was neither the time nor the place to get involved in a dispute with a loud Australian who, strangely, appeared to be in command of an American unit.

Very odd! But there would be plenty of time to get to the bottom of that and sort out their differences later.

Brandon's remaining sailors quickly got organised and began moving the wounded down to the launch, which Smallman had turned around so that it was sideways on to the shore, making it easier to lift the injured on board, none of who were able to walk. The loading of the wounded took place amidst a hail of bullets and constant mortar fire, which miraculously caused no further casualties.

Whilst Brandon felt that by moving the launch around Smallman had done the right thing in view of the number of casualties, he was acutely aware of the fact that the

launch also made an extraordinarily big target lying broadside on to the beach. It was certainly receiving the
undivided attention of a large number of enemy soldiers
who were fortunately not having a great deal of success in
their attempts to hit their temporarily stationary targets. As
soon as the wounded were all on board he shouted to
Smallman to bring the launch around, facing seaward with
its stern as close to the shore as he possibly could.

By this stage rifle and light machine-gun bullets were
whistling around the launch and a steady stream of mortar
explosions seemed to be gradually creeping down the beach
in their direction. Like all servicemen Brandon had been
trained to recognise the sound of enemy weapons, but for
the first time he was in a situation where the training meant
something. He thought back to the time at battle tactics
school and the words of the petty officer firearms
instructor.

The AK47 has a very distinctive sound compared with
the standard US weapons. He found himself laughing out
loud at the thought. Who gives a shit how it sounds, for
Christ's sake. By the time you've heard it, it's probably hit
you.

★

Out in the darkness of the river estuary the ship kept up its
fierce bombardment of the hills, and in return was
obviously receiving some considerable attention from the
enemy as several small fires could be seen blazing on
various parts of the ship.

To Brandon's annoyance the Australian and the small
black man had disappeared into the jungle while the
wounded were being moved. The last time that he saw
them both, crouched down and heading away from him
into the dense tree line, he saw something that amazed him.

It was the black man. Not only was he wearing a pistol and carrying an M60, with sufficient ammunition to conduct a war on his own, but on his back was slung a bag which, if Brandon's eyes didn't deceive him, held an M72 LAW: a light anti-tank weapon which had the very special and convenient quality of being disposable. It was a folding bazooka, complete with shell, that you used once and then threw away.

By the time Brandon had everyone else on board the launch, bullets and mortars were bracketing the beach. The launch was out in the open and terribly exposed. He was anxious to get away from what seemed like a certain death trap but could not leave without the two men who apparently were the senior ranking people of the mission. He was beginning to get pretty angry about the situation.

'Where the hell have they gone?' he said to nobody in particular. 'We'll give them three minutes, Smallman,' he said to the wounded coxswain, who with the light of the explosions on the beach could be seen to be in great pain. 'Are you all right, boy?' he asked the young sailor. 'Because when I tell you to go I want you to give it all you've got.'

'Fine, sir! Don't you worry about me. I won't let you down.'

'Good man. I know you won't.'

Two of the seamen had leapt out into the sea and were crouched down in the water alongside the launch, ready to push her away from the beach. They had started to return fire into the tree line but Brandon had ordered them to cease fire in case they hit the two men from the special unit.

The mortar shells were still exploding at regular intervals over a wide area, but luckily the creeping barrage that had seemed so threatening a few moments before had receded. It appeared that the mortar gunners had lost the target. Their vision would certainly be obscured by the intense dust and smoke that was being created by the constant explosions around the beach.

The three minutes were long up, and just as Brandon was about to give the order to push off the two missing men came hurtling out of the tree line on to the beach. The small black man was first in the boat. He ran so fast he seemed to almost run across the surface of the water. One of the sailors crouching in the water laughed out loud at the sight. Brandon noticed that the black man was still carrying that bloody heavy machine-gun, although the pack was missing from his back. He threw his leg over the gunnels of the launch immediately alongside Brandon, who then noticed a very large and ugly-looking knife strapped to the man's right leg, just below the knee. The thought immediately flashed through Brandon's mind that out there in the bush were probably several unfortunate North Vietnamese soldiers who had come into a more intimate and deadly contact with that knife.

The big Australian was not as lucky as his heavily armed associate. He was about fifty feet from the launch when a mortar shell exploded immediately behind him and he was hurled twenty feet, ending up in a crumpled heap on the sand. The air was instantly filled with smoke and flying dust and grit. For a moment Brandon couldn't see him. Then he saw where the body had landed and despite the protests of the rest of the men in the boat he leapt over the side of the launch into the water and ran up the beach to where the Australian lay.

As he ran through the swirling dust and smoke, bullets spurted into the sand around his feet. He thought to himself, What the holy shit am I doing this for? The man's dead.

Just at that moment the Australian lifted his body into the crouch position then collapsed again. Brandon reached him in a flash and somehow managed to get him on to his shoulder in a fireman's lift.

He was just about to make his way back to the launch when the Australian screamed out, 'Don't leave that kitbag, for God's sake. It is vital.'

Brandon looked down and saw that the Australian was indicating a dark-coloured duffel bag.

'What's so important about it?'

'Take my word, mate.'

'I wouldn't take your word if you told me we are in Vietnam, you crazy prick,' Brandon shouted, as his anger at being kept waiting on the beach for so long suddenly got to him.

The Australian screamed and then fainted with pain as Brandon, still carrying the man across his shoulders, bent down and tried to pick up the duffel bag. It was about 3 foot 6 inches long and it was very heavy. Brandon was already staggering under the heavy weight of the unconscious man and he hurried back to the launch, fortunately downhill, half carrying and half dragging the bag. He thought to himself that whatever was in this duffel bag had better be damned important. As he staggered towards the water's edge the mortar and rifle fire intensified and he wondered how it was he was not hit.

Unknown to him, however, the Australian was hit by two more bullets which probably would have been lethal to Brandon had they not hit less important parts of the unconscious Australian who, sprawled across Brandon's shoulders, was acting as a unwilling flak jacket.

Later Brandon was to review the event and marvel at how he was able to carry the Australian and that damned heavy bag. He put it down to abject fear causing a rush of adrenaline giving him the strength to achieve what surely would have been impossible under normal circumstances.

As he reached the waterline he realised that the little black man was alongside him, helping him get the wounded Australian on board. Brandon, by this stage totally exhausted, then felt himself being bodily lifted over the side into the launch. He later recalled thinking that whoever was doing it was exceptionally strong. He collapsed on the deck of the launch while still held in the vice-like grip of the little black soldier.

He shouted, 'Smallman, get the fuck out of here.'

His efforts were wasted however, for Smallman was already steering the launch away from the shore at a very fast rate of knots, and zigzagging it dangerously in an attempt to confuse the enemy gunners who now seemed to be concentrating all of their energies on the fast-receding boat.

Brandon lay back in the launch as it bucked and reared across the waves, which by now had become quite high. He looked up into the sky and saw a mass of tracer and shell bursts above them. He then became conscious of the loud boom of the ship's guns firing non-stop into the hills. He could also hear the sound of the ship's anti-aircraft and machine-guns in operation.

'Give the bastards hell,' he shouted and found himself laughing out loud.

Suddenly there was a massive explosion from the shore behind them. Brandon steadied himself against the side of the launch and looked back towards the land. The whole hillside had erupted like a volcano and the jungle was a mass of flames and minor explosions.

'Roasted your balls, you slit-eyed bastards,' screamed the little black special forces man, laughing with great abandon. Then, as if to explain his outburst he turned to Brandon and shouted, 'Me and the boss left them a few calling cards while you guys were loading the wounded into the launch, Commander.'

'You sure made a great job of it,' laughed Brandon, over-come with the sheer excitement of the moment. 'Those cards of yours must have all been aces of spades.'

He noticed that the firing from the hills had almost ceased now, and eased himself down on to the deck. He looked at his watch. It was just over thirty minutes since they had left his ship yet it felt like a lifetime.

'What the hell!' Someone was kicking him in the leg. He rolled over and realised he was lying next to the Australian who was barely conscious and kicking at him feebly, apparently trying to attract his attention.

'Did you get the kitbag, Commander?'

'Yes! Don't you worry about it. How do you feel?'

'Don't worry how the fuck I feel, that bag is really important. It must not get into anyone else's grasp, Commander. You've got to hide it until we reach Saigon. Do not hand it over to anyone but me, whatever you do. Promise me you will do that. Both of our futures, both of our lives depend on it. Believe me. If you don't, a lot of men will have died for sweet fuck all.'

'You're not going to be in any fit shape by the time we reach Saigon.'

'Then hang on to it until I am in fit shape, and am able to take it from you personally. Nobody, I say nobody, no matter what rank they have, must know about this, mate. For the time being just you and me. Got it?'

'We'll talk about it later,' said Brandon, suddenly realising that he was whispering at the same level as the Australian.

'We talk about it now, Commander. If that bag leaves your hands we all die,' said the Australian, furiously grabbing Brandon's collar. He looked into Brandon's face with a pleading, desperate look and then slowly released his grip and collapsed into deep unconsciousness.

We all die? thought Brandon, and at that moment a cold shiver ran through him.

The duffel bag suddenly took on a whole new meaning for him. He dragged it over towards himself and tried to examine it more closely. It was too dark to see much, except for the occasional explosion which momentarily lit up the sky. It was an ordinary, military issue duffel bag, dark in colour, although that may have been dirt, and it was locked with a large heavy padlock. Whatever was in it, it was packed very tightly and it felt firm but soft. No sharp edges and no metallic feel about it.

He was beginning to get very worried about the duffel bag, but his worries were abruptly interrupted when the launch thumped against the side of the ship.

# Chapter Nine

The injured Smallman had managed to steer the launch back to the port side of the ship out of sight of the shore and in the cover of the larger vessel. The scrambling net was still hanging over the side and Brandon climbed up on to the deck, having ordered the rest to stay in the launch while it was winched back on to the ship. This would make it easier to recover the wounded and would ensure their transfer to the sickbay in the quickest and most comfortable manner.

He immediately headed for the bridge at a fast run. He need not have hurried for Lieutenant Junior Grade Peter Best had things well under control. The launch was back on board and being secured and the ship was already under way by the time Brandon had reached the top of the gangway.

'Casualty and damage report, Best.'

'Two cooks and one steward dead. Eight seamen wounded, gunner's mate Davis, seriously. He lost a leg. The surgeon is working on him now.

'Six hits to the ship, sir. Five of them caused superficial damage to decking and one lifeboat. The sixth exploded in the galley causing the fatalities and severe damage. It put the galley out of commission.'

Brandon tightly gripped the rail of the bridge and felt quite sick for a moment. Four of his men, including the seaman, in the launch, were dead. Nine of his men were wounded, one of them crippled for life if he lived. He felt like screaming out loud but knew that whatever the circumstances he must retain his composure.

He then realised that Lieutenant J.G. Best was looking at him rather strangely. He must have looked an awful sight. He was soaking wet and dirty, his clothes were torn and his jacket was covered in blood. No wonder Best was staring at him. But he wasn't exactly looking at him. He was looking at something he was holding in his right hand.

Brandon looked down and saw that he was holding the Australian's duffel bag – tightly. So tightly that the knuckles on his right hand had gone white. Oh my God! What am I doing? he thought to himself.

'Oh, by the way, sir, the EO is going to be okay. Apart from a lot of open wounds he has a few broken ribs, a broken arm and collarbone and a badly fractured jaw, but the surgeon says he will be up and about in two or three weeks. Lucky beggar will probably get a trip to Manila, or better still stateside.' The young J.G. seemed quite envious of the wounded John Tincey.

Brandon knew that in reality, because of operational requirements John Tincey could probably only expect a week or so in hospital, followed by several weeks of light duties. Whatever light duties are in a battle zone with a bloody great war raging.

Later he would have to compile a full report on the entire mission, and specifically note the circumstances of the deaths and injuries. This would involve reports in the ship's log and numerous other special reports for the Navy Department. There would most likely be an official inquiry into the mission, during which it would be decided whether any glory, or more than likely blame, should be attributed to anyone.

Brandon was Navy to his boots, but even he sometimes wondered whether the admirals behind their plush desks had ever been to sea, and if they had, whether any of them had ever participated in hazardous operations such as the one that he and his crew had just experienced. As for the Navy Department bureaucracy, those guys really shitted him off.

Luckily for both Tincey and the efficiency of the ship, the *James Cunningham* would not be called on to participate in any hazardous operations for a while. The ship had suffered quite a hammering in the brief engagement and would not be fit for further active service until considerable repairs had been carried out.

With any luck, thought Brandon, we'll have to sail to Hawaii or Manila for repairs and refitting.

\*

Brandon stayed on the bridge until the *James Cunningham* was well out into the open sea and steaming southwards at top speed. He had ordered that the ship remain at action stations, for the enemy might consider avenging themselves against the vessel that had inflicted so much damage on their troops. It would therefore be some time before he could be sure that they were out of danger.

Over the tannoy he briefly commended the crew for their excellent work in the battle. He wanted to tell them of their bravery and how proud he was of them, but felt that this may sound a bit hollow at this time when they would all be mourning the loss of close friends. He would do that later, when the ship was back safely at its moorings.

It would probably be done in conjunction with a memorial service for the dead seamen. With the Vietnam War policy of flying all dead servicemen home to the US for burial by their families, the ship would not have the opportunity to say farewell to its dead in the traditional naval fashion.

As soon as he had given his brief message to the crew he left the bridge and made his way below to the sickbay to check on the condition of his own wounded and those from the special forces unit.

He stopped at several posts on the way to speak to members of the crew. It was the appropriate and correct thing to do, but it was also a caring thing to do for his men under the circumstances. Even though David Brandon was basically a loner, he really did care about the welfare of the men who served with him on the USS *James Cunningham*.

# Chapter Ten

In the sickbay the situation was fairly chaotic. The Surgeon Lieutenant, David Schwarzer, and the ship's own sick berth attendant Pirelli were very busy dealing with many wounded at once. As he entered he could sense the fear and the pain of the injured men. The sickbay was permeated with the stench of blood and other bodily smells. He could hear loud groans from several of the wounded men, and gunner's mate Davis was screaming like a banshee as Schwarzer and Pirelli worked like madmen to stem the flow of blood from what remained of his right upper leg, in preparation for surgery.

Several other crew members had been directed to the sickbay to help, and they were doing the best they could to make the remaining wounded comfortable whilst they waited for their turn to be treated by the overworked medical staff.

Just to the left of the entrance a young radio operator sat on the floor cradling his unconscious buddy's head in his lap and rocking him gently while he mopped a dribble of blood away from the wounded man's mouth, but the blood kept coming. Brandon felt a hard lump in his throat when he recognised the tune which the sailor was quietly humming to his friend as he nursed him. It was a lullaby that his mother used to sing to him when he was a small child.

As he stood in the entrance he realised that he was shivering once more, however this time it was definitely not because he was cold and wet.

Commander David Brandon, US Navy, was really terribly frightened for the first time in his life. More frightened than back on that beach. He found that he could not stop the flood of tears that ran unchecked down his face. He felt so utterly helpless and consumed with the conviction that he, and he alone, was responsible for those of his crew that had been killed and for those unfortunate sailors who were suffering agonies before his eyes.

I shouldn't have left my ship, he thought to himself. If I had sent someone else in charge of the shore party I could have prevented all of this from happening.

Slowly but surely he was being overwhelmed by awful feelings of guilt, recrimination – of self-doubt. What if?

He turned away and started to hurry out of the sickbay. He had to get back on deck. He needed some fresh air. He couldn't allow anyone to see him like this.

'Captain! Come here quickly.' It was Schwarzer, the surgeon, and he wasn't requesting.

He was commanding. 'Quickly!'

It felt to Brandon as if he had received a sharp kick. Instantly he was in control again.

'What gives?' he called as he threaded his way around the mass of wounded and helpers towards the end of the room where Davis was being operated on. 'What can I do to help?'

'That's more like it,' whispered Schwarzer. 'You looked as if you were about come apart back there.'

'Sorry, Doc. It's the first time I've lost men; and to lose so many... '

'Cut it out, Captain, self-pity is not on the menu today. Not in front of these guys, anyway,' whispered Schwarzer as he looked around the compartment. 'If you think you owe them, then this is where you pay back.'

Then very loudly he said, 'Thanks, Captain, I sure could use an extra steady hand.' Loud enough for anyone to hear, if they cared to. Then, even louder he said, 'Scrub up and get back here asap, Captain. We've got a few lazy bastards trying to work a trip stateside. Have I got news for those guys. When Schwarzer's cut and tuck is finished with them they won't know they've been wounded. I suspect the only injuries most of them have are the social kind they got on their last trip to Kim Lau's massage parlour, back in Saigon. There are not too many Purple Hearts, just a lot of brown underpants.'

Brandon glanced at the sea of faces around him and saw that even through their pain many of the injured men were smiling.

This is one hell of a doctor to have around when the going gets tough, he thought as he quickly scrubbed and dried his hands and arms, then held them out while Pirelli helped him with a pair of surgical gloves.

From then on it was just a continual flow of people and wounds of all types and severity. Brandon need not have been there. In fact, he shouldn't have been there under the circumstances, but being with the wounded at this time helped him greatly. He was deeply moved by what he saw. The patience and courage of the injured men who had endured all types of agony whilst waiting for treatment made him feel ashamed of his earlier self-pity and the selfish tears that he had shed.

The surgical team completed their work on Davis, having had to remove the remains of his leg up to the base of the buttock. Schwarzer was not happy with the results and asked Brandon to request a Medevac helicopter immediately, even though the ship was still considered too close to enemy positions and the fear of attack; and at extreme range for a helicopter dustoff.

The request was made and fortunately the hospital ship USS *Panama* was close enough to safely lift off a medical unit, and agreed to do so because of Davis's critical condition. At the same time arrangements were made to medevac the remaining wounded to shore as soon as the ship was in reasonable range. Meanwhile they would each be given the expert attention of Doctor Schwarzer's *cut and tuck* team.

The Australian was treated immediately after Davis. He had some major shrapnel wounds in the back, which according to Schwarzer had just missed the spinal cord. His right arm was badly broken in two places, probably due to the combination of impact from splinters from the mortar bomb, and hitting the ground after being lifted so high into the air by the explosion. He also had three bullet wounds, two in the right shoulder and one just below his left thigh.

One of the shoulder wounds had been caused by a high velocity bullet and the result was quite frightening. Massive internal injuries had been caused to bones, muscle and tissue, and the exit hole was enormous. The Australian's wounds were diagnosed as critical and the patient was in a state of advanced shock. He was earmarked for evacuation at the same time as Davis, as he required treatment that Schwarzer was unable to provide under the crowded circumstances and with the limited surgical facilities and lack of intensive-care medical support available. Schwarzer commented to Brandon that the man was in superb physical shape, which probably saved his life.

'Anyone less fit would have died as the result of that high velocity bullet, let alone all of his other wounds,' he advised the Captain.

'Shit, I feel that I should spend more time on him, but I have got too many other men to deal with. I hope that helo comes quickly, for both of their sakes.' He was referring to the Australian and Davis, the amputee.

Schwarzer had also decided to evacuate the stoker who had broken both legs during the storm. It seemed that one of the legs had gone badly wrong and the man also required treatment that couldn't be provided on the USS *James Cunningham*. Without such treatment Schwarzer feared that the man might also have to lose his leg, at the very least.

The doctor advised Brandon that due to the limited space and facilities available the EO had been returned to his own bunk, where he would receive regular house calls from designated crew members. He was assured that Tincey was unlikely to suffer any permanent disability from his wounds.

Shortly afterwards, a tragic event occurred. One of the special forces men, who had received a bullet in the upper chest but seemed to be managing quite well and whose body signs were considered satisfactory under the circumstances, suddenly keeled over and died. He had been sitting on the floor in the corner talking to the other wounded around him, and generally reassuring them, when he coughed and fell over, dead.

Brandon stayed on in the sickbay, and following the instructions of the doctor and the medic, helped as best he could, until news was received of the impending arrival of the hospital ship's Medevac helicopter.

It was still pitch dark and the sea was pounding into the bows of the ship as she surged southwards to home and safety. Brandon decided that he should take the con for the duration of the tricky and delicate landing of the helicopter on the floodlit landing pad at the stern of the ship. This was particularly essential as the landing pad had received a direct hit from an enemy mortar during the action and only two-thirds of it was useable for a landing zone. It was to be a tricky manoeuvre but at least two men's lives depended on it being carried out successfully.

In the event the sea calmed suddenly and the helicopter dropped cleanly out of the sky and landed safely. It had a small medical team on board, and after a brief discussion with surgeon Schwarzer the team collected their three wounded charges together with their medical files and clambered back into their aircraft.

Brandon was just about to leave the area and return to the bridge when one of the helicopter medical team ran up to him and beckoned him to the helicopter. He climbed on board and was directed to the stretcher of the Australian, who was by now fully conscious and appeared to be in a state of great distress. Brandon knelt down beside him and strained to hear the Aussie above the noise of the helicopter's engines.

'I hope you have still got the bag, Commander. You have to keep it for me. Do you understand? If it gets into anyone else's hands we are both going to die.'

He grabbed at Brandon's coat front and looked into his eyes. 'Brandon, you do this for me and I'll guarantee you a great future. If you don't there will be no future, for either of us.'

With that he collapsed back on to his stretcher, exhausted.

'I don't even know who you are; what's your fucking name?' shouted Brandon.

'Yes you do, it's Senator! That's all you need to know. It's not as if I'm going to marry you, for Christ's sake,' grimaced the Aussie, who then lapsed into unconsciousness.

Brandon watched the helicopter disappear into the distance and stood staring into nothing for a long while before he was shaken back to reality by the tannoy calling him to the bridge.

During the following hours the ship was moved in and out of battle stations on several occasions as contacts were made with shipping and a lone aircraft. The aircraft failed to identify itself and was probably an enemy reconnaissance plane. It was too high and too far off to be sure, or to engage even if it had been positively identified. Just in case, however, Brandon changed course and moved to the east to confuse any surface vessels that may have been directed towards his ship by the plane.

★

The engineering officer had had a working party of welders on the helipad for over two hours, and had certified it as serviceable less than ten minutes before the arrival of the Medevac helicopter units for the remaining wounded and the dead. Brandon had never seen filled body bags before, and the sight of that neat row of bags laid out on the perimeter of the helipad awaiting the arrival of the helicopters sent a chill through his body. He could not shake off the thought of how close he had come to occupying one of the bags just a few short hours before.

Brandon knew what would happen to the body bags. They would be forwarded to a special unit where the bodies would be cleaned up and prepared. All the documentation would be carried out by the war graves unit, then these sad casualties of war would be placed into shiny aluminium coffins and transferred to Tan Son Nhut airbase. At the base they would be towed across the tarmac on trailers, just like passengers' luggage at an ordinary airport. The coffins would be loaded into the cavernous fat hull of a C141 Starlifter air freighter and transported back to the States. When they arrived home the coffins would be offloaded and then distributed to cities and townships throughout the country, where they would be claimed by their loved ones and buried. All of this at the expense of a grateful country.

Generally the first thing that a soldier saw when arriving for duty in Vietnam was a row of coffins being loaded on to a C141, going home. A great morale booster for raw recruits who probably had a premonition of death anyway, just by being there.

This daily transportation of the war's dead was a regular TV feature during periods when the war slowed down too much to satisfy the bloodlust of the media and the public. That was how Brandon saw it anyway. He also tended to think that Uncle Ho, up in the north, would see this act of returning the bodies home as a sign that the American military did not consider that they had a permanent role to play in Vietnam and, furthermore, that they did not wish to leave any evidence behind to show that they were ever involved. The North Vietnamese regime probably saw this as a premature admission of defeat by the Americans.

He had returned to the sickbay on two further occasions since his earlier, traumatic induction into the world of surgery, and was pleasantly surprised to see how well Schwarzer and his group had dealt with the other wounded men. Once the two critical cases and the stoker with the broken legs had been flown off, the pressure had been removed and the medics were able to attack the job of treating the remaining cases in a systematic way.

He took his time speaking to the men in turn and sharing a mug of coffee and a cigarette with two of the least injured sailors who had been wounded in the mortar attacks on the ship.

One of the special forces men was awake and seemed to be quite talkative – until Brandon arrived, that is.

'What's your name soldier?' said Brandon, offering him a cigarette.

'We are not allowed to give our names to anyone, sir. No disrespect, but that is the fact of the matter,' answered the soldier, taking a cigarette and leaning forward to accept a light.

'Surely I am entitled to know. After all, we saved your arses and we're taking you home,' said Brandon, feeling somewhat annoyed by the man's attitude.

'Sorry, sir, but them's the rules, and I am not allowed to tell you spit.'

'But what about the Australian, your commanding officer?'

'I don't know who you are talking about, sir,' said the soldier, lying back and feigning sleep.

Brandon had no right to be annoyed. He knew the rules better than anyone. These special forces guys were doing some pretty scary things, and if the media could brand the average serviceman in Vietnam as a murderer, rapist or whatever currently sold papers or got TV ratings, what the hell would they do with these guys if they got the chance. Regardless of that, however, he was annoyed, bloody annoyed, and it was all to do with that Australian or whatever he was.

Who the hell does he think he is, treating me that way. And as for that bag: what the hell is in it?

He made up his mind that he was going to open it up and examine the contents at the earliest possible opportunity.

He carried on his rounds of the wounded men, and eventually ended up having a mug of coffee with Schwarzer, who was taking a well-deserved break.

'How did it go, Doc?' asked Brandon. 'You seem to have done a wonderful job on these men.'

'They were all pretty much the same in terms of the severity of their injuries, so I sort of treated them alphabetically – A to Z,' said Schwarzer, laughing out loud and making light of the excellent work that he and the others had done.

'By the way, Captain, that medic of yours, young Luciano Pirelli. He is brilliant enough to graduate from John Hopkins. His ability with surgical procedures and handling the knife is better than most surgeons I know. I just wish there was some way I could help that kid get into medical school. He has the makings of a fine surgeon, and that could all be wasted if he stays where he is.'

Brandon was interested and pleased to hear this about his crew member, who he now saw in a different light. He assured Schwarzer that he would speak to his commodore about it, and see what could be done to get Pirelli, a nine-year regular seaman, a scholarship of some sort.

He wondered how it was that Schwarzer, in such a short time, whilst up to his neck in wounded, was able to find the time or raise the interest to discover the first name of an enlisted man. Pirelli had served under Brandon for almost a year and he knew nothing about the man, except that he was a medic of the not-too-navy variety.

He made a silent pledge to himself to bone up on the crew's records and find out more about them.

★

The Medevac helicopters arrived on time, together with a high flying escort of fighter planes. Probably the earlier reported sighting of the recon aircraft had given them cause to be that extra bit careful.

The small black special services man who had met them on the beach was also evacuated with the wounded. He was the only remaining member of that unit and had no place on the ship. It was appropriate for him to leave with the others. Brandon had enough problems dealing with his damaged vessel, especially now he was short-crewed. He still had men who were injured in the storm and not yet fit for duty. The last thing he needed was a lone soldier, particularly a special forces one, left on board and getting in the way.

Just after the Medevac dustoff Brandon was walking towards the bridge when a cold shiver ran down his spine.

Oh my God! The duffel bag! That Aussie's fucking kitbag. Where the hell did I leave it?

The last time he saw it was immediately before the evacuation of the Australian and gunner's mate, Davis. It had been standing in the corner of the sickbay, to the right of the entrance. However, he didn't recall seeing it when he was in the sickbay prior to the recent medevac.

Holy shit, regardless of what I think of that Aussie, I had better find that duffel bag. Didn't he imply that it could be a matter of life or death? thought Brandon as he hurried back to the sickbay. As he reached the entrance he deliberately stopped and made an attempt to calm himself down. He now felt sure that there was something terribly wrong about this whole situation, and he did not wish to show his concerned feelings to anyone else on the ship. If this did go wrong he wanted to be in a position to disassociate himself from the Aussie and his mystery bag.

To his concern the duffel bag was not in the sickbay. It had disappeared. He retraced his footsteps taken during the previous hour or so, but without any luck. The duffel bag was gone.

He suddenly felt desperately tired and after checking out the bridge, he advised the officer of the watch that he would be retiring to his cabin, and should be called immediately should anything out of the ordinary occur.

He entered his cabin in a confused state. He couldn't remember the last time he felt this concerned.

Over what? A secret bloody duffel bag, belonging to a secret bloody foreigner, from a secret unit on a secret bloody mission?

Then he saw it. The duffel bag! Lying on his bunk. There were also four other bags, standard army backpacks. He recognised them as the ones worn by the four injured special forces troopers.

He sat staring at them for nearly an hour. Who had put them there? What was in them? Were they really that important, and to whom were they important?

What the hell am I letting myself in for? he asked himself as he stowed the duffel bag and the four backpacks away in a locker, having decided to follow the mysterious Australian's instructions to the letter.

## Chapter Eleven

Things had been hectic since arriving back from the mission. Rather than send the USS *James Cunningham* back to Hawaii for repairs the admirals had decided to do the work where it was. In terms of battle damage it was agreed by the powers that be that the ship was relatively lightly damaged. Thus for three weeks it was crowded with engineers and fitters, both Navy and Army. Oxyacetylene torches flamed and sparked all over the ship while the damage, particularly to the flight deck, was repaired.

Brandon had many exhausting days of intelligence debriefings, and suffered inquiry after inquiry regarding every single incident, both storm and battle related, that had occurred on the *James Cunningham* throughout the mission. His greatest traumas, however, related to the extensive enquiries into the deaths connected with the mission.

He had moved into quarters ashore, and though he could never really explain why, he had hidden the duffel bag and the backpacks which he had placed in two very large holdalls in the loft space just above his wardrobe, having first checked the loft out for rats and other vermin. He had decided to do what the Aussie had demanded. No more. No less. Virtually to pretend that the bags did not exist and to hand them over as instructed when the time came. Other than that, he did not want to know.

The bags were nothing but trouble. They had become the source of sleepless nights and had caused him to resort to the uncharacteristic practice of drinking. He found himself more and more turning to the bourbon bottle for solace. He felt more lonely than he had ever felt before, and this reflected on his work and his increasingly strained relationships with his officers and crew. As for the officials and engineers who were working on his ship's repairs, they were daily harassed and harangued by Brandon, whose level of tolerance was at an all-time low.

Initially he had tried to track down Senator or whatever his name was, putting on an act of being a concerned officer considering the welfare of a fellow officer who had served with him, and whose life he had saved. This ploy did not work, as it seemed that nobody knew the whereabouts of the Australian. Senator had apparently vanished off the face of the earth; or that's how it seemed.

When, in a moment of near desperation, he had discussed the matter with his immediate superior he had been advised to forget all about it.

'Leave it, David. It was just another mission. I know it went very badly for you and your crew, but things are not going to be made any better by trying to find a scapegoat for what happened. You're under a lot of stress, boy. Perhaps you should see the Doc about some R and R. Your EO Tincey is up and about again. Perhaps he can take care of the ship while you take a few days off somewhere.'

So that's what they think is wrong with me. Stress? Battle fatigue? I had better shake out of this pretty quick or they are going to take my command off me, he thought as he left the boss's office and made his way back to the ship.

After that incident he worked hard on containing his emotions and put a lot of effort into his relationships with both crew and contractors. His act was obviously convincing because word got back to the office of the Admiral that he was getting over his problems and was pretty much back to normal.

That was how it appeared to everyone he dealt with during working hours. However, each evening when he returned to his own private space in his apartment the curtain of gloom and doom fell once more on David Brandon, and he retreated into himself and into the bourbon bottle.

The bags? Well, they just stayed in the loft where he had put them, where they seemed in his often drunken state to hang over him like the sword of Damocles.

The call came a month later, by which time his nerves were shot to pieces and he was beginning to panic about the duffel bag, wondering what he would do with it when he moved back on board in a few days' time at the end of the refit and repairs.

The phone rang at 6 a.m., waking him from a fitful, disturbed sleep.

'Brandon here,' he said curtly. 'Who the hell is this at six in the morning?' he continued, suddenly feeling anxious and hoping it was not a senior officer, or even some poor sailor merely doing his job.

'Good morning, Vietnam,' came the distinctly Australian voice. 'Senator! I trust that you still have my property, David.'

Brandon could not believe the gall of the man.

'Yes, I have your fucking property. Just who the hell do you think you are?'

'Shut up and listen. I will collect the bags at eight o'clock tonight. Leave your front door unlocked and turn off all lights. Have the bags ready and do not ask any questions. Whatever happens, you will only hand them over to me, do you understand?'

Brandon was on the verge of telling him to get fucked, but decided against it. Something told him he was on very dangerous grounds, and that Senator was not a man to trifle

---

with. In any case, the phone went dead while he was trying to think of a suitable retort.

He couldn't get back to sleep, and before his jeep arrived to pick him up at 7.30 a.m. he had checked out the bags in the loft, twice.

During the day his nerves were so bad and he looked so pale and drawn that several people commented on how unwell he seemed. He somehow managed to maintain the outward good nature that he had worked so hard to portray over the previous weeks since his boss had suggested he see the doctor. He laughed it off and told everyone who asked that he had had an unfortunate disagreement with a bottle of bourbon, and the bourbon had won.

Knowing his reputation for not drinking too much or too often, everyone accepted this story with a sympathetic smile. What they didn't know was that he was now a heavy drinker and his battles with the bottle had become a nightly reality. However, no hangover in the world could have caused Brandon the pain and concern that he presently felt.

By the time he got back to his apartment at six o'clock that evening he was a nervous wreck. He immediately got the bags down from the loft, dusted them down and checked them for damage.

For the first time since that night on the beach when the Australian had handed him the first bag he began to think about its weight. At least once in the past month or more he had thought back to that night on the beach and marvelled at how he could have carried both the Aussie and this very heavy bag. Not once until now had he considered how much it really weighed. He carried it into the bathroom and dropped it on to the scales that the previous tenants had left when they returned stateside.

Forty-four kilos? Shit, what's in this fucking duffel bag?

He then weighed the four backpacks and discovered that they each weighed between fifteen and twenty kilos.

The backpacks were each locked in a similar way to the duffel bag.

Once again he was tempted to try to pick the locks and examine the contents, but instinct told him that would be a stupid thing to do. They would be off his hands in a couple of hours and then he could forget all about the Australian, the mission and the bags, and get on with his life once more.

He concealed them behind a sofa, making sure that they would not be seen should he have any unexpected visitors.

'Unexpected visitors? Oh God, what if someone does call on me? Don't be so paranoid, Brandon. Who the hell would visit you? You've been such a miserable, unapproachable bastard that you're hardly likely to be on anyone's visiting list,' he said out loud to himself as he checked once more to see if the bags could be seen.

However, just in case he decided that the best thing to do was to turn off all the lights in the apartment and hopefully give the impression that he was out. He then settled down with a glass, a bucket of ice and bottle of bourbon and waited. It seemed like the longest wait of his life.

Just before eight o'clock he quietly unlocked his front door, then moved back into the lounge room and returned to his seat and the bottle of bourbon which by now was half empty. He shook the bottle and smiled to himself.

Be positive, David, it isn't half empty, it's half full. He chuckled out loud, quite pleased with his clever humour.

# Chapter Twelve

'What's so funny, Commander?'

Brandon was so shocked that he leapt up out of his seat, knocking his glass over and sending the bourbon bottle flying across the matted floor.

'Jesus Christ! You scared the shit out of me.'

'Sit down man and calm your nerves. Your drunken paranoia is giving me the shits.' Senator's voice came at him from the darkness. There was no doubt in Brandon's mind that this was the voice of a person who should be obeyed without question. He sat down quickly.

Suddenly he could see him. He was across the room, sitting in a wheelchair of some sort. There was another person standing alongside him. A small, slightly built man. The extreme shock of finding the man Senator in the room had temporarily caused Brandon to lose his night vision but as he calmed down it was quickly returning.

The man with Senator was the small black soldier who had been with him on the beach that night, the only one of the mission team who was not wounded. For some unknown reason, the first thing that came to Brandon's mind was that it must have been this man who had placed the duffel and other bags in his cabin during the confusion of the helicopter evacuations.

Senator – Brandon wished to God that he knew this guy's real name – was leaning slightly to his right side, and his left leg was encased in plaster from the thigh to below the knee and was stretched out in front of him resting on a metal framework protruding from the front of the chair. He was wearing a sling on his right arm which was extended across his chest with his hand resting up by his left shoulder. He was dressed in what appeared to be pyjamas, with the left leg cut away to allow for the heavily plastered leg, and had a dressing gown splayed across his shoulders.

'What are you doing here in that condition?' asked Brandon, badly shaken by the appearance of the man.

'Well, David, I am extremely touched by your concern for my health, but I'm really not here. I'm too sick to be moved, and at this very moment I am in bed under sedation,' chuckled Senator, 'and there are two witnesses to that fact who really believe it is me in that bed. I understand that you have been asking after me, Davey boy. That was a pretty stupid thing to do, and you will never do it again, will you?' His tone was most threatening as he spoke the last two words.

'The kitbag, David, or the duffel bag as you yanks call them, and the backpacks!' demanded the Aussie with an authority that seemed out of place for a man in a wheel-chair. 'I know you still have them and that you haven't tried to open them. Lucky for you that you didn't. You see, the duffel bag has a nasty little device concealed inside that bloody great ugly padlock, and just in case you, or someone else, tried to cut the bag open it also has little wires threaded around the material which all connect up to that same nasty little device I mentioned. If you had tried to force the lock or cut the bag open you would have lost your family jewels and a few other major working parts. Poof!

'Oh, by the way, talking about poofs, are you aware that some of your officer club friends are putting it around that you are a shirt-lifter, a horse's hoof, or as you yanks put it, gay. I could never get used to the idea that those bastards have stolen one of the nicest words in the English language to describe themselves.

'Don't worry, David,' he continued as he saw Brandon open his mouth to protest. 'We know that there is nothing queer about you, boy. By the way, that little Vietnamese girl whose nose you broke was doing all right. She got her nose fixed with all that money you chucked at her but alas, just last night she had a road accident. It seems that some bastard ran her over with a truck and failed to stop. That's war, isn't it? It breeds some unscrupulous bastards.'

Brandon slumped back into his seat with shock as he thought about the poor girl and what he had done to her on that awful night.

'Why did you do that to her? She did nothing to you,' he sobbed.

'What makes you think I did anything to her, David?' Senator sneered, 'I was just giving you a traffic report. Now grow up! That girl was a threat to your future, to our future. She can't hurt us any more so stop snivelling and get those bags. Now!' The last word came out with a ferocity that shook Brandon.

He quickly rose to his feet and walked across the room to the settee, still shocked with the news that he had just been given. Not just the death of the girl, but the fact that Senator had been keeping such close tracks on him. He seemed to know everything about him, and obviously knew more about the so-called accident than just reporting the traffic news. Senator had arranged for that poor kid to be killed and it was all tied up with this crazy duffel bag and the other bags that he was now handing over.

He took them out from their place of concealment behind the settee and made to hand them to Senator, but he was intercepted by the black man who said, 'Careful, Commander, we don't want to hurt my man, do we?'

Brandon looked towards the man in the wheelchair who nodded. 'Give them to Felix.'

At last one of them had a name, something Brandon could relate to.

'Do you know what is in these bags, David?' asked the Aussie. 'A hundred kilos of the finest grade heroin I have ever had the pleasure of obtaining. This is the first of many consignments that you and I are going to handle, and we are both going to be millionaires.'

Brandon gasped in amazement at what he had just been told. He couldn't believe that this was happening to him. Suddenly he was involved in drug trafficking, and possibly murder. His whole life was falling apart at the seams, yet he had done nothing wrong. He had merely obeyed what he had believed at the time were legal military orders.

The anger welled up inside him and suddenly he could contain it no longer. The thought went through his mind that if he could get the drugs back and hand them over to the authorities he might be able to drag himself out of this mess. It all happened so fast. His brain seemed to be bursting. He lunged at the wheelchair in an attempt to grab the duffel bag.

Suddenly his world went white; he felt as if he was floating on a large fluffy cloud. Then it all went black, jet black.

## Chapter Thirteen

Brandon was vaguely aware of the darkness. A black face. The face was close to his. His brain was swimming and he started to feel pain in the back of his head. Violent pain.

The face became clearer. It was the man called Felix, and the man was pouring something over Brandon's face, something cold. The room was no longer in darkness. The drapes were drawn and a small table lamp was casting an almost eerie light across the room and on to the out-stretched leg of Senator, whose upper body and face were still in the shadow.

'He's come back home, boss.'

'That was a pretty dumb thing to do, David. Felix is one of the most efficient killers in Vietnam. Fortunately for you he only gave you a gentle kiss this time. If ever you even think of touching me, harming me, I will give him the word, Davey, and that word is, kill.

'The only reason that you are still alive is because I owe you for saving my life back on that beach. I am really grateful to you. That is why I have decided to cut you in.

'No self-righteous protestations now. I've got you by the short and curlies, David. I own you and you had better get used to the idea,' Senator said with a snarl. 'You really had better get used to this, mate, because if you don't, I may have to arrange another hit and run, only with Felix around I won't need to hire a truck.'

Brandon felt a cold chill engulf his entire body.

The Australian threw a small parcel into Brandon's lap. 'Before I tell you what this is all about, and how you fit into the story, I want you to open that parcel and contemplate your future.'

Brandon looked at the parcel and then back to the big man in the wheelchair who snapped, 'Open it! Then let's start again from scratch. I don't often give people second chances, David.'

Brandon fumbled nervously with the wrapping, but was finding it difficult. His head was throbbing with pain and he still felt somewhat disoriented. At last the parcel dropped open, and as it did his jaw also dropped open, very wide!

The parcel contained wads of new American banknotes. Lots of them.

'Fifty thousand bucks, David. Your share of instalment one, and the first of many such payments in the future. You have the potential to earn millions of dollars within the next few years, and all you have to do is act as the ferryman for my boys. I want you to be my deliveryman. I'm not asking you if you are in or out, David. I'm telling you that you are definitely in, because there isn't any future for you in being out. I'm sure you know what I mean.'

Brandon cowered back in his seat. He had no doubt what Senator meant, and he really believed him. He had no alternative but to co-operate, at least for the time being. What else could he do? Anything was better than incurring the wrath of this man and Felix, his personal ambassador of death. He nodded, still stunned by the amount of money that he held in his hands.

'All right, David, I am going to tell you all that you need to know and no more. If ever you make enquiries about me, other than directly from me, I'll instruct Felix to handle the answers to your enquiries. Understand?'

Brandon nodded quickly. There was no point in antagonising the man. He was very frightened and still struggling to come to grips with the situation that he found himself in.

Senator continued, 'Firstly I do not have a name as far as you are concerned. If ever you speak to me, you will call me Senator. Got that?'

Before Brandon could acknowledge him, the man continued.

'As you know, my people are not supposed to be here any more. In fact, I'm definitely not here. Believe me.' He laughed. 'According to the records in my country I am presently somewhere else in the world involved in a commercial project that is making big export dollars for Australia. Commercially, posterity will record that I am a good bloke doing his bit for his country. I have a man representing me in that area who, believe it or not, actually looks like me. Poor sod!

'For a few years I served Queen and Commonwealth doing all sort of nasty things in a unit that would make the green berets and the SAS look like the boy scouts. Most of the work I did was so hush-hush that even the Government didn't know about it. Believe me, it was cloak and dagger, but without the decency of the cloak. The man who ran the show had got it down to a fine art. A former military leader and Cabinet Minister, he knew his way around the Government and bureaucracy and he had somehow managed to screw a budget out of some obscure branch of some obscure government agency. Then under the guise of operating an overseas aid agency he set up the enterprise, mainly to make money for himself.

'Mostly he employed ex-special forces men who were too over-the-top, even for their own people. Everyone was carefully selected and screened, and the unit commanders were specially headhunted, if you'll excuse the expression,' he chuckled to himself again, and Brandon noticed that Felix, if it was really his name, was also smiling widely, 'from senior positions around the world.

'His business was so dicey that in many cases candidates who turned down the offer to join were terminated. This was particularly the case with relation to recruitment of commanders. It was really this factor that led to his ultimate downfall.

'Anyway, as I said, I had been a senior officer in a special forces unit, and had also done a few freelance jobs in Africa, when I was approached and recruited. I didn't really want to join the firm, but decided that it was better to be in than dead. You see, David, they put this little bastard on my case.' He pointed at Felix and they both burst into laughter. 'I've had to put up with him ever since. Nine years now.

'Each of the units comprised five or six men, and during my time with the firm my unit operated solely in South-East Asia. It was mainly contracts, termination, that sort of thing. Sometimes one person, and sometimes whole units were removed.

'Coming from the conservative background of the Navy, you would be surprised how many people, for power or personal gain, will pay for the permanent and violent removal of their opposition, military or civil. Sometimes we carried out jobs and left clues that would lay the blame at someone else's door, more often than not merely to obtain political brownie points. You know what I mean. This sort of deception has always happened in the Asian region. It still does.

'Payment was always in heroin, gold or diamonds, or whatever. Never money! It can often come back to haunt you.

'Anyway, our boss man back in Aussie got too greedy. In order to expand his business he decided to set up more units and it was during this exercise that they put the finger on him.'

'Who were they? I'm not sure that I understand what you mean,' interrupted Brandon.

'Shut up and you'll find out. It is important for our future business relationship that you learn to listen, not talk.'

Brandon was still nursing a very bruised and aching head, so he decided he had better sit back and let the Australian get on with it. He sat back in the chair, resting his throbbing head on a cushion while Senator continued.

'Unknown to any of us, the boss had had far more refusals in his recruitment campaign than were good for business. His hit squads were very efficient and the people concerned never got a second chance to consider the offer. Even our unit sometimes hit people who had probably committed the sin of refusing the boss. Ours not to reason why, and all that shit. However, far from ensuring the security of the business it set the dogs on his trail. Virtually every special forces outfit in the world was not only losing some of its best people, but many of those people were eventually turning up dead.

'The Yanks, Brits and French got their heads together and established a team, code-named "Seeker". You can imagine, they were the very best. What an outfit. Within eighteen months they had totally wiped out seven of our units. Two more had dispersed and gone to ground, most of them were knocked off, one by one. One unit defected to the French and shopped the boss. Poor stupid bastards. They all died in a very nasty way when the minibus they were travelling in just south of Bangkok was hit by a runaway gas tanker that exploded and burst into flames. Some fucking accident. Still, serves the bastards right. They should have known better.

'The boss fell out of the top floor window of a high-rise hotel in Sydney. Funny that. He wasn't even staying at the place. They put it down to suicide. The Government was so blissfully unaware of his business interests that it gave him a right old send off. Honoured citizen and all that crap.

'Unfortunately he left squillions of dollars in a Swiss bank account that we have not yet been able to get our hands on. We will eventually though.

'However, the saddest blow of all was when my unit was totally wiped out.' This comment was met with loud laughter from Felix who had just returned from the kitchen, having made everyone a cup of coffee.

'Felix got on to them first,' said Senator, stirring sugar into his coffee. 'He recognised a guy called Louis Leverdier, an ex-legionnaire he had served with in some obscure African revolution. Sadly on the wrong side, eh Felix? Tell David what happened while I drink this. I'm out of condition. Not used to all this exercise and excitement.' He chuckled to himself as he raised the cup to his lips.

'Well, we was in a place called Siem Reap in Cambodia. We had just bumped off a mess of bad guys and made it look like it was done by the good guys, so the other bad guys could then start a little war with some respectability. You know, David, the usual sort of shit.' He chuckled at the confused look on Brandon's face.

'I recognised Louis straight off. I was with him in Angola when he caught a big splinter from a grenade deep in his right thigh. He was hurt real bad and lost lots of blood as well as one of his balls.' The memory of this seemed to amuse Felix tremendously. 'I carried the big ungrateful French prick for thirty miles. We were fighting a rearguard action all the way, before we were picked up by our boys. Seventy guys went in, and only five of us flew out. Well, at first there was six of us and the pilot, all packed into a one-engine Cessna, with every bastard in Africa firing at us.

'One of the guys got a stray bullet in the back of the head so we chucked him out at three thousand feet. He was a big bastard, so I hope he fell on someone important. Anyways, when you've been that close to a man like I was to Louis, you don't forget him. You even get to know his smell and recognise the sound of his breathing.

'Anyway, I recognised him and knew that he must be after us. That's fucking gratitude for you. I mean, I saved that bastard's life, man.'

'Get on with the story, Felix. None of your black dramatics, thank you,' interrupted Senator with a smile.

'Yeh, boss! Right, David! That night our team was due to fly out in an old DC3 freighter, and head back south to Pnom Penh. About an hour before we were due to fly out, me and the boss here,' he indicated Senator, 'hid out and watched Louis and his pals sneak in and fix something to the undercarriage of the plane. Then they just got into their four-wheel drive and hit the road south, probably not wanting to get caught up in the war that we had just helped start. The boss and me checked out what they had left for us and found it was a big bastard with a timing device that was set to go off a couple of hours after take-off.'

*

Having finished his coffee Senator now resumed the story. 'It was important for our survival that Leverdier and his mates believed that they had wiped out our unit, and the only way this could occur was for the team to die. They were expendable you see, David.'

'But what about your two?' asked Brandon. 'I can see that you saved your own skins, but from what you say these guys are not stupid, so they must still be tracking you.'

'They probably would have been if we hadn't arranged for me and Felix to die in the plane as well.

'Luckily for us, earlier that week we had come across two backpackers in the town. They were doing the usual hippy thing, taking an R and R on junk. It's the only tourist attraction in that area. Only deadbeats and people like us go to those parts of the world, you see.

'Unfortunately for them they were pretty much our size, and very conveniently one was blackish. Americans or Canadians we think. They were high on booze and drugs when we found them that night. We terminated them with our hands. Couldn't risk them being found with wounds. We took them to the strip and hid their bodies, dressed in our clothes of course, in the rear of the plane amongst some freight.

'Just before the flight was due to take off I received a pre-arranged radio message from the guy we had just worked for. This message helped us to convince the other members of the unit that our contact had given us another small job to do. I instructed them to proceed without us and arranged to join them later in Pnom Penh. They accepted the story and were happy to get the hell out of there, so the plane took off.

'Apparently, fortunately for Felix and me, the plane caught fire and burned out when it crashed after the explosion, but all the bodies were accounted for. We were later told that there was a big Frenchman with a bad limp who arrived out of nowhere and volunteered to assist the authorities. He vouched that the bodies were those of his friends who he had seen off at Siem Reap.

'A couple of days later Leverdier and his mates were caught in a small ambush on the road to Pnom Penh, and before they could escape Leverdier was shot and killed. The ambush was blamed on the Khmer Rouge, but in fact it was carried out by our associates who had been paid well to ensure that Leverdier did not remain in circulation.

'After all, David, if we are to be dead, it would be pretty dumb to have someone floating around in our line of business who can identify my shadow here. Don't you agree?'

'You are a cold, heartless bastard. They were your own men you had killed.'

'For a start I didn't have them killed, someone else did that. I just made sure that we weren't killed with them, Davey boy. Definitely a preferable and sensible alternative scenario.

'Anyway, Felix and I know our way around South-East Asia like the backs of our hands. We each speak at least two of the languages fluently, and get by with most of the others. I've got a large number of top Vietnamese officials, military and civil, on both sides of the border, by the balls. I also have similar contacts in Cambodia, Laos and Thailand, and am developing a few useful contacts in the People's Republic of China.

'I am in a position with each of them to either tighten my grip on their balls or cut them off, and they all know it because of information and evidence that I hold. I have got access to a large pool of money and other resources, and quite frankly I am generally seen as being a fucking good bloke to have on one's side. The end result is that I have many serious business partners all over South-East Asia.

'Because of my experience, influence and contacts your top brass have taken to me like a pig to shit, and have contracted me, so to speak, to lead special forces teams into places where it would not be appropriate or wise for their guys to go. You see, to them Felix and I are expendable. For that dubious privilege your government pays me a heap of money.

'That mission that we'd just completed, the one you picked us up from, was to assassinate a top NVA general, name of Kwan. The military here thought it was a bloody good idea. Incidentally, what they didn't know was that their views on the demise of General Kwan were shared by another NVA boss, General Hieu, whom I know from way back. Hieu was having the screws put on him by his chum Kwan over his drug running extra-curricular activities.

'I visited my mate and did a deal on the understanding that he would set up the target for me at an appropriate time. The US military, for whom I work as a mercenary, Christ, I hate that word,' he laughed noisily, 'provided me with a team of men, paid me well for the deal and provided the transport and support, both in and out.

'My NVA chum, Hieu, contacted me with the details of when and where I could hit Kwan, who incidentally was very important to the North Vietnamese war effort, but a far too ethical and dedicated communist for my friend's liking. I went in and did the job on our poor unfortunate general. My mate paid me in heroin, which you now know all about, and we got the hell out of it. Your people paid me too, but what the hell?

'Sadly, we didn't allow sufficiently for one factor. General Kwan's troops were pretty pissed off about losing their boss and came after us with a vengeance. We had been given the wrong intel, and believed that Kwan's regiment was involved in an offensive to the west, and too far off to cause us any immediate concern. While we were in transit to the killing zone, however, the whole fucking regiment had returned home from its war games.

'Their commander, a Colonel Lo, a bloody good soldier by the way, caught some of my men and did some God-awful things to them to try to find out what we were doing and where we were going. A dreadful waste of time and energy on his part for they knew nothing, and a damn shame for those soldiers to have to die in that terrible manner. We could hear their screams from miles away.'

Senator's voice trailed off into silence for a moment. He then cleared his throat loudly. 'I have vowed that I will kill Lo some day. He will die in a manner that no man has experienced since medieval times. Take my word for it, David, that man is already dead. When I have finished with him he will not be admitted into heaven or hell. Now, where was I?'

Brandon was reeling with shock, and he was physically shaken by the venom in Senator's voice as he told of his plans for the ill-fated Colonel Lo.

'Yes, David! You are to be our deliveryman. I have acquired a very special and important friend in your Navy Department who will ensure that you get all of the shit jobs that relate to our missions. Incidentally, in case you were wondering, that is why you were specially selected for the last mission. It was also why your pleas for escort boats went unheeded. I couldn't afford to have too many sight-seers around the place. By the way, the Navy man does not know that you are involved, just that your ship is to be used.'

Everything started to fit into place now for Brandon. Shit, his Navy Department friend must be very high up in the system, he thought.

'You have already shown that you have the skills and the balls for such work, and it did not take much for my, ah friend, to convince his fellow top dogs that this should be so.'

'Just who the fuck do you think you are? You can't direct the US Navy, no matter how influential you think you may be in this region.'

'Can't, David? Can't is not in my vocabulary. I've already done it and will continue to do. Heroin currently has the most influential voice in the world, David, and don't you forget it.

'Your job is to ensure that I get in and out no matter what the risk to your ship and crew. You are going to become most, what do you yanks call it – gung-ho? Yes, that's the word. You will become renowned for the risks you take and the terror you strike into the hearts of the enemy, David.

'My friends and I are going to make sure that you become a war hero, and super bleeding rich into the bargain.

'What I have paid you tonight is only the tip of the iceberg. As long as this war continues we are in the money. And don't forget, David, Felix and I are taking the greatest risks. You are mainly just the deliveryman, the taxi driver, so to speak, but an extraordinarily highly paid taxi driver.

'You are also going to get all the kudos and the medals. That will probably help your ego and overcome your stupid anxiety. Look upon yourself as sort of modern-day privateer, David. Like they used to, you'll be doing all sorts of dangerous and exciting things, outwardly for honour and glory, but really for your own personal gain.'

'What if I tell you to go to hell, and that I'm not interested?' shouted Brandon, almost foaming at the mouth with anger.

'You will die, David. Quickly and without mercy. And, should you be stupid enough to share the knowledge with anyone else, they will die too. Believe me, matey, you are already in this up to your arse, and there is no way out.'

David Brandon felt a terrible chill engulf his entire body as he slumped back into his chair. He had never felt like this before in his life. He was a defeated and ruined man.

Senator continued. 'That girl. The one that you belted up. We had no choice. You see, she had found herself a lover boy, a stores major who we know to be involved in all sorts of graft. We are pretty sure that she hadn't told him about you, because he was overheard telling another officer that if only she would tell him who beat her up he would fix him.

'Anyway, she had to go just in case she did decide to talk. It really was a road accident, or that is what the police reports all show. We'll keep an eye on our stores officer chum for a while, just in case.'

Brandon was still shaking as the result of what was happening to him, and his voice came in a sob when he next spoke. 'Why are you telling me so much, and why me? Why did you pick on me?'

'Quite simple, David. We need a ship's captain. It has to be a ship that can be used for missions such as ours. The man had to be good at his job. You were a perfect choice. You are a bit of a loner. You have no commitment to a woman, family, or anyone else it seems.

'You are a bit pissed off with the Navy at the moment, which incidentally we do not want to continue. Our plans require you to become a very happy sailor chappie once more. That is most important to our plans. You will stop your incessant moaning and complaining and get back to being the sort of bloke you used to be; not too long ago, we are told. War heroes cannot be miserable bastards. It's somehow out of character.

'However, your pissed-offness with the Navy was a bonus to me as it made you vulnerable and an easier target for us. I'm sorry, David, but that's how things are.'

'What do I do now?' queried Brandon, still struggling to come to grips with the situation.

'You do absolutely nothing. Just what the Navy tells you, and of course, whenever we meet you, or if I contact you, you will obey my instructions to the letter. If you are worrying about the bags, then rest your mind. That will never happen again. It was just because I copped this packet of aggro that I had to put that chore on your plate.

'Felix has got up the noses of a few people whom we work for. He has a bad posture that man.' Both he and Felix laughed. 'Mainly because of this he could not have carried those bags ashore as easily as you, so I had no alternative. Considering what a paranoid bastard you are I suppose you did quite well under the circumstances.

'I have to go now, David, but before I do I have one instruction for you, and it relates to tonight, or what is left of it. Listen to me and do exactly what I tell you. Your mates, Captain Andrew and Commander Neville, the ones who are putting it around that you are a poofter, have been invited to a special evening of fun and games. The sort of games that they will probably enjoy very much. Lots of very young girls, and boys. Just children really, but exactly what your mates are after. It's mainly because you don't share their enthusiasm for that sort of sport that they are trying to destroy you.

'Well, they are all going along to this special shindig and it is important that you have a watertight story about where you are and what you are doing this evening, and throughout most of the night. You see, David, whilst these grubby bastards are enjoying themselves with those little kids, and sadly for the kids we will have to give your mates a head start, they are going to be raided and caught. Not by their navy buddies who might be inclined to cover up for them, but by a very nasty-minded bunch of South Vietnamese police who are currently tracking down the organisers of a paedophile business amongst the US military here in Saigon. The shit will be flying high and will reach the Pentagon and even the White House by morning.

'I do not want you to be anywhere near, or for anyone to think that you were either involved in the party or in shopping your mates. You see, the police have been notified of the party by an informer with an American accent.

'It will be known by the powers that be that both Andrew and Neville have reported on you at some stage. That is the only, if not very vague connection between them and you. But someone might try to put two and two together and we don't need that sort of problem.

'Your executive officer, Lieutenant Tincey, is out of hospital and presently kicking his heels in his quarters. I have it on good authority that he has promised himself an early night tonight.

'You are going to change his plans for him, David. I want you to tidy yourself up, put on your uniform and call on him. Take him to the officers' club, which incidentally is at the other end of Saigon to where your mates will be finding themselves in deep shit. Treat him to a great, boozy night out to welcome him back from the dead, so to speak.

'Lay it on like a special tribute to a war hero from his commanding officer. After all, he will be getting a Purple Heart for his little escapade. Involve as many of your fellow officers as you can and spend a bit of money on them. Not too much, but enough for them to remember your presence and your generosity tonight. Regardless of what happens you must stay at the club until at least 2 a.m. Don't get yourself too pissed and be tempted to go out on the town. That is a definite no-no! Got it?'

Brandon was totally confused, but he nodded his head.

'No matter if you have a bad head tomorrow. Do as I say and you will be the last person who could possibly be suspected as an informant in what will turn out to be just about the messiest thing the US military has ever been involved with. Believe me, David, there will be so much embarrassment over this episode that there is bound to be someone who will believe and try to prove the existence of a whistle-blower within the service.

'Unfortunately, it will also be very good press for the anti-war lobby, but our little business is far too important for that to get in our way. These people who are trying to get at you can undermine our whole future now that you are part of the firm, so to speak. They have got to be destroyed. We have no alternative.'

Brandon felt quite sick and excused himself, saying he needed to go to the john. When he returned to the living room the Australian and Felix had gone. All that remained to convince him that he had not dreamed it all was that little paper package, torn open and with its contents spread all over his armchair and on to the floor.

Still in a daze he returned to the bathroom where he took a long cool shower, allowing the streams of water to hammer over his still-throbbing head. He then went into his bedroom and removed a uniform from his closet and slowly dressed himself.

★

At 10 p.m. that evening he entered the officers' club leading a surprised and rather flattered John Tincey. Brandon was pleased to see that the club was full. He spoke to the head steward and ordered champagne for anyone who cared to join him in congratulating Lieutenant John Tincey on his Purple Heart, and welcoming him safely back to active duty on the USS *James Cunningham*.

The word quickly got around about the party which was later joined by two captains and an admiral. The party continued at the officers' club until about 4 a.m., and was a great success from everyone's point of view, particularly the Senator's.

*Part Two*

Ajax Bay
San Carlos Water
Falkland Islands

June 1982

# Chapter One

Everything was a red haze, and the pain was unbelievable.

Jesus Christ! Will somebody please help me. Someone please stop the pain.

He had never known such intense pain. Everywhere! All over his body. He knew that he was badly hurt, but had no idea how badly and what sort of injuries he was suffering.

Where the hell am I? Why am I here? What has happened to me? The questions roared through his brain. The fact that he could not answer them only made matters worse.

The man could hear voices and moans of pain coming from all around him, and was aware that he was lying on something soft. A bed? Surely not a real bed. What bliss after all that time sleeping in the cave and the cellar. He must be safe at last.

He tried opening his eyes and focusing on his surroundings. Through the haze and the pain he felt sure that he could see a ceiling above him. Yes! He was inside a building of some sort. The ceiling seemed quite low and was a dull, dirty grey in colour. Grey? Concrete grey? There were large rusty hooks hanging from this strange ceiling.

Who the hell has large rusty hooks hanging from their bedroom ceiling? a voice inside his confused mind asked.

Then there was a real voice. It came from outside his head. It wasn't his mind playing tricks on him. Whoever it was appeared to be speaking with some authority. The voice was close by and getting louder. It was a man, and he was speaking in English. He had a broad London accent.

Thank God, I'm not a prisoner. The Argies haven't captured me, he thought, his spirits suddenly lifting as he realised he was with his own people. The Brits!

He felt sure that the man was speaking to him but he was unable to move his head towards the voice. Exactly who was speaking to him, and where this concrete bedroom was, puzzled him greatly.

He tried hard to speak, to communicate with this man, but couldn't manage a single whimper. Every move he made was agony and he felt as if someone was gripping his mouth shut to stop him speaking.

Why the fuck would somebody want to stop me speaking? he thought to himself, just as a wave of pain sent him hurtling into the strange, hazy red surreal world of mental oblivion. Fortunately unconsciousness also brought with it relief from the terrible agonies that his badly savaged body was suffering.

'Poor bastard's gone off again, boss.'

'Thanks, Chief. I'll look in on him later. Meanwhile, apply some fresh flamazine to those chest and shoulder burns. Christ! He barely has any skin left to grow back. Thank goodness his back wasn't burnt as well. At least the poor sod has got something to lie on. Not like those Welsh Guards boys coming in from the *Galahad*. I must go, Chief. It's a nightmare out there. Do what you can for this one, then come on over to the admission ward.'

The Lieutenant Commander and the Chief Petty Officer both laughed out loud. Admission ward? What a joke!

★

It was 8th June, 1982, and the Falklands War had been going for well over a month. The medical unit in which the Chief Petty Officer worked was a pretty basic and ramshackle affair. It was set up in a disused meat works on the shore of Ajax Bay. On the door of the building had been painted the legend, *Welcome to the Red and Green Life Machine,* and that was precisely what the place was, a life machine.

It was the life centre for many wounded men, both British and Argentinian, where they were patched up and made comfortable, and in many cases where they underwent substantial emergency life saving surgery before being lifted off by Casevac Wessex helicopters. Their destination the SS *Uganda*, the Red Cross hospital ship, fondly known as Mother Hen.

Had the soldier in question been capable of understanding he would probably have gained some comfort from the fact that this small, temporary front-line medical unit had not lost a patient.

Sometimes, however, *Uganda* was not readily available. Owing to her Red Cross status she was required to stay within the battle exclusion zone several hundred miles offshore. In bad weather, and there really wasn't much of any other sort of weather in and around the Falkland Islands in June 1982, it was often not practical or safe for helicopters to risk such long journeys.

The Navy had already lost Harrier Jets that had apparently lost their way in the white-out conditions and eventually run out of fuel.

In the event of the non-availability of *Uganda* the wounded were transferred to one of several Royal Navy vessels, closer by, that were equipped with full surgical facilities. Some were sent to the SS *Canberra* that had brought so many of the combat troops from the UK to this almost forgotten and many would believe, godforsaken part of the world. *Canberra* was now used as a hospital ship.

Whilst it was a medically sound decision to get the wounded to the best facilities at the earliest time, if they were placed on warships they were still subject to the rules of war that related to that ship at that time.

At this point in the war the British were losing too many of their front-line ships with such medical facilities, and because of this they tried not to leave wounded men on warships for too long.

At the moment though, there were no spare helicopters available, otherwise this badly wounded and burnt soldier would have been on his way to one of those better facilities. Instead he would have to continue lying in pain in that abandoned concrete meat works that his pain-ridden mind was telling him was a bedroom, and that had seen much better times.

The man had only arrived that morning, having been brought in by helicopter from somewhere in the west of the islands. The man had been accompanied by some paras and another dirty and dishevelled man who had declined treatment for a wound to the hand. The Chief Petty Officer had tried to insist but the man refused, and did so with some authority. The manner with which the paras deferred to him indicated that he held a senior rank, so the matter was not pursued.

At the moment the helicopters were all far too busy, frantically trying to lift survivors off the blazing decks of HMS *Galahad*, and from the sea nearby. She had received several hits from Mirage A4 Skyhawks of the Argentinian air force, the Fuerza Aerea Argentina, which had made a daring and almost suicidal attack at sea level across San Carlos Water. The *Galahad*, a large, troop-landing vessel was ill-equipped to repel such a ferocious attack.

Although several other ships engaged the aircraft, trying to prevent them getting at the *Galahad* at the critical time of disembarkation of its cargo of fresh troops to the beach head, the ship was hit several times and was on fire and mortally damaged.

*Galahad* carried the Welsh Guards, and the wounded being brought ashore were mostly suffering burns, many of them very serious burns, far worse than the soldier whom the Lieutenant Commander had just been treating. There were also several soldiers with other critical injuries, including missing limbs.

The soldier in question at the Red and Green Life Machine, whilst just another casualty of the war, was a casualty with a difference. The difference started with his long, unkempt dark-brown hair, and the pierced right ear, which in another place and another time would have sported a stud or a ring. In this war, however, nobody questioned the physical appearance of certain soldiers. He wore no badges of rank or unit, but he obviously belonged to one of those secret and special units. SAS? SBS? Who cared? He was a British soldier, wounded in a pretty nasty little war that was gradually wearing the British military down to the point where it was touch and go whether they could carry on so far from their main bases and reserves.

He could have been a corporal or a colonel, but nobody in the Red and Green Life Machine knew, nor was it their business to enquire. Their objective was to get him well enough for transfer to a hospital ship, or at least some better and safer facility than this one, at the earliest possible time.

These special soldiers, and surely that was what he was, were never debriefed in the same manner as others in the aftermath of combat. They answered only to the highest ranking officers, and to specific high-ranking officers at that.

It was not surprising to the medical staff of the Red and Green Life Machine therefore, that regular enquiries were made of this particular wounded soldier by no less than a Brigadier.

Being complete professionals they were also not surprised by the written order that stated that when the man regained consciousness, no other person, of whatever rank, was to speak to him about anything other than his physical well-being.

The order went on to state that the moment this soldier returned to consciousness the Brigadier was to be informed. The man would then be immediately evacuated by the Special Boat Squadron, destination probably unknown. Under no circumstances was he to be processed with the other wounded soldiers. Meanwhile he was to be kept segregated from all other personnel.

'They must think we are running the fucking Ritz down here. How in fuck's name do we segregate him when we are all living on top of each other?' mumbled the Sub Lieutenant who took the radio message.

'We'll just have to hang a blanket around his cot, Sub,' acknowledged the more experienced petty officer medic.

'As long as we are not expected to provide room service I'm sure we can handle that stupid little request. After all, *sir*,' he emphasised the word 'sir', 'we are the Royal Navy, and we've been fucked around by the Army for centuries. I mean, it was probably the Army sharpshooters in the rigging of HMS *Victory* who really shot Nelson, not the frigging French, so why should we get upset about a stupid little fucking signal like this one?'

The Sub Lieutenant smiled. 'You're lucky there are no Green Jackets amongst the gravel crunchers down here, Chief, or they would be having your balls for that. It was the 60th Rifles who were the sharpshooters on *Victory*, and they get pretty shitty with anyone who says what you just did. I should know, my brother's in that regiment.'

★

The wounded soldier who was the reason behind the conversation had slowly started to get his bearings and to understand pretty much where he was and roughly what his injuries were. He was a highly skilled field operative with extensive first aid and battle injuries knowledge and experience, and had served in some very nasty places, some of which the British army strenuously denied ever having been involved in.

He overheard the earlier conversation between the Lieutenant Commander and the Chief Petty Officer and was very concerned. He had a close friend attached to the Welsh Guards as an intelligence officer. If the Welshmen were on *Galahad* then perhaps his friend was too.

The sudden return of violent pain interrupted his train of thought regarding the possibilities of what may have happened to his friend. He must have called out in agony, because the Chief was suddenly alongside his cot.

'Going bad for you, friend? Don't worry, I'll fix you up.' He was only gone for a brief moment and when he returned he was holding a hypodermic syringe.

'Don't worry, soldier, this will take you off to some exotic play land for a while,' he whispered as he gently injected the needle into the man's right forearm. It worked almost instantly, but as the soldier relaxed into unconsciousness he heard the Chief Petty Officer's voice echoing in the distance.

'If you find a handsome bird with big knockers while you're out there in cuckoo land, give her one for me, mate.'

The soldier rapidly became deeply unconscious and did not hear the Chief finish the crude remark with a loud chuckle.

'Don't forget to let me know if you find that bird. If you do, and you get your end away, I just might have to take a shot of that stuff myself.'

The Chief Petty Officer moved off to tend to other wounded men thinking to himself, I wonder who he is, and what he has been up to over here. He's not one of your ordinary gravel crunchers, that's for sure.

The sailor was dead right. The man was no ordinary soldier. In fact, until just a very short time before the man had been doing a very different sort of job, for Queen and Country.

## Chapter Two

Belfast – Northern Ireland

On 11th March John Millane had arrived at work at the premises of McQuillan and Son, Civil Engineers, Wesley Street, East Belfast, at his usual starting time of 7 a.m.

Millane was a fitter and turner; a very good fitter and turner, and because of his high level of skills he generally got the high quality, big bonus jobs that were of the greatest importance to the firm. He was a top craftsman and was respected for it.

He hung his coat in the locker and placed his sandwiches in the tearoom fridge alongside the more elaborate, container-packed lunches of his workmates. Unlike them he didn't have a wife to prepare him such delicacies.

His workmates all knew he was single. They all knew that his sandwiches were bought each morning from the café at the end of the street where he regularly had his breakfast at 6.30 a.m. It was also well known that Widow Flaherty, the café owner, had a soft spot for him, and that she used to give him the very best of everything whenever he ate there.

It was not, however, a subject that Millane's workmates joked about, because Mrs Flaherty was a supporter of the Protestant paramilitary group, Belfast Regiment.

The workers also knew that he was one of her latest recruits, and quite fanatical about the cause. When dealing with people who were dedicated to taking on both the IRA and the British Army, if needs be, you just didn't joke about it. Like smoking, it could sometimes be detrimental to your health.

Millane was a loner, but quite a likeable type if, of course, you kept off politics. It was fairly easy to do that at McQuillan & Son, for the boss only employed Protestants, and the long-standing differences between the Protestants and the Catholics were the only politics to speak of in this neck of the woods. McQuillan didn't give a stuff about the equal opportunity crap promoted by the British Government in London, and refused point blank to comply with it.

McQuillan's family tree went right back to the Apprentice Boys of the great Battle of the Boyne, and it was no secret that he hated all Catholics and republicans with an intensity that most people, even the most ardent loyalist, found hard to believe.

It was rumoured that Widow Flaherty and the boss had got together to fix Millane up with the best job in the firm.

'But then that can't be true, 'cos isn't he after being a shit-hot tradesman, better than any of the rest of us here, and him being only twenty-seven years old. So why would anyone have to fix him up with the job when he is the only one with the skills to do it? I sure as hell couldn't do what he does, and I've been in the trade for yonks,' was the comment of one of the old hands when the rumour was put to him.

Nevertheless it really was true. McQuillan had arranged the job after a heart to heart with Mrs Flaherty. He and the widow woman were long-time intimate friends, and he was a dedicated financial supporter of the Belfast Regiment paramilitary. Neither of these facts were known to anyone other than Moira Flaherty and Michael McQuillan.

Millane had come to Moira Flaherty's attention when he stood up in a Catholic pub not too far away and had taken on two burly young IRA supporters who had burned a British flag on the floor of the public bar.

Millane had beaten them both senseless but had been done over badly for his sins and crass stupidity by the remainder of the pub's male clientele, and a few women as well. At least two of his less visible scars could be attributed to the stiletto heels of a couple of drunken and very vindictive good Catholic girls.

Moira had traced him to the local infirmary and, after a few visits, during which she brought him the usual hospital fare, fruit, chocolates and the like, she began to establish a close friendship. During their many conversations she discovered that he had recently been discharged after serving five years in the parachute regiment. An Ulsterman, and one-time staff sergeant, greatly disillusioned regarding what he saw as the biased and pro-Catholic stance of the British Army in Northern Ireland, he had declined to re-enlist. He had finished his tour of duty and had moved back to Belfast to fight for the Protestant cause in his own way.

During his final two years in the Army he had had many scrapes with both the military and civil police because of his violent approach to Catholics or anyone who appeared to sympathise with the IRA cause.

Moira had a contact in the Special Branch of the Royal Ulster Constabulary. A sympathiser of the cause, the Detective Inspector had done a full check on Millane, and had verified that he was on the level regarding his history. He was also able to fill in some of the other, less than military, exploits of this unhappy soldier.

The Inspector was known to be an informant, and over a period of years the Special Branch had used him in instances like this. At some future date he would be brought to book for his disloyalty and treasonable involvement with the Belfast Regiment, meanwhile he was extremely useful.

Not only was he responding to requests from the Regiment, but he was also feeding them fairly useless information deliberately made accessible to him by the British High Command and his own Special Branch bosses.

From there it was a relatively straightforward process for Millane to be approached with the view to him becoming a fully fledged member of the Belfast Regiment.

The first inducement was the offer of the job, which because of his background was right up his alley. In reality he was a highly qualified mechanical engineer with very special capabilities when it came to making intricate timing devices and things that went off with very nasty bangs. But that was a side to his life that the Detective Inspector was never to find out about.

★

His induction was fast and violent, although to his surprise and relief there were no incidents involving firearms or death. He made sure that the Regiment knew that he had some personal moral standards that he hoped he would retain until such time as it became essential to the cause that he relax them.

He was most definitely not all that he appeared to be. Knowing that he had been followed constantly during the first few months, he made sure that everything he did and said would satisfy the people who were overseeing his probationary period.

His mission was to infiltrate the organisation by what-ever means he considered appropriate, short of 'causing death or high-level violence', whatever that was supposed to mean. It seemed to be a cop-out on the part of his superiors. However, as an experienced soldier he felt that he knew how far was far enough.

As part of his duties to the cause he was involved in a few fights and private beatings of Catholic ne'er-do-wells, who would have probably been done over by their own in due course. On a couple of occasions he was also involved in exercising summary jurisdiction over Protestants who were either not doing their bit for the cause, or were too chummy with the RUC or the Brits. This involved some old-fashioned, hard physical violence.

In these incidents he gave it his all. At least he appeared to be doing that. As a highly trained commando he knew the ways in which one could beat another without causing any permanent damage. Nonetheless, the superficial wounds he inflicted looked bad enough to satisfy the Belfast Regiment, anyway.

It concerned him that he was assisting in the brutalisation of members of the public, a small number of whom had committed no greater sin than verbal support of the other side, a basic human right that as a child and throughout his Army service he had always been taught to uphold.

He was prepared to carry on though, for he wanted to work his way to the very top in the Belfast Regiment. If it meant beating a few people senseless to prevent the para-militaries killing others, then so be it. He knew that Moira Flaherty and Michael McQuillan were only pawns in the game; mere lieutenants of the real movers and shakers.

It was those movers and shakers, the top people, possibly high-ranking political figures, whom he really wanted to meet. If he was to move up through the system it would be that level of people that could make it happen, not the Moira Flahertys and Michael McQuillans of the world. They were a starting point for him, an introduction, and for that he was grateful. However, that was all they were.

## Chapter Three

The 11th March was just an ordinary day in terms of Millane's work at McQuillan's. He was working on a special job, making some parts for a very exclusive and expensive veteran car. The car, a 1918 Daimler, was fairly unique, and original parts were just not available any more.

During the time that he had worked for the firm he had proved his ability, and indispensability, time and again. Give him a blueprint, an accurate set of specifications and the right tools and materials, and he could make just about anything.

McQuillan was a clever businessman, and had quickly assessed Millane's skills. He came to a special financial arrangement with him, and within no time at all his company had become the main resource in Northern Ireland and other parts of the United Kingdom for those unique spare parts that nobody could obtain elsewhere. He even had a pool of well-paying clients in Southern Ireland, which amused him greatly.

Sure, he paid Millane nearly double the tradesman's wage, but he was worth every penny of it, and on top of everything he was a loyal and dedicated soldier to the cause. He could think of no better combination of qualities for a man to have when working for McQuillan & Son.

Just before lunchtime Millane found himself without a piece of special material and some parts that were essential for the job he was working on. McQuillan had screwed up again, and there was a deadline to meet if he was going to satisfy the client and get the fat bonus that was up for grabs.

He walked into the boss's office without knocking, a sure sign to McQuillan that his best worker was not happy.

'John, my boy, sure and haven't I spoken to that silly bastard, Kelly, at least three times about this, and hasn't he promised me on stacks of bibles that he would have the stuff here for me by now?'

'Cut the bullshit, Mr McQuillan; if I don't get it by this afternoon you won't get the job done, and the main reason that concerns me is that my bonus is on the line. You'll have to get on to it straight away or it just won't happen. There's at least three hours' work to do if the job is to be completed on time.'

'Okay, John, I'll arrange to get it couriered here straight away. Meanwhile, why don't you go and get yourself a cup of tea. Take a bit longer for your lunch and I'll have it here by one o'clock. On second thoughts, why don't you go to the widow's for a cooked meal, and I'll stand the cost of it. I can't be fairer than that, now can I, Johnny boy?'

He knew that he was wasting his time pursuing the matter further, so decided to take the boss up on his offer. He put his hand out, palm upwards, and was pleased to see a five pound note placed there.

'Thanks, boss! I'll keep the change,' he said with a chuckle, and headed straight for the back door. The thought of a hot cooked meal made him feel quite good. He turned left out of the alley into Wesley Street, and strolled towards Flaherty's café. The walk would take about ten minutes or so, but he was in no hurry.

★

He was about a hundred yards away from the café when the armoured personnel carrier pulled in front of him. He hadn't noticed it until then, but why should he? Wasn't it a fact that the Brit patrols were a standard everyday part of Ulster life these days?

Six armed paras leapt out of the vehicle and took up defensive positions on the footpath, surrounding him.

'John Millane?' came the challenge from the seventh soldier who had climbed out of the front passenger door of the vehicle. He wore the badge of rank of company sergeant major, a crown on his lower sleeve.

'Who the fuck is asking? You English pig!'

'Watch your mouth, you bog Irish git.'

Millane looked around quickly for a place to run. There was nowhere he could go. He was trapped.

'I asked you a question, Paddy boy. Are you John Millane?'

'If I was I wouldn't be wasting my time talking to filth the like of you,' he replied, lunging suddenly at the Sergeant Major, hoping to push him aside and make a bolt for an alleyway opposite.

The butt of the soldier's Stirling machine-gun swung up like a flash and caught him on the jaw, knocking him to the ground.

Just at that moment a young woman came around the corner by Flaherty's café. She was wheeling a small push-chair laden with shopping bags. The moment she saw Millane on the ground she left the pushchair and ran forward past the soldiers surrounding the prostrate man. Like a mad person she leapt at the para standing over Millane, tearing at his face with her fingers and screaming abuse at him.

'You dirty English bastards. I saw what you did, and I'll be saying my piece to the press before this day is through. Mark my words, you pigs,' she screamed as the Sergeant Major grabbed her by the shoulder and pushed her roughly to the ground.

'Piss off, you Irish whore,' he spat back at the woman, putting his hand to his face to stem the bleeding from two deep gouge marks left by the woman's fingernails. Then without any warning he landed a kick in the woman's stomach, throwing her across the footpath into the gutter.

Enraged by what he had just seen Millane leapt to his feet and head-butted the Sergeant Major across the bridge of the nose causing blood to splatter everywhere.

He would have pursued the fight further had it not been for the two young paras who leapt on him from behind and dragged him off. The last thing he remembered seeing was the young woman getting up and running away down the street dragging the pushchair and her shopping behind her. At that moment a well-aimed blow from the butt of a rifle rendered him unconscious. The two soldiers who were restraining him dragged him to the rear door of the APC and roughly threw him inside.

The vehicle did a screeching turn in the narrow street and roared off down the road in pursuit of the young woman. As they drew alongside her she stopped and put her hands up. She was dragged into the rear of the vehicle with little ceremony, landing on the unconscious body of John Millane. Had he been awake at that moment he probably would have seen, and no doubt been surprised by, the slight smile that creased her pretty young face.

## Chapter Four

His return to the world of the living was quite painful. His head was ringing, and he was aware of voices echoing in his brain. The back of his skull felt like it had been hit with a sledgehammer.

'Sorry about this, John my dear chap. Hoped we would not have to drag you out in such a bloody hurry, but we were desperate, and couldn't chance doing it as originally planned.'

His head was starting to clear. His eyes began to focus, and the echoes had started to recede from inside his head.

'Colonel Davis? What the blazes am I doing here? You've fucked up my whole operation. It will be impossible for me to get back in there again. I had the bastards eating out of my hands. What in heaven's name got into you? Five months' bloody work totally wasted.'

'Calm down, Lieutenant Millane. We had no choice, and the result was that we saved your life.' It was a woman's voice from behind him.

He sat up and turned round, every little movement an agony. What he saw surprised him very much. The young woman with the pushchair. She was now dressed differently, and her coarse, broad Ulster brogue had been replaced by a quiet, cultured London accent.

'Who the hell are you? What the blazes do you have to do with my assignment?'

Colonel Peter Davis, Army Intelligence, and John Millane's reporting officer since the commencement of his deep infiltration project, spoke again.

'She is right, John. By the way, meet Detective Inspector Joan Mulders, Special Branch. She has almost certainly helped to save your life.'

'What the hell are you on about? I was in no danger. They hadn't the faintest idea that I was anyone other than the man they thought I was. We had an arrangement about contact and withdrawal, Colonel. You have completely screwed everything up now.'

'Yes, we did have an arrangement. The arrangement would have got our message to you by 6 p.m. tonight. However, we needed you now. On top of which fate took a hand. If we had waited until our designated contact time it would have been precisely six hours and ten minutes too late, John. I can assure you that we would not have prejudiced the mission other than in an emergency, and this is one such emergency. Perhaps Inspector Mulders can explain to you what happened.'

'It had better be good,' Millane snapped angrily.

Five minutes later they were sitting at a table in a small interview room. Millane knew that they were in one of the Special Branch safe houses south of Belfast. He had operated from here during the days prior to his insertion into the crazy world of Catholic versus Protestant terrorism.

A young man with long hair had brought cups of tea and coffee into the room and then left, locking the door after him.

Probably Special Branch, thought Millane, watching him leave. The young police inspector sat down on the other side of the table and lit a cigarette. She inhaled deeply, then blew three perfect smoke rings, which curled slowly to the ceiling before dispersing.

'Very impressive, Inspector. Now let's get on with it.'

'I'm glad you like it, Lieutenant Millane. Sure, and isn't it my favourite party trick.'

She had reverted to the coarse Belfast dockland accent that he vaguely remembered from the incident in the street.

'Why don't you stop feeling so fucking self-righteous and sorry for yourself, Lieutenant. If we hadn't done what we did your arse would be in a sling. Worse, you wouldn't have an arse to put in a sling. You would be long fucking dead.' The words seemed so much harsher in the brogue that the woman affected so well.

'I have been working on this case since June last year. Over ten bloody months, Lieutenant.' She had now reverted to her own voice, or was it just one of her other vocal disguises?

'During that time I have been working with the opposite team to you. The Provos! They are a sick bunch of bastards, but I have managed to get my feet under the table, so to speak, reasonably high up in the pecking order.

'This morning I was doing some shopping for the team that I work with, and purely by chance I was in the vicinity of your workplace. Like you, I had planned to go to Flaherty's café to have a bite to eat for lunch. I do that quite often, just to keep an eye on you. Just one of my special projects.

'You never even noticed me though, not once. Not very flattering for a girl like me, especially when the place only seats twenty.'

She smiled to herself as she dashed her cigarette stub into the ashtray. The room remained deathly quiet for nearly two minutes while she finished drinking her cup of tea. She placed the empty cup on the saucer and continued.

'While I was doing the shopping in the supermarket I was slipped an urgent message. It told me that the Colonel needed you out pretty urgently, and that there was a fixed procedure for doing that which he could not wait to implement. I was also told that your withdrawal was far more important than anything I was doing at the moment. I hope they were right, Lieutenant, because I have really stuck my neck out for you.

'I suggested the paras pick you up in the manner that they did. I also suggested that I should become involved for two reasons. One to make it look good for the locals who may be watching. Mainly though, I thought that if you were a true officer and a gentleman, you would respond more authentically if I put my oar in and set you up, so to speak.

'The soldiers in the patrol didn't even know who I was until just as they were chucking you in the back of the APC, when the Colonel's people got a message through to their radio operator. That was why they picked me up so ignominiously.

'I had already seen you coming away from the factory, so I hurried up the next street in order to get to the café before you, and then to intercept you and set this thing going. I wasn't sure how you would react to the patrol turning you over. You can never be too sure when you're in my line of business. I couldn't be sure that you would leap to my defence, so to speak. I had to take the chance though, because it had to look very good to anyone who may have been stickybeaking. Anyway, you fell for it, hook, line and sinker, just like a raving bloody novice.'

He flinched at this brutal attack on his professionalism, but decided to keep calm, and find out what else this arrogant young woman wanted to tell him.

'I knew it would take you about ten minutes to walk to the café. I also knew that if I didn't do this right I would probably blow my own cover, let alone yours.

'Anyway, the Colonel had arranged for you to be picked up. The soldiers in the patrol were not told who you really are, they were only told your name and that you were a dangerous man who they had to bring here, soonest. They were instructed to ignore army regs and protocol if need be to achieve this end.

'I hope you believe in fate, First Lieutenant Millane, because if the APC had taken a minute or more longer to get to you, you would have been dead. You know? Three shots over the grave and goodnight nurse.'

Millane's mouth dropped open in shock. 'What the blazes do you mean?'

'What I mean, Lieutenant Bloody Fantastic, is that my mates the Provos had, unknown to me, arranged a nasty surprise for Mrs Flaherty and her clients. Not my group, but another one from south of the city who must have had it in for one of the poor unfortunates who was having lunch there. We haven't sorted out the connection yet, but we are working on it.

'The first that was known about it was when an anonymous phone call was made to the local police station, but as the call was being made, the place blew up.

'The timing was most fortunate, for you anyway, because at the time of the big bang you were in the APC sleeping it off, a couple of blocks away.'

'What was the casualty list like?' Millane asked quietly. He felt quite shaken by the information that had just been given him; even though he knew Mrs Flaherty and a fair number of her customers were no good, strangely he still felt concerned about them.

'Luckily it was a bit before the start of the lunchtime rush, but the explosion still killed four people. Ironically, the person whom they probably had as one of their main targets, Widow Flaherty, was in the backyard having a smoke. She lost her right arm, and probably her sight as well. The cook, Sean Kelly, was killed instantly. He won't be missed much by us though. He was top of our list for the drive-past killing of a man and his little daughter last week.

'The other three fatalities were customers. We haven't identified them yet. The fire brigade and the investigation boys are still there. Let's hope they don't find any more bodies under the rubble.'

'What sort of explosive device was it?' Millane asked in a subdued voice. The shock was just beginning to set in.

'We think it was TNT, with a clockwork timer. Pretty crude stuff. It was all packed in the boot of a Renault parked in front of the café. It was a massive explosion. It destroyed the houses either side of Flaherty's, but luckily they were both empty at the time.'

He sat quietly for a moment, taking the news in, and trying to think how he could regain the ground he may have lost due to the coincidence of his departure at the precise moment of the explosion. He was also wondering whether it was safe for him to go back in again. The Colonel broke the silence.

'I know that you had to put up some sort of display of righteous indignation about being turned over by the patrol, John, but why on earth did you do it so violently? I have a pretty sad and uncomfortable sergeant major nursing a badly broken nose, thanks to your performance. It hasn't helped the pain much for him to find that he was bringing home an SAS officer from undercover.'

'I know, sir. I will have to go and see the man. It was a bad decision of yours from my point of view though. Everyone and his or her dog gets turned over once in a while by the army in this area. It is, however, rare for anyone to be taken away.

I am so well placed in the system that there could be people who may consider my arrest at that particular moment to be too much of a coincidence. I may easily be their number one suspect for the bombing.

As for my response to the patrol's actions, I just felt that I had to make a show of some sort, for the natives you see. On top of which I really saw red when the Sergeant Major kicked our Inspector friend here. Christ, I have obviously been away from the Army and civilisation for too long.'

The Police Inspector spoke next, after lighting herself another cigarette.

'You are probably right about reinsertion into the area. It would take a lot of convincing for those people to trust you, especially in the light of what happened at Flaherty's. Unless...'

'Unless what?' questioned the Colonel.

'Sorry, Colonel, I was just thinking out loud. But it isn't a good idea. Not a very good idea at all.'

'For Christ's sake, what are you burbling on about?' shouted Millane, his depression at the turn of events rapidly changing into anger.

'Well, First Lieutenant John Millane,' she replied, reverting to the Belfast brogue once more. 'I think the Sergeant Major and his merry men should be given the opportunity to beat the holy shit out of you. If he roughed you up and put you in hospital for a few days your friends may not smell a rat. I'm bloody sure he would enjoy getting even with you for spoiling his good looks so dramatically.'

'Oh! Fucking hell!' was all that Millane could think of saying. 'Fucking, bloody hell!'

# Chapter Five

In the event, it was not the Sergeant Major and his men that worked on Millane. It was a skilful army doctor with some very fine surgical tools. His work was also done whilst Millane was mercifully under the influence of some very powerful local anaesthetic and, to the annoyance of the doctor, a couple of stiff Scotch whiskies.

The end result was perfect in every way, except of course from the point of view of Lieutenant John Millane, Special Air Service. Once the anaesthetic wore off he was faced with the same painful after-effects as if the beating had been real. The wounds that he bore were a broken nose, deep lacerations to the head and face, and two cracked ribs.

The wounds were sufficiently authentic to satisfy the young doctor in the casualty department of the infirmary where he was unceremoniously dumped by the Colonel's men. In fact the wounds were bad enough to convince the doctor that he should call the Royal Ulster Constabulary and register a serious complaint about the conduct of the British Army.

Not that the RUC would investigate the alleged assaults too carefully. After all, the victim had already become known to them as being involved with a suspected terrorist group, and as such could suffer as many beatings as came his way, for all they cared.

★

Before undergoing his strange surgery he had been advised of the real reason for his hurried and unorthodox withdrawal. Something nasty was brewing in the South Atlantic, in the Falklands. The Argentinians had opened hostilities, and his unit, presently scattered all over Ireland on undercover duties were being recalled and reformed. A specialist SAS communications unit, their role was apparently going to be critical to future British actions to regain the Falklands.

★

Inspector Mulders also suffered a minor beating before being released on to the street. She, however, did not visit the hospital. She went instead to the offices of Sinn Fein, the political wing of the IRA, and between tears told of her ordeal.

It was to be a further two weeks before she was completely cleared of any suspicion and returned to her unit, if only as the fetcher and carrier. It was this suspicious nature and the tendency to be extraordinarily careful that had helped make the IRA such a successful and elusive force over so many years.

★

Although he was required back in his unit, it was imperative that Millane could walk out under his own steam, with the complete trust and support of the Belfast Regiment.

Whilst nobody with any sense believed that the military exercise in the South Atlantic would be a pushover, the powers that be did expect it to be over soon. On the conclusion of the hostilities Millane would need to go back into Northern Ireland if that was at all possible.

From his hospital bed, where he feigned considerably greater pain and discomfort than was really the case, he managed to get a message out to Michael McQuillan telling him where he was, but it was two days before he visited him. Millane expected this, as he felt sure Michael would be suspicious and would investigate the matter thoroughly before making a move.

Widow Flaherty was in the intensive-care unit of the same hospital, and McQuillan felt safe to visit her as it was well known that they were friends. His relationship with Millane was less well known outside his company and the Regiment, so he made his enquiries and bided his time.

Several people had in fact witnessed the interception by the British patrol, and had given graphic descriptions of his rash actions towards the soldiers. This, together with the news of the violence he had suffered at their hands later, and the eyewitness account of the extent of his injuries given by a supporter of the cause, made it quite clear that Millane could not have been involved with the bomb.

His interception and arrest had been a simple coincidence, and but for his stupid, vile temper would have probably ended with him being permitted to go on his way.

However, the British soldiers did him and the cause a big favour by taking him into custody. Otherwise he would have continued up to the café, and would almost certainly have died. It was at the table where he usually sat that two of the victims had died.

*

This was the final analysis of the Belfast Regiment's security team, backed up strongly by their Detective Inspector contact in the RUC Special Branch. Once again he had proved useful to Colonel Davis's people who had carefully fed him the information that they wished to get back to McQuillan and his associates.

What really clinched it was Millane's behaviour towards Michael McQuillan when he arrived with flowers and fruit at the start of the evening visiting hours' period, four days after Millane's admission.

'Hullo, John my boy, and how are they looking after you?'

'Don't you fucking John my boy me, you murdering bastard,' Millane hissed between clenched teeth.

McQuillan was dumbstruck by the venom in his voice and the hate in his eyes.

'What the blue blazes are you talking about? Have you lost your senses, man?'

'Lost my bleeding senses is it, and you being the one who specifically sent me down the road to the widow's to have an early bite to eat.

'It was the very first time you ever did that, McQuillan, and just by coincidence that happened to be the very day and the precise moment that the Provos – or was it just made to look like the Provos?' he spat out the words. 'Was it the Provos, or was it you, you bastard? It's too much of a coincidence, and when I get out of here I am going to get to the bottom of this, if it's the last thing I do. Mark my words, if you are involved I'll kill you with my bare hands, so help me.'

McQuillan was visibly shaken, and he stepped back, dropping the flowers and the bag of fruit on the floor.

'Surely you can't be serious, John. Me? Christ! The widow and me are that close. I love her. Don't you see, man, I couldn't do anything that could possibly hurt her. I'm shattered, and here she is, as we speak, in danger of losing her sight and even her life.

'God, man, you have got it all wrong. You don't know how wrong. I know you are hurt, John, and you are in great pain, but you mustn't think crazy things like this. I'm your friend, and you are one of us.'

Millane knew at that moment that he had him in his grasp.

'Well, where the hell were you over the past few days? Why haven't you been in before now, you bastard?'

'Things have been pretty scary, John. We have been in a state of turmoil. We've had the RUC and Special Branch all over us like a rash. On top of that we have had a few urgent security issues to sort out.'

'What you are really telling me is that you have been checking up on me again. Isn't that right! Haven't I proved time and time again that I'm a real brother of the cause? You pack of bastards. Is this what I just took a terrible beating for? Will you look at me, Michael. Look what they have done to me.' John buried his face in his hands and began to sob quietly.

McQuillan was obviously moved, and convinced. In a noticeable state of embarrassment he explained. 'Okay, John, you are right. We did do a bit of extra checking. Not just on you, but on everyone in the Regiment. Even I was checked out. Some cheeky sod broke into my house and searched it from top to bottom. Nothing was stolen, so I am pretty sure it was one of the company commanders checking if I was clean. It would have been senseless if we hadn't done a thorough internal check on everyone.

'We thought that we may have been compromised from within, or even infiltrated, you know. These Special Branch and SAS bastards are moving in everywhere.

'But I promise you, John boy, we were not just doing you over. Not at all. Some of the enquiries about other members are still continuing.

'There are a couple of the lads who cannot or won't substantiate where they were and what they were doing at the time of the bombing. They were probably out screwing, or perhaps committing crime, but whatever it was, once we find out about it they could be in serious trouble. They will be disciplined anyway for failing to come clean.'

John shuddered at the thought of the disciplinary action that they would face.

The poor sods are in for one hell of a hiding for their sins, he thought, remembering the few occasions he had helped administer such discipline for the cause.

'We don't need cowboys in the Regiment,' Michael continued solemnly. 'If we are going to win through and get rid of the IRA and the bleeding Brits we must have absolute discipline and loyalty. Yes, John! We know you are one of us, and it's your sort of discipline, loyalty and dedication that I want to instil in the rest of the lads. I'm saddened and hurt that you could have believed that I was responsible for what happened to Moira, and to you. You are a dear friend, John.'

Millane had gradually became less hostile, and McQuillan responded readily to his more friendly tone. Within minutes they were discussing the issues surrounding the bombing, and what had happened to him on the 11th.

He also told Michael that his clothes had mysteriously disappeared from the hospital, and that he was convinced it was part of a Brit plot to harass him. He shared with him his fear that the paratroop sergeant major who took him in on the morning of the bombing was out to get him because of the broken nose he'd received for his sins.

'Haven't they bloody bashed you enough, John?' his boss asked in despair.

'It seems not, Michael. Some very strange things have happened to me since I got here, and the soldiers from that patrol have poked their heads in here several times.'

He left Michael McQuillan in no doubt that with good cause he was really beginning to fear for his life.

The man stayed for over an hour before excusing himself to visit the widow, Moira Flaherty, in intensive care. By the time he left Millane was convinced that his story had been accepted. The first part of the elaborate plan to get himself back with the Regiment whilst enabling him to temporarily get out of Northern Ireland had worked.

McQuillan promised to call in and see him the following morning with a change of clothing and shoes which he would pick up from his lodgings. He also said that he would work out a way to smuggle him out of the hospital to safety.

What his boss did not know was that Millane was not going to let things wait until the next morning. Part two of his plan was going to be implemented that very night.

## Chapter Six

The hospital was quiet and still. Most of the patients were asleep, naturally or drug induced. Millane was wide awake though. He had to be fully alert when the next part of the plan commenced. He had to be able to play a very convincing part in what was about to happen.

At five minutes after midnight six men in uniform entered the ward and hurried to his bed. Their role was not to inflict any further violence but to add authenticity to his next move.

The other patients in the ward were woken up very suddenly by the sound of shouting and threatening voices. Even though the ward was in darkness they were able to tell that the commotion was coming from the bed of the man who had been beaten up by the British Army.

The story of how he had arrived at the hospital had spread like wildfire soon after his admission. His reported exploits with the patrol had given him an air of notoriety amongst staff and patients alike.

'Don't think you are going to get away with a simple fucking hiding, you Irish git,' one of the group of soldiers was quite clearly heard to say, as was intended.

'You're a dead man, Paddy,' said another man.

'We're going to get you, you bog-trotting bastard,' came a third voice.

'Help me. For Christ's sake get help. They are going to kill me,' Millane shrieked at the top of his voice. 'Please help me.'

Suddenly he was grabbed by one of the men and he ended up on the floor, surrounded by his bed linen.

Almost as suddenly as they had arrived, the soldiers disappeared. They were, however, seen by all of the men in the ward, in silhouette only, and just for a brief moment as they moved out into the dimly lit corridor.

Within minutes the hospital night staff had been fully alerted, and the Royal Ulster Constabulary notified. They attended and took details, particularly the excellent descriptions given by some of the other patients. It was amazing just how remarkably graphic and precise some of the descriptions were. Even Millane had seen no more than shadowy outlines of the men, and he was wide awake at the time.

He found it difficult not to laugh but dared not as he had to portray a man fearing for his life.

He stuck to his story of being suddenly woken, and only seeing shadowy figures looming over his bed, shouting out their threats. He said that they may have been wearing army uniforms but couldn't be certain because it was so dark.

As it transpired he didn't have to be certain. His fellow patients, almost to a man, provided the police with all the evidence they needed to satisfy them that a group of soldiers had entered the ward and threatened the life of the patient, John Millane. Whilst the individual descriptions varied so much as to be totally useless, the RUC were left in no doubt that it was a fair bet that soldiers of the British Army were after this man.

*

At 3 a.m. Michael McQuillan received a coded telephone message.

'Michael, the darts match has been cancelled. I'll let you know what the new arrangements will be.'

The routine was well established. Such a call meant that he was to go to a pre-arranged public call box and await a call. This was an essential precaution as his home telephone calls were often intercepted by the authorities.

The call, from the Special Branch friend of the Belfast Regiment was brief and to the point.

'The Brits came after your friend John tonight. If you want him alive you had better get him out of Ulster.'

The plan had succeeded. Not only would Michael McQuillan get him out of the hospital, he would have no choice but to help get him out of Northern Ireland.

At 6 a.m., dressed as a ward orderly Millane left the hospital in a laundry van. He was driven to a small airfield and flown to Rhyl in North Wales where he disappeared from sight with strict instructions from Michael McQuillan to keep in touch.

# Chapter Seven

## Friday 9th April, 1982

The SS *Canberra* was a beautiful ship. Even now, stripped of all her luxurious fittings and fixtures and packed solid with troops and their battle equipment, she still had an air of sophistication about her.

Beneath her decks, now cleared of deckchairs and the playthings of the rich and famous, were billeted the troops of the 3rd Commando Brigade, comprising 40 and 42 Commando, and the 3rd Parachute Regiment. They were off to war.

Exactly a week earlier on Friday 2nd April the Argentinian army had invaded Port Stanley, the tiny capital of the Falkland Islands, Britain's most distant dependency. The island was defended by a largely ceremonial force, a small but gallant group of men, the Royal Marine-Naval Party 8901.

Their position was hopeless, and within a short period of time they were directed from Whitehall to surrender to the invading forces.

From that moment the entire resources of the British military were committed to preparing an invasion task force for the recapture of the Falklands.

The *Canberra* had been commandeered from her owners, the P & O Line and immediately commissioned for the purposes of the invasion to become one of the key players in the naval task force.

She sailed from Southampton on 9th April together with the Royal Fleet Auxiliary ship *Tidepool*.

Isolated in the forward part of the ship, well away from the bulk of the troops was a group of three men. They were different from the rest of the military on board, but nobody ever questioned their difference. It was taken for granted that they would be there.

There were in fact several such groups of men throughout the ship, some in larger numbers. They came from the Royal Marine Special Boat Squadron, the fabled SBS, and from the more widely known Special Air Service, the SAS.

Most of these men had been hastily withdrawn from various undercover operations throughout Britain and Europe, and the balance from specialised training in various parts of the UK. Their importance to the forthcoming operation was such that several well-advanced operations had been blown part-way through in order to release them.

Their roles were to be crucial to the war effort, and the work that they were about to do would create havoc behind enemy lines and provide opportunities for the military units that would follow them in.

*

This three-man team stayed below decks throughout the first stage of the *Canberra*'s voyage which took eight days and ended in Sierra Leone on the west coast of central Africa, where she and her consort RFA *Tidepool* refuelled.

The journey was uneventful, or it seemed that way to all except the most senior officers on board. The troops' days had been filled with endless drills and exercise sessions that were part and parcel of military life.

Fortunately, only the leaders of those men were aware that the voyage to date had been a constant concern to the British Government and the High Command, and that they had been under constant surveillance by satellite, reconnaissance aircraft and submarines.

There had been grave fears that the Argentinian Navy had a submarine stalking *Canberra* throughout the latter part of her journey to Sierra Leone, waiting for the right time to strike. In the event that proved not to be the case.

Had such an attack occurred it would have had a disastrous effect on the planning for the military encounter that was to follow.

At Freetown, Sierra Leone, the SAS unit comprising Major Douglas Marven, First Lieutenant John Millane and Sergeant Eric (Yettie) Smith was smuggled ashore in a large shipping container that was lowered on to the wharf in the early hours of Saturday 18th April.

Smith had earned his nickname as the result of a skiing accident whilst training with Norwegian Alpine troops two years before; Yettie being the slang name given to a skiing mishap of any sort.

Millane's nickname had temporarily become Punchy in view of the still badly swollen broken nose that he had acquired from the enterprising army surgeon in Belfast.

As for Major Marven, he was known as Boss, standard for the leaders of any SAS team.

Shortly afterwards the container was to be lifted up and moved further down the wharf and then hoisted on board a dirty-looking freighter, the SS *Halwood*.

However, the container was not immediately moved as planned, but remained on the wharf in the blazing sunshine and heat for eight hours. For Marven and his men this was not what they had originally understood would be the case.

The roof of the container was fitted with a large fan and extractor operated by a heavy-duty truck battery. It was designed to regulate the temperature to an acceptable level, or at least to keep a steady flow of fresh air pouring into that sweltering sweat box; but only for a limited period of time. But, two things went badly wrong.

Firstly, somebody on the wharf loaded another container on top of theirs, completely blocking the vent to the fan and disabling it within minutes. Then the mobile wharf crane that was due to lift up the container and convey it along the quay to where *Halwood* was berthed broke down.

It was only as the result of the intervention of Captain Bridges, the skipper of the SS Halwood, who had soon realised what had gone wrong, and his timely production of three bottles of Jamaican rum, that the maintenance engineers agreed to work on the machine, which fortunately was repairable but would take several hours.

Whilst this critical wheeling and dealing was taking place the conditions inside the hot metal box were deteriorating by the hour. Marven knew that unless the container was cleared of whatever it was that had been placed on top of them, and moved to where it could be put on board SS *Halwood*, he and his men only had a few hours before they would have to take drastic action.

He quickly calculated that the air inside their temporary home would become unbreathable within seven hours or so, and directed his team to lie down, conserve energy and sleep, if at all possible.

They were given regular and reassuring reports on what was happening outside, thanks to a person who identified himself as a crew member of *Halwood*, and who tapped out regular Morse code messages on the metal body of the container. Being signals experts they each understood the messages.

★

Prior to leaving Southampton Marven and his team had been fully briefed and trained on the emergency exit procedure should the container not be picked up on time, or if some form of accident occurred that made it essential, such as a fire.

However, nobody had anticipated that something as simple as loading another container on top or the breakdown of a crane would cause such a serious emergency to occur.

One end of the container had two large doors that were held closed externally by a horizontal steel bar which was locked with a giant padlock. In the case of an emergency the container was supplied with a special toolbox. This contained a cordless drill and some plastic explosives and detonators. There was a small area marked on the inside of each of the steel doors near where the padlock was located, which was made of thinner than normal steel. In each of these areas were painted two large fluorescent white dots.

In dire emergency holes were to be drilled through the door at these dots, and the plastic explosive material which was rolled into long thin strips would be threaded through the top holes and lowered to the point where they could be pulled back through the bottom holes. The material would then be tied together loosely and detonators inserted.

Having achieved this the men would then retire to the opposite end of the container, and concealing themselves behind the mattresses and blocking up their ears, would detonate the explosives which would blow the steel bar and padlock off the container, hopefully opening the doors.

In the eventuality of this action having to be taken, the radio would be used to alert the *Halwood* of their intentions, giving five minutes' warning; the only time that use of the radio from the container would be authorised.

The crew of the freighter would immediately create a diversionary disturbance on the dock, long enough for the three men to escape the container and mingle with the seamen involved in the disturbance. Should the SS *Halwood* people not be able to receive or carry out their role other SAS units on board *Canberra* would come ashore and take whatever action was deemed necessary.

This all looked fairly simple on paper, which was where it had remained. There had not been time to practice the escape routine. But then, nobody had expected such an emergency to occur anyway.

However, even on paper it had several shortcomings, some of which could be highly dangerous for the people inside the big oven-like metal box on the wharf.

There was a danger that the main force of the explosion would blow back into the container and injure the men. It was also possible that the explosion would merely buckle the door and cause it to jam, or not even blow the steel bar and padlock off. There would not be a second chance.

Marven and his men were not relishing the thought of having to take this extreme action.

The heat had become so intense that they were reaching the point where they had virtually exhausted the oxygen supply in the confined space inside the container. Marven discussed the matter with Millane and Smith and told them to prepare for an emergency breakout. The power drill was prepared, and Yettie commenced the delicate task of making the holes. Delicate that is in terms of the need to make as little noise as possible, and to ensure that the drill bit did not protrude too far out from the metal wall as it cut its way through. He had just completed the second hole and was aware that he was feeling dizzy through lack of air. Millane was preparing the plastic explosives, and was so weak that he had fallen to the floor, where he had sensibly decided to remain.

Yettie wiped rivulets of sweat from his head, and was just about to commence work on the third hole when he heard a voice. Someone outside on the wharf was speaking through one of the holes.

'What the bloody hell are you doing? Cover those sodding holes up or you'll give the game away.'

Major Marven pushed Smith aside and placed his mouth near the holes.

'We have no fucking air in here. I have no choice. Within a few minutes we will be passing out.'

'Sorry matey, but you will have to bloody well wait, and pass out if necessary. Just five minutes, I promise you. The skipper is just finishing pouring rum down the throats of the engineers and the crane driver. You'll be on your way real soon. Better go or someone will think I'm nuts. Just how long can you spend doing your boot laces up when you're wearing slip-ons?'

With that assurance Marven ordered the men to lie down on their mattresses once more and try to relax. There was a lot of banging and other loud noises outside the container, and within a few minutes the obstruction above them had obviously been removed, because the fan immediately began to work.

*

The SS *Halwood* really was an awful-looking ship. It was registered in Panama and looked dirty, dingy and extremely rusty. In fact, it looked as if an average sort of storm would sink it outright.

However, she was intended to look that way, but looks can often be deceptive, and they certainly were in this case. *Halwood* was a sturdy ship with incredible seagoing capabilities. She was not meant to look any better than she did.

The dirt was purposely stuck to her superstructure with liberal coatings of grease, and the rust effect was created by a special commercial paint product that gave the final appearance of age and disrepair to the ship, which was exactly what her owners wanted.

She was owned by a company called Atlantic Image. Even if one had conducted the most thorough research on the company it would never have been disclosed that the real owners were an obscure government-funded agency based in London, and under the control of senior officials in Whitehall.

The ship conducted certain highly confidential and nefarious activities in various parts of the world that the Government would not want to be seen to be operating in, but mainly in the mid and southern Atlantic regions. At the same time it traded quite successfully as a tramp steamer, picking up small cargoes and ferrying them to distant ports of call.

*Halwood* was crewed by a hard-looking group of men who few would suspect were in fact serving and ex-Royal Navy personnel. Their captain, who went under the name of George Bridges, was a recently retired Lieutenant Commander of Her Majesty's Royal Navy. He looked even worse than his crew, sporting a rough shaggy beard and a brightly coloured rugby jersey under his grimy jacket. He had the outward appearance of a cut-throat pirate of olden times.

'Welcome aboard, gentlemen. I am sure we will be able to make you feel at home for the few days you are with us.' The Captain was leading his bedraggled charges along a spotlessly clean passageway which opened up into a beautifully appointed wardroom. The below decks' appearance of the ship was most definitely Royal Navy.

The deck crew who they had first met bore no resemblance to the men who greeted Marven and his team and assisted them in getting settled into their large three-berth cabin in preparation for the next stage of their journey.

They had not been briefed on exactly what to expect, other than that they would transfer to a less noticeable ship, so the interior of SS *Halwood* came as a most pleasant surprise.

The major was led off to a communications room which was fitted out with modern radio, radar and electronics equipment of the calibre that he had grown used to in the most sophisticated of environments. Within minutes he was communicating with Hereford, from where he received his latest instructions.

He then returned to the cabin where Millane and Smith were already making up their bunks. He was pleased to see that someone had already made his, even though in the SAS it was a rule that each man looked after himself, regardless of rank.

# Chapter Eight

Saturday 17th April, 1982

First Lieutenant Millane was responsible for the first aid and medical welfare of the small team. Amongst his long list of qualifications and skills he was a highly skilled paramedic with battle wounds' experience and a hundred per cent success rate. However, his record run was interrupted in Sierra Leone as the result of the mishap with the container.

During the eight plus hours that the team was trapped in the metal box standing in the open under the remorseless tropical sun all three men had become disoriented and unwell. Regardless of the constant fluids that they had taken during their incarceration Millane and Yettie Smith had become dehydrated and nauseous. Marven, whilst unwell and suffering from diarrhoea remained the fittest of the trio and became their temporary medical support person as the result of Millane's inability to perform that duty.

All three were a sorry sight when, once the container was loaded on to the *Halwood*'s deck, they were released from their temporary prison. Immediate showers and changes of clothing went part-way to easing their discomfort, yet even a good night's rest in their cabin did not prepare them for what they were about to suffer.

The ship weighed anchor and put to sea whilst the *Canberra* and *Tidepool* were still being refuelled. The timing could not have been worse for Millane and Smith. In the brief period since they had arrived on *Canberra* the Atlantic Ocean had developed a particularly large swell – or so it seemed to those two unhappy men.

Whilst the sea had become slightly more aggressive, their real problem was that they were now travelling in a much smaller vessel than they were used to; a vessel with no structural mod cons such as stabilisers or the like. In fact, whilst extremely well appointed below decks with the best of amenities for the crew, and with the latest space-age technology for navigation, communication and surveillance, the SS *Halwood* was very poorly equipped in terms of her ability to handle anything but the calmest of waters without causing extreme discomfort to her shipmates. This was especially so when the shipmates concerned were already as unwell as First Lieutenant John Millane and Sergeant Eric Smith. The result of *Halwood*'s conflict with the large swells of the Atlantic was a day and a half of unremitting sea sickness for both men.

Smith admitted to being a poor sailor at the best of times, and in the past had often joked about being sea sick in a rowing boat on Regent's Park Lake. Millane was different, having never before been sick at sea. In fact, he was an accomplished sailor having skippered several successful yachts at Cowes. His illness therefore caused him considerable anger as well as discomfort.

Major Marven was the only member of the team not suffering the ravages of seasickness. On the advice and under the instructions of his Lieutenant he was eventually obliged to administer intramuscular injections of Stemetil to both men.

Within twenty-four hours their conditions had improved considerably but they each had a badly swollen arm as the result of their boss's lack of experience with a hypodermic needle. This was to become a concern later in the operation, but at the moment was the subject of some good-natured banter between the men.

'Stop moaning, you miserable sods. What would you rather have, a sore arm or seasickness?' he challenged them when the complaints were made about his heavy hand with the injections. 'I was just practising to get into the darts team once we get back home.'

There was no response from Millane or Smith who decided to let the matter lie; for the time being anyway. Each was most grateful for the relief from the constant sickness and diarrhoea that had incapacitated them for thirty hours. They each pondered the various ways that they would get back in a fun way at their well-liked boss at some later time.

★

Once over the immediate effects of their illness the three men were fully occupied in unloading the container and checking the equipment that they would take ashore with them once they reached their destination.

As soon as everything was stowed below decks the container was dropped overboard into the sea, where it quickly sank to the bottom of the ocean. Prior to its disposal large holes were cut into its walls with oxyacetylene cutters. Captain Bridges explained that it was the only way he could hope to prevent pockets of air being retained in the container which could bring it back to the surface at some future time.

'The crew don't like the hard work involved, and a lot of my peers think I am being overly paranoid about such things, but I've seen plenty of these monstrosities floating around the oceans.

'If a ship of our size or less hit one under a full head of steam it would sink us, so I always spend that little bit of extra time cutting the bloody things up so that they can't float, not easily anyway.'

Millane was most impressed by the man's concerns for the ocean's environment, whilst Yettie Smith tended to sympathise with the crew members who sweated it out with the cutting equipment.

'Waste of time if you ask me. How can it possibly float? It's too sodding heavy.'

'This ship is heavier than that, and we're floating,' Major Marven snapped as he walked away from where the container was being cut open.

The Sergeant stood there with a vacant look on his face.

'Shit, we are too. Never thought of that.'

There was a lot of gear to be taken to the shore. It comprised a portable radar unit and direction finder, radio transmitters, tents, digging tools, two inflatable rafts and small portable heaters and stoves, together with sufficient fuel for a two-month operation. They had been assured that their stay would barely be more than two weeks, but in typical army style they provided more than enough. The men would not argue with their decision, after all, it was always considered better to have too much than not enough. There was also a medical kit that was well enough equipped to deal with everything from sore throats to substantial field surgery if the need arose.

As with the general equipment, there was enough food of the compo rations, concentrated food variety to last well beyond any period of time that they should be required to stay in the operational zone. They only had a small supply of water because it was so bulky and heavy to carry, however they had been assured that there was plenty of natural water where they were going to be based. The Major had joked that with their luck they would probably have to hack it out of the ice cap and boil it before it could be used. He was only half joking, because he had seen the weather forecasts for the area they would be operating in. The usual purifying tablets and water sweeteners had been added just to be sure.

In terms of weaponry, each man had an automatic pistol and a self-loading rifle, (SLR). They had a general purpose machine-gun, (GPMG), hand grenades and sufficient ammunition to fight off the entire Argentinian Army, or so it seemed. Their armoury was enhanced with a rocket launcher, for which they carried ten missiles.

To ensure their personal safety and comfort each man was equipped with a bullet-proof jacket and heavy-duty winter clothing to help them stand up to the extremely low temperatures that they would certainly experience. Their Bergens, the compact army rucksacks, were filled with tightly rolled, vacuum-packed woollen socks, replacement thermal underwear and personal medical and first-aid equipment. There would be few, if any opportunities for washing clothing during the operation to follow.

★

After three days at sea Marven called the men together to discuss their destination which had been kept from them until now, and to brief them on matters such as transferring their equipment and supplies ashore.

Their destination was a small island named Skull Rock, fifty miles north of Jason Island, north-west of West Falklands. The rock was uninhabited except for a crofter who would endeavour to meet with them shortly after their landing and assist them in establishing a well-positioned and secure base.

Their role was to act as a forward observation unit to warn of the movements of enemy aircraft, surface vessels and troops, particularly aircraft which could be so threatening during any attempts at troop landings. Even the finest troops in the world were helplessly exposed and completely vulnerable whilst in landing craft between ship and shore.

Skull Rock was not the prettiest place in the world to be based, but it was sufficiently far from the main Falkland Islands for a reasonable period of warning to be given regarding any potentially threatening aircraft.

They examined the maps of the small rocky island that the skipper of *Halwood* had produced, and realised why they were to land at the point that had been designated. Quite simply, it was the only place. The remaining coastline comprised sheer cliffs and razor-sharp rocks hammered constantly by thundering seas. The small cove that they were to enter had a steep shelving beach and the sea was generally very rough with huge breakers pounding the shore.

'How the hell are we expected to get in there with all our equipment, Boss?' Millane asked quietly.

'Well, we are assured that on each turn of the tide there is a one-hour period of relative calm. I must admit, John, I am not overly happy with the word 'relative'. That could mean anything, and probably does. Anyway, that's the story. They tell me that once a year a bloody great barge is run in on the beach to pick up the sheep for the abattoir on the main island. I suppose if they can do it, we can.'

'The only catch is that we have got to do it in little rubber boats, not a bloody great barge, Boss. How are we going to get all of our stuff ashore in an hour?' Millane continued, 'There are only three of us with two boats. We have already decided that it will take at least two trips for each boat, and that is based on having a reasonably accessible beach in terms of water conditions.'

'Good point, John, but we will have a little bit of help in that regard. There is one other thing that I haven't told you both, which I am sure will please you no end being the complaining buggers that you are.'

Millane and Smith both smiled at that remark.

'We are leaving this most hospitable but gyrating rust bucket at 0600 hours on the 24th, and transferring to a submarine which will take us the rest of the way to our destination in far greater comfort.

'When we get there, at the appropriate time the Jolly Jack Tars will assist us in getting our gear to the beach, and up on to dry land before the tide turns. Any more questions?'

'Yes, Boss.' Yettie Smith was scratching his neck, always a good sign that he was concerned about something. 'You know I am always a starter for any sort of operation, but I just can't figure this one out. Why couldn't they have just got themselves a Royal Signals Corps team and put them in. They've got some crash hot blokes in that outfit. This just doesn't seem like it's our sort of job.'

'I agree with you, Yettie, or I did at first. However, there are a few good reasons why we are going to be here rather than in the main punch-up. We are a specialist radio unit both in terms of being technicians and operators, but that is where our similarities to other regiments ceases.

'Whilst we are getting a bit of help to get ashore in the first place, we may have to get out under our own steam, and in a hurry. That means without waiting for the tide to turn. This requires a team with the sort of special small boat skills and rough water experience that we've got and most others haven't.

'The sort of weather that I have been warned to expect is something that we are trained to work with and withstand. Not many other units have that level of training and endurance capability. Think of Brecon Beacon.'

Millane and Smith both shuddered at the thought of the agonies they had suffered on that godforsaken piece of

Welsh real estate. They were both aware of men who had failed because of their inability to stand up to the extremes they were expected to overcome, and of the several men in elite military units who had perished there even though only engaged in peacetime war games exercises.

Marven need not have said any more, but he continued anyway. He seemed less than pleased to have been asked the question in the first place.

'Finally, Smith.' It was then that Yettie really knew he had upset the boss. 'The most important reason why we are here is because if needs be we are able to disperse and blend into the countryside, and individually conduct our own style of guerilla warfare, without the need for direct support. The Argentinian Army, or a platoon of their Marines could arrive on our doorstep, and incidentally those guys are no slugs. If that happens it will be pointless taking on what is very likely to be a superior force, using standard military tactics.

'This is our bread-and-butter work. This is what the SAS is all about, Smith. All right?'

The Sergeant lowered his face slightly. 'Thanks, Boss. I apologise. I guess I just wanted to be in on the big one.'

'So did we all, Yettie. So did we all.'

★

Marven and his team had been up for over an hour super-vising the stacking of their equipment and supplies on to large, rope net squares laid out neatly on *Halwood*'s heaving deck. At the appropriate time these squares would be drawn together at the corners and would be hoisted up by the ship's derrick and lowered down on to the deck of the submarine.

Over the past few days the men had practised for this transfer again and again. The business of preparing their equipment and supplies so that when the transfer was completed they would know exactly what was where was something that the three men were experts in.

However it was important that each individual load should contain sufficient amounts of each item to enable the men to perform their tasks ashore, if only for a limited time.

It was of critical importance that if one or more loads were either lost overboard during the transfer, or left on board the *Halwood* in error, they would not contain all of one or more specific items, for instance, all the ammunition, or food.

Many a battle had been lost in the past because the soldiers involved had been unprepared in this way, and found themselves short of a vital part of their equipment or supplies whilst having an ample supply of something that they did not need.

★

At exactly 0600 hours the submarine suddenly appeared out of the waves one hundred metres or so from the freighter. It was painted a matt black and bore no numbers or insignia. It seemed amazing to John Millane that these two vessels could move so close to each other in such a heavy sea without colliding. He was also surprised that under these very difficult circumstances the large loads from *Halwood* would be lifted on to the submarine's deck and then speedily unloaded and carried into the bowels of this enormous underwater warship without mishap.

As it turned out neither he nor his team mates would see any of this happen. They were the first to be transferred to their new transport. One by one they were winched down to the submarine where they were grabbed and quickly led to an opening in the deck and on to a ladder which took them to the level below. They were then taken to a small cabin and the door was shut behind them.

Millane noticed that none of the seamen he saw wore any uniform or badges of rank. Each man wore jeans or overalls over plain T-shirts. He saw nothing to indicate the name of the submarine, so he decided he was not meant to know. They were used to operating under these circumstances in their own unit.

'Nothing like *Morning Departure*, Punchy,' Yettie called to him across the cabin.

'I hope not, you daft sod. If I remember rightly, in that film the submarine sunk.' Millane good-humouredly threw a pillow at him.

★

The following three days were very limiting. There was little or no space to exercise, and apart from their personal weapons they were not able to get to the rest of their gear. The three men slept a lot, and took great care not to eat too much of the excellent food served on board the submarine. They had to be trim and ready for extreme physical exertion, not only after they reached the beach, but in getting to it in the first place.

Few people spoke to them during their time on board but each man in the team had the distinct impression that the submarine had something more important to do than act as transport for such an insignificant little group of gravel crunchers.

The accommodation was so comfortable that all three men were disappointed when informed that they had arrived at their destination.

★

They had worn wetsuits for the trip from the submarine to the shore, which was just as well, because they got a thorough soaking on several occasions while bringing their inflatable boats on to the beach.

The submarine had launched three more inflatables to enable the transfer to be conducted in the fastest manner possible. One of these capsized in the surf and lost all of its load. Its two crewmen righted the boat and headed for the beach fast. Reaching it before anyone else they dragged their now-empty boat on to the beach and prepared to assist the others.

This was just as well, because the two most difficult stages of the exercise were at the moment just prior to landing when the paddlers stepped out of their boat into the treacherous undertow, and then at the point when, with no water beneath it, they had to drag it beyond the range of the thundering surf. The two extra men were able to help considerably, and no further cargo was lost.

Thank goodness we plan these things thoroughly, Millane thought, paddling like mad to prevent his boat from being caught by a rogue wave crazily coming at him from a totally different direction to the rest of the sea. The power of the wind was tremendous and was increasing the hazards as it tried to lift the inflatable into the air. He was carrying the lightest but most important pieces of radio and electronic equipment and was managing his boat alone. The Major and Sergeant Smith had heavier loads, as did the sailors in the two other craft struggling their way through the surf, hence the need for two people to handle each of these boats.

Millane was grateful for the help of the two sailors who were waiting on the beach, and very relieved to feel the restraining influence of the extra two pairs of hands on his fragile little craft.

The submariners did not wait around. The weather and the sea conditions were worsening fast, thus as soon as all the boats were unloaded and their cargo dragged up the beach beyond the reach of the grasping tide, they said farewell to the SAS soldiers and hurriedly took off back to their submarine and the comfort of the quiet and still world below the waves. Luckily they suffered no mishaps getting back through the raging surf.

★

'Shit, I'm frozen, Boss.' John Millane was standing half naked on the shingle beach, in near freezing temperature, his wetsuit unzipped and rolled down over his hips. He was frantically trying to towel his upper body dry. The wind was fierce, and blowing little particles of sand and salt in each droplet of spray coming in from the ocean. It was a hopeless task, yet each man was fully aware of the need to achieve the maximum level of dryness and warmth in the fastest possible time. The temperature was well below freezing, but that was to be their least problem. More than anything they dreaded getting fully dressed in their thermal underwear and winter clothing, only to discover that they had left itching particles of sand on their body that would rub and cause irritations and festering sores over the days to come.

Marven came to their aid. The most experienced member of the team in these conditions he had quickly thrown a parka over his wetsuit, and while his partners were struggling with the seemingly impossible task of drying their bodies he had opened one of the wooden boxes, releasing a large canvas sheet.

Yettie Smith had immediately understood what he had in mind, and without a word being spoken he had grabbed one end of the stiff material and held it upright. It took just a second or so for Millane to understand what was required of him. He instantly stepped into the area of limited but temporary shelter provided by his team mates, and in a short while had completed drying himself thoroughly and put on the vitally important protective clothing. He then took over from Marven, allowing him to do likewise.

Yettie took much longer than expected. He appeared to be unable to bend his right arm. He also seemed to be disoriented.

'Sorry guys, but I haven't been able to do much with this arm since the Major tried to tear the bastard off with that syringe the other day,' he shouted to be heard above the roar of the wind and waves. His humour was obviously faked, and he appeared to be in some distress.

Seeing that he was unable to complete dressing himself and aware of the effect that the low temperature would be having on him Millane stretched out his arm and grabbed the other end of the canvas sheet. Marven understood what he was intending, and letting go of his end he snatched the towel from the distressed Sergeant and began to rub his body dry. That completed, he quickly dressed the man and helped him on with his socks and boots. This took several minutes, by which time all three men were visibly shaking with the cold which was made even more severe by the wind-chill factor. Smith's condition had noticeably deteriorated to the point where Marven was beginning to get worried for the man.

This is not a good way to commence an operation. Yettie is not at all well. We must get him to cover.

Reading his commanding officer's mind, Millane leaned forward and draped the canvas sheet over the shoulders of the two men.

'Wait one! Hang on to this, I wont be long.' With that he turned and ran off up the steeply rising shingle beach and out of sight. He was back a few minutes later and, raising his voice to be heard over the roar of the wind he shouted encouragement to the Major and Smith.

'There's a shallow cave in the cliff round there.' He pointed back to where he had come from. 'It's out of the wind, and we should be able to light a fire and warm ourselves up.'

'Good stuff, John. Yettie, get your arse up there with this sheet and a couple of heaters. Punchy and I will start bringing the gear up. I expect the place to be looking and feeling like the fucking Ritz by the time we get there. Okay?'

'Got you, Boss,' replied the less than enthusiastic Sergeant Smith, knowing full well that he was getting the cushy job because of his bad arm and his generally poor condition. He felt guilty and inadequate for leaving his partners to do the dirty work, however he really felt unwell, and knew that the right decision had been made. Under similar circumstances he would have made the same decision, and had done so in the recent past.

Within two hours Major Marven and Millane had transported all of the equipment and supplies up the beach and into the shelter of the cliff. The cave was not sufficiently large for it to be used as a storage centre, so the majority of their gear was stacked in a shallow and dry-looking gully nearby and sheeted over for protection from the elements. Large rocks were placed all around the edge of the canvas, and it was generally agreed that this would withstand, at least for the time being, whatever the weather was likely to throw at them.

Meanwhile, regardless of his unwell condition Yettie Smith had done them proud. He had managed to erect the canvas sheet across the entrance to the cave, with just a small area able to be moved for access. The material was secured by several rock-climbing pitons hammered deeply in to the surrounding rock face. A master in the art of camouflage, he had covered the canvas sheeting with rope netting interwoven with grass and ferns from the surrounding landscape. But for the few articles of equipment still left outside, the other two men would not have been able to see the entrance when they finally made their very weary way to it after completing the transfer of supplies from the beach. Marven was very satisfied with the results.

The cave was just large enough to enable the three men to spread their sleeping bags close together for extra warmth. The few items of equipment and supplies that Yettie had brought into the cave were stacked against the canvas sheet which was tucked underneath the boxes. This was helping to hold it securely on the ground. The boxes also acted as extra windbreaks.

The Sergeant had managed to take the chill off the air by lighting one of the portable heaters, and by stoking up a small stove, on top of which stood a large billycan of boiling water. The three men were soon enjoying a scalding hot cup of tea, topped up with a large spoonful of sweetened condensed milk. In spite of this, and the slightly warmer temperature of the cave they were still very cold.

The cave was not very roomy or comfortable, but they sat back on their poncho capes and wallowed in the sheer luxury of the moment. After what they had just endured this was something special. Beyond their flimsy protective cover the roar of the wind was now deafening, so every word had to be shouted if it was to be heard.

'Yettie, get your head down. You too, Punchy. I'll take first watch.'

Nobody argued with the boss, and within moments the two soldiers were asleep, their thermal sleeping bags zipped up over their heads.

Two hours later Millane was woken up, and handed a steaming cup of tea.

'Your shift, John. Yettie has been very restless. I think he is probably not going to be a lot of good to us for a day or so. I've decided that you and I will do the watches, at least until you have had the chance to look at him in the daylight.'

'He won't like that, Boss. You know how bloody determined he can be.'

'Yep! So can I, John. So can I.' The Major was sound asleep seconds after he had finished speaking.

# Chapter Nine

Dawn came in a most unwelcome manner. The wind had turned to the east, and was battering into the canvas sheet protecting the entrance to their tiny home. Marven and Millane fought to hold it in place for over an hour before they were forced to give up the fight. The moment they let go, the canvas tore into three pieces with a loud crack. One strip, still suspended from the side wall of the cave was suddenly caught by a fierce gust and whiplashed across the cave, hitting Millane in the side of the head, splitting the skin and knocking him flying.

'Where the hell is that bloody crofter?' He was in pain and wiping blood from a cut above his right eye.

'If he's not here by now, I doubt he is coming,' replied Marven, quickly checking his watch. 'He should have been here several hours ago. How's Yettie?'

'I don't know, Boss. He is really unwell. I can't work out what's wrong with him. He is feverish and has a bloody high temperature but his body is cold. I reckon we have got to get him to somewhere warm and dry very soon, otherwise we may have to write him off as far as the operation is concerned.'

'Stay with him. I'll do a recce and come back later. Give me an hour, two at the most.'

Millane pulled the remains of the canvas sheet over the sick man, and laid alongside him, pulling the man's cold body close to his own, hoping to pass on some of his body warmth. The wind eased momentarily, but when it built up once more it brought with it a flurry of snow which quickly covered the two men huddled together in the open cave.

★

Marven was not very pleased with what he found during his recce of the island. Stumbling around in the now fierce snowstorm he discovered two huts – or what remained of them. One of them appeared to have been blown to pieces, and by the size of the crater in part of the foundations it was almost certainly caused by an air to ground missile of some sort. Picking around in the debris he made a gruesome find: the burnt and mutilated body of a man. He had to assume that this was the crofter who had been going to assist them.

Fifteen minutes' walk away he discovered a second hut on the top of a slight rise. This one had been burnt out, but two blackened rock walls remained. He briefly checked the snow-covered wreckage to see if there had been any further casualties. Finding nothing, he was just about to move on when he stubbed his toe on something hard in the rubble beneath his feet. Bending down he discovered a very large iron ring embedded into the floor. Clearing the snow-layered ash and debris from the vicinity of the ring, he realised that it was a handle to what appeared to be a trapdoor.

It took him ten minutes to prise the heavy wooden door open. It was charred as the result of the inferno that had gutted the hut, but the burning was superficial. What he saw beneath the door delighted him. The trapdoor opened exposing a narrow staircase which led down to a room about twelve foot square with thick timbered walls and a heavy log timber ceiling. It contained two narrow beds and a large wooden cupboard. The floor was concrete and a thick dirty carpet covered most of it.

In the corner of the room was a small alcove containing a chemical toilet and a makeshift handbasin with a small hand pump above it. Out of curiosity he tried the pump and was amazed to find that it worked, although the water that it disgorged was a dirty brown. There was a pipe leading up out through the ceiling which was probably a ventilation shaft of some sort.

In the cupboard wrapped in plastic and canvas bags were blankets and several sets of old but clean woollen clothing. Under the beds he found kerosene and chemicals for the toilet. The room was equipped with kerosene lamps and a large heater.

I wouldn't want to use those in this confined space, he thought to himself as he continued exploring. The room was obviously designed to protect the crofter when the weather conditions became so bad that the hut above was in danger of being blown down.

It was only half a mile from the cave and would be ideal for their purposes, if only to enable Sergeant Yettie Smith to be nursed back to full health in some sort of comfort. The room was as cold as an icebox but he knew how quickly such a space could be heated up by the portable heaters that they had with them. At least down here the sick man would be protected from the cutting sub-zero wind. It was likely to be the extreme wind-chill factor that would present the greatest danger for Yettie.

Making the decision to move into the cellar was easy. He set off back to the cave as fast as he could manage in the blizzard-like conditions, his head down to protect his face from the cutting sleet and ice.

'Grab as much gear as you can, John. You and I can manage Yettie between us. Once we get him up there into bed we will be able to transfer the rest of the gear at our leisure. Believe me, old son, the place is like a bloody

Butlin's Holiday Camp compared with this hole in the rock.'

It had only taken a moment to describe what he had found to the delighted John Millane.

*

It took the rest of the day, mostly in darkness, to move all of the equipment and supplies up to the hut and into the cellar below. By the time Millane took the first watch and the others had settled down for the night they were established in their new base, and almost ready to commence operations.

Between the trips back and forth to the cave and the gully where the equipment was stored they managed, whilst taking breaks from the intense cold, to do some essential housework. The outlet to the ventilation pipe was found and cleared out, and the room was swept free of dirt and dust. The two beds were pulled together to give extra floor space and to enable all three men to lie down at the same time should the opportunity arise.

It had taken several hours to set up the radio equipment. This was the first scheduled task for the team, and Millane knew that there would be several operators in various locations waiting to pick up their signal advising that they were established and operational. A long aerial was fed through the trapdoor framework, across the floor of the burnt-out building and up one of the surviving walls.

He had carried out numerous tests, and managed to tune into several radio wavelengths. He hadn't managed to transmit yet, but felt confident that with a few minor adjustments there would be no problems once the appropriate time arrived. Their instructions were to transmit on every other even hour commencing at 2200 hours on the first day until such time as they made contact.

The submarine would have already advised that the party was ashore in one piece.

In one piece, he mused as he looked across at Yettie stretched out on the newly extended bed. Christ knows what is wrong with him. He's burning up with fever. I hope he isn't heading for pneumonia.

Glancing at Major Marven lying fast asleep next to the sick man, he smiled to himself as a frivolous thought came into his mind. For your sake let's hope the boss doesn't have a horny dream while he's cuddled up that close to you, Yettie.

Checking the Sergeant one more time he pulled on his balaclava, drew the hood of his parka over his head and pulled the drawstrings tight so his chin was covered securely. A brief check of his weapon and the magazines in his pockets, then pulling his gloves on he climbed the stairs to the trapdoor above.

He crouched below the door listening intently for any sound of danger. In fact he was very sure that every sound he could hear was dangerous. The wind was continuously screeching across the ruins above his head. He could hear another unpleasant, yet strangely comforting noise. It was either heavy rain or sleet. He was not looking forward to going out in such weather, but knew that it was important to ensure that the island was free from danger to his group. The comfort came from the knowledge that such weather was more likely to deter the enemy if they were about, than himself.

His patrol was uneventful other than for the discovery of several smashed and empty cases, some wooden and some heavy-duty cardboard, that had once contained compo rations and equipment from the inflatable boat that capsized. The ravages of the sea had long since smashed them open and discharged their contents to the depths. He picked up all of the pieces of cases that he could find, and taking them well away from the surf line he buried them deeply in the shingle.

It was pitch dark, and very difficult to see much, but the crashing surf created a glowing phosphorescence on the edge of the beach which had made it possible for him to just see the give-away debris that had been thrown from the sea. He felt sure, however, that a further search in daylight would be likely to reveal other items that if found would immediately indicate the presence of British troops on the island.

He would report his find to Major Marven on his return. They were not expecting visitors, but it would be folly not to prepare for that eventuality.

★

'Thanks for the tea, John. No joy with the radio yet?'

'No, Boss. Could be atmospherics, but I think it more likely that it took a knock from something while I was bringing it ashore. I'll try it later when you wake me up for my next stint.'

Marven was sitting on the edge of the bed with his hands cupped around a large tin mug full of a substance that no self-respecting tea company would be likely to claim as its own, but it was sweet and steaming hot.

'I'm off to the beach to see if I can find any more of the stuff that was lost overboard. I'll take a torch with me. It'll be pretty safe to use it in these weather conditions.' He was talking to himself though, as Millane was already curled up on the bed, sleeping soundly.

Over the next few days this routine became the norm. Radio contact had been established and the first aircraft sightings had been reported. Millane had also had several brief discussions with a naval doctor regarding Yettie's condition. He was now showing signs of either pleurisy or pneumonia.

A week after their arrival the boss made the decision that the team could not chance having the sick man with them any longer and sought an evacuation at the earliest possible time. Millane's careful nursing had had no effect on the Sergeant, whose condition, if anything, appeared to be getting worse.

Eventually they received a message advising them that a submarine would attempt to rendezvous with them on the following Saturday, just three days off, but the vessel would not be able to stop for more than a few minutes. Therefore Marven and Millane would have to get an inflatable boat through the surf and out into the open sea in order to make the transfer. There was no question of waiting for the favourable tides; they would have to chance it, and all three men would have to travel in the same boat. It was not a job that could be done by any fewer than two men paddling. On their own the two officers could have done it with relative ease, but with a seriously ill man with them it would be touch and go.

They didn't debate the issue. The boss said it would happen, and Millane accepted it as just another thing to be done. The SAS had the reputation of looking after its own, so Sergeant Smith would be taken to the submarine where he could receive the best of medical treatment for whatever his illness was, come hell or high water.

*

Air traffic to and from Port Stanley had become quite heavy, and the subsequent frequency of radio broadcasts from the team had become a concern to both Marven and Millane.

'The Argies aren't stupid. If we keep this up we are going to get sussed before long, Boss.' Millane had just signed off after reporting the westward travel of a squadron of Canberra bombers escorted by three Mirage, and three A4 Skyhawk fighters.

'They've got a bloody big air force for our lads to compete with when they get here, John, so anything we can do to keep them informed and warned has got to be worth something.'

'The Fuerza Aerea Argentina is a good outfit. I met some of their guys a few years back, and they were real good at what they did. Whatever eventuates I am willing to bet they will put up a bloody good show. The thought of what they could do to our mob if they catch them out in the open scares the shit out of me.

'Anyway, let's hope they don't home in on our signals; if they do we'll just have to make a run for it.' Both men laughed at the thought of them paddling their inflatable boat at a speed sufficient to outrun the Argentinian Air Force.

Their latest concern, however, was not whether their signals would be identified and homed in on, it was more the chance of being seen by one of the many planes flying in and out of Port Stanley while they were sitting out in the open sea on Saturday, waiting for the arrival of the submarine.

'Why the fuck does it have to be in broad daylight, Boss?'

'Well, they did say they couldn't afford the luxury of waiting for the tide, and they also warned us that they couldn't hang around for long.'

'But what if one of those squadrons of Mirages or Skyhawks spots them as they come up. They will screw us well and truly if they are half as good as you say they are.'

'They will probably only come up high enough for their sail to be above water. You and I have practised this often enough, John. Let's not be negative about it before it happens. Our biggest, and probably only danger is going to be getting through the bloody surf and out to where the sub will hopefully be. If the weather is true to form of late, the clouds will be so low that the Argie Mirages will have to be bloody water-skiing to see us.'

★

The following days were occupied mainly with looking after Yettie Smith and keeping up the constant fitness regime that was essential if they were going to survive their stint on the island, let alone the surf on Saturday.

One of the boats was recovered from the gully near the beach where they, after being carefully deflated and packed into large canvas bags, had both been buried. It was dusted off and examined for damage. There was none visible, but there was no opportunity to inflate it and do the job properly. This would only be done at the last moment in daylight on Saturday afternoon, and if the worst came to the worst, repairs would have to be done on the run.

The weather was unbelievably bad. It was blowing a blizzard and the sleet and snow was coming in sideways on. The surf pounding on to the steeply sloping beach was higher than they had seen it before. When they inflated the boat it turned out to be in perfect condition. They tied it down securely to ensure that it didn't take off in the hurricane force wind that was lashing the exposed slope.

Marven and Millane were again dressed in wetsuits, with plenty of outer clothing over the top. Regardless of this they were extremely cold before they even got to the shore where it was all about to happen. Prior to leaving the cellar to head for the beach and prepare the inflatable they had dressed Smith similarly to ensure that he would be spared the ravages of the weather and the sea as much as was possible. He was delirious and incapable of helping himself in any way.

Spare clothing had been sealed in heavy-duty plastic bags and loaded into the boat, just in case they sank and were washed up on to the rocks somewhere away from the beach and their cellar hideout. Both men knew that regardless of their extreme fitness the prospects of survival without adequate dry clothing were remote in the hideous conditions that they were exposed to.

It took them ten minutes to carry Yettie Smith to the beach. They placed him inside a zip-up waterproof sleeping bag and carefully lay him in the bottom of the boat. To ensure that he couldn't fall out they secured one end of the sleeping bag to the boat with a rope. Then they untied the lashings and commenced dragging it down the beach, their unconscious colleague inside. It was harder than they had expected it to be. The gale force wind was so strong that it kept lifting the raft up from the ground even with Yettie inside.

Marven and Millane paused just before the point where the surf hit the shingle and waited. The sea was very angry and the high-walled breakers were following each other in closely at regular intervals, then pounding down like drumbeats on to the shore. The undertow was so fierce that it made a high-pitched screaming noise as it dragged hundreds of tons of shingle back into the base of the next breaker. They had calculated that it would not be wise to allow themselves to enter the water in the undertow, which would merely pull them under the next wave. Their plan was to hit the water at as fast a run as they could manage, just as the surf landed, and to try to ride it out before the undertow took hold.

They were just about to commence their run when they experienced a remarkable bit of luck. A large breaker had just landed but before it could start to recede it was immediately followed by two further breakers, totally out of sequence and appearing to come from completely different angles to their predecessor. The result was that, while the water was raging in a tormented dangerous manner, for a few seconds there was no undertow.

'Now, John. Now! For fuck's sake.'

Millane needed no second telling. He was already running like mad, his left arm almost being torn out of its socket by the weight of the boat and the force of the wind tearing at it and trying to drag it out of his grasp.

Up to his knees in the water he saw that the undertow had still not started to drag the mad water back down the beach. He leapt on to his side of the boat, aware that the Major was already inside. Now they were paddling like mad; strong and deep even strokes. A huge breaker appeared ahead of them, but they were no longer quite so vulnerable as they had been moments before. Leaning all of their weight forward they paddled hard into the wall of water. They had practised the techniques of dealing with such seas on numerous occasions, both in training and on active service in different parts of the world. The only difference now was that the water was much colder and they were competing against blinding sleet and snow as well as a savage sea. The giant wave was upon them, lifting them high into the air.

For that brief moment they were in the lap of the gods. There was nothing they could have done that could possibly have had any meaningful effect on what would happen to them when they hit the water again. They hung on grimly as their fragile craft hovered in the air for what seemed like ages before it landed. Fortunately when it did it landed flat on the surface in the trough of the wave which was dragging them back with it towards the shore. To overcome this their paddling had now increased in momentum. Both men knew that if they worked hard enough and moved the boat at sufficient speed they would not only be able to minimise the effect of the waves' dragging force, they could also get close to the next breaker before it formed fully into a curving wall of roaring water.

They didn't quite make it, and again found themselves being dragged backwards in the wake of the giant wave. Time and time again they had their work cut out struggling to get to the point where they would be able to beat the next breaker.

They had to fight over a dozen such waves; each one becoming less high and fierce, until eventually they found themselves in the open water out of the clutches of the fearsome tide. Now all they had to contend with were six foot high waves and swells, the horrific wind, and the ever-constant danger of capsizing.

Both men were exhausted and very cold. During the previous minutes they had both inwardly harboured the secret fear of not being able to last out to this point. Now they could take it relatively easy, with one man at a time paddling to hold the inflatable boat into the wind, and upright; the other man taking the opportunity to get down under the boat's cover for a brief period of shelter.

Yettie was not handling the gyrations of the boat too well. He was now so delirious that he had to be constantly restrained to prevent him toppling it over.

'Over a bit to the left, John,' Marven shouted to enable himself to be heard over the noise of the wind and sea. 'As far as I can judge, we have to be at a point level with that high rock over there to the west. They had better come soon though; they said 1400 hours. It's 1430 now. It took us twenty minutes just to get through that bloody surf. I am not looking forward to going back through it again.

'I don't think Yettie is going to last the night out if we miss them. He's really off the planet at the moment. Right! You take over in here. You know what to do in these sorts of circumstances. I'll take over with the paddle.'

'Thanks, Boss. That'll be great. Have you put the kettle on?' Then suddenly, 'Holy cow!' he shouted at the top of his voice. 'The Navy's arrived. Jesus, they scared me witless. Stupid bastards. Stupid, lovely bastards.'

Just a few feet to his right the submarine had appeared, its massive sail lifting out of the water and soaring above them. The skipper was obviously sure of himself in the terrible overcast weather conditions. It was highly unlikely that too many aircraft would be flying in such a storm. The vessel had completely surfaced, its enormous black hull acting both as a windbreak and a baffle against the waves. The small boat was temporarily becalmed, a weird sensation after all that the men had endured for the previous hour.

The barren deck was suddenly full of parka-clad sailors. Millane was joined by the Major and they quickly paddled to the submarine, where they were dragged on to the flat and strangely still deck.

A man who identified himself as the ship's Number One led them to a hatch in the side of the ship's high sail. Inside they climbed down a ladder to the control room where they were given towels and a cup of hot cocoa.

Stripped down to their wetsuits they soon became warm again. The officer advised them that the submarine was going to submerge for a short while.

'During which time you can have a wash and brush up, if you wish to.'

The invitation was too good to turn down, and so both men took a luxurious but very brief shower. During their ablutions they both experienced a very strange sensation as the vessel submerged back below the waves.

Once they were showered and dried they were given fresh wetsuits and winter clothing. When they were dressed once more they both felt stifling hot in the confines of the ship. It didn't occur to them until shortly afterwards that stifling hot was a luxurious condition to be in under the circumstances.

Yettie had been removed from the inflatable and hurried to the sickbay where he had been stripped and put into bed under the watchful eye of a naval doctor who had already injected him with something to bring the fever down and help him sleep while he examined him further and made a diagnosis.

★

'That's one very sick soldier we have there, gentlemen.' The Captain had just put down the telephone. 'That was the doctor. He says that your Sergeant certainly has pneumonia. We'll do everything we can for him. Unfortunately we are not due to rendezvous with the task force for several days, so he is stuck with our sickbay and its relatively limited resources.'

'We know you will do everything you can, Captain. We thank you. He'll be a damned sight better off here than with us on that godforsaken rock.'

Ten minutes later the sub had returned to the surface and they were soon once again in their vulnerable little craft which looked even more so now they were back in the water and dwarfed by the massive black ship. The comfort of their windbreak soon disappeared as the vessel sank quickly below the waves with barely a sound, not that one could be heard too well above the roar of the sea and the howling wind.

Pleased that they had been able to ensure that Yettie Smith was in safer hands, and feeling much more comfortable after their shower and change into fresh wetsuits and clothing, both men felt that they could handle anything that came their way.

That was until it hit them – or rather their inflatable raft. A large piece of driftwood the size of a power pole thrust into the soft side of the raft and immediately tore it to pieces.

They had not been prepared for their sudden immersion, and were soon in great difficulties trying to divest themselves of their boots and cumbersome clothing. Just as Millane came to the surface he saw a large partly submerged plastic bag bobbing nearby.

'Shit! The spare clothing. Better get it. We are sure going to need it now.'

Later he was to realise what a wise decision this had been, although at the time he merely did it on an impulse. There were actually two bags but they had been tied together at the top, and luckily at the time the bags had been packed they had not been completely emptied of air. The consequent ballooning effect kept them sufficiently afloat for him to recover them after several attempts were thwarted by large waves.

Major Marven was alongside him instantly. This was a relief to Millane because the boss's skills in water were legendary throughout the SAS. He was one of the most powerful swimmers in the regiment.

'It's about time for the turn in the tide, John,' the boss screamed into his ear. 'Let's head for the beach as fast as we can. We should be able to get in quite easily if my watch is right and the tide is turning.' Without another word he set off at a fast freestyle followed by Millane at a much slower pace, and being slowed down even more by the two heavy and only just floating bags he was trailing behind him.

If we are going to get ashore okay I might as well dump these. They're only getting in the bloody way. There are plenty more back in the cellar. If only the bloody things floated a bit better, he thought as he struggled with the two cumbersome bags. Yet he found himself unable to make that decision for some unaccountable reason, so he floundered on with great difficulty.

They were about three hundred yards from the shore when, to his amazement, over the top of a giant wave he saw Marven pounding back towards him. He stopped swimming and trod water, wondering what was wrong. He felt sure that the boss wasn't just coming back to give him a helping hand.

'Argie marines,' Marven shouted above the roar of the elements. 'About thirty of them in half a dozen Zodiacs. God knows where they have come from. There must be a ship out there. I'm buggered if I know how they missed our sub.'

'More to the point, Boss, how did our sub manage to miss them?'

'Probably under orders not to engage anything at any cost; after bigger fish no doubt. Anyway, we can't land on the beach. At the very least they will have sentries keeping an eye on the boats. Also we have to keep out of their way regardless. We mustn't get involved either. Looks like we have got to head west towards those rocks. If we get ashore we are going to need those clothes you are dragging along with you. Well done, John.' The Major's voice was hoarse through shouting.

'Aren't those rocks bloody dangerous? Wasn't that why we had to chance the beach anyway?'

'Buggered if I know, John. We have no choice, so let's go. We sure as hell can't stay out here all day. I'm beginning to feel numb with the cold. Are you sure you can manage those bags?'

Without waiting for a response he turned in the water and set out for the rocks in the distance. Realising there was no alternative Millane struck out after him.

As they approached the rocks they really did look dangerous, with razor-edged splinters jutting threateningly upwards towards the sky. A certain death trap for any form of boat but, as with the beach, the turning tide had also made the sea much calmer in this area. In the event both men were able to time their arrival on the rocks, waiting for a suitable swell to take them in as slowly as possible. Millane followed the boss, ending up clinging to a tall spike of rock only a few feet away from him. The art was not to get washed off again by the next swell.

They carefully made their way through the maze of sharp pointed rocks to the foot of the cliff, hanging on tightly as each wave roared in, threatening to lift them off and drag them back into the sea, or worse still, on to the sharp rocks. They were still up to their waists in surging water, and knew that for safety's sake they had to get above the waterline before the tide turned fully and the sea resumed its full ferocity.

*

It took them ten minutes to find the first foothold above the waterline, by which time they were both beginning to feel the effects of exposure. They had to get up the cliff and change out of their wetsuits into dry clothing as a matter of urgency.

It was Marven who found the fissure that was to be their exit from the rocks. A long, chimney-like split in the cliff face, it also took them out of the direct force of the icy wind until they were almost to the top, by which time their physical exertions had brought some warmth back to their bodies; if only temporarily. The fissure was only shoulder wide but there were sufficient hand and footholds to enable the soldiers to climb to the top with ease. The biggest problem was getting the bags of clothing up with them. They achieved this by separating them and carrying one each.

At the top they quickly reconnoitred the area to ensure that the Argentinian marines were not in the vicinity. They weren't. Finding a small, reasonably sheltered opening in a rock face the men took the opportunity to change out of their wetsuits. In the plastic bags were three full sets of long thermal underwear and top clothing. This included gloves and socks, but unfortunately no shoes.

Millane had had the foresight to include a towel in each bag, so they were able to dry themselves as much as possible before putting the clothes on.

Marven had equipped himself with a diver's knife strapped to his leg over his wet suit. He used this to cut sections out of the lower legs of both wetsuits which each man slipped on over their feet and up past their ankles. Whilst not as secure and warm as boots, they were functional and provided a degree of warmth as well as a layer of latex between the feet and the rocky surfaces on which they would have to walk.

'I wonder what those bloody marines are up to. Surely they couldn't have found us this easily, John.'

They were making their way carefully along the top of the cliffs to a point overlooking the beach. Taking shelter from the snow and sleet under a rocky outcrop they observed what was happening below them.

The marines had spread out and worked their way up to the top of the hill where the burnt-out hut and its secret cellar was situated. Even in the half-light they could see that the men were rummaging about in the debris of the hut but did not appear to have discovered its secret.

'They must be bloody blind, Boss, how could they miss it?'

'Look around you Lieutenant Millane,' the Major responded sharply. 'Whatever happened to field craft? Use your bloody eyes and your fucking head, man.'

Millane could have bitten his tongue for being so stupid. Since just before they left the cellar earlier in the day it had been pouring with sleet and snow. The ground was covered in a bleak white carpet.

The men at the burnt-out hut were walking on several inches of snow. Of course they wouldn't be able to see the cellar entrance unless they knew it was there in the first place.

'Sorry, sir: stupid slip. It won't happen again.' He knew that the boss's sharp retort was meant to remind him that even though it was not critical at this moment, such a basic, stupid oversight on their part at some later time could result in failure, capture and even death. He promised himself that he would remain more alert in future, and not open his mouth until he was sure his brain was connected.

'I wonder if the Argies know about the tide, Boss.'

'If they don't they are in for one hell of a rude shock when they try to get out of here. Which, incidentally, I hope will be soon. I am in urgent need of a sit on that portable loo, and I'm pretty sure that if I dropped my pants here my balls would freeze off.'

Both men laughed. Millane knew that this was the boss's way of breaking the ice after the reprimand. He also knew that they were both in great need of some warmth and hot food that the cellar and its amenities could provide.

Their question was answered for them when the marine nearest to them suddenly pointed out to the sea which had started to dramatically change in character, and shouted something up the beach to the men nearest to him. One of the soldiers was carrying a radio and he spoke into his handset.

It was like watching a ghostly mime, as no sounds other than those provided by nature could be heard.

They saw the men at the top of the hill turn and begin to trot downwards towards the beach. Once they got there they lined up in true military fashion whilst one of the figures who remained out in front of the squad appeared to address them.

'The silly bastard will want to inspect them next.' Marven chuckled out loud.

Then, as if to prove to him that he was wrong the marines broke up into six groups and headed for the boats. They were well disciplined, and obviously very well practised. Within minutes all six Zodiacs were through the heavy breakers and on their way out to sea.

Marven and Millane were impressed with the excellent displays of seamanship that they had just witnessed.

'If their fighting ability is anything like their seamanship we will have to watch out for those boys if they return. Come on, John, I want to get home as quickly as possible. I'm freezing my knackers off lying down here.'

They were on their feet and down on the beach within minutes. From there it was only a short distance to the comfort of their hideout which they reached just as the last touch of light disappeared, leaving them in darkness of the sort that few people ever experience in their lives.

'I can't see them coming back tonight, John. To do so would be bloody stupid. I think we can dispense with mounting a watch. Let's build up a nice bit of warmth, then eat and get our heads down. We both need it after what we've been through.'

## Chapter Ten

Their lonely vigil continued until well into May without any further excitement. The steady flow of air traffic to and from Port Stanley continued non-stop. They had perfected the art of making speedy transmissions, and decided that the Argentinians were not equipped to intercept and trace transmissions in the way that the British forces would be. Alternatively, they believed that the British hadn't arrived in the area yet, so they were not operating in a combat state of readiness.

★

On 19th May disaster hit the Special Air Service. A Sea King troop transport helicopter transferring SAS personnel from one ship to another crashed into the sea. A large number of men died. This tragedy changed many of the plans that the task force leaders had developed over the previous weeks.

The following day a special force of SAS made a diversionary attack near Goose Green striking terror into the hearts of Argentinian soldiers, mostly conscripts, who had never experienced war before, let alone war with such a special force. On that same day Millane received a message advising that the operation at Jason Island was to be aborted and that they were to commence preparations for closing up shop. They would be picked up by a submarine within a few days and returned to the main task force.

Both men were pleased to be leaving their tiny island. They were anxious to get back to the main force and into the real action, although concerned at what they might discover when they saw the casualty list from the Sea King disaster. Doubtless each would find themselves mourning the loss of friends.

★

Captain Fernando Braun was sure he was wasting his time. He had been directed to make a reconnaissance of the bleak rock that was coming up on his port wing. He had flown over it so many times over the past four weeks since his squadron had been transferred to Port Stanley.

He was excited about his country's victory over the British, and the fact that the Malvinas were now back in the hands of their rightful owners. For too long the imperialist British had strutted around the world, stealing land rightfully owned by other sovereign states. The Malvinas which the British insultingly declared to be their property and had unlawfully named the Falkland Islands, had stood tantalisingly out of the reach of his countrymen until Presidenti Leopoldo Galtieri had made his brave and momentous declaration that they would once again become part of Argentina.

He was very proud of his country's action which resulted in bringing the Malvinas back to Argentina, and wondered if other countries similarly treated by major powers would follow suit.

★

He remembered his grandfather telling him how, after the Second World War, the British had treated the Germans so badly after they had fought such an honourable war. He remembered the stories that he had been told as a child, both by his grandfather, and more recently his father, about how the now deceased and sadly missed Colonel Braun had fought with distinction in the SS and had managed to escape to Argentina just before the final days of the war. He was also told as a child not to believe the outrageous stories that were told by the British and their allies regarding the alleged atrocities conducted by the Germans, the SS in particular, according to Grandfather.

Fernando had never thought to question the enormous wealth that his family possessed, nor had he even considered how his grandfather had managed to escape and get halfway across the world at such a difficult time.

In reality Colonel Braun had not existed. The name and immediate rise in status to colonel had been adopted by the SS man whose real rank and name was Lieutenant Carl Krieg. The adopted name change to Braun had been part of his escape plan: the escape that brought him riches beyond his wildest dreams.

Unknown to any of his family, for he had never divulged the true story of his wartime exploits, he had been entrusted with a large cache of Nazi gold and other treasures that had been smuggled out of Germany in the final days before the fall of Berlin. He and six storm troopers had guarded the cargo day and night throughout its journey on the dilapidated cargo steamer, *San Paulo*, across the South Atlantic where, two hundred miles north of Buenos Aires it was anchored in a deserted cove.

Several hours before that the crew had been rounded up and locked in a cabin under guard and the ship's control was taken over by the Lieutenant and his men. Krieg and his SS troopers were all accomplished seamen, specifically trained from the beginning of the war to perform such an important task for their beloved Führer.

These treasures were intended to be set aside for funding the triumphant return of the Führer and his armies when the time came. Each of the men had sworn an oath to serve the Führer to the death if necessary, and they were all proud to have been given the honour that had been bestowed on them.

When the ship was ten miles from the shores of Argentina Krieg ordered the engines to be stopped and the anchor dropped. One by one the crew were brought from the cabin to the main deck and shot. Their weighted-down bodies were thrown overboard into the shark-infested waters. No trace would be found.

This task completed, the ship was steamed up once more and commenced on the final stages of its journey to the pre-selected cove. It had in fact been chosen by Krieg himself on a trip from neutral Spain to Argentina earlier in the war. He had also purchased a warehouse in a small town just north of the cove and had supervised the building of deep concrete cellars below its floor.

★

Once anchored in the cove Krieg and his men spent two weeks unloading the ship on to a small jetty and transporting the gold and treasures to the warehouse in a truck that Krieg had purchased. The cargo was stacked into the cellars which were then bricked up and plastered over, leaving the warehouse looking as it had done when it was first purchased.

Krieg and his men were billeted in the warehouse for a short period while they waited for further instructions from Berlin through the Embassy in Buenos Aires. As it transpired the Embassy was never contacted by Berlin, so Krieg received no instructions.

He was the only one of the team who spoke the language, so he made himself personally responsible for the purchase of provisions in the small town.

It was whilst purchasing food in a local store that he heard a radio news broadcast announcing the fall of Berlin and the death of Hitler. In shock, he walked down to the beach and sat on the sand in a daze, wondering what to do next. Six hours later he had made up his mind.

That night while his men were asleep he shot them one by one with a silenced Luger pistol.

*

Now, thirty-seven years later his grandson, oblivious of his family's sordid past, was a playboy pilot in the air force. Money was no object to him and the life offered excitement and glamour. His wealth ensured that he always had many beautiful women to call on whenever he wished.

He therefore resented the simple chore that he had been given this morning. To closely observe a bloody desolate lump of rock, just because some bloody stupid square-bashing soldier claimed to have intercepted one strange radio signal from that direction.

'Haven't they ever heard of atmospheric interference?' he shouted out loud as he banked to the left and lost height rapidly for a sea level approach towards the one and only beach. The Pucaro turboprop aircraft he was flying was a wonderful machine for such a task. It was able to fly at a slow speed which made it perfect for inspections of this sort.

Nevertheless it was not the job for a captain, certainly not Captain Braun. He couldn't understand why they hadn't sent one of the young lieutenants. Another thing that annoyed him was that Pucaros usually hunted in pairs which was much more fun, and certainly not as lonely and boring.

His boredom was to be his downfall. He wasn't concentrating properly and had passed over the top of the man almost before he noticed him. The man was wearing military fatigues of some sort.

'Shit, he must be British. We don't have any people on this island,' he called out excitedly as he increased power and put the plane into a steep climb, banking to the left to go around for a second approach. Switching off the safety he prepared his weapons for what was to come. He felt elated that at last he would have the opportunity to right the wrongs that the British had done to his grandfather.

I am about to avenge you, my dear grandfather. This is for you, he promised his revered ancestor, whilst crossing himself and looking up to the heavens.

'Alpha four to base. Alpha four to base. British military personnel on Skull Island, I am going in to attack. Over.'

Had he not switched his radio off at that particular time he would have heard his squadron commander ordering him to take no action, but to circle the island out of range of enemy fire, keeping observation until relieved or reinforced.

Braun guessed that Colonel Emelio Hernandez would be likely to give this order, which was why he switched the set off the moment his transmission was concluded. He wanted to get his first battle kill. He would be the first one in the squadron. Hernandez would have wanted that privilege for himself.

Later, when he had covered himself with glory for being the first in the squadron to claim victory in combat, he would explain how his set had malfunctioned at that critical moment.

'Hernandez won't take this from me, the fat lazy bastard. It's all mine,' he shouted as he lowered his flaps to reduce his air speed to the minimum, and flew up the beach at ground level towards the hump at the top, where he had last seen the man.

★

Millane was taken totally unawares by the sudden appearance of the Pucaro. The wind was whistling around the cliff face so noisily that the aircraft sound had been muffled.

'Shit, I must have been dozing. Fuck it, we're blown,' he screamed at himself as he rushed back to the cliff face and to the small cave where the machine-gun was set up, facing down the beach. The weapon was strategically placed to deal with a seaborne attack up the beach by foot soldiers.

He knew, however, that to fight against an aircraft from this location would be stupid. Owing to the height of the plane above the ground it would be able to fire directly into the cave with its cannon. Even one well-aimed cannon shell into such a confined space would be fatal.

He didn't even stop to think about it. He snatched up the weapon and a belt of extra ammunition and ran out towards the top of the beach. There was a water-filled ditch just behind the brow of the hill. He would set up the gun just there and catch the bastard as he came over the top. He knew that the Major would have heard the aircraft and would be on his way, but was sure that he would arrive too late for this little confrontation.

Just as he leapt into the ditch he heard the Pucaro coming towards him. Knowing how slow they could fly he didn't want to give the pilot too much of a target, so he slumped down low.

'These buggers always fly in twos. I wonder where his mate is,' he spat sand from his mouth.

Just then he saw the nose of the Pucaro coming over the rise at the top of the beach, less than one hundred yards from him. He knew he only had a split second to act, but was trained for such an eventuality as this. He squeezed the trigger and sprayed the aircraft from the nose, down under the belly and along the side of the cockpit.

Captain Braun was hit by five of the hundred or so bullets that hit his aircraft, and died at precisely the same moment that the fuel tank exploded. The Pucaro disintegrated in mid-air, its burning fuel tank hitting the ground and bouncing and skidding along the beach directly towards where Millane was lying. He had no time to move. He knew this was the end, so he just lay there watching, mesmerised by the sight of the large ball of flame racing towards him.

The tank hit the ground a few feet in front of the small ridge that he was hiding behind and exploded. The force of the explosion tore a large crater in the shingle in front of the ridge. The powerful blast threw him backwards into the ditch where he landed unconscious on his back in a foot of water with his head completely immersed. If he hadn't have been wearing a small pack on his back he may have fared better than he did, however, the bulky pack caused his chest, stomach and upper legs to arch upwards, preventing his body from being completely immersed in the slimy water.

Even though he was unconscious at the time he screamed out loud as the burning fuel engulfed him, the scream only terminating when his mouth and nostrils became full of the thick brown sludge in which he lay.

★

'The idiot has switched off. The silly bastard's after glory. I hope he finds it, but he may have bitten off more than he

can chew. Get Marine HQ and tell them what has
happened. Tell them to get some of their boys out there.
Then prepare the squadron for take-off. We're going out
after the useless sod. I'll court martial him for this.'

Colonel Emelio Hernandez turned and left the control
tower at the double, taking the stairs two at a time.

★

Marven was only two hundred yards away from the
machine-gun post in the cave when he first heard the
engine noise of the Pucaro. He had just completed a full
circuit of Skull Island looking for any signs of enemy
shipping. He had a nagging concern that the Argentinian
marines might return at some stage. He immediately broke
into a fast run and reached the cave just as the Pucaro
commenced its second run up the beach. He couldn't see
the plane, but even though the wind was howling at a high
level of decibels he could hear the engine noise, and could
tell that it was almost upon him.

He made the same decision as Millane had done just a
brief moment before. The cave was too exposed from the
air. He knew he had mere seconds to get across the stretch
of loose shingle to the ditch. His weapon at the high port
ready for action he kicked off and zigzagged across the
exposed flat beach, reaching the ditch just as the Pucaro
came over the top, appearing suddenly through the gusts of
snow about one hundred yards to the south of him.

It was at precisely that moment that he saw Millane. He
was lying flat on his face, his automatic weapon firing
directly at the aircraft as it closed on him. He could see the
bullets peppering the fuselage alongside the cockpit. Then
it was suddenly over. In a split second the Pucaro seemed to
jerk backwards in flight, its nose turning skywards. There
was a massive explosion, and it disintegrated into hundreds

of pieces which sprayed out in every direction. A ball of flame leapt forward from the centre of the fireball which had been the Pucaro. It hit the shingle and skidded and rolled forward towards where Lieutenant Millane was lying. A warning shout died in the Major's throat, as he realised it was far too late. The flaming part exploded just in front of the ditch and flames carried onwards, engulfing John Millane.

From start to finish the terrible incident took barely five seconds. Within that brief time both Millane and Captain Braun had died horrible deaths.

Douglas Marven stayed put.

'Where's the other bastard?' he asked himself out loud, because just like Millane he expected the Pucaro to have a partner out there supporting him. Before leaving the UK they had all been well briefed on the types of aircraft used by the Fuerza Aerea Argentina, and the tactics they were likely to adopt. The briefing officers had been quite specific about the Pucaro turboprop, they always hunted in pairs.

One minute later he had decided that this particular pilot must have been alone. Scanning the overcast sky to reassure himself he ran along the top of the ditch to where the body of Lieutenant Millane lay. He would get his identity tags and quickly bury him. It wouldn't take long in the loose shingle and sand on this beach.

The Pucaro, or what was left of it, was still burning in several locations within a hundred yards or so from where it had first exploded. He saw the cockpit section which probably still had the pilot in it. He decided to take a look after he had dealt with John Millane's body.

Glancing down into the ditch he saw the torso and upper legs which were still burning. The murky water was covered in a film of fuel which was also burning dimly with a bluish hue.

## Chapter Eleven

He was not looking forward to dragging the remains of his friend from the ditch, and then looking for the other body parts, but knew that he had to do just that. This was one of his men, and he had a duty to perform.

Stepping into the slimy liquid he waded towards where the man lay. Splashing the smelly water over the body to douse the flames, he was just about to grasp the corpse by the shoulders when it shook violently. He instantly thrust his hands below the surface of the water and lifted the head above the surface. Checking the rest of the man's body he was relieved to find that his first thoughts were misplaced. John Millane was in one piece, and miraculously he was still alive. Coughing and spluttering out mud, and terribly wounded, but still alive.

Getting him back to the cellar looked like being impossible. Millane was seriously burned from the chest down to the knees, and the left leg was badly broken. He ended up dragging him to the cave, feeling sure that at the very least he would not be able to be seen from the beach. He laid him over in the lateral position to ensure that he didn't choke on the slime that was still pouring from his nostrils and mouth. Building a mound of sand and shingle behind Millane's back to hold him securely in that position he then took off his outer coat and laid it over the injured man. After one last check of the man's pulse he then sprinted through the stormy wind and snow to the cellar.

Tipping the first-aid kit on to the bed he rummaged through it to find morphine and flamazine, that marvellous cream which had proved to work wonders on burns injuries. He was relieved to find several syringes of morphine and a large container of the precious cream. There were no splints, so he dragged a shelf from the cupboard and using his knife split it into two long pieces. Placing the morphine, flamazine and several bandages into his pack, he snatched up a sheet of canvas and wrapped the splints and two blankets inside it. As a last minute thought he threw a bottle of water into the bag.

On returning to the cave he was relieved to find that Millane was still alive, and that he had been sick, vomiting a large mass of mud and slime on to the sandy floor.

'Better out than in, John. Stick with me, boy. That is an order.'

The first thing he did was to try to clean as much of the mud and slime from the badly burned part of the Lieutenant's body. Gently pouring the water from the bottle he was quite successful. However, not knowing much about such injuries he was concerned that the filthy water could cause infection. Such was his concern that he made one further hurried trip back to the cellar and collected three more bottles of water.

Once he was satisfied that he could not clean the wounds any more under the crude conditions that he was working under, he gently administered the flamazine. John Millane screamed constantly throughout the process.

The Major had put off administering the morphine, for fear that it might run out before he could be moved to safety, but now he had no choice. Shortly afterwards Millane mercifully lapsed into unconsciousness. Marven was grateful for the silence, as the constant screaming had completely unnerved him to the point where he began wondering if he could continue with the first-aid work that was essential prior to moving the man to the relative comfort of the cellar.

Ten minutes later, his leg roughly splinted, and wrapped in blankets, Millane was laid on to the canvas and dragged slowly up the hill to safety. The weather was relentless, but the snow helped save the day by creating a soft blanket between the canvas and the rocky surface below.

'Thank God you don't have any burns on your back, John, otherwise I don't know what I would be able to do,' he shouted above the storm to the unconscious man. He then smiled to himself. Christ only knows why I am talking to you, you poor bastard. If you could hear me I guess that would mean you would be conscious. Then you would be in trouble being dragged around in this barbaric way. Sorry, old son.

Getting him down the stairs into the cellar was a nightmare. Eventually the weather took a hand in the proceedings. The storm became so severe that with the cellar door open the room below was being filled with snow. Knowing that this would not be a good thing once it thawed and turned into water on the floor below, Marven took the Lieutenant by the shoulders and dragged him backwards down the stairs, his backside and splinted leg bouncing on every step. Fortunately he did not regain consciousness. Once he had managed to lay him on the bed Marven cleared up the floor and threw out the snow that had fallen into the cellar, before closing down the hatch and returning to his patient.

There was no way of knowing if there were other injuries, he just concentrated on what he could see. Aware, however, that his knowledge and skills were not at the appropriate level to nurse his very sick colleague he decided to use the radio to seek medical advice and aid.

His emergency call was received by a ship of the task force, and he was told to terminate the transmission, and wait. In the meantime he took Millane's temperature and pulse, details which he felt sure would be sought by the medical adviser to whom he would later be speaking.

★

The cellar was slowly freezing up as the result of the blizzard that had developed outside. That was the bad news. The good news was that the enemy would not be able to reach the island whilst the storm continued. This would give Marven some respite, and allow him to try to stabilise his patient in preparation for the next phase, his removal from the bleak Skull Rock.

The message, when it eventually came, was most timely, as Millane had begun to develop a high fever and was shaking violently. The Major had lit two of the heaters and had managed to retain the temperature at a steady two degrees above freezing point.

The doctor at the other end of the transmission was most helpful, but his advice caused great concern for Douglas Marven. There was a need to administer more flamazine, otherwise major infection and scarring could occur. The flamazine was already used up. The contents of the medical kit were designed for first aid only, not lengthy periods of treatment. It was also obvious from the advice of the doctor that the morphine supply he had would not be sufficient.

Some hours later he received a call from a senior special forces officer whom he had worked with in the past. The Colonel recommended that the only course of action may be to surrender to the Argentinian forces if and when they arrived.

'There's no way we can get to you, Douglas. Sorry old chap, but we are stretched to the limit since we lost all those boys in that chopper crash. Over.'

'Fucking charming, James. The only problem with your advice is that we have got a storm going here that is likely to close us in for over a week. That was certainly what I was told in my last discussion a few hours ago with the medic. Lieutenant Millane won't last that long. I'm out of flamazine and nearly out of morphine. The poor sod will scream himself to death unless I can do something for him in the next day or two. Over.'

'I don't know what else I can offer you, Douglas. We really are in the shit at the moment. Over.'

'What about that sub that picked up Sergeant Smith? Is she around anywhere? What if I can get my man out in the inflatable to where they picked us up last time? Please, James. It will be his only hope. Over.'

'You'll never get off that beach, Douglas. If I remember rightly from the briefing it's a bit of a bastard, isn't it? I know you managed it last time with Yettie, but there were two of you working the boat then. This is not possible. You couldn't do it on your own. No way. Over.'

'Let me make that choice, James. It's John's only hope. I owe it to him to give him that chance. Over.'

'I'll call you back, Douglas. I promise I'll do my best. Out.'

\*

Three hours later the call came. The submarine was twelve hours away, and was already heading in the general direction of Skull Island. The Colonel was quite blunt about the point that if it hadn't already been heading that way, it would not have been specially redirected just for this purpose. Marven understood that, and accepted it totally. He was a professional soldier and would not have expected it to be any different.

The message also made it quite clear that, as before, the submarine could not be at the island at a time that coincided with the turn of the tide. Marven would have to be at the designated location exactly on time, or the sub would have no alternative but to leave without them. Marven concluded the message with just one final request.

'For Christ's sake, James, please ensure that they let us know if for any reason they cannot make it. I shall hit the water about an hour before pick-up time. If they don't arrive we will both be dead. Thanks for all your help, James. Over.'

'Good luck, Douglas. I know you will make it. You always were a jammy bastard. Out.'

★

The storm was horrific. The rock was snowed in completely and the conditions were white-out. It was impossible to see more than a yard in front of his face but Marven had to go out into the elements; he had to find the second of their buried inflatable boats. It was a very difficult thing to do. The landmarks were completely obliterated by several inches of snow. He knew that unless he found the boat on this occasion he would never be able to do it later. The conditions were such that the snow would be a foot deep within the hour.

He had to find the shallow cave that they had first moved into after arriving on the island, but the snow was drifting towards the cliff face and had probably been filled in by the storm.

Head down and leaning into the gale force wind he trudged up and down several times over a period of two hours. He was beginning to suffer the effects of hypo-thermia, but he recognised this and knew that he was in trouble.

He had just decided to give up and return to the cellar when a sudden gust of wind hit him. It was so strong that it blew him sideways and off balance. In trying to remain on his feet he put his right leg out too far, lost his footing, slipped and fell over on to his back, skidding backwards down a slight slope and colliding with the rock face. He was about to pick himself up when, looking up, he saw something flapping in the wind.

He couldn't believe his uncanny luck. It was a small piece of the canvas sheet that had been wrecked by the storm during that first night on the island. It was about six inches long and connected to the rock by a piton that they had overlooked when they moved to the cellar. The severity of the gale had dislodged the snow that had been covering it, just at that precise moment that Marven looked up.

'There is a God after all. Thank you, God,' he shouted out loud.

Within minutes he had located the place where the inflatable had been buried. He carefully burrowed into the snow and shingle, taking care to scrape rather than dig. There was no way he could have repaired the boat should it be damaged. It appeared to be in good order but he realised he could not check it out in the storm so he decided to take it back to the cellar. He would return to the beach later and inflate it. There was plenty of time.

The decision was a very wise one to take, as the white-out conditions worsened to the point where it took Marven over an hour to find his way back to the burnt-out building and the safety of the cellar. He only achieved that by walking into one of the stone walls which he had not seen from only three feet away, that was before he turned right and smashed his face into it.

The boat was in good condition, which was more than could be said for Major Douglas Marven. He was definitely suffering from the early stages of hypothermia. He felt very unwell, and could not prevent his body from shaking. There was only one thing to do, light the kerosene stove that was in the cellar when they arrived.

'The worst that can happen to us is that we'll suffocate, John.'

As it turned out they did not suffocate, even though the room filled with acrid smoke which could only be cleared by opening the cellar door on regular occasions. However, the heater worked wonderfully well in terms of heat. Within an hour the temperature had risen by twenty degrees and Marven felt much better, although he dreaded to think what would happen to his body when he was once again exposed to the frightening conditions outside.

Every so often John Millane woke in pain, and on more than one occasion broke into a scream as he unwittingly moved his ravaged body, subjecting himself to intense indescribable pain. Knowing that the rendezvous was soon to occur, for he was sure that he would manage to get the boat out through the surf, the Major decided to restrict the use of the morphine to whenever his charge appeared to be suffering the very worst sort of pain. He had no idea how he would make that decision, but decided to play it by ear.

In the meantime he decided to get some rest himself, since in a few hours he would be faced with the seemingly impossible task of getting the flimsy inflatable boat through the tortuous breakers out into the open sea, with a cruelly injured man on board, without any help.

★

He woke with a start. His patient was screaming at the top of his voice and was throwing himself about on the bed. Marven had to grapple with him in the hope of calming him down, but in doing so was obviously hurting him even more. The morphine was finished. What the hell could he do to help calm the man down? Just then he saw it.

'Idiot! Bloody idiot, Marven. The compass. The beautiful bloody compass,' he shouted loudly as he leapt across the cellar and grabbed the compass that they had brought ashore with them. It was a heavy-duty naval type that was full of pure alcohol. He tried hard to try to remember what the function of the alcohol was, but just couldn't think straight. All that he knew was that it was one hundred per cent proof.

Taking a saucepan out of the cupboard he held the compass over it and smashed the glass with the butt of his pistol. The colourless alcohol dripped into the saucepan together with pieces of broken glass. There was about a cup full. He then carefully decanted a small drop of the liquid into a mug and took a small sip. The burning sensation of the super-strength alcohol brought tears to his eyes.

'Shit, I might as well lay him out in the snow. This stuff will surely kill him.'

Looking around he suddenly remembered the tins of pure fruit juice in the compo ration packs. He quickly found a tin of orange juice and, opening it, topped up the cup. It was almost frozen solid, but soon began to melt in the alcohol. Stirring it vigorously he carefully took another sip.

'I've a good mind to drink this all myself, John. It's great. I hope you appreciate the sacrifice I am making for you, my boy. I'm going to get you well and truly pissed. No brain, no pain, or so they say. For your sake I hope they are right.'

Even in its diluted state the drink was very potent. It took Marven over twenty minutes to slowly pour dribbles of the orange-flavoured alcohol into Millane's mouth. At first it was difficult, as the man tried to spit it out, but after about five minutes he had acquired a taste for it and began sipping the alcohol quite happily. At last he was quiet, if only drunkenly so.

His drunkenness, whilst quietening him down, also worried Marven, whose new concern was that he might be sick and choke on his own vomit. Once again he found it necessary to lay him on his side, in the lateral position, to ensure that this wouldn't occur. As it turned out, John Millane was a happy drunk for whom alcohol had the magical effect of deadening pain. Most types of pain, at least.

★

Looking at his watch he decided it was time to go. He had just peeped out of the cellar door, and to his horror the weather had not eased at all. If anything it was worse, the snow was certainly heavier. The wind had changed and was now coming across the island from the north, which meant that it would be hitting the exposed beach from the left, making things even more difficult.

He had no choice; it was now or never. He could certainly hold out, but unless John Millane received urgent skilled attention he would die. There was only one choice.

★

He reached the beach quite soon after leaving the cellar. The wind change had left the now exposed cave free from direct wind. Taking full advantage of this Marven inflated the boat inside the shallow hollow. He then lashed it down to the ground with rope and large steel pegs that were part of their equipment. Just to be sure he took advantage of the piton that was still hammered into the rock above the entrance to the cave, and tied a spare rope from that to the rowlocks of the inflatable.

It'll probably take off like a kite before I get back! He grimaced at the thought.

Returning to the cellar be began to prepare the now unconscious man for his move to the beach. Firstly he gently rolled him in three blankets which he tied around with lengths of rope to ensure that they did not come loose. They also had the added purpose of keeping the patient as still as possible. He then stripped one of the mattresses from the bed and laid it over the stairs. He climbed up to the cellar door and opened it wide. Then, dragging the mattress up behind him he threw it onto the snow outside, in the shelter of the remaining north wall.

Returning to Millane's side, he gently slipped his arms under the blanket-wrapped body and lifted it up. It took every ounce of energy to carry the dead weight up the stairs, and even more to pass the unconscious man through the hatch opening and out on to the snow. Climbing out he then carefully slid Millane to where the mattress lay, then falling to his knees and taking a deep breath he gently lifted Millane on to the mattress, finally covering him with a sheet of canvas.

The mattress had been prepared earlier, when Marven had pierced holes in two of the corners and threaded a rope through it. He was now ready to leave. Taking one last look into the cellar which had served their needs over the past weeks, Marven rose to his feet, grabbed hold of the rope and began to drag the mattress across the snow like a sledge. Stopping about twenty yards away he ran back to the open trap door.

For a moment he stood over the opening looking down into the cellar, the only safe place on the island.

'This is a complete act of faith, John my old son,' he yelled back to the unconscious man, 'let's hope the Navy turns up trumps.'

Then, from his pockets he took two hand grenades. Pulling the pins he pitched them both into the hole and slammed the trapdoor shut. He then ran to where he had left the mattress, and quickly continued dragging it towards the beach. He had gone just a few yards when the ground erupted beneath the cellar door which was blown high into the air. Before leaving he had poured the remaining kerosene out on to the floor. This had ignited and a substantial blaze had taken hold. Marven was sure that whoever found the cellar would not be able to make use of anything that was left there. He had already smashed the radio, having heard no more regarding the arrival of the submarine. The explosion and fire would merely finish off the job. From now on he knew that it was a case of get off the island, or die.

★

Getting to the beach was an ordeal. Twice Millane had rolled off the mattress and had to be put back on to it with little regard for the pain it might inflict on him. The second occasion was the worst of the two, because the moment he rolled off the mattress it took to the air in the powerful wind. It took all of Marven's strength to pull it down to the ground and keep it there long enough to drag his wounded companion back on to it. The exertion had exhausted him to the point where he found it extremely hard to complete the haul to the cave. When he did reach it he collapsed on the ground alongside Millane.

He wasn't sure how long he had laid there. All he knew was that he was numb with the cold, and both he and Millane were completely covered in snow.

He looked at his watch.

'Oh, my God, John,' he said to the unconscious man, 'we have missed the sub, and I have wrecked the fucking cellar. Our only means of survival has just gone up in flames.'

He brushed the snow off the blankets in which Millane was wrapped and lay down alongside him for ten long minutes.

'Boss? Let's give it a go. We've got nothing to lose now. Perhaps the sub is waiting for us.' The voice was a mere whisper, but Millane's face was close to his.

'John, you are awake. Sorry, my friend, I have screwed up this time. Looks like we have missed our connection.'

'Let's try it anyway, Boss. I'd hate to snuff it here on the beach. Please?' The talking must have exhausted him, for he groaned out loud and lapsed back into unconsciousness.

'Okay, John. If you say so, old son. Then let's give it a nudge.'

It took several minutes for him to unlash the boat and roll Millane into it. Pulling the canopy up over the unconscious man's head and zipping up the opening, he began to drag the inflatable down to the point where the surf began to recede. He stopped and gazed out to sea. The waves were so high that he knew he would never make it. Short of a freak wave like the time before, he could see them both drowning in the undertow. Still, he continued waiting for an opportunity. His hands were frozen solid and he found it hard to hang on to the paddle and the rope securing the boat. He began to feel weak and giddy, and his legs felt very strange, almost as if they didn't belong to him. Suddenly he sank to his knees. He knew he couldn't go on.

Stop feeling sorry for yourself, Marven. You are responsible for a fellow officer. You can't give in now. A voice was screaming at him inside his head.

Dragging himself to his feet again he began to pull the boat down into the tide. He was now ankle deep and already the undertow was beginning to pull him down towards the thundering, crushing breakers.

Just then the water got beneath the boat and it started to float downwards.

'Now's your time, Douglas,' he shouted, and began to run down the beach dragging the boat behind him.

★

The black Zodiac powered over the top of the breaker and crashed on to the beach immediately alongside Marven and his little boat. Six wetsuit-clad men leapt out into the surging torrent of water and within seconds had dragged him and his boat back up the beach, bringing it to rest alongside theirs.

Marven felt numb. This far, only to be nabbed by the bloody Argie marines. He also couldn't help himself once more grudgingly admiring their skill with their bloody boat. One of the men stepped forward and clasped him by the hand.

'Major Marven? Jarvis, Special Boat Squadron. We just happened to be on board the sub when we were advised about the condition of your friend here. We thought you wouldn't mind a bit of extra help from the Navy.'

Marven clutched the man's hand tightly, tears welling in his eyes.

'God bless the bloody Navy. Thank you!'

★

The high-powered outboard of the Zodiac and the exceptional skills of its SBS crewmen were more than a match for the violent breakers, which even though they appeared to be trying their best to tear the craft apart were soon left behind. Marven strained his eyes, hoping to see the outline of the submarine, but the snow was so heavy that he was unable to see anything beyond the bow of the boat.

Suddenly the large black shape of the submarine appeared in front of them. The coxswain expertly steered the Zodiac towards the stern of the ship which was slightly awash, and drove it right up on to the deck. As if by magic the stern then lifted higher out of the water leaving them high and dry. Within seconds willing hands were helping to lift John Millane down to the sickbay of the submarine where the ship's surgeon and his attendants were waiting to work on him. Minutes later the submarine submerged and got under way.

Marven was greeted by the skipper, whom he immediately recognised. It was the same submarine that had picked up Yettie Smith.

'You seem to be spending a great part of your life helping me and my men out of the shit, Captain. Thank you very much.'

★

Major Marven declined the invitation to clean up and take a shower. Instead he sat down on the deck just outside the door of the sickbay, waiting for news of John Millane's condition. He was so exhausted that he immediately fell asleep with his back against the bulkhead. Nobody disturbed him, even though he was blocking part of the passageway. Instead, some kind soul draped a blanket over him and left him to sleep on.

Several hours later the submarine surfaced once more, and the Zodiac carried Marven and the deeply sedated Lieutenant Millane ashore to a small flat rock about half a mile from the coast of West Falklands. He had been cleaned up, his burns covered with a fresh dressing of flamazine and he was heavily bandaged on various parts of his body. His leg had been reset and encased in plaster of Paris, and he was securely strapped on to a stretcher. The surgeon had advised Marven that there were several shrapnel-type wounds which needed attention, and that pieces of metal and other foreign bodies were embedded in Millane's body and would require surgery to remove them. Otherwise he felt that he would make it.

On the rock they were met by a helicopter. There were six tough-looking paras on board, two of whom were medics. They took control of the wounded man, whilst once again Marven fell asleep on the floor of the aircraft.

He woke up as the helicopter was coming in to land alongside a large, flat, concrete structure that looked as if it known better days.

The paras quickly lifted the stretcher out on to a flat concrete pad which was broken in many places, the cracks filled with weeds and grass. Marven followed them towards the entranceway of the building, above which someone had hand painted the words:

'Welcome to the Red and Green Life Machine.'

*Part Three*

# The Coral Sea, off the East Coast of Queensland, Australia Southward Bound

January 8th, 1997

# Chapter One

The *Palminto* sailed southwards through a calm sea beautifully tinted with shining blues and greens. A light westerly breeze was coming from the coast of Queensland on the ship's right. He drew in a deep breath and felt he could almost smell the perfumes of the lush forests along the distant coast. He enjoyed this stretch of Australia's coastal waters whenever his ship passed through them on its way to and from Melbourne in the south.

She was a beautiful, sleek-looking ship, painted a brilliant white with the red and black colours of the company emblazoned on the single, low, swept-back funnel. A funnel which, apart from enhancing her general appearance and acting as a billboard for the company colours, had no technical function on such a modern ship. Apart from her deck configuration of hatch covers and computer-operated derricks, in many ways she had the appearance and lines of a luxury liner rather than a cargo vessel, but cargo vessel she was. The *Palminto* was a fine ship.

Technologically she was one of the most advanced ships of her kind in the world. Certainly the most advanced operating in the southern hemisphere. She was fitted with the very latest space-age computerised equipment and systems. Most of the technology was centred in and operated from a control room located high above the main deck, just below the bridge, which like most modern freight-carrying vessels was situated at the stern of the ship.

Such a ship required very few people to operate it, but those who did were all technically qualified in one way or another.

Her crew were also all young and very fit, and specially selected through a process unlike any other in the merchant service.

This seven year old vessel regularly sailed into Melbourne in Victoria, Australia with her high value, hi-tech cargoes, consisting mostly of new technology equipment and parts from Japan, Taiwan and South Korea. She usually on-loaded Australian machine parts which she delivered to major ports in the Philippines and China.

*

The *Palminto*'s Captain, David Brandon, stood silently on the starboard wing of the bridge, gazing forward along the broad deck, admiring his ship's immaculate appearance. He was also watching a small group of crew members practising soccer on the deck just below the bridge, in a compound surrounded by netting to prevent the balls going overboard. He was very proud of his ship and his crew, and had every right to be so.

*Palminto* was an exemplary ship in every way. She was always maintained to the highest level of cleanliness and efficiency. Her crew, mainly Filipinos, never fell foul of the authorities in any port that she entered. On the contrary, they had a reputation of being most welcome at her various ports of call. The ship had an excellent soccer team and regularly participated in charity events whilst ashore in the major cities she visited.

Whenever *Palminto* sailed into the Port of Melbourne, Brandon utilised the services of a small public relations company in St Kilda. Their role was to keep him advised of which high public profile charitable events were taking place whenever the *Palminto* was in port, and to ensure that as much good publicity as possible was given to the ship and her crew for their participation in those events.

The reputation achieved by Brandon was good for the ship, and good for the company's business. The company happily wallowed in the reflected glory of both the business and social achievements of their captain and his crew.

However, from Brandon's point of view it was the social and sporting activities of the ship's crew, and their general popularity, that seemed more than anything to place the ship in the position of being beyond reproach in the eyes of the Port of Melbourne Authority, Her Majesty's Customs, and the Victoria Police.

Not that there was ever anything illegal on board the *Palminto* whenever she sailed into Melbourne. She was always steam cleaned and squeaky clean by then, just like the image that David Brandon had maintained throughout his service in the United States Navy, and since joining the company.

She was, however, a sort of Dr Jekyll and Mr Hyde ship flying under false colours. You see, she was not only the finest and most reputable ship in the fleet of the White Shores Line of Hamburg, she also acted as the international deliveryman for the most efficient illegal drugs operation in the Pacific region. Brandon was, and had been for some years, the key player in the Senator's international narcotics enterprise. He was the chief deliveryman of some highly sought-after and controversial items of cargo.

The crew members were somewhat unique in that whenever ashore they never got into the usual troubles that many merchant seamen tend to get into in foreign ports. Their behaviour was exemplary. This was part of the ship's code of conduct laid down by Captain Brandon, and obeyed to the letter. The crew appeared to be proud of their ship and the company, and more often than not they tended

242

to wear the issued T-shirts or bomber jackets with the company emblem displayed prominently.

★

The ship was to all intents and purposes a credit to her owners. Indeed, the company was most reputable in every respect, renowned for its excellent, safe and well-maintained ships, and for its reliable service to its clients. It was also internationally respected for its scrupulous adherence to maritime law and the laws of the countries into which its ships sailed. The company was proud of its commercial and safety record, and its reputation for speedy transportation of cargo. The White Shores Line was particularly proud of its ships' captains, whom it went to such great pains to select and train in the company culture.

However, even though the captains of all of their ships were considered to be among the best, throughout his fourteen years with the company Brandon had earned the reputation of being better than the best. This, his latest ship, was considered by the White Shores Line to be the company's flagship, and Brandon was the highest paid captain in the company fleet in recognition of that fact.

Now, at the age of fifty-five he was a healthy, fit and active man, still pursuing his love affair with the sea and with ships. He was considered by all who served under him to be a fine captain, if not still a bit too 'navy'. However, none of his crew ever complained. Without exception they considered him to be the very best skipper they could ever serve under. He was very fair and treated them well.

And then there were the special bonuses which made them the best paid crew members in the whole of the company, and arguably the best paid merchant seamen in the Pacific region, if not the world.

Those bonuses, which incidentally the company had no knowledge of, were paid by Brandon for productivity, loyalty and a code of absolute secrecy. They were for services above and beyond the call of duty, and were large enough to ensure that each and every crew member would retire early – and by their standards, rich! Extraordinarily rich!

The bonuses also paid for a code of silence and honour that if breached could result in their termination – in more ways than one.

Thus, the crew turnover rate on the *Palminto* was extremely low, much lower than most other ships in the south-eastern oceans. In fact, it was virtually non-existent. In seven years only three men had left the ship. Everyone on board was aware that those crew members had departed after apparently incurring the wrath of Captain Brandon, and who, strangely had never been seen again.

These disloyal characters were never discussed, but the circumstances of their jumping ship and apparent disappearances were a source of nagging concern to each and every clear-thinking crew member. When it came to issues that affected their well-being every one of them were very clear thinkers. Consequently they were concerned enough to ensure that they didn't do anything to cause them to fall foul of the Captain or to think of deserting the *Palminto*.

In fact, desertion was just about the last thing on their minds. They were making a great deal of money which would allow them to do all the things that they had never dreamed possible. Their bonus monies were paid into special bank accounts arranged for them by the Captain, and they were cautioned not to touch that money until they were finally paid off.

Brandon monitored each of the accounts and gave regular verbal briefings to each of the crew on the status of these special funds. This ensured that not only were the crew advised of the interest that their bonuses were earning, thanks to the careful and caring stewardship of their Captain, but they were quietly reminded that Brandon would know if any one of them was tempted to tap into the funds, contrary to his wishes. Meanwhile their higher than normal company rates of pay allowed them to develop comfortable lifestyles back home.

Brandon had advised them well regarding the bonuses and the investment accounts into which they were paid. It would cause many raised eyebrows if they were seen to have suddenly come into greater wealth than one would reasonably expect of a merchant sailor, even a sailor on a larger than normal rate because of the highly technical nature of his role on the company's flagship. The crew were constantly reminded that investigations by the wrong people could cause considerable harm to everyone.

The good Captain Brandon had assured them all that at the appropriate time they would be paid off, and given appropriate letters and documents to prove the authenticity of their new-found wealth. They could each then return home to their families and establish themselves as important and influential people in their own communities. A dream come true. There was no way that any of the crew members would do anything to jeopardise this dream. It also ensured that each one would keep a close eye on his fellow crew members to see that they were keeping to the code that they had all so readily embraced.

The crew of *Palminto* had one other very good reason to follow Captain Brandon's rules. Every one of them had been hand-picked. Firstly, they each had the technical skills essential to carry out their particular role on such a modern ship. There was also one special extra attribute that each of them had in common. They each had a background of criminal activities which Brandon had documented and locked away in a secure place.

None, however, had a formal police record as such. This was either because they had been too clever to get caught, or more likely because they had developed a liaison with certain police or military personnel who ensured their continuing freedom for a cut of the profits of their criminal enterprises.

★

The Senator and Felix had been most thorough in their recruiting campaign for the crew of the *Palminto*. The Senator's team had spent months following up leads and information, then staking out each man, one by one, in order to confirm the information received and to develop a comprehensive dossier on their nefarious activities. The subjects were then each approached and advised of the special opportunities that existed for them if they joined the crew of the *Palminto*.

During the recruitment period Felix had occasion to arrange accidents of various kinds for three individuals who offended the Senator. Two of the men got too smart for their own good and tried to tail Felix's men, apparently with the view to obtaining more information than it was desirable for them to have. The third man, not too keen on the idea of going to sea and leaving his lucrative sidelines ashore, thinking that the person who had approached him was an easy mark tried to rob him at gunpoint.

Unfortunately, for him that was, he picked on Felix of all people. Which, if nothing else, only went to prove what a bad judge of character that stupid man was.

Felix dealt with him efficiently and terminally. The man was later dropped on the roadway, to all intents and purposes the victim of a hit and run. The Senator had actually warned Brandon back in Vietnam all those years before, that anyone tangling with Felix would end up looking like they had been hit by a truck.

How was that unfortunately stupid felon likely to know that, however? He had not had the good fortune to be party to the Senator's earlier counselling session.

Once the willing crew members were signed on, Brandon made sure that each one was immediately made aware of the detailed record he had on his criminal background; and further, that he would not hesitate to place this information in the hands of the appropriate authorities should the need arise. None of the men doubted Brandon's word regarding the dossier on their crimes, nor questioned his ability to carry out his threat to expose them.

David Brandon was pleased with the control he had over his crew. He had them all by the balls and they knew it.

Not one member of the crew had, to the knowledge of the Senator or Felix, ever killed anyone during the commission of their crimes, or been involved in a crime which resulted in death. The Senator was most thorough regarding that aspect of his subject's past criminal activities. Murder is the type of crime which in South-East Asia, and in most parts of the South Pacific, is likely to bring retribution upon the person who committed it, often from the family or friends of the deceased.

The last thing that the Senator or Brandon needed was the kind of publicity that could result from a member of his crew being on the losing side in any sort of vendetta.

During the crew selection process the Senator was also careful not to recruit people who were, or had been members of, or were in any way associated with known criminal gangs or syndicates. He did not even consider people who could in any way be implicated as the result of an investigation into some other criminal elements.

Brandon was most satisfied with the criteria the Senator and he had established for the recruitment of his crew, and was particularly pleased with the requirement not to have been involved with gangs or syndicates. During his military career he had become aware of too many people who had been arrested as the result of an obscure investigation into somebody or something else, which by pure fluke had led the police to their door. Anyone with any knowledge of the way police work knew that cops throughout the world relied on this element of luck in their daily chores.

Yes! *Palminto* was squeaky clean, spotless in every respect. The Senator and Captain David Brandon could not, and would not, chance the slightest bit of dirt coming her way. As added security and insurance Felix was also lurking in the shadows to deal promptly with the offending person should such a problem occur.

## Chapter Two

As he leaned on the rail on the starboard side of the bridge, he looked out to where, although he could not see it, he knew the lush green coastline of Northern Queensland lay. A thought occurred to him, that in all the years that he had been sailing into Australian ports he had never once visited Queensland, though he had thought about it often enough.

Queensland, with its Great Barrier Reef stretching for most of its coastline is a most unique part of Australia. The Barrier Reef is one of the wonders of the world, and is the home of some of the most exotic species of fish and underwater life on the planet. The authorities and environmental bodies are constantly concerned for the future of the reef and its magnificent inhabitants. One of their greatest concerns is that ships travelling along the east coast of Australia will discharge oil and other contaminants into this environmentally sensitive underwater wonderland. Such happenings could undo in days what had taken millions of years to develop.

Consequently shipping lanes are quite clearly defined and are some distance to the east of the Reef, and a considerable distance from the shore. The penalties for going too close to the Reef, or discharging anything illegal into these ecologically pristine waters are severe. Brandon always believed that they were not severe enough. He had little time for the cowboys, travelling in the guise of seamen, who did so many environmentally unfriendly things to the sea which was their home and their livelihood, and was his closest friend.

In many ways the distance of the sea lanes from the shore was a blessing, in that the extra-curricular activities of the ship were less likely to be observed. Furthermore, the authorities are generally so preoccupied with the maritime activities in and around the Reef that Brandon's ship was less likely to be given any special attention.

However, the distance from the shore was also a curse, in terms of the difficulties that this caused a certain person who was shortly to rendezvous with the ship.

Brandon looked down again at the crew members playing soccer, and thought about the control he had over them. In a way it scared him a bit, but it also excited him to think that he was part of an exclusive group of influential people who could make instant life or death decisions about the future of men who disobeyed the rules.

Just at that moment the ball smacked against one of the uprights of a port side derrick. He looked across at the derrick and was immediately reminded of the morbid fact that a derrick looks a bit like a gallows.

In reality the ship's derrick was named after a celebrated official hangman of that name, who used to operate his deadly and terminal craft at Tyburn, London, during the early nineteenth century. It occurred to Brandon that in many ways he had the same level of power as that gruesome historical character.

★

He was a warm to hot weather man, and felt sure that the climate of Queensland, particularly its northern regions, would appeal to him greatly. He decided that as soon as he was able he would visit Brisbane, and then take a long and leisurely trip northwards up the coast to the Barrier Reef and beyond.

Most of his voyages were into Port Melbourne, via Sydney. Although he was very fond of the city of Melbourne and its beautiful lush parks and nearby hills and forests, the weather in southern Victoria was not his favourite. In fact, he would normally have felt cold the whole time that he was in Melbourne if it hadn't been for the adequate clothing that he had purchased over the years specifically for his visits to that part of the globe.

While he knew that he could never live there permanently, Melbourne held a strange and wonderful fascination for him; so much so that he had purchased an apartment, quite a luxurious apartment, overlooking Albert Park, one of Melbourne's most beautiful landmarks. The apartment was well situated with regard to Brandon's wish to place himself in the most appropriate position in the pecking order of Melbourne's rigidly structured social set.

The Australians amused him regarding their attitude towards any form of social structure. They were always slinging off about the English, whom they called Poms, and their historically rigid class system. Brandon had, however, found to his amazement that the Australians were as class conscious as most, even though they went to great lengths to deny it.

He really enjoyed the Melbourne social scene but knew that, regardless of the Aussie protestations to the contrary, he was only able to become part of this elite group because of his status in the international commercial sector, and his obvious wealth.

The Albert Park apartment was beautifully decorated and appointed, and enabled him to entertain in keeping with the image that he had developed. It was looked after by an agency that also provided the most wonderful cook/housekeeper, who lived nearby in Prahran, a short tram journey away. Mrs Reynolds was a gem. Although he only required her direct services for a few days of the year, she regularly visited the apartment and ensured that it was in spotless order for the occasional visits by special out-of-town business guests for whom Brandon had agreed to make the facility available.

Most of these guests were associates of the Senator. Brandon never met these people, nor was he intended to. The military style need-to-know principle was most important to the Senator's security, and was rigidly adhered to.

★

He had also wisely invested a considerable amount of money, although negligible in terms of his overall wealth, in an exclusive, upmarket restaurant on the South Bank. The South Bank was a newly established, highly prestigious and successful hospitality and entertainment area. It was situated on the south side of the Yarra River which ran through the centre of the city of Melbourne. The restaurant was located close to the world-renowned Entertainment Centre, and the newly built Crown Casino and its adjacent one thousand room hotel. The restaurant was already renowned as one of the major eating places for the discerning, and had become a must for the rich tourists from overseas, especially the Japanese gambling tourists for whom money appeared to be no object.

Business was booming and the financial projections were for an even brighter future. His financial interest was anonymous, and his business affairs relating to the restaurant were conducted through his Swiss bank. He often asked himself why he had become so intimately involved with Melbourne when in his heart he was sure that he could never have a future there, not a safe one, anyway. He had always believed that the only form of secure retirement he would enjoy would be one as far as possible away from the Senator and Felix.

★

Brandon had made several good friends in Melbourne, mainly highly successful business people from the upper echelons of Melbourne society whom he had worked with over the years since he joined the company. Not unexpectedly, they all tended to complain constantly about the Melbourne weather; yet with few exceptions they had voluntarily gravitated to Melbourne from warmer parts of Australia, mostly Sydney and Brisbane.

He had, periodically, during times of inclement weather tackled each of them about their dislike for the climate, and why they chose to live in such a comparatively cold place when in most instances they could have easily moved elsewhere in Australia within their respective businesses. The replies had all been very much the same. They hated the weather and felt it their God-given right to complain about it loudly whenever they wanted to. However, to Brandon's great amusement, even though they often exercised that right, each of them obviously loved Melbourne passionately and could probably never leave it.

Strange people these Melburnians, he thought, but likeable.

He mused over the events that brought him to *Palminto* and into the way of life that he now led. His future was secure. Certainly not because of the guaranteed relative pittance of a pension from a grateful company, but with wealth beyond his wildest dreams of years earlier. People often say it is an ill wind that blows nobody any good, and this old adage was so appropriate for David Brandon.

\*

He was especially contented at this time, as owing to circumstances beyond his control it had been decided by the Senator that it was to be his last voyage. In four months' time he would have been retiring with an honourable discharge from the company anyway, at which time he would receive their totally inadequate joke of a pension, together with their inevitable patronising acknowledgement of his loyalty and success.

Brandon chuckled to himself at the thought of the company pension. He looked forward, however, to the official function that would be laid on for him by the directors in September, and was amused by the thought of the praise and platitudes that would be heaped on him for the extraordinary services that he had rendered.

Little did they know just how extraordinary his services had been. Whilst carrying out such excellent work for the company, he had also been indulging in a very special form of private enterprise which would ensure that his pension would be supplemented by a private fortune in various secret bank accounts around the globe.

He was wealthier than all of the company's directors put together. He would, however, accept their praise and their pension with extreme gratitude, and would end his mercantile marine career with an outward display of pride and humility befitting a man of honour and integrity. Not that either of those words were in any way appropriate to Commander James Brandon, US Navy retired, now Ship's Master of the *Palminto*, and the Senator's chief deliveryman.

Yes, all things considered Brandon was very pleased with himself. Who would believe him if he told them just how wealthy he was? How on earth could a ship's captain achieve that? But David Brandon was a mega-rich man, and he owed it all to the Vietnam War.

No! That was not quite true. He really owed his wealth and his future retirement to a mysterious man he had met under the most weird and frightening circumstances during that war. The wild and secret Australian, known to him only by his wartime code name 'Senator'.

He turned inwards towards the bridge.

'Slow ahead both, Mr Raman,' he called to his First Officer, 'and tell the special deck crew to stand by.'

'Aye aye, sir,' replied Raman, signalling the speed change to the engine room, whilst at the same time picking up a telephone and relaying the Captain's instructions to the mess deck below.

Brandon walked back to the rail and stood with the cool sea breeze ruffling his slightly greying hair. He stared ahead and contemplated his future.

Four months to go and I retire for good. I'll never need for anything again, he thought.

He looked at his watch and noted that it was 1110 hours. He had just fifty minutes before the pick-up. There was plenty to do, but his men were really proficient at preparing for a rendezvous such as this.

\*

*Palminto* was a successful ship in every respect, but in terms of her illegal activities her success was due mainly to immaculate organisation and timing, and of course to the fact that Brandon's ship never carried its illegal cargoes into Australian ports.

Those illicit cargoes always left the ship while she was still at sea, and before she reached Sydney. He could never envisage a situation that would lead to the authorities wishing to search his ship whilst she was at sea. After all, she was a clean ship and the pride of the company's fleet. That was how she would continue to be seen by Her

Majesty's Customs, and all of the other mostly unnecessary bureaucracies that Brandon had to deal with in the course of his duty.

How many times he had done this over the past fourteen years? With never a hitch!

Well, there had been those three unhappy occasions when the loyalty of certain crew members had come into question. In each case the persons concerned had been suspected of attempting to steal some of the special cargo that was bound for the Australian streets. Action had to be taken to remedy the situation. The contracts of the crew members concerned had been terminated – in a very permanent way. Those crew members, as far as the rest of the crew were concerned, had deserted the ship.

On each of those three occasions the rest of the crew had been subsequently notified of the desertion of their colleague. They were also reminded of the considerable advantages to be accrued in return for their continued and unwavering loyalty to their Captain. They were further reminded of the terrible disadvantages that each could suffer if they were disloyal. Brandon never ever mentioned the manner of the disadvantages that they would face. He didn't need to. With men coming from the backgrounds of those selected to crew the *Palminto* there was never the need to spell it out chapter and verse.

Even though desertion was the official and publicly stated reason for the sudden departures of those crew members, Brandon was sure that every man on board understood the full implications of the ship's termination clause perfectly well.

The terminations had been conducted on shore by persons not known to David Brandon. This unpleasant business was carried out by people working under the directions of the Senator. Felix probably handled the nuts and bolts of that type of dirty work. In all probability he had carried out the terminations himself. He certainly appeared to enjoy violence. However, Brandon had not become involved, and the less he knew about anything like that the better he felt.

\*

The Senator. Brandon's relationship with this man was indeed strange. He had only met him on a few occasions over more than twenty years, and he was only just beginning to get used to the idea of referring to him as the Senator. At those infrequent meetings with the man he tended to call him sir, in the military style.

Brandon only used the name Senator on rare occasions, and then generally only as an identification code. The name still struck him as being overly dramatic. The Senator's instructions usually came in sealed orders, delivered by Felix, who after all this time still put the fear of God into him. Brandon's communications to the Senator were made through a secure telephone line, the number of which changed constantly, those changes being advised to him in his sealed orders.

He recalled way back, those many years before when in his apartment in Saigon he had been confronted so suddenly by the man, code-named Senator and his dangerous shadow, Felix. Even though confined to a wheelchair with those serious battle wounds, the Senator's instructions never to seek to discover his true identity were so convincingly threatening and violent. Even now, occasionally Brandon woke up in the middle of the night sweating with the memory of that frightening event.

Such was his fear, and his genuine belief that to disobey the Senator really would mean death that Brandon had never even given it a moment's consideration.

He had good reason to believe that the Senator was in a position of great power, but whether this was because of his drug-created wealth or for some other reason, he neither knew, nor cared.

Since that night in Saigon he had witnessed first-hand the ruthlessness of the Senator's orders on numerous occasions. This had given him even greater cause for keeping the faith, as Felix put it. There was no way that his services would be terminated like those three greedy, stupid sailors from the *Palminto*. No way!

The arrangements that had been made by the Senator for any subsequent terminations were tidy and efficient, and to Brandon's complete satisfaction. He was pleased to know that in the event of such a further problem all he had to do was to immediately inform the Senator through his secure line and the matter would be taken care of.

David Brandon was not without personal courage. In fact he was a brave man by most men's standards. His bravery had been proven in many dangerous situations in the Navy back in Vietnam, particularly after he became involved with the Senator. However, he had never personally killed another human being, face to face. He certainly did not relish the thought of having to do that sort of work himself.

By leaving that sort of thing to the Senator he was able to retain a warm and comfortable feeling of non-involvement. Even though the disloyal actions of a wayward crewman could threaten his entire future, he had the satisfaction of knowing that there was someone else on the end of a phone who would resolve the issue for him, on request.

The Senator insisted that neither Brandon nor his ship could be seen as involved in anything even slightly dubious. This pleased him very much. It was the perfect situation. He had the best of both worlds.

He would, however, be glad when this final voyage was over. In less than a month the company would receive his formal resignation with effect from the end of the current voyage, which ended in Manila. Three months' notice, while far greater than the company's requirements, would be in keeping with the company-man image that he had always outwardly portrayed.

Under normal circumstances he would have expected to ship into Manila about three weeks earlier than that, but the company had arranged for some refitting and upgrading of the ship's electronics to be carried out whilst in Melbourne. This would mean that Brandon and his crew would be kicking their heels for a short time. He was not concerned about this, as it would give him the opportunity to visit friends in Victoria and across the Bass Strait in Tasmania. There was plenty for the crew to do, both on painting and general maintenance of the ship, and in social and sporting activities ashore.

He also knew that in his absence the ship and each member of its crew would be under twenty-four hour surveillance by Felix and his dangerous associates.

A relief captain would be waiting to take over his ship in Manila. In all probability the relief captain assigned to the ship would be James Prescott, a stern-faced, completely dislikeable Welshman. He was reputed to run his ships with a particularly harsh form of discipline, supported by regular biblical sermons, often whilst under the influence of a large amount of malt Scotch whisky.

However, Prescott was a highly skilled and experienced master mariner with an excellent record of success in his profession. The company was not, however, aware of his propensity towards a particular brand of double malt Scotch whisky. If they had, Prescott's career would have already come to a sudden end. Brandon casually considered the possibilities of what he could do to ensure that the company did become acquainted with this information, without him personally becoming involved, of course. Perhaps he would discuss this with the Senator at some stage, and seek his views on the Welshman's future career.

Why should I care who takes over the ship after I have left, even if there was a ship to take over? he thought.

'Because Prescott is a self-opinionated, self-righteous prick,' he said out loud in answer to his own question.

'You called me, sir?' asked Raman, the First Officer, suddenly appearing at the doorway of the bridge.

'Sorry, Mr Raman. Just thinking out loud,' replied Brandon, feeling slightly embarrassed by his stupid outburst, but smiling to himself at the thought that Raman may have assumed that he was referring to him in that manner.

'By the way, get those men moving a bit faster down there,' he said, pointing towards the deck, and indicating the men who were dismantling the netting that had surrounded the area where they had until just recently been playing soccer.

'Aye aye, sir.'

Well, Prescott, thought Brandon, I will screw your career anyway, if only because I don't bloody like you. As for *Palminto*, well, you will have to wait a bloody long time for her to arrive, my whisky drinking, self-righteous, bible-punching friend.

# Chapter Three

A lot of things, good and bad, had happened to David Brandon since that frightening, fateful evening in his quarters in Saigon, back in 1972.

After the Senator and Felix had left he had sat in the living room of his small apartment for a good fifteen minutes, staring at the fortune in bank notes that lay strewn around him. It was all too unreal for words.

Finally he glanced at his watch, then snapped back into reality with a start. 'God! I have got to get to the officers' club. John Tincey – I must call him or it might be too late,' he said out loud to himself, suddenly feeling very frightened once more. Even though the Senator and Felix were long gone, he still felt chilled by the deadly sincerity of the Senator's threat to kill him if he did not do as he was told.

A loner by nature, he preferred to be on his own, and had never in his life, even as a small child, longed too much for the company of others. Now, in the wake of that chilling meeting with the Senator and his psychotic henchman, Felix, he actually felt lonely for the first time in his life. Very, very lonely.

However, he had no choice but to follow the Senator's strange and worrying instructions, and picking up the phone he dialled the quarters where most of the junior officers lived whilst ashore.

'Lieutenant John Tincey, please,' he requested of the duty seaman. He hoped and prayed that Tincey had not changed his plans and already left. He desperately needed the man as the reason for the party that Senator had directed. Without him Brandon would have great difficulty in convincing others to join in what would have to be a raging all-night drunken affair. After all, with his reputation of not being a drinking man, who in their right mind would want to join a party thrown by him. No, it was well known that this sort of thing was not his style at all. But with the well-liked party man, John Tincey, as the draw card, things could be very much different. They would be! They had to be!

He waited for what seemed ages, and was just on the verge of panic when he heard Tincey's voice at the other end of the phone.

'John! David Brandon here, your intrepid leader. Get yourself booted and spurred young man. We are going to celebrate your return to duty, and your Purple Heart. I have decided that as you are now a real live hero, the very first one for the *James Cunningham*, that fact should be recognised. So you, me, and as many of the other officers as I can get hold of are going to the club, John. We're going to hang one on, like we have never done before. Well, let me re-phrase that. Like I have never done before,' he said with a chuckle. 'I'm pretty sure that you may well have, on numerous occasions.' A further chuckle. 'Now! Get ready and I'll pick you up in half an hour. That is an order, Mr Tincey.'

'Aye, aye, sir,' came the enthusiastic, if somewhat bemused reply.

*

The party was a great success. Brandon had managed to contact six of the other officers from the *James Cunningham*, all of whom seemed delighted, though somewhat surprised by their Captain's plans for John Tincey. To save anyone feeling left out of things he left messages for the remaining officers who were not available at the time. One by one they joined the party at various stages during the evening, and into the small hours of the following morning. The party achieved exactly what Senator had wanted it to.

Also, apart from being a bloody good party it was a key factor in the development of a very special camaraderie amongst the officers of the *James Cunningham* that was to make the ship stand out above all others in the flotilla during the years that followed.

By midnight the party was going full steam ahead, with some fifty or more officers in attendance. Brandon had also been pleased to open its doors to several army and marine officers. They had a ball, and were so delighted to be included that they had between them purchased three cases of bourbon as their unsolicited entrance fee.

He had been concerned at the thought of spending too much money on the party, because Senator had quite rightly warned him not to. Splashing too much money around could bring unwelcome attention to himself. After all, commanders in the United States Navy were not overly well paid.

*

At the beginning he had despaired at the large numbers of officers who were joining in, and began to wonder just how he could get around having to spend a large sum on the food and drink that was obviously going to be consumed during the night, without questions being asked. However, he soon discovered that his fears were unfounded and the party was not costing him an outrageous amount of money after all. In the tradition of the Navy, and the armed forces in general, most of the participants were bringing bottles, and sometimes cases of drink into the party with them.

It soon became obvious to Brandon that the real need of these people was to find a temporary haven away from the war, if only for a brief moment. Such opportunities, other than on lone drunken binges, were all too rare in Vietnam at that time. Without intending to do so, and without realising that he was doing it, Brandon had provided the perfect opportunity and achieved the right result for everyone present.

The manager of the officers' club was delighted with the roaring trade that he was doing in the sale of alcohol, and showed his pleasure by providing much of the food, with the compliments of the club. All too often he, an older Lieutenant Commander who had missed quite a few promotion opportunities, had had to resort to minor and major black market activities in order to make the club run at a reasonable profit. Profit was necessary, not only to satisfy his masters, but also to add to his own private nest egg which he had established to pay for his fast looming retirement.

He felt quite justified in privateering in this way, for as the manager of the club he had developed a liking for the good life which a navy pension could never support.

As he often reminded himself, For a non-combatant working in the service industry, so to speak, war is one hell of a good investment.

All in all, things were going according to plan for Brandon, and it appeared that everyone was enjoying the occasion. John Tincey certainly appeared to be having a wonderful time.

There were several female officers present from all branches of the services, together with a fair sprinkling of nurses from the many military and naval hospitals in and around Saigon. How they heard about the party he neither knew, nor cared. This was the very first time he had personally experienced the military social networking system, and there was no doubt that it worked wonderfully well. He pondered that, but only very briefly, before deciding that all that really mattered was that dozens of the right people were at the party, and that he, David Brandon, was being credited with getting them there.

Much later, during the latter part of the evening he was made aware of how so many people knew of the function. He was approached and congratulated by several people for having had the foresight and good sense to place invitations on the noticeboards of the hospitals and all of the officers' quarters. He accepted the many compliments with some embarrassment, for he would never have thought of doing such a thing in a thousand years.

It was obvious that the Senator was a very enterprising and well-organised man, and equally obvious that this event was of significant importance to the man.

\*

Brandon recognised many of the females as being the ones that regularly attended the parties laid on by officers. He felt sure that 'laid' was the operative word for such occasions. He guessed that some of the guys there would probably score before the night was over. From what he had been told in the past about the goings on at and after those officer functions, at least some of them would have no choice but to score.

Getting into the mood himself, he had been watching a very pretty young nurse for most of the evening and wondering whether he should make a play for her. She was really cute and had a great body which was only just contained by her rather tight uniform.

He realised that much as he would like to try his luck with the girl it would be a pretty dumb thing to do in view of his responsibility to keep the party on the boil, and ensuring that it kept going at the club premises.

Suddenly the music was turned up very loud and to Brandon's surprise the nurse he had been giving so much attention to leapt up on to a large table. Then, gyrating to the tune she performed a delightful striptease, right down to her panties and bra, much to everyone's delight. A minor problem occurred when a drunken young army officer leapt also on to the table and as quick as a flash stripped down to his underpants and proceeded to grab the girl, who at that stage was dancing erotically to the loud applause of the party-goers. Two of his army colleagues intervened, but not before the drunken, and horny, young man, an erection pushing out from his underpants, had managed to rip her bra off and fling it into the crowd of happy and laughing spectators.

The show ended abruptly at that point. The young officer was carried off by a couple of his highly embarrassed and apologetic army colleagues, and was not seen again that night.

The nurse, looking very sexy and slightly bemused by what had just happened to her, got down from the table and circulated around the bar for a few minutes longer. She was still only wearing her extremely brief and largely see-through panties, and was also displaying her adequate and very shapely breasts to anyone who cared to look, which at a party of that sort meant almost everybody.

Even David Brandon, who as the instigator of the party had been somewhat embarrassed by the incident, could not keep his eyes off the girl's breasts. He noticed that the nipples were large and prominent and deep brown in colour. He found to his further embarrassment that he was beginning to feel sexually aroused by her almost naked appearance.

The issue was resolved for him when some of her nursing friends whisked her off when it became apparent to everyone that she was also quite happy to be touched by anyone who cared to. Several young officers obviously did care to and had taken advantage of the opportunity, which was why the girl had been removed by her colleagues.

Brandon noticed her back in the bar about half an hour later. She was fully dressed and looked as if she had sobered up quite considerably. He thought that he might try looking her up at some later date.

*

At about 1 a.m. Admiral Stone arrived. He told Brandon how relieved he was to be there after an earlier formal function at the US Embassy in Thong Nhut Street. Whilst at that function he had been notified that his men were laying on a real hooley-dooley of a party at the officers' club, and that he also been invited. Brandon instantly realised that this must have been another of Senator's initiatives. However, as with the others the Admiral was giving him the credit.

Stone insisted that this was more his style, completely different from the starched shirt evening he had just suffered. He introduced three highly inebriated Embassy officials who had accompanied him and congratulated Brandon on the fine thing he was doing for young Tincey and his other officers, and for the Navy in general. Having made his little speech he then proceeded to forget he was an admiral and joined the party with a vengeance. Things were shaping up just as the Senator must have wished.

When told that he had just missed the striptease the Admiral suggested that the young nurse should be encouraged to do her act again. Brandon was not sure if the girl was approached on the subject, but he was certainly was not game to do so. In the event she did not repeat her performance, not at the party anyway.

At one stage of the evening Brandon saw young Best, the Lieutenant J.G. who did so well on the bridge during the recent battle with the shore guns and mortars. He was doing well on this occasion too, with a tall blonde nurse who had a reputation throughout the naval base of being a sure thing. The Base Bike! There was even a story doing the rounds that she had got herself laid by over a dozen officers in one night at a recent marine function. It was alleged that most of the sexual gymnastics had been performed on the bar in front of everyone, including several women. He toyed with the idea of warning Best about her, but decided against it in case the young officer felt that his captain was questioning or doubting his maturity.

Some weeks later he was to regret his decision when Best was taken ill and later diagnosed as having a particularly virulent strain of syphilis. The news of Best's illness caused considerable panic in and around the naval base for some time. If it hadn't been such a serious matter he could have laughed at the number of officers he knew, many of them quite senior and all married, who were making regular visits to the MO. Brandon never saw the tall blonde nurse again and it was generally assumed that she had been shipped out in a hurry.

Shortly afterwards a rumour circulated the base that Best had attempted suicide whilst in the officers' contagious diseases ward of the naval hospital. He was immediately flown stateside.

Thinking back on him and his misfortune Brandon recalled that night of the mission, on the bridge of the *James Cunningham*, when Best had expressed such envy at the thought of John Tincey getting a trip back home because of his wounds.

Well boy, he thought sadly, it was you who got the trip home instead, only they don't give Purple Hearts for your sort of wounds.

When General George Washington had decreed that soldiers honourably wounded fighting for their country should wear a purple decoration, he almost certainly had not considered social diseases to be placed in the category of honourable wounds.

Best was never to return to the USS *James Cunningham*.

\*

The party finally concluded at about 4 a.m., by which time the bodies of drunken officers were lying all over the place in the officers' club. There were no women left. It seemed that they had either taken off with male officers, or more likely had helped each other home. They had a pretty good reputation for looking after themselves and each other on such occasions. Whatever, Brandon was relieved that he was not faced with the more difficult task of delivering intoxicated women back to their quarters. That always had the potential of being an embarrassing problem, or so he had been told by fellow officers who had taken on that responsibility in the past.

Brandon and a few other less worse-for-wear officers helped each one of the less capable participants of the party into the various types of transport that he had commandeered, using the Admiral's name. Instructions were given to the drivers regarding the destination of each of their sorry charges, and a case of beer was included for each driver to induce them to keep their mouths shut, with a big 'or else' clause attached to the deal.

Fortunately Brandon did not have the embarrassment of having to make travel arrangements for the Admiral himself. He had left at about 3 a.m., allegedly accompanied by the young stripper.

'The horny, lucky old bastard,' said one of the officers helping Brandon with the walking wounded survivors of the night's festivities.

John Tincey and he were the last to leave. Tincey was not aware of this fact however, as he was deeply unconscious due to the amount of alcohol he had consumed. He had been fêted by his peers and his senior officers and had been treated as a sort of hero, which delighted him immensely. He would later insist that he virtually had no choice but to get drunk, in view of the fact that everyone present wanted to have a drink with him. For many of them it was numerous drinks. He would also protest that he did it for the honour of the ship, and the Navy, though at the time of his departure from the club he was incapable of saying or of doing anything.

Brandon thanked the sailor who had driven them to the officers' quarters. He then half carried Tincey to his room and left him lying fully clothed on his bed. He sure was a sorry sight, and would later feel much sorrier than he looked. Leaving specific instructions with the duty seaman that Tincey's early call, listed for 6 a.m., was cancelled and that he was not to be disturbed he then made his way back to his quarters.

As soon as he reached his apartment he put himself to bed having decided that he would give work a miss. After all, he was the ship's Captain, and if he couldn't have a sleep in, then who the hell could?

As it happened he was so violently sick that he got very little sleep, and eventually at about 11 a.m., feeling like he had a truck driving around inside his head, he made his way to the ship. Because of his inability to handle alcohol, and due to the rather large amount that he had consumed, he had totally forgotten the reason why he had arranged the impromptu party.

★

He was soon brought back to reality, and into the real world of sober people when he reached the base.

The shit had hit the fan, and how. Rumours were rife throughout the base that a major international incident had occurred overnight. Not only were several US army and navy officers and high-ranking Vietnamese officials in custody, apparently charged with the crimes involving young children, but that two US naval officers were dead. The rumour was that the officers were from the base, and that Captain Andrew and Commander Neville had not been seen since the night before. Many Vietnamese police and soldiers had also died in what, if only half the stories could be believed, was a real live gun battle. A battle of great proportions.

It was all too incredible to really believe, but the fast sobering David Brandon believed it totally. His belief was assisted by the inclusion of the names of Andrew and Neville in the rumours. He felt sure that the Senator was somehow involved. He also felt sure that the previous evening's celebrations were linked to the terrible things that had happened, and knew that he had obviously helped that man, Senator, make all of this happen. The mere thought of it scared the shit out of him.

It was alleged, and believed by all, that an international political and diplomatic shitfight was already on the plates of the governments of both the United States of America, and South Vietnam. All military units were brought on to full alert. It was almost as if the US High Command was anticipating the start of hostilities – between the Allied Forces in South Vietnam.

David Brandon couldn't help thinking that Uncle Ho must have been having a field day.

Holy shit! he thought, shaking with fear. Oh my God! What the hell have I done?

## Chapter Four

At about the same time as the young nurse was contemplating her meteoric rise to naked stardom on the table at the officers' club, the first of a stream of cars were arriving at a country residence about five miles south-east of Saigon.

It was a large mansion in several acres of grounds with a high security wall surrounding it, appropriately named The Retreat. In happier French colonial times it had been the residence of a Monsieur Paul Lebrocq, an ex-army colonel, registered as a reserve officer. Lebrocq, a wealthy rubber planter reputed to be worth many millions of dollars, was, like so many Frenchmen during times of national crisis, a patriot and an incurable romantic.

His romanticism was proved to all the world when in November 1953 he volunteered, together with his entire reserve unit and thousands of other French soldiers, to parachute into a place, little known until that time, called Dien Bien Phu. He had never made a parachute jump before, but then neither had most of his men. The action taken by Lebrocq and his fellow Frenchmen was completely in vain. History would later prove that the attempt to relieve the beleaguered garrison, which was surrounded by the Vietminh Army under General Giap was hopeless, and stupid in the extreme.

The brave Paul Lebrocq was never seen again. Not one man in his battalion survived the terrible Battle of Dien Bien Phu.

It was hoped that they all died bravely in battle, but the reputation of the Vietminh with regard to their treatment of prisoners of war was less than good, and they were not a party to the Geneva Convention. However, that same convention that the French were signatories to had all too often been ignored and abused by the French themselves during that wicked colonial war.

Lebrocq's distraught, panic-stricken wife, like so many other French nationals in Indo-China at that time had seen the writing on the wall and on receiving news of the fall of Dien Bien Phu immediately abandoned all of her husband's business interests in the country. Together with her children, and carrying a few of her most valuable possessions, she walked out of the beautiful home that her husband's family had lived in for over one hundred years and returned to the safety of mother France.

★

Shortly afterwards the French gave up Indo-China to the Vietminh and concentrated their efforts on their rapidly diminishing empire. This was the decade when colonial empires throughout the world began to crumble at a very fast rate.

The house and its estate were taken into the safe keeping, a nice way of saying stolen, by a South Vietnamese general who claimed that he was already a part owner of the property, and that the Lebrocq family departed owing him large sums of money. He produced documentary evidence to the court to prove his claim. Although the judge knew that the evidence was forged, in those days judges didn't argue with conquering generals. Now, nearly twenty years later it was owned by his son, also a general. General Diep.

A massive and beautiful flat-roofed and stuccoed Mediterranean-style villa, it had originally been part of a very large estate, but over the years Diep's father had subdivided it on numerous occasions. He had made many millions of dollars on the transactions, but by the time he died all that remained was the house and a relatively small acreage. It was none the less still a substantial property, very much in keeping with the important position held by the General.

Diep owned several rich homes in and around Saigon, as did most if not all of his senior military colleagues. Most of these homes had been obtained by corrupt means, but then corruption was a way of life in this part of the world.

He was married and was the proud and doting father of four children, three boys and a girl, all under the age of ten years. His family did not live in The Retreat. For security reasons, after all there was a war in progress, they lived in Saigon itself in a palatial residence not very far from the American Embassy, a prime and prestigious location for a man who had ambitions to enter parliament at the conclusion of the war. The house was under twenty-four hour guard, which was not only essential, but at that time was considered the norm for a military officer of his seniority and prominence.

It was close to the expensive private schools that his children attended, as well as being quite near the barracks of General Diep's Infantry Division. Perfect in every way.

The Retreat was used for special holidays for the family, but at all other times it was maintained by Diep as a private sanctum for entertaining his fellow generals, senior politicians and other important dignitaries.

The house was beautifully appointed with twelve fully contained suites, most of which had private access from outside. The building was not originally built this way, but had been adapted over the years to meet the confidentiality requirements of Diep's special visitors. In the manner of a senior businessman he always referred to these visitors as his honoured guests.

The honoured guests, from all walks of life, regularly visited the mansion and paid large sums of money in order to participate in the most discreet manner in an activity which it was necessary to keep absolutely secret. Their jobs and probably their lives depended on this secrecy being maintained.

Being a general, even with the official trappings, together with the high level of corruption that was open to someone of that rank, could not possibly provide the level of income that Diep required to pay for his ultra-lavish lifestyle. Therefore some years before, initially to impress and meet the special and exclusive needs of senior officers and officials of the South Vietnamese regime he had established a private enterprise venture. The enterprise was a great success, which whilst providing for the needs of that special clientele had brought him great financial rewards.

When the United States Government entered the war it opened the door to a much wider, influential and often affluent range of clients. This, together with the US policy of twelve month tours of duty in the Vietnam war zone, guaranteed him a constantly rolling over, ongoing and thriving business which produced wealth beyond his initial plans and expectations.

*

Diep was a paedophile. He had discovered that he had different sexual preferences quite by chance whilst serving as a young officer in the north-east of the country many years before.

He did not see himself as being perverted, but rather looked upon himself as a normal man with normal sex drives, but with a liking for younger, much younger girls.

Like an alcoholic who refuses to accept that he has an addiction to alcohol Diep would go to great lengths to deny being a paedophile, and would become very angry with anyone who dared suggest that he was such a sick person. After all, he was an officer and being the father of small children he outwardly expressed his abject disgust for such people.

On one occasion during a recent battle against the NVA he had personally executed two soldiers who had been caught raping a small girl in a village they had captured from the enemy. Having declared them guilty without anything vaguely resembling a fair or reasonable trial, he had them forced to their knees in front of the entire unit. He then shot both of them in the back of the head.

★

His sexual feelings regarding small girls came into the open when during an anti-terrorist operation he had captured a small-time gangster who was conducting armed hold-ups in the region. The man was the sole survivor of a shoot out with Diep's platoon.

In an attempt to bribe Diep in order to gain his freedom the man had offered him his six year old daughter, who he assured him would satisfy his sexual needs better than any grown woman. Diep had been so angry and sickened by the man's suggestion that he had drawn his revolver and summarily executed him on the spot.

The thought that a small child could be offered for sex played on his mind for days. He was disgusted by the thought, yet at the same time he could not stop the strange, yet enticing fantasies that invaded him constantly.

It was not by chance therefore, that some days later he found himself unaccompanied outside the home of the dead gangster. He entered the house and met the man's wife, who was accompanied by a small girl. The woman was quite ugly, and the child was very much her mother's daughter in terms of her looks. He advised the woman that her husband had died whilst resisting arrest. She was obviously terrified that she would be killed also, and screaming hysterically she pleaded with Diep to spare her life. Then, to his utter amazement she also offered him the sexual favours of her child.

He was furious with the woman and so badly shaken by what had happened that he beat her severely, leaving her unconscious on the floor. He then ransacked the house looking for arms or anything relating to her husband's crimes but found nothing. In the kitchen area after the search he found a bottle of local wine which he drank. He was so confused by what had happened to him that he drank the coarse, peasant liquid far too quickly, and soon began to feel quite unwell. Finding a couch he sat down for a while, hoping that this sick, giddy feeling would soon pass so he could be on his way.

He dozed off, and again his mind was attacked by the weird fantasies that had plagued him over the previous days. He awoke slowly, a strange relaxed feeling overwhelming his entire body. He was being fondled in the most sexually satisfying way by the child.

He was to return to the house and to his child lover regularly during the remaining months that he served in that region.

★

During the following years, initially with the help of his father, he moved rapidly up through the ranks, mainly by buying the favours of his senior officers and politicians. As he gained more power and became trusted he was discreetly invited to become a member of a secret group of men, mostly senior army officers who enjoyed the same perversion as himself.

It was, however, an extremely expensive perversion. He resented the payments he was required to make, because unlike the other men in the group he did not believe that he had a sexual need for young girls.

I am not a paedophile. It is just that I rather enjoy the experience of sex with little girls, he used to remind himself constantly.

In fact, he genuinely felt sickened by these other men.

But then who am I to be the judge of their moral standards?

Yes, the cost was outrageous, but he could see no alternative if his desires were to be satisfied.

On his inheritance of The Retreat he immediately saw the potential for a private enterprise operation that would not only meet his own personal sexual needs, but could also be financially rewarding.

Throughout the planning phase of his enterprise he kept reminding himself that he was different to the others. However, he was convinced that if he did not exploit those sick bastards somebody else would. So he decided to set up a business at The Retreat, and to offer the most expensive, but guaranteed to be the most discreet, service in the country. As he had anticipated he never found himself short of honoured guests.

Whilst the war was not going particularly well, the Americans and their allies were pouring ever-increasing men and matériel into the conflict, obviously determined to win. Even more, they were totally convinced that they could not possibly lose.

Diep felt secure, both militarily and commercially. The war was going to be won.

Who am I to question the military might of the United States? he would ask himself.

Consequently he was sure that his entrepreneurial enterprise could last for ever, if he played his cards right.

*

So it was on that night, the night of the party for Lieutenant John Tincey, that The Retreat was fully occupied by honoured guests. They were Vietnamese politicians and senior public servants, and high-ranking officers from both the South Vietnamese and the United States military. Diep was also there.

In their expensive private luxury rooms the honoured guests were enjoying themselves with their young sexual partners, most of whom Diep would have claimed were there as willing participants.

According to him, the majority of the children were willing in that they, or their parents or guardians, were being paid a small amount of money for their services. Not that that made them any better off than the rest of the small boys and girls who had been kidnapped and detained in The Retreat that night.

Those small children were destined to face horrific abuses, both physical and sexual, of the very worst kind.

## Chapter Five

Colonel Quen was a totally dedicated police officer. However, unlike most senior police officers he was totally dedicated to two causes.

His first cause was a purely political one, a dangerous political one. He had seen his country torn apart by corruption and greed, and had also witnessed the invading armies of America, earlier helped by their allies from Australia and New Zealand, destroy the culture of the land and corrupt the morals of its youth.

Quen had been a convinced and committed communist for many years since his university days, and the changes that had occurred in his country, particularly since the arrival of the foreign military forces, angered him so much that he swore to support the cause of the north to the death, if needs be.

Unlike many of his communist comrades he had kept his political beliefs to himself. Those who had openly professed their support of communism had all died. Some of them had just disappeared, never to be seen again. Others had been branded as subversives and terrorists, and in many instances had been summarily and publicly executed for their political beliefs.

Quen had decided to keep quiet and wait. He was not afraid to die for the cause, and would willingly do that if he felt it was worthwhile. No! He would wait until his life, or his death could be more sensibly given to the cause.

The war was being won by the North so he wouldn't have to wait too long. Meanwhile, because of his senior position in the police service he had been able to secretly establish an active cell of Vietcong freedom fighters. With the intelligence information that he was able to provide them they had been highly successful, particularly in bringing terror into the hearts of American servicemen, many of whom had seen friends and colleagues killed whilst indulging in drunkenness and debauchery in the bars and brothels that they had created in Quen's beautiful homeland. The news of the bombing exploits of Quen's battle unit had been received with great joy by his brothers of the North Vietnamese Army.

He accepted that some of his VC comrades had died too, but he knew that they had each been happy to do so. Theirs was the ultimate sacrifice and gift to the future People's Republic of Vietnam. In most instances their deaths had had some purpose, and they would always be recognised as heroes and martyrs. Quen, however, had made a personal pact with himself that if he was to die for the cause, it would be in the act of doing something so important and heroic that it would go down in the annals of Vietnamese history.

*

His other cause was a strictly police-related matter that was being given the highest priority. It was the detection and destruction of a massive paedophile network that had been established in and around Saigon. From snippets of reliable information that he had received he felt sure that it was operated by a South Vietnamese military officer of senior military rank. He was equally sure that the success of the paedophile group was mainly due to American money and the involvement of American officers. In this latter assertion he was wrong. The American involvement was relatively small compared to that of his own countrymen.

\*

Much of his bitterness towards Americans stemmed from the fact that two years before, whilst leading a police vice patrol in one of the areas mostly frequented by US servicemen, he had discovered a small girl, only five years old, dumped by the side of the road. The child was terribly battered and was in a bad way. She had been reported as kidnapped in broad daylight from outside her home earlier in the week. Barely able to speak, she had managed to tell him that she had been taken in a van to a place that had very big rooms, high ceilings and four-poster beds. Then, over two days she had been savagely raped and beaten during a continuing sexual orgy.

So severe were her injuries, both internal and external, that she died in his arms before an ambulance arrived. Quen had held her closely and gently rocked her in his arms humming a lullaby to her.

Just before she died the child had opened her eyes and called out, 'Please don't let them hurt me again, Daddy.'

He held the child closely to his chest, and with tears rolling down his face he whispered into her ear, 'I promise you that Daddy will never ever let anyone hurt you again.'

She did not hear his solemn promise as she was already dead. But in a way, by dying she had helped him keep his word, because nobody ever could hurt the poor child again.

The death of this child and the manner of her demise affected him more than he could possibly describe. The fact that the child was discovered in an area used by Americans was, however, a ploy to cover up the fact that she had been kidnapped by Diep's men and had suffered her injuries at The Retreat.

Quen was determined to catch the people who did this terrible thing. Later, at the child's graveside he made her a further promise that he would find and kill as many of the people involved as possible, regardless of what happened to him as a consequence.

The limited information he had was that membership of the paedophile cell was open to senior officers in the military, and to senior government officers and politicians only. This was no ordinary organisation.

If he could break it open wide, it could possibly lead to the downfall of the government, which would most certainly cause enormous embarrassment to the American military and their government back in the United States. It might also, but this was almost beyond his wildest hopes; it might also create a massive rift between the South Vietnamese Government and the United States which could undermine their joint war effort.

To help him achieve this end, on top of his normal police resources, he had been given substantial financial support from his contacts in the north who recognised the strategic importance of uncovering this criminal conspiracy. The money enabled him to pay informants and to bribe officials, but so far that had not been enough. He still had not traced the leader of the cell, or its centre of operation.

*

It was therefore with great pleasure, but a certain amount of suspicion and apprehension, that he received the anonymous information regarding The Retreat.

The information came in a telephone call to his office. He had already worked a straight twenty-four hours and was about to go home to bed. It was, however, only ten o'clock in the morning and although he was in no mood to get involved in anything else when he was so tired, he grudgingly felt that he couldn't really refuse to take a call at that time of the day, specifically as the caller asked for him by name. It might also be important. It was!

The voice at the other end of the line was that of an American. From the way that the man spoke and the expressions he used Quen formed the impression that the man was probably a Negro. He had had a great deal of experience in dealing with American Negro servicemen, and they tended to adopt a peculiar slang, and affect a style of speaking that separated them from most other American servicemen. Yes! The man was almost certainly a military person, or someone involved closely with the military, for he spoke at great length about American officers who were going to attend an orgy involving children.

He called them 'Lil kids', or something really American like that.

In fact, not only did Felix tell Quen about the intended orgy, but he also informed him that this was the paedophile cell that the he had been trying to track down for so long. He was startled by the fact the informant claimed to know of this particular investigation.

Whilst Felix passed on the information to Colonel Quen, his boss the Senator sat opposite him in his wheel-chair, sipping at a glass of whisky and quietly nodding his head. Felix gave Quen the location of The Retreat and the details of the owner, together with the approximate times that the officers and other participants would be arriving at the mansion to commence their evening's sick entertainment.

He also pointed out that General Diep had dozens of heavily armed army non-commissioned officers performing security duties at the estate, which with its high walls would be easy to defend if it came to a fight. He emphasised to Quen that if the raid commenced before 2 a.m. he could lose most of the key players.

He tried to arrange a meeting with his informant, but Felix just laughed and told him to do the job right and not to worry. He then wished the Colonel good luck and rang off.

\*

So excited that he could hardly breathe, he was also extremely suspicious of the fact that the information was from an anonymous source and that it was so comprehensive, and so readily given.

Can it be a trap? he thought to himself as he mulled it over in his mind again and again.

He was even more concerned when he began to digest the news that the owner of The Retreat and alleged ring-leader of the cell was none other than General Diep, one of the most influential of the Army's generals. If this was false information, then a man as powerful as he could destroy Quen for good. To falsely accuse such a high-ranking officer of such a terrible crime could lead to the sudden end of his career, even to his death. Such was the power of a man like Diep.

The thought that it could be a trap played havoc in his mind for some time whilst he considered the people he knew, both in the criminal world and elsewhere who could possibly want him out of the way. He came up with a complete blank, but that didn't stop him worrying.

Then again, if the information was correct, it would be a wonderful coup for him, and also for the cause of the VC and their comrades in the NVA. If he could trap influential politicians and military leaders, particularly Americans, under such circumstances the repercussions could have a vital impact on the course of the war, perhaps even leading to the withdrawal of the American military from Vietnam.

The excitement gripped him.

If this information is correct and I uncover this ring of disgusting gangsters I will be striking a great blow for my people.

He lifted his head with pride and smiled to himself at the thought of how the news of his success would be received by his leaders.

General Diep and his sick friends. The fools! The stupid fools! The irony will be that the imperialistic forces of the corrupt government of South Vietnam will be helping me to achieve that end.

His excitement and happiness at his obvious good fortune was so great that he immediately dismissed all of his early negative thoughts regarding the validity of the information from the anonymous American. He would immediately act on the information and to hell with the consequences. As an experienced policeman he was used to acting on intuition, and his intuition told him that this was going to be the big one.

He picked up the telephone and dialled an internal number.

'Captain Lee! Come to my office and bring Lieutenants Huen and Than with you. Before you come I want you to recall all men in the unit. This is a priority! Also contact Captain Nguyen at 3rd Division. I want his entire unit as well. I will be conducting a briefing for all officers on a major and top secret mission at 1100 hours.

'Now! My office – five minutes. Got it?'

*

Within the hour he had brought his own officers, and the officers of the 3rd Division up to speed with all that he knew regarding the paedophile ring. He made a specific point of advising them of the important positions that many, if not all of the people involved in this ring could hold.

Quen was an honourable man with a great respect and an almost fatherly regard for the men who worked for him, even though he sometimes found this hard to reconcile in view of the fact that they were working for his blood enemies.

Because of his special regard for them he also warned them that if the information that he had been given turned out to be false there would be a lot of shit flying; very dangerous shit! To dispel any misgivings caused by this warning he assured them that at the final briefing later in the day he would issue each of them with written instructions signed by him, which would hopefully cover them in any subsequent inquiry.

As one, his officers protested that this was not necessary, but Quen smiled and said, 'Thank you all, but it is obvious that none of you have ever really been in deep shit before, and you certainly don't deserve to be in it because of me. If this goes wrong the shit will be too deep to swim to the shore – believe me. My written instruction will act as a sort of lifebelt for each of you.'

He laughed out loud at his clever play on words, and they all joined in.

Quen need not have bothered about offering this safe-guard to his men. Most of them later threw his memo away, such was their faith in their commander. In most cases the officers who took that action would live to regret their decision in that regard.

Without exception all of his small, hand-picked team of officers were dedicated policemen. As honest cops each one of them had good reason to detest the sort of people that they were hoping to arrest in the forthcoming mission. They all held Quen in high regard and had no concerns about following his orders to the letter.

I wonder what they would do, and how loyal they would be to me if they knew who I really am, thought Quen grimly as he glanced around his office at their young, eager and excited faces. Regardless of their misguided political beliefs and allegiances Quen really cared for these young men, and promised himself that he would do everything in his power to protect them when the great day of liberation finally came.

★

Captain Lee had a close relative in local government. Through this source, during the course of the afternoon he was able to confirm that the owner of The Retreat was indeed General Diep, and that the premises were used by him on regular occasions, rather than rented out to tenants. His relative was also able to provide him with a plan of the premises at the time of the most recent subdivision, together with a map of the neighbourhood.

While the plan was some years old and did not necessarily reflect the present interior layout of the building, it did give the general exterior layout of The Retreat and its environs. Regardless of its possible short-comings it enabled Quen and his colleagues to work out a reasonable and workable plan of attack on the premises.

Lee had taken a special observation unit to reconnoitre the exterior of the estate and as much of the interior as possible. In two nondescript cars they had managed to film most of the perimeter walls, and had by sheer luck got a shot of the main driveway up to the front of the house. Just as they were making a pass along the main road fronting the estate a delivery van was leaving, and at the precise moment that they passed the main gateway the large solid gates were wide open. Shortly afterwards they were closed by an elderly and bent man in workers' overalls. He was assumed to be the caretaker. There was no sign of any guards at the gate, or nearby.

Not that Quen would have had a problem if the gate hadn't been open. He had managed to cover all possibilities by getting Captain Nguyen, a skilled helicopter pilot, to borrow a military machine from his brother, an air force colonel at the nearby airbase. With a police cameraman on board Nguyen had overflown the east and west perimeters of the estate at a reasonable height so as not to arouse suspicion. His cameraman had obtained some excellent footage of the main house and all of the luxury outbuildings.

★

Later, with all of his officers and senior NCOs present, Quen presented his plan of attack. The films taken of the estate from both the air and the ground were excellent – far better than he had hoped.

The stakes were so high for General Diep and his honoured guests that the security men who the informant had referred to would certainly be trusted and seasoned soldiers. A man of Diep's intellect would obviously take the highest level precautions to cover up his criminal activities, and this meant that his security guards would be top quality troops, probably non-commissioned officers from his own elite unit.

Quen's plan seemed pretty foolproof, but just in case something went wrong the assault units would be heavily armed and prepared for the worst scenario. Both his team and that of Captain Nguyen were highly trained para-military police units, and the teams that would scale the walls were designated as commandos, such was their military reputation.

The estate was surrounded by a four metre high wall which would be scaled with ladders in six specially selected locations by police commando assault teams, each comprising six men. These locations were selected because of their close proximity to dense bush and undergrowth. A small river, about fifty metres wide, ran along the north and east sides of the estate. It was deep and very fast running which tended to make those sides of the estate less probable escape routes. However, they would need to be covered, but this could be done by a relatively small number of men.

This task was given to Lieutenant Huen with a squad of ten men and two vehicles mounted with searchlights and heavy calibre machine-guns. He would also receive the support of a river police speedboat, just in case.

Huen realised that in the position that he was allocated there was unlikely to be much chance of seeing any of the action, which disappointed him very much. His respectful protestations and requests for a more active role were received with howls of laughter from his colleagues, and a good-natured pat on the back from the Colonel.

Lieutenant Than, with a squad of twenty men in three vehicles, was to cover the west wall which contained the side entrance of the estate which, like the front entrance, appeared to have an electronically controlled gate. As with Huen, all of his vehicles would have searchlights and machine-guns, but in his case they would be armoured personnel carriers, better equipped to handle any attempt at a vehicular break-out from the estate.

The police commando units were to be led by officers and senior NCOs of Captain Nguyen's unit which was specially trained in such work. Two units would scale each of the west, north and east walls simultaneously. They would infiltrate the grounds, taking out any guards, preferably without resorting to killing, as the evidence of such people would be vital in any subsequent trial. Each man was equipped with two pairs of handcuffs for the purpose of restraining such prisoners.

Exactly five minutes after the commando units had scaled the wall, Quen, with six armoured vehicles and thirty men would assault the front gate and drive straight up to the front of the house. Then the building would be surrounded and entered, and the criminals rounded up.

From the local maps they had obtained from Lee's relative Quen was able to allocate positions for all of his units that would enable them to keep under cover until such time as the assault commenced.

The whole exercise was being given the planning and precision of a full-scale military assault. Quen was not writing off the possibility that the assault could become a violent one, but in the event of that possibility he was well prepared. He was using over one hundred highly trained and well-armed police officers, most from special para-military units. He felt sure that if Diep was involved in the criminal activity that he believed he was, he would be taking extraordinary precautions to safeguard his interests and those of his clients. After all, he was a general, so those precautions would certainly be of a military nature.

*

Quen's units began to infiltrate the area as soon as darkness fell. By midnight everyone was in place, and well out of sight of the walls and gateways of the estate. Then began the long wait.

Phase One, the infiltration by the police commando units over the west, north and east walls was to commence at exactly 2 a.m. The assault on the main gate by Quen and his men would follow at exactly 2.05 a.m., unless the commandos met with armed resistance, in which case Colonel Quen would take immediate action.

# Chapter Six

Diep was reasonably happy with the plans for the evening. He was expecting fourteen honoured guests. Of the Vietnamese guests attending, one was a Cabinet minister, and three were senior government officials. Two generals, one army and one air force, would also be attending, together with four army colonels. The remainder were senior US military officers. All of the guests except two had visited The Retreat previously.

The two new guests were naval officers, one a commander and the other a full captain. They had both been recommended by General Ngy, whom Diep had worked with for many years. Their payments had arrived that morning through the pre-arranged channels, and according to Ngy both of these officers were loaded, to use the Yankee idiom.

Diep had already inspected the spacious luxury bedrooms and was satisfied that his guests would be delighted with the quality and presentation of the amenities. In the villa's fabulous gourmet kitchen the staff were busy preparing the exquisite food that would be available for guests throughout the night, and delivered to their rooms on request. Likewise the bar staff were polishing glasses and silver ice buckets, ensuring that everything was ready for the guests who would be arriving from midnight onwards.

He had previously checked the security guards patrolling the grounds. They were all specially screened and selected senior NCOs and warrant officers from his regiments.

These men were paid very well for these special duties. The two senior warrant officers in charge of security were also guaranteed special free privileges of the sort enjoyed by the guests, but which they would enjoy after the guests had left the following morning. Like Diep, they and their men were fully aware of the penalties for people involved in the sexual exploitation of children, so they were not likely to be indiscreet. They were all totally loyal to the General. It was a matter of having to be, as the alternative was not something to be considered lightly.

★

Downstairs in what used to be cellars, but which were now converted to dormitories were the main attractions of the coming night's entertainment. Twenty-eight small children, boys and girls, were being scrubbed clean, rubbed in exotic-smelling oils and perfumes and dressed in provocative clothing that was especially chosen to thrill and excite the paying guests. Some of the children were handcuffed to their beds, and all of them appeared strangely quiet and submissive, considering the fact that the majority of them knew what the evening had in store for them.

At this stage few of them were in a condition to care, and the drugs that had been administered to them during the course of the evening would guarantee that they did as they were told. The fact that they were drugged would also ensure that they would cause no great problems for the men who were shortly to abuse their frail young bodies.

There was, however, one matter of concern to Diep. Until recently there were always plenty of people willing to offer children for virtually any form of employment. As a rule they were paid a reasonable sum of money for the child and no questions were asked. Those people were probably not even related to the children in question. There were so many orphans of this war that children had always been relatively easy to procure.

However, this easy access had largely dried up. It was now very difficult. The authorities, both South Vietnamese and American were anxious to close down the child sex business and were going to great lengths to achieve this. As the result Diep had found himself short of children for this night's activities.

With far too few young subjects to satisfy the needs of the honoured guests he had sent out some of his men to procure at least six more from the streets and sidewalks of Saigon.

★

The men had been largely unsuccessful in their endeavours, and had only managed to find and kidnap three children. Then, on the way back to The Retreat a disaster occurred. One of the children, a girl aged about seven, had tried to escape by climbing out of a hole in the roof of the van. She had hit the road when the vehicle was doing about eighty kilometres an hour and had bounced into a roadside power pole, dying instantly.

From the point of view of the kidnappers the tragedy had nothing to do with the death of the child. It merely related to the fact that they would have one subject less to hand over to General Diep. They were sure that he would be very unhappy with them, and soldiers who displeased the General usually lived to regret it, even sergeants and warrant officers.

To compound their potential problems with the General, the men stupidly picked up the child's body and brought it back with them to The Retreat, thus creating the very real problem of having to dispose of it in the morning. Their assumption that the General would be displeased proved to be correct. In fact General Diep was more than displeased. He was extremely angry with them, and promised them that he would decide on their fate later.

Diep just hoped that none of his clients would be too violent with their tiny partners during the coming hours, as replacements were so hard to obtain. However, his concern for the children's welfare was merely a commercial one.

★

Back at the naval base Captain Peter Andrew and Commander Al Neville were having a few drinks in Neville's quarters prior to leaving for a very special function. They had heard that a party was being held at the officers' club, but had dismissed it as small fry in comparison to the one that they would be attending. On top of which they had also heard that it was being run by that fairy David Brandon, and they both agreed that it would not do to be seen in his company too much.

Whilst dining out the evening before, they had been really surprised and pleased when they had been given invitations from their host General Ngy to attend what he described as a private, and very discreet, gentlemen's evening.

Ngy, the commanding officer of a South Vietnamese Army division worked very closely with the American Forces, and as a result was well known in American officer circles and was often a guest at their functions.

He had met them purely by chance, or so it was made to appear, at a cocktail function in Saigon. He had been quite insistent that they be his guests for dinner at a very high-class restaurant later that evening.

Flattered by his attentions they had spent the evening with him and had not only enjoyed excellent food and wine, but had also enjoyed some time with the beautiful hostesses that were provided as an adjunct to the meal.

He was a charming and generous host, and during the course of the evening he had told them of a special function the following evening at which the girls would all be the most beautiful in Saigon. He also advised them, with a sly smile on his face, that they would also be somewhat younger than those one would find in the normal clubs and hotels. The discussion centred around this forthcoming function for a while until Neville broached the subject of admission to the event.

'Gentlemen, it so happens that I have an invitation for two. I was personally planning to attend with one of my colleagues, but unfortunately this damn war has got in the way and I must return to my unit first thing in the morning.'

He gave a big theatrical sigh, then laughed out loud.

'You have been such delightful company that I would be most happy if you took advantage of my invitation and attended on my behalf. I feel sure that you will enjoy yourselves, and as experienced military men we all know how helpful it can be for one's career to mix in the right places, with the right people.'

He laughed again and nudged Captain Andrew in the side.

'That is very kind of you, General,' said Andrew, but we really couldn't. Surely you have colleagues of your own who would be more appropriate to represent you.'

'Sadly, no! You see, they will have all received recall notices to the unit just the same as their esteemed General. If they haven't I shall kick someone's arse.' He laughed, and they both laughed with him.

Andrew looked across to Neville who nodded his head and mouthed the words, Let's go.

'Okay, General, we will be delighted to attend. I can't tell you how much we have appreciated your hospitality this evening, as I know we will tomorrow night.'

'Good! Then that is settled. Here is the invitation, and I will explain how to get there before I leave you this evening.'

He gave Captain Andrew a card embossed with Vietnamese wording. He assured them that this would be accepted as an invitation for both of them. He also assured them that he would phone The Retreat and tell the host that they were attending on his behalf.

After bidding his guests farewell Ngy made two telephone calls from a private room in the restaurant. One was to General Diep explaining that he had recruited two American officers for the following night's function and giving him their details. He advised Diep that their entrance fees would be paid in the usual way the following morning, and also told him to look after these officers as they were both very rich men.

The next phone call that he made was to an unlisted number, and was answered by a man with an Australian accent.

'They took the bait, Senator, and will be there tomorrow night. I haven't the faintest idea why you should wish to involve two insignificant American naval officers in this, but I'm sure that you must have good reasons. However, they had better not screw up the arrangements that you are making on my behalf. The main thing is to get that bastard, Diep. You have had your payment, now make sure that he is dealt with.

'I obviously want him out of my hair, for business reasons, so to speak, but even if I didn't I would want to see him punished for his disgusting trade in children. Surprised, Senator? I do have some standards, you see. Especially when children are involved. I will pay the attendance fees for these officers tomorrow morning in the usual manner. Diep will not suspect, and your American friends will go, how do you say, like lambs to the slaughter?'

The Senator replaced the phone on the hook.

Slaughter being the operative word, my friend, he thought.

'I believe that we have another satisfied customer on our hands, Felix, or we will have by tomorrow night. Fancy that old bastard being so self-righteous about the sex trade when he is up to his arse in heroin trafficking. We know he's been to The Retreat on several occasions, and he didn't go there to sample the local wines. Mind you, it serves Diep right for trying to muscle in on Ngy's drugs business. If he had been contented to stick to his sordid child abuse nonsense Ngy wouldn't have paid us so handsomely to get rid of him. All in all, we are the only real winners, Felix my boy.'

Felix laughed out loud.

'The bit that amuses me the most,' he replied, 'is that by involving these two sailor boys we are drawing Brandon tighter on to the hook. I mean, sure they are putting it around that he's a queer. So what? Nobody really believes them. They couldn't have done him any harm in the long run.'

'That doesn't matter, Felix. What does matter is that Brandon thinks they are a danger to him and his precious bloody career. We have helped him along in that belief. He's shit scared they are going to go to the top with some trumped-up charge against him and that he'll be chucked out. But we need him on board, Felix, so we fix his mates and he is eternally grateful, as well as being eternally shit scared of us.

'You've heard of the stick and the carrot principle? Well, this is sort of like that, except that in Brandon's case both the stick and the carrot will be shoved right up his arse if he steps out of line.'

Their laughter was so loud that it would have been heard in the next house if it had been closer. However, the next house was a full half kilometre away and was surrounded by a four metre high wall. The Senator and Felix could therefore be absolutely sure that nobody at the neighbouring house, The Retreat, would hear their laughter.

★

At midnight Andrew and Neville arrived at the entrance to the walled estate known as The Retreat. Andrew handed the invitation card to one of the two uniformed army guards on duty outside the gate. It was examined and handed back. The soldier saluted smartly and as he did so the large gates opened wide allowing Andrew to drive through and up the tree-lined avenue to the large mansion at the end.

'Well, my friend, we have at last hit the big league,' Neville said as their car pulled up outside the front door of the magnificent main house.

## Chapter Seven

Colonel Quen was feeling very pleased with himself. It was 1.45 a.m., and so far his observers, hidden in a small garden opposite the front gates had reported that twelve cars had entered the estate. It appeared that at least fourteen passengers had arrived for the evening's activities. Because it was dark none of the visitors had been identified, even with the infrared scopes that they were using to assist them in their task. Quen didn't mind about the lack of identification. Within half an hour or so all would be revealed.

Already he had been informed that there were probably six armed soldiers at the gate, two of them outside. If he needed confirmation that the information about this evening's activities inside the walls was correct, the fact that the gate was so heavily guarded went a long way to convincing him.

Yes, he was very satisfied with the way the operation was going. He was probably in the minority in that regard because the weather had developed into a tropical storm and at least half of his men were concealed out in the open with little to protect them from the elements. Still, they were trained to withstand this sort of discomfort, and it would soon be over. He was quite worried about visibility though.

'Don't worry, Colonel. If we can't see them too well, then chances are they won't be able to see us. You see, we at least know that they are there, but they're not expecting us at all: or I hope that they aren't,' said Captain Lee.

Lee was sitting half in and half out of the car, balancing his night scope on the top of the car door. He was soaked through to the skin but didn't really feel very wet as his excitement had taken full control of his body. Mere physical things like wet clothes would probably concern him later when it was all over.

'Thank you for that little bit of homespun philosophy, Captain,' chuckled Quen, feeling quite comfortable as he at least had not yet had to get out of the car. 'However, much as I admire your philosophical dissertations I would be much happier if you were to confine yourself to reporting on the dispositions of the men that you can see. Also, if you get pneumonia don't blame it on to me. Why can't you get back into the damn car and shut the door?'

'I can't see through the windscreen in this rain.'

'We do have windscreen wipers you know, Captain Lee,' replied Quen.

'But they'll make a hell of a noise, sir.'

'Don't be such a bloody idiot. In this downpour, not to mention the thunder and lightning, we can hardly bloody hear ourselves think let alone hear the fucking windscreen wipers. Come back inside man.'

A worrying thought suddenly came to him. He grabbed the handset just as Lee shut the door.

'Nguyen from Control. Over.'

'Control from Nguyen. What's up, sir?'

'I don't know about you, but from where I am, thanks to this damn storm, I doubt if I could even hear gunfire, particularly if it was at the other end of the target area. You will have to ensure that your men use their radios immediately if fired on. I daren't risk the possibility of us not knowing if they have been intercepted.'

'Yes, sir. I understand. Each team has a PR though, and they have all been briefed. However, I'll contact them on their wavelength and ensure that they understand your instructions. Nguyen out.'

I wonder why the Colonel is panicking all of a sudden, Lieutenant Nguyen thought as he replaced the handset of his radio.

'Bloody nuisance their personal radios not being on our main wavelength. We just didn't have the time to set the communications up exactly as I would have liked. Still, hopefully Nguyen has it all under control,' Quen said, to himself, but out loud.

Soaking wet, and by now very uncomfortable, Captain Lee decided to remain quiet.

The rain continued to pour down in torrents and the thunder and lightning was continuous, and earth shaking. Visibility was virtually down to zero, except for those brief moments when lightning lit up the landscape. Even without the violent sounds of the electric storm the rain was drumming so loudly on the roadway, the ground, the trees and especially on the roof and bonnet of the car in which Quen and Lee sat, that it was impossible to hold a conversation without shouting at each other.

They could no longer see the armoured personnel carrier which was parked only ten metres away to their right. This was to be the lead vehicle for the assault on the front gate – the vehicle that Quen and Lee would transfer to a minute or so before the front entrance attack was made. The Colonel wasn't enjoying the prospect of getting out of his warm and dry car and running across that gap of mud and water to the rear of the APC, but it would have to be done, and very soon.

Meanwhile the rain continued to come down heavier and heavier, and even for Quen who was born and bred in this area and used to the tropical storms that were prevalent to the region, the noise was unbelievable.

The deafening noise of the storm was to be the cause of the terrible things that were to happen on that dark, angry night.

★

At 2 a.m. precisely the police commando teams rose like ghosts out of the undergrowth where they had been hiding for over an hour. With a long bamboo ladder carried between each two men, three ladders per team, they raced through the fast-flooding undergrowth to the sections of the wall selected for their respective assaults.

Team One was to scale the east wall just in front of where Lieutenant Huen's jeep was hidden in the bushes, some thirty metres away. He watched them as they reached the base of the wall. One of the men pushed the ladder up against the wall, whilst the other turned and with his automatic rifle at the port, kept momentary guard whilst his number one began to climb. Huen noticed the first man appear to pause on the top of the wall, then he slid over. The second member of the team started up the ladder. The other two ladder teams were slightly behind the first, as was planned. At that same moment the same scene was being re-enacted in five other locations around the walls of the estate.

★

Sergeant Major Lin, a veteran paratrooper, and one of General Diep's personally selected guards was crouching under a small lean-to against the east wall. He had been on his rounds checking the guards along the east and south walls when the storm had suddenly intensified. He had dived into cover, and was trying hard to keep himself, but more importantly his cigarette, dry. This sort of weather really pissed him off but he was being paid a month's wages extra for working this weekend so he couldn't complain. Then he would get the chance to enjoy himself for a few hours with one of those kids. Real officer's perks, he thought to himself.

Lin had enjoyed the rape and pillage aspects of military combat in the South Vietnamese Army for some years. It was during one of those post-combat, highly illegal but very common, interludes that he discovered that he enjoyed sex with young kids. Since then he had risked his career, and even his life, on many occasions to enjoy his perversion. He acknowledged that he was a pervert but really didn't care. He was a very basic man who just wanted it as often as he could get it. General Diep had somehow learned of his sexual preference two years before and had put the heavy word on him. At first Lin had been scared witless about the danger he was in but his fears turned out to be unfounded. All that Diep wanted him for was to ensure that he and his honoured guests weren't disturbed whilst they did the very same thing, but in greater style.

Suddenly, above the roar of the storm, but during a brief lull in the thunder and lightning, he heard a clatter against the other side of the wall and thought that he heard a voice. Moving out from under the shelter he looked upwards, and just at that moment he saw two vertical pieces of wood appear above the ridge of the wall.

Shit! A ladder!

He immediately cocked his automatic rifle and at that moment saw a dark figure appear and momentarily lie flat along the ridge of the wall above him.

Lin slowly sank down against the wall, silently lowering his rifle to the ground and drawing his bayonet from its scabbard. The figure on the wall slid down and landed almost alongside him. Grabbing the man around the throat from behind he pulled him towards his body, at the same time thrusting the bayonet deeply up into the man's back, piercing the heart. He lowered the dead man to the ground and was removing his bayonet from the body when he heard a voice call from the top of the wall.

'All right, sergeant?'

'Sure!' Lin called back, lunging forward at the throat of the second man just as his feet hit the ground. The upward thrust of Lin's knife severed the man's windpipe, killing him instantly. Lin looked down at the two bodies and noticed that the first man he had killed was carrying a personal radio of some sort. He bent down and fumbled for the switch, turning it off.

Better safe than sorry, he said to himself as he touched the transmit switch of his own radio, whilst at the same time retrieving his rifle from the ground.

'All units! All units! This is Lin. Emergency! Trespassers in the compound. I repeat, trespassers in the compound. Armed to the teeth. I have just terminated two. Scaling walls with ladders. Sound the alarm. I repeat, sound the alarm. We have big trouble.'

Just as he finished his message, through the torrential rain he saw two other men dropping down from the wall into the gardens, one about five metres from him and the second man about the same distance further along the wall. He guessed that, as with the first team he had terminated, these two men would also have back-ups, so he waited for the next intruders to appear. He was right. Two further men dropped from the wall, each joining their partner on the ground in a crouch position.

Lin was an old campaigner who had seen a lot of action during his twenty years in the army. His instincts told him that this was the time to strike, before they had time to organise themselves. He aimed his weapon, and with short accurate bursts dispatched all four men in just seconds. It surprised him just how easy it had been. What surprised him even more was that the noise of the storm was so loud that he had hardly heard the sound of his own weapon.

Checking the bodies to be sure that the men were all dead he noticed a badge on the shoulder of the black one-piece uniform that one of them was wearing. He recognised it instantly.

'All units from Lin. Six intruders now down. We're in deep shit. They are from one of those special police units. I repeat, they are police. Inform the General immediately.'

★

Three things then happened almost at the same time. The emergency lights at the base of the wall near him suddenly came on. This gave him a fright and caused him to momentarily step back from the light and into the open, away from the shelter and protection of the wall, a most unsoldierly action for an experienced man like Sergeant Major Lin.

He then heard the distinct but dull sound of automatic fire coming from further along the wall. He assumed that the lights were on all around the compound, but could not see any because of the intensity of the storm. However, he had done all he could where he was so he decided to head towards the sounds and to help his men who were manning the other guard areas.

At that very moment the third thing happened. A bullet entered his head just above his right eye, and exited at the base of his skull taking half of the back of his head with it. He died without even knowing what had happened.

Had Sergeant Major Lin had time to think, he would probably have wondered how an experienced old soldier like him could get caught out in the open like this. He would also have thought that this was a bloody stupid way to die.

*

The shot came from the top of the third ladder of Team One. Sergeant Lo, the second in command of Lieutenant Huen's unit, had been concealed closest to Team One. As the last member of the six-man team had slid over the top of the wall Lo heard a noise which he thought sounded like gunfire. Unfortunately the noise occurred at the precise moment that the area had been shaken by an enormous thunderclap.

He was confused, but still convinced that there had been another noise. Ex-army and a veteran of several major engagements he was used to acting on his first impressions and his soldier's intuition. This was probably why he had survived those very nasty battles when others had not.

He knew, however, that his orders were quite specific. He and his group were to stay put unless ordered by Lieutenant Huen to do otherwise. The Lieutenant was just as pissed off as he was that they had drawn the short straw and had to take up positions on the side where the action was least likely to be.

Lo also knew that if he disobeyed Huen's orders, and by doing so blew the operation he could kiss his next promotion and probably his career a fond goodbye. That would probably be the least that would happen to him, but he was certain that the noise he had heard had been gunfire. If he was right, that could only mean that his men had been intercepted going over the wall. Gunfire or not, he had to make sure, and throwing caution to the wind he ran towards the nearest ladder and dropped to the ground at the base of the wall.

Apart from the thundering of the rain he could hear nothing. Not a sound of any life on the other side of the wall. Surely at this very moment the sergeant in charge of Team One would be gathering his men together ready to assault the house, and if they were obeying their instructions they should be huddled up in the shadow of the wall, probably only inches from where he lay listening.

Even those guys would have to make some noise. They made enough noise going over the wall to wake the dead, he thought.

He quickly decided to climb to the top of the wall and take a look for himself, first glancing back to where he knew Huen's vehicle was concealed. He couldn't see it through the wall of water descending from the skies, and he hoped like hell that as he couldn't see Lieutenant Huen at this particular moment, the Lieutenant would not be able to see him.

What if I've made a mistake? What if the noise I heard was merely the storm?

However, he had just started to climb the ladder when he heard the sound of gun fire again. This time he was absolutely sure. This new sound came from further along, in the direction of where he knew Team Two would have been.

He was halfway up the ladder when he heard the second noise, a man's voice giving instructions to someone, probably on a radio. He was giving a warning to someone that they were the police.

Lo raised himself level with the top of the wall and carefully looked over. A wall light just below the top of the wall came on just at that moment, and lit up the area immediately below him. What he saw shocked and stunned him. Just below him stood a man wearing an army beret, and a poncho cape to protect him from the torrential rain. He was carrying a gun of some sort and held a personal radio to his mouth. Spread along the base of the wall were six bodies, the bodies of Team One. All of them? Lo couldn't believe his eyes. An entire team wiped out in just a few seconds.

The man with the radio was definitely not from one of the police teams, he was dressed differently. He lowered the radio and looked as if he was going to move off. Lo was in deep shock, but he knew that he couldn't let this man escape, not after what he had done to Team One. He cautiously raised himself above the wall, lifted his gun, took aim and fired a short burst of three rounds at the head of the soldier below.

Panic-stricken, Lo scrambled back down the ladder and ran to where he knew Lieutenant Huen's vehicle was standing. Almost hysterical, and with tears rolling down his face, he informed his officer what had happened. On hearing his incredible story the Lieutenant glanced at his watch and immediately tried to call the Colonel. It was 2.05 a.m.

★

At exactly 2.05 a.m. Quen's armoured vehicle hit the main gates on the south wall, shattering them from their hinges. The two soldiers on duty outside had fired on the APC which had returned the fire, dropping both men to the ground. The vehicle rolled past the gateway and stopped halfway up the paved drive. It had hardly come to a halt when the rear doors were flung open and the police officers inside hit the ground running. They had only just left the vehicle when a heavy machine-gun opened up from behind them, just inside the main gateway, cutting them down in seconds.

Quen had forgotten the guards inside the gate, and in doing so he had also forgotten a very basic military rule.

Never open the doors of an APC when they are facing towards a potential danger. Always try to place the vehicle broadside on, in order to get the greatest protection from the armour plating for the soldiers inside the vehicle.

The radio inside the cab of the vehicle burst into life just as the vehicle's horrified machine-gunner began to return the fire.

'Huen to Control. Caution as you enter. We appear to have been blown.'

'Thanks! Thanks a fucking lot,' Quen screamed out, to nobody in particular.

★

The battle at The Retreat lasted for nearly forty minutes, during which time Quen's unit suffered forty casualties, eighteen of them killed. Also killed were twenty-one officers and NCOs of the South Vietnamese Army; one of them, half naked, was later discovered to be a three-star general. Also found dead inside the mansion were one Cabinet minister and two senior government officials. Near the gateway on the west wall lay the bodies of two semi-clothed officers of the United States Navy.

Six small children were also found dead in the shattered villa. Strangely, one small girl appeared to have suffered multiple fractures and other injuries, none of which appeared to be consistent with what just happened at The Retreat. According to a doctor who examined the bodies shortly afterwards, this little girl had been dead for some hours and her injuries were the sort one would expect to result from being involved in a road accident.

★

General Diep and Colonel Quen both died in the battle. Quen had made it his personal responsibility and duty to find and dispatch the General. He found him half naked in one of the magnificent bedrooms. He was frantically trying to dress himself as Quen burst through the door. Also in the room, cowering beneath the bedclothes, was an hysterical small girl.

He kept his weapon pointed at the obviously frightened Diep who had obeyed the Colonel's command and was lying on the floor with his arms and legs extended. At the same time Quen coaxed the terrified young girl from the bed, explaining that he was a police officer and assuring her that she was safe and would come to no more harm. After a while the child climbed out from under the sheets and stood naked and trembling in the corner of the room. He saw to his horror that the lower part of her body was streaked with blood, stark evidence of the abuses that she had suffered.

He ordered the girl to wrap herself in a sheet and leave the room immediately. While suffering from extreme shock the child understood what she was being told to do and nodded dumbly. Then, with a bloodied sheet draped around her fragile little body and dragging along the floor behind her, she opened the door and walked out into the corridor. Quen backed towards the door and slammed it shut with his foot.

By this stage the General had regained some of his composure and adopted a threatening attitude towards Quen, whilst at the same time starting to rise from the floor.

'I don't know who you think you are, soldier, but you are in real trouble. By the time I have finished with you you'll wish that you'd never been born—'

He never finished the last words of his threat. Quen had stepped close to where he was kneeling, and at point-blank range he had aimed his pistol between Diep's legs and fired one round. The bullet removed the man's penis and testicles, smattering blood and gore across the large bed behind the General who let out a long, piercing scream as he looked down to where his manhood had been. He then fainted and collapsed to the floor.

Quen immediately stepped forward, and placing his pistol against Diep's temple he administered the *coup de grâce*, doing so with a feeling of great pleasure. He had kept his graveside promise to the little girl.

The killing of the General had been quickly and efficiently carried out. Sure, he had indulged himself a bit in the manner of his death, but the General had died far less painfully than the evil bastard deserved.

He left the room and ran back to where he could hear the battle raging. Soon after he was caught in the open by one of Diep's guards who emptied half a clip from his automatic weapon into Quen's upper body, inflicting massive injuries to the head and chest, but he did not die instantly.

He lay in agony watching and listening to the massive gunfight going on all around the compound. Moments before he died he was joined by one of his sergeants who endeavoured to make him comfortable and stem the flow of blood which was pumping furiously out of his body.

It was obvious to the police sergeant that his Colonel had a very short time to live, so he decided to stay with him to the end, just so that he would not die alone. Quen knew the sergeant well, having served with him for many years. He understood exactly what the man was doing for him, and he gripped his hand in gratitude.

Quen knew that he was going to die and he had no regrets. However, he really did not want to be alone at the moment of his death.

Just as his life ended he spoke to the sergeant, slowly, but quite clearly. The words he spoke confused the man, who later decided that his leader must have been delirious at the moment of his death. Out of great respect for his Colonel he never reported those last words to anyone.

'Sergeant, we have done many good things together. You are an honourable man, and for that I respect you. But real honour will only come to our country when it comes under the control of the people who really care for our future. The North must and will win.'

He tried to say more, but his voice faded and he departed this world feeling sure that what he had done would help hasten the ultimate victory and bring him great honour amongst his communist comrades.

*

The others killed in the battle had died as the result of what was later described at the courts martial of Captains Lee and Nguyen, and Lieutenants Huen and Than, as undisciplined and indiscriminate fire. According to Quen's men, any indiscriminate fire came from the criminal defenders of the compound, and from the men who were involved in the crimes against the children, not from the police units.

Their protestations would fall mainly on deaf ears, for although they had uncovered and destroyed a disgusting child sex coven and released many small children from their bondage, they had also laid bare a highly embarrassing situation for the governments and military of both South Vietnam and the USA.

No medals or praise would be awarded for the actions of these police officers. On the contrary, a lot of very senior people were embarrassed and angry, so someone would have to pay.

The courts martial of Quen's brave men ensured that they were the ones who would do the paying.

There were many people in very high places on both sides of the Pacific Ocean who would have preferred that General Diep's enterprise had remained undetected, regardless of the moral implications of what he was doing.

★

Half a kilometre away the Senator and Felix listened to the battle being fought on their behalf in the walled compound of The Retreat. Even above the sound of the storm the heavy machine-gun and crackle of automatic fire could be heard distinctly.

'Well, Felix old son,' said the Senator, 'not only have we done for General Diep, for whatever happens he is a goner, and our mate General Ngy will be delighted and most generous I am sure, but our paranoid friend Brandon will be convinced that he started it all. What with that and his guilt feelings about his involvement with the last lot of heroin, we have really got him by the bollocks.

'Yes, Felix, I think we have just got ourselves a US warship and its captain to help in the business. Not a bad day's work for a couple of bad buggers like us.'

The two men raised their glasses and drank a toast to David Brandon and the USS *James Cunningham*.

'The deliveryman and his ship.'

# Chapter Eight

For over two weeks Brandon was both physically and mentally tormented by the deaths of Andrew and Neville. As predicted, he felt completely responsible because of his involvement with the Senator.

Although he constantly reminded himself of the fact that the two dead officers had been his enemies, and that there was no doubt that they were trying to destroy his career, this gave him little relief. He had helped to kill two colleagues, fellow navy officers. The feeling of guilt was weighing very heavily on him, and his problems weren't helped much by the atmosphere of gloom and doom that prevailed over the whole base.

The deaths of the two officers had helped compound what was already a grave international situation between the two allies in the Vietnamese conflict. The situation was made even worse by the fact that the Vietnamese police had fucked up and started a mini war between themselves and their own army. So many people had died that the top brass on both sides were looking for scapegoats. It was obvious that the Vietnamese were going to make examples of the survivors, both army and police.

On top of that, they had a major international scandal on their hands. A prominent army general running a paedophile ring for senior people? A Cabinet Minister and a Lieutenant General involved and dead? It was too hard to push under the carpet, particularly because of the extraordinarily high casualty list, and the status, both political and military, of many of those casualties.

The Vietnamese authorities had two US army colonels, apparent participants in the orgy, in custody and weren't letting them go. They refused to waver regardless of the demands made on them by the US High Command, and by politicians at the highest level. This, together with the fact that two dead US naval officers had also apparently been involved in the child sex scandal, gave the Vietnamese authorities a lot of clout.

Despite the considerable evidence to clearly prove Diep's role in the affair, they protested vigorously that the US officers were the ringleaders of the scandal, and that the Vietnamese nationals present at The Retreat were virtual innocent bystanders. Ridiculous though this story was, it had only helped deepen the rift between the Allied Forces and their respective governments which did nothing to enhance the war effort.

*

On the American side the finger of scorn was being pointed at the Navy, particularly at the base from which Andrew and Neville had operated. It was suggested by certain sections of the media that virtually everyone at that base was under suspicion. Although that was nonsense, the suggestion resulted in everyone, particularly the officers, being under enormous stress. Tempers were frayed and it was difficult to get much work out of officers or enlisted men. The latter were particularly angry at the sour treatment that they were getting from their leaders.

All female personnel had been transferred to other bases. This was done on the assumption that only men would be involved in a scandal of this sort. All personnel were confined to base, and all of the officers with quarters elsewhere were ordered to immediately billet themselves back inside the base, or on board their ships until such time as the political heat subsided. The refit and repairs being almost completed, Brandon returned to the USS *James Cunningham*.

The situation was not helped by the sudden arrival on the base of a special Navy investigations unit that had been sent over from the States to examine the allegations that other naval personnel may also have been involved in the 'child sex slave trade', as the media had named it.

★

Then, one day some weeks later all the officers on the base were summoned at very short notice to be addressed *en masse* by the Admiral. The hall was packed solid with men who, expecting the worst, sat silently and glum faced waiting for the tirade of abuse that they were sure would come. Admiral Stone was not known for mincing words when things were not going as he wished.

Brandon was particularly nervous and distressed as he sat waiting for his arrival. He feared that Stone was going to publicly announce his involvement in the affair, and that his career would end dramatically with a long term in the brig.

'Atten hut!' came the command from the rear of the hall.

Everyone sprung to their feet and stood rigidly to attention as Admiral Edward Stone strode to the raised dais at the front.

'At ease, gentlemen,' he commanded, removing his hat and flinging it on to a nearby chair.

'You'll all be pleased to know that the investigation team has completed its work and has given this base – that means all of you guys – a clean bill of health.

'The media people won't like it one bit, I know. I can see the headlines now. Whitewash is the word that I'm sure will sum up their protestations. So you and me will have to put up with even more crap for a while.

'Frankly, I don't give a shit. The dogs have been put back on their leashes and will leave this base today. Their report will probably have a few nasty innuendoes in it, but I have been advised that basically it will vindicate all of you from any involvement in this nasty, disgusting business.

'I feel ashamed that you have been put through this nonsense, and that you have each probably felt that you have been under suspicion. Well, in my book none of you have been suspects, and you will not be insulted in this way again.

'As for those two sick members of our officer corps who disgraced themselves, the US Navy, and our beloved country in such a terrible manner, all I can say is that they got their just desserts. They are better off dead, and I never wish to hear their names again. Be warned, all of you. Woe betide any officer who I ever hear trying to excuse or lessen their disgusting crimes. No! As far as I am concerned, whoever shot them did the United States Navy a very good turn.'

Stone stood silently for a moment to allow the officers to absorb his words.

'Now, regarding the discipline situation, I am fed up with seeing and hearing about the piss-awful behaviour of officers on this base. I know that you are all angry, and you have every right to be so, but the time has come to stop feeling sorry for yourselves.

'If you are looking for sympathy it's in the dictionary, somewhere between shit and syphilis.'

A murmur of laughter came from the assembled officers.

'Tear those chips off your shoulder, or I will do it for you. Stop taking your anger and frustrations out on your sailors. Start being good officers again, and if any one of you is brought to my notice in a negative way in this regard I'll have you out of this man's Navy and into some God-forsaken fucking infantry unit up north. Do you understand?' he shouted.

A mumbled response came from the crowded hall.

'I said, do you understand?' he shouted again. His face was bright red and he was obviously angry at their lack of response. He spat out the words, bombarding the officers in the front rows with his spittle.

'Aye aye, sir,' came the resounding roar.

'Good! Now hear this,' the Admiral said, his voice returning suddenly to a normal level, 'Commander Brandon has kindly offered to arrange another one of his excellent parties at the officers' club this Saturday. All of those present who are not on duty will accept his invitation. There will be no absentees. That is not a request, it is an order. Do you all understand me?'

'Aye aye, sir,' they all shouted in chorus.

The Admiral then called out, 'Where are you, Brandon?'

Several rows back, where he had hoped he would remain inconspicuous, David Brandon stood up quickly, his mouth still wide open in surprise.

'Here, sir!'

'Damn good idea of yours, David,' called the Admiral with a chuckle.

'Shall we say 2000 hours? By the way, I have no other engagements that night, so I would be most pleased to accept your magnanimous invitation to join you and your fellow officers. Thank you!'

'Aye aye, sir, you are most welcome,' came the startled reply.

By now most of the officers in the hall had realised that this was the first that Brandon had heard of the party, and many of them were cheering and laughing loudly. The ice had been broken.

His officers were suddenly beginning to look and sound like officers of the US Navy should, thought Admiral Stone, and he was pleased and greatly relieved.

★

A short while later, back on board the USS *James Cunningham*, Brandon entered his cabin and locked the door. He threw off his jacket and made for his bunk. He was emotionally exhausted. The sudden release from his anxiety had been all too much. He desperately needed a rest.

It was then that he noticed a small parcel sitting on his bunk. It was gift-wrapped in red and gold striped paper, with a silver ribbon tied up in a bow. He felt his body suddenly go cold.

'Oh, my God,' he said out loud. 'What the hell is it this time?'

He picked up the parcel and nervously opened it. It was a repeat of the experience that night at his apartment. The parcel contained money, only this time there was $25,000 in brand new bank notes. A small note accompanied the money. It read:

*Dear David,*
*Thanks for your help. It gets better. Trust me!*
*Senator*

He decided not to make inquiries regarding the delivery of the parcel. He just knew that nobody on board would have any knowledge of the parcel or of any visitor to the ship.

★

The following Saturday, as ordered by Admiral Stone, there was a massive party at the officers' club. This time it was confined to navy officers, from the base only. The only guests were female, and included most of those who had attended the party for John Tincey, together with numerous colleagues from the hospitals and administration units in the region. It was a really good party at which everybody let their hair down with the sheer relief of knowing that things were back to normal, at least within the base.

Although it was obvious that the shit would continue to fly for some time to come regarding the battle at The Retreat, at least the navy officers present were able to feel reasonably comfortable in the knowledge that things on their own doorstep were cool. They could all get back into the business of fighting and surviving the war.

Over the previous few days since the announcement from the Admiral the entire atmosphere in the base had changed. Officers and enlisted men were communicating with each other again and morale and discipline had very much returned to its earlier good level.

The party was well under way by the time that Admiral Stone arrived. He was accompanied by the pretty young nurse who had kindly divested herself of her clothing for the guests at the previous function. However, she remained the pillar of virtue throughout the evening, and to the great disappointment of most of the officers at the party did not remove one single small item of clothing.

Well, certainly not prior to leaving with the Admiral at about 2 a.m.

# Chapter Nine

It had recently become imperative that the ship's extra-curricular activities cease, and the final voyage of the *Palminto* had been planned down to the last tiny detail.

Some six months earlier the Philippines Government had conducted a purge of its Customs Service in Manila, and as the result of this unfortunate turn of events it had become obvious to both Brandon and the Senator that this would have to be the last voyage. At first they had both hoped that the problem would die down and go away. Alas! That was not to be.

In the sudden and unprecedented purge almost all of the port's senior officials and most of the operational staff had been suspended and their work temporarily taken over by selected civil servants and military personnel.

The people who Brandon had worked so closely with were suddenly no longer available to provide the special services that were so important to the deliveryman operation.

No longer could the special cargo be driven straight on to the wharf and loaded on to the ship as in the past. It had all been so unbelievably simple. For thirteen years, hundreds of kilos of pure heroin were delivered to *Palminto* prior to each voyage from the port. It was all so well organised.

During this time none of the customs officials had ever had any direct dealings with Brandon. A Filipino agent delivered the cargo and personally dealt with the customs officials, so he and his crew were to all intents and purposes not involved. So discreetly was the operation run that a good lawyer could have argued a very strong case that they were not only not involved, but that they were totally unaware of the nature of these particular cargoes. The arrangements had been considered foolproof, until now anyway.

As a result of the clamp-down things had become very worrying for Brandon, and reached a critical point one day when he suddenly got the strange feeling that he was being tailed whilst doing some general shopping and business around the city area.

At first he had wondered whether or not it had a been a figment of his imagination, but he then became sure that something was wrong when three times in the one morning he had seen the same man. On each of the occasions the man was apparently reading a newspaper, but obviously watching him. In a city as densely populated as Manila, to meet up with the same person twice would be an extremely rare occurrence, but for it to happen three times in different parts of the city would be nothing short of a miracle.

The seemingly miraculous third occasion occurred after Brandon, feeling sure he was being tailed, had hailed a cab. He had directed the cabby to drive around numerous backstreets in the eastern suburbs for over twenty minutes before returning to the city.

He then entered a restaurant some four miles away from where he last saw the tail. Ordering a coffee, he had barely had time to sip at it when the same man entered the restaurant, sat at a table on the opposite side of the dining room and began reading his newspaper once more.

Brandon was scared, but suddenly, for a very brief moment he couldn't help but smile to himself.

The stupid bastard is holding the newspaper upside down.

For one crazy moment he thought of going over to where the man was sitting and turning the paper up the right way.

Isn't that what spies would do in the movies? he asked himself.

Regaining his senses, he became frightened again and decided against that silly, foolhardy course of action. Instead he forced himself to finish his coffee, taking his time over it. Plucking up courage he strolled as casually as he could to the phone booth in the foyer of the restaurant, trying hard not to stare at the man. Once in the booth with the door shut, he placed himself in a position whereby through the small mirror on the wall behind the phone he could see the table at which the man was sitting. To his relief he was still sitting down, pretending to read his newspaper.

Once he was satisfied that the man could neither hear him or read his lips; he had once read that CIA agents are taught to lip-read, he telephoned a city number.

Felix was always somewhere to be found wherever the *Palminto* was in port. He constantly changed address and telephone numbers, but Brandon was always notified of the changes, even though often at short notice. The number that he rang had been given to him by the driver of the cab that he took when he had first left the ship earlier that morning. Felix was highly organised in that regard.

'What's up, Doc?' queried Felix, knowing that it could only be Brandon on the end of the line.

'Shit!' was his first word after Brandon had advised him what had happened, and where he was.

'Stay where you are for a while, David. Be natural. Order a meal or something. Keep an eye on our man. I want to know if he makes a call or contacts anyone. I'll get a message to you instructing you what to do within the hour.

*Bon appetit*, Captain, and keep your cool, man. Everything will be fine. Leave this guy to me.'

Keeping his cool was almost as difficult as pretending not to know that the man was watching him. Harder still was eating the food that had been placed before him, let alone trying to pretend to be enjoying it. It was less than average and not to his liking at all. However, he had to stay put for as long as Felix took to get a message to him.

★

It took just over an hour, a very long hour, relieved only by a brief moment of humour when, after twenty minutes of deep concentration on his newspaper, the visibly embarrassed watcher realised that it was upside down. His frantic attempts to correct the situation resulted in several pages of the broadsheet ending up on the floor.

Brandon was amazed by his own ability to find humour in a situation which really frightened him. Perhaps it was pure nerves, or was it his absolute belief that Felix and the Senator were invincible and that they would rescue him from this situation without there being any trouble? After all, nothing had been too difficult for them in the past.

Just as he was beginning to wonder what had happened to Felix, a waiter appeared alongside him and handed him a piece of paper on a small tray.

'Your bill, sir.'

He was about to protest that he hadn't finished when he noticed that the paper did not look like a bill. It was stained and roughly folded. He thanked the waiter and very carefully unfolded the paper. Scrawled on it were three words.

*Follow the waiter.*

Brandon stood up and placed the note in his pocket. Withdrawing his wallet at the same time he removed a few bills and placed them on the table. Turning casually he walked towards what appeared to be the door of the kitchen, through which the waiter had just disappeared. Out of the corner of his eye he saw his tail get up and start to follow him. The man looked very confused, and to Brandon's surprise, even a little afraid.

The waiter continued walking through the kitchen and out into a narrow back alley. He seemed to be in a great hurry so Brandon increased his pace to match. The people working in the kitchen appeared not to notice them, and as he walked through the door into the daylight he saw that the waiter was standing close to the wall on the right of the door.

To Brandon's horror he was holding a vicious-looking machete in his hand which was raised up high against the wall. He indicated that Brandon should go to the left and to make it fast.

Everything happened very quickly from then. The man who was tailing Brandon came rushing out into the alley brandishing a pistol in his right hand. The waiter launched himself from the wall and brought the machete down on to the man's extended right arm. Brandon saw a flash of red, and to his horror the gun fell to the ground, still held tightly in the man's severed hand. Without even pausing, the man, who by now he realised was no ordinary waiter, had brought the machete upwards in a vertical sweep that caught the man under the throat, nearly severing his head.

The body had barely hit the ground before a small van screeched to a halt alongside. The driver got out and helped the waiter bundle the body, together with the severed hand and gun, into the rear of the van. The bogus waiter then quickly removed his heavily bloodstained white jacket, threw it over the body and slammed the rear doors of the van shut.

Both men then leapt into the front of the vehicle which drove off with a screeching of tyres, leaving him standing there shaking violently with terror and shock.

He immediately turned towards the wall and brought up his awful lunch. His horror was so great that he was unable to stop himself urinating in his trousers at the same time.

At that moment a man wearing a chef's hat came out of the kitchen and casually began hosing the blood and vomit down a nearby drain. He appeared not to notice Brandon, and having tidied up the area and removed all traces of the recent killing he returned to the kitchen without saying a word.

Brandon was paralysed with horror. He could not bring himself to believe what he had just witnessed. Within a matter of a minute or two a man had died a most horrible death, and all trace of the crime and the man had been erased. It was almost as if he had not existed. He felt terribly ill. He was shaking like a leaf, in shock and totally confused and frightened.

Suddenly he felt someone pulling at his sleeve.

'Come with me, Commander. Let's get out of here. Jeez, bro, look at the state you're in. I hope you don't mess my car up, man. I've got a date tonight,' snapped Felix, dragging the shaken Brandon along the alley towards the main street.

★

Felix drove Brandon to a drab hotel on the city fringe. The desk clerk looked up as they entered, then turned to the board and removed a key which he handed to Felix without a word being exchanged. They took the elevator to the third floor and entered a surprisingly well-appointed room in the front of the building with views of the bay.

Felix threw Brandon a dressing gown, then he spoke for the first time since leaving the restaurant.

'Okay, Commander, get out of those filthy clothes, then give it to me chapter and verse. Where and when did you first notice him? Did he meet anyone? Did he have a car? Did he telephone anyone while you were in that restaurant? Don't miss out anything, no matter how trivial it may seem to you. Our arses could be in a sling over this.'

'Well, I never saw a car at any stage, and he definitely never spoke to anyone or used a phone, not to my knowledge anyway,' Brandon replied, shaken even more by Felix's apparent casualness regarding the man's awful death. He then went on to describe as best he could, everything that he had happened up until the time when Felix's machete man had approached him in the restaurant. Felix occasionally interrupted the story to clarify various points, while he made notes in a small pocketbook.

At one point the phone rang and Felix listened to some-one for about five minutes. The only words he spoke were, 'Are you sure about that? He was definitely a customs department special officer?'

He put the phone down and turned to the still-shaking Brandon.

'Looks like we killed ourselves a customs spook, Commander.'

'I never killed anyone,' hissed Brandon with venom. 'Don't involve me with you and your fucking disgusting friends.'

'Now you listen in, and listen good, you ungrateful, self-righteous arsehole. Whether you like it or not you are involved, up to your neck. As far as the law is concerned you were party to the murder of that customs cop, and if they catch you they will hang you by the balls just as if you used the knife yourself, so don't get smart-arse with me, do you hear?

'Over the years you have been involved in a hell of a lot of killings, Commander. How else do you think we have survived so long? Those officer friends of yours back in Saigon. Where the fuck do you think you would have been now if we hadn't got them off your back? They were going to screw you, and would have done it if it wasn't for us. Then all those other guys who died that night, soldiers and police, and those poor lil kids. Do you think you had nothing to do with that either? All of them, and the guys on *Palminto*'s crew, and plenty of others, sailor boy. All dead! To save your skin as well as ours.

'You are a rich son of a bitch, Brandon. You've got millions stashed away in secret accounts and it's all thanks to the Senator for adopting you. You also owe me too, Commander, for saving your white arse and doing the cleaning up after you, you useless prick. Now get out of my sight and take a shower. You smell of piss and spew. I'll have your suit cleaned.

'And David, I am going to have to make some urgent calls to see if we can't salvage the mess you appear to have got us into.

'Meanwhile, my man, keep out of my way. It's not beyond the realms of possibility that you may have outlived your usefulness. You may not be a religious man, but you should probably say a prayer or two right now, 'cos if this doesn't work out I may still get the chance to do a job on you. Understand?'

He had never seen Felix angry in all the years he had known him, but he sure was worked up now and Brandon felt he had every reason to be scared. He decided to do exactly as he was told, and having showered he retired to the bedroom and stayed there, worried sick about this sudden reversal of his fortunes.

★

Felix was on the telephone for almost two hours. Brandon could vaguely hear his voice through the closed door but was unable to hear what he was saying. Not that he thought it was a good thing to know too much at this moment.

Then after about ten minutes of silence there came a knock on the bedroom door.

'You awake, Commander?' called Felix as he entered.

All signs of his earlier anger had disappeared and he looked very relaxed and pleased with himself. In his hand he held Brandon's suit and shirt on a hanger and wrapped in a plastic cover.

'Here you are, my man. Room service at its best. I have been talking to the Senator and things are starting to look a bit better now. He will be making some arrangements and I have got some people to call on, but it looks as if we can get out of this shit you have gotten us all into. It looks like the Manila end of the business is completely blown though, and we will have to close up shop pronto. Things were getting a bit hairy anyway. The Senator says to tell you that you may be coming up to an earlier than expected retirement.'

'Early retirement?' He suddenly felt dreadfully cold. Then he plucked up courage and turned to face Felix.

'Is this going to be one of your enforced retirements, Felix? Have I outlived my usefulness?'

Felix looked at him and seeing how pale and frightened he looked suddenly realised that he had incorrectly mistaken the mention of early retirement as a threat. He chuckled out loud.

'Lordy no, Commander. If anything happened to you now it could raise too many eyebrows. On top of which, the Senator has got plenty more for you to do. No, my man, pay no heed to the ranting and raving I did earlier.

That was my way of shaking you out of your shock and self-pity. I think you are a genuine pain in the arse, but for some reason the Senator honestly thinks the sun shines out of your fundamental orifice. You got nothing to fear from me. You'll be spending all your hard-earned, ill-gotten money soon. I promise!'

David Brandon was not totally convinced. In fact he was not convinced at all. It was to take many days for the fear to wear off and for him to return to his normal feeling of well-being, or what passed for well-being when you worked for the Senator.

## Chapter Ten

The next few days were quite worrying for Brandon, who stayed on the ship for fear of being tailed again. He wondered what the customs authorities would be doing about the disappearance of their agent and why they had decided to tail him in the first place. Whenever he saw a customs officer on the wharf he began to panic. He constantly felt that someone was going to come to the ship and arrest him. He spoke to Felix on several occasions to try to find out what was happening and to receive instructions. On each occasion Felix reassured him that everything was okay, but warned, 'Stop being a pain in the arse!'

He told him that his informant had reported that the authorities were sure that drugs were being brought through the port, but that they didn't know which ship or ships were being used. It seemed that many people were being kept under surveillance, generally for no particular reason.

'We needn't have killed that man, Commander. He was merely one of a large team of customs cops who were keeping an eye on dozens of ship's officers and crew members at the same time. Never mind though, we couldn't take the chance. Incidentally, his body was found at the scene of a nasty gangland battle where several guys got chopped up a bit.' He laughed quietly to himself.

'It was very considerate of them to arrange it for us. His bosses in the Department of Customs will think he was involved in some criminal enterprise that went wrong. It cost us a hell of a lot of money, but all's well that ends well, as they say.'

*

What did become clear over those days was that the authorities were definitely clamping down in the port, and there was no way that the usual delivery of drugs could possibly be made. Police and customs officials were everywhere, and they were heavily armed.

Something that was even more disturbing to Brandon was the large number of army patrols on the wharves and at the dock gates. They were obviously expecting some sort of trouble, and seemed intent on causing some of their own along the way.

One of his crew members was badly beaten for answering a corporal back when being asked about the contents of his duffel bag. The man really required hospitalisation, but under the circumstances Brandon thought it wiser to pay for a doctor to attend the injured man on board the *Palminto*.

The *Palminto*, as with every other ship in the port, was searched from top to bottom; twice. The customs officers and police involved, whilst in no way open to bribes like the previous regime, were most polite and professional in their dealings with Brandon and his crew.

This was obviously not the case with all other ships, as Brandon had witnessed himself. From the bridge of the *Palminto*, which was higher than on many other ships, he had a good view of most of the docks' area, and from this vantage point had witnessed the searches on two other nearby ships that had been given a very rough time by comparison.

The squeaky clean reputation of the *Palminto*, its skipper and crew, and its smart appearance was obviously having some effect on the attitude of the authorities. However, regardless of the slightly less aggressive approach by the customs and port officials it was definitely not going to be possible for the *Palminto* to do anything other than leave port with her legal cargo only.

Brandon was convinced that the Senator was not going to be happy with that outcome.

It transpired that Felix and the Senator had devised a contingency plan for the delivery of the scheduled secret cargo which was particularly large and expensive, and had already been sold to an eager customer in Australia.

*

The method of delivery of the cargo was of great concern in terms of how it was to be carried out. It involved the *Palminto* being intercepted at sea by a very fast launch and the cargo being winched on to the launch and stowed away whilst both vessels were still moving.

During his service as a US naval captain Brandon had gained considerable experience in transferring fuel and supplies at sea between moving warships. However, because of the vastly different sizes of the two craft involved in this operation, together with the lack of specific training on the part of the captain and crew of the delivery launch, the cargo transfer operation was fraught with danger. Not only was there the possibility of simply dropping the cargo whilst it hovered between the launch and the safety of the *Palminto*'s deck, there was also the distinct possibility of discovery by the authorities, because by necessity the transfer would have to take place on a usually well-patrolled stretch of coast. In the event of discovery the cargo would have had to be dumped into the ocean.

The prospect of the loss of several million dollars worth of heroin was not built into the plans of either the Senator or Captain David Brandon.

Twelve hours out of Manila the *Palminto* was steaming south at fifteen knots when the transfer took place. Luckily the weather was good, although the sea was fairly rough, which did not make the operation an easy one. The *Palminto*, which was still in territorial waters that were busy with incoming and outgoing traffic, could not be seen to slow down or stop. To do so could have brought instant attention from a multitude of sources.

It was essential that the ship continue at her normal speed. However, at fifteen knots, a vessel the size of the *Palminto* created a substantial bow wave, which caused a strong swell along the length of the ship on both sides. As well as having to contend with the rough sea, there was a large ocean swell sweeping in from the Pacific on the port, seaward side of the ship as she travelled southwards. This, combined with the general condition of the sea and the turbulence caused by the forward movement of the ship meant that the seaward side would be hardest for a small craft to approach. However, because of the need for the approach to be made out of sight of the land and the constant possibility of prying eyes that was the side on which the transfer had to be made. Dislike it or not, he had no choice.

*

Because of the amount of traffic in the sea lanes the launch had been forced to shadow the *Palminto* for over an hour before the all-clear was given for it to commence its approach. This in itself was a risk, a target for sea watchers, of which there were many along the nearby stretch of coast. At the time of the transfer the sun was low over the horizon and darkness was beginning to fall. Whilst this was a blessing in terms of the possibility of the transfer being witnessed it did not make the operation any easier.

Brandon looked down from the rail at the tiny, sixty foot boat struggling to retain its station under the most awkward circumstances. A boom had been swung out over the port side and a cable lowered. The Filipino skipper of the launch was a capable seaman, but even so it took several attempts before he could place his launch below the boom sufficiently long enough for his crew to hook their precious load on to the *Palminto*'s cable.

Brandon noticed that the container was packed in polystyrene so that if it went overboard during the transfer it would float. That was the good news. The bad news was that in the event of discovery the package would have to be ditched anyway as a matter of self-preservation, and that wouldn't be too easy with it wrapped up in polystyrene. As it turned out the floatability or otherwise of the package was not required to be tested. The load was winched aboard and the small launch increased speed, and turned out towards the ocean and quickly disappeared eastward.

*

The next morning Brandon received a coded signal from the Senator that, with regret, the decision to cease the *Palminto*'s extra-curricular activities at the end of its current voyage was definitely confirmed.

It appeared that a message had been received from Felix that three hours after its rendezvous with the *Palminto* the delivery launch had been intercepted by a patrol boat of the Philippines Navy. Fortunately for the Senator and Brandon, the skipper was conducting some other, fortunately unrelated criminal activity at the time, and the launch had been blown out of the water with the loss of all hands whilst trying to make a run for it.

Felix had also stated that he had received certain other information that made him sure that it would not be long before the authorities started to put two and two together, and come to the conclusion that *Palminto* was worthy of closer scrutiny.

Thank goodness there were no survivors, thought Brandon as he considered the information about the launch. He was aware of the manner in which criminal suspects were interrogated in that part of the world, and under that sort of duress it would have been highly likely that the secret activities of *Palminto* would have been disclosed had any of the crew survived.

Oh my God! What have I become? he asked himself, suddenly realising that he was applauding the deaths of other human beings.

The Senator's message had also advised him that he would receive further information the following day.

Within twenty-four hours he had the information that he was promised.

His resignation and early retirement from both the White Shores Line, and from the Senator's employ were to be a reality, and were imminent.

He was to retire and the *Palminto*'s criminal activities cease. But how could the continuing loyalty of the crew be guaranteed once they ceased to receive the extra pay and bonuses that they were used to? Once the special operations ceased there was no way that the Senator would continue to pay them for services they no longer rendered. The alternative was to pay them all off completely, but even then there was no way that their silence and loyalty could be guaranteed once they had been paid off and allowed to go their own ways. Even though Brandon held damning information regarding each crew member, who was to say what each individual would or could do once out of the immediate control of their esteemed Captain?

So, quite businesslike and cold-bloodedly the Senator decided that the only course of action open to him and his operation was to terminate the contracts of the entire crew simultaneously. Even Brandon, with his intense disgust at the thought of being involved in further killing could see no other viable alternative.

The plan for the termination of the contracts of the crew was soon to be put into operation. Whilst in Melbourne one of the Senator's operatives would secretly board the ship and place high explosive charges in key points in the bilges and in other key locations throughout the ship.

Brandon would not know in advance how or when this was to happen. He already had first-hand experience of how easy it was for Felix to board a US warship without being seen. If that could be achieved at a time when the most stringent wartime security precautions were in place, then boarding *Palminto* in Melbourne would be a piece of cake.

The explosives, which would be sufficient to totally destroy the ship, would only be able to be detonated with an electronic device that would be placed in a secret compartment in the floor of the wardrobe in his cabin. At a predetermined place on the return voyage to Manila, *Palminto* would disappear without trace. Her destruction would of necessity take place at a point where the sea was at its deepest and salvage would be out of the question.

★

Brandon began firming up the operational plans to ensure that the Senator's wishes were followed, and that the *Palminto*'s deliveryman activities ended efficiently; and with a bang.

Naturally all hands, with the exception of the brave Captain Brandon, would be lost with the ship. It was vital to the plan that all crew members would be locked below deck to ensure that there would be no survivors. This would easily be accomplished for some twenty-four members of the crew, and the remaining six from the bridge and the engine room could be disposed of separately by Brandon. Whilst he had some qualms about having to personally carry out the killings, as plans go it was really quite simple.

Looking somewhat the worse for wear, with burnt and torn clothing, he would spend a few days in a life-raft before his rescue which would result from the sighting of his raft by a private aeroplane, organised by the Senator. On leaving the ship Brandon would take with him a pocket-sized electronic beeper which, when activated, would send out a signal on a wavelength that could only be intercepted by the Senator's people, whose aircraft would alert the nearest rescue authorities. Once the rescuers were in sight, Brandon would commit the device to the deep together with any remains of the excellent food and warm blankets that he had taken with him into the raft to make his lone voyage as comfortable as possible. He would carry heavily weighted bags in the life-raft for this specific purpose.

Once rescued he would feign the considerable distress that a hungry and dehydrated survivor would be expected to display, and eventually he would probably be fêted as a hero, at least by the company whose ship he had just sunk. It would all be so easy, and it would resolve both the immediate problems facing the Senator and Brandon in an efficient and most permanent manner.

A story was devised of how the ship collided with some underwater obstacle whilst travelling at her highest speed, and how she sank, nose first, within seconds. As he thought about this his face broke into a frown. He saw the necessity of it all, and quite frankly he would have never been able to really enjoy his wealthy retirement if any of the crew remained alive. He would have always had the fear that one of them might talk and that it would lead to his own arrest and imprisonment, something he could never have faced up to. He would rather die than rot in jail.

No, his misgivings had nothing to do with the demise of thirty crew members, however loyal they may be, but the thought of sinking so beautiful a ship really caused him great concern, even pain. It all seemed such a pitiful waste.

What a long while ago since Saigon, thought Brandon. How I have changed. Whatever happened to the nice guy I used to be?

Meanwhile *Palminto* sailed southwards on that beautiful day, moving ever closer to her first pick-up point, and ultimately to her rendezvous with death. The sudden and violent death of thirty dispensable Filipino crewmen, and one beautiful ship.

## Chapter Eleven

The single engine Beechcraft banked slowly to starboard as the pilot pointed its nose toward the south-west and throttled back in preparation for landing at Brighton Hill. To be precise, at the Brighton Hill Aero Club, just fifteen miles out of Cairns on the north coast of Queensland. It was small and fairly isolated. Not exactly the sort of place that you would expect to find a Qantas or Golden Wings Club. In fact, it wasn't the sort of place where you would expect to find too much of anything, let alone luxury amenities.

This was one of the reasons why the pilot of the Beechcraft continued to renew his annual membership of the flying club, and more to the point why he operated part of his tourist flight business from the small and dusty airstrip.

His business was located in a small hangar at the far side of the airfield. The hangar was just large enough for one aircraft, and built into its interior was a small office and a workshop.

The pilot was a tourist company proprietor who operated from Cairns and from two other country flying clubs like Brighton Hill. He had often wondered why it was called Brighton Hill, as it was on one of the very few completely flat pieces of land for miles.

★

Edwin Grant was fifty years of age and had learned his trade flying small spotter and special mission aircraft as a lieutenant in the US Army Air Corps in Vietnam. He had done some pretty interesting and stupid things in those days. Not the least stupid of which was to fly into hostile territory and pick up messages and packages from the ground without landing.

This very dangerous practice was an extension and refinement of the activity that was originally perfected in World War Two in Europe when Lysander aircraft of the Royal Air Force had swept into fields in occupied Europe and delivered and picked up urgent dispatches that couldn't be transmitted by radio.

The pick-up part of the operation was achieved by suspending a hook from the belly of the fuselage near the tail unit. The hook would catch on a line suspended between two upright poles like a clothes line. One end of the line was anchored to its pole by a catch which had a certain breaking strain. This would cause the hook to drag the line in from the other end, on which would be the message or the package. Once the hook reached a point near the load it was to uplift it connected with a small metal plate which activated a lock on the hook unit. The lock would immediately close up tight on the line and the package would be secure and able to be hauled into the aircraft, which by then would be well away from the pick-up zone.

From the moment that the hook first connected with the horizontal line to the moment that the lock closed on the line and harnessed it to the aircraft was only a split second or so. It didn't always work first time round, but the ultimate success rate was very high, and much safer than landing the aircraft and taking off again. It was also a very speedy operation.

When Grant and the bunch of crazies he worked with weren't picking up and delivering messages they were doing something less safe just to prove how crazy they really were. They were actually landing their aircraft by the light of torches and flares and delivering and picking up people, mainly military people, and usually people in deep shit at the time.

Those were the days! It still surprised him to this day that he had survived just one of those hair-brained, hair-raising missions, let alone the hundreds that he had successfully completed. He chuckled to himself when he thought of those missions being hair-raising, as he had since lost most of the hair from the top of his head.

Hair-raising my arse! he thought, that's what made me lose my hair, not raise it.

He wasn't too sure which was really the most stupid practice of the two, picking up packages in flight, or landing on those tiny little handmade temporary strips. In Vietnam he had picked up many items, but had had some bad experiences when suddenly finding his little plane being dragged backwards out of the sky because some stupid prick on the ground had decided to send a real heavy load without the pilot's knowledge. To counter this very real danger he had developed the skill of increasing engine revolutions at the precise moment when the aircraft was about to take the full force of the weight of the load.

★

Now, twenty-five years later with the much more advanced technology of the two engine Cessna, and the aid of nitrogen-filled bags to lessen the actual weight of the pick-up load it really was a piece of cake. Edwin Grant owned three such aircraft.

He lived in Brisbane, where under his own name he was a respected tourism entrepreneur, also owning and operating several luxury coaches and a small fleet of tourist launches.

His bona fides were so good that he did not need to pretend he was someone else in order to conduct his less public, but much more lucrative deliveryman flying business for the Senator. After all, he was a tourism industry businessman and a returned war hero pilot. Nothing was more natural for someone with his special background than to utilise his flying skills in conjunction with his successful tourism business. He therefore ran small tourist flight operations from Cairns, Townsville and Rockhampton, with resident pilot-managers at each centre. He operated one of his three Cessnas from each of these airfields.

Grant also kept an aeroplane, a Beechcraft, at Brisbane airport for local tourism work. In this plane, about five or six times a year he flew up to his operation centres in the north and spent half a day or more with his local pilot-manager.

On these visits he made a point of checking over the Cessna based at each airfield and then taking it up for a flight for an hour or two, both to satisfy himself that the aircraft were running well, but mainly to keep his hand in. That was the story that he told his staff anyway.

These visits were planned weeks ahead, and the local pilot had to ensure that on the days of his visits the aircraft was not to be booked for tourist business, but left available for Grant's own personal use. On these days he usually gave his local pilot the rest of the day off, commencing from the moment that he had completed his initial check of the books and the aircraft. Edwin Grant was looked upon by his pilot employees as a bloody good bloke.

In reality he really was a bloody good bloke, but more to the point he was a bloody shrewd bloke, because most of his visits to his regional operations were timed to coincide exactly with the shipping timetables of the SS *Palminto*.

He had been most thorough when selecting his aircraft. They had to be appropriate and powerful enough for his work for the Senator, but first and foremost, in order to maintain the correct image of the tourism-related flying business they had to meet the special needs of that work. It was vital that the front image of the enterprise was the right one. There were dozens of modern small aircraft within his price range that would have met his needs but he had a particular liking for the Cessna. Most pilots have a favourite type of aircraft that they enjoy flying the most and this was his favourite.

The twin engines were an obvious attraction from the point of view of his tourist industry work. Two engines are safer, is the perception of the average tourist, who is somewhat overawed by the thought of defying the natural laws of gravity in a heavier than air machine and leaving the safety of the ground under the power of only one engine. In fact, many people would argue that the gliding ability of a single engine plane makes it much safer than a two engine craft which without power has the tendency to fly like a brick.

Nonetheless, Grant's aircraft had a much higher occupancy rate than any of the other aircraft at Brighton Hill which were all single engine, a fact that pleased him well regardless of the reasons behind it.

*

Since first establishing his business some fifteen years before, initially as a front for the Senator's work, the tourism side had become so successful that it was now a substantial income source. This was in sharp contrast to the early days when the tourist business barely came out even. Yet even in those days he had managed to make a healthy profit by supplementing his income through the extra work he did for the Senator, the hard-nosed bastard he had first met whilst landing in a dried-up paddy field in Vietnam. Their meeting took place in the middle of the night, whilst a major shit fight was taking place all around him.

★

His aircraft on that mission was a specially designed and equipped six-seater that was going to have to lift out a team of up to seven special forces men, together with all their equipment. Six-seater meant five plus the pilot, but if the entire team arrived for pick-up there were going to be two too many passengers and far too heavy a load. It would be touch and go if he made it off, even assuming that he managed to get down in the first place, a point he had made loud and clear to the duty major in charge of operations that night, but to no avail.

The Major had merely replied, 'Grant, my experience with these special forces guys is that most of the poor bastards aren't going to make it to the strip, if indeed any of them do. You may even find that nobody is there to pick up anyway. However, having said that, my man, this is the only plane serviceable at the moment so I have no fucking choice. We will rip out all the seats for you to lessen the load but in the end it is up to you just how many of those guys you feel you can safely lift off. You will just have to assess the situation when you get there.

'Be careful how you turn any of them down though, 'cos those guys are crazy enough to chuck you out and fly the fucking plane home themselves.'

*

Grant had circled the pick-up zone for ten minutes, and remembering the major's comments about the likelihood of the mission being blown was almost ready to call it off when he received the radio signal indicating that the mission team was ready to be lifted off.

He was instructed to come in from the south and land along a strip that would be indicated by intermittent bursts of red tracer. This was a fairly normal and acceptable procedure and generally worked quite well as long as the mad bastards on the ground remembered not to fire the tracer along the landing strip, but alongside it.

It probably would have worked well on this occasion too, but for the attentions of an evil-minded NVA with a heavy machine-gun firing green tracer who was intent on destroying young Edwin Grant, trying to show him the permanent way out rather than the safe way in.

The friendly red tracer was firing in short bursts from the southern edge of the clearing and was aiming due north. His instructions were to land in a direct line just to the left of the tracer markers where he could be reasonably confident that there would be a good firm base for touch-down.

That was fine, except for the green tracer which was firing from the opposite direction and immediately into his landing path.

The red tracer continued coming so he decided to give it a try, but to be ready to boost his way out of there if things got too hot. Lowering his flaps, cutting back the engine revs he lost both height and speed very rapidly, and putting the nose down he strained his eyes for the next burst of red.

Once it came he got his bearing and immediately aimed for the stretch of ground to the left of the intermittent line of red light and made his final approach. The enemy's green tracer intensified and was gradually creeping up towards him as his wheels hit the ground with a sudden crump. The plane bounced into the air just as a burst of enemy fire sprayed the ground in front of its nose. But for the heavy landing and the bounce into the air he was sure that his plane would have been totalled by the last burst, which appeared to go under him.

He was back on the ground and braking hard as the aircraft bounced along the rough surface towards to the far end of the clearing where he knew the enemy machine-gunner lay in wait.

A strange and stupid thought went through his mind as he prepared to turn and head back towards the south end of the clearing.

Somebody has got this all arse about face. Green is supposed to signify safety, and red danger. Why then is that green bastard trying to fucking kill me?

Even before the aircraft had come to a halt he was turning it around to face south, and was increasing throttle ready for a headlong dash back to the safe end of the landing zone. Just then he saw the green tracer arcing towards him from the forest nearby.

My God, it's coming straight at me. Shit!

He kicked the rudder hard to the left and thrust the throttle forward. The aircraft leapt forward and sideways in such a violent manner that he felt sure it would turn over on to its side. The first burst of enemy fire had missed him, just.

Here they come again, he thought. 'Throttle! Go for it you wonderful little bitch,' he shouted at his aircraft.

Just at that moment he was conscious of a stream of flame hurtling past his tail unit into the hostile jungle, right down the line of the repeating green tracer. There was a tremendous explosion and burst of flame, and the angry searching green tracer ceased in a flaming moment of death.

Momentarily blinded, Grant was so excited by the sudden demise of the green tracer man that he found himself screaming a string of obscenities out loud.

Such was the ferocity of the explosion that Grant's aircraft was blown sideways into a stand of high tussock. Luckily he was still in full control and he had his hand down hard on the throttle, and because of his increasing forward momentum he was able to steer himself back on to the hard ground and once more follow the red tracer markers which were now immediately to his left, and very, very close.

At the end of the clearing he throttled back and turned once more into the direction for take-off. Out of the dense bush suddenly appeared a group of running men. He counted four. They were alongside the plane in a second or so and took up defensive positions. Nobody spoke a word, but just knelt down and looked outwards into the bush and the forest.

'Will you guys get the fuck into the plane,' he shouted, straining his voice so that he would be heard over the engine noise.

The men ignored him completely and remained crouched in their defensive positions, weapons ready and staring into the darkness. This continued for what seemed like an age. Grant was beginning to get very nervous and irritated. He just wanted out of that place.

Suddenly, two of the men leapt to their feet and rushed off into the darkness. The remaining two stayed where they were and barely moved a muscle. Grant strained his eyes to try to see what was happening out there in the darkness but to him it was just a blanket of impenetrable blackness.

Just as suddenly as they had left the two men returned, only this time they were helping a wounded man, half carrying him up to the doorway of the aircraft. Then, still without a word being spoken the wounded man was lifted carefully on board and the remainder of the men clambered in.

Grant checked his instruments and began to increase the throttle, at the same time yelling to his passengers to hang on tight.

He was just about to release the brake and commence his take-off run when he felt some thing cold and hard against his neck.

A deep, strangely accented voice said, 'If you move this plane before I give the order, I'll blow your fucking head off. Do you hear me, sonny?'

Grant nodded his head and sat rigidly still, his heart pumping. A little voice inside his head was telling him that he had been wrong, all this time thinking that he worked for the crazies, 'cos these weird fuckers behind him were the real crazies.

For about thirty seconds – it seemed much longer – he nervously awaited further instructions. Then he heard the hammer of the weapon click back and felt the pressure lift from his neck. Just at that moment a small figure leapt into the aircraft and crawled up behind the pilot's seat. The man leaned forward and amidst roars of laughter from his comrades shouted into Grant's right ear.

'Okay my man. My name is Felix, and this is a hijack. Fly me to Cuba.'

How they got off the ground that night he would never know. Followed by masses of rifle and machine-gun fire, which seriously wounded two of his bloodthirsty passengers, Grant managed to literally hop the aircraft into the air and over the high trees at the end of the clearing with only inches to spare.

I hope to fuck that nobody down there has got any of those nasty little ground-to-air missiles pointing my way, he thought nervously.

Edwin Grant had had his baptism of fire with, and had been introduced to the Senator and his right-hand man Felix in the manner that all of their subsequent business dealings were to be made. Very violently.

★

Over the following months he found himself involved in an inordinate number of missions with the Senator and his team. The fact that he was chosen for each of the missions was too much of a coincidence for his liking. These missions, as with everything concerning the Senator, were highly dangerous. However, most of them did not involve physical landings. Grant's job was to pick up packages from bush clearings using the Lysander hook-up routine. Lots of the packages contained military documents and enemy equipment for delivery to the military analysts of the top brass.

Most of his pick-ups, however, were of a different variety and belonged personally to the Senator. Each pick-up generally involved several loads being transferred to the aircraft from the ground using the difficult hook routine. It was dangerous business, but Grant neither asked what the loads were, nor did he care. All that mattered to him was that he had suddenly become a very rich man.

His selfless bravery – or was it stupidity – on that night when he first picked up the Senator and his team had earned him a place on the firm. It also earned him a steady flow of multi-figure dividends, all paid in hard cash. All he had to do was survive the Vietnam War and he would be made for life.

Meanwhile, the Senator was obviously pulling the strings of someone very high up in the system. Whoever it was, and however he was doing it he would never know. What he did know was that he had virtually ceased to work for the Army and was really working for the mad Australian and his little black associate, Felix.

There was only one catch, however, and that was the fact that to work as a deliveryman for the Senator raised the danger level of his operations by about one thousand per cent.

## Chapter Twelve

Grant's pilot-manager at Brighton Hill was an ex crop-duster named Bill Wallis. Bill was an easygoing kind of man who got on extremely well with the tourists. His main claim to fame was that he was able to turn a basic sight-seeing flight into something bordering on exciting, or that was how the tourists saw it, without really doing much more that a few steep banks and a bit of slightly illegal wave hopping. He was an excellent pilot and not one to take any unacceptable risks.

He was also a first-class aero-mechanic and kept a tidy set of books, so he was considered by Grant to be quite an asset to the company.

Perhaps one of his greatest attributes from Grant's point of view was his enthusiasm to get the hell out of it whenever Grant visited and gave him his extra day off. Whilst he was a long-time married man rumour had it that he was involved in some extramarital activity with a lady who lived in the outback somewhere. The Aussies had this wonderfully descriptive but crude expression for it. Bush Leg-Over.

Once Grant gave him the okay after checking the aircraft and the books Bill Wallis was off like the wind, and it could be guaranteed that he would not be seen until the following day.

More to the point he would not be around to see what Grant was doing, because what Edwin Grant did on Bill Wallace's days off was private, very personal, and highly illegal. This was one such day, and immediately Wallis had left and the dust cloud from his car had faded into the distance Grant got to work on the Cessna.

★

He first removed a square floor panel immediately behind the pilot's seat exposing a fairly large hatchway. Each of his aircraft had this hatchway which Grant had had installed to enable him to do aero-photography work. He really did do such work on a regular basis for local authorities, mining companies, map-making companies and the like, and it was a regular form of income for him. The hatchway was, therefore, an essential adaptation for this sort of work. However, nobody had ever thought to query why the hatches on Grant's aircraft were so large, certainly much larger than was necessary for camerawork of any description.

He then began assembling the hook pick-up apparatus which he had unloaded from the Beechcraft. Once assembled the hook was attached to a fine, endless steel cable that was rigged around two pulleys; one on a triangular frame suspended under the aircraft and the other on a framework now erected on the floor behind the pilot's seat and just forward of the open hatchway. Attached to the inside pulley was a winding handle which when operated would turn the pulley wheel, thereby winding the cable anticlockwise between the two pulleys and bringing the hook up through the hatchway into the aircraft. The hook had a sensitive automatic lock built into it which would close up tight when subjected to a certain weight.

The tension in the automatic lock could be adjusted to suit different weights. The apparatus was fixed into bolt-holes that already existed in the aircraft's bodywork. Grant was very methodical and took his time, the assembly operation taking thirty minutes to complete.

He checked the system out and satisfied himself that the apparatus was firmly secured and that the pulley system and the hook and its locking device were working correctly, and that they would take the necessary weight. He then immediately took off and commenced what had become his regular flight pattern whenever visiting Brighton Hill.

Whilst he had no reason to believe that Bill Wallis had the faintest idea what he was really doing, Bill was no fool and everything that Grant did had to appear authentic. This was not just for Bill Wallis's benefit but also the dozens of other people who lived in the wider area, who knew Bill and talked to him. This was a country area, and country communities were very closely knit. They talked to each other about everything and nothing all the time. It was pretty hard to keep secrets in such communities. It seemed that everyone knew everything about everyone else's business, even to the point where everybody except Bill's wife knew all of the blow-by-blow details of his Bush Leg-Over activities.

Edwin Grant was very conscious of this fact in everything that he did and said.

He had set routes that Wallis knew he flew over in order to test his flight instruments. Bill also knew that he then always set off to examine existing and future tourist flight routes and locations. At the completion of each flight he would later meet with Bill and discuss possibilities and more often than not would provide him with a written plan of some sort to consider and report back to him on.

His cover was perfect. He was merely a first-class businessman doing his best to increase his market share, which could only be a good thing for Bill Wallis.

Developing and reinforcing his cover in this way meant that Grant had to spend well over an hour in the air before finally positioning himself, well away from prying eyes, for his run out to sea and his timetabled rendezvous with the Senator's seagoing deliveryman, *Palminto*. He had advised Bill that he was going to check out the numbers of craft that were visiting the Reef, and where they were mainly concentrated, as this could be a subject of extra interest for the sightseers who paid such good money for time in the air with Grant's company.

★

Brandon checked his watch for the twentieth time. It was a nervous characteristic that he had acquired in Vietnam, and it seemed that he would never be able to cure himself of the habit.

Five minutes to go.

He looked forward across the deck. His crew were as efficient as usual and everything was set up. Two large poles had been erected, the first about one hundred feet forward of the bridge and the second about twenty feet nearer the bow. They were each about twenty feet high and suspended across the top of the two poles was a fine nylon line which was fixed to the top of the forward pole with a small aluminium peg. The line lay in a shallow groove running fore and aft across the top of the second pole and suspended a further five feet down the side. Attached to that end of the line was a fairly long and large box-like package. It contained thirty kilos of the finest heroin. It was carefully packed and sealed and inserted in an inflatable bag that was filled with helium. Whilst making the package quite cumbersome this lighter than air gas lowered the physical weight of the consignment considerably. One of the crew was standing on a stepladder, which was bolted to the deck, holding the package steady to prevent it from ballooning out in the fresh sea breeze and lifting its retaining line off the aft pole, across which it was so precariously suspended.

At the foot of the stepladder crouched two other crew members who were holding down three similar packages, each attached by a hook to one end of a twenty-five foot fine nylon line. The other end of each line was attached to a small aluminium peg.

On top of each pole fluttered a small, bright yellow flag. These would help the pilot locate and target the fine nylon line.

A very high-powered and fast launch had been lowered part-way down the port, seaward side of the ship just above water level. Two life-jacketed seamen were already sitting in it in case of an emergency. If the aircraft dropped any of the packages into the sea they would float because of the inflatable bag in which they were contained. The launch would be dropped on to the sea and would pick these up and return them without the need for *Palminto* to stop or slow down.

Until ten minutes earlier these packages had been sealed in a steel container about 2.5 metres long, 1.5 metres high and 1.5 metres wide, which was clamped to the deck just forward of the pick-up site and against the port rail. The container contained several more of the packages, already sealed in their inflation bags, but at this stage deflated and therefore about one third of the size of those that were awaiting pick-up.

On the floor of the container underneath the packages were six strange-looking objects. They appeared to be made of blue fibreglass or plastic, and were roughly 2 metres long and 1.25 metres wide. The objects were about twenty centimetres deep, and were shaped like squat, extra wide surfboards, and at the front of each was what looked like an air valve.

As with the packages they had been delivered to the *Palminto* in their present form during the ship-to-ship transfer off the Philippines. They were in fact custom-built containers, and like the packages they contained pure heroin. Each container contained one hundred and fifty kilos, and also like the packages they were designed with an air-proofed outer casing which could be pumped full of helium to make them sufficiently light and buoyant to be manoeuvred underwater by two scuba-divers.

Each of the heroin consignments had been hermetically sealed under laboratory conditions and multiple wrapped in a bid to make them sniffer-dog proof. However, such was the unlikelihood of this working well that Brandon had decided to seal all of the packages and containers in the airtight steel container on the deck. The men who dealt with the initial receipt of the drugs all wore overalls and gloves which were burned immediately after the container was sealed. The air inside the container was then extracted and the exterior steam cleaned. At each stage of the offloading of the heroin the same procedures would be followed, and after the final consignment was offloaded the container would be dropped overboard on the seaward side of the ship away from prying eyes. Then the deck in the vicinity where it had been kept during the voyage would be thoroughly steam cleaned and finally painted.

Short of an intensive examination of the ship by a scientific team both Brandon and the Senator felt that the integrity of *Palminto* was well safeguarded.

★

Looking eastwards, Brandon was straining his eyes in the bright midday light for a sight of the visitor who was soon to briefly rendezvous with his ship. He did not know who the pilot was although he had been doing business with him for many years. He had never met the man and never would, and although in the early days he had longed to know who this very clever pilot was that wish had long since worn off.

The pilot was just one other important link in the Senator's network. He was one of the people charged with the responsibility of removing all incriminating evidence from *Palminto* before she arrived in Melbourne. That was one of the security precautions taken by the Senator. The aircraft could easily be identified. There was no way to avoid that as any steps taken to disguise the well-marked, and locally well-known aircraft would immediately arouse suspicion in the minds of any locals who saw it.

Certain contingency plans had been arranged to cover Grant if ever any investigations led the authorities to his tourist air company. However, no matter what happened to *Palminto* later on neither Brandon nor his crew would be able to identify the pilot of the aircraft that carried out the pick-up.

★

At exactly twelve noon Grant saw the *Palminto*. She was ploughing southwards through the Coral Sea at a steady ten knots, slower than usual, but nobody would notice that, for any lost time would be made up within an hour of the pick-up. *Palminto* was about twenty miles from, and out of sight of the Great Barrier Reef.

Grant had been conducting a low sweep out to sea to ensure that there were no other ships or fishing or tourist boats of any description within visual distance of the rendezvous. Satisfied, he switched the Cessna on to autopilot and left his seat for a brief moment to check out the equipment. He wound out the hook until it was hanging as far to the rear as it could go without snagging against the rear pulley wheel. Then locking the handle in place he returned to his seat and again took control of the aircraft.

The normal procedure, which he had successfully completed four or five times a year for many years, was quite a simple one. He would make only four passes and pick-ups just in case the ship was being monitored on someone's radar, although at the height he was flying it was unlikely that this would happen.

However, it was highly irregular and illegal to pass low over a ship on the high seas so the less chance of the act being monitored electronically the better. In all, his pick-ups from *Palminto* would take less than five minutes, and then he would be long gone.

In any case, one hundred and twenty kilos were not to be sneezed at. Some of it would satisfy a large part of the Brisbane market for a while, especially that part of the market that dealt with the needs of tourists. Grant would later carry out the same exercise from his bases at Townsville and Rockhampton, four pick-ups on each occasion. Three hundred and sixty kilos in all, most of it destined for markets much further south than Brisbane.

Each of his approaches would be from the west, passing over the ship and then climbing and flying out seaward. He came in behind the ship and banked to port, turning on to an easterly course and flying at almost sea level, aiming the aircraft directly at the ship. Seeing the two yellow flags he corrected his course and height. He then approached the *Palminto* quite slowly, concentrating hard on maintaining the correct height.

Brandon watched the aircraft as it banked left and straightened up for its run at the ship. He was acutely aware of the delicate nature of the operation and was great in his praise for the skill of this unknown pilot. To actually connect a hook suspended from the belly of the aircraft with a line suspended between two poles on a moving ship was a remarkable feat in itself. Add to that difficulty the factors of wind and weather and the various movements of the ship on the surface of the sea, then what this pilot was doing was quite extraordinary.

There was, of course, no guarantee that he would succeed on each of the four runs, if on any at all. The arrangement was that he would be permitted one extra attempt only; five pick-up attempts at the most. If all else failed there were emergency pick-up points further south, apart from the two other scheduled ones.

The final objective was to offload all of the packages well before the ship passed Brisbane. If this was not possible for any reason, the packages remaining would be weighted and dumped into the sea. No risks could be taken. Such were the strict rules of operation for Brandon and the *Palminto*. However, the dumping of such valuable cargo would only take place in dire circumstances.

Affected by the tension of the operation he gripped the rail of the bridge wing and watched the aircraft heading for his ship at what appeared to be an overly fast speed for the pick-up. He smiled to himself briefly when he realised that he had been thinking these same thoughts on every previous occasion that these pick-ups had been made over the years, even though the pilot had rarely failed to collect his load accurately.

The aircraft seemed to be aiming straight for the side of the hull, when suddenly it went into a slightly nose-up posture and with a deafening roar of its twin engines, zoomed across the deck at exactly the correct height. A cheer broke out from the crew on the deck below. Brandon suddenly realised that he was cheering as well, and he felt slightly embarrassed.

★

At the precise moment that he passed over the starboard side of the ship Grant pulled back on the stick and put the aircraft in a nose-up attitude, increasing the throttle. The Cessna surged forward and he instinctively knew that he had collected the load. He levelled off at two hundred feet and switched to autopilot. It took just a few seconds to wind in the package as far as the hatchway. It was too large for the hole, but Grant was prepared for this and holding tightly on to the hook on top of the package he drew a knife from his pocket and carefully slashed the outer packaging which released the helium gas with a rush. He then carefully stowed the now much smaller, and heavier package into one of two massive reinforced holdalls sitting on a rear passenger seat restrained by the seat belt.

He smiled to himself as he thought how fortunate it was that he didn't have to speak to anyone at that moment for he knew that some of the helium gas would have entered the cabin, and that inhaling it had an effect on the vocal cords which resulted in a high-pitched squeaky voice for a few seconds afterwards.

While Grant was gathering in his catch and resetting the hook equipment the crew members of *Palminto* were setting up the next package for pick-up by the Cessna. It took just over ninety seconds from the moment of the first pick-up to when Grant aimed his aircraft at the suspended line ready for the second load.

★

Just four minutes later he flew eastwards away from *Palminto* with the fourth and final load on board after four successful passes. He wound in the final package and having deflated the outer bag he placed the package in the holdall with the others, and flew eastward out to sea until *Palminto* had disappeared from sight behind him. Then changing course to the north he continued for ten minutes before he made his final turn, setting course over the Reef for Brighton Hill.

He circled the field twice before landing, looking for any tell-tale signs of something being wrong, but everything appeared in order. There were no cars parked near any of the flying club buildings on the far side of the field so he brought her down and taxied straight into the company hangar.

Shortly afterwards, having disconnected all of the hook-up equipment he replaced the hatch cover and touched up the screw heads with quick-drying enamel paint. Nothing could be left to chance, and even Bill, relaxed as he was, would soon notice the paint missing from the heads of screws and might become suspicious. When he was satisfied that everything looked in order he called Bill Wallis on his mobile number. When he heard the sleepy voice of Bill on the other end he smiled to himself, visualising his Bush Leg-Over encounter.

In fact, Bill had only just started to relax after a hectic forty-five minutes of wild lovemaking in which he had exhausted, and twice repeated, his very limited repertoire of positions. He was lying alongside his woman with his face snuggled between her ample sweating breasts, wondering sadly why his wife never seemed to enjoy sex, whilst this woman just couldn't get enough and always made herself available at a moment's notice.

Naively Bill believed that he was her only man. She knew that this was what he believed, and could see no point in him knowing about the other lovers in her life and the financial arrangements she had with them for her services.

Mavis liked Bill very much. He was kind and generous, and although not terribly skilled in bed he was gentle and considerate in his lovemaking. He genuinely loved her and told her so whenever they were together. This somehow gave her a feeling of comfort and security which she had not experienced before. This was why she had never charged him for her services as she did the other men. If Bill had known about her private enterprise attitude to sex he would have been devastated and would have walked out of her life. The thought worried her greatly, so much so that she had begun to gradually reduce her business activities so that she could be available for Bill whenever he needed her, which was almost daily these days. She had certainly developed a great need for Bill and was beginning to realise that life without him would be pretty bleak.

'Sorry to disturb you when I gave you the afternoon off, Bill, but something has come up and I have to head south sooner than expected. I'm just going to use the ute to go to the petrol station on the highway and pick up some cigarettes before I fly out. I have got a few ideas for a new tourist run taking in the boats doing the Reef run. I will leave the notes on the desk and perhaps you could give me a call in a few days' time. Is there anything you need from Brisbane?'

Bill did not seem overly happy at being called, but he covered up pretty well.

'No thanks, boss. You caught me at a bad time, I have got a headache. See you later.'

I've heard it called some strange things in my time, but never a headache, thought Grant. I thought that was what women suffered from when they didn't want any.

He smiled to himself as he picked up the first of the extremely heavy holdalls, collected the keys to the pick-up, and struggled out towards where the truck was parked. A minute later he had also loaded the second bag into the truck.

# Chapter Thirteen

The two holdalls were extremely heavy and it was a strain for Grant to lift them on to the passenger seat. He then climbed into the driver's seat. He was hot, his body was shaking and he was sweating, which was how he always felt after these pick-ups. The sensation wasn't entirely due to the exertion of carrying the holdalls. In fact, that was only a small part of the reason. The sheer excitement and exhilaration of carrying out those intricate and dangerous aerial manoeuvres so close to the ship while it was pitching and rolling had virtually the same effect on him as a sexual encounter. He was still trembling with excitement and was on a high that he would need to come down from before he flew again.

The drive in the ute would help ease him back to normality, yet that wasn't why he was using the truck. He was moving the consignment on to the next stage of its journey. Where it went to after that he neither knew, nor cared. All that he knew was that a large sum of money would be transferred to his bank account, and that it would be explained away as a payment for special tourist services.

He took a pack of cigarettes from his shirt pocket and lit one. He had plenty more in the Beechcraft. His story to Bill about using the ute to go to the highway to buy some cigarettes was all part of his cover to ensure that everything he did was normal, and was seen to be normal by anyone who might notice the well-known vehicle out on the highway or at the truck stop.

He would in fact purchase some cigarettes from the shop and spend some time gossiping with the young woman who manned the truck stop during the day. That wouldn't be too much of a chore anyway. She was a good-looker, whom under other circumstances he would probably have enjoyed getting between the sheets. He had the distinct feeling that she could be available as at times she appeared to be throwing herself at him. She made no bones about the fact that she had an ambition to get away from the area and was prepared to do almost anything for a ticket south to Brisbane, or Sydney. However, there was no way that Grant could get involved. What a pity!

The drive to the highway was pleasant enough. He passed three vehicles travelling in the opposite direction towards the airstrip and made a big show of waving to the occupants, two of whom he recognised as employees of the aero club.

On reaching the highway he turned left and headed south towards the truck stop, nine kilometres away. He had travelled for six kilometres when he saw the lane off the road to the left, concealed behind a large clump of trees. Just to the right of the entrance to the lane was a small gully, virtually invisible from the road.

He slowed down as he reached the lane, and after a last minute check to ensure that there was no traffic in sight he pulled the ute over on to the edge of the hard shoulder, and leaning over to his left he opened the passenger door. Sitting back behind the wheel, he stretched out his left leg and pushed hard with his foot against the heavy holdalls that were sitting on the front passenger seat. The bags toppled out into the gully and rolled out of sight. Grant then accelerated hard, gradually steering the ute back on to the roadway, and the force of the forward acceleration caused the open door to slam shut.

It was 2.15 p.m., and he was dead on time. His next job was to carry on to the truck stop and his friendly liaison with the pretty young girl. This would complete the final part of his reason for taking the ute and would establish his credentials for being on that part of the highway. Once back on the highway he continued on southward, not even looking in his rear-view mirror. He didn't need to, for he knew that his consignment had been delivered safely and that it would soon be on its way on the next leg of its journey.

He would be passing on two further loads in this manner, many hours and miles further south at Townsville and Rockhampton.

★

The truck was immaculate. What wasn't bright red in colour was beautifully polished chrome. It was a long-nosed Mercedes with a large number of horses under the bonnet. The articulated trailer was refrigerated, and was carrying beef carcasses south to Brisbane.

The driver was a short wiry man with a shock of red hair and like many Australian truckies he wore a distinctive uniform of black singlet and shorts whilst on the outback roads. He had an immaculate pale-blue shirt and shorts on a hanger in a plastic zipper bag hanging in the sleeping compartment behind the driver's cab. He changed into this uniform when he neared the main centres where he had to meet with clients of the company.

Yes! He was a good image for the company, a good and reliable company man. He had been working as a sub-contractor for the same major national company for twenty-five years since purchasing his first truck after returning home from his third and final tour in Vietnam.

He had driven trucks in Vietnam for the Australian Army, which was where he was spotted by one of the Senator's talent scouts who recognised him as an entrepreneur. While he was driving for the Army, he was also driving for anyone else who needed transport for whatever goods they wanted delivered, to wherever they wanted them delivered.

Phil was bright enough to understand just how much he could get away with and who he could rip off the easiest. After his first tour in Vietnam he knew everyone who was worth knowing, and had been there and done that in terms of knowing his way about the systems of both the Australian and the US military.

In the earlier stages of his first tour in Vietnam he had started his first, very lucrative petrol business with a Maori sergeant in the New Zealand Corps of Transport. This was how he got started, but the Kiwis, being so few in number, tended to be more careful than most, and their racket was tumbled. Phil managed to get out of it unscathed, thanks to the very tight-lipped Maori who didn't involve him, even when the shit started to fly.

Shortly afterwards, whilst the Kiwi military inquiry was still underway the Maori sergeant disappeared in Saigon and was never seen again. It was rumoured that he had ripped off his major client, a South Vietnamese police colonel who had dealt with him summarily.

After his disappearance the Kiwi inquiry ceased and the heat was off young driver Cartwright.

However, the Senator's talent scout learned all about Phil from a Kiwi military policeman who talked too much when offered sufficient Bacardi and Coke, and the freedom of the house in a remarkably friendly and clean Saigon brothel.

Whilst the initial meeting with Felix was quite disturbing, Phil found that all that was required of him was a slight variation to the criminal activities that he was already engaged in. The only difference was that he had to follow some very strict rules about what he could or could not do.

At first being told what to do got up his nose a bit. Phil was, however, much brighter than the average so he soon got to realise that the risks were less, for far less work, and best of all, for far greater pay. The result? He became a deliveryman.

It was the payments that he received from Felix, for he never did learn about the Senator, not even to this day, that set him up in this very worthwhile trucking business. He was working for himself in a legitimate business, except for an occasional deliveryman job for Felix. Such jobs were highly illegal, but quite safe and extraordinarily lucrative.

★

Phil Cartwright was sitting in his cab relaxing. He had been parked off the road for about twenty minutes. He appeared to be doing some light maintenance on the dashboard of his truck, or that would have been his story if approached by police.

That wouldn't have concerned him though, because everything was in order. He had a full load of refrigerated carcasses on board and his container was officially sealed with an aluminium company seal. He had a timetable to meet and it was important, both for his business and for his personal well-being, that he stuck to it rigidly.

At precisely 2.45 p.m. he had turned right off the highway into the concealed lane and parked his truck. He picked up a coil of rope from behind the passenger seat, and climbing out of the cab he quickly walked towards the stand of trees between his truck and the road. Whilst he knew that his truck was invisible from the highway he still stopped and crouched behind a large old gum tree and waited and watched.

This location had been carefully chosen for its isolation and for its large field of vision. From this point Phil could be sure that there were no witnesses to what was about to happen. This was the only risky part of the operation, for he had to expose himself to view from the highway for a full minute. This was how long it would take him to get down into the gully, retrieve the two holdalls, and then struggle back up into the shelter of the trees with the very heavy loads.

He satisfied himself that the road was clear in all directions before he launched himself into the gully, stumbling on the way down. He fell and landed on his back in the deep tussock grass that had appeared recently after heavy rain. He lay there for a brief moment getting his wind back. Then he crawled across to where the bags lay and lifted the nearest one with some difficulty as it was extremely heavy. He tied one end of the rope around the handle of the holdall, then holding the other end he struggled back up the bank. He reached the top and slung the rope around the base of the gum tree for leverage. Then pulling hard he dragged the holdall up the bank of the gully into the shelter of the trees, where he collapsed, panting and sweating. Shortly afterwards he repeated the exercise for the second bag.

He checked his watch. Three minutes exactly.

Not bad for a wicked old bastard like you! he chuckled to himself.

He then got back to his feet, and carefully parting the bushes he once again checked the highway for any sign of life. He had learned over the years that one just couldn't be too careful when playing Felix's dangerous games.

Satisfied that everything was clear he took hold of the rope, and winding it around his shoulder he dragged the second bag towards the back of the trailer. It took him exactly one minute to break the seal on the rear doors of the refrigerated container and open them. He unzipped the holdall and hoisted each of the two packages into the container. Returning to where he had left the first holdall he dragged it to the truck and repeated the exercise before leaping up into the trailer.

Near the rear doors there were four large beef carcasses hanging on the extreme right hanging rail that were specially marked. Phil was able to recognise the marking anyway, and that was all that mattered. To the untrained eye, these four were just a few amongst many large, cold and stiff dead animals on their way to the market.

Wrapping each of the packages in white muslin bags that he had brought with him from the cab he placed one package inside each of the four carcasses. There was plenty of room, as these carcasses had been specially pre-prepared at the abattoir by some unknown employee of Felix.

How they would be collected, and by whom, he didn't wish to know. All that concerned him was that they would be removed from his charge at the appropriate time and that he would then be on his way home, a far richer man.

Within five minutes Cartwright had dismounted from the container and closed and resealed the doors with a special bit of equipment supplied by Felix. This enabled him to replace the seal with a duplicate that would have fooled even the most professional of people in the business.

The holdalls and the original door seal he buried in a hole that he had dug nearby, having first liberally sprayed them with acid that would burn them beyond recognition. The entire operation from start to finish had taken ten minutes, during which time no other vehicles had passed.

He climbed up into his cab and started the engine. Ten minutes later he pulled on to the forecourt of the Sandhills

Truck Stop where he would wash his hands and buy a cup of tea and a sandwich before continuing on his way.

★

Like Grant, from the start he had also considered the sexual possibilities of a liaison with the attractive young woman behind the counter, and like Grant he knew that to play around whilst working for Felix could have lethal consequences. However, unlike Grant, he had from the start decided that if he used his head there would be no way that Felix or anyone else need know about a little bit of harmless fun. He had, therefore, stepped over the forbidden line nearly twelve months before and had formed a close and very intimate relationship with young Dolly. To cover himself he was making it financially worth her while to be as discreet as he was about their sexual gymnastics.

Yes, he mused, a bit of extramarital nooky never did a bloke any harm, and she sure is a great lay, and what a great pair of knockers.

As he pulled onto the forecourt of the truck stop the ute driven by Grant drove out on to the highway and headed northwards. They waved to each other as country drivers always did.

★

Grant was completely unaware of who the pick-up person was, or how the load that he had dumped earlier was to be picked up and conveyed on the next leg of its journey south. He assumed that it would be picked up by a truckie, but there were hundreds of them using this road every day, and frankly he didn't wish to know which one it was. He was being very well paid for his work, and secrecy was part of his job specification.

However, first and foremost he was scared witless of that man, Felix. On the occasions that he had been obliged to meet with him he found that the mere presence of the man caused a cold shudder to run up his back. What was that old expression? Wasn't it about someone walking over your grave? That was definitely the effect that Felix had on him, so there was no way in the world that he was going to do anything to offend the man.

Why should I? he thought, Christ! he has made me a bloody rich man.

## Chapter Fourteen

Phil Cartwright, however, was a different sort of man. He definitely knew about Grant, or at least that he was the guy who dumped the consignments that he then picked up and carried south.

For a year or two now he had started to become very nervous about how well the operation was running. A realist by nature, he felt sure that this state of affairs could not last for ever. Since his first tour in Vietnam he had lived on the fringe of the so-called underworld, though he wasn't a full-time criminal. He had his own quite lucrative business, and enjoyed the lifestyle of the truckie, even if it was not his intention to stay in the job for too much longer. Next birthday he would be fifty. You can't drive a truck for ever, or he certainly didn't intend to.

Actually, whenever he thought about his age, he was reminded that Felix was of roughly the same vintage, perhaps a bit older. It amused him to imagine that all of the other people involved in the trafficking were probably of the same generation and that before long this substantial drugs enterprise would be operated by a group of geriatrics.

He had seen too many people in the drugs-related criminal fraternity fall foul of their associates and the law. The majority of them were lucky and merely ended up in gaol. However, several that he had known that had been involved with drugs had mysteriously disappeared, some being discovered later minus some important parts, and very much dead.

It seemed to him that people who committed drugs infidelities generally ended up the victim of some form of ritualistic murder.

He knew for sure that the drugs bosses intended each such gruesome death to play a major part in ensuring that similar infidelities did not occur again. By and large the threat was effective and most people in the drugs game abided by the rules. After all, the pickings were great, and generally very little hard graft was involved. That alone should have been a great incentive for maintaining a very tight lip and being loyal to the cause.

Unfortunately the business of drugs was so lucrative that it had the effect of making some greedy individuals venture into the private enterprise world, often with the hard-earned products of their boss or of the syndicate that ran the show.

★

Cartwright was not one of that sort, and if nothing else he was extremely loyal to the people who provided for his retirement. It was, however, his retirement or the thought of it that was causing him the greatest headaches. He had a massive nest egg stashed away for the day that he could at last hang up his driving boots.

He had even developed a pretty much foolproof plan for laundering his money in a way that would make it totally legal and useable. There were still ways in which one could use the casino system for that purpose if you planned it well.

When he and his wife headed off into retirement he did not want his money to become a problem for him; though the thought of spending his retirement with his wife worried him because their relationship was no longer a good one.

But, and it was a very big but, he had never heard of anyone that had ever retired from the drugs game. Was it even possible? He lay awake at nights worrying about the issue. Was the thought of a rich retirement a childish daydream? How would he broach the subject with Felix? How would Felix take it? Would he end up as another drugs statistic, headless in a dirty quarry somewhere off the beaten track? He was concerned because he knew that Felix was a brutal killer.

Every time he had to meet the man his stomach churned over with worry, and he always felt fantastic relief whenever his meetings were concluded and he was back on the road once more. It was almost as if Felix had given him a reprieve from the death sentence, but that he was the potential and probably ultimate executioner.

*

It was during one of his frequent sleepless nights that he suddenly decided to insure himself against the likelihood that his retirement plan might be terminated. It was almost as if a massive load had been lifted from his shoulders. Even his wife, who wasn't known for her sensitivity, noticed a remarkable change in his demeanour. He became bright and chirpy once again, just like he used to be back in the good old days when they first got married.

It occurred to him that if he obtained evidence regarding the other links in the drug delivery chain, documented it, and then took steps to have the documents safeguarded in a legal way, then not even that crazy black man, Felix, would chance his arm against him.

He decided on that fateful night to take every possible safe step to discover as much about the network and the other deliverymen as possible, then once he had done this he would place the evidence in the hands of several lawyers in both Queensland and New South Wales, as well as in a safety deposit box in his bank's vault.

The extremely elaborate plan that he designed included arranging with each of the lawyers and with his bank manager that should anything nasty happen to him each of them would distribute the documentation to a pre-determined list of people. This list included the police in all eastern states, and the National Crime Authority people down in Adelaide, South Australia.

His list of organisations and individuals that would receive the evidence would also include every major newspaper and important and influential politicians, both state and federal throughout Australia.

The plan also included spiriting his wife into hiding to somewhere safe so that she would not become a victim also. They no longer hit it off together, but he felt duty-bound to ensure she suffered no harm.

He did not consider that his decision to take this action was in any way disloyal. Far from it, if nothing nasty happened to him the plan also ensured that in the event of his death by natural causes all the documentation would be destroyed.

Surely nobody could construe that as being disloyal, he told himself as he put his pen down after working out his security plans.

All I am doing is looking after my personal interests, not challenging or attacking the interests of Felix or his bosses.

But, he said to himself with a wry smile, I promise that if Felix or his crazy fucking mates do anything to me or mine, their balls will be hung out to dry.

*

Over the next few weeks Phil Cartwright spent every spare moment that he could find writing down everything that he knew about Felix and the drugs movement, at least that part of the movement that he was currently responsible for. He did it in longhand rather than run the risk of anything being able to be picked up off his computer. He had always been thorough in that regard over the years.

He wasn't sure how he should go about approaching lawyers with the view to setting them up as part of his contingency plan, and tormented himself worrying about how to do this without raising suspicion and causing the police to be informed.

Then one evening whilst staying at a motel south of Brisbane on one of his legitimate meat transportation trips, he watched a lower than B-grade movie on the TV, which was awful in every respect, except that it solved his problem for him. In the movie this guy went to several lawyers and got each of them to prepare a will for him. One of the conditions of the will was that in the event of his death under suspicious circumstances they would each recover documents from the vaults of the local bank and follow the instructions included with the documents.

Cartwright couldn't believe his luck. It was perfect, so he decided to adopt the general plot and adapt it to suit his own needs. Then choosing six main centres on the way south, three in Queensland and three in New South Wales, he extracted from the Yellow Pages the names and addresses of six fairly significant law firms that he felt would be reputable enough to trust with such an unusual mission as his. During his next three trips south he established contact with those law firms and in each instance they prepared his will exactly in the manner that he asked.

In each instance the lawyers were concerned regarding the peculiar nature of the clause that referred to his demise by foul means. He covered this aspect of his will by telling each of the lawyers a story about screwing the wife of an influential man in the general area of the main centre that he was in at the time, which was why he was dealing with a lawyer there rather than in his home town.

The fact that he was admitting being unfaithful to his wife was also an understandable reason for dealing with a lawyer elsewhere. This aspect of the story seemed to ring true to each of the lawyers, who Phil made sure were all men.

The story went on to explain that Cartwright feared that his extramarital sexual gymnastics had been discovered by the irate husband, whose continental origin demanded some form of retribution.

It was purposely designed to be fairly elaborate and sufficiently paranoid in its plot to satisfy each of the lawyers that they had some form of minor harmless nutter on their hands. In each instance the lawyers went to great lengths to arrange for the establishment of a security box with the local bank to satisfy their client's strange requests. After all, he was paying well for the service, and there was nothing illegal about the arrangement that Cartwright was making with them, even if it did relate to immoral activities.

Most of the lawyers thought that his story was improbable enough to be quite amusing, and he knew that at the very least they each thought him a bit strange. That was what he wanted them to think, so he acted out the part as best he could.

All in all he felt very satisfied with the way in which he had conducted himself and how cleverly he had ensured his future security.

# Chapter Fifteen

Over the following months he honed his contingency plan to a very fine point. He became quite convinced that in the event of his retirement plans being challenged by Felix and his bosses, once he advised them of what he had done to safeguard his future interests they would have no choice but to allow him to go ahead and retire safely.

After all, he intended them no harm and was not threatening them. He felt sure that as men of the world they would have the good sense to see things his way. If they didn't they would unwittingly set off a chain of happenings that could bring their entire enterprise falling around their necks.

Not that Phil looked forward to this eventuality, for it would certainly mean that he would be dead, and just as certainly that he would have died in a very painful, and less than natural manner.

*

The plan finally began to shape up in the way that he intended in September 1995 when he received a phone call from Felix instructing him to go to a certain telephone booth in the local shopping mall and await further instructions.

In fact Felix merely said, 'Be there in forty-five minutes, or else!'

Cartwright knew what he had to do. He had been well trained by Felix over the years so he understood fully such cryptic messages and the need to obey them implicitly.

The instructions he received that day related to the next consignment that he would pick up from the gully alongside the highway just south of Brighton Hill. Felix was very precise, which was what Phil had come to expect over the years. In this business nothing could be left to chance. The only difference was that on this occasion he would be taking certain actions not in Felix's game plan, and only he would know about them.

Firstly he would be taking steps to see and then identify the person who was placing the consignment in the gully ready for his pick-up. Next, if at all possible he would then try to discover how that person got hold of the drugs and from whom, but he didn't fancy his chances in that regard. This entire operation had always been kept tight.

Tighter than a duck's arse in fact, he thought.

Still, he would give it a go and see what eventuated.

He knew that if he was found out it would result in his immediate death. However, he felt sure that risking death in this way was the only way to ensure that he would not die at Felix's hands at some later date.

★

On the day of the pick-up he arrived at the Sandhills Truck Stop a bit earlier than usual, and after checking out his truck and parking it he went to the back of the truck stop buildings and into the men's toilets which were hidden from sight from the rest of the complex.

After first checking that nobody was around he ducked into the nearby bush, waited for a moment to make sure that he wasn't being followed, then headed off across the hills to a small stand of native trees and high grass that he had located on an earlier foray. It was not too far from the truck stop, but out of sight of any nosy person who might happen to be gazing up towards the hills.

From this location he had a perfect view of the highway below. The gully from which he would later recover the drugs was clearly in view and only one hundred and fifty metres away.

He had stopped alongside the pick-up point before driving to the service station, and on the quite public pretence of relieving himself into the gully had checked to make sure that the consignment hadn't already been delivered. He didn't think it would as Felix was the sort of guy who would plan things in a way that would ensure that the consignment wasn't left unattended for too long for fear of it being discovered by a truckie answering the call of nature as he himself had pretended to do earlier.

Truckies, particularly those from the bush did tend to stop and relieve themselves by the roadside without too much concern about privacy. Felix's planning, however, would certainly be such that the discovery of the consignment in such a casual manner would be a most unlikely happening.

Pity the poor bastard who did happen to find it just because he needed a piss. He'd be in deep shit, he thought with a hint of a smile.

He didn't have to wait for too long. A grey ute came southwards along the highway. He knew the ute, and had seen it often along this road. He felt sure that it was something to do with Brighton Hill airfield a few clicks north. As he watched it approach he was aware of the fact that he was sweating profusely, yet at the same time shivering. It wasn't a particularly hot day, but he certainly wasn't cold. He was really wound up, and excited in a way that he hadn't experienced since his army days back in Vietnam.

What the hell am I doing? Jesus, Cartwright, you're not a kid any more. Grow up and control yourself.

His feeling of excitement grew more intense as the ute slowed down and pulled to the side of the road by the gully. It didn't stop though, and Cartwright started to feel a sudden surge of disappointment as it appeared that nothing was going to happen. Suddenly, the passenger door of the ute flew open and two large objects hurtled out and tumbled into the long grass of the gully and out of his view.

The ute accelerated fast and turned back on to the road, continuing on in the direction of the truck stop.

'Cartwright old son, you are a real clever bastard,' he said out loud. Then laughing almost hysterically with excitement he was on his feet and running hell for leather down the hill back towards the truck stop less than a kilometre away. He had to get there before the ute drove past.

He knew that if he hurried he should just make it. The highway twisted and turned around the hill that he had kept observation from and then made a left-hand dog-leg turn before commencing the straight stretch that led to the truck stop.

It was vital that he saw the driver, for the next stage of his plan was to find out who it was and where he, or she, came from. Without that information he would almost certainly have to wait until the next consignment, the following January or February.

★

The run down hill, weaving in and out of the fairly dense bush took much longer than he had anticipated, and things were made worse when he stumbled and fell headlong into a stand of tussock grass which was occupied at that moment by a red-bellied black. Although not the friendliest of snakes at the best of times it was a toss up who got the greatest shock, Phil or the snake. Both retreated rapidly from the point of encounter. Cartwright was badly shaken and it took him a full half minute to regain his composure. He had seen many men die from snake bites in Vietnam and had a deep revulsion for the creatures which he could not overcome.

Knowing that the ute would have by now passed the truck stop he slowed down to a walking pace until he reached the toilet buildings once more, and feeling rather dejected he strolled casually from the rear of the buildings on to the forecourt by the fuel pumps.

He couldn't believe his eyes. The ute was parked on the forecourt and a tall, well-dressed man was walking away from it and heading into the café and shop area.

From here he could see Dolly who was busy serving tea and coffee to a couple of truck drivers who were making no pretence of hiding their endeavours to look down the front of her blouse. She was laughing with them, and encouraging them a bit by leaning forward over the counter for much longer than was necessary. He suddenly felt a mixture of jealousy and anger. He wasn't sure why, because he was pretty certain that he wasn't the only truckie she was sharing her bed with.

Suddenly he was annoyed with himself.

'What I am I doing feeling this way over a bit of skirt, even if she is fantastic in bed?' he murmured to himself.

As he walked up to the counter he glanced over to where the driver of the ute was sitting. The man didn't seem to fit in this place. He was far too well dressed even though he wore casual clothes, and he had the look of an executive of some sort. Not the sort of bloke that you would normally expect to see in a truck stop place.

'Who's the posh guy, Dolly? I've never seen him in here before.'

'That's Mr Grant. He's a Yank, up from Brizzie. He comes in every so often. Something to do with Brighton Hill Flying Club I think,' she replied, without looking up from the toast she was spreading with masses of butter.

'Give me the keys of your car, luv. I've got to call on a bloke and I don't want to unhitch the trailer. It's such a bloody performance with all that frozen gear in it.'

'Out getting your leg over elsewhere are you, Phil?' laughed Dolly, at the same time pushing her car keys across the counter.

'Me? Be unfaithful to you, the love of my life? I'm deeply hurt,' replied Phil feigning shock and anger.

'I'll deeply hurt you if I find you are doing the job on anyone else, you horny bastard. I'll cut it off for you,' she whispered as he moved towards the door of the café.

She was not smiling when she spoke, and there was an unusual hint of unpleasantness in her voice.

A look of concern came over Phil's face as he realised suddenly that he had just been on the receiving end of a less than veiled threat.

Wow! This could be difficult. Don't tell me that she's gone and fallen in love with me. Jesus! I don't need that sort of aggro at the moment. Bloody women! I'm buggered if I can understand them.

Quickly dismissing the thought he hurried across the car park and after fumbling with the door lock which was prone to jamming, he climbed into Dolly's dilapidated Toyota Corolla. As he did so he nearly did himself an injury similar to the one that Dolly had just virtually threatened him with because he had failed to adjust the seat back before attempting to climb in. Cursing his stupidity he pulled the lever which released the seat lock, then settling himself as comfortably as he could he started the engine.

He had planned this day for a long time, but even though he knew exactly what he had to do and how he was going to do it he still could not suppress the excitement welling inside him.

He was shaking so much that he nearly forgot to check the fuel gauge.

Stupid cow has forgotten to fill the tank. Christ above! After all this I am going to miss him. The dozy bitch.

His mind was full of obscenities about Dolly, who after all wasn't intending to go anywhere, and she did live at the truck stop so why the hell should she worry about filling the car?

As he pulled up alongside the petrol pump he suddenly began to feel pretty unkind, and somewhat stupid.

Poor little Dolly. Sorry kid! Why I'm taking it out on you I don't know. Never mind, I'll give you a tank full to make up for it.

He smiled to himself as he filled the car, thinking of later that day when he hoped to do more than just fill her petrol tank. Out of the corner of his eye he saw the tall man, Grant, coming out of the café and strolling towards the ute. He paid for the fuel and was just pulling out of the forecourt on to the highway when Grant climbed into the ute and started the engine.

★

In his earlier planning for this eventuality he had decided that if this opportunity arose he would move off in front of the subject vehicle.

He had heard the police use that expression when he had tuned into their wavelength on some of his long runs. All truckies did it to give themselves an idea of where the cops were likely to be, or not to be when they were speeding.

Anyway, having a good idea where the vehicle came from, now pretty much confirmed by Dolly, he felt it was a good plan to tail him from the front. He'd first learned about this technique in a thriller that he'd read some years back. It seemed to work well for that hard-shot private detective from the Bronx, and he'd done it in heavy New York City traffic.

'Surely it has got to be easier out here in the bush,' he mumbled to himself as he straightened the car up and slowly headed in the direction of Brighton Hill.

He worried a little at one point when the ute slowed down considerably, causing him to fear that it would pull off and take a different route. However, his fears were unfounded, and as he turned off at the road to the airfield he was relieved to see in the rear-view mirror that the ute was following. He felt sure this was a clear indication that Grant, or whatever his name was, was not suspicious of him.

*

On arriving at the airfield there was only one place for him to go without causing undue suspicion, and that was to the flying club building which was the only semi-public place on the airfield. All the other buildings and hangars were privately owned by various aero enterprises and he would have little or no legitimate reason for going to any of them.

He parked the car outside the flying club and strolled around the building as casually as he could. His heart was pounding inside his chest and he felt almost faint with apprehension. If anyone approached him he would pretend to be enquiring about introductory flying lessons. As it was, the area was deserted and the building was locked.

He took advantage of that fact and sat down on a wooden bench on the front verandah of the building. From his position he could see every other building around the airfield, but was sure he could not be seen in the deep shadow that the verandah offered. It was perfect.

Grant had pulled up almost opposite his position and was backing the ute into a large shed, which from Phil's vantage point appeared to have an office of some sort attached to it. Alongside the office was an aircraft hangar with the front doors shut.

A plane was parked in front of the office. Parked? Cartwright was never sure if that was the right terminology to use when referring to aircraft. It was a very neat-looking aircraft that even to his untrained eye looked quite expensive. Certainly more so than some of the old string bags that he knew flew out of this paddock. His biggest worry was that he didn't know one aircraft from the next, so identification was going to be more difficult for him than for others more versed in the flying game.

He had prepared himself for this sort of eventuality, however, and from his pocket he took a small compact Pentax camera. It had a zoom lens which would enable him to take shots from a longer distance and compensate somewhat for his lack of knowledge of aircraft and memory for special features. Most of all it would enable him to relive this experience later with the benefit of the excellent photographs this camera would provide.

Setting the zoom lens he took several photographs of the office and shed hoping that these would reveal the name of the owner. He also took two shots of the parked aircraft knowing he would have to take more if and when it moved.

Bloody hell! What do I do if this Grant bastard doesn't leave? Why am I so sure that he is going to fly out? What if he heads back to the road? It will be bloody difficult to track him out on the highway again. He is bound to suss me, and then I could really be in deep shit.

Those worrying thoughts began to disturb him to the point where he was considering leaving his cover and heading closer to the building that Grant had disappeared into. He rose to his feet, closed the lens of the camera and carefully placed it back into his pocket then moved back deeper into the shade of the verandah. He was considering the best direction to take to get back to the car, when Grant came out of the office building and appeared to lock the front door before strolling across to the aircraft. He walked around the plane, apparently checking it, and then he climbed in and seated himself in the pilot's seat.

Cartwright panicked a little thinking that the plane would take off before he could prepare the camera. He snatched the Pentax out of his pocket, and in doing so dropped it on the wooden decking of the verandah. Stooping down he picked it up and checked it. Luckily it appeared to be okay.

What the hell do I know about cameras? It could be wrecked, he thought as he took it out of its leather case and prepared to take more shots.

Just at that moment his luck changed. Grant got down from the aircraft and walked over to the hangar where he appeared to fiddle with the lock on the small door set into the one of the large hangar doors. The door opened and he disappeared inside and came out a moment later, locking the door behind him. By this time Phil was raring to go.

Leaning on the verandah rail to steady himself, and with the zoom lens on full range he took several frontal shots of Grant as he walked to the plane, and one perfect side-on shot as he paused before climbing back into the pilot's seat.

*Let's hope this bloody thing really is working*, he thought as he prepared himself to get some sideways shots of the aircraft as it taxied off.

★

Grant was a professional pilot and in no great hurry when it came to air safety. Having completed his pre-start cockpit check he then started the engine of the Beechcraft. He then called the flying club on his radio to check if there were any club aircraft in the vicinity, and in particular planning to land. Although he could see that there were no aircraft movements on the ground air traffic regulations required this action. The flying club only manned its small control tower, more of a glass-fronted shed, when club activities were in progress, but the safety procedures had to be followed at all times.

Because of this he called the tower three times before deciding to taxi to the south end of the field and turn into the light breeze coming from the north-east. As he increased engine power in preparation for take-off he tried the tower once more. Getting no reply he made one final visual check to the south before he eased off the brake and the aircraft began to accelerate forward.

Immediately after leaving the ground he banked steeply to the right and in doing so flew directly over the roof of the flying club. There was a car parked outside the club-house and he couldn't recall if he had seen it there before on previous flights into Brighton Hill. He knew all of the aircraft owners and pilots, and a fair number of the casual members but had never seen that particular car there before. It was too old and battered to belong to any of the people he knew.

He also wondered why, if someone was in the club-house, they hadn't replied to his radio calls. It had always been common practice at this airfield for whoever was in the building to monitor and respond to calls.

As he gained height he headed towards the nearby coast before setting a course southwards to his next pick-up location. He wondered about that solitary car for a minute or so before becoming totally absorbed in his flying and in his plans for the next stage of his deliveryman work.

Phil had used up the complete roll of film before Grant banked over the clubhouse and headed out towards the coast. He was delighted with the way things had gone and just hoped that the camera was working correctly.

In a couple of days' time while *en route* south he would have the film developed and printed in some obscure camera shop where the pictures that resulted would mean little, if anything, to the person who carried out the work. One further smart move on his part to ensure his ultimate security and safety.

He would then show the shots to a mate of his in Brisbane. The man was a flier who did light freight work for the mines up north and occasionally for Phil. He would be able to identify the aircraft and probably even be able to help him to identify this American, Mr Grant. It would only cost a couple of slabs of beer, and perhaps a night at one of the better class of table-top dancing clubs that he liked to patronise whenever he was in Brisbane.

Everything is fitting neatly into shape, he thought as he packed the camera back into its case and returned it to his jacket pocket.

Once satisfied that the aircraft was safely out of sight and unlikely to return he walked back to the Toyota and drove round the airfield to the buildings that Grant had just vacated.

Parking the car at the rear of the small hangar where he felt it would be unlikely to be seen he walked slowly around the building keeping close to the wall, at the same time keeping watch on the entrance road to the airfield to ensure that his activities were not noticed by prying eyes.

The hangar had no windows, and both the main doors and the smaller door were locked. However, the hangar door comprised two sliding doors which did not fit too well. It looked as if a vehicle had collided with one of the them as it was slightly buckled in the middle. As a result he was able to see through a fairly substantial gap at the south end of the hangar. It was dark inside but he could quite clearly make out an aeroplane. It was larger than the one that Grant had flown off in and it had two engines. He caught a strong whiff of paint but thought nothing of it.

Perhaps all aircraft hangars smell of paint, he wondered.

Returning to the car he rummaged in the boot and found a small tool roll. Opening it up he discovered very few tools of any consequence.

I hope for her sake she never has a breakdown, he thought.

What he did find was a small coil of very strong wire. Using the rusty pair of pliers that appeared to be the main tool in the kit he quickly shaped the wire into a peculiar-looking implement which he felt sure would satisfy his requirements.

Not the best-looking key I've ever seen, but it will open that old lock for me, he thought as he made his way back round to the hangar door.

He was a man of many skills, not the least of which was opening doors that he wasn't supposed to, something he had learned in the Army and perfected in Vietnam.

It was dark inside the hangar but he was not game to turn any lights on, just in case. As he got closer to the aircraft the smell of paint got stronger. He was inquisitive about that smell.

It must be fresh paint, why else would it be so strong? he thought.

He couldn't see well enough to identify where the paint smell was coming from, so he gently felt around the body of the aircraft with his hands, starting at the engine cowling and working slowly and carefully backwards towards the tail.

As he moved back past the cockpit door he touched something sticky on the underside of the plane. He got down on the floor, and taking out his cigarette lighter he snapped it on briefly, and immediately saw where the paint smell was coming from. There were blobs of it, quite neatly done and almost dry. He could plainly see that someone had painted over several bolts. Very recently!

Making a mental note of where the paint marks were he slid out from under the belly of the aircraft and rising to his feet dusted himself down, at the same time cursing loudly when he realised that he had a large oil stain down the side of his trousers and several paint marks on his shirt front.

Locking the hangar door was harder than opening it, but he eventually managed and was soon back in the car and out on the open highway.

As earlier in the day when he was observing the gully where the drugs were to be deposited he was sweating profusely, and shivering at the same time. It wasn't the result of being cold though. It was definitely through sheer excitement.

As yet he didn't know what was going on at the airfield, or what the American, Grant, was up to with that aircraft in the hangar, but he knew instinctively that the man was another of Felix's deliverymen. He was also sure that those paint marks had something to do with Grant's role in the deliveryman business.

*

By the time he arrived back at the truck stop he had made up his mind to keep an observation on the airfield when the next delivery was due in some months' time. Then suddenly a cold shudder crept down his spine when he thought of the danger he could be risking if Felix got wind of what he was doing. All his planning could go down the drain if that happened, and if it did he could end up dead and buried before he even got a chance to present his insurance policy.

Who the fuck do you think you are, a member of the S I fucking S? he mused as he parked the car.

No mate! You stick to the plan, Cartwright my old son, he thought, answering his own question.

My pilot mate in Brizzie will suss out what's going on when I show him where those paint marks were, and when he identifies the type of aircraft, and possibly who it belongs to.

★

He rolled over in the narrow bed and looked down at the slightly thin, but none the less beautiful body of Dolly lying alongside him. He had been sitting with his bare back propped against the wall, smoking silently whilst she gently caressed his body. He had a lot on his mind, and just couldn't stop thinking of what had happened to him earlier and wondering what he would uncover when he got back to Brisbane. He was convinced that it was all part of a strange jigsaw puzzle that when solved would strengthen his case with Felix for his safe and healthy retirement.

Dolly had started by stroking his lean, muscular chest and had slowly worked her way down to his thighs. He could feel himself being aroused as she gently played with his penis and testicles with her long slim fingers, and with the tip of her tongue. He was ready and so was she.

Stubbing his cigarette in the ashtray alongside the bed he turned back towards her and raised himself on his knees, at the same time pulling her on to her back and gently lifting her legs up and tucking them under his armpits. He was erect and very excited as he moved himself inwards between her legs and paused for a moment whilst he gently rubbed his penis in a slow rhythmic motion up and down against her vagina. She moaned quietly and almost growled the words he was waiting to hear. The words that he knew from past experience he would coax from her as he stroked his penis against her pulsating, thrusting vagina.

'Phil! Now! Please, I need you now, my darling. Right now.'

She was tense for a moment as he entered her and thrust himself deep inside her waiting body. Then, as he began to slowly move in and out she relaxed and began to croon softly, a beautiful lullaby-type tune that he was never able to identify but always promised himself that he would ask her about at the end of their lovemaking, yet never did.

Suddenly she said, 'Phil, why did you need my car today?'

Taken back by this sudden enquiry at this particularly inappropriate moment he felt his manhood shrinking inside her.

'Can't it wait till later? I'm concentrating. I mean, do you want nooky or a bloody debate?'

'Don't be so crude with me, Phil. I'm just interested,' she snapped indignantly, pulling herself backwards and away from him, causing his now shrunken member to withdraw from her and droop dejectedly.

'I'm sorry, love,' he said, gently stroking her face, trying like mad to concentrate on becoming erect once more, but knowing that he was fighting a losing battle.

'Let's just say that I was out sorting out a bit of personal insurance.' It was coming back. He could feel his penis rising once more, the thought of today's adventure acting on him like a sexual stimulant.

'Oh! I wish you had told me. I could have helped you out. I would have introduced you to my insurance man. I'm with the Prudential, you know.'

His erection disappeared instantly. The thought of a rat speedily disappearing up a drainpipe came briefly into his mind. It was all over, done! Not to return that night. Not, however, that it would have mattered if it had, for Dolly would not have had anything more to do with him that night anyway.

After all, what self-respecting girl wants to make love to a bloke who, when he was at the most crucial and exciting moment of their lovemaking, started laughing and didn't stop for two solid hours.

The stupid, inconsiderate bastard.

## Chapter Sixteen

Grant touched down in Rockhampton at about 3 p.m. on the following day, and after a few brief air traffic formalities he picked up a hire car and headed towards the city. A short while later he registered at his usual motel, situated five miles out of town. After a brief discussion about the weather with the wife of the proprietor he went to his room. He was so tired that he didn't even bother to shower. He just stripped off his clothes and dived into bed, falling asleep almost instantly.

At about 8 p.m. he woke and showered and dressed, feeling quite refreshed. The last two days had been very wearing.

Thank goodness I only have to do this a few times a year. If it was more often than that I would end up a nervous wreck, he thought as he ate the sandwiches that he had arranged to be delivered to his room.

He was about to meet with Felix and was not looking forward to it, but knew that he had no choice. The man frightened him intensely, and this had been the case ever since that night in Vietnam when Felix had leapt into the plane, joking that he was a hijacker and that Grant had to fly him to Cuba.

Everyone on board had thought that very funny except for him. He had taken one brief look at the man and instantly decided that even though there were probably several VC out there in the jungle who were going to try their best to kill him and the others during their hair-raising take-off, this black man Felix was more to be feared than all the enemy put together. Throughout his dealings with the man over the many years since he had found no reason to change his mind in that regard. The mere thought of him made Grant nervous. Meeting with him, although it had now become routine, still scared him more than he could explain.

However, he always met with Felix after his final pick-up. The meeting was always of short duration, and was merely a debriefing of the three pick-ups. This time it was unusual in that Felix was asking to meet him before the final pick-up had taken place.

This had happened once before though, but that had been because of a mechanical fault on the ship which had caused the third pick-up to be delayed by a few hours. He assumed that this out of sequence meeting was probably due to a similar circumstance.

He thought about the two earlier pick-ups and had no concerns about them as they had been carried out to perfection, even if he said so himself. Both Cairns and Townsville had gone as smooth as clockwork.

He had experienced no weather problems and the drop-off leg of the double had gone smoothly in both instances. He knew that his professionalism could not be faulted, but that was not what was nagging at him. It was the fact that he had to meet this man face to face; Felix, who for reasons beyond his control frightened him half to death.

The meeting took place in a lay-by a few kilometres north-east of Rockhampton on the road to Yeppoon, as dictated in the instructions that he had received in the note slipped under the door of his motel room.

Grant pulled off the road into the unlit lay-by, and opening the bonnet pretended to be examining the engine by the light of a torch.

This was all part of the game plan devised by Felix, who enjoyed making such occasions fairly dramatic.

He knew that Felix was already there and could sense he was close at hand, such was the evil aura that surrounded the man. He also knew that Felix's arrival would be as dramatic as the plot for the meeting, so he tensed himself for the moment when he would announce his presence, hoping that his fear would not show.

'How're they hanging, my man?'

Grant nearly leapt out of his skin, and immediately found himself resenting the man even more for the frightening influence he had over him.

'Why the fuck did you have to do that?' he snapped, jumping backwards in fright. 'Why can't we meet like other civilised human beings, somewhere reasonable?'

'Why, Edwin, my dear friend, I didn't know that you cared. You just referred to me as a civilised human being. That's the last thing I would have expected to be called by you. You are obviously getting to like me, and that is good.'

'Cut the bullshit, Felix, and let's get on with the business. I feel ridiculous meeting you like this. Just like a couple of flakes who haven't come out of the closet yet.'

Felix chuckled out loud. The sound of his laughter made Grant shudder.

'Don't kid yourself, my man. You're not really my sort,' he growled.

Just at that moment Grant realised that the only thing he could see of the man were his brilliant white teeth shining through the near absolute blackness of the night. It seemed almost surreal, as if the teeth were the only things present, with no body attached to them.

Without a further word, Felix got into the front passenger seat of Grant's hire car and lit up a cigarette. Grant looked over the raised bonnet into the front of the car just as Felix inhaled. His face was lit up partly by the glow of the burning tobacco, and for a brief moment Grant saw a startling likeness to the devil in that evil black face.

He joined Felix in the car and they both sat silently in the darkness for nearly five minutes before Felix spoke. Grant was expecting this, however, and knew it was all planned to add to the dramatics of the meeting and to reinforce his fear of Felix, of which the man was very much aware.

Felix explained the reason for the unscheduled and unusual get-together.

'We are not sure, but we have a suspicion that someone may be tracking us from the sea. If that is the case, to make sure that we are not caught in the act I want you to meet the ship one hour earlier, due east of Cape Townsend.

'Make sure that this is the most perfect of all your perfect pick-ups, Edwin, then head due north before turning left across Broad Sound. Once you hit the land head back to the drome and make the drop off in exactly the same way as always.

'Once this is done I have one further job for you to do before you head back home to Brisbane. If we are being tracked, and we have good reason to believe that this is a possibility, the tracking is being done by a trawler fitted to the gunnels with all sorts of electronic gismos. This trawler has been traced as being in almost every sea lane and port that we have since March 1995. It is bright red, so you can't miss it. Its name, although you will not get close enough to verify that, is the *Sea Knight*.

'If it has been tracking us, it has been doing so electronically, and from a distance. Sure, they will have sussed out that somehow *Palminto* is meeting up with an airborne vehicle of some sort, but they will not have seen it happen. If they do believe that, then chances are that they will assume it is a helicopter. I mean, how on earth could a real aeroplane pick something up from a moving ship on the high seas? The pilot would have to be some sort of crazy fucking magician, wouldn't he!'

Felix chuckled to himself, and even Grant saw the funny side of that statement. He was anxious to ask some questions, because the thought of the enterprise being blown really scared him. He knew from past experience, however, that one did not interrupt Felix when he was talking. Not if you had any sense, that is.

'Now, this trawler, if our calculations are right and if we are not being too fucking paranoid, should be out there tomorrow morning. We estimate that by the time you have delivered the goods to the drop-off point and get back to your plane, the nosy bastard should be about twenty miles due west of Heron Island. We need to know if he is there.

'Your extra job, therefore, is to fly out there and take a look-see before you fly back to Brisbane. I'll contact you when you are back in your office, and you can let me know the worst, or the best. Whatever the case may be, the Senator and I need to know.

'Now, I don't want you doing anything stupid like flying low at the bastard. On the contrary I want you to head out across Heron Island, towards where we think he may be, as high as you can possibly go. Just check if the ship is where we suspect it may be, then as soon as you sight it turn right and get the fuck out of there.

'Once I know whether we are imagining this or not I can work out a strategy for the future. Now, Edwin my man, any questions?'

Grant was surprised and pleased that he was getting the opportunity to clear up a few points, because if the *Palminto* was being tailed and monitored he had every reason to be really concerned about his future.

'How did you find out about this ship?'

'Sorry, man! Need to know applies here.'

402

'Okay then, what happens to our operations if this ship is for real and we are blown?'

'Well, that depends on who is doing the job on us. So far we have managed to track down the owners of the ship, and they are real cool. What we don't know yet, is who is paying them and pulling their strings.

'If we have been blown, then we will put into operation the withdrawal plans that we have discussed in the past. We can then all disappear and get on with our new lives in the style that we have only dreamed of to date. There is nothing to fear, Edwin. I promise you that it is not in the Senator's best interests for anything to happen to any one of us.'

The discussion lasted a further five minutes during which time Grant was debriefed on the previous two pick-ups in Cairns and Townsville. Felix seemed well pleased with the way that they had gone.

Then with a brief, 'Keep the faith, Edwin my friend', Felix left the car and disappeared into the blackness.

Grant waited a further ten minutes as he had been instructed before leaving the lay-by and driving back to his motel.

That night he had a very restless and disturbed sleep. The thought of imminent capture and imprisonment by the authorities worried him very much, but not half as much as the premonition of death which he just could not shake off.

★

The Senator was working very late that night. His office was in darkness other than for the reading lamp that sat on his desk by his telephone. At midnight exactly the phone rang.

'The man has been told, and will do what is required.'

'I'm sorry, but you obviously have the wrong number.'

'Everything is arranged and the contract termination has been set up to the satisfaction of all parties.'

'I haven't the faintest idea who you are. I've told you, you have the wrong number.'

'Sorry pal! I've made a mistake. Sorry to have bothered you.' Felix put down the receiver.

No bother at all, the Senator said to himself. I doubt, Felix my old friend, that our associate Grant will be satisfied with the contract termination arrangements that we have made.

★

The pick-up and drop-off went exceptionally well and Grant was very relieved to find the *Palminto* exactly where Felix assured him she would be. At least that part of the story was genuine. He had had a bad night, not only worrying about the possibility of arrest, but also fearful that Felix had something nasty up his sleeve for him.

The normality of that first sight of the *Palminto* removed most of his fears, so much so that he began to feel quite foolish for being so suspicious of Felix.

Once he had hidden the load in the usual place behind the derelict barn that was the site for the Rockhampton operation, he headed straight back to the airfield.

Getting all of the necessary clearances he took off shortly afterwards, and headed eastwards towards Heron Island. From there he would start to climb to his maximum height and set a course which would either lead him to the *Sea Knight*, or better still prove Felix's fears to be groundless.

The aircraft was still climbing when the explosion occurred. It was only a small explosion as explosions go, but it was big enough to wreck the front of the plane, smashing all the instruments and radio equipment whilst at the same time blowing off Edwin Grant's legs from the knees down.

He took a few moments to die, by which time the aircraft, or what was left of it, was in a screaming death dive. The only part that was reasonably intact when it hit the sea was the cabin section. Grant was dead by then and entombed in the cabin of his plane, his body eventually coming to its final resting place five hundred feet below the surface of the sea.

It would never be found. For security reasons Grant had registered a flight plan indicating his return to Brisbane by the most direct route. There would be no reason to search this part of the ocean for the missing Beechcraft, and it would have been unlikely that the explosion would have been heard or seen that far out to sea and at that altitude.

Felix had planned this well, both in terms of the size of the charge, and the timing device that would activate the detonator. He had also selected the position of the bomb to ensure that as well as disabling the craft in the most permanent way it would also destroy the instruments and radio. Yes, he had done his job well.

At the moment of his death, Edwin Grant had even commented on how well Felix had done his job. Well, sort of.

'Felix, you bastard. May you rot in he—'

His final word was not completed, because at that very moment a part of the cabin door was blasted off by the air pressure caused by the high speed that the plane was descending. The flying door part sliced off half of Grant's head, part-way through that final curse.

★

The Senator rang Felix on his secret number, using a scrambler phone in his office.

'Status report please, Mr Black.'

'Only one contract remains. The unsatisfactory road transport contract will be dealt with shortly.'

Replacing the telephone the Senator sat back in his large leather chair with a very satisfied smile on his face. Things were going extremely well.

*Part Four*

# Manly
# New South Wales

March 1997

# Chapter One

*Palminto* was enveloped in ghostly silence. It was nearly midnight and David Brandon had just given the order to stop engines and lower the anchor. He could see the bright lights of Manly Beach off to the right of his ship.

'Nothing on radar, sir,' came the report from the bridge officer.

'Thank you. Commence operations, Mr Raman.'

'Aye aye, sir.'

A bell rang below where he was standing and within a minute Brandon saw two groups of men suddenly appear on deck. One group ran forward to the large container at the bow of the ship. The second group made their way to the port, the seaward side of the ship.

The men were all dressed in black, not that it made much difference. The ship was four kilometres from the shore and it was pitch dark. What was about to happen on board *Palminto* could not have been witnessed by anyone outside the ship, but he never took chances.

The first group had reached the container and were unbolting the rear door, revealing the six blue surfboard-like containers. These were carried to the port rail of the ship where the other group had already suspended a rope ladder over the side and firmly secured it.

Once the six heroin-filled containers had been carefully laid on the deck the forward group returned to the large deck container and began the slow and laborious task of unbolting the brackets that secured the container to the ship.

There were seven men standing by the ladder which was swinging quietly against the side of the ship. They were dressed in black scuba-diving suits and hoods and wore black air tanks and equipment. Attached to each man's diving hood was a powerful headlamp. Their flippers were hung from their weight belts.

One by one the men climbed over the rail and descended the rope ladder to the water level. Hanging by one hand they used the other to release their flippers and put them on prior to entering the water. Each man then made the necessary equipment adjustments and trod water awaiting the commencement of their task.

Above them an electric crane quietly whirred into life. Two other men on the deck connected one of the surfboard-like containers to the four hooks suspended from the cable of the crane. Slowly the container was lifted over the rail and gently lowered to the sea below. As soon as it reached the water two of the divers swam forward and took up positions on opposite sides of the container, each man holding two handles. A third diver was checking to ensure that the men had control of their cargo before releasing each of the four hooks from the crane. The divers holding the container were very proficient and well practised in their tasks, and once it was released they immediately tilted it nose down and sank below the surface with their load.

As soon as the men submerged their headlamps came on automatically creating a strange underwater glow.

They guided their load under the ship and slowly headed downwards to the seabed. Their personal lights provided powerful beams which once clear of the confused surface water clearly illuminated the seabed ahead of them, giving excellent visibility for a distance of ten metres.

Twenty minutes later they came to a stop, poised above a massive oblong concrete block. There were six of these blocks in close proximity to one another and they were each attached to an anchor to help secure them against the fierce power of the tides. The men lowered themselves on to the block which had four chains attached to it, each of which had a large shackle on its end.

The divers connected each shackle to one of the four handles on their load. Once the object was safely secured to all four chains the men turned back towards the ship and after fifteen minutes began ascending slowly to the surface. On their way upwards they passed two other divers bringing another load to be secured to one of the concrete anchor points.

As the first two divers surfaced against the port side of the ship the third container was just being released for its journey down to the seabed.

The first team of divers waited patiently for their next load which was being lowered down towards them, together with replacement air tanks. The man whose job it had been to release the containers was also responsible for assisting the divers with the tank exchanges. The whole exercise went like clockwork.

*

Back on deck the group of men working on the big container had already unbolted the brackets holding it in place. Next, large holes were cut into the sides of the container with acetylene torches. Then a second crane was brought into action which lifted the large metal box and swung it out over the side of the ship where it hung suspended. The workmen then replaced all of the large bolts into the deck plate and tightened them down hard. The whole area was then hosed down with a high pressure steam hose. Later in the night that deck area would be dried and heavily spray-painted. No trace of the container would be discernible to man or beast. The paint contained substances that were designed to confuse and disorient sniffer dogs that tried to pick up any scent should that worst scenario eventuate.

By the time the steam cleaning was finished the seven divers had completed their tasks and were back on board. Their gear had been cleaned and their diving suits, hoods and gloves placed in the suspended container. The deck crews removed their outer clothing and gloves and these were also put into the container.

Petrol was sprayed on to the clothing and a lighted match was tossed into the container. The items burned fiercely for a short while, after which the large metal door of the container was slammed shut and the securing bolts pushed into place.

The container was then swung out away from the ship and lowered to the water. When it was just below the surface the crane operator paused the machinery momentarily to allow it to fill with water. He then released the load which sank slowly to the bottom of the sea. Yet again David Brandon had left nothing to chance.

Less than two hours after commencing the operation the order was given to start engines and move on. The rattling sound of the anchor chain pleased Brandon more than he had thought possible.

*Palminto* was squeaky clean once more, and on her way south. He was very relieved. This was his final run. He would never have to take such enormous risks, ever again.

## Chapter Two

*Samuel Frederick Thomas Alfred Peter Marven. What a mouthful!*

Sammy pondered over his great misfortune to have three uncles in a family that by tradition named its male members after the grandfather on the father's side, the grandfather on the mother's side, and any extraneous uncles that were hanging around at the time. The family also generally threw in the child's father's name. Luckily, his dad must have realised the great embarrassment that his only son would have to suffer throughout his life anyway, let alone saddling him with yet one further useless name.

He might as well have though, thought Sammy, as he laboriously worked his way through the immense document that he had received from the Immigration Department in Canberra. He was faced with two problems. Firstly the document was almost too difficult to understand, and secondly, there was not enough room for all his bloody names.

The penalties one has to pay for enjoying oneself. He forced a chuckle, and got back down to the complicated, and seemingly endless document.

He had arrived in Australia from Britain ten months before, intending to go everywhere and do everything. The trip had been paid for by his father, Lieutenant Colonel Douglas Marven, MC, DSC, retired, late of the Special Air Service, as a reward for obtaining his Bachelor of Arts degree in Ancient Greek History at the London School of Economics.

The Colonel had never stopped wondering why his only son, considered by others to be a reasonably bright specimen and proven to be a fine young athlete, had not followed him into the army. Worse still, why he had farted around at the LSE, known in his circles, the Army circles, as 'Rent-a-Riot', doing a degree that would be next to useless if ever Sammy decided to try to settle down. He thought that a long overseas trip, sowing some wild oats, would do the boy some good and if nothing else it might bring him back into the real world.

He suggested Australia to his son, because in his thirty years in the Army he had got to know numerous Australians, liking them as people and admiring them as soldiers. He was always amused by their irreverent approach to authority; their apparent determination to thwart the system, and perhaps the most important factor that Aussies seemed to consider as their creed; *mateship*. He had decided that a year or so living and mixing with these sorts of people would do his son the world of good. Specifically relevant also, was the fact that Australia was just about as far away from England as one could get.

To his delight Sammy had leapt at the idea and within weeks he was on a British Airways flight to Sydney, armed with a twelve month visa and work permit, obtained at very short notice with the kind assistance of a Special Branch friend of the Colonel who owed him a special favour. The favour was owed as the result of a particularly dangerous undercover operation that the SAS had carried out in conjunction with the Branch some years before when Marven was a captain. During the early stages of the operation things went frighteningly wrong and the Special Branch policeman's cover was blown. The actions taken by Marven and his men to try to salvage the situation had not only saved the reputation, but possibly the life of that particular Special Branch friend. Due to those circumstances the policeman had stated that this particular small favour was merely a freebie between friends which in no way could repay the debt. The Colonel, however, had insisted that the slate was now wiped clean.

★

Colonel Douglas Marven had good reasons for this attitude. He felt sure that he would need no further favours as that very morning his doctor had confirmed the results of tests that had been conducted over a three week period at a clinic in Harley Street, London's elite address for the nation's top medical consultants. His cancer was not operable. It was terminal.

'How long have I got, Doc?'

'If you do as I tell you, and if you are a wee bit lucky, possibly as much as a year or more.'

'What sort of quality of life will I have?'

'Apart from the pain, and the side effects of the treatment we will be giving you, you should be able to get about reasonably well for six months or so. After that there will be a steady deterioration in general health and mobility, a massive reduction in body weight, and ultimately it will lead to you becoming completely bedridden around nine months from now. From then on things will happen pretty fast, I'm afraid.

'I wish I could give you even a faint glimmer of hope, Douglas, but I cannot.' The doctor shrugged his shoulders, and getting out of his chair he walked across the room to look out of the surgery window at the windswept footpath below.

'How is Sammy managing things at the moment, Douglas? Christ! It was only a year or so ago that I sat with you in this room telling you that Samantha was dying. I remember all too well how badly he took his mother's

death. God only knows how he will cope with seeing you
going down hill fast and knowing that you are going to die
as well.'

'It's all under control, Doc. I have arranged for him to
have an extended working holiday in Australia for a year or
so. I pulled a few strings and jacked it up on the quick.

'I'm not totally stupid, my friend. I watched my wife
fade away to become a pain-racked skeleton, suffering the
extra agony and discomfort of the treatment, and the
indignity of having her body and its functions seize up on
her. I was too close to it not to pick up some of her feelings,
and to see how much Sammy suffered with her, especially
after her death.

'So it wasn't too long after my pains arrived that I knew
what was wrong with me. At least that it was something
critical. Then when I saw the look on the face of that
specialist bod in Harley Street I just knew that it was all up.
I've spent the last three weeks preparing myself for the
inevitable, and considering how best to help Sammy
through this. You are right, Doc, he wouldn't be able to
handle it at all. We are as close as father and son could ever
be, even closer since his mother died.

'Anyway, with him in the Antipodes and me here, with
our communications of the long-distance variety, he may
never cotton on. Until the very end, that is. I can put on a
good act and save him from all this provided that he doesn't
see me. None of my friends will let me down and we don't
have any family here in England. All I need is your
assurance that you won't let on, and I'll be home and
hosed.'

The doctor returned to his chair and sat pondering for a
minute or so with his chin resting on steepled fingers.

'Okay! I'll go along with your charade, but under great
protest. He's not a child and he is going to be rather pissed
off with someone when you do give up this mortal coil.

You are not going to be around to face his wrath, so guess who will be the patsy. Don't give me all that nonsense about privacy and patients' rights, and so forth. After all, I have known you and your family since you were a snotty nosed second lieutenant. I was at Sammy's bloody christening, for God's sake. Doesn't that give me some quasi-family rights?'

'Don't try that one on me, my friend. Sure, you are just about family, but this deal is between you the doctor and me the patient. Let me down and I'll sue the living shit out of you.

'And by the way, Doc, if you're claiming family rights I'll give you them, but with them goes family responsibilities. Get it?'

# Chapter Three

On his father's recommendation Sammy had intended to use Sydney as a base from which he would travel the length and breadth of the continent. In making this recommendation, not only had his father failed to understand the sheer enormity of such a feat but he had also misunderstood what moved and motivated his son.

The young man had learned to surf back in England on the rugged and treacherous coast of northern Cornwall, in surf that was more often than not a mass of roaring foam in which individual waves were indiscernible. As the result he was an accomplished rough sea surfer with better than average skills in staying on the board. He took one look at the beautiful, clean, and by English standards, enormous waves at Manly Beach and he was hooked. Coming from a place where the sea was invariably cool to downright cold, he also marvelled at the warmth of the water and its beautiful clean blues and greens.

Not only was Manly a fantastic beach for surfing, but if for any reason the sea was too rough or too smooth there were a dozen or more alternative beaches either north or south of Manly that could be accessed by road quite easily. He mainly stayed on the northern beaches, because to get to the southern surf one had to traverse Sydney Harbour and the city in order to reach them. He had transport, but the green Beetle VW he owned, whilst just about the most noticeable vehicle on the eastern seaboard of Australia, was not the most reliable and he was loathe to take it too far.

His love for the water had extended to the point where he had also recently taken up scuba-diving. With some basic guidance from a surfing friend who was also into diving, and the regular use of his gear, Sammy had become quite proficient.

However, in a phone conversation with his father a month or so before he had told about his underwater exploits and had been surprised at the forceful manner in which he had been reprimanded and cautioned about diving again until such time as he had been properly trained, and kitted out with his own reliable equipment.

His father's advice with regard most things physical, but especially diving, was not to be taken lightly. Sammy was fully aware that as a long-serving officer in the Special Air Service he was a professional highly skilled diver and advanced instructor, proficient in the use of some of the most advanced equipment in the world and experienced at great depths. Consequently, he had promised to do what his father told him.

The Colonel was concerned that Sammy might not be able to afford the training and the gear so he immediately arranged for a suitable sum of money to be deposited into his bank account. He hoped that this would take some pressure off his son, and that it would also create one further good reason for his son to continue his holiday.

The last thing that he wanted at that moment was for his son to terminate his stay in Australia, return home and discover his emaciated and bedridden father and realise that he had been lied to.

*

He need not have been concerned, because back in Manly nothing was further from Sammy's mind. This was why he was struggling so desperately with the complicated form that might enable him to extend his stay.

He was sitting astride the sea wall close to the boat ramp at the northern end of North Steyne, the Manly Beach esplanade. He had strategically placed himself in that position, partially to use the wall as a base on which to rest the form that he was endeavouring to complete, but mainly because there was always a possibility that some kind soul might recognise him and offer him a ride in one of the numerous speedboats, sailing boats and fishing boats that entered the water at this point daily.

There's that bloody boat again, he thought, looking up suddenly as a sporty-looking launch, blue and gold in colour, with the title *Jetset* emblazoned on the stern was being manoeuvred backwards on its trailer towards the water's edge by a late model 4WD Jeep.

I wonder if it has that weird hole in the back again. He recalled the three previous occasions that he had seen the boat and his curiosity was aroused.

There were several strange things about the boat and its occupants that caused him to remember it. It had an inboard jet engine with a massive Johnson auxiliary hung on the back, but it did not speed when in the water, certainly not in his sight. Furthermore, on each of the previous occasions he had seen it launched it had only been in the sea for a maximum of one hour.

The boat was manned by three men, all fully kitted up with dive suits, and there was a lot of very expensive-looking gear in the launch. However, in his opinion they were never out there long enough to justify the cost and trouble of a dive, and they did not appear to be equipped for fishing.

There was an even more significantly strange thing that he remembered. On each occasion that he had seen the boat enter the water there was a very noticeable oblong open slot at the stern, just below the waterline. It was almost as wide as the hull of the boat and about twenty centimetres deep. He had no idea what this was for, and had spoken about it to boat enthusiasts that he knew, only to find that they did not know what he was talking about. Some had suggested that he must be mistaken, because in their opinions such a hole would serve no useful function and could even hinder the craft's performance.

The real reason why he was so concerned to discover what this strange opening in the hull of the boat was for, however, was that on each occasion that the boat returned to the boat ramp after its brief excursion the open slot had disappeared.

Well, it hadn't actually disappeared. It was still there, but some object had been placed in it, filling up the hole. Now, as before whenever the boat was being launched, the open slot was quite visible.

There has got to be some simple and logical reason for it, he decided. But then, what in hell's name do I know about boats?

He wondered what his father would say if he told him all about this.

He'd probably tell me I'm a bloody idiot and to mind my own business.

He decided that he would tell him anyway, when he phoned him next.

Meanwhile, I'll do a bit of detective work and find out exactly what these guys are up to. He almost said out loud as the boat began to move slowly away from the ramp, heading out towards the open sea.

As on past occasions the boat disappeared out of sight northwards at a very slow speed. He remained in his position astride the wall and tried his hardest to concentrate on completing the form. It didn't work very well though, and it was with some relief that he saw the craft coming back around the headland, moving in towards the ramp. As it approached the ramp the boat swung around on a wave, and it was no great surprise to him to see that the slot was again filled with an object exactly the same colour as the boat.

★

The men on the boat eyed him suspiciously as they performed the task of winching the boat back on to its trailer. They were obviously aware that he was watching them. Seeing this, he smiled at them and gave them a friendly wave. One of them, a small man with very dark skin, possible a Negro, although he could not see properly as the man was wearing a diving hood, waved back and flashed a broad, white-toothed grin.

The boat secured, the crew all climbed into the Jeep which turned south along North Steyne and was soon lost to sight amongst the traffic.

Sammy checked his watch. As on each of the other occasions, the mystery men, because that was how he now categorised them, were back on shore in just over sixty minutes from the time of launching the boat.

Something very strange is going on here. Perhaps it's even illegal. I'll check it out further the next time I see that bleeding boat, he decided.

★

The very next day Sammy saw the Jeep and trailer, complete with boat and crew, heading once more toward the boat ramp. It was 11 a.m. and he had just returned from the Department of Immigration where he had lodged his application for the extension of his visa. He was in his VW, some way from the boat ramp and travelling in the opposite direction when the Jeep passed by. He was sure that they hadn't seen him so he did a quick U-turn and followed them.

He had already planned what he would do if he saw them again. The evening before he had sat in his bedsitter with a Sydney street directory and had plotted a radius of about four kilometres from the boat ramp. He felt sure that was the maximum distance that they could have travelled, dived, and then returned within the hour, as was their normal pattern of operation. He then decided that as the boat always turned north around the headland and that the trip was always of approximately the same duration there must be a specific location that they were heading for on each occasion.

He had shared his thoughts with a few of his pals and without exception they all thought him somewhat stupid, and like fair dinkum Aussies they told him so.

'The thieving sods are ripping off some poor bugger's cray pots,' was the general consensus.

'Stop being a Sherlock Holmes, or someone will be kicking your nuts in, you stupid Pommy bastard,' was the generally agreed recommendation to Sammy, a recommendation that he chose to ignore because he felt that something more interesting was going on.

★

Having made up his mind to find out what these men were doing he had continued working on his plan well into the night. Consequently when he woke up he felt quite tired. However, the sight of the Jeep and the fact that he was in pursuit, so to speak, revived him quite considerably. He was fired up and ready for whatever was to happen. Adjusting his rear-view mirror he checked out his diving gear and the pair of borrowed binoculars on the rear seat and smiled to himself. This was what he had really come to Australia for – adventure!

He drove past the boat ramp without even glancing to his right. He didn't need to. He knew they were there preparing to launch the boat, *Jetset*. He also felt sure that he knew where they were headed for, and proceeded on up round the headland to a quiet cul-de-sac overlooking the cliffs above the northern end of Fresh Water Beach, the next beach up from Manly. He had discovered this route to the cliff top from the street directory he had examined the night before.

Having made the decision to use this as his lookout point he was greatly relieved to find that the cul-de-sac had a footpath out on to the cliff edge. He felt sure that from that location he would be able to see the boat coming around the headland from Manly.

If his calculations were as accurate as he felt they must be, he should be able to see where they went to and perhaps even get some idea about what they were up to. The weather was perfect and visibility was at its best.

He parked the VW and made off towards the cliff edge, the binoculars slung over his shoulder. If anyone was watching him they would presume he was just another holidaymaker, or even a birdwatcher.

He mused over the birdwatcher theme.

Ornithology is not my thing, but birdwatching is right up my street. He chuckled to himself, thinking of the kind of birds that flocked to the northern beaches, particularly to Manly.

★

Sammy positioned himself near the cliff edge against the safety barrier at a point that gave him a magnificent view of the stretch of sea to the south that the boat would have to cross coming around from Manly Beach.

He didn't have to wait for too long. Only minutes after settling down at his observation point he saw the boat cruise sedately around the headland and move slowly up the coast heading directly towards where he was hidden.

Whilst he felt sure that they would not be able to see him he drew himself down closer to the ground, an old army trick that his father had once taught him. He also recalled him advising, 'Never point a pair of binoculars towards the sun, or any other form of bright light, Sammy. The reflection of the light on the lenses will give your position away to the opposition, no matter how well you are concealed.'

He must have been about eleven years old when his father gave him those instructions in what he referred to as field craft. He remembered it so well. It was on Dartmoor, and they were on holiday. They were playing hide and seek, but it was a rather sophisticated version, as they were using camouflage and binoculars. The opposition on that day were his grandfather and his mother, both of whom had since died tragically. Mum and Pops were really not that good at it so he and Dad gave them all sorts of chances and still won.

★

The boat was travelling northwards, parallel to the beach and about two hundred metres offshore.

They've got to do something soon. They must be ten minutes or so out of Manly. If they are going to do whatever they do and get back within the hour they have got to make their move now.

The boat was almost below him and it appeared as if it was going to cruise straight past, when suddenly it did a sharp ninety-degree turn to the right, picked up speed and headed out to sea. It got smaller and smaller. Even with his very powerful binoculars he was finding it increasingly difficult to pick out detail on the boat. Then, he came to the conclusion that the boat must have stopped. He would not normally have been able to tell from that distance whether it was moving or not. However, he decided that it must have stopped and dropped its anchor because it had swung around with its bow pointing into the southwards moving tide. Then he saw movement on the deck followed by a few splashes in the water alongside the boat.

They've gone over the side, he decided.

At this moment he was frantically thumbing through the pages of the street directory which he had brought with him. Once he found the correct page he drew a straight line out to sea from the point on the map where he calculated he was hiding. He wasn't a good judge of distances, but felt certain that the boat was just over a kilometre away from the shore. Even though he wasn't completely sure of his calculations he was very sure of the line which the boat had taken when it did its sharp right turn from the shore.

It suddenly dawned on him that he was lying on the grass in front of a four storey block of holiday flats. That was probably the marker the helmsman of the boat had used when he carried out that critical manoeuvre. Sammy felt that things were looking more sinister by the minute and he was becoming quite excited. His throat was extremely dry and he desperately needed a drink. This was how excitement normally affected him. He also needed a pee. He had brought nothing to drink, but he was at least able to roll over in the grass and discreetly satisfy the most urgent of his needs without breaking cover or being seen from the houses and flats behind him.

He was quite proud of this gymnastic feat, because throughout he had not taken his eyes off the boat. Then suddenly, he couldn't be sure if he was imagining things, but were there black figures bobbing in the water behind the stern of the boat?

Moments later the boat turned its bow towards the shore. With the tide as it was, Sammy knew this meant that it was again under power and heading back towards him. He was now shaking with excitement. Stage A of his plan had worked out exactly as he had planned. Even if he did not know what they had done out there, the timing was immaculate. They would be arriving back at the boat ramp in twenty minutes time. He would be there to tail them to wherever they went. Only he would not be in his VW. If they suspected him in any way they would be looking out for that car. He had borrowed a Holden ute from one of his surfing friends and it was parked just up the road from the boat club where they would hitch up to their trailer and recover the boat.

★

Sammy was delighted with the way in which his plans had turned out. He was sure these men were up to no good. Even if they were only ripping off someone's cray pots, he would have caught them at it, and that was exciting stuff. He had already decided that he would take no further action if that was all that they were up to. The Aussies have a sort of code about what they refer to as 'dobbing', and Sammy did not want to breach that code. He was sure that to do so could lose him friends.

However, he felt that he would take a lot of convincing that this was all that these very well-equipped men were up to.

I mean, it's sheer common sense that you wouldn't invest in a boat of that sort, have such obviously expensive equipment and a crew that large for a few crayfish. The bloody things are so cheap in the restaurants that this can't be what they are doing. It just doesn't make sense, he told himself while he sat in the ute waiting for the return of *Jetset* and its crew members who by now he was convinced were up to something sinister.

The Jeep swung out of the boat club into North Steyne and headed south. What Sammy then did he had seen done on the TV a thousand times. He already had the engine running, so he slipped the brake and moved off. To ensure some form of anonymity and be less conspicuous he let two cars get between himself and the Jeep and trailer, and kept way back. At South Steyne the Jeep turned off from the seafront and headed inland. It had only travelled a kilometre or so when it turned right into a small industrial area. As he drove past the intersection Sammy saw the tail of the trailer disappear into the entrance of a factory yard about one hundred metres or so from the main road.

'Frederick Street!' He spoke the name out loud, and noted it with the view to looking it up in the street directory later. He drove straight on without looking back.

★

He had completed Stages A and B of his plan. Stage C would happen that night after dark, when he would have a look inside the factory or whatever it was that the 4WD had entered, and examine that boat and trailer from close up.

That would probably be tricky because he had no breaking and entering experience or skills, and he might have to do just that to achieve his objective that night.

Whilst he wasn't looking forward to this particular adventure, he was sure that Stage D would be the really tricky one. That would take place the next morning. For this stage he had borrowed a dinghy with a 60 hp outboard.

He was going to see if he could find what it was they were diving for out there.

It would be quite difficult and probably even stupid, because all he had was a rough pencil line on a Sydney street map to indicate the course that the boat took from the shore, and his very rough guess as to how far out the boat went before it stopped. It was all very hit and miss.

How deep is it out there? What if the current is dangerous? he asked himself as he pondered his crude map.

If I am as much as half a degree out in my estimations I will miss the spot by a bloody mile, or at least enough to make it impossible to find whatever it is that they were diving for. That's the bloody point that you are missing, Sammy, he told himself.

What if the dive they made today removed the last of whatever it was they were after? What is the point in looking for something that isn't there any more? he thought.

Common sense told him that he was almost certainly wasting his time, but then Sammy was the sort of person who, once he got his teeth into something, would not let go regardless of the dictates of common sense.

I've got this far, I might as well go the whole way, he told himself. Didn't someone once say something about it not being the destination, but the journey that counts. Jeez! Now I'm getting all philosophical about it. This is nonsense.

At that moment he arrived outside the house which contained his bedsit, and became preoccupied with trying to find somewhere to park the ute in a street already crowded with old cars and vans mostly fitted with roof-racks adapted for carrying surfing gear. The plan was that his friend would pick it up later whilst Sammy was doing late shift at McDonald's. He had to be careful not to park illegally as a parking ticket was definitely not part of the arrangement.

# Chapter Four

The evening shift went very slowly for Sammy even though the store was extremely busy with masses of holidaymakers, mainly with young kids enjoying a cheap evening snack before making their weary way home to their holiday flats or hotel rooms.

He found it very hard to concentrate on what he was doing because of the excitement that was building up inside him. Stage C of his elaborate plan was to involve breaking into the yard of the premises at Frederick Street where he had last seen the Jeep and its trailer. He was fully aware that if caught by the police he would be treated as a criminal. They were hardly likely to be as convinced as he was that something unlawful was being carried out by the men with the boat, but would concentrate their efforts on ensuring that the illegal breaking and entering that Sammy was about to do was punished.

He considered all the pros and cons and was disturbed by the fact that the cons far outweighed the pros. In fact, the more he considered Stage C the more he became convinced that there were no pros at all, and that if he proceeded with his night's plans he would end up in the hands of the New South Wales Police – well and truly nicked.

So intent was he on his plans and the probability of them being a disaster that he failed to perform very well for McDonald's during the late shift, and he incurred the wrath of the shift manager.

'Get your bloody act into gear, Sammy, or you are for the chop. There are plenty of people out there looking for a job like yours,' said the manager after the third mistake that he made.

'What's wrong with you, man? You're behaving like a bloody zombie. Wake your ideas up, or else.'

The threat was more than implied, which caused him to concentrate a lot harder than he had been doing so far during the evening. Concentrate on the boss's business, that is.

Sammy was genuinely concerned about the possibility of losing his job. He knew that he had only got it because he was recommended by a few of the staff who were in the surfing fraternity. He was in fact considerably older than most of the other employees even though he was only just twenty-two. He was also a Pom, the Aussie name for English people, which in some ways made him more vulnerable when dealing with a few of the shift managers.

The guy on at the moment was all right. He was only twenty years old and his father was of English origin, so he had been prepared to give Sammy a go. Tonight was a different matter altogether though for he was behaving most strangely. The manager had even considered the possibility that he was on drugs, but discounted the notion because of Sammy's reputation for open aggression towards anyone who was into that scene.

In the event he decided that perhaps Sammy wasn't well and gave him the benefit of the doubt; for that shift anyway. At the completion of the shift he made quite a point of ensuring that Sammy was left in no doubt about his future work prospects if he behaved in a similar manner again.

Thanking him for his consideration Sammy assured him that it wouldn't happen again. Back in the car park he sat in his car for quite a while going over his plans for the exercise he was about to embark on. He was suffering from an acute attack of last minute nerves. However, his anxiety to find out what was happening eventually got the better of him. He started up the engine and drove off towards Frederick Street and whatever he may discover there.

★

He had already planned to park a few streets away and approach the factory on foot. If things went wrong he didn't want to be traced because his car was seen at the scene. He smiled to himself as he recalled the detective series where he had seen that plan being carried out by a crook. However, the memory of that series renewed his worries about being caught in the act and the thought of him being considered to be a crook and what this might do to his relationship with his father was his main concern at that moment.

What would Dad say if he knew what I am about to do? he asked himself. Blimey, he is in the SAS so he must have done this sort of thing a hundred times over. Sammy tried to justify his intentions.

Parking the car near to, and facing into an intersection was the next part of the plan. This was also borrowed from the same TV series, but was nonetheless good common sense. If he had to make a run for it he didn't want to find himself hemmed between other vehicles when he returned to his car.

What the bloody hell am I thinking of? Make a run for it in this clapped-out old heap? Get wise, Marven. Stop kidding yourself that this is like on the TV. What you are doing is pretty bloody dumb, he told himself for the tenth time that evening.

Nonetheless he was still determined to do it and the plan for parking the car was most sensible, he was convinced. At least he would be able to leave the area without too much hassle once Stage C was over.

It was not that easy. Every street within a couple of blocks of Frederick Street was jammed solid with parked cars. Every one of the streets had vehicles parked right up to the intersections. He was surprised that the police hadn't purged the neighbourhood the same way that they had done on a few occasions where he lived.

They obviously hadn't though, and his cleverly planned strategy with regard to parking was about to be abandoned when to his surprise he saw a small truck driving away from the street he was turning into leaving a very good space for him to slip the VW into, right alongside an intersection. Making sure that the car was locked securely he made off towards Frederick Street to try to find the premises that the Jeep and trailer had entered.

★

Luck was again with him, for when he reached the factory area he noticed that the street lights were out at the end of the street where he was going to have to conduct his criminal activities. In the dark there would be less chance of being discovered, he hoped.

Unfortunately he found that the darkness also had a negative side in that he couldn't tell exactly which gateway the Jeep had driven into. There were four gateways alongside each other, the middle two leading to factory premises built on rear plots of land. Not having any previous experience in this sort of thing he hadn't equipped himself with a torch to cover this eventuality.

Shit! I'll have to climb over the first fence and work my way along if needs be. He cursed himself for not doing a reconnaissance during the daytime. How stupid of me not to bring a bloody torch. How am I going to see what's inside the building, if I ever find it?

Climbing over the gate was easier said than done. The first one was very high and did not feel very secure. It was pitch dark, so it wasn't until he was halfway up that he noticed that the top was covered with some very evil-looking rusty barbed wire. He decided that it was not worth risking injury, or even tearing his clothes, so he climbed back down and moved along to the next gate.

This was a lot better. A big sturdy gate with a crossbar halfway up that made it very easy to scale. Within seconds he found himself on the ground on the other side of the fence and knelt and waited for a while in case the noise made by his exertions had disturbed any person or animal.

He hadn't even thought of this possibility before which made him feel angry with himself, and not a little bit stupid. He sized up the inside face of the gate to plan the best way to climb back over in the event of being confronted with either dog or human. It was even better than the outside face of the gate in that it had two crossbars, which gave him some relief.

He remained still for what seemed like an eternity, but was probably only a couple of minutes, by which time he felt pretty sure that the factory yard he was in was not guarded by man or watchdog. Feeling secure again he started off along the driveway towards the large warehouse-type structure he could just make out at the rear of the land.

As he approached the building he began to feel nervous again but it took just a few seconds to realise that his fears were unwarranted. The building was open, and empty.

Which way now? he wondered. If I try the one on the left I might have to contend with that bloody barbed wire on top of the gate. The thought of it was sufficient to convince him to go to the premises on the right.

As luck would have it there were several large holes in the fence leading into the yard of the premises.

Probably due to the fact that the neighbouring business is empty, he surmised. No point in securing the fence. Thank God for a bit of good luck.

He reached the building in a low crouch and flattened his body against the wall. Even in the dark he could see that these premises were very well maintained and obviously in regular use. He looked around to get his bearings and realised that he was crouching in the middle of a well laid out flower bed. This startled him because he didn't want to leave footprints anywhere. He realised, however, that he was panicking unnecessarily as the ground was rock hard. Apart from some small damage to a few plants he would not be leaving any evidence that could identify him.

After waiting for a moment he rose to his feet and began making his way around the building which looked like it could be a warehouse. There were no windows and the main entrance comprised two very large hanging doors that were large enough to give access for a substantial-sized truck. Everything was locked very securely and there was no way that he was able to see inside the building. He was disappointed, but after going around the building once more and finding no other means of access he decided to try the next building to the right. He felt sure that this would have to be the last one that could possibly have been used to house the Jeep and its trailer.

Approaching the adjoining fence he saw that a waste disposal dumper bin was positioned quite close to the boundary between the two premises. He looked through the wire mesh fence and although it was dark he was able to see that the ground on the other side was covered in thick grass and did not appear to have any nasty things concealed in it that could injure him if he landed on them. This was important to him, as he had made the decision to climb on top of the bin and use it as a launching pad for a leap over the top of the fence. He was a fairly fit and agile young man and could see no problem in completing the jump safely, even in the dark.

The dumper bin had two lids, one of which was open. He climbed up on the side framework intending to close the lid prior to climbing on to the top of the bin. Just as he was about to close the lid the moon appeared from behind a cloud and lit up the area quite brightly. It was so sudden and so bright that Sammy felt totally exposed. Temporarily panicking he dived down into the open end of the bin where he discovered that he was lying amongst piles of waste paper and cardboard. He quietly murmured a prayer of thanks that that he was not sharing the bin with anything nasty or smelly. He stayed there without moving a muscle, waiting for the darkness to return.

The moon had almost gone behind a cloud and he was about to climb out of his hidey-hole when something caught his eye. In the corner of the bin nearest to him lay a yellow life jacket. As soon as darkness returned he pulled the jacket towards him and tried to examine it as best he could in the bad light. It was torn and had obviously been discarded as rubbish.

So it's a life jacket. So what? he pondered. Everyone and his dog has got at least two of the bloody things here in Manly. It doesn't mean a thing.

He was just about to throw it down when the moon suddenly reappeared with a vengeance. The light was brighter than before, and he found himself once again digging down into the rubbish trying to blend with the contents of the bin. Then he saw it. He was still clasping the life jacket and was holding it very close to his face. He couldn't believe his luck. The word *Jetset* was roughly inscribed on the inside of the article with a felt pen of some sort.

'Got you!' He started to shout out loud, suddenly lowering his voice to a whisper. 'Got you! Got you! Now we'll really find out what is going on around here.'

How though? His senses suddenly returned as he realised that he must have made a loud noise. You can't get into the bloody building, Sammy boy. So, smart-arse, what now?

Without thinking he leapt to his feet and with no further consideration for concealment he climbed out of the bin and ran to the nearby wall of the large building. The moon was still illuminating the area very brightly as he took off at a jog around the perimeter walls. He knew that he just had to find a way into the building while he still had some light, and had almost circled the building when he saw what he was looking for.

At the base of the wall was a small trapdoor about a metre tall. From its position he was sure that it would give access into the main building, but sadly it was secured with a hefty steel padlock. He tried to force it open with his hands.

He chuckled to himself. Okay, Mr Puniverse. Who do you think you are kidding? It will take a very heavy hammer to break that bugger open.

He was now suddenly aware that he was standing in virtual daylight, such was the brightness of the moon, in full view of the rear of a row of houses in the street backing on to Frederick Street.

All I need now is to be seen by an insomniac with as vivid an imagination as I have, and I'll be deep in the proverbial shit. Time to go home, Sammy old lad. He looked down at the padlock and sighed.

I'll tackle that lock later when I have the right tools for the job, he promised himself as he darted back to the hole in the fence that he had entered through. Within a minute he was over the front gate and back on to the street just as the moon helpfully ducked behind a cloud once more, leaving the area in darkness. He checked his watch. It was exactly forty minutes since he had parked his car.

★

He saw nobody after leaving the warehouse, not that he really expected to at that time of night. He took no chances though, and moved back and forth between the darker parts of the streets that he hurried through. The VW was where he had left it. He laughed at himself for even thinking that it wouldn't be. Christ above, who would steal this old bomb?

He was on a big high by the time he reached the car. What he had just done was really scary, yet it was also the most exciting thing he had ever done in his life. His hands were trembling as he fumbled to get the key in the door lock. As he sat down in the driver's seat the trembling got worse and he began to sweat profusely and feel very uncomfortable and insecure. It occurred to him that he was probably suffering from delayed nerves, bordering on shock. He certainly was in no condition to drive the car so he decided that he had no choice but to sit back and wait for the shakes to subside.

Later, as the shaking sensation wore off he began to feel more in control. He then began to feel quite foolish about the manner in which his body had reacted to the events of the evening.

So much for thinking you're a hard case, Sammy, he thought, as with hands as steady as a rock he placed the key into the ignition, started the car, and drove off towards home and his bed.

# Chapter Five

Phil Cartwright was very tired but he knew that if he did not make it to Bondi before dawn he would be exposed, and very vulnerable. Ever since he'd begun making his plans to safeguard his future he had been almost regretting what he'd done. That was, however, until a few days earlier in Brisbane.

In Rockhampton he had collected the holdall from the hole in the ground behind the derelict barn as he always did at that pick-up. He then stashed the bags of heroin inside the meat carcasses in the normal way, locked and sealed the refrigerated container and drove south towards Brisbane where two days later he visited his flying friend, taking with him the photographs that he had taken of Grant and his plane at the Brighton Hill Flying Club outside Cairns. He had had the film developed and printed at one of his stopover towns on the way down.

He was quite satisfied with the results, not that the photographs meant much to him, they were just photos of an aeroplane and a man, but they were good quality pictures which was all he had been aiming to achieve. He needed his pilot mate to be able to identify the man in the photographs, tell him something about him and advise where he could be found if the need arose.

Phil was totally convinced that Felix would kill him if he knew what he had been planning, yet he was also convinced that once he had outlived his usefulness Felix would kill him anyway. This was precisely why he was arranging his

440

special sort of insurance policy. Whilst he felt sure that there was no way that Felix could have known what he was up to he still couldn't help feeling apprehensive as the days progressed.

I'll identify this pilot from Brighton Hill then I'll lie low for a while. Go somewhere for a holiday perhaps. Somewhere where Felix will never think of looking for me, even if he cared to. He tried to reassure himself with this thought, particularly the bit about Felix not caring where he was.

If only I could really believe that, he had thought at the time.

★

His friend John was very pleased to see him again. This was due to the fact that whenever Phil required a favour he always repaid it in a worthwhile way, either in cash or special favours, sometimes both. On the last occasion Phil had taken him to a strip club for a night out. John had never seen table-top dancing before and couldn't believe his eyes when he saw what it was all about.

A married man, with a pretty but boring wife who made no secret about her dislike for sex, he was thrilled by the sexual encounters of that evening.

Not only did he have naked women displaying their personal attributes from very close up, but at one stage one of them straddled him and simulated the sex act, to the great delight of the rest of the club's male clientele. Simulation or not, it was almost better than the real thing for John.

The favour he had done for Phil had involved a special flight which had saved the man a considerable amount of money. On top of which the stuff that he was transporting from Queensland was ripping off the taxman in New South

Wales, a highly illegal and dangerous pastime. Phil had, as always, paid him cash in hand. The evening out, however, was a special favour between mates and thrown in as a bonus.

John decided that night that Phil must have made more on the deal than he had anticipated, because halfway through the evening he arranged for a move into a back room where two of the table dancers performed privately for them, ending up in a very wild sexual interlude which by John's standards was an orgy of great proportions. He could not get over what he had done, and what had been done to him during that evening by both of the young women at the same time.

That night when he eventually got into his own bed his wife had frigidly turned her back on him, as usual. However, he could not repress the enormous smile of contentment that engulfed his face as he immediately lapsed into a deep sleep.

*

Phil had already briefed John by phone about the photographs and what he wanted him to do with them. He didn't explain why, but then he never did explain his business affairs. John neither expected him to, nor would he dare think of asking. He knew that whatever Phil was up to was certain to be illegal, but even though he did certain little jobs for him John never saw himself as being a criminal also. He felt sure that if the worst came to the worst he would be able to satisfy a court of law that he genuinely thought he was carrying out normal commercial contracts whenever he did such work.

He invited Phil into his little office and offered him a beer. This is bound to be a boozy day, so we may as well start early, he thought to himself as Phil sat down, pulled the top off his stubby and took a long swig from the bottle.

Taking a Kodak envelope from his jacket pocket Phil passed it across the table.

'I want you to identify the bloke in these pictures and tell me all about him, and where I can find him if I need to. There's two hundred in it for you and I might be persuaded to take you out on the piss again if you do a good job of it.'

John enthusiastically opened the envelope and took out the wad of colour prints which he laid out on the table.

'Beechcraft! It's a Beechcraft four-seater, late model, say a year old. It looks in good nick. I don't recognise the livery though. The colours aren't from one of the major contractors, nobody that I work with anyway.'

At that moment John stopped dead. The hand lifting the second print froze in mid-air. Phil saw with surprise that all of the blood had drained out of his friend's face which was now deathly pale. Then he began to shake as if overcome by a violent fever.

'What the fuck are you involving me in, Phil? I don't know what you are into but count me out,' he blurted, throwing the print back across the table and pushing the remaining photographs away from him as if they were diseased.

Phil was physically shaken by the man's violent reaction: to what? What was he so distressed about?

'What are you talking about, John? What's up, man? All I want you to do is identify a bloke. What's so bloody terrible about that?'

John was on his feet now, and grabbing at the pile of photographs he shoved them into Phil's hands and pointed towards the door.

'If you think I am going to get involved with murder you have another think coming, Phil. Get the hell out of here and leave me alone from now on. I know I have been a soft touch, but not any more.'

By now Phil was getting pretty mad. 'If you don't tell me what you are talking about I'll punch your bleeding head in, you dopey bastard,' he snapped, grabbing at John's shirt front and pushing him back into his chair.

'Tell me what you are talking about, or else.' The threat in his voice was very real.

Suddenly it occurred to John that Phil really didn't know what he was talking about.

'That bloke. The one in the photo. He's dead! Some bastard has done him in. They can't find him. The word going around the pilots is that somebody bumped him off for welshing on a drugs deal,' he choked out the words.

Phil sat down with a start.

'Oh Christ!' was all he could say.

★

In the following ten minutes or so John explained to Phil that the pilot in the photograph was a man named Edwin Grant. He had been flying out of Rockhampton, strangely out to sea and not on his registered flight path, when his plane disappeared.

'That doesn't mean that someone has murdered him, you idiot.'

'Listen to the rest before you write the story off,' demanded John.

'The guy was flying way above what a plane of that sort, on the sort of tourism business he was into, would normally fly. There would be no need to fly above three thousand feet, and he was at about fifteen thousand or more. For a start that is very strange. Secondly, the plane was actually seen to blow up. This guy I know was doing a

bit of illegal fishing when he saw the thing go up in flames.
It was him who told me how high the plane was.

'Not much of the plane stayed afloat, but he actually
picked a bit of the wing out of the water. Now believe me,
Phil. This bloke was in Vietnam about the same time as
you. He was an explosive expert in the engineers. He said
that the explosion wasn't caused by no aviation fuel, but
dinkum explosives of the nasty variety. He chucked the
debris back into the sea and pissed off pretty smart.

'Now, I know that the bit of wing was recovered and
was looked at by the air safety experts. They should have
been able to suss out what happened to that plane with all
their scientific whiz-bangery, but nothing has been said. I
think this is a bloody great cover-up, so whatever happened
they have got to be involved in some way.

'Oh, and another thing my mate told me which is also
very strange. He has this bit of crumpet at Rockhampton
where he lives. Naturally his wife doesn't know anything
about her. To make sure it stays that way he takes her out
in his car and they get their rocks off out in the bush, off
the road somewhere. Well, the night before Grant's plane
went up my mate was parked one hundred metres or so off
the roadway near a lay-by on the road to Yeppoon. He
heard a couple of cars arrive at the lay-by, so went to have a
look, just in case it was his wife and her brother coming
after him.

'He saw this white bloke who he swears was Grant,
from the pictures on the TV. He was having a less than
friendly chat with a little black man who sounded as if he
was a Yank. It seems like the black guy was in charge and
was laying the law down to Grant. From what my mate saw
the white guy Grant was scared shitless. That may not
amount to much to you, Phil, but as far as I'm concerned
that Grant fella was murdered. If you have some interest in

or involvement with that poor bastard then I can no longer afford you as a mate.'

Nothing Phil could do or say would change John's mind. Even an offer of a larger than usual amount of cash was no good. He was real scared and made no bones about it. Eventually Phil had to leave, and even as he walked out John was throwing things into a large bag, and it was obvious that he was clearing out, at least for the time being.

# Chapter Six

That meeting had played on Phil's mind ever since, and he was beginning to feel as scared as he had ever been. Driving through Manly at this time of night was not altogether smart, but he wanted to keep off the main routes as much as he could. He knew that no matter what happened he would have to go through the Harbour Tunnel. However, once he had achieved that he should be fairly safe.

He was supposed to deliver the consignment no earlier than 6 a.m. that day. All he had to do was reverse into the loading bay of a certain freezer warehouse in the southern suburbs and deliver the designated carcasses as if they were a normal consignment of meat. The cold store man was probably the person responsible for moving the stuff to its next location, but Phil wasn't really interested any more. He felt quite sure that he had stuffed things up enough already by poking his nose in where it didn't belong.

He hoped and prayed that if he had, and if Felix got to know that he had, the steps he had taken to insure himself would be enough to save his life. However, his doubts about that had grown stronger by the hour.

*

Just at that moment he saw a green Volkswagen come screaming out of the road to his right. He had been day-dreaming about his concerns and hadn't been fully concentrating. The result was that the big truck was just slightly over the centre line of the fairly narrow roadway. The VW driver was driving far too fast and didn't quite make the left turn that he was obviously intending. The tiny car smashed broadside on into the rear wheel of the prime mover of the articulated truck and was thrown off towards the kerb where it ploughed into a lamppost, this final collision bringing it to a violent halt.

Suddenly Phil Cartwright was wide awake. He brought his truck to a standstill within metres as he hadn't been travelling very fast when the collision occurred.

Christ almighty! he thought as he leapt down out of the cab. As if I didn't have enough fucking worries, without this.

He ran across to where the crumpled VW stood. He noticed that the right wheel arch was smashed in where it had collided with the rear wheels of his prime mover. The driver's door was wide open, probably sprung open by the force of the impact with the lamppost. The driver, a man, was slumped over the steering wheel, and Phil immediately noticed that he had his seat belt done up.

'Thank the Lord for that,' he grunted as he leaned forward into the VW. Stretching across over the driver he undid the belt. As he did this the man fell sideways towards him, making it very easy for Phil to lay him down on the roadway immediately alongside the car.

Shit! Aren't I supposed to leave him where he is? Too late now, he thought as he gently moved the man, who he decided was probably only about twenty-one years of age. He was deeply unconscious and bleeding quite badly from a large wound on his forehead. Phil had forgotten most of what he felt he should have known about first aid, but he did remember that unconscious people should be laid on their side in the foetal position, or did they call it the lateral position these days? He had only just completed this act when a police car came to a sudden halt beside them.

★

It didn't take long for the police officer, who was probably even younger than the unconscious driver, to check the young man's injuries and call for an ambulance. By this time a small crowd had begun to gather. Most of them were the worse for alcohol, and had probably turned out of local clubs, or were making their way home on foot after disembarking from one of the very late ferries from Sydney. It amazed Phil just how many people were out and about in the middle of the night. He wasn't used to this up north where he came from.

A breakdown truck appeared, seemingly out of nowhere, and the policeman arranged for the crashed car to be moved. For some reason he went to great lengths to explain to Phil that he was moving it rather than leave it where it was to be stripped down by the local thieves, many who were almost certainly amongst the crowd of onlookers. Phil was very surprised to be given this level of information, but having been on the road most of his life he guessed that the breakdown man would probably see the cop all right for a few dollars for giving him the tow job. That was really the way of life out on the road.

Everyone makes a buck. He smiled to himself at the thought. And why shouldn't they?

★

The ambulance arrived before the policeman could take all the notes that he needed for the accident report so he directed Phil to accompany him in the police car to the hospital. He wanted to decline because of the troubles he had anyway, not the least of which was that this meant leaving his truck parked with a fortune in drugs stashed away inside frozen meat carcasses. However, he knew that if he did not co-operate with the police he could end up in a lot of extra unnecessary grief, on top of that which he already had.

Grudgingly, and with some serious misgivings he got into the police car. The cop had assured him that the truck and its contents would be looked after by the police.

Yeah! Whoopee! Phil thought. You bastards will steal half the fucking meat and leave the rig with no wheels if you get a chance.

He hoped that the street yobs who were eyeballing at the scene would stick around until he got back from the hospital. The thought of any of the carcasses with the drugs inside disappearing brought him out in a cold sweat.

At the hospital he gave his details and was given a piece of paper by the policeman on which was written the name and address of the young VW driver, a Samuel Marven. After nearly half an hour of generally being stuffed around Phil was told he could either go, or wait for the cop to finish his work, at which time he would give him a lift back to his truck. He chose to go and telephoned for a cab from the foyer of the casualty department.

While he was waiting for the cab to arrive he decided to have a look into the cubicle where the young man, Marven was. He was interested to discover whether he had regained consciousness. Not that he felt overly full of the milk of human kindness, but he did want to be sure that the guy wasn't permanently damaged in any way.

If he's conscious I'll give the silly bastard a piece of my mind.

As he approached the cubicle he heard a voice calling out. The voice had a strong, refined English accent. He recognised the accent immediately, having served with a lot of Poms in Aussie units in Vietnam. A nurse drew the curtains back into place as she walked out of the cubicle.

'Don't worry. He is still not conscious, but he will be all right. He's slightly delirious at the moment. He keeps talking about a little black man and a boat, and something about diving too. I can't let you in there though. Sorry!'

Phil thanked her and was halfway to the outside door of the casualty department when a bombshell hit him.

Oh my God. It can't be. It's got to be a coincidence. No, it's too much of a coincidence. Sweet Jesus! That guy knows Felix? He must do. How many little black men are there in this sodding place?

Having been given Sammy's name and address by the police officer Phil made up his mind to contact him at some stage to find out more about his little black man, if only to satisfy himself that it either was or wasn't Felix.

Meanwhile, he decided to warn the kid as discreetly as possible. To make sure that the young man got the message directly Phil scribbled a brief note on a scrap of paper and tucked it into the top pocket of the shirt lying over the chair near the bed. The message merely read:

> *Keep away from the black man. He is dangerous. I will contact you.*

Phil Cartwright was cold yet sweating when he got out of the taxi, climbed back into his truck and continued on his journey.

# Chapter Seven

His instructions were that he was to drive to a certain freezer warehouse in Sydney's south. The warehouse was open all night, but he was not to deliver before six. He was instructed to park the trailer in a specifically designated bay and connect up to the power supply on the wall of the bay. He then had to drive away from the premises sounding three short and two long blasts of his horn as he drove out of the gateway of the yard. It was always the same routine. The only difference on each occasion was the venue to which he had to deliver. This information was always passed on to him over the CB radio the evening before.

He assumed that at the truck horn signal the next stage of the process would commence, and that another delivery-man would take possession of the heroin and move it on to its next destination. Until very recently he had never concerned himself with what happened to the consignment once he had left it. Now he was beginning to wish that he had not changed that approach, and kept his nose out of Felix's business.

Not too many days before he had decided to watch what happened after he had deposited the trailer, to add strength to his well-planned insurance policy. However, things had changed dramatically since his startling meeting with his pilot mate, John.

With the news of Grant's sudden demise, which like John he was now sure was murder, he felt that his turn could be next. It all made sense. Felix and his boss had obviously decided to chuck it in and cut their losses, for whatever reason. If this was the case then people like him and Edwin Grant were an inconvenient liability for them. He tried to put himself in their shoes, and decided that in their circumstances he would also probably feel more comfortable if everyone else was out of the equation. Yet he doubted that he would have had the guts to follow through with any terminal action like that which caused Grant's premature demise, not unless his own life depended on it.

He went over every possible scenario time and time again and always came to the same conclusion. From the moment he delivered that trailer and sounded the signal on the horn he would be open to attack of some sort, but it was logical that Felix would be more likely to wait until he was well away from the delivery zone before taking any action.

What if I just dump the load? No, that's no good! That would definitely lead the cops to the dope, which would open up a hornet's nest for me, and everyone else concerned. That would certainly make me a marked man, if I'm not already.

'What if I have got this all wrong and Grant's death was an accident? If I do anything unexpected and that is the situation, then I will drop myself in the shit for nothing. No! I must cover my tracks, just in case Felix is fair dinkum. But I must do it in a way that at the worst looks like an oversight. I'd better fake a breakdown that prevents me from doing the delivery as per my instructions.

However, after hours of mental torment he decided that the best plan of attack was to deliver the trailer, pretty much on time, but not quite. He also decided not to sound the horn signal. His excuse for not sounding the horn would be that it malfunctioned at the critical time. To support this story if that became necessary he doctored the mechanism so that it would not work. If examined by anyone but a real expert it would look like a genuine breakdown.

If his concerns really were misguided, at least this story could possibly get him out of any trouble with Felix.

★

He arrived at the freezer warehouse half an hour early and pausing outside the gate he had a good look around. Everything seemed quiet. There wasn't even a security person in the gatehouse, so he put the truck into low gear and as quietly as possible moved slowly into the yard.

Backing into the bay and uncoupling the trailer was carried out in far less time than he had ever managed before. He was sure that he had disturbed nobody. The sounds of the freezer motors and fans inside the warehouse were very noisy, and he felt sure that they would certainly have blocked out the sound of his truck. His only danger of being seen would be if one of the freezer workers came out into the yard for a quick smoke. He was in luck and never saw anyone.

So, at 5.40 a.m. precisely he moved forward to the exit side of the gateway. Just in case he was being watched he went through the motions of pulling the toggle of the horn. He even put on a small charade, feigning concern at the lack of noise from the horn.

You may get killed, Phil my old son, but you'll probably get a bloody Academy Award while you are at it. Even though he felt terribly tense at the time he managed to force a wry smile.

From the warehouse he took a devious and well-planned route to his final destination, an empty warehouse in Bondi that he had used in the past for certain of his other illegal activities. He had planned to abandon the prime mover there until he was sure that Felix was not after him.

The location was perfect in every way, and the building was just tall enough for his prime mover which fitted in with only centimetres to spare. From the outside it seemed a very unlikely place to find a truck as it just did not look big enough. It was situated in a street of commercial premises, so Phil was reasonably sure that he had not been seen entering the building.

Once he had stowed the truck he locked the doors of the building from the inside and stretched out on the bed in the rear of the vehicle cabin. He was asleep within minutes and stayed that way for nearly twelve hours.

*

The warehouse was equipped with a very basic toilet with a wash handbasin and power point. After washing and dressing he changed into a clean set of clothes. He had a suitcase packed with sufficient clothing and toiletries for a ten day stopover, which was what he planned to give himself.

That evening after dark he let himself out of the warehouse and double-locked the door behind him. He walked two or three kilometres, changing direction several times to ensure he wasn't being followed before hailing a cab to Sydney's Kingsford Smith Airport. At the airport he checked in under the name of Dennis Jardine.

Just prior to boarding his flight to Melbourne he made two phone calls. The first was to his wife. He told her that his business had been extended and that he had picked up a load to take south to Victoria. This was nothing unusual for someone in the trucking business and his wife merely accepted this news as the norm when you are married to a truckie, not that she cared too much. He promised her he would call her later in the week.

*

His next call was to a man named Kevin O'Reilly who occupied an office at King's Cross. His business was import and export, or that was what the shingle on the office door implied. Phil had been conducting some interstate import and export work on behalf of O'Reilly for some months now. The work was just as illegal as that he did for Felix. Some people might see it as even more illegal as it involved the movement of firearms and explosive materials.

He had no idea what O'Reilly did with the stuff, but he was paid well enough not to want to know. The man had a broad Northern Irish accent and Phil had the vague idea that he was involved in Irish politics in some way because of various comments he had made from time to time in relation to media reports on violent incidents in that part of the world.

O'Reilly had been expecting him to pick up a special consignment on his behalf the following evening. Phil had already been instructed that the job was important and urgent but in view of the Grant affair he did not dare hang around in Sydney any longer.

As expected O'Reilly was not pleased, and like Felix he was not a man to be taken for granted. He was obviously aware that he was not Phil's only client but was not in the least interested in those other clients. He merely wanted his own business carried out without any hitches. During the conversation he became so threatening that Phil felt it wise to make some form of explanation as to why he couldn't do the job. He hoped that the Irishman would understand and not give him any further aggro.

'Look, Kevin, I am involved in some other business that handles some very nasty stuff. I think the organisers have decided to close up shop, and me with it.'

'So why should I fucking care, Phil? We have a deal, and you have a job to do for me. If you don't do it I could have you kneecapped.'

'Christ, Kevin. Give me a break. What these guys are likely to do to me will make kneecapping look like something worth having. They've already bumped off another one of their deliverymen. I'm going to be next.'

'I'll look after you, Phil my boy. Tell me who they are and I'll fix 'em for you. Me and the boys will stop their farting in church, I promise you.'

'You don't understand, Kevin. These are major league players. You and your blokes wouldn't stand a fucking chance against them. This is why I have got to go somewhere quiet for a while.'

This made O'Reilly very angry.

'My boys are professional soldiers for the cause, Phil. Not part-time hoods who hang around the Cross. I don't like being insulted like this. There's nobody in Sydney whom we couldn't handle, and you know it for sure.'

'Get real, Kevin! Your boys are bloody babes in arms compared with the guy that's after me. He is one nasty little black bugger who I am not going to wait around for whilst you and your bog Irish pals get themselves done in. I'm off, whether you like it or not. Cheers, Paddy.'

Red with anger Phil Cartwright slammed the phone down and stormed away from the phone booth towards the departure area.

Stupid Irish prick! Then after a moment's thought, Stupid bastard yourself, Philip Cartwright. Now everyone wants to kill you. When will you ever bloody learn? he thought as he stormed through the gate towards the plane.

A few minutes later he was airborne, in a window seat looking down at the lights around Botany Bay as they receded into the night. Ninety minutes later he walked out of the airport buildings in Melbourne and caught the first of five cabs. He criss-crossed Melbourne several times before catching the final cab which, once he was sure he was safe would eventually take him to his hideaway for a week or so, a small secluded hotel overlooking Port Phillip Bay.

## Chapter Eight

Sammy's condition was not as bad as was first thought. He had a nasty concussion, and the cut in his forehead required twelve stitches. Generally he felt less than good, but once he started to become aware of where he was and what had happened to him a feeling of great relief overcame him. It occurred to him that colliding with a large truck was not the best thing to do in a little VW Beetle and that he was probably very lucky to be alive.

Some hours after admission he was transferred to a trolley and taken to a ward where he was unceremoniously put to bed after a rough and ready bed bath by a not too friendly male orderly. It seemed to Sammy that the guy was not at all pleased about having his night disrupted.

Hard bloody luck, you miserable sod, Sammy thought as the man stormed off after completing his chore. It's not as if I did this on purpose. Me? I'm the sodding victim.

Back in casualty the doctor who had admitted Sammy, Dr Talufa, a Fijian by birth, noticed that the orderly who wheeled Sammy off had forgotten to pick up the shirt hanging over the back of the chair in the cubicle. He picked it up and carried it to the general office meaning to arrange for it to be delivered to the ward at some later stage during the night. As he did so the note that Cartwright had placed in the shirt pocket fell out on to the floor. He picked it up and opened it.

He just couldn't believe his eyes as he read what he had written.

*Keep away from the black man. He is dangerous. I
will contact you.'*

He was fairly hardened to racism, having been subjected to
it for most of his life, but believing that he must be the
black man the note referred to he felt that this was probably
the most blatant form he had experienced for a long time.

He knew that the truck driver had written something on
a scrap of paper and placed it in the patient's shirt pocket.
He had seen him do it. In his opinion it could only be him
whom the note was accusing of being dangerous as there
weren't any other black men around.

His first impulse was to go after the truck driver and
have it out with him and he was quite capable of doing that.
Talufa was a very big man with a hard look about him. It
was rumoured that he played Rugby Union.

He showed the note to the senior staff nurse who was
horrified at what she saw written on the scrap of paper.

'Perhaps he is one of those neo-Nazi types,' she offered.
'Those people are so bigoted they will do and say anything.
Best leave him alone, Doctor. You never know what he
might be capable of doing to you.'

This caused Talufa to rethink his original idea of going
after Cartwright.

'You may be right. Better to forget it. He isn't worth it.
Thank God I stopped the note from getting to the patient.'

The staff nurse agreed with him.

He resolved to report the incident to the hospital
management but later during the night his anger subsided
and he decided to forget about the whole matter and threw
the note into a rubbish bin.

★

Two days later Sammy was released from the hospital with a very stern warning about the dangers of doing anything stupid for a week or so, or at least until his GP had cleared him with regard to the concussion. He casually raised the subject of a gentle bit of scuba-diving.

'Do that and you will probably drown yourself,' Talufa warned him.

Having been told by a ward nurse about the doctor's high-level skills on the rugby field Sammy decided not to push his luck.

A big guy like him would have no choice but to do everything at a high level. Much higher than me, anyway, thought Sammy, smiling to himself as he stretched his neck to look up at the man.

So when he leaned over and whispered in Sammy's ear, 'And if you come back here too soon I'll break your bloody legs for you', Sammy took the hint and decided to do as he was told.

It was not going to be too easy for him. He knew that the urge to follow up his investigations and proceed with Stage D, the investigatory dive to try to discover what they were diving for half a mile from the shore was likely to get the better of him, but under the circumstances he would just have to fight it.

★

At the same time that Sammy was waiting for the taxi to take him home the mystery boat, *Jetset*, was anchored off the coast in exactly the same spot that he had seen it on that day that he had kept observation from the top of the cliffs. One crew member was left on board the craft which was making very heavy weather of the huge swell coming in from the Pacific. He was sitting in a slowly revolving swivel chair looking intently through a pair of huge binoculars mounted on a cradle in front of him. In the event of any other craft coming within half a kilometre he would give the signal over a specially designed speaker system relayed through a long line extending down to the lead diver, Felix.

Felix and two other divers were diving down towards a large concrete slab which was anchored to the seabed. The slab was about three metres long by two metres wide, and about half a metre deep. It was massive, but even with its enormous weight it was no match for the mighty tidal currents that swept the area at that depth. The anchor was therefore of vital importance to the operation.

Hovering above the slab was the remaining one of the six surfboard-like containers from the *Palminto*. It was locked on to the concrete by four heavy-duty chains, each attached to a handle recessed into the sides of the container by a large shackle. The shackles were necessary because of the natural buoyancy of the container which even though it was packed with one hundred and fifty kilos of heroin was made of material that was designed to have flotation capabilities. It was also designed to be lightened by pumping helium into reinforced cavities in the bodywork.

Felix directed the operations to ensure that there was no error. Even though the other divers had carried out this exercise on numerous occasions in the past, one small mistake and a container could be swept away by the fierce tidal flow. The men took up their positions on opposite sides of the container, each holding the two handles on his side. Once Felix was satisfied that they both had a firm hold he swam around the object releasing the shackles one by one, and the container rose very slightly on release. Felix then turned the small valve at the front of the container and a plainly audible hissing noise came from the valve together with a few small bubbles. Within seconds compressed helium was released into a series of chambers in the container which began to lift slowly in the water. The two divers then began to steer their lighter load forwards and upwards following closely behind Felix who was using the boat's anchor line to guide him on his way up.

About halfway to the surface the three men stopped and secured themselves and the container to ropes and shackles fixed securely to the anchor line. They were professionals and each man was highly trained and fully conversant with the tables that dictated the decompression times necessary when diving at any given depth. After the appropriate period of time for decompression Felix signalled that they should once again proceed upwards. He released himself first and headed upwards very slowly. The other divers followed, but not as closely as before. They were waiting for the signal from Felix that the coast was clear and that it was safe to surface. They were also watching for his hand signals which would direct them to the rear of *Jetset*.

Their next task, and the most difficult of all, was to manoeuvre the container into the open slot at the stern of the boat. This was not an easy thing to achieve in calm water but with a heavy swell running it would take all three of them together with the crewman on board, all of their energies to achieve this task. Just as they thought they had the container running straight into the slot a particularly large swell lifted the boat suddenly and they found themselves nearly half a boat length away from *Jetset*'s stern. The second attempt was successful but cost them a great deal in terms of energy and physical pain. As soon as the container was stowed inside the slot the man on board lowered a small lever and it was locked firmly into place. To all intents and purposes it appeared to be part of the craft.

With some help Felix and his two fellow divers clambered on board and lay exhausted on the deck for several minutes before the little black man lifted himself to his feet and gave the order to weigh anchor and return to the shore.

★

Two hours later the Jeep and boat trailer and boat were back in the warehouse at Frederick Street. Felix's crew members had already removed their diving suits and were once again dressed in their street clothes. Without a word being spoken Felix gave each of them a sealed envelope which none of them opened. They were aware what the rate was for the job. They had no reason to doubt the man who had always paid them well in the past. Once paid they left the premises on foot at five minute intervals. They had strict instructions not to leave a vehicle within a kilometre of the warehouse, a long-standing instruction that they always obeyed to the letter.

Not until the last man had left the building did Felix remove his diving gear and diving hood. Whilst he knew that the divers who worked for him would know that he was black-skinned, they would be less likely to be able to identify him out of diving gear. That was his sincere hope anyway. Not that it really mattered any more as the Senator had given Felix quite specific instructions regarding the crew members of *Jetset* and he had already planned how he would carry out these instructions.

★

The following morning one of the two divers who accompanied Felix was out diving, doing a regular routine contract job on one of Sydney Harbour's multitude of private piers when he disappeared. He was diving alone which is not a sensible thing to do, but was why he was always able to submit the lowest tender for the work. His corpse was recovered ten days later, and the post-mortem revealed there were large pieces of fishing net tangled around it. It was decided at the inquest that he had died by misadventure, the victim of an encounter with underwater flotsam.

Felix knew the *modus operandi* of his fellow diver, and was aware that the man obtained a very lucrative living from diving alone. The man was so engrossed in his work that Felix was able to attack him from behind just as his air supply was running out and he was about to conclude his dive and refill or replace his tank.

It was all a matter of timing. Felix watched him drop into the water and dive down to conduct his work. Then he merely sat there with his stopwatch ticking over. At exactly the right moment he quietly slipped over the side of his rented outboard dinghy and plunged down to the litter-strewn bed of the harbour.

His victim was totally unaware of any danger. Wearing a diving mask gave one tunnel vision and removed all peripheral sight. Taking advantage of this Felix approached from behind and without any great effort wound the netting around him. Once the subject was secured, even though struggling violently, it was a relatively simple job to tow him down to the seabed. Felix then stood guard until the unfortunate victim's air supply was completely exhausted, occasionally stepping in to prevent any chance of escape from the web of nylon mesh.

*

That same evening the second diver was last seen staggering along North Steyne Promenade, apparently the worse for wear. Locals would later testify that he was upset by the disappearance of a diving mate and had had a few drinks too many. In fact a sedative had been dropped into his second drink of the evening. Felix, dressed in a wetsuit with a hood, had followed him from the beach as he made his way along the promenade. When he was satisfied that nobody was watching he dragged him on to the beach and across the sand into the heavy surf of Manly Beach. Using his enormous strength he held him underwater until he stopped breathing. He then swam several hundred metres out from the shore towing the man behind him before letting the fierce ebb tide take the body out to sea. This was no mean feat for any man, but then Felix was not just any man.

★

The third crew member who had acted as helmsman on *Jetset* lived on his own in a caravan park at Mona Vale, north of Manly. In the early hours of the following morning the gas tank that supplied the cooking stove of his dwelling exploded and enveloped the caravan in flames. The man died instantly and his body was incinerated.

At 6 a.m. that morning Felix telephoned a short message to the Senator.

'The garage sale was a great success. I got rid of the three lots of gear we didn't want.'

The Senator replaced the receiver, smiled to himself and returned his attention to the report that he was writing.

Felix, invigorated but exhausted from his energetic day of killing, rolled over and within seconds was soundly asleep.

## Chapter Nine

In Melbourne, nine hundred kilometres south of Sydney, later that same day Phil Cartwright decided to try to trace the boy whom he had been involved in the accident with. Ever since leaving the hospital he had been really worried after hearing that the injured boy had been calling out about a little black man.

If that poor bloody kid is involved with Felix, he is in it up to his neck, he thought, as he waited for directory assistance to give him the correct number for the hospital. Concerned about the obscure possibility of the call being traced he had purchased a phone card from a newsagent shop nearby and found a phone booth from which he was making the call. He wrote down the number and replaced the handset.

What if I have got it all wrong? What if he was talking about some other black guy? Why should I take this risk? All of these thoughts were racing through his mind as he dialled the number of the hospital.

He asked for the casualty department and was put on hold.

'Casualty. Dr Talufa speaking.'

'Ah Doctor, you are just the bloke I am looking for.'

He started to explain to Talufa that he was seeking advice on the young man who had been involved in the accident when he suddenly sensed that something was wrong. The doctor had gone very quiet at the other end of the line.

'Are you there, Doctor?'

'I'm still here, Cartwright, and I think you have got a damn cheek calling me after that disgusting note that you left for the boy.'

'What are you talking about? What note?'

'You know perfectly well what I am talking about, Cartwright. The note in which you warned him about me. The one in which you told him I was dangerous. You rude bastard!'

Suddenly Phil realised what the doctor was talking about. The note he had left in the boy's shirt pocket.

Shit! The doctor thinks I was referring to him. No wonder he's pissed off with me.

'You've got it all wrong, Doc. You're one of the good blokes. I overheard that young fella mumbling about someone while he was still unconscious. From what he said I think that we have a mutual acquaintance, and if I'm right he may have a problem. The black man I am talking about is not you. No way, Doc. My black man is one mean son of a bitch. I'm sorry if you are offended. Now, what about that young bloke?'

Whilst not totally convinced that he was being told the truth Talufa decided to back off and take the matter no further. With some reservations he explained to his caller that Sammy Marven was all right and that he had been discharged. Due to hospital rules he declined to give Sammy's phone number over the telephone even though he felt sure that as the other party in the accident Cartwright was probably entitled to receive it. He purposely adopted a negative and unhelpful stance due to his dislike of the man resulting from the wording on that rough note that he had found.

Sensing that he was being given the cold shoulder and reluctantly accepting that fact he brusquely thanked Talufa for his advice and terminated the call. However, he promised himself that he would track down Sammy Marven on his return to Sydney, just in case his black man was Felix.

★

It took Sammy nearly two weeks to get the damage repaired on his VW, and to overcome the occasional bouts of nausea that resulted from his concussion. He felt really pleased with himself when he at last collected his car from the panel beaters.

★

Cartwright had extended his stay in Melbourne by a further eight days, mainly because he was scared. He was still convinced that Felix was trying to kill him, and there was no way that he could shake off that fear.

Bloody hell man, you've been in hiding for over two weeks, scared of your own shadow. You have got to go back and face up to life at some stage. Why not now? he argued with himself.

Finally he came to a decision. It was not one that pleased him too much but he knew that he couldn't hide for ever. He rang Qantas and booked a flight to Sydney later that day.

At about the same time as Sammy was making the final check on the repairs to his VW prior to accepting it back, and paying the bill for the insurance excess; Phil Cartwright, again using the name of Dennis Jardine, was boarding his flight and settling down for the eighty minute flight back to Sydney.

★

Also at that same time a third person was taking some action in relation to Cartwright. A tall, dark-haired man was making a phone call to a silent number in Sydney. He was very relieved to be making this call having just spent twelve days, ten hours a day sitting around Melbourne Airport as one of a four-man team that was covering both domestic and international arrivals and departures around the clock.

He and his associates had studied several photographs of Cartwright, none of which he was even aware had been taken of him. They had been taken quite recently by Felix using a high-speed telescopic lens camera. The decision to take the shots had been made in case Phil got wind of being in danger, as he most certainly had now. If he decided to try to run for cover the photos would help Felix's contacts around the country to trace his whereabouts. It had worked.

Felix was delighted with the news.

'Good man! Get the other boys out of there, pronto. Get back to doing whatever you are supposed to be doing, and ensure that your cover story is still intact.'

'Yes, sir,' came the reply. The man who made the call was very pleased with himself as he activated a beeper which he knew would bring the other three lookouts hurrying to meet him in the bar near the Qantas domestic check-in counters. They would each be as pleased as he was. Not only was their long surveillance over, but they would each be richer to the tune of $10,000. That was the going rate for this sort of job.

None of the men mentioned the job, or the money. They were too professional for that. They knew that the cash would be delivered within the next two days and that they could meanwhile get on with their lives.

After downing their drinks two of the men went to the escalator and headed towards the short-term car parking area. The other two men waited for the courtesy bus for the long-term car park. Within ten minutes the four men were in two cars heading along the Tullamarine Freeway towards Melbourne City. They were relaxed and confident that their extra-curricular duties had not been noticed. After all, why would anyone in their right mind challenge four detectives of the Victoria Police?

★

Elsewhere in Australia other lookouts were being contacted by Felix cancelling their long surveillances. These people also knew that they would be paid a substantial amount of money even though they had not personally been successful. That was how the system worked. Their payments were in cash, delivered by ordinary couriers. The system ensured that nobody ever dealt with Felix, the paymaster.

They had each carried out such tasks for their unknown boss on several occasions in the past, but none had ever met the man. They knew him by voice and name only and that was sufficient for them. The tasks that they performed were quite legal if you discounted the tax evasion aspect. The job was mostly comfortable, if not boring. All they were required to do was to endeavour to locate certain people whose photographs and personal details were sent to them on occasions by the man with the American accent. Some of them were licensed private detectives, but most of them were serving police and customs officers who were supplementing their main income in a most lucrative way.

None of them realised how lucky they were never to have met Felix face to face; because of this there was no reason for them to die.

★

Once Felix had got the news and called off the surveillance teams he made two further calls summoning a small team of picked specialists to meet him at Kingsford Smith Airport, Sydney. They were instructed to be there in time to meet the incoming flight from Melbourne.

He now knew exactly where and when Cartwright would be arriving and he carefully placed his men to ensure that the interception could be carried out with the least amount of fuss. His plan was quite simple. Once Cartwright had been clearly identified he would be followed and, at the most suitable time, terminated.

Felix was an expert at selecting suitable locations and times for such events. In this instance he intended to take full advantage of the bustling airport crowds. Getting close to the target would be impossible for him personally because of his distinctive appearance which would make him more vulnerable to identification once police enquiries got under way. With this in mind he selected a contract hit man with a reputation for close-quarter killings such as this. The man, carrying a jacket and a briefcase in order to blend in with the rest of the aircraft passengers, was instructed to get close enough to Cartwright to shoot him dead using a silenced handgun.

It would probably appear at first that the victim had merely collapsed, and others would rush to his aid. In the confusion that would follow the killer would melt into the crowd and disappear. Felix would settle with him later, as the man could not be permitted to live.

Felix was under strict instructions from the Senator to leave no possible loose ends. That meant disposing of all those with whom he had had direct face-to-face contact.

Having strategically placed his men he found himself a position just outside the exit doors of the baggage reclaim area. He would be the backstop just in case something went wrong. Whatever happened Cartwright must not be permitted to disappear again. It had already cost a small fortune to trace him on this occasion.

Felix was not happy about this because all such costs came directly from his own budget. This had made him all the more determined to get him, once and all.

'You're dead, you bastard. For sure!' he mumbled to himself through gritted teeth.

Nobody was nearby at the time. If they had been they might have noticed that Felix's eyes changed dramatically for a brief moment, with the pupils almost completely disappearing from sight. Then he smiled and suddenly his appearance returned to normal.

⋆

The big jet came to halt alongside Gate Lounge 1, and the crew performed their landing rituals, disarming doors and cross-checking. Meanwhile, before the seat belt sign had been extinguished most of the passengers were on their feet unloading bags and clothing from the baggage lockers above their heads. At this particular moment at the end of every flight there was a certain amount of confusion, amongst the passengers, anyway.

Phil took advantage of this to ensure that he was the first passenger in the gangway at the head of the economy class passengers. A flight attendant stood in front of him preventing him moving further until the first and business class passengers had disembarked. Once the flight attendant moved aside he raced to the door and exited on to the disembarkation walkway, nearly knocking the purser over as he rushed through the door. Within seconds he had caught up with the business class passengers and mingled with them just as they turned sharp right and headed up the walkway to the exit door into the gate lounge.

Nobody even noticed him slip off his jacket and place it into his holdall. Nor did they notice him place a large headset over his ears. If anyone had bothered to look, what they would have noticed was that he was now wearing a blue bomber jacket with the word 'Qantas' emblazoned on the rear in large stencilled figures and would have assumed he was a member of the airline's ground staff. This assumption would have been reinforced had they noticed that instead of turning right and following the other passengers through to Gate Lounge 1, he opened the exterior door situated at the bend and exited the walkway, running down the stairs on to the tarmac.

*

No. Nobody noticed Phil's strange method of departure from the Qantas flight. However, it was late and they were all preoccupied with their own affairs and anxious to continue their journey to wherever they were going.

On reaching the tarmac Phil ran under the main lounge walkway area and headed along the wall of the terminal building towards the central area of the airport complex. By this time there were several airline personnel, both ground and aircrew, heading in that direction, so he caught up with them and followed them through the door into the terminal building.

Within seconds he was out on to the roadway in front of the airport buildings and heading at a fast walk towards the Ansett terminal to his right. Whilst walking he removed his jacket from his holdall and put it back on. The earphone headset had long since been removed and deposited in a rubbish bin. Once again he looked just like any other weary traveller rushing to get home.

As he came to the covered area outside the Ansett terminal a large blue Ford Fairlane sedan with dark tinted windows screeched to a halt alongside him. The rear passenger door was flung open and a very large man leapt out. He grabbed Phil by the left arm and threw him into the still-moving vehicle where he lay still across the rear bench seat. The large man jumped back into the car which roared off at a very fast speed.

For two whole minutes there was absolute silence in the vehicle. Then a man sitting in the front passenger seat spoke.

'Okay, Phil, you can get up now. So what the fuck is this all about? Why in God's name I should be helping you after you let me down the way you did I shall never know. Perhaps it's my Irish sense of black humour,' said Kevin O'Reilly with a sly smile. 'However, you were after giving me a substantial gratuity, were you not?'

# Chapter Ten

It didn't take long for Felix to realise that something had gone badly wrong. He knew that Cartwright had boarded the aircraft in Melbourne and that Sydney was its only stop.

He was also sure that he couldn't possibly have walked through the passenger terminal to any other exit door as he had two other men watching inside the terminal who would have spotted such a move and reported it on their mobile phones. He could not have stayed on the plane because the flight crew would have soon evicted anyone who tried that. However, regardless of all of the precautions taken Cartwright had somehow escaped his net, again.

Felix was so mad that his two associates did not even dare to come back to see him. They merely rang in at the end of their fruitless searches then made their individual ways back to Sydney, each very worried about their future employment opportunities. Little did they know that this should have been the least of their concerns.

The hit man had also departed immediately after a brief mobile phone discussion with Felix. A rendezvous was arranged for later that day to discuss the next step. He didn't know it, but Felix's next step was to kill him. There would be no discussion on the subject. It was not negotiable.

An hour later Felix rang an unlisted Canberra number and reported the circumstances to the Senator. His message was brief and cryptic. It was highly unlikely that anyone could have been listening in, but had they been they would have been unable to understand what was going on.

'The dog's escaped again. I will be calling out all of the boys to help catch it.'

The Senator slammed down the receiver.

'Shit! This bastard is going to screw it all up if we are not careful,' he snarled to himself as he let go of the handset.

★

The Ford Fairlane was now winding around the secondary roads of the Blue Mountains to the west of Sydney. Phil Cartwright had been blindfolded as a security measure soon after being dragged into the car. Due to the heavily-tinted windows of the car nobody could see in so there would be no disturbing reports to the police of the sighting of a blindfolded person in the rear seat of a motor vehicle.

Kevin O'Reilly was determined to safeguard the location of his safe house property which was absolutely top secret. It was used for some very strange and highly illegal activities that would not have pleased either the Australian state or federal police authorities had they known of them. The governments of Britain and the Irish Republic would have also been deeply concerned at what went on at this location.

Meanwhile, Phil sat back in comfort, sure that he was perfectly safe; at least for the time being. He was interested in knowing what his destination was but accepted O'Reilly's requirement for secrecy as it was one of the best guarantees for his own personal safety. He knew, however, that he must be somewhere in the mountains because of the angle of climb that was evident even in a luxurious and well-sprung car like the Fairlane. He had also assessed the time that he had been travelling, and calculated that the

Blue Mountains were the only range of sizeable hills within that time of travel from Sydney.

He did not like the idea of wearing the blindfold because of the personal discomfort but accepted that he was unlikely to have it removed until they arrived at wherever it was that Kevin had decided to take him.

★

He had negotiated a rent with the Irishman on the first occasion that he telephoned him from Melbourne. It was considerable but he had been assured it included personal bodyguards and the highest form of security.

His main objective, for the short term at least, was to stay alive and figure out a way of disposing of Felix. He figured that as long as Felix was alive he was the greatest threat to his safety. Probably with the assistance of O'Reilly and his associates, and certainly at considerable extra expense, he would sort out this matter before retiring into obscurity with a new identity. Kevin had even suggested that he could provide the latter service: naturally it also came at a very high cost.

He sat quietly in the front passenger seat of the car with a broad smile on his rugged face. He rather liked Phil Cartwright. He was a nice guy. However, at the moment his most redeeming feature was the fact that he was involved in some form of enterprise that was so illegal that it had apparently made him excessively rich, and had also put a price on his head.

O'Reilly had very soon realised that he had the opportunity to benefit from that wealth and to reap a very rich reward for the services he was about to provide for Phil. The Irish Cause needed that sort of money. It would be filtered back into Northern Ireland in the form of cash and hardware of the military type.

Yes, Phil, my old darling. You are safe with me, boy. Nobody is going to get within a mile of you without me knowing. You are worth nothing to me if you are dead so come hell or high water I am going to keep you as safe and well as in your dear mother's arms.

With that happy thought in his mind he continued to gaze out at the darkness of the mountains. He knew that their ultimate destination was only three kilometres away and that they had driven past it once already. He also knew that they would continue driving for at least another half an hour to ensure that their passenger was completely disoriented and would have no way of knowing where he was. This was not due to any mistrust of Phil Cartwright but because so much was invested in maintaining the secrecy of the safe house location.

However, the thought that Phil would never know where he was rather amused him.

★

Cartwright also had a smile on his face at the time, not that anyone would have noticed it in the darkness of the car. He was amused by the fact that so many left turns had been made it was obvious that they were driving around in circles trying to confuse him. Whilst amusing him it also satisfied him because he could tell that they really were seriously security conscious, not just playing at it.

Perhaps they might be a match for old Felix after all. He played with the thought for quite a while during his blind journey.

Thirty minutes later the car did a sharp left-hand turn and stopped. Phil could hear a gate creaking open and the buzz of the electric window of the driver's door as it wound down. He then heard muffled voices outside the car.

The window sound came again, and they drove on. Now they were obviously off the public road and driving on a rough unsealed surface which tested the suspension of the car to its fullest. A few minutes later the car stopped again. The four doors of the car opened and Phil could feel the coldness of the evening mountain air. He was helped out of the car and the blindfold removed. Owing to the darkness it took him just a few moments to regain his vision and he could see that they were in a large courtyard with a high wall surrounding it. The car had come to a halt outside a large stone and brick building with a most imposing ornate front door.

'Come inside, Philip my man,' said O'Reilly, pushing the door open and leading the way into the brightly lit hallway.

'This is going to be home from home for you; for a short while at least,' O'Reilly continued as he led the way into a large lounge furnished with luxurious armchairs.

'I'll pour some drinks for us. Now it's Scotch for you I believe, Phil.'

Cartwright nodded whilst stretching out in one of the chairs.

Handing him a drink O'Reilly continued. 'Now these are the house rules, Phil. Break them and we'll break you and then throw you back to the wolves you are hiding from. We've got a lot more going on in this place than just playing mother to you. So listen in, old son, and don't interrupt.'

# Chapter Eleven

Samuel Frederick Thomas Alfred Peter Marven was not a good patient, mainly because he had no patience. He had always wanted things to happen now, and could never stand having to wait for anything. This was especially so with events such as birthdays and Christmas. There were times as a small child when he had driven his parents to distraction because of this particular trait.

He had not improved with age, and so it was with great difficulty that he faced the prospect of not being able to do the fun things such as surfing and scuba-diving. He was particularly concerned that he could not dive because he was anxious to complete his planned Stage D and discover what it was that those guys were diving for.

He gave this matter a lot of thought because he had a considerable amount of time on his hands. Sure, he was able to do his work shifts, but even that caused him some difficulties as he occasionally felt dizzy and had to sit down. The shift managers were more tolerant of him now though in view of the fact that he had been involved in the road accident. However, the dizzy spells, combined with the earnest belief that Doctor Talufa was telling the truth about the dangers helped control his reckless enthusiasm. At least for the time being.

What if I had a bad spell whilst underwater? Jeez, it's bad enough having one on land. I had better take notice of the doctor, or else. He even threatened to break my legs for me. Sure, it was a joke, but he is a big bugger and I don't feel like taking the chance. All of these thoughts raced through his mind as he grappled with the boredom of the enforced inactivity caused by his accident.

★

He reviewed Stage C which hadn't been a crash hot success as he hadn't even got into the building or been able to see what was inside the place. However, there was one positive result. He did know that he had the right location otherwise why would that life jacket have been there?

Until now his memory of that night had been pretty hazy, thanks to the bang on the head. He concentrated hard trying to bring back the memories of what he had done in Frederick Street, then suddenly it all began to surge back in his mind. He recalled the trapdoor in the bottom of the wall and remembered the size of the padlock that held it closed. He also remembered that he had decided to revisit the building and take a hammer or something to force the padlock open so that he could gain entry and look around.

After reviewing the situation time and time again over several hours he made up his mind that this was a task he could complete without it being life-threatening if he had another one of his dizzy spells.

Stage D, which should have been the dive would now be relegated to Stage E. The new Stage D would be a return to the warehouse building in Frederick Street, suitably equipped for a real bit of criminal breaking and entering. He then realised that compared with his previous visit to that building, on this occasion he was relatively relaxed about doing it. He was not suffering the bad nerves that he remembered having on that earlier night.

That bash on the skull has knocked out whatever remaining sense you had in your head. You daft bugger, he told himself with a smile.

*

Shortly after midnight he entered the yard of the Frederick Street premises and quickly located the trapdoor. It was pitch black with a heavily overcast sky and a weather forecast that promised bucketfuls of rain very soon. He knew that he had to make it quick.

He was appropriately dressed on this occasion wearing dark clothing and carrying a small black shoulder bag. He had purchased the bag that morning at the ferry end of The Corso, the pedestrian mall that ran between Manly Beach and the wharf from which the Sydney Harbour ferries operated. He felt sure that James Bond would have been quite proud of him. In the bag was a very heavy hammer, a large screwdriver and a hand torch. It also contained a Mars Bar and a bottle of mineral water. Hardly the most sophisticated tool kit for a burglar, certainly not in the super-crook league but it would have to do. The Mars Bar and the drink were for after the crime. He felt sure that he would need such a reward after the successful completion of his task.

It took him a long time to pluck up the courage to give the first hammer blow to the padlock, and when he did it sounded like a bomb exploding. He wondered how anyone in the neighbourhood could have slept through such a racket. He lay flat, his heart thumping wildly and his hands shaking uncontrollably.

You've done it now, Sammy. The cops will be here any minute.

He was so sure of this that he got to his feet and quickly packed the hammer back into the bag with the other items, and he was about to take off when there was a horrendous clap of thunder and the skies opened. It began to rain as suddenly and heavily as it can only rain in Sydney. The 'let's build an ark' type of rain that few mortals other than

Noah and Sydney-siders had ever experienced. Within seconds he was soaked through to the skin and depressingly cold.

'Stuff it, we're going in,' he spoke out loud as if addressing a group of followers.

A minute later he had smashed the top off the padlock and with the help of the screwdriver had prised open the trapdoor which was clogged with coats of old paint.

On his knees and completely oblivious of the fact that he was now crouching in an ever-growing pool of mud and water he shone the torch into the hole. It opened directly into the building. He was in luck.

He got down and crawled through the small entrance, pulling the trapdoor closed behind him. He rose to his feet and stood still for what seemed like an age but was probably only thirty seconds or so. The building was in total darkness, much darker than outside due to the lack of windows. Gradually his night vision improved and he was able to get his bearings. Fearful of falling over something or down a hole he switched on the torch and carefully shone it around the interior of the building. It appeared empty except for two things, the boat trailer and the craft named *Jetset*.

He searched the boat thoroughly and found nothing other than life jackets and a half-full jerrycan. He removed the cap and sniffed the contents. There was no smell so he guessed that it must be water. He decided to make a thorough check around the walls to see if there was anything left on the many shelves which he could vaguely see by torchlight from where the trailer and boat were standing. As well as the shelves, at the opposite end of the building to the main doors he saw what appeared to be a platform.

Starting at the right-hand side of the large doors he moved anticlockwise around the perimeter walls, checking each shelf as he went.

A close-up inspection of what he had first thought was a platform proved to be was a stack of items covered with a tarpaulin sheet. Not expecting to find anything of any importance he nonetheless dragged the tarpaulin clear. What he saw puzzled him greatly. There were six large, flat, blue containers shaped like oblong surfboards, but much wider and more square at the front and sides. They were about 2 metres long, 1.25 metres wide and twenty centimetres deep and appeared to be made of some sort of plastic or fibreglass. He assumed that they must be containers, because the top one had a one metre by half a metre opening in its top face, exposing a recess which extended for most of the length and breadth of the container. Each of the containers had two handles set into each side. One other thing that really puzzled him was the valve-like appendage that stuck out of the front of each of the containers. They looked exactly like the tyre valves on his car. A closer inspection with his torch revealed that the valves each had a large nut on the top. He grabbed the top one and turned it. There was a loud hissing noise which surprised him so much that he jumped backwards. He quickly turned the nut in the opposite direction and the hissing ceased. His brain was working overtime trying to figure out what the hissing noise was.

Sure that he could do nothing further he carefully replaced the tarpaulin sheet and headed back towards the trapdoor having decided to return once more the following night with a flash camera. Whilst he didn't know what the containers were he felt that if he showed the photographs around someone else might be able to identify them.

★

He was just passing by the front of the trailer and boat when it suddenly hit him like a bolt out of the blue – the reason why the boat had puzzled him in the first instance. He quickly moved round to the stern, and there it was; the answer to the question he had been asking himself all along. The open slot in the back of the hull. It was almost certainly the same size as the rear end of each of the containers under the tarpaulin.

That's what they are. Those bloody containers or whatever they are slide into that hole in the rear of the boat. That's it! The boat goes out with the hole empty. Somewhere, somehow, it picks up one of those containers, slides it into the hole and brings it home. Then the bastards go out again and again until they have picked up all of whatever it is they have got in those containers. The hissing noise must be some sort of gas that lightens the container and counters the weight of the load.

He was both excited and proud of himself for working it out.

It must be drugs, Sammy boy. The hole in the top of the container is not deep enough to hold anything else. In fact, the whole container isn't big enough.

Slow down, old son. You had better check it out.

Throwing caution to the wind he rushed across to the pile of containers and once again removed the sheeting. He leaned across the top container and tried to lift it. It was fairly heavy, but he grabbed the two handles nearest to him and pulled hard. It slid off the pile and hit the ground with a loud crash. He then dragged it across the floor to the rear of the boat.

One end of the container appeared to be narrower than the other, so Sammy decided that that must be the end that went into the hole first. He lifted the container up at that end and dragged it closer to the boat so that the narrow end was leaning against the bottom lip of the hole in the hull.

So far he had managed to hold the torch throughout his exertions. He realised that he would have to put the torch down whilst he continued his work, because to find out whether the container fitted into the hole required both hands and the container was not light. He left the torch switched on, but the light was only splaying dimly across the floor as the batteries were beginning to give out.

'Shit! I should have brought some spare batteries. Dumb sod!' he shouted out loud in frustration.

It took about five minutes of struggling and cursing before the narrow end of the container suddenly slipped into the hole. Sammy stopped for a moment to regain his breath whilst he leaned against the rear end of the container.

He bent down to recover the torch just as the batteries went dead and the light went out. Standing up quickly he collided with the back of the container which suddenly slid all the way into the hole in the boat with a loud double click.

At first he thought nothing of it as he fumbled around in the dark trying to get a finger hold on the rear of the container in order to pull it out again. It was in tight, and it was flush with the rear wall of the hull, which was obviously how it was supposed to be.

There must be a locking device, was his first thought as he clambered on to the rear end of the boat, trying frantically to find a lever of some description. It was a hopeless task in the dark, and if he had been able to see he would have realised that he was feeling in the wrong place anyway. The release lever was on the top rear edge of the boat, not down on the deck where he felt sure it must be.

★

At that moment Sammy sensed that apart from the fact that he had locked the container into the boat something else was very wrong, and to his dismay it occurred to him that he could see the light of dawn showing around the large main doors of the building. He glanced down at the luminous face of his watch.

Shit! It's nearly five o'clock. I've been in here for hours. Bloody idiot I am.

In view of what he had discovered, the thought of being seen or caught leaving the premises frightened him very much. Panic set in at that moment. He hurried across to the far wall and once more replaced the tarpaulin. He could do nothing about the container locked inside the boat. He would have to leave it.

Perhaps they won't notice it, you stupid sod. You are really in the shit now, Sammy, he raved to himself as he crawled out through the open trapdoor. He pulled the door to and tried to force the broken padlock shut but it wouldn't go. He left it hanging loosely on its hook. It was plainly obvious even in the semi-darkness of dawn.

*

By the time Sammy got back to his car it was far too light for comfort. He was very scared. He had stumbled on some form of crime which appeared to be drugs related but he wasn't sure. He was convinced, however, that it must be pretty serious with the cost of all of the resources involved.

He couldn't go to the police for fear that they would arrest him for breaking and entering.

He knew that unless they were totally stupid the owners of the boat would soon discover that the building had been broken into and, more seriously, that someone had sussed out what the containers were for, or at the very least that they fitted into the boat.

He drove directly home to his bedsit and tried to get to sleep, but without any success.

You've really done it this time, Sammy. Dad will know what to do though. You had better come clean and tell him all about it, he told himself as the morning sky grew lighter and the hot sun started to blaze in through his window.

It was a day for doing things in the water but Sammy was not going to do that today. In fact he was not leaving his little flat at all, for anything. For the first time in his life he was really concerned for his safety, perhaps for his life.

Eventually he did manage to doze off to sleep, having promised himself that he would telephone his father that evening, which was morning in England.

\*

Felix was very jittery. It was not normal for him to be concerned about anything. That was not his style. However, he had just arrived at Frederick Street and entered the warehouse to discover that someone had been in the building. There were muddy footprints all over the place. It only took him a moment or so to realise that the entry had been achieved through the trapdoor, so he quickly examined the exterior of the building to see if he could find any clues regarding who had been there, and how they got into the compound.

Apart from the muddy footprints there were no obvious signs that would have assisted him in discovering who the intruder was so he returned into the warehouse to see if anything was missing or disturbed. His first thought was that everything was in order and that perhaps this was just the act of some young hooligan either searching for petty cash or somewhere to bed down for the night. He had started to feel relieved about the whole issue when he noticed the rear of the boat.

To his horror one of the containers was in place, inserted neatly into the slot of the rear of the craft. Panic hit him. He knew for certain that when he last saw the craft the slot was empty and that all of the six containers were neatly stacked against the wall covered by the tarpaulin sheet.

Who could have done this? Was it the police?

Whoever it was, Felix knew that they were rumbled. He knew that he would have to find out who it was who entered the warehouse and track that person or persons down.

His current assignment was to tidy up all the loose ends. To date he had achieved that most successfully, other than in the case of Phil Cartwright, but he was working on that. Yet here was another loose end. A very big loose end, a real problem that he was going to have to solve and resolve before he could safely report to the Senator that all was well. This problem could wreck everything.

He pondered whether to report this disturbing incident to the Senator but decided not to. He knew that his future depended very much on the complete success of his activities in closing down the whole deliverymen system. To inform the Senator of yet another hitch in his programme would be counter-productive and could cause him problems, perhaps even terminal problems.

*

Felix nailed up the trapdoor and then secured the warehouse tightly. He again looked around the compound for clues, finding none. After locking up the gate at the Frederick Street entrance he drove back into Manly and called into a restaurant for lunch. The restaurateur was a most helpful man who had offered many facilities to Felix over the years, and on this occasion whilst his meal was being prepared he was given the use of a small office. It was a room he had used in the past when he needed to make secure telephone calls.

He made several calls during the twenty minutes or so prior to eating. When he had finished he returned to his table, where his meal was delivered to him instantly.

He had just set many wheels into motion having contacted his entire city-based network, setting the hounds loose amongst the underworld to discover who was responsible for the break-in at Frederick Street. He had also arranged for an exercise of incendiarism to take place that evening at the warehouse to destroy all the remaining evidence within the building and prevent any further busybodies poking their noses into his affairs. Next to Cartwright this most recent problem was probably his biggest.

His instructions to his network were quite specific.

'Someone is interfering with my business. Find the bastard and there is big dough in it for you.'

He needed to give no further advice to his associates. Within hours questions would be asked all over the Sydney region, particularly amongst the younger criminal set. No stone would be left unturned, and it was highly likely that if the act had been committed by somebody with a criminal background their identity would ultimately be discovered.

★

Felix also sought to identify the younger hooligan and criminal elements in the general Manly area. One specific phone call that he had made was to a police station in central Sydney. His message was very brief and explicitly commanding. Some twenty minutes later, having completed his lunch, he was sitting back drinking a glass of cool beer when he was joined at the table by a tall portly man in his forties.

'Okay, Felix, what's your problem? I hope this is important because I've had to put a lot of important things on hold to get here.'

'Don't be a smart-arse with me. I pay you big money, so whatever I want you to do takes priority over everything else, get it?'

'Yes! But you don't realise—'

'I don't have to realise anything. You just do as I tell you. Now shut up and listen. Somebody broke into our warehouse in Frederick Street and there are a lot of things in there that we just do not want anyone to see, if you get my drift.

'My first question, Mr Copper, is: was this a police operation and if so why the hell am I paying you to keep them off my back?'

The big man went to speak but Felix waved him silent with a slight movement of his hand.

'My next question is: how fast can you establish a house-to-house operation within a one kilometre radius of Frederick Street? I want every household in that entire area visited and every person, and I don't care how many there are in the house, every person spoken to. This is a closely knit community of bedsitters. Everybody has got a car and they are constantly arguing and fighting with each other over car parking spaces. Everyone is jealous of their own car parking territory. Someone must have noticed some strange movements, a motor vehicle or a stranger to the neighbourhood.

'This is very urgent, Copper, so don't give me any of that crap about your own police work commitments. I pay you big bucks and therefore your total commitment is to me. Are you with me, friend?'

The policeman sat silently. He was looking pale and drawn.

'Okay, Felix. I'll do my best.'

'You will do more than your fucking best. You will do everything I want. If you don't, then you and I will be having a difference of opinion that you will not enjoy. Do you understand me? I am not going to ask you any more. Are you sure that you understand me?'

'I guess I have no choice. You've put me on the spot, Felix. I'll set up some sort of operation right away. Perhaps I can do it on the basis of it being a community policing thing. Leave it to me, I'll come up with something. I promise. Please don't do anything that could jeopardise my professional situation.'

'That's entirely up to you, Copper.'

Shortly afterwards the policeman left the restaurant. Felix sat back sipping at his beer. He felt fairly satisfied that the net he had set would soon close in on the Frederick Street intruder.

He also came to the conclusion that this particular policeman must not be allowed to reach retirement age in the force.

# Chapter Twelve

Sammy had eventually overcome the fears which he had experienced following the episode at Frederick Street, but it had taken a while. In the aftermath of the event he really did suffer very badly from nerves and sleeplessness. However, his bravado had now partially returned and he was determined to proceed with his plans. He also decided not to bother his father.

Due to his voluntary isolation for several days he had not kept up to date with local news. Had he done so he would have probably heard about the massive fire in Frederick Street. The fire, fanned by a strong sea breeze had destroyed several warehouses and factories. Police had reported that there were no suspicious circumstances. Had Sammy been aware of the fire he would have felt nothing but suspicion, and would also have been terrified and fearful for his life.

He had not had a dizzy spell for four days, and on a recent visit to the hospital Doctor Talufa had told him he was looking good. He never mentioned anything about Sammy not diving but he also never said or implied that he could go diving. In fact, the subject had not even been raised. Why should it be? How could Talufa be expected to remember some chance remark that Sammy had made on the day that he had been discharged from the hospital after his accident?

He felt quite smug, but couldn't help also feeling slightly guilty about using the doctor's failure to raise the subject of underwater activities as an approval to go ahead and do it. However, that was what he intended to do regardless of the consequences.

During the evening before he had once again reviewed his discoveries at Frederick Street and ended up spending nearly an hour memorising the shape, size and features of those strange containers that fitted into the slot at the rear of the boat. He even drew himself a picture of one of the containers as a visual reminder. He was sure that if he did find anything during his exploration of the seabed, whatever it was would in some way relate to the design of those containers. There would just have to be some connection between them.

You're kidding yourself, Sammy. What if there is nothing there anyway? What if you dive and miss the location altogether? What if the divers met other divers underwater and merely passed on the containers from person to person? Christ! This is getting more stupid by the minute.

He frowned as he considered the possibilities, and the ever-increasing probability that he was imagining everything. However, he knew he wasn't imagining the fact that on the occasions he had seen the boat it had always left the shore with an open slot at the rear, and returned to shore with something filling that space. He also now knew that those containers were designed to be carried in that space.

He had one remaining and major concern. Diving on his own! However, he had no choice. He was just going to have to dive alone. Firstly, he did not want to involve anybody else. Secondly, nobody else would have believed him enough to want to join him on the dive anyway. He recalled too vividly how all of his friends had written him off as some sort of idiot for even considering pursuing the matter further.

Hadn't they all decided that his *villains* were merely stealing crayfish from other people's pots? Even though Sammy now knew for sure that that was not the case he would have achieved nothing by raising the subject again, not amongst his circle of friends anyway.

★

So it was on his own that Sammy launched the six metre runabout he had hired for the morning and set off north-wards around the head towards the place where *Jetset* had done its sharp right-hand turn outwards towards the open ocean. The sea was quite calm as he steered around the headland and sailed northwards with Fresh Water Beach on his left-hand side.

This was the difficult bit, because when he had watched them perform their right-hand turn he had been up on the cliffs further north looking southward towards them. Now he was in a boat trying to emulate what they did and it was going to be really tricky. He had already considered the frightening reality that if in completing his turn he missed the right spot by a few metres, or if in sailing out to sea he was half a degree off course, he would completely miss whatever it was they had been diving for.

At the spot that he felt they had been when they turned he performed a turn to the right and slowly headed out to sea. He constantly looked over his shoulder back towards the shore to try to judge whether or not he was going out at a ninety-degree angle from the beach and was satisfied that he was doing quite well.

His next difficulty was going to be to judge just how far from the shore he needed to go in the runabout before throwing an anchor overboard and going down for a look on the seabed. He had no way of knowing exactly where to stop as the view from water level in the runabout was completely different to his previous view from the top of the cliff. However, he took an educated guess and, stopping the engine, he threw the anchor overboard. It was now or never.

Sammy spent quite a bit of time putting on his diving suit, tank and equipment, taking great care to ensure that he was correctly rigged and ready to go. Whilst safety was a key factor in diving he was knowingly about to ignore the paramount rule of scuba-diving by going underwater on his own, so his best and safest bet was to ensure that everything was in excellent order before he risked dropping over the side.

★

After twenty agonising minutes, by which time the sea was beginning to develop a small swell, he decided it was time to go. Sitting on the side of the boat facing inwards he allowed himself to fall backwards into the water.

His head above the surface, he quickly made one final check of his equipment before commencing his dive to the sea floor.

He had adopted the same routine that Felix and his crew had followed on all of their previous dives to the seabed in that general area. As with most experienced divers he followed the anchor rope down, taking his time and warily looking out for any underwater hazards.

He had still not got used to the idea that while diving in Australian waters he could encounter sharks and other underwater creatures that could be a danger to him. He was aware that in the last six months there had been a couple of reported encounters with big whites, considered just about the most dangerous creatures in the sea. On both of these occasions, the divers concerned had not been attacked. It seemed that they were lucky, probably because the sharks had already eaten.

Even though he was now well trained with many hours of diving behind him he had a constant fear of sharks, so he felt very relieved when he at last reached the seabed, and holding on to the anchor rope he slowly did a three sixty degree turn to examine the surrounding seascape. There was nothing in sight.

And why should there be, you dopey bastard? he thought to himself as he let go of the anchor rope and moved to his right to commence his search routine.

I've probably missed the right spot by miles. Still, nothing ventured, and all that crap.

He had planned the search quite carefully and was determined to see it through. It would be quite easy for a lone diver to lose himself out there so far from the shore. If anything went wrong he may never be found. His plan was to swim around the anchor rope, slowly spiralling outwards to increase his circle of search, yet at all times remaining in sight of the rope, which prior to commencing the search pattern he had tied some bright red and yellow fluorescent tapes to. He was convinced that, providing the water stayed reasonably calm, he would have clear visibility of the anchor rope and its fluorescent accessories from quite a distance.

To his relief this was the case as he slowly circled outwards from the anchor rope, while straining his eyes, seeking some clue of what those strange men were doing down here under the sea.

He was very conscious of the time constraints on him regarding the air in his tank. He constantly checked his watch because he knew that he would have to leave ten minutes of air at least to allow him to slowly rise to the surface whilst decompressing on the way. He had spent a considerable amount of time studying the tables that dictated the speed and time of ascent from various depths as his father had impressed on him the dangers of rising to the surface too fast. The too-sudden lowering of pressure on the body could result in the formation of bubbles in the blood, causing a condition known as the bends which could lead to death.

He was just about to the limit that he had permitted himself in his plans when off to the right he saw something that did not seem to fit into the seascape. Feeling quite excited but determined not to allow this to affect his breathing and the manner in which he was handling the dive routine he moved off towards this sighting.

At first all he could see was a square mound which was certainly not consistent with the undulating shape of the bottom of the sea, but as he came closer to it he saw that it was a large concrete block. The block itself must have weighed a tonne and was sitting on the seabed and was anchored down. Regardless of its weight, however, it still moved gradually as the tide gently pulled back and forth, and it was straining against the anchor chain.

He swam around it a couple of times and noted that there were four chains attached to this large flat object. His eyes lit up and his excitement increased because the chains were placed in a way that they coincided with the spacing of the four handles on the containers that he had seen in the warehouse. Each of the chains had a large shackle on the end which could quite easily be used to connect it to one of the handles. Not far from this concrete block were several other identical slabs of concrete.

He had cracked the case, as he'd heard them say on numerous occasions in the movies. The containers were obviously brought to this point by someone else, chained to these blocks by those four chains and shackles and left there for pick-up. Then the black man and his associates conducted their dive and unshackled the objects, taking them up to the surface where each container was slotted into the rear of the boat and brought into shore, one container per trip.

★

His excitement was so great that he had lost track of time, when suddenly he realised his mistake and glanced at his watch. He knew that he was in real trouble for there was no time to return to the anchor rope. His air supply was so limited that an immediate ascent to the surface was imperative. Somehow he would have to fit in a short decompression stop before finalising his rise to the wave tops. Decompression was, however, a precise operation, and in a constantly moving sea it was difficult for an inexperienced diver to stay at exactly the same depth in order to achieve the required waiting time without something to hang on to; but he had no choice. He began rising to the surface as slowly as he dared, realising that his tank was running dangerously low and at any moment could run out.

His heart was in his mouth. His gauge could be wrong. If it was wrong in his favour it could give him that vital extra minute or so, but if there was less air in the tank than it indicated he could die within the next few minutes.

He reached a point that he guessed was halfway to the surface and started taking the necessary action to tread water and stay at the same level, but did so as gently and casually as he could manage in order to use as little of his precious air as possible and to maintain his normal body rhythms. He watched his air gauge closely, at the same time keeping a steady eye on his wristwatch.

Time was fast running out. He had no choice; not only was his air supply on its last gulps, but the fear and excitement of his danger was causing him to breathe heavier and therefore use a greater amount of air than was necessary or safe whilst diving, particularly at such a critical time.

One more glance at his air gauge showed that it was empty and he knew he had to get to the surface immediately or else. He kicked hard upwards and quickly released his weight belt, letting it sink to the seabed. Common sense told him he had made the correct decision on the basis that one could always buy another weight belt, and this was good thinking for an inexperienced diver in the dangerous situation that he was in. His speed to the surface immediately increased with the loss of the weight belt, but then his air ran out.

Irrationally he tore out his mouthpiece and let it dangle loose over his shoulder as he increased his breaststroke arm movements upwards. His lungs were bursting and he was starting to feel dizzy and experienced violent pains across his chest. He knew that he was losing consciousness.

Then suddenly he reached the surface with a blast. His speed was such when he hit the surface that he felt as if he was going to leap out of the water.

Luckily he surfaced facing in the direction of the boat, which by now was nearly one hundred metres away. He knew he had to reach it but also knew that he had no energy left and that he was possibly suffering an attack of the bends. Having identified this difficulty he had the good sense to inflate his life jacket in order to give himself some extra buoyancy. He did this by turning the valve on the small pressure tank attached to the jacket which inflated it almost instantly. With this buoyancy aid he lay back for several minutes, floating on the surface. He felt sure that he should also jettison his tank, but he was now hallucinating and illogically decided not to do so because of the expense of replacing the equipment.

The cramps and violent pains resulting from his fast trip to the surface began to slowly subside. By then he had drifted even further away from the runabout and realised that as a matter of urgency he must try to reach it before anything further happened to him. With a gentle breast-stroke he set off towards the boat which seemed to remain a constant distance from him, regardless of how hard he swam.

He must have passed out for a while because the next thing he knew was that he was bobbing against the side of the boat, his air tank clanging against the aluminium hull.

Slowly removing the tank he reached up and dropped it over the side into the boat. He then hung on for several minutes more whilst he built up the energy to lever himself over the side, eventually managing to drag himself out of the water.

He lay in the boat for a considerable time, falling into a deep sleep of exhaustion.

★

He woke up with a start, feeling very cold and disorientated. It took him a minute or so to recover his senses and to actually realise where he was and what he was doing. The sea was beginning to get rougher and the sky had become very overcast. Looking at his watch he realised that he had been asleep for over an hour and that there was an urgent need to get back to the shore.

He found it very difficult to pull up the anchor rope, his body was so tired. He considered cutting the rope but decided against that in case he need to drop the anchor again on the way back to the shore. He was relieved to realise that he was again thinking logically. Eventually he did manage to drag in the anchor and after two pulls started the outboard motor and turned the boat back towards the shore. Once he was within a hundred metres or so from the beach he turned sharp left and increased the revs of the engine, hurrying as quickly as possible southwards around the headland towards the boat ramp and safety.

Sammy realised that he had just had a very close encounter with death and was having great difficulty in coming to grips with that fact.

## Chapter Thirteen

It was with great relief that he arrived at the boat ramp and ran the runabout straight up on to the concrete surface. Turning off the engine he sat back in the boat for some five or ten minutes, regaining his composure and wondering what to do next.

Securing the boat at the side of the ramp he lifted off the outboard engine and with difficulty managed to return it to the shed owned by the hire company. After collecting his deposit he wearily made his way to the car park where he had left his VW, struggling under the load of his tank and diving gear. On arrival at the car he unlatched the boot at the front and carefully placed his tank and diving gear inside.

He was suddenly conscious of someone alongside him and before he knew what was happening he had been grabbed from behind and was pulled into the rear of a large van standing nearby with its doors open. He tried to call out for help but something had been tied firmly around his face. He was so weak from his earlier exertions that the role of his assailant was made considerably easier.

He struggled as much as he could and started to kick the side of the van but quickly realised that this was a pointless exercise. The vehicle was on the move and he was being restrained by very strong hands. Then he felt a sharp pain in his left arm.

My God! They've stuck a needle in me. What the hell is going on?

Sammy did not have much time to think any more about what was happening to him as he lapsed into a deep, drug-induced sleep.

★

Picking Sammy up had been pretty simple, after all he was only an amateur. The detective police officer to whom Felix had given such strict instructions spoke to two of his subordinates who had worked with him on Felix's projects before.

Within a couple of hours a door-to-door inquiry had commenced covering all properties within a kilometre radius of Frederick Street. It was not such a tall order as was first expected because the majority of the premises in that area were industrial and commercial. The real difficulty lay in the fact that most of the residential buildings were occupied by more than one family or were broken up into individual bedsit units. Some of the houses had as many as ten to fifteen tenants.

During the period in question five incidents had raised the suspicions or the annoyance of certain residents. One incident that was reported which took place on the evening prior to Felix discovering the break-in related to a green Volkswagen car.

It had been parked at a location where this particular resident normally left his vehicle. The man was so annoyed about it that he had vindictively made up his mind when he saw the vehicle again anywhere within the area to do something nasty to it. He decided he would either damage it or let the tyres down to repay the inconsiderate driver for the inconvenience he had caused.

The man was able to describe the vehicle very well to the police officer and did so with undisguised pleasure, believing that the owner of the vehicle was in some form of trouble with the police.

The green VW was one of four motor vehicles reported to this particular police inquiry. Each was followed up vigorously by Felix's police associates to discover why they were in that particular neighbourhood at that particular time. Each of the other drivers had satisfactory reasons for being where they were on the nights in question.

However, nobody was home on the three occasions when the police officers called at the house where Sammy boarded. In fact he was at home but not answering to the knocks on the door. On the third occasion a nosy neighbour reported that the owner of the VW had left that morning with some diving gear. He further reported that he often used to hire a boat from the boat ramp at the northern end of North Steyne. This information was reported to Felix within the hour.

Immediately on receipt of this news Felix was sure that he had his man, remembering vividly the nosy young fellow who seemed to be spending far too much time watching what they were doing at the boat ramp. He also recalled seeing the green VW parked in the car park alongside the boathouse. It may possibly have been a coincidence but it was worth following up.

Half an hour after receiving the call an associate of Felix broke into Sammy's bedsit room and after a thorough search of the premises found two scraps of screwed-up paper in the rubbish bin. They contained drawings that the searcher thought might be of interest to Felix.

Once he was shown Sammy's drawings of the containers he knew for sure that he was the man who had broken into Frederick Street, and he was going to find and punish him.

★

Felix recognised Sammy immediately he saw him walking up the boat ramp towards the car park and directed his driver to reverse the van up close to the VW. The rest was easy. Sammy was preoccupied with loading his diving gear into the bonnet boot of his VW and was taken from behind with little effort.

Once in the rear of the van he was injected with a drug that immediately put him to sleep, but which would wear off within the hour. The van then drove to premises in North Sydney and into an underground car park where Sammy's unconscious body was carried into a side room.

'Put the bastard on that,' said Felix, pointing to a large table in the corner.

His associate lifted Sammy's limp body and unceremoniously dumped him on his back on the table top.

'Now let me know the minute the bastard wakes up.'

Thirty minutes later Sammy started to come around, and a brief phone message to Felix brought him back to the basement room within a few moments. His captive was helped into a sitting position with his back against the wall and was given a glass of water.

'Okay, boy! What have you been up to?'

Sammy was really not in a position to understand what was going on at that stage but realised that this must be something to do with the warehouse in Frederick Street. He knew he was in great danger and was scared witless.

'I don't know what you are talking about, sir. I really don't understand what this is all about.'

'Well, sonny Jim, I'll put it to you nicely. Someone broke into my warehouse in Frederick Street and touched things that I didn't want touched. Now I want to know who you work for and what you're doing, and above all why you did it. Now, don't even think of telling me lies because if you do I will break every bone in your body. Do you read me, kid?'

Sammy was fully conscious now and looking around nervously for some way of escaping. He guessed that the door was locked and that the black man and his accomplice were obviously more then he could handle on his own, even if he was fit and well; which he wasn't.

'I really don't know what you are talking about, sir. You've got the wrong person. Please let me go. I really don't know what you're talking about.'

He barely got the words out when a fist hit him in the mouth, knocking him flat against the wall and smashing his head violently. Sammy could feel blood welling in his mouth, and tears started to roll down his cheeks. The tears were more from the shock and horror than from the pain inflicted by the punch.

He thought briefly about his options and decided that they were not very good. Realising that he could not escape, and hoping that if he told the truth they would let him go with nothing more than a good hiding, he relaxed and started to tell his story.

Felix sat quietly throughout with eyes fixed firmly on the boy's face. He just could not believe that his carefully planned enterprise had been uncovered and analysed so cleverly by this inexperienced young man. He was convinced the boy was telling the truth particularly with regard to his insistence that he had passed no information to anybody else, and he was also satisfied that the police were in no way involved.

He knew what he had to do. Leaving the room he came back five minutes later with a small bag.

'Hold him still. He's going back to sleepy-byes,' he said to the other man, who immediately grabbed Sammy firmly and held him down.

It only took a second for Felix to fill the syringe and inject the dose into Sammy's right forearm. Within a few minutes he was delirious and behaving very strangely.

'Okay, this is the story. You've got to systematically pump this kid full of heroin until he is history. He lives in a bedsit. He appears to have no relatives or close friends. He is apparently a foreigner from Britain or somewhere like that, so if he ends up an overdosed junkie who in hell is going to care?'

The other man nodded and sat back in a chair in the corner, waiting for further instructions.

'Give him a shot every twenty minutes. Don't give it to him all in one go otherwise if some smart doctor examines him they might be able to suss out what happened. Make a mess of his arms as well. Smack him around a bit. I want this boy to look like a real junkie. Get it?'

Again the man nodded. Felix, obviously satisfied with the result of his efforts instructed the man to call him when the deed was done.

★

Samuel Frederick Thomas Alfred Peter Marven never did fully understand why this was happening to him as he never regained consciousness.

Twelve hours later his badly abused body was dumped in an alley in an area where junkies were known to congregate. It was raining hard at the time and within minutes of being left there the clothing on the corpse was soaked and filthy, and the torrential rain poured on to Sammy's open and unseeing eyes.

When he was found he would be treated by the police and medical authorities as a dead drug addict, a junkie.

Felix was sure that the investigation into the boy's death would be brief, and the results a foregone conclusion. This was partly because he paid certain senior police officers well to do his bidding, but mainly because he knew that it was unlikely that anyone would care too much anyway.

His views on human nature were proved to be correct. Nobody did care. Nobody in Australia, that is.

## Chapter Fourteen

Major John Millane walked hurriedly towards the battalion office. A sergeant had called him away from the range where his team were undertaking some very difficult and violent exercises.

'The Colonel wants you in his office, sir. He said to make it quick. I get the feeling he's got the shits with someone, Major.'

It took him ten minutes to reach the battalion offices which were situated a considerable distance from the rifle range and the exercise complex. Considering he had a bad limp as a result of his injuries in the Falklands War that was pretty good going. It would have probably taken any other man of his age twice that time to cover the same distance. However, he wasn't just any other man, he was a major in the Special Air Service, the famed SAS, and this was Hereford, the headquarters of that elite unit. Soldiers at Hereford didn't do anything slowly, they did it at the double, and in view of the urgency implied in the Colonel's message Major John Millane headed for his destination in double quick time, regardless of his limp.

The limp was one of the few immediately noticeable results of the battle wounds he had acquired in the Falklands War. The severe burns to his chest, abdomen and legs, together with a very serious compound fracture of the right hip had resulted in his right leg being slightly shorter than his left. This ensured that he would never walk again without an irritating lean to his right. It only hurt him occasionally, but it annoyed him intensely, particularly when he was in uniform.

However, once he had learned to adapt to this aggravating disability it did not interfere with his speed and general agility. In fact, there were many of his SAS peers who were willing to attest that, if anything, he was sharper and more deadly now than he had ever been.

It was only when he was stripped down that the full extent of his burns and bodily disfigurement was fully visible. It had taken many months of hospitalisation and painful skin grafting to get him back on to his feet and return him to operational duties in the regiment.

★

At first it seemed to him that it was possible that the SAS would have to retire him because of his injuries. He was then reassured somewhat by the fact that once he arrived back in England from the Falklands he was placed in a private hospital rather than a military one.

This was not because the SAS didn't have faith in the military medical system, far from it, but if their men were ever to eventually go back undercover they had to remain a certain discreet distance from the normal Army. Their medical credentials had to be impeccably civilian, in the same way that their bogus identities and history had to be.

He spent the first few weeks in a very private and exclusive nursing home in an outer suburb of south-west London. The nursing home was located quite close to Roehampton Hospital which was renowned for its specialist burns unit. The doctor who treated him in the nursing home was also a senior consultant to the Roehampton Burns Unit, and worked for the government in confidential cases such as that of John Millane. As such his security clearance was of the highest order.

During his hospitalisation, in conjunction with the burns specialist and Special Branch at Scotland Yard, the SAS came up with a plan for his return to operational undercover work. The plan would satisfy any enquiry that his injuries had been acquired in a relatively normal manner, other than battle. If successful it would enable him at some appropriate time to resume his contact with Michael McQuillan of the paramilitary Belfast Regiment.

★

At about the same time that he was lying unconscious in the temporary medical unit at Ajax Bay in the Falklands, The Red and Green Life Machine, a disused warehouse in River Road, Barking, a town to the east of London, had been burnt to the ground. Two unidentified men had perished in the fire, and the investigating officers had decided that the men, both believed to be in their twenties or thirties had probably been vagrants or unemployed people using the building as a place to bed down. They had apparently been sleeping in an upstairs room above what used to be the administration offices of the building during its better times.

A third man had survived the fire but had received extensive burns to his body and legs, and fractures to his legs. He was a young man in his late twenties who had no identification on him at the time and during his hospitalisation had steadfastly refused to answer police questions regarding his identity.

He had an accent which seemed to be part American, part Irish, but this did not assist the police in identifying the man. For the want of a better name he was known in the Roehampton Burns Unit as Mr Smith. Smith was a very sick man who, at the time when his burns injuries were beginning to respond positively to treatment, became seriously ill with pneumonia.

★

By then, not many miles away Millane was responding well to his burns treatment, but was suffering from fluid on the lungs which turned into a mild case of pneumonia. The specialist was keeping a close eye on his condition, but was not unduly concerned.

The medical similarities between Mr Smith and John Millane were, however, of particular interest to the specialist who reported his thoughts to Millane's masters. They, in turn, were interested in the similarities of the unidentified man's age, general body size, and in particular his accent.

The development of a plan to insert Millane back into the civilian world was immediately commenced. At an appropriate time the anonymous Mr Smith and Millane would be switched. The American-Irish accent of Smith would be a bonus in the switch as Millane would have to revert to his Northern Irish persona. The accents, whilst not identical, were near enough to satisfy the immediate concerns of the planners of the switch. The nuts and bolts of the task were left in the hands of the experts in the dirty tricks business. One thing was for sure, they were determined not to lose the contacts and advantages that Millane had created in Northern Ireland prior to his departure for the Falklands.

It took a few days to finalise the plan, and a bedside briefing was conducted to ensure that he was fully conversant with all aspects of his temporary role.

On the same day as the briefing Mr Smith was transferred to nearby Kingston Hospital for intensive-care treatment for his pneumonia which had become very serious. This move was arranged carefully so as not to raise anyone's suspicions, for Roehampton also specialised in illnesses such as pneumonia which often followed serious burns injuries.

In fact the ambulance took the man called Mr Smith a great distance from Roehampton to a small private hospital where he would receive top-class treatment and much later be discharged. Smith, or whatever his name was, would be completely oblivious to what had happened, but perhaps would wonder why he had had the good fortune to have been so well looked after.

The patient who arrived at Kingston Hospital was in fact John Millane, now to be known as Mr Smith. The shift was made at a time when Millane's pneumonia had worsened and he was very ill.

The briefing officers had expressed the concern that perhaps he was not well enough to go through with the move and the change of identity, but even though very ill he had told them to get a move on and get the show on the road.

After a week or so of intensive medical care at Kingston Hospital he was starting to pick up. He felt much better in himself and was getting used to the pain and disfigurement caused by his burns. He had also learned to live with the pain of his fractures. The temporary plaster cast applied to his badly damaged leg back in the Falklands had been removed because of the severe burns on that part of his body, so he was harnessed to the bed in a way that ensured as little body movement as possible in the trunk and upper leg areas.

The transition back to his Ulster accent had been simple. To assist in the switch of characters he had slurred his speech during the first week or so then gradually moved into the real Northern Irish, Ulster accent. The change had been so deliberately gradual that nobody even noticed it.

He ensured that apart from his refusal to divulge his personal details, an aspect of the character he was playing that he stuck to rigidly, he became the perfect patient. He very soon endeared himself to all the staff at all levels, particularly the young female nurses. He took every opportunity to flatter and flirt with them. The result was that he was looked after extraordinarily well and his wish to remain anonymous became accepted readily. However, to retain his friendly image he made the concession of admitting to having the first name of John, which pleased everyone.

As a model patient he got into the habit of moving around constantly without ever being challenged. Firstly it was in a wheelchair, and later on crutches. This enabled him the freedom he needed for his next move. One morning in the waiting room of the casualty department he took the opportunity to make a long-distance call to Michael McQuillan in Belfast.

He told Michael the story of hiding out in the disused building which caught fire and how he was burned and broke his hip. He explained that he was masquerading under the name of John Smith, which Michael thought was very funny.

He made a point of asking after Moira Flaherty who was so badly injured in the bomb blast at the café. He was genuinely pleased to hear that she had regained the sight in one of her eyes, and was getting used to wearing an artificial arm. Michael assured him she was definitely on the mend.

Having said all the right things he then asked for Michael's help in getting enough money to tide him over when he got out of the hospital. McQuillan assured him that he would look after everything for him.

He was true to his word and in less than a month John Millane was discharged from Kingston Hospital and into the care of an Irish family who lived in nearby Surbiton.

From then on he was back on the payroll of the Belfast Regiment.

★

Since that time sixteen years before he had firmly established himself as an agent of the paramilitary and had travelled back and forth between Britain and Northern Ireland working for both the Belfast Regiment and the British authorities. He had been given credit for various happenings that disadvantaged the British military and gave a boost to the morale of the paramilitaries and was generally seen as a loyal supporter of the cause.

★

Thinking that the Colonel must have urgent Irish business to discuss he found himself thinking of these past events as he hurried to meet with his commanding officer.

# Chapter Fifteen

He was shown into the Colonel's office without delay and was told to sit down. His commanding officer did not look very pleased with life.

'John. Colonel Marven. Wasn't he with you in the Falklands? Saved your life? That gives both of us the incentive to help him in his hour of need. He is one of us, which is why I am doing what I am doing.'

'What exactly is it that you're doing, and why is it you're doing it, sir? In fact, how does this affect me? I really don't know what you're talking about, Colonel.' Millane looked very confused.

'Marven is terribly sick.'

'Yes Colonel, I know. I visit him quite often. He has terminal cancer.'

'Well, John, he has just received some other bad news as well. His son has just died in Australia and he is quite naturally very upset about the whole thing. The boy is reported to have died from an overdose of drugs, but Douglas Marven does not believe that and says that he needs your help.

'I understand that you probably would have died if he hadn't brought you back to Ajax Bay so you obviously owe it to him; on top of which you know what the attitude of the SAS is towards helping our own people. So, if Douglas Marven wants your help I am going to release you to give him any assistance he needs.

'But make it prompt, John, we have got too much on at the moment to lose valuable officers for too long a time. Let me know what your needs are in terms of leave and so on.'

Millane sat there stunned. Douglas Marven only had one son. His name was Sammy and he knew him very well. A likeable lad. His father had shifted him off to Australia to get him out of the way because he didn't want him to know that he had cancer.

Shit! That poor man is going to be in hell of a state. Sammy was such a good kid. What on earth did he do to end up this way?

'Colonel, I really appreciate this, sir. I'll get down to London straight away and see what I can do to help. I'll let you know what he requires of me and if it means I will have to take leave.

'This is going to be very difficult, sir. As I said, I used to visit him, but a couple of months ago he directed me never to visit him again. I think he was embarrassed about his physical appearance as he deteriorated with the cancer. I ring him occasionally but haven't spoken to him for a week or so now. Poor Douglas.'

★

Within four hours Millane was in London. The drive from Hereford had not been without incident. An MGB GT sports car attracted quite a deal of attention at any time, but on a motorway travelling at a speed slightly over the limit it tended to attract the close scrutiny of police officers. This certainly was the case today. He was so preoccupied with his sadness of the news of Sammy's death, and his puzzlement about what it was that the Colonel wanted him to do that he was not concentrating fully.

The sound of the police siren and the blue flashing light on the roof of the car alongside him brought him back to reality with a jolt. The police officer seemed to be in a friendly and relaxed frame of mind and Millane felt sure he was only in for a telling off and a caution. He was wrong.

The constable looked over his shoulder into the rear of the car and noticed the uniform jacket across the rear seat with the badges of rank of a major on the epaulettes. He immediately changed his approach. The smile disappeared and he became very formal.

Bloody hell! An ex-serviceman with a chip on his shoulder about officers. What a damn nuisance, he decided.

This opinion was confirmed within a very short time. Fifteen minutes later, and with a speeding ticket and fifty pound fine to pay he was back on the road. The policeman tailed him for many miles before finally becoming bored with being a bloody nuisance. He pulled over, leaving him to travel on alone.

★

The Colonel was confined in a private hospital in Putney on the south bank of the River Thames. Had he been able to get out of bed he would have probably been pleasantly surprised by the beautiful view of the river and the large number of black swans just below his window. He was, however, totally bedridden and barely able to move, such was the advanced stage of his illness.

Millane's anger at the vindictive action of the police officer melted instantly when he saw his ex-boss and friend lying there in such a pitiful state. The Colonel was asleep so he sat down in a chair by the window and quietly waited for him to wake up. He felt it would be unkind to rouse the man and he had nowhere else to go until such time as he was told what the Colonel required of him.

His mind wandered back to the days when he served with Douglas Marven. A six foot, strongly built fellow who was capable of outpacing all of his men during their regular exercise and training sessions; once a brave and capable soldier he was now a mere shell of a man, gaunt and emaciated. The thought of the tragic series of blows that had struck this man over the last few years caused tears to swell in his eyes.

It was barely two years ago that his beautiful wife Samantha had died of cancer after a very short illness. He remembered how badly Douglas Marven and his son Sammy had taken her death. Now, with only a short time to go before his own death, to discover that his only son had died in less then normal circumstances far away on the other side of the world might be more than he could handle.

Perhaps it would be just as well if he faded away in his sleep right here and now, he mused, gazing out of the window across the river below.

★

Suddenly he was shaken from his thoughts by a clear and commanding voice.

'John! Thank God you are here at last.'

Startled, Millane swung around quickly and leapt to attention, purely out of habit. In doing so he knocked over the chair that he had been sitting on. The incident brought a soft gentle smile to the face of the sick man, which relaxed him instantly.

'Colonel, I am shattered to hear about Sammy. How ever did he get involved in drugs? Surely that was not his scene.'

'He wasn't on drugs, John. I have never been more sure about anything else in my life. Something does not ring true. If Sammy died of a drugs overdose, and I can only accept that that is a fact, it was either an accident or some-body else administered the drugs to him.'

'You're talking about murder, Colonel,' he said with a shocked voice. The thought of Sammy being murdered surprised him very much, and a cold shudder went through his body.

Christ! The cancer and drugs have twisted the old man's brain, was his immediate thought.

'I am serious, John. Sammy wrote to me weekly, some-times more often. His letters were bright and lucid and very cheerful. He telephoned me often. He seemed to be in with a bunch of great kids, all full of life and the thrill of living. He couldn't have been shooting himself up with heroin. Yes, that's what they say it was, John, heroin, but he was writing such long informative and loving letters. It really does not ring true. I will not accept it.

'I know you probably think I've lost the plot. You probably think I've had too much of whatever it is they are pumping into me to ease the pain. Well, John, I promise you that that isn't the case. In fact I am not in their good books in this place because I am currently refusing to take the drugs. I would rather suffer the agony.

'Now, if you think I have been a pain in the arse bringing you down from Hereford, then I am sorry. However, I'm afraid I haven't even started being a nuisance to you yet. I want you to go to Australia for me, John, to Sydney. I want you to do two very special things that I should be doing, and would be doing if I was well.

'Do you realise that you are the only person on this earth that I am close enough to to ask to do this for me? The first thing that I want you to do is to send Sammy's body home to me. I have had my lawyer make up all the legal papers for this to happen. I want you there to ensure that it happens in the right way. I have a bad feeling about this business, John. A real bad, bad feeling.

'When I get his body home I have arranged for a private post-mortem to be conducted before I bury him with his mother. My lawyer has already done all that is necessary for that to happen as soon as Sammy arrives back here.

'God! There I go again.' The Colonel began to sob quietly, tears rolling down his face.

Out of respect for this man that he cared for so much Millane turned his back and walked towards the window. A minute or so later the Colonel spoke again.

'I'm sorry about that, my friend. I find that I haven't got used to talking about him in the past tense. Every time I think of Sammy I think of him being alive. Then the reality hits me, and it hurt bad, worse than all the cancers on this earth.'

Millane turned around to speak to the Colonel and was surprised to see that he had his eyes closed and appeared to be sleeping again.

The poor sod has exhausted himself. I better leave him and come back later.

Just as he was about to turn towards the door the Colonel opened his eyes again.

'Did I doze off? Every so often I wear myself out. It is knocking the hell out of me, John. Now, where was I? Ah yes! As I said, arrangements have already been made for a post-mortem to see if we can figure out exactly what happened to my boy.

'Then the second part of your job for me in Sydney is to find out what happened. I mean, what really happened, John. I want you to investigate the whole affair from start to finish. I need to know exactly how my son died, why he died, and who was responsible. I cannot go to my grave not knowing the truth. Now, that puts a very tight deadline on you because I don't have much time left.

'My own doctor gives me a month at the outside. The people here, well, they just want to drug me into cuckoo land so I don't feel a thing. That's not my style, John. Definitely not my style. When I go I want to go fully alert with my wits about me and aware of what is happening.'

The Colonel smiled again. 'I mean, when I arrive at the pearly gates I don't wish to be so drugged out of mind that I don't recognise where I am, do I?'

John Millane smiled with him. At this very moment he realised just how much he loved this man and why he had been his close friend and role model for so long.

'As I said, I have resisted drugs until now, and I will continue to do so until I no longer have the ability to make that decision. I am told that a time will come when the pain will affect my thinking and that my brain processes will just seize up. At that stage they will start pumping drugs into me, probably just for their own convenience.

'Christ! I am being heartless about them because I know they really mean well. Anyway, if you haven't come up with the goods by then I don't know what I will do. I suppose you will have to look forward to a visitation one dark and windy night.'

Both men smiled at each other at the thought of the Colonel's ghost returning to haunt him to discover what he had found out in Australia.

\*

Millane sat very silently while the Colonel spoke. Quite frankly he was stunned by what he was being asked to do. Sure, he was willing to go to Australia to arrange the return of the boy's body. He felt duty-bound to do so, particularly in view of the fact that the Colonel had virtually designated him the sole surviving 'family member'. To carry this out was the very least he could do for the man who had saved his life in battle.

But staying on and investigating a murder which, regardless of what the Colonel had said, appeared to him to be a figment of his imagination? Were these the ramblings of a dying man, a man whose mind had obviously been affected as a result of the cancer and the violent and continuous pain that he was forced to endure? This was really expecting too much of him, Millane thought.

'Colonel, I know just how much of a tragedy Sammy's death must have been to you, but if the authorities in Australia had told you that he died from an overdose of heroin, surely to make such a statement must mean that they have investigated it fully. I can't imagine that a death reported in this fashion would not have been investigated both medically and by the police.'

'John, you obviously think I'm crazy. What's that lovely army expression of ours? A few shillings short of a pound? But I know I'm right, John.' The dying man's voice hardened and his eyes lit up with anger and determination.

'I had hoped never to have to do this but you leave me no choice. What I am about to do I would have considered not very long ago to be dishonourable. I saved your life in the Falklands, Major Millane. Do you remember 1982? I saved your life and you owe me for that. You owe me, Major Millane. If I could do this on my own I would.

'Look at me, man. I have had it. God alone knows I am ashamed to do this, but I am calling in the debt that you owe me.

'You are the only person I have; on top of which you have the skills of penetration and investigation that you have perfected over many years in Northern Ireland and elsewhere. If I am right, and I know I am, you are the one person who can uncover the truth for me, for Sammy.'

The Colonel appeared to suddenly collapse. Tears poured from his eyes and he sobbed uncontrollably.

'Please, John. I beg of you, as my friend, as Sammy's friend. Bring my son home and find out who caused him to die, who murdered my boy.'

The room was silent for several minutes except for the sound of the Colonel sobbing quietly.

After a while Millane broke the silence.

'Right, sir! When and where do I have to go?'

'Good man! I knew I could rely on you, even though I had to be a bastard about this whole thing,' came the firm reply.

The Colonel leaned over to the bedside cabinet, obviously with great difficulty. He groaned with pain as he opened the drawer and lifted out a small package. He held it out to John Millane, his friend.

'It's all here, John. My solicitor helped me put it all together. I have taken it for granted that your passport is in order. So, here is a return British Airways ticket to Sydney, together with the necessary entry permits and so on. I have enclosed some reading material giving you all the information that I have to date. I have also included some expense money for you.'

John Millane opened his mouth to object to the inclusion of money but was stopped in his tracks by a dismissive command from his ex-boss.

'Do not argue with me, John. I am taking awful liberties with your life. There is no way that I could permit you to pay for doing my bidding.

'I have also taken a further liberty that I trust you will forgive me for. Knowing your domestic situation, I have booked you on a flight out of Heathrow at 5 p.m. tomorrow.'

The Colonel was referring to the fact that Millane's marriage had come to a final end just a year ago after many years of bickering and fighting between his wife and himself, and that he had no other family.

'Please keep in touch with me, John. I need to know what is happening. I will try my hardest to keep alive until such time as you can find out the truth. Good luck, my friend. God bless you.'

Millane realised that he was being dismissed from the room, just like the days when he served with the Colonel. It was strange, yet after all of his years of military service the dismissal process between different ranks never ceased to annoy him.

He still had a hundred questions to ask and as many comments to make but he was virtually being forbidden that privilege because the Colonel had dismissed him. He looked hard at the withered body lying on the bed and was tempted to stand his ground and ask all the questions that were rolling around his brain.

It then occurred to him that he was being unfair and unkind to the man. The Colonel probably wanted him to leave so that he could suffer his pain and anguish alone.

So, without a further word he came to attention and nodded his head, the nearest to a bow he had ever made to any man. He had no idea why he did it, but it just seemed the right thing to do to his old friend, the man who had saved his life. The man whom he might never see again.

★

Even though his plane was leaving the next day he had no choice but to drive back to Hereford. He needed to pack and make final arrangements for the temporary handover of his command. He was both confused and angry at the same time but he knew that he had no choice other than to do Colonel Marven's bidding even though it was an intrusion into his life. He resented even more the manner in which the Colonel made it non-negotiable, even referring to the fact that he was no longer attached: the implication being that the Colonel felt that he had no obligations or responsibilities to anyone else.

Whilst worrying about all of these issues he was none the less convinced by the Colonel's logic. He was in fact Marven's only choice. He did owe him his life and therefore was the most appropriate person to do this.

★

The next morning he rose early and made his way to the battalion headquarters. The Colonel was busy but postponed an appointment in order to see him. He felt obliged to tell his boss the whole story. After all, he was going to the other side of the world and had no idea when he might be able to return.

The Colonel sat quietly during the ten minutes it took to explain the situation.

'I can see that you are less then happy about this, John. You don't like other people ordering your life, do you? Well, hard shit! You are a soldier and Colonel Marven is one of the regiment's heroes.

'Good gracious, man, he saved your bloody life. As far as I am concerned you owe him, and so does the regiment. Take it that you are on official regimental business from here on, Major. That means that should you need assistance, even though you are in Australia, you should contact me direct. Do you understand me?'

Whilst Millane did not say so, he did not really understand how an officer in the British SAS could be on official regimental business in another country, even a Commonwealth country. He knew that these sorts of incursions could only officially take place with the agreement of the government of that country. He was quite sure that no such diplomatic agreement would be sought over an incident such as this, which after all was a straightforward civil affair.

*

Eight hours later he had still not resolved all the issues in his mind. However, it was now too late. He was seated comfortably in a first-class seat in the British Airways 747 that was to take him direct to Sydney, Australia. He had no idea what he would discover once he arrived but had an unsettling feeling that all was not going to be straight-forward. In fact, he had a nasty premonition that for him the shit was about to hit the fan.

*

Because of his gut feeling that Sydney was going to be a bad experience, just prior to boarding the aircraft Millane had made a last-minute telephone call to a secure telephone number in Belfast. His message on a recording machine was brief and concise.

'This is Millane. I am obliged to go on a brief holiday to Sydney, Australia. The Brits are after me again. I hope you have contacts over there in case I need help. I'll call you later in the week.'

*Part Five*

# Sydney – New South Wales

Late April 1997

# Chapter One

Tuesday – 8.30 a.m.

Sydney's Kingsford Smith International Airport came as quite a surprise to John Millane. After the seeming chaos of London's Heathrow with its blatantly obvious military and police presence and intensive security arrangements this Australian airport was comparatively calm and relaxed. Even the customs officials were polite and helpful, and to his further surprise were extremely efficient in the manner with which they dealt with him and his luggage. It was quite a dramatic change from his recent experiences when travelling through airports in Britain and Europe.

Thank God terrorism hasn't caught up with the Aussies yet, he thought as he made his way out of the International Terminal.

The cab rank was much the same as cab ranks all over the world. Hassled and tired people waiting anxiously to get to wherever they were going. The immediately noticeable difference was that the queues were much shorter and the cabs were in greater abundance than back at Heathrow.

After only a few minutes it was his turn for the next cab and the driver leapt out and opened up the boot. Millane's first disappointment of Australia came when he saw that his luggage was expected to share the boot with bags of vegetables and what looked like a bundle of dirty oily rags. He stepped back, slammed the boot shut and walked further down the line of cabs to the next one, much to the amazement of the driver of the first cab who was still standing at the rear of his vehicle.

The driver of the second cab seemed surprised at what had happened and insisted that he must take the first vehicle on the rank. However, Millane was a seasoned campaigner when it came to dealing with cab drivers. Within moments he was relaxing comfortably in the rear seat and experiencing his first Australian cab ride. It was almost as if there were no road rules for this particular driver who seemed determined to get to the Berkley Hotel in Sydney and get rid of this difficult passenger at the earliest possible time.

Not normally a nervous man by nature, he had to admit to being somewhat concerned about his fate during the hair-raising journey. So after a couple of minutes he fastened his seat belt, later realising this was a legal requirement anyway.

Even if it wasn't it would be a bloody good idea with this guy.

*

On arrival at the Berkley the driver leapt out and was most helpful in assisting with the bags. Unfortunately he tried to be too helpful and within a few moments had begun to be a nuisance to Millane who made a point of paying him the exact fare. The man looked very put out by this and stretched out his hand.

'Oh, do you want a tip? Well, I'd plant your peas early this year: it's going to be a hard winter.' With that he turned on his heels and hurried into the foyer of the hotel leaving the cab driver standing on the footpath gaping in surprise.

After the usual registration formalities he was given a room key, and declining the offer of assistance with his baggage made his way to the lift and then to his room where he was planning to stay for a few days at least.

The sheer luxury of first-class travel with the better quality airlines was such that the exhaustion factor inherent in flying was considerably less than for the people travelling economy class. The trip had been extremely comfortable and relaxing, and apart from having a couple of glasses of wine shortly after taking off from Heathrow he had slept for the majority of the journey, having first advised the cabin crew that he did not wish to be disturbed.

He was, therefore, refreshed and felt capable of getting on with the job that he had come to Australia to do.

*

Having left his key at reception he made enquiries of the doorman how best to get to Manly and was advised of two choices. One, to take a cab all the way, which the doorman insisted would be a long journey and quite boring, or alternatively to get a cab to Circular Quay, the harbour's central ferry terminal and from there take a ferry direct to Manly.

The thought of a trip on Sydney Harbour rather appealed to him, so thanking the doorman he hailed a cab to Circular Quay where he arrived a few minutes later. He eventually found his way to the ticket kiosk where he purchased a return ticket to Manly and was directed to Terminal 3 where he boarded a ferry that was about to leave.

The weather was superb so he decided to sit on deck at the bow of the ship and enjoy the best view possible between Sydney and Manly.

Unfortunately Sydney Harbour had other plans for him in that the seemingly smooth trip suddenly changed as the ferry moved across a large opening to the ocean on its right.

There was a massive swell running in from the Pacific Ocean and the ferry turned into the swell for a minute or so causing fairly large waves to splash over the bow of the ferry where he was sitting, alone.

It's no wonder I am the only stupid sod sitting out here, he thought as he hurried back towards the comfort of a forward-facing glass screen. Look at all those people grinning out at me. They must know I'm a bloody tourist. Even he saw the funny side of it though. Regardless of the unexpected soaking he thoroughly enjoyed it.

This beats the hell out of bussing around London.

On leaving the ferry terminal he crossed the road and walked along a very pleasant pedestrian shopping mall called The Corso, which to his surprise led to the open beachfront of the world-renowned Manly Beach. Although an experienced traveller he had never seen such a beautiful beach so close to a town centre. It all looked so friendly and inviting. The main promenade was lined with Norfolk Pines which only added to the colour and character of the area.

★

He found a small café on the main esplanade, South Steyne, and ordered a pot of tea. Whilst waiting for the tea he undid his briefcase and once again examined the instructions from Colonel Marven. The waitress was most helpful to him and quickly directed him to the undertakers where Sammy's body was currently being kept. She insisted it was only five minutes' walk away.

'Thank heaven I'm a fit man, otherwise this would have bloody killed me,' he said out loud, still walking some fifteen minutes after leaving the café. Then he saw it.

Wilkinson and Son was situated in a large stone building which had the appearance of having once been a church.

He rang the bell on the large wooden, church-like door and waited. After a moment or so the door creaked open and a tall, sombre-looking man dressed in a dark grey suit invited him inside and led him into a sparsely but nicely appointed reception area where he directed him towards a luxurious high-backed leather armchair. The man sat down behind a large mahogany desk, and clearing his throat enquired how he could be of help.

Millane explained that he was here to pick up the body of Sammy Marven and placed the legal documents that the Colonel had given him on to the highly polished table.

The mouth of the man opposite dropped open and his eyes nearly popped out of their sockets. The blood drained from his face and Millane recognised the look of fear in the man's eyes.

Quickly regaining his composure the man said, 'There must be some terrible mistake. Mr Marven's body was cremated this morning.'

Leaping out of the seat Millane snarled at the man. 'What the hell do you mean, cremated this morning? I have all the legal documents. They are there in front of you. The body of Samuel Frederick Thomas Alfred Peter Marven was to be kept by you in your mortuary, in your care, pending my arrival to take the body back to England.'

'Well, yes, that was the original arrangement, but then Mr Marven's lawyer turned up. Surely you must know all about that.'

'Which bloody lawyer? The only lawyer involved in this business is the lawyer who signed those documents I've just given to you, and he's the lawyer of the Marven family who I assure you is back in England. You had better do some quick explaining, Mister, because unless you have a damn good story I am going to call the police and stir some very deep shit for you,' he snapped angrily.

'Well, sir, yesterday I got a visit from this black American gentleman. A small man. He claimed that he was the lawyer for the Marven family and produced all of the documentation to prove not only that he was indeed their lawyer, but that he had the authority to direct that the body be cremated. Some of the forms he produced were the same as those you have there.'

He picked up one form and frantically waved it in the air.

'This form is the official document authorising the removal of the remains of the deceased from this country. I will shortly show you the identical form that he gave me. However, his differs in clause C which is the clause that states the manner in which the body will leave the country. I assure you, sir, that the documents the man presented to me are genuine and I have no cause to believe them to be otherwise.'

By this time Millane was both angry and deeply puzzled. He was convinced that there was no way that the Colonel's lawyer could have made such an error. However, this raised the question of who else would authorise such a thing to be done, and why?

The undertaker left the room for a moment and returned with a folder in his hand. He opened it up and removed a small wad of documents. He handed them to Millane. Whilst he was not a legal man the documents seemed to be of the legal type and most of them were similar to those that he had been given in England. They certainly appeared to direct the undertaker to conduct a cremation and to await instructions regarding the removal of the ashes.

Millane was not an indecisive person but on this occasion he was completely thrown by the events that had occurred. He did not know what to do.

'Can you please give me a copy of those documents?'

'Well, sir, that is not normal practice,' Wilkinson replied nervously, then he looked into Millane's eyes and his blood ran cold. 'However, under the circumstances I believe I have no alternative but to accede to your wishes. There has obviously been a very bad mistake made by Mr Marven's lawyers in England. Whilst it is not unusual for me to receive two sets of instructions from the same family, or the same organisation, this specific sort of problem has never happened to me before.

'I really do hope this is not going to cause any problems for my company. In my line of business we have to be most careful. After all, we are dealing with families in the midst of their grief, probably at the most tragic period of their lives.'

Millane knew that the man was lying though his teeth but decided to let him continue in the hope that he would say something useful.

'I am sure however,' Wilkinson continued, 'that you will find that everything is in order, and that subsequent to your departure from England Mr Marven's plans were changed for some reason or another. Meanwhile, sir,' he stumbled over the word sir and looked most distressed, 'what shall I do with the ashes?'

'Hang on to them for me for the moment, Mr Wilkinson. Do not, I repeat, do not under any circumstances hand them over to anybody else without my authority,' he snapped at the man.

'If that lawyer returns with the correct documents I will have no choice.'

He leaned forward over the mahogany desk and shouted into Wilkinson's face.

'I have done with stuffing around with you, you lying little bastard. You will have a choice, so don't kid yourself. The only choice you will have will be to do exactly as I tell you, otherwise I'll break your scrawny little fucking neck. Do you understand me, Wilkinson?'

His threat seemed to have done the trick as the man slumped back into his chair and began to shake violently.

★

Five minutes later Millane was thumbing through the photocopies that Wilkinson had provided for him, whilst the undertaker sat in front of him gazing into thin air, obviously in shock.

Millane noticed that one of the documents bore the crest of the British Consulate-General, and was signed by a Mr Basildon.

'Why is this form necessary?' he snapped at the undertaker.

Wilkinson glanced at the sheet of paper. 'That is a normal routine document when the deceased is a British citizen.'

Having examined the documents thoroughly he placed them into his briefcase. He then asked the man for directions to the British Consulate-General Offices, discovering to his dismay that he would have to return to Sydney once more. Looking at his watch he realised that it was just after 1 p.m. He had been in Australia for just over four hours.

'How long will it take me to get back into Sydney if I go by cab?'

'I suppose if you paid the driver well enough he could get you to the Consulate-General Office within half hour or so. It really depends on the traffic,' Wilkinson replied sullenly. His voice had almost failed he was so afraid of this threatening man. All he wanted was for him to leave.

Millane picked up his briefcase and made to depart, but just before he did he lifted the man out of his seat by the collar of his coat and reminded him just what would happen if he failed to obey the instructions he had been given.

'I'm at the Berkley if you change your mind and decide to tell me the truth.' He almost felt sorry for Wilkinson when he saw tears welling in his eyes.

★

He was in luck. Just as he walked out onto the footpath he saw a cab discharging a passenger a short way down the street. At first the driver did not seem interested. In fact he appeared to be quite opposed to the idea of a fast drive into Sydney. However, when Millane thrust a twenty dollar bill into his shirt pocket and advised him that the money was merely a down payment his face lit up. After giving him the address and reminding that speed was of the essence Millane collapsed back into the rear seat and fastened his seat belt.

His previous cab journey had been worrying enough, but was nothing compared with this one. The man was positively certifiable. The chances he took were really over the top, but having instructed him to get there as fast as possible Millane decided he should just lie back, shut his eyes and relax as much as he could, under the circumstances.

★

'It's Wilkinson here, sir, the undertaker. Now, you told me that everything was in order and that there would be no trouble. Well, you were wrong. You've got real trouble. I have just had a snooping Pom in my office who has just arrived from England this morning. He had all the correct legal documents to take that boy's body home.

'This man is no fool, sir. He's a nasty bastard too. He threatened me with violence. Now, I know you paid me well, but I'm not in the business of being threatened, and I think you should—'

He didn't finish the sentence. Felix had listened to him enough. He dealt with him in the same way that he dealt with all people he considered inferior.

'Shut up! You stupid idiot. Stop talking shit and tell me more about this fucking Englishman.'

The undertaker gave him all the information he required, including a very good description of the man. He also advised him that he was on his way by cab to the British Consulate-General Office where he would probably arrive within half an hour or so. Almost as an afterthought he told Felix where Millane said he was staying.

'You were paid well for your services, Wilkinson, so keep your big mouth shut. You are not to speak to that man again. Do you understand me?'

Wilkinson was now really scared. Within ten minutes he had been physically threatened by both the Englishman and the little black American. The difference between his fear of Millane and that for Felix, however, was that in Felix's case he feared for his life. He had no way of knowing just how justified he was for feeling this way.

# Chapter Two

Tuesday – 2.45 p.m.

The British Consulate-General Office in Sydney was usually very busy. However, Millanc arrived during mid-afternoon and the place seemed almost empty of people, on both sides of the counter.

It appeared that today was a day that the office closed at 3 p.m. for some reason or another, and the clerk whose attention he eventually managed to raise apparently resented this late visitor and tried his hardest to ignore him. Millane was used to this sort of petty bureaucrat, and once he realised he was being given the cold shoulder treatment he put on his best Oxford accent and loudly demanded to be attended to. It worked immediately.

The clerk was obviously easily intimidated and probably thought that the pushy customer with the posh Pommy accent was likely to be important.

Experience over the years had taught Millane that in such circumstances the louder the voice, the better.

He asked to speak to Mr Basildon, the person whose signature was on the form he had viewed in the under-taker's office, and a copy of which was in his briefcase. After much stalling he was shown into the man's office.

'Leave the door open,' the man instructed sharply.

Millane closed it with a bang and sat himself down at the desk.

Basildon was a tall, slim man with hawk-like features and very dark eyes. He was immaculately dressed in what appeared to be a Savile Row made suit. The style was certainly similar to that worn by most officers from the Brigade of Guards and it was certainly of that superior quality. He also wore what appeared to be a Guards' Brigade tie. Millane was later to decide that this latter affectation was a lie, and that the man had probably never even served in the military.

His instant thought from Basildon's demeanour was that the man knew he was coming to visit him, and also knew what the visit was all about. The bureaucrat then proved this to be the case within the first minute by referring to the very document that had brought Millane to his office.

'How did you know that I was enquiring about Mr Marven?'

'My clerk told me of course. We are not that inefficient here, Millane.'

He was immediately on the alert. He had not discussed the purpose of his visit with the clerk. It was obvious that Basildon had been contacted by Wilkinson, or someone he had since spoken to, as he was the only person in Australia who was aware of his interest in Sammy Marven.

Basildon made no pretence about his feelings regarding his visitor. He was angry about being disturbed at this time of the day and told Millane so. However, his anger could not disguise his obvious nervousness which caused his right eye to twitch repeatedly. He was definitely displaying signs of being concerned about the presence of his caller.

★

As a highly trained and experienced undercover operative John Millane had a high level of skill in assessing people.

His life had depended on his ability in this regard on numerous occasions in Belfast and elsewhere.

He had a nagging feeling that his life was probably at risk on this occasion, although he was sure that Basildon could not be a threat to him. It was the people who the man was working for in assisting in the disposal of Sammy's body who he would have to be wary of. They were almost certainly high-powered people if they could get support, however unofficial, from a place like this.

Now he was sure of Basildon's complicity he immediately got down to the subject of the illegal cremation of Sammy Marven's body. The mere use of the word illegal startled the man who went strongly on the offensive, threatening legal action if the allegation was not withdrawn immediately. He was rattled and he showed it.

Basildon was loud in his defence and in defending the reputation of his department. Millane smiled to himself as he played with the thought that the bureaucrat had probably been taught by the same man who told him that the loudest voices were always the most intimidating.

However, in this instance it was wasted effort as he was up against a professional who already knew that he was lying and trying to cover for someone else.

In his endeavours to achieve his objective of bullying Millane into submission the man became more and more nervous as he realised that he was not succeeding. His eye twitching had increased dramatically and he also started to stutter. Taking advantage of the control that he now knew he had, Millane asked, 'So who is this lawyer who brought in the documents for you to sanction?'

'What lawyer? I don't know what you are talking about.' By now Basildon had begun to cough and choke. His speech was almost incoherent.

'The little black guy. The American. You know very well whom I am talking about, Basildon, so stop fucking me around. I have it on excellent authority that a black American claiming to be a lawyer, a small man, came to you seeking authority to claim the body of one Samuel Marven, and have it cremated. I have copies of the document you signed in this briefcase.

'Now don't bullshit me, Basildon. You signed the form that was given by this black man to the undertaker, a man named Wilkinson, over in Manly. Or are you telling me that he wasn't a lawyer after all?' He decided to go for broke and really lean on the man.

'I also have proof that the black man paid you for services rendered.'

Basildon's face dropped. He was emotionally shattered. His face was bright red and he appeared unable to speak.

Millane was concerned that he may have a heart attack and he didn't want that to happen. Not that he was in the slightest concerned for the health or welfare of the man who he had already decided may be directly or indirectly involved with Sammy's death, or at least involved in the conspiracy to cover up the facts behind it.

His only concern for Basildon's health was that he wanted him alive and well and able to assist in his enquiries that were already beginning to lead somewhere significant.

'Speak up, man. You know what I'm talking about, and more to the point you know bloody well whom I'm talking about. I want to know who the black man is and where I can find him.'

At last Basildon seemed to be trying to bring himself under control. 'I don't remember who it was. I cannot be expected to remember every detail about every minor matter that comes across my desk. Good God, man, I see dozens of people every day.'

The suggestion that Sammy Marven's death was a minor matter infuriated Millane. He leapt up in anger and grabbed

Basildon by the Guards' Brigade tie and pulled him towards him so that their faces were almost touching.

'A young lad who I was very close to has died here in Sydney under very suspicious circumstances. I was sent, together with all the genuine documentation, to collect his body and take it home to his dying father who is my closest friend. How dare you refer to that as a minor matter?

'Thanks to you issuing the final authority his body was claimed by a bogus lawyer, an American whom you fucking well know. The boy's body was cremated, for Christ's sake.'

Basildon started to sob uncontrollably, but Marven did not release his grip on the necktie. On the contrary, he pulled it tighter until the man began to choke.

'That authority was signed by you only two days ago and already you are claiming to have forgotten the entire incident.

'For a start, Mr Basildon, I ought to break your fucking legs just for suggesting that Sammy Marven's life and death was a minor matter. Secondly I will not tolerate people lying to me. Those who do get severely punished and I'm sure you don't want me to punish you, because I am very good at it and I don't believe in half measures.'

By this stage Basildon was sagging at the knees so Millane let him fall to the ground. He was in a state of complete collapse. Millane was suddenly aware of a strong smell of urine. He let go of the tie in disgust.

'You make me sick, you disgusting bastard. You are lying through your teeth for some reason. I intend finding out why you are doing it. More important, Mr stinking pissing Basildon, I am going to find out whom you are doing this for.'

The official had ceased to twitch. He was staring up at Millane with a pleading look on his face which had turned a sickly, pasty grey. A small dribble of spit was running down his chin and the tears were flowing freely.

'Get me the complete file on this matter, Basildon. Now don't fuck with me or I will make you sorry you were ever born. I'll cause you more trouble than you have ever dreamed of in your worst nightmare. Don't even think of sounding the alarm or calling for help. Do so and you will be doing yourself terminal harm.'

Basildon sobbed loudly for a few moments before choking out the word, 'I can't give you the file. It's in the night safe. It's on a time lock that doesn't deactivate until morning when the office opens. The only person who can open it otherwise is the Consul General. He has the coded numbers to bypass the time lock.'

Millane was sure he was telling the truth, but, at that very moment he heard a noise outside the office and decided that it might be appropriate to get out as quickly as possible. To be detained for violence in this place would be extremely difficult for a serving British Army Officer to explain.

'You are a lying bastard, Basildon,' he hissed between closed teeth, barely able to stop himself from hitting the man. 'I know you are lying and I can prove it, but I am going to leave you alone. Until tomorrow morning, that is. By that time I will have stirred up enough shit in London to guarantee that you will be flying home, economy class, on the first available flight. The sort of shit I am capable of stirring, and the strings I can pull in high places will destroy your career and probably put you behind bars for a while. I kid you not.'

The man looked as if he was going to pass out, when Millane turned on his heels and stormed out of the office slamming the door behind him.

'Mr Basildon does not wish to be disturbed,' he told the security man who opened the front door of the building and let him out on to the street.

★

He stood there for some while seething with anger. Then, turning back towards the building he spoke out loud, 'You'll keep until morning, Basildon. Then I'm coming after you. Just watch me, you bastard.'

Out of the corner of his eye he saw a cab coming towards him, and stepping into the road he waved it down. Directing the driver to his hotel he slumped back into the seat in the rear and closed his eyes. This seemed the best way to experience a Sydney cab drive, whilst mentally reviewing the things that had happened to him since his arrival in the country.

He looked at his watch. It was just after 4.30 p.m. He had only been in Australia for eight hours and already his entire mission was a disaster.

You were right, Colonel. Sammy was murdered, but I don't know why. I will find out though. I promise, he said to himself as the cab raced on to its destination.

★

They careered through the streets, the driver seemingly behaving as if he had a death wish, but Millane did not notice just how fast the vehicle was going. His eyes were fixed firmly on the car that was following them.

The passenger side rear mirror was jammed outwards at an angle that provided him with a perfect view of the traffic behind. He noticed this immediately on getting into the cab, and thought how stupid the driver must have been for not correcting it. He was about to make an observation concerning the way the mirror was facing when he first saw the car that was following them.

The white Holden was maintaining the same speed as the cab, which was not an easy thing to do. The cab driver was behaving like a maniac, weaving in and out of the traffic as though his life depended on it. Yet the Holden remained close to its tail.

★

Blessed with exceptional eyesight he was able to pick out detail at a distance that most other people, even those with above average eyesight, could not. This ability had saved his life and the lives of associates on a few occasions in the past. He took advantage of this now and concentrated hard on getting a visual fix on the driver of the car, and any other occupants.

There was only one person in the Holden, but he or she was hard to see as the head only just showed above the dashboard. The person was either very short or was purposely bending forward to prevent being seen.

Just at that moment the cab driver braked hard to avoid a pedestrian who had foolishly stepped out into the road. The pursuing driver did not anticipate the sudden deceleration and ended up skidding broadside on towards the rear of the cab with its driver side closest.

Millane saw the driver full face for a brief moment. It was certainly a man. He was very dark and he did not appear to be crouching down. He was a small black man.

'The little black American,' Millane shouted out loud.

'What was that, mate?' asked the cab driver.

'Never you mind. Just get us out of here, and fast.'

The cabby didn't need telling twice. Within seconds he had accelerated forward leaving the Holden and the little black man way behind. Millane felt sure that the man had not resumed the pursuit as he had not appeared again during the remainder of the journey to the Berkley Hotel.

# Chapter Three

Tuesday – 4 p.m.

Shit! Why are you so surprised, John? You've only been in the country for eight hours. Sammy's body has been illegally cremated. You've uncovered an obvious conspiracy to get rid of whatever evidence Sammy's body might have held. You have been lied to by a senior British government official. You've been tailed by the little black man, and he appears to be the link to everything.

Now this. Jesus! Whoever did this was a determined bastard.

He gazed angrily around his hotel room which was a complete shambles. The drawers of the dressing table were thrown around the floor, and the bed and armchairs had been upturned and their bases ripped out.

His two suitcases, which he had not bothered to unpack on his arrival, had been forced open and the contents were strewn across the room. Someone had obviously been searching for something important, because as well as causing damage to the furniture the intruder or intruders had also sliced open the linings of the leather cases and ripped off their top covers. They were totally destroyed. Complete write-offs.

★

This wasn't the first time that Millane had had his living quarters done over by people searching for information. It had happened to him on two occasions whilst involved in undercover work in Ireland.

The searchers on those occasions had also been very determined to check out his credentials, but his property had never been subjected to this level of destruction.

He came to the conclusion that this was probably not the intruder's full-time occupation as it smacked too much of amateurism.

'The bastards,' he shouted out loud as he rummaged through his gear to see if anything was missing. He was relieved to see that as far as he could tell all of his property was still there.

He knew that his documents were all safe as he had been carrying them in the briefcase that he had taken with him earlier.

Just then a wide smile came over his face. He had suddenly started to think about what would happen if he put in a claim under his travel insurance. The smile quickly vanished as he remembered the bureaucratic nightmare he had experienced when he had made a travel insurance claim once in the past.

Well, Colonel, it looks like you were doubly right. This is really no coincidence. My visits to the undertaker and then to our Mr Basildon have really frightened somebody. They were probably searching to see if I had any evidence pointing to them.

His mind was working overtime as he picked up his clothing and other personal belongings from around the room and piled them neatly on a chair.

They have no idea what I really know, and what I may or may not have on them, whoever they are, he pondered as he completed his clean-up operation, but if these bastards are anything like the bastards that I know and love so well, then they will be back.

This disturbing thought was generated from his personal experiences in the past, and his clear understanding of what his next step would be under similar circumstances.

He remembered with a rare tinge of guilt the people he had made return visits to after such unsuccessful searches. He recalled the beatings that he had felt obliged to give to some of them in order to obtain the information or property that he was after and didn't want to be on the receiving end of such treatment.

★

This whole episode had reinforced his belief that Sammy Marven's death had been less than accidental, and most certainly not self-inflicted.

People wouldn't go to such lengths to harass someone who is looking into the circumstances of a genuine suicide or overdose, now would they? What would be the point?

He was puzzled as to what the intruder might have been looking for, but had already made up his mind that it would not be healthy to hang around to ask questions personally. His instincts told him that if he did he would be in extreme danger. He would have to get out of the place and find a more secure base from which to continue his investigations.

'Continue my investigations? Christ! I haven't even started them yet,' he shouted out loud as be grabbed the edge of the upturned bed.

He needed to make a phone call. He found the telephone and within minutes he was nibbling on a large steak sandwich and sipping at a double Scotch supplied by room service. He made sure that the young man who delivered the tray had not seen inside the room. There was nothing to be gained by alerting the hotel management that one of their prime rooms had been trashed.

Having righted the bed and other furniture, and replaced the drawers of the dressing table, he was sitting in an armchair dialling an international number. Whilst he was aware that the number he had dialled would show up on the hotel's records, he was quite sure that Michael McQuillan's secure line system would electronically prevent anyone from tracing the call that he was about to make.

'Michael, my man,' he said in his affected Irish accent, 'I'm in the shit, big and deep so I am. I think that my life may be in danger at this very moment. Some real bad buggers are after me, Michael, and only because of my loyalty to the cause.'

'What could you possibly be doing in Australia that would in any way be of benefit to the cause, John lad?' Michael asked with a low chuckle.

'It's not a joke, Michael. Here I am in grave danger of being terminally screwed and you are after treating it as some sort of fun. Michael, I wouldn't be calling you from the other side of the world if it wasn't terribly serious, now would I?'

'Probably not, John, but don't piss me about, boy. If I am going to help you I need to know the complete story. I am not treating this lightly, John, but our international network is crucial. I can't risk compromising it in any way.

'The people I am going to contact are not the sort to be fooled around with. If things are not exactly what you say then are they are going to get awfully pissed off with you, and I don't mean maybe.'

Millane had already considered the probability that Michael McQuillan would need to be assured that he had a good excuse before contacting his people in Australia on his behalf, and had already worked out a story that he felt sure would do the trick.

'Michael, on my very first day here I have come across a scam for getting hold of defence force surplus weaponry that virtually makes it legal.'

McQuillan interrupted him sharply. 'So what's so bloody clever about that? Surplus gear is relatively easy to acquire anywhere.'

'You are right, Michael, but this stuff isn't as surplus as it is made out to be. The Aussie military would not like it to be leaving their hands this long before its use-by date. Anyway, there's another bunch of lads who have decided that I am muscling in on their territory. If that wasn't bad enough they seem to think that I am either a federal copper or one of their own New South Wales boys.

'I have already had my room torn apart and I suspect they will be coming back after me. I know I would if I was them. I do not want to be around when that happens, Michael, but I have no place else to go. I need some back-up, or at least a temporary hideout.

'Think about it, Michael, this weapons scam could be ours for the picking. It is the best I have ever seen, and you know I am good at smelling out these sorts of things. But I have got to find some way of discouraging these other lads before they get to me.'

'I sincerely hope you aren't fucking with me, John, because I have got to take some pretty drastic action on your behalf. It will mean accessing a very important cell of the organisation, and these Paddies are real nasty buggers, believe me. If they decide to look you up, before they take you on, they will check you out so closely that it will be almost like having sex with them, if you know what I mean.' Michael chuckled once more.

'Suits me, Michael. Aren't I a loyal member of the Regiment? I have got nothing to hide, my friend. In fact, after what those bastards have done to me so far I have got nothing. Period!'

'Give me your number, John, and stay put. If you have to get out fast, take as many precautions as you can to ensure that you aren't tailed. Then head for somewhere that you know. Somewhere public, out in the open air where nobody can sneak up on you. Can you think of such a place, John?'

'Tell them the ferry terminal at Manly. If I have to bolt before you phone back I will be in the concourse of the Manly ferry terminal. Tell them I'll be carrying two white cotton bags.'

'Cotton bags? I don't understand you, John, and if I don't they sure as hell won't either.'

'The bastards destroyed my suitcases, Michael. So if I have to leave the hotel in a hurry I shall be carrying my gear in two pillowcases from the hotel room.'

'I've got you,' Michael acknowledged. 'Now, don't leave unless you have to. I'll be as quick as I can. Oh, and by the way, John, this phone number will no longer be obtainable. I'll give you the new one later. God be with you, boy.'

★

The line went dead, and Millane returned to his steak sandwich and whisky feeling slightly more reassured than when he first called Michael McQuillan's number.

It took him just a few minutes to pack all of his belongings into the two pillowcases that he removed from the pillows on the bed. Luckily they were quite large and he was able to tie the tops thereby securing his property in the event of his having to escape in a hurry.

Whilst doing this he had left out a tie which he used to secure both of the pillowslips together. This was to enable him to carry them over his shoulders should he have to run or climb during his escape.

When packing back in the UK he had anticipated some leisure time while in Sydney so he had included a pair of running shoes. He quickly changed into these as he felt sure that they would be more practical if he had to make that quick exit. He then started to plan for that eventuality.

★

Checking the corridor outside his room he satisfied himself that there was nowhere that anyone could conceal themselves. He also examined the stairwell, but discounted that avenue of escape as it could be blocked too easily and he would be too vulnerable.

His room had a small balcony. He saw that there was one floor above his, and that the balcony above could be reached relatively easily, although he would be left hanging in mid-air for a short while if he climbed up that way.

He then noticed a large pipe attached to the wall close to the balustrade of the balcony. The pipe extended up to the rooftop and would be quite easy to climb if that became necessary. Whilst he didn't relish the thought of being trapped on the roof, at least that was one option. It could also give him an advantage in that from there he would be occupying the high ground should the opposition choose to come up after him.

He examined the pipe once more to see if there were any alternative exits if he selected it as his avenue of escape. To his dismay he saw that both the pipe and the balconies of the lower rooms ended some five flights from the ground. Still, entry to one of the rooms below him was also an alternative to consider if all else failed.

Once satisfied that he could not be trapped in the room he placed the two pillowcases on the balcony as this would be his immediate escape route whether he went up or down.

He then spent the next five minutes securely jamming items of furniture up against the door of his room to help prevent access from the corridor.

★

Whilst he was doing this he noticed that the door handle was made of a shiny grey metal, probably steel for strength and security. A sudden idea came to him. There was a table lamp lying on the floor in the corner of the room. He pulled the plug out of the power socket in the wall. Then, using a small pocket knife which he always carried on him he cut the cable of the electric blanket at both ends. He then stripped the ends of the cable leaving the three wires exposed with the wires at one end much longer than at the other. He then cut the cable of the table lamp at the lamp end and stripped the wires of that end in the same way as with the electric blanket cable.

He joined the wires of both cables together, making sure that none of the individual bare wires were touching.

He now had a cable some ten feet long with a three pin plug at one end and three very long exposed wires at the other which he securely twisted around the door handle.

Having done that he replaced the three pin plug back into the power socket, making sure that the switch was in the off position. Should anyone try to force entry into the room he would switch the power on before making good his escape, which he had now decided would have to be upwards to the roof.

Anyone touching that bugger will get a nasty shock. Millane laughed at his play on words. He knew that the handle would be perfectly safe while the power was switched off. However, once he turned it on it would be a completely different story, and he would only activate the switch if somebody tried to force the door.

John Millane, you are a resourceful, evil-minded bastard, he said to himself. Then out loud he added, reverting again to his Irish drawl, 'But wouldn't the Belfast Regiment be proud of you, Paddy.'

★

As a final precaution to ensure fast response should McQuillan return the call in time he pulled the telephone as near to the open door of the balcony as he could, and then sat down on the floor beside it and waited. Fifteen minutes had now elapsed since he had spoken to Michael. It seemed like hours.

He continued to sit and wait patiently for the call he wanted urgently to receive before the inevitable return of the intruders or their associates. When the phone did eventually ring it startled him. He snatched it up and spoke urgently into the mouthpiece. 'Yes, Michael.'

'It isn't Michael. Now, this had better be for real, Millane, 'cos we don't like people who fuck us around.' It was a broad Belfast voice on the other end of the line.

'I promise you it's for real. I'm in a very dodgy position and I need some back-up quickly. How can you help me?'

'Well, it's for sure that we are not stepping foot into that hotel. If you as deeply in the shit as Michael said you are then get out of there and head down George Street towards The Rocks. We'll be looking out for you. We understand you will be carrying a couple of pillowcases with your stuff in them.

'When we're sure you are not being followed we may take action, but we will decide that out on the street. Now, get the hell out of there and into the open where we can assess you.' With that the caller cut off.

*

At that moment he heard a noise outside the door, then saw the handle being turned and the door vibrate as if someone was exerting pressure on it. He briefly checked that the furniture piled against the door was still secure. It looked as if it could hold out for a minute or two, which was all he would need, he hoped.

The pushing against the door had temporarily ceased and he could hear two men taking outside. He threw the pillowcases over his shoulder then rushed to the power point and switched it on. Immediately there were sparks and the strong smell of burning but he was not concerned as he was already out on the balcony.

Reaching over towards the large pipe he launched himself at it. Just at that moment there was a loud scream, and the lights in the hotel room behind him immediately went out.

Gripping the pipe firmly he began his climb upwards. He was a highly trained and fit soldier so despite his gammy leg the climb was very easy for him. It took him less than a minute to reach the roof, by which time he could hear very loud noises coming from below. The intruders were obviously having another attempt at breaking the door open and by the sound of it were not having too much success.

*

Clambering over the wall and on to the flat roof he quickly took stock of the situation. Apart from two skylights and the lift housing, the roof was flat. It was much higher that the roofs of the neighbouring buildings, not that he had ever considered jumping from roof to roof. That sort of nonsense only ever happened in the movies.

He ran to each of the skylights but to his dismay discovered that they were both heavily barred. The brick building that housed the lift machinery had one steel door on to the roof. This was locked, but within seconds he had gained entry with the aid of some small strips of metal called jigglers that he had acquired from the expert locksmith who helped train SAS operatives. To date his success rate with the jigglers had been one hundred per cent. He was relieved that his record was still intact.

Once inside the building he was able to look down four lift shafts on to the top of the lifts which were on various floors. All of them appeared to be in service and one was stationary on the floor that he had just hurriedly vacated in such an unorthodox manner.

★

He decided that he had no time to lose and reached out for one of the cables that operated that lift. He grabbed it and hastily lowered himself on to the roof of the box-like container that was the lift. Crouching down low he slowly lifted the access trapdoor a centimetre or two and peered inside.

A man was standing in the lift, the door of which was open. Even from above he could see that he had been successful in booby-trapping the hotel room door. The man had a towel wrapped around his hand and was leaning against the back wall of the lift, groaning and talking loudly to a man in the corridor who could not be seen from the top of the lift.

'Let's get out of here. The bloke's gone. He's done a runner. We ain't going to catch him now. For fuck's sake, Derek. I need to see a doctor. I feel like shit.'

'Stop bleeding whinging, you useless bastard. We've got to get him. Felix will do his nut if we report that we have lost him. I'm going to try to get up on to the roof. That's the way he must have gone. You get down to the foyer and make sure he doesn't come out of any of the lifts, or the stairs, and for Christ's sake take that fucking towel off your arm. You'll bring attention to yourself, and we need that like we need a hole in the bloody head.

'We can't afford to alert the hotel staff. That would embarrass the shit out of us,' ordered the second man, obviously the senior of the two.

The man in the lift pressed a button and the lift commenced its journey downwards. It was to be the last thing that he would remember doing before regaining consciousness some five minutes later. Millane had taken advantage of the slight noise of the lift descending and had dropped through the trapdoor, landing alongside the injured man. He only hit him once, but he was a past master at putting people to sleep with apparent ease.

'Nightie-night, friend. I hope it is going to be really embarrassing for you when you are discovered, whoever you are.'

He started to search the man for some form of ID, but found nothing in his jacket pockets. Just as he started to roll the man over to check in his trouser pockets the lift came to a sudden halt and the door opened. Two elderly ladies were about to enter as Millane rushed out.

'That man is injured, ladies,' he said in the best Aussie accent he could manage. 'I'll inform the people at reception.'

The two women stood there with their mouths open as he rushed past them and headed to the reception desk. He looked most strange carrying two bulky pillowslips over his shoulder.

The reception clerk looked equally startled when he spoke to her using his Ulster accent to create the greatest confusion. He spoke loudly.

'What an unsatisfactory place this is. I only arrived this afternoon, and already someone has broken into my room and wrecked the place. Oh, and by the way, there is a man in the lift who needs some medical attention. I think he's been attacked. You'd better call the police.

'It's obviously not safe for anyone to stay here. You'll be hearing from my lawyer.'

# Chapter Four

Tuesday – 6.30 p.m.

Within seconds he was out of the door and on to the main street. Stopping a passer-by, in his best Oxford English accent he asked the way to George Street. On receiving directions which included the way to The Rocks, he continued on his way.

He felt that he had escaped the hotel in the best possible way under the circumstances. The man, Derek, who the guy in the lift had been addressing had been most concerned about raising the attention of the hotel staff. Whatever his reason was he would now be the centre of attention, or at least his associate would be. He hoped that this would keep them occupied for quite a while.

Once he reached George Street he slowed down and kept to the shop doorways as much as possible, trying to give the impression that he was a tourist doing some window-shopping. At the same time he was taking full advantage of the mirror-like reflections in the large windows to see what was happening all around him. He had calmed down after the initial excitement of the escape and was now in an anti-pursuit mode.

★

After five minutes of walking he removed his jacket and tie and stuffed them into one of the pillowcases. Even this slight change in appearance would give him a small advantage over any would-be pursuers other than Michael McQuillan's people. They would be looking for a man carrying two filled pillowcases.

It seemed as if he had been walking for ages when he saw a slow-moving car apparently following him along the street. He stopped and looked into one of the shop windows, and the car also stopped. He noticed that there appeared to be only one man in the car, a green Toyota. He moved off once more and saw that the car had followed suit.

Ahead of him he saw a sign indicating the entrance to Wynyard Railway Station and he decided to get off the road and take the rail option in the hope of shaking off his pursuers prior to continuing towards The Rocks as he had been instructed to do.

Wynyard Station did not look very impressive from George Street. It was even less impressive as he entered and found himself in a long passageway with closed shops either side, each one of which had one or more large rubbish receptacles standing outside. He broke into a run, intending to get to the end of the passageway before the Toyota reached the George Street entrance. Thirty seconds later he found himself in a large open concourse that was the real station entrance. He was about to continue running through when from behind him a voice spoke his name.

'For fuck's sake, Millane, will you stop practising for the 2000 Olympics and come with me.'

From the accent it was obvious that the man was from Northern Ireland, almost certainly Belfast, which reassured Millane considerably. He remembered to revert to his Ulster accent once more.

'How do I know you are my friend?'

'You can rest assured I am not your fucking friend, but luckily for you a friend of mine is Michael McQuillan's friend, so stop acting the fool and follow me closely.' Without a further word the man hurried off.

The man was small and wiry, and even though Millane was extraordinarily fit he found it difficult to keep up with him; on top of which, after all of his recent exertions his leg was hurting him very much. He was also conscious of his limp which had become more pronounced after his short sprint through the passageway to the station. He had learned to live with this over the years but was angry with himself that his old wounds were playing up at such an inappropriate time.

They reached a pair of escalators, but only the down side was operating.

Wouldn't you bloody believe it. I certainly don't have the luck of the bleeding Irish, he cursed inwardly as he commenced the climb in pursuit of the little Irishman.

The escalator was very steep, with high steps, and seemed to go up for ever. Millane was tiring fast and his leg was hurting him badly, and he was beginning to wonder if he would ever get to the top. He had lost sight of the little Irishman which caused him some concern, and was conscious of how exposed he was, wondering if he was being led into a well-laid trap.

You're being a bit paranoid, John. They could have done for you in a dozen places if they had wanted to, he tried to reassure himself.

However, this did not ease his concern. There was nobody on the fast-moving down escalator so he prepared himself to dive across the gap and roll down to the bottom if confronted with an ambush. It was an exercise he had practised on numerous occasions during training in pursuit management techniques.

He did not relish the thought of doing it though, as it was highly physical, bone-crunching and dangerous stuff.

Suddenly he was at the top, and coming out of the escalator as he had been trained to do, at the run in a low crouched position, he nearly collided with the Irishman who was standing, hands on hips, and laughing out loud.

Millane was feeling somewhat stupid, and the little man was capitalising on his embarrassment.

'Okay, Superman,' the man laughed. 'Come with me, and for Christ's sake walk upright like everyone else or people will think you're a fucking gorilla.'

The man was obviously enjoying Millane's embarrassment and was trying to make a big issue of it. Even though the man was really pushing his luck to the limit Millane decided to keep silent, although inwardly seething with anger. He would have dearly loved to punch the Irishman's face in, but realised he was not in a position to do anything other than obey instructions. However, he made himself a silent promise that if ever he got the opportunity to get back at his little tormentor he would do it in a way that the man would not forget in a hurry.

★

Moments later they were out on the street where, to Millane's surprise, the green Toyota was standing with its engine running. The Irishman led him directly to the vehicle and opening the rear nearside door he ushered him inside.

He was directed to lie down on the floor behind the front seats with his face down and stay there until told. He heard the front passenger door open and close and assumed that the little Irishman had got into the car also.

★

Whilst this was happening, a few kilometres away in his exclusive luxury apartment overlooking the harbour, Felix was feeling very angry with the person he was speaking to on the telephone. It was Derek, the more fortunate of the two men who had tried unsuccessfully to get to Millane in his hotel room shortly before.

'What do you mean, he got away? Jeez, you are supposed to be highly trained cops; skilled operators. And how come your partner had to identify himself as a cop? That was a stupid fucking thing to do.'

Felix waited while Derek tried to explain the circumstances that had made it unavoidable to do what they both did as the result of his colleague being attacked in the lift, explaining that if they hadn't identified themselves the police would have been called to the scene which would have complicated matters even more.

'As it is the bastards in Internal Affairs have managed to find out and they will be after us.'

'Who is this guy? The way you describe him you make him sound like some sort of special services man. You and your pal have fucked up badly, Derek. I thought I was sending men to do men's work. Instead you have performed like a couple of inexperienced Boy Scouts.'

The worried man at the other end of the line tried to interject.

'Shut up and listen. Don't ever interrupt me when I am speaking, my man. I am giving you and that stupid fucking partner of yours another chance. You've got until tomorrow morning to find and eliminate him, or I will eliminate you.'

'Eliminate? Shit! Listen here, Felix, you can't threaten us like that. Don't forget who we are.'

'I told you to shut up, and I shan't tell you again. You are already up to your necks in that level of shit anyway, so get real, man. If this guy is some form of government agent, and from what you tell me he is a cross between 007 and the Caped Crusader, then it means that you have probably blown it.

'Either you fix him or he will fix us, and that means you two especially. I have no intention of going to jail because of idiots like you two. As for remembering who you are, I sure do. You are crooked cops and if you are caught you will go away for so fucking long that they'll probably throw the keys away.

'So, get this man. It is not negotiable. That is an order.'

With that Felix slammed the phone down. He was as mad as he had ever been.

He rose from the chair and walked across the living room of the apartment to his well-stocked bar. Pouring himself a generous measure of bourbon he walked out on to the spacious balcony. The view was magnificent.

Things had gone so well for so long, and there had never been any hitches. Now, all of a sudden, ever since the unfortunate clamp down by the authorities in Manila everything seemed to be falling apart.

*

He watched the brightly lit ferry as it passed by on its way back from Manly to Circular Quay and thought back over the things that had happened to him since he moved to Australia, and the wonderful lifestyle that their enterprise had given him. He knew that it was nearing an end and that everything would have to change. He was also convinced that he would have to leave Australia, probably for good. This disappointed him greatly for he had grown to enjoy his way of life.

He found himself increasingly frustrated by the problems that were confronting him as the result of the Senator's instructions to close down the business and to leave no loose ends. Unfortunately the loose ends were continually multiplying, especially since the arrival of this mystery man, Millane.

He would have to terminate the undertaker, Wilkinson. He was a loose cannon who was scared witless and couldn't keep his mouth shut. Then there was the pompous official, Basildon, at the British Consular Office. He had been far too easy to buy and because of that was a big problem. Over the years Felix's experiences with that sort of person were that they were always likely to be open to a higher bidder, or could be vulnerable to threats of exposure which could harm their status. He would certainly have to go.

The two stupid cops were also a worry. He would get them to fix this Millane guy then he would have to kill them too. He felt sure that the New South Wales Police would never miss them. The thought of these terminations caused him to smile happily. He really enjoyed killing people. It gave him a satisfaction the equal of anything else he had ever experienced, including sex.

Unfortunately there were just too many things for him to do, and finding the time to fit everything in was his greatest problem. He had to fly down to Melbourne the following day to finalise the matter of the *Palminto*. The sinking of the ship had to be planned and timed to perfection.

'I know that nobody said that life was meant to be easy,' he said out loud to himself as he strolled back to the bar to pour himself another drink, 'but why the hell does it have to be quite so fucking difficult.'

★

Back in the car Millane was feeling cramped and silly lying on the floor with his face down. The car had maintained a normal speed and had made numerous right and left turns. At one stage it also made what was obviously a U-turn.

Whoever they were, they were going to great lengths to ensure that they weren't being followed, whilst at the same time also guaranteeing that Millane would have no idea where he was.

From his position on the floor of the car, even facing down, he could see that the light was fast beginning to fade outside. It then got dark very quickly. He was getting concerned about the lack of light during the next stage of whatever these people had planned for him. Normally an undercover operative found comfort in darkness but this was usually because he knew the geography of the area he was working in. Here in Sydney he was totally unfamiliar with the landscape, and therefore the darkness was likely to be more of a hindrance than a help.

After about twenty minutes of driving the car came to a halt and the rear nearside door was opened. Millane was instructed to get out. They were in a quiet street alongside a small corner reserve dotted with trees and shrubs.

'Do you see that park bench over yonder, Paddy? Well, go and sit on it and wait until you are spoken to. Under no circumstances are you to try to see whoever it is who speaks to you. Do you understand me?'

Millane nodded his head.

'Disobey and you could get a bullet in the head for your sins.' It was the little man who was giving the orders and on this occasion he was not smiling.

He seemed like the sort of person Millane had got used to taking most seriously back in Belfast, but he found it hard coming to grips with the fact that these same sort of people were also here in Sydney, Australia, ten thousand miles away from the dirty backstreet war of Northern Ireland.

By now it was very dark and the small park was lit with the gentle light from a cluster of bud lights that adorned the tree above the bench. He sat and waited patiently for over twenty minutes, beginning to think that their assessment of him had not been a favourable one and that perhaps he should take advantage of the poor light and make a bolt for it.

★

'So you are John Millane, are you?' The sudden sound of the voice after so long a period of silence startled him. 'I have been having further talks with Michael and he speaks very highly of you, John. He says that you aren't afraid of giving the Brits a hard time, and of getting punished for doing so.' It was an Ulster voice, coming from the shrubbery behind him.

He sat still, not daring to move a muscle. There was no way of telling if the man had a gun, or other accomplices who would shoot him if he disobeyed his instructions. What he did know was that under the same circumstances back in Belfast they certainly would not hesitate to do just that, so he was not about to take any unnecessary risks.

'In case you are wondering about my credentials, John, I have been told to tell you that the widow Flaherty is coming on fine and that she is managing the artificial leg with great skill.'

'It was her arm she lost in the blast, not her leg, and that was fifteen years ago.' Millane smiled at the amateurish way that the man had tried to catch him out.

'Oh, so it was, to be sure. If that isn't enough to convince you that I am Michael's man, then I can tell you even more. Like the day that you acted like a bloody fool and got yourself arrested and carted away in an army APC, all because the Brits roughed up a young colleen. Very noble of you.' The man laughed softly. 'The day of the explosion, I think it was.'

'All right, I believe you are Michael's friend. My question is whether or not you are my friend, 'cos I need one now more than I have ever done before, and I am not kidding.'

'Tell me what you want, John, and I'll see what I can do for you. Incidentally, whatever we do for you is for Michael, and the only payment we demand is your absolute discretion. The slightest slip in that regard and we will classify you as an enemy and deal with you accordingly. Do you understand and accept those terms, John?'

Millane readily accepted the conditions laid down and then he told the man the story about the military arms purchase scam that he had related to Michael McQuillan. He knew that he had to be precise in every respect and that his story had to be exactly the same as he had told to Michael. This would be the final part of the test for him. He knew that a man such as this would be interested in access to military hardware, just as Michael had been. He guessed that this was probably one of their main activities here in Sydney so far from Ulster, and the cause.

He then related the story of the little black man who had tailed him and then had his room torn apart before sending his cronies to get him. He knew that the latter part of the story could and probably would be checked out with the hotel and he was sure that these people would check that matter very thoroughly.

His only concern was that they might speak to someone who was on duty when he registered. At that time he was not using his assumed Ulster accent.

The Irishman seemed most interested in the description of the black American, and it seemed as if he either knew him or knew of him.

'Go back to the car, John. My men will take you to a place to put your feet up for the night. They will also supply you with a bag. You look pretty stupid walking around Sydney carrying your worldly possessions in two pillowcases.

'Once you get there you must stay put and wait for me to come back to you. Until I say so you must have no further contact with the outside world. Do you agree with those conditions?' Millane had no choice but to agree, and without a further word being spoken he returned to the car.

★

Once again he was directed to lie down with his face to the floor, and once again he was taken on a complicated tour of Sydney, or so it seemed by the number of times that the car made left and right turns. Eventually, after driving down a steep slope for a short distance they stopped somewhere very dark.

He was directed to get out and stand still. Although it was pitch black he quickly gained his night vision having been in darkness for most of the evening. He was sure that they were in some sort of underground car park. The floor was concrete and he could vaguely pick out painted white lines.

One of the men walked off into the darkness and his footsteps echoed back off the walls. He returned shortly afterwards and whispered something to his associate. Millane was led to a door which opened into a lift. It was very small, barely large enough for the three men. They did not appear to rise very far when the lift stopped and the door opened.

He was led into a large room which was comfortably furnished. It had no windows and only one other door which led to a medium-sized bedroom and a bathroom and toilet. These rooms were also windowless. Wherever he was he felt quite safe, but also realised that he was their prisoner should they choose to treat him as such.

★

The little Irishman who had guided him out of Wynyard Railway Station told him that he was to be left on his own until the following morning when someone would return to negotiate his future. After showing him the facilities and advising him that there was no way out, other than by the lift which would be locked from downstairs, both men left. He heard the lift opening and closing below before he made any move.

After ten minutes of checking he was satisfied that the place was not bugged, or if it was it would have to be highly sophisticated. He doubted that such a group would have access to such stuff. He certainly knew that Michael McQuillan's group back in Ireland did not have such equipment.

He was sure, however, that the little Irishman was correct when he stated that there was no way of getting out of this place.

He had no choice but to do the only sensible thing. He had a hot shower and got into bed. His leg was now very stiff and was causing him some pain, and he had not realised how exhausted he was after the day's exertions. Within minutes he was sound asleep.

# Chapter Five

Wednesday – 6 a.m.

Millane woke with a start and lay still for a moment wondering what it was that had roused him. Then he laughed at his own stupidity. It was the absolute silence that had brought him out of his deep sleep. He couldn't remember the last time, if ever, that he had experienced complete silence. It was strange.

He looked at his watch and was surprised that he had slept for so long. He decided that it must have been a combination of the jet lag, even though this was dramatically reduced by the luxury of first class, and the stress of the previous day's hectic events. Whatever the reason he had enjoyed nearly twelve hours of dreamless, uninterrupted sleep.

He felt good and was completely refreshed and ready to go, but under the circumstances he had nowhere to go. He was locked in and completely at the mercy of the Irishmen who had effectively become his captors.

*

He had two hours to wait before he was revisited by the men who had brought him to this place. In that period he was gainfully employed. He soaked himself in a bath of scalding hot water until it was virtually cold, then finished off with a luxurious shower, finishing his ablutions with a leisurely shave.

As promised his hosts had left a large canvas sports bag for him, so he carefully packed all of his belongings, then sat back and waited. He decided to complain to his land-lords regarding the lack of kitchen facilities and provisions as there was not even a jug or pot to boil water, let alone the makings for a cup of tea or coffee.

At 8 a.m. on the dot he heard the lift door open and close below. In anticipation of the worst scenario, that the Irishmen had discovered that he was not really one of their friends, he concealed himself behind the settee in the lounge room. Not immediately in sight of the lift door, but close enough for him to attack his visitors if things came to the worst.

The lift doors opened and he sensed that at least two people had entered the room, but lay still, ready to leap out at the intruders, if that was what they turned out to be.

'Okay, Millane. Stop playing hide and seek. Breakfast is served, so will you come and get it,' came the broad Ulster voice of the little Irishman he had taken such a great disliking to the previous evening.

This man is really pushing his luck with me, he thought as, much to the delight of his tormentor, he stepped out from behind the settee.

'Just one more word, you little git, and I'll break your fucking legs for you.' He spat the words out with great venom.

The man merely laughed.

'Now isn't that a lovely way to treat a friend who has just brought you a bacon and egg sandwich and a thermos flask of lovely Irish Breakfast Tea.'

It suddenly occurred to him that he hadn't eaten anything since the sandwich he had had in the hotel room the day before, so he grabbed the tray that was offered to him and attacked the food and the tea with enthusiasm.

In the conversation that followed he was informed that he had come up trumps as far as their boss's enquiries about him were concerned. However, their group was involved in a major operation at the moment and were already looking after the security of one other person. As they were only a small group and their resources were stretched to the limit, all that they were able to provide was overnight safe house protection until the end of the week, together with transport morning and evening to and from pre-arranged locations.

This seemed a perfect arrangement to Millane who had already decided that he did not relish the thought of the twenty-four hour company of the little Irishman; on top of which he always preferred to be freelance in whatever he did, as the fewer people around him the better if it came to any nasty business. He also understood that the additional offer of transport to and from the safe house was not a service offered out of the kindness of their hearts, but merely to ensure that the location of the premises was kept a secret.

Having agreed to this arrangement he asked his new-found allies to drive him to The Corso at Manly, and to pick him up in the same place at 7 p.m. Once this was agreed to he was subjected to the same precautions as on the previous evening, only on this occasion because it was daylight he was required to wear a bag over his head. As before he was most impressed with the arrangements to retain the security of the safe house.

As soon as the car had performed the mandatory thirty or so right- and left-hand turns he was advised that he could remove the bag and sit up. They were just turning on to the Harbour Bridge and heading towards North Sydney. It took nearly forty-five minutes in the heavy morning traffic to reach Manly. He hurried away from the car and watched it drive off. Making sure he wasn't being followed he walked towards The Corso and was soon lost in the morning shopping crowds.

★

He called into a small restaurant on the esplanade over-looking Manly Beach, where over a pot of tea he reviewed the situation to date and planned his next moves. While he was pouring a second cup he noticed a fire engine racing north along South Steyne, its lights flashing and siren blaring loudly. It was followed closely by a police car. In the background he could hear several other emergency sirens, but thought nothing of it until a bread delivery man entered the premises, apologising to the proprietor for his late arrival.

'There's been an explosion a few blocks away and the whole town has been closed up by the police and the fire people.'

'Where exactly was the explosion, Geoff?' the woman behind the counter asked.

'Well, I never exactly saw it for myself and I may have misunderstood,. but a bloke told me that it had completely destroyed the funeral director's place. You know, the one in that lovely old stone building. What on earth would there be in an undertaker's premises that could cause an explosion?'

The teapot remained poised in mid-air. Millane was stunned by the news.

Shit. What about a bomb? was his first cynical thought.

'Excuse me, I couldn't help overhearing what you said, but is that the premises of Wilkinson and Son?'

'That's what I was told,' the bread man answered. 'They say a man was killed in the explosion.'

He felt a chill run down his spine.

Christ, this has got to be something really massive for them to go to these lengths, he thought as he rushed out of the restaurant and hurried towards the place where Wilkinson and Son was located.

★

After five minutes of hard walking he reached the next intersection to the premises, but was unable to go further due to the blue and white checked tape that a young policeman was stringing across the road in front of him.

He didn't need to go any further anyway as he could see all he wanted to see. Wilkinson and Son no longer existed. The entire building had collapsed and the rubble was flaming furiously. Fire officers were directing their hoses at the blaze in an attempt to prevent the fire from spreading to neighbouring premises. Several streets were filled with fire engines, police vehicles and ambulances.

'Excuse me, Officer.' He addressed the young policeman in his best Oxford English accent. 'I had an appointment with Mr Wilkinson, the proprietor of that place.'

'Well, sir, unless you are an undertaker yourself you won't be much use to the man, as he was killed in the blast. His body was recovered by the fire guys soon after they arrived. Thank your lucky stars you weren't early for your appointment, that's all I can say. Now, I'm afraid I shall have to ask you to move on.

'If you have any enquiries to make you should pop into the station tomorrow, by which time someone should be able to help you out.'

Thanking the young officer for his most helpful advice, Millane headed off to his next destination, the hospital. It had occurred to him that there might be someone there who could fill in some of the more specific details of Sammy Marven's death.

Now that all of the other evidence had gone, including the evidence he felt sure he could have dragged, even if reluctantly, from the late but definitely unlamented Mr Wilkinson, he would have to search further afield.

He was looking for something that would prove conclusively that Sammy was murdered, a fact he was convinced of already, but that would also point towards the killer.

★

On the way to the hospital he suddenly thought of the man, Basildon, at the British Consular Office. If Felix or his mates were so quick to kill Wilkinson then Basildon's life was definitely in danger. The last thing he wanted was for that line of evidence to disappear also.

He found a phone booth, and seeking directory assistance he was put through to the Consular Office. The news he received, whilst not surprising, was none the less disturbing.

Posing as a colleague from the Embassy in Canberra he managed to get through to a senior person. The bogus identity he had assumed was sufficient to convince the man to pass on information that would not normally be given over the phone.

'He threw himself out of the window of his apartment early this morning. Nobody knows why. He must have had some real bad problems; he lived alone, you know. Nobody would have expected him to commit suicide.'

Thanking the man, and promising to pass the information on to the Ambassador he put the phone down.

Suicide, my arse. Someone was pretty quick off the mark in getting rid of those two. These people are really nasty bastards. You'll have to watch yourself, John, or you could easily be next.

# Chapter Six

Wednesday – 4 p.m.

He had already decided that if he could find the evidence to prove who killed Sammy that person would have to die.

He thought briefly about the several people he had killed during his specialist army career, both with his bare hands and by other, less physical, remote means. Most of the men he never even knew. They just happened to be the enemy and were there at the time.

Sammy was real though, and he knew that he would feel no remorse in killing the person or persons who had wasted him. In fact, he was sure that he would get some real satisfaction from achieving that end. First and foremost, however, he had to be fully satisfied that he knew for sure who had committed the crime. Hardened killer he may be, but in the absence of a lawful command he felt morally obliged to make sure he had the proof that he could live with.

★

On arrival at the hospital he went to the Casualty Department. A pretty young nurse at reception greeted him with the sort of smile that used to make him go weak at the knees when he was a much younger man. He explained that he was enquiring about the death of Sammy Marven and gave her his full name and the date that Sammy was brought to the hospital. She turned to her computer screen and keyed in some details.

'Well, he was apparently dead on arrival and was certified dead whilst still in the ambulance. The doctor who dealt with the incident was Doctor Barker, but he is on leave at the moment. Other than the ambulance crew and the mortuary attendant I doubt if anyone else saw the body.'

Millane was saddened by the reference to the death of this nice young man as an incident, whereas if had been alive on arrival at the hospital the matter would have been referred to as a case, or something similar. The nurse checked the computer further and explained that the mortuary attendant who had received the body was currently on night shift and would not be on duty until 7 p.m. that evening.

He thanked her and turned to leave when she called out to him.

'Are you interested in the other time he was in here?'

'What do you mean? What other time are you referring to?'

Well, about a month ago he was involved in a road accident and spent a few days here suffering from severe concussion and some other injuries. Doctor Talufa was the person who dealt with him. If you want to talk to him he is on duty at the moment. If you wish I can page him for you.'

'That would be very kind of you, nurse,' he replied, wondering what on earth he could possibly get out of talking to the doctor.

He heard her speaking to someone on the telephone. She then turned back to the computer and pressed some more keys. There was a gentle whirring sound that he assumed was the printer operating.

★

'Mr Millane?' The voice came from behind him. 'I am Doctor James Talufa.'

Turning, Millane was most impressed with what he saw. The doctor was a tall, well-built man. He looked fit and capable of handling himself. He was walking out from behind the reception desk and was holding a sheet of paper in his hand.

'Thanks, Jenny,' he said to the nurse. 'I'll take it from here.'

The young woman smiled back at him with the look of a cat that had just swallowed the canary. Millane smiled to himself as he glanced from the nurse to the doctor. The body language between them was pretty powerful stuff.

Who's a lucky bastard then? he said to himself, quietly hoping that he was right for both of their sakes, and at the same time wishing that it was him and not the doctor who was the recipient of the young nurse's attentions.

'I remember this young man. He tried to take on a large articulated truck in his VW, and lost the contest. A young English guy, very interested in rugby if I remember rightly. I had to put the fear of God into him to stop him from running off and scuba-diving too soon after the bash on the head. If you're after his address I can give it to you, provided you can convince me you have a right to ask for it. What is he up to these days?'

'He's not up to anything any more, Doctor. He is dead. Your young lady here has just been telling me about him being pronounced dead on arrival by your colleague, Doctor Barker.'

Talufa looked visibly shaken by the news.

'Sorry, man, I really didn't know. Please accept my apologies. I hope I haven't upset or offended you. What happened to him? I hope he didn't go diving too soon.'

'No, Doctor, he didn't go diving. He died from a drug overdose.'

'Bullshit! What the hell are you talking about? I checked that young man out from head to foot. He was as clean as a whistle. No way was he into drugs. Christ, man, there are plenty of ways of picking that sort out, not just by the holes in their bodies alone, and incidentally, your man Sammy had none at all. There was no way on this earth that he was a candidate for an overdose. He was full of life and far too well balanced for that.'

'You saw him a month before he died. How can you make such sweeping statements this much later?'

He was angry with the doctor for making his assumption, even though he felt sure that the man was right.

'Aren't you guys supposed to base everything on medical facts?'

'I have been a doctor for quite a few years now, Millane, and one gets the feel for such things, or I do anyway. I have rarely, if ever, been proved to be wrong in this regard.'

'Well, Doctor, your colleague, Barker said he died from a drugs overdose. Are you saying he was wrong?'

'Certainly not. He's a fine doctor. Your young lad obviously did die from an overdose. What I am saying is that I cannot accept that he would have taken drugs willingly. Someone must have hit him with them.'

Overhearing this conversation between the two men, the nurse pushed the computer buttons again. A minute or two later she handed Doctor Talufa two sheets of paper. He quickly read them through.

'It seems that Doctor Barker had some suspicions about the boy's death. He reported that the body was covered with needle marks, but that they all appeared to be of very recent origin. It is easy for a doctor to pick out the new wounds from the old ones. He felt that the drugs might have been administered by some other person than the deceased and he reported the matter to the police. This is a copy of that report. It was sent to a Detective Senior Sergeant Brickly-Davis.'

'I think that Mr Brickly hyphen bloody Davis and I are going to have a talk about this matter. Things are starting to make some sense to me now. I had better go now, Doctor. I have things to do, but I'll get back to you soon.

'We should get together for a pint or two. I'm a rugby fan also. I used to play for Combined Services in my younger and fitter days,' he said with a wry smile.

★

He was halfway out of the door of the Casualty Department when Talufa's voice rang out.

'Do you know anything about a black man? Not me, another black man. A little man, I think.'

'Why do you ask?' He was struggling not to show his excitement.

'Well, the man whose truck he collided with heard him moaning something about a little black man. He must have known the guy, or thought he did, because he left a note warning the boy about the black man. I read the note, misunderstood it and thought he was talking about me. I was pretty pissed off at the time.

'I tackled the truck driver about it when he phoned in to enquire about the boy a couple of weeks later. He assured me that it was someone else he was talking about, and that the guy was in some way dangerous.'

'Doc, this little black man has suddenly become a key person in this whole tragedy. He has cropped up so many times. Late yesterday the bastard was tailing my cab and nearly collided with us. He had my hotel room trashed and then sent two guys after me. I've got the distinct feeling that it was he who had Sammy murdered.'

'Murdered?' Talufa sounded astonished.

'Yes, Doc. I've known all along that he was murdered. Wasn't that what you meant when you said that somebody else must have administered the drugs to him? Wasn't that why your Doctor Barker sent the report to the police? My job is to discover why, and by whom. That's what I am here to find out and things are now beginning to move on in that regard.'

'Are you some kind of policeman, Mr Millane?'

'No, Doc. You really don't want to know who I am. I would rather it stayed that way as I have got to do things that would offend your Hippocratic oath, or something. I'm just about as close as you can be to being Sammy's next of kin though. One thing you can believe is that I am probably nastier than the little black man could ever be. You can put money on that.'

With that he hurried out of the hospital, now quite certain that he would never be able to keep that date of a few beers with Doctor Talufa. When he had done what he intended to do he would probably not be able to have a beer in public with anybody, certainly not in Australia, anyway.

## Chapter Seven

Thursday – 8 a.m.

Felix had arrived in Melbourne the night before and had booked into a small, nondescript hotel where nobody asked any questions.

He had now managed to get on board the *Palminto* without being noticed by anyone, including Captain Brandon. The ship was berthed in the Port of Melbourne having just completed some refit work that had been scheduled by the company to be carried out prior to the next voyage.

Brandon had been startled when he suddenly appeared on the bridge where he had been examining reports on the refit. Felix was annoyed when he advised him that there were still two crew members on board. They were engineers working on the rudder equipment at the aft end of the ship.

'I told you I needed the ship clear today. Don't you understand plain English?'

Felix was not pleased that his orders had been disobeyed and made sure that Brandon understood why. He needed approximately eight hours to complete his work on the ship, and the last thing he needed was the possibility of being disturbed by men as smart as engineers might be.

He was about to install the explosives that were to cause the sinking of the *Palminto* as it cruised northwards off the east coast of Australia a week or so later.

Brandon had been terrified of Felix ever since that night in Vietnam when he and the Senator had visited his apartment to collect the bags of drugs. In fact, the mere presence of the man was sufficient to make him feel extremely uncomfortable.

Still, he was heartened by the fact that this was to be his last voyage, for much as he loved the sea he longed to be free of the Senator's line of business, lucrative though it was. It excited him to think that he was actually going to retire and start to really enjoy the money that he had made over the years.

'Get rid of them, James. Send them somewhere. Find them a couple of whores ashore. Pay for a dozen whores if you have to. Do anything that you like, but get them off this tub within the hour. At nine I will be having company, and they are bringing some lovely little goodies with them. Nobody, I repeat, nobody must be around to see my pals, and especially the luggage they are going to bring on board. Now, do it.'

'Sure, Felix. I'll ring Rent-a-Whore. They'll be a great help. Now, will they be under R for Rent, or W for Whore?' Brandon mumbled as he turned to leave the bridge on his way to find the two engineers. Much as it annoyed him to have to do Felix's bidding, he knew better than to defy him.

★

In fact, getting rid of the men was very simple. He had never thought of himself as being an inventive man, but the story that flowed from him about why he needed to be on the vessel on his own until nightfall surprised even him. He never actually told them anything of any substance, but the manner in which he wove the tale left both men in no doubt that their self-righteous skipper was about to embark on some sort of sordid sexual fling to celebrate his final farewell to Australia.

The clincher was the five, crisp, one hundred dollar notes that he handed to each of them whilst suggesting that they find themselves some top-class female company.

One of the two men actually did that in a rather exclusive brothel on the opposite side of the Yarra River to the Crown Casino, where afterwards he frittered away the remaining dollars until well into the night.

He decided from Brandon's tale that his Captain was bringing some special ladies on board, and that secrecy was really in keeping with his general behaviour.

The other man whose name was Roberto was a few years younger. He visited a gay bar in South Yarra and ended up with two, very young, gay men in a small flat in Carlton, where he stayed the night indulging in a range of sexual activity and smoking pot. He arrived back on board well after dawn, but nobody seemed to care.

When Brandon had handed him his bribe money he automatically took it for granted that because the Captain was unmarried and a loner by nature, he was probably going to be dealing with the same sort of people as himself. The thought of it brought a wide smile to his face.

★

Felix was surprised and relieved when he saw the two men climb into a cab and head off towards the dockyard gate, and the city.

The goodies, as Felix called the luggage brought on board by the two men who arrived at nine were a large amount of an explosive substance shaped in oblong blocks that looked and felt like plasticine. There were four large crates of the stuff, together with a bag containing fuses, a mass of wire and several electronic devices to assist in the timing and co-ordination of the charges which would explode simultaneously in key places throughout the ship.

Brandon did not know the men, nor did he wish to know them. They were Felix's special people and that was good enough. However, Felix made sure that he never got close enough to them to even see their faces. They were in fact serving soldiers in an elite army unit. To make quite sure, Felix ordered Brandon to retire to his cabin and stay there until called.

★

The explosives that they had brought with them were, according to army records, still sitting on the shelves of a deeply placed underground munitions store at a military base an hour or more north of Melbourne.

The stuff that now sat on the shelves in its place, if ever used, would prove to be a great disappointment to whoever risked his life to position it.

Armed with plans of the ship the men worked down in the bilges and other dank places doing their work. While they were busily employed Felix spent some time underneath their van. To any viewer it would have appeared that he was probably doing some routine maintenance. However, Felix had made very sure that nobody had seen him. He was far too smart for that.

By 4.30 p.m. the work on the ship was complete. Felix's two helpers were each handed an envelope containing a great deal of money, the equivalent of a year's pay for each of them. Neither checked the contents of their envelope, certainly not in front of the little black man. They had dealt with him in the past and knew that whatever they had been given would be more than they could have hoped for working for anyone else, even for anything as unlawful as this.

Felix caught the 6.35 p.m. flight back to Sydney, and was asleep within seconds of sitting down in an economy class seat towards the rear of the aircraft. Nobody ever noticed a black man in economy, but Felix knew from experience that this may not necessarily be the case in first or business class, even in multicultural Australia.

★

At about the time that Felix boarded his flight to Sydney the van carrying the two explosive experts was driving north on the Hume Highway approaching their camp. They were both feeling very satisfied with their day's work. Both men had killed before in hand-to-hand situations, so neither of them gave a moment's thought to the fact that their work that day would result in the destruction of a ship, and kill the whole crew.

They had stopped in a lay-by outside the city and had examined Felix's reward money. Each of them had $50,000 in used notes, wealth they had never dreamed of before. Previous jobs for Felix, which usually involved blowing up empty business premises, had generally earned them $10,000 each, but this was really big time.

They turned into the entrance to the camp and had just driven under the raised barrier at the Guard Room when the explosion occurred. The van and its two occupants disintegrated into thousands of tiny pieces which rained down on the people and buildings within half a kilometre radius.

The Guard Room just wasn't there any more. Where it had once stood there was now a large crater about a metre deep.

Miraculously nobody else was killed. The young military policeman who should have been manning the Guard House was a hundred metres away at the time, sheltered behind a rifle range wall. At the precise moment that the explosion occurred he was about to withdraw from the excited and grateful young woman lying beneath him.

Their encounter had been unplanned, at least by the MP, who would have had a contraceptive in his wallet if he had known how his day was going to pan out. He was normally better prepared then this, but didn't tell her that. He felt that there was no point in her knowing that she was merely one of the many he gave his favours to. In fact he had the reputation of being the best stud in the camp.

He wanted it badly, but didn't wish to chance it without a sheath just in case anything went wrong. He was sure that if he revved her up a bit she would be anxious for the real thing as soon as possible.

But, one thing had led to another and the next thing he knew the woman was screaming for him to go inside her, whilst at the same time pleading with him not to go all the way.

Suddenly it all went wrong, for both of them. He was just on the verge of pulling away from her when the explosion occurred. Instead of pulling back the shock wave that accompanied the explosion threw him forward and back on to her before he had time to withdraw. He climaxed with a massive shudder. She screamed out with a mix of extreme satisfaction and abject horror.

He leapt to his feet, pulled his trousers up, and ignoring the woman's screams began to run to the spot where the Guard Room had been just a short while before.

He never heard the obscenities that the young woman directed at him. All he could think about was how he would explain being absent from his place of duty.

★

Felix would have seen the funny side of that sequel to the explosion had he known about it, but all he knew was that there had been an explosion in an army base in Victoria and that two soldiers had died. It was more than he ever hoped to achieve. He heard the news on the radio of the cab on the way from Sydney Airport to his apartment.

He had been sure that the soldiers would return to their base directly and had set the timer accordingly, but had estimated that the explosion would probably occur while they were on the open highway somewhere near their camp. After all, his sole objective was to get rid of the men; the loose ends that the Senator wanted tidied up, and which were haunting him at the moment.

The fact that the explosion occurred in the precincts of a military base was a bonus for him. His experience of the military was that they tended to look for the worst scenario under such circumstances, and the worst scenario for them would be terrorism. He smiled to himself at the thought.

'If those stupid bastards want to run around looking for terrorists it suits me fine,' he mumbled to himself as he opened the door to his apartment. 'Shit! But I'm no fucking terrorist. I am just a simple businessman trying hard to make a buck.' With that he broke into loud laughter which continued for some minutes.

# Chapter Eight

Saturday – 2 p.m.

Millane was angry and anxious to get out and continue his search for this black man, and whoever else was involved in the murder of Sammy Marven. Unfortunately for him he had been locked in the safe house location since Wednesday evening.

The Irishmen had arrived on Thursday morning, but only to bring supplies and to advise him that they had another special operation on and could not look out for him for a few days. He had protested that he was big enough and ugly enough to look after himself, and that he didn't need their help.

'I agree that you are ugly enough, Millane, but don't try to be a smart-arse with us. The other day it was a matter of life or death for us to look after you. All of a sudden you don't need us. Grow up, man.'

The little Irishman who he had taken such a disliking to was most specific about his instructions.

'My boss says if you leave here without us you can't come back. We will wipe our hands of you. On top of which, if you do that and this place gets blown, then you will have us after you as well as this little black man you keep on about.

'Sure, and isn't it us who are after being your fairy godmothers? Why the fuck would you want to leave here? There's food galore in the fridge. There's tons of grog, and you've even got a telly. What sort of head case would be wanting to leave a paradise like this?'

Millane got the distinct impression that the choice for him to leave, regardless of the terms stated, really wasn't a choice after all, and that he would be in real strife if he suggested that he did want to take that option. He decided to accept the inevitable and take advantage of the break to catch up on his sleep and to hone himself up with some really hard and constant physical exercise.

Now, more than two days later he was feeling in better shape than he had done since leaving England. He was tingling with energy and raring to go. What he really felt he needed was the opportunity to have a long, hard run, say ten kilometres or more. With this in mind he decided that as soon as the Irishmen had dropped him off in Manly again, for he was sure that this was the place where it would all happen, he would buy himself a tracksuit, some swimming togs and a couple of towels.

*

His Irishmen eventually arrived, and an hour later he was in Manly where he made his purchases. Having placed his clothes in a neat pile on the sand below the promenade wall, he set off back and forth along the long beach at a fast pace which he kept up for nearly two hours. At the end of that time he felt sure he had run more than twenty kilometres. This was the equivalent of his usual daily exercise and he felt much better for it.

He had a bad feeling about the future and was convinced that he was going to encounter the sort of problems that only the fittest of men would be able to handle.

He knew, however, that he had more going for him than most super-fit people. He was also highly trained with weapons and explosives, and his vast array of personal skills extended to the martial arts. They also included the not-so-noble art of killing fellow human beings. He had done this before and was prepared to do so again to save his own life, but certainly would do so to avenge Sammy Marven's death.

After the run he plunged into the surf and swam hard for twenty minutes. Returning to the beach he washed himself under a cold water shower point extending out of the sea wall, standing under the icy water until his body was chilled and numb. He then towelled himself down, dressed and headed back to the shopping area.

His first visit was to the McDonald's restaurant where, according to the Colonel's briefing, Sammy had worked. He spoke to several of the young staff, but apart from confirming his belief that Sammy would not have been into the drugs scene they were not able to provide any clues as to what happened to him.

★

His next visit was to the police station where he asked to speak to Detective Sergeant Brickly-Davis. This was the man who, according to the hospital report, Doctor Barker had reported his suspicions to about all the needle marks being of recent origin.

He was led to a waiting room where he was left for nearly ten minutes. Because he was suspicious why this policeman had apparently not followed up the doctor's report, he decided to use his Ulster accent. It tended to throw people somewhat, and seemed less threatening. The last thing he wanted to do at this point was to give the policeman cause to think that he was in any way a danger to him. If the man had been involved in Sammy's death, or was involved in covering up it would not do to raise his suspicions.

Derek Brickly-Davis seemed a very unlikely name for the character who entered the waiting room. He was tall and stocky with a large stomach that extended over his waist belt. His nose had obviously been broken at some stage giving him the look of a boxer. The policeman attempted a smile, and kept it up until Sammy's name was mentioned. Then the shutters came down instantly and the smile was replaced with a scowl.

'And what has Samuel Marven got to do with you, Paddy?'

The way in which the man suddenly began to talk down to him annoyed Millane intensely, but he felt sure that his simple Irishman act had probably lessened the likelihood of the confrontation becoming too great. The man had formed the opinion that he was dealing with an inferior person, and as the result had weakened his position.

'Well, sor.' He spoke in the broadest accent that he could muster having decided to really play the part in style. 'Well, I'm a friend of the family, and I just happened to be over here in Sydney on holiday, so I agreed to ease the minds of the dear people by finding out as much as I could about the poor boy.'

'Poor boy, my foot,' the man replied with a snarl. 'He was a druggie, and they're a bloody nuisance around here. If they want to kill themselves that's their privilege and a blessing in disguise to me and society at large.'

Millane immediately changed his tack. He had intended to ask about the nature of the puncture wounds but decided that it was a lost cause with this man.

'I thought I would ask to see the hospital doctor's report. He's away on holiday it seems, and I can't get any joy from the people at that place.'

'What hospital report? The only report we have is one that certified life extinct due to a massive overdose of heroin. That's all I can tell you. Now, if I was you I'd let sleeping dogs lie. The real story about what a hopeless bugger this boy was will distress the family even more. Leave it alone, Paddy. It's not worth pursuing. Now off you go and carry on enjoying your holiday.'

Before he could say another word Millane was physically pushed out of the waiting room and into the street. The detective turned on his heels and stormed back into the police station.

'You don't get away with it as easy as that, mate,' Millane growled as he walked off down the street. He made his way to a nearby restaurant and settled himself by the window where he could watch the front door of the police station. Ordering a sandwich and a pot of tea, he waited and watched.

He was convinced that not only was the man lying through his teeth, but he was also hiding something of great importance to his investigation into Sammy's death. He had also decided that given an opportunity he would make the detective regret calling Sammy a hopeless bugger.

★

'Felix, I've had an Irishman here at the station asking about that boy, you know, the drugs one.'

Brickly-Davis had called Felix the instant he got back into his office. The mere fact that someone was making enquiries about a matter that he had been assured was over and done with frightened him. Apart from destroying the report from that Doctor Barker he hadn't even thought about the boy since the night he dumped his body in the alleyway.

Felix had promised him that there was nobody in the world who would be the slightest bit interested in the case once the body had been cremated.

If that really was correct, then why was the funeral director's place blown up and old Wilkinson killed? He was sure that Felix had done that but couldn't understand the reasoning behind it. All he knew was that a simple business which had earned him twenty grand had suddenly become more of a public issue than he was told it would be.

He was also nervous about the deaths of the three divers in such a short period of time. Accidental though they may have appeared, and that was certainly how the Coroner had recorded them, he considered it all too much of a coincidence.

He was sure that at least one of them used to go out with Felix in his speedboat.

Then the boat was destroyed in the warehouse fire. It was all too convenient for his liking, and he was beginning to feel frightened for his personal safety.

'So who is this Irishman? Anyone we should be worried about?'

'I don't think so. His name is Millane. He seems like your average bloke, but a bit too nosy for my liking. He's got a bad limp.'

Felix was very excited. At last the man had come back out into the open. He had had dozens of people looking for Millane for several days since that ill-fated attempt to get at him in the hotel. Even though it was Brickly-Davis and his associate who had cocked up that particular exercise it suddenly occurred to him that neither of the men had actually·seen him face to face.

Felix had seen Millane that day he had followed him. He also knew that Millane had got a close-up view of him when he nearly skidded into the rear of the cab. This guy was really pushing his luck, but it was fast running out for him.

'This is the man whom I sent you after at the hotel. Didn't you realise that? Jesus! You are a dumb son of a bitch at times.'

'Are you sure, Felix? This man didn't seem too bright. He just seems like an ordinary sort of guy trying to do a favour for the boy's family. He's got a very bad limp so he can't be much of a problem.'

'For a guy who doesn't seem that bright he sure made fools of you and that useless prick of a pal of yours. Wake up to reality, man. We have a professional on our hands here, and I just wish I could figure out who he is and why he is on to us.'

Felix was concerned that anyone should be asking after the boy at all. If nothing else it meant that someone had the money and the initiative to follow the matter up in Australia. It was a long way to come from England, so at the very least this man Millane must be a private investigator of some sort. Whatever he was Felix had already realised that he must take him seriously, limp or not, which was why he acted so promptly after the man had nosied around the funeral director's premises and the British Consular Office.

'Get rid of him. He's a real determined bastard so do it soon. I just can't take any chances on this matter.'

Brickly-Davis didn't like being spoken to in this way by anybody but he had to accept what Felix had said. If this was the guy from the hotel he had made complete fools of himself and his partner, and for that he would welcome the chance to fix the man up, permanently. The thought that the Irishman probably recognised him from the hotel, yet still went through the charade of acting out the friend of the family asking after the boy routine, really pissed him off. From being extremely worried about the man's seemingly innocent enquiries just a few minutes ago, he was now feeling very angry with himself for being taken in so easily.

He felt pretty stupid for bringing the subject up at all, thus giving Felix the opportunity to insult him.

The thought of getting even with Millane for the indignities that he and his partner had suffered at his hands just recently was extremely attractive. However, it was not sufficient to replace the fear that was paramount in his mind, that Felix was intending to kill him and his partner, even if they managed to carry out his wishes.

Death seemed to be the guy's solution to everything. Now the detective was even more convinced that the other deaths that had occurred over the past week were the American's doing. One other thing that he was completely sure of, however, was that the only way to keep on the right side of the man was to obey his instruction, to the letter. Millane would have to die. He didn't like killing but felt he had no other choice. There was no doubt that the man had become a nuisance, and he deserved to die if only for what he did at the hotel. That was definitely something that he wanted to get even for.

'You're right, Felix. He will have to be got rid of. I will try to do it today while he is here in Manly. Leave it to me.' From the moment he had spoken Brickly-Davis felt safer.

Felix's voice sounded very friendly when he replied. 'Good man! We mustn't overlook any of these little problems or they will become big ones. I'll fix you up with a nice little bonus when you complete this job. You had better get someone to help you with this one. Is your friend Arthur's hand better yet? If it is then take him with you. He'll probably be quite pleased to get his hands on the bastard who tried to electrocute him,' he said with a sly chuckle.

# Chapter Nine

Saturday – 6 p.m.

The thought of Millane possibly being an investigator of some sort had put Brickly-Davis on the alert. If that was the case he knew that there could be a chance that the man would be attempting to keep him under observation. He immediately rang his partner, Arthur, from the bungled hotel exercise and filled him in on what had transpired. He advised him that Felix had ordered that extreme action must be taken against this troublesome snooper. He also advised him that he was concerned that the Irishman might possibly be intending to tail him.

He told Arthur what he wanted him to do, then he sat back and waited.

In the restaurant down the street from the police station Millane was becoming bored and anxious. The man had not left the station. Not by the front door anyway.

Stupid sod, Millane. Of course, police stations have also got rear doors, and it's at the rear where they park their bleeding cars, he mumbled to himself in anger.

You've wasted three sodding hours drinking awful tea by the gallon, and the man's probably gone home to his wife and kids.

He was mad with himself for not being professional. Sure, he knew that he could only be at one place at any one time, but common sense should have told him that the most likely point of exit for a person as mobile as a police officer would be from the rear where the car park would obviously be.

He immediately paid his bill and left the restaurant. He had no idea where he would find the policeman, so decided to leave that avenue of enquiry alone for the time being regardless of how attractive it appeared to be. He decided to follow up his enquiries amongst the young people whom Sammy knocked around with, for he had been given several names and addresses whilst talking to Sammy's workmates in McDonald's.

★

'It's definitely him, Derek. I only saw him for a second in the lift before he knocked me cold, but I'd recognise that bastard anywhere. I'm following him northwards along North Steyne. I saw him coming out of that little tearoom just up from the station. No! Of course he hasn't seen me. Do you think I'm completely stupid?' Brickly-Davis's associate Arthur reported over his mobile phone.

He had followed his partner's instructions and had checked out all the streets surrounding the police station. At first he had been unsuccessful, but not being a person who gave up easily he started around once more in the opposite direction. Feeling frustrated and angry he had almost arrived back at the front door of the police station when he saw Millane walking out of the restaurant. Arthur noticed that he did not appear to be in a happy frame of mind.

Wasted a few hours have you, mate? Didn't expect Derek to come over and have a cup of tea with you, did you? He smiled at the thought of Brickly-Davis and this mystery man Millane, little fingers poised in the air, drinking tea from bone china cups.

He's a coffee and beer man actually, you Irish prick. His only thoughts were of taking revenge against this man who had hurt him so badly, twice. Once with the electrically rigged door handle, and then with that vicious rabbit punch in the lift. He had been to the doctor twice to try to get relief from the extreme headaches that he had suffered since, and the tablets that had been prescribed had done little to relieve the pain; instead they made him feel nauseous.

His biggest problem since the attack had not been his headaches though, but rather the leg-pulling, mostly unpleasant, that he had suffered from his fellow police officers. He knew that he wasn't liked by his colleagues. Most of them realised he was up to something crooked, but fortunately for him they either didn't have any proof, or more likely didn't want to get involved.

The quickly constructed story that Brickly-Davis had given to explain the fact that they had been in the hotel in the first place, and how his partner had been found unconscious with a burned hand in a lift had not been very convincing to either their police colleagues or their senior officers. Currently the entire force was constantly under attack as the result of evidence being submitted to a Royal Commission on Police Corruption. Such was the paranoia throughout the force that Brickly-Davis and he were both now under investigation as the result of the hotel incident.

When Derek had told him of Felix's instructions to terminate the man, Arthur had almost drooled with anticipation of the pain he would inflict on the Irishman before finally putting him out of his misery. Whilst he knew that he would receive payment for the deed, this had become such a personal thing that he would have happily done it for nothing.

'Keep him in sight and call me back on the mobile at regular intervals. Meanwhile, don't let him suss that you are following him. I'm going to get the van, then I'll rendez-vous with you at some appropriate place. I'll work out a plan of action, and then we'll do it. Okay?'

'Right on, Boss,' came the excited reply.

★

Millane picked up his tail almost as soon as the man commenced his surveillance, as he was leaving the restaurant. They couldn't have made it easier for him. It was the guy he had knocked out in the lift at the hotel. To make it even more certain, and from a professional point of view even more stupid, the man had one hand heavily bandaged. Millane couldn't help but smile to himself.

He assumed that this man was a police officer colleague of Brickly-Davis, which amused him even more.

Where do these blokes get their training? This one is pathetic.

He thought seriously about losing the tail but decided that the most productive thing to do was to encourage the man to come closer to him. Experience had taught him that the best way to achieve this end was to pretend complete ignorance of the pursuit. This generally made the opposition more daring than discretion should allow and resulted in them coming close enough for physical action to be taken, should the opportunity arise.

He continued with his plan and called at some of the addresses that he had been given. As it turned out this exercise proved fruitless because none of the young people he asked after were at home. He wasn't too concerned though, as his primary objective was to create the opportunity to come face to face with the man who was tailing him. Perhaps this time he would get the chance to find out exactly who he was. He recalled that when he dropped in on the man back in the lift his attempt to discover his identity had been prevented by the untimely appearance of the two elderly ladies, so he was determined to ensure that his next close encounter with his victim would be under more favourable circumstances.

He was so amazed at the poor quality of the surveillance that was taking place that he lowered his guard and made some very bad errors of judgement. Firstly he concentrated too much on the tail and not enough on the wider environment, which is a critical factor under such circumstances. Specifically he failed to check for possible ambush sites. His SAS associates back at Hereford would have been astonished at the lack of professionalism that Millane was displaying here in what was, both during exercises and in real live situations, a vital survival skill.

The fact was that he had become so intent on trapping his pursuer that he forgot the basics. He paid the price.

★

Derek Brickly-Davis had parked the van ahead of Millane and his pursuer, Arthur. He had opened the rear door, clearly permitting Millane to see that it was empty. This, he hoped, would cause the man to relax momentarily and give him the edge for his next move. The sliding passenger door of the van was also open, and the detective crouched on the seat facing outwards, watching Millane's approach through the wing mirror. He grasped a large piece of timber in his hands and waited, unable to believe how simple it was. Millane just walked past so casually he never even saw his attacker leap from the van.

The heavy block of wood hit him hard on the back of his head, but the pain was brief. Everything seemed to burst in a flash of light. Then, nothing.

★

Arthur was within fifty metres of the van when Brickly-Davis struck. He broke into a fast run and was soon alongside the vehicle, where his colleague had hold of the unconscious Millane under the armpits. He immediately grabbed the legs, and moments later their victim was inside with the door slammed shut.

Taking no chances the men hurriedly tied Millane's hands and feet with lengths of thin nylon cord that had been brought along specifically for that purpose, and Arthur's handkerchief was pushed into the mouth of their prisoner to prevent him making any noise. Only when this task was completed did the two detectives sit back and relax.

'What's the plan, Derek? How are we going to get rid of this bastard? I want a piece of him before we do for him. I've promised myself that. If you don't have a plan I'd just as soon kick the bastard to death,' Arthur growled through clenched teeth.

Derek chuckled at the thought of how much pleasure his partner would get from that. He even felt like doing that himself, but he had a better idea which he quickly related to Arthur. The only part of the plan that neither of them liked was that it couldn't be carried out until after dark which was still half an hour away. They discussed this and both agreed that it was as easy to sit it out here as to drive somewhere else, so they sat back on the floor of the van and made themselves as comfortable as was possible under the circumstances.

At one point Millane started to come round, but Arthur dispatched him back into unconsciousness with a violent crack on the head with his police service revolver.

# Chapter Ten

Saturday – After Dark

Millane painfully opened his eyes. It only took him a few seconds to work out his situation and to realise that he was securely bound. He vaguely recalled being hit over the head the second time so he decided that it was far better to keep still and wait until an opportunity arose that he could take advantage of.

It was pitch black but he realised that he was on the floor of a fairly large van or truck. He decided that it must be the van that he had been passing when he was attacked.

They'll be proud of you back in Hereford, Major Millane, I don't think. He cursed himself for his absolute stupidity.

Occasionally the glow of street lights and the headlights of passing vehicles flickered into the rear of the van. His night vision had begun to return and he was able to see that he was alone. He realised there were at least two men in the front of the vehicle as he could hear them talking. However, whilst he could hear their voices they were muffled by the engine noise and he could not make out what they were saying. He realised that even if he had been able to hear their conversation, and perhaps even discover what they had planned for him there was nothing that he could have done under the circumstances. He was tightly bound and gagged, and outnumbered at least by two to one.

He was also painfully aware of the fact that he had been on the receiving end of quite a vicious beating. He felt weak and disoriented, and decided to try to get some sleep if he could, and wait and see what they had in store for him.

Just lie back and think of England, John my old son. You stupid, useless bastard. He berated himself as he lay still, pondering his fate. He didn't have to wait very long.

He hadn't managed to get any sleep due in part to the movement of the van and the hardness of the floor, but mainly because of the severe pain in the back of his head. It felt as if a heavy tank was driving around inside his skull.

He realised that the van had turned off the road, and that it was driving over an uneven surface. It was very dark and there were no longer any vehicle or street lights shining through into the rear.

Just then the van stopped. He heard the men get out and then the rear doors of the van were flung open. Two hands grabbed his feet and he was dragged from the back of the van landing very heavily on his shoulders and the back of his head.

At that moment it became obvious to Millane that he was about to die. These men had absolutely no concern regarding his physical well-being, which they might have done had they had any intention of interrogating him. Had that been their intention they would probably be trying to keep him in as reasonable physical condition as possible until after they had discovered what it was they wanted to know. That would certainly have been the way Millane would have handled such a situation. No! He was sure that these men wanted him dead.

Almost as if they knew what he was thinking, to reinforce his views one of them kicked him viciously in the kidneys. The pain was so intense that he momentarily blacked out.

He came to with voices hammering in his brain.

'What the fuck did you do that for? Do you want to have to carry him up there? If you do that too often then you're going to have to.'

'I really don't give a shit, Derek. After what he did to me I want to hurt him as much as I can. He's not going to get his the easy way.'

Millane lay still waiting for the next blow. He reluctantly decided he should resign himself to the fact that death may be imminent.

Up there? I wonder where I am, and where they are going to take me before I die. He really wanted to ask them a few questions. Why and how did Sammy die? Why have I got to die? Who the fuck is the little black man?

That final question was perhaps the one that intrigued him the most. He was, however, still gagged with the handkerchief and could barely make a sound other than a groan whenever the pains in his head and his kidneys became too great.

The pain was not the main thing concerning him though, it was the fact that he was going to die without knowing why and what this was all about.

'Why don't we undo his feet? At least then we can make the bastard walk up those stairs.'

'Don't be stupid, Arthur. This guy is some sort of professional, that we do know. Felix thinks he is anyway, and that's good enough for me. I'm not taking any chances. So, mate, as far as I'm concerned you can kick the holy shit out of him right here and now if that will ease your warped mind. But it's you that is carrying the bastard up there anyway. You are twice my size and a lot younger. And by the way, arsehole, I outrank you.' Both men burst into laughter at that remark.

'Well, in that case I might as well make the most of it. That's for my bleeding burnt hand, Millane, and that's for the king-size fucking headache that you gave me in the lift.'

The first kick was in the kidneys, and the one in repayment for Arthur's headache was intended to give Millane the same result. That kick was in the right side of his head and it rendered him immediately unconscious. This was a blessing for Millane, since Arthur didn't stop there; he continued to kick the unconscious man until he became bored.

At that point he bent down and lifted him into the traditional fireman's lift position over his shoulders, and with hardly any effort carried him across a dirt yard to a high scaffold. He then began to mount a series of steep steps that eventually ended three flights up, where he casually dropped his load on to the plank flooring of the scaffold.

Brickly-Davis had accompanied him just in case he needed any help. However, once he reached the top he turned around and made his way back towards the stairs.

'You tip him in and I'll start the mixer up, Arthur.'

'Okay! Take your time, Derek. I'm going to make this bastard squirm if it's the last thing he does, which it sure as hell will be.'

Both men again laughed at Millane's misfortune.

As soon as Brickly-Davis left, Arthur bent down and removed the gag from Millane's mouth. Once this was removed he was violently sick which seemed to amuse Arthur even more.

Millane would have loved to punch the man's leering face, but even if he had had his hands and feet untied he was too weak and badly injured to be able to make any movement at all without experiencing immense pain.

A less fit, ordinary man would probably have been already dead as the result of the beating that he had received. Momentarily Millane cursed his luck for being so fit as it had merely served to extend his suffering. If this was the end he wanted it to be as quick as possible.

Please God, make it quick, I beg of you, he thought to himself, determined not to plead with this man who was the source of his agony. He thought back to all the men he had killed and hurt in his life, and could think of no person to whom he had behaved in the way that he had been treated by this man, Arthur.

★

By now he had become accustomed to the darkness and could vaguely make out his surroundings. He was on a flat plank platform at the top of a scaffolding of some sort. Immediately alongside him there was a large, wooden-boxed framework. Hanging over it was a large pipe, on the end of which was what appeared in the dark to be a canvas nozzle. Just then an engine burst into life down below them, and at that moment Arthur bent down and once again lifted Millane over his shoulders. He walked to the edge of the wooden boxing and bodily threw his victim over the edge into the darkness.

Purely by chance Millane landed on his feet, and although they were tied together he was still able to absorb some of the pain by rolling over into a parachute roll. He came to a halt against the side of the wooden framework, and with some difficulty managed to lift himself to his feet. He looked up and could see his executioner leering at him over the edge of the framework a mere two metres above his head.

At that moment he learned what the canvas nozzle was for as it began pouring liquid concrete at a very fast speed. He was to be buried alive in concrete inside some structure, where his final resting place would never be known.

He decided there and then to try to upset part of their plan anyway, and smiled to himself as he realised what a pathetic, futile gesture this was. However, he shuffled his way to the edge of the framework, thinking that if he could retain this position his body, or at least his clothing would be seen from the outside once the boxing was removed.

Perhaps they'll cut me out and I'll get a reasonable funeral after all, he thought as the wet concrete began to fill the boxing and now reached as far as his waist. He looked up again and saw that Arthur was still looking down at him.

'You want to hear me beg for mercy do you? Well, you're wasting your time, shithead,' he shouted out in defiance.

The man merely smiled back at him.

## Chapter Eleven

Just as the wet concrete reached his chest two very strange things happened. The smile on Arthur's face appeared to freeze, and something began to pour out of his mouth on to Millane's upturned face. Then it started to spurt out of a very strange, ever-widening hole that suddenly appeared in the man's forehead. That was before the front of his head exploded, and seemed to disappear.

It was at that very moment that Millane realised that his face was covered in Arthur's blood and a large portion of his brains. Irrationally he ducked under the concrete to wash off the terrible mess.

At that very same instant the flow of concrete through the nozzle stopped. Even though his head was under the surface of the wet sludge John Millane was aware that the engine noise had ceased. He raised his head and looked up, and even though his head and face was covered in the concrete his eyes were relatively clear.

Much to his horror and amazement he saw that Arthur was not dead. His head had not exploded and he was still there, alive and smiling down at him. He wanted to scream.

Then a strange voice said, 'Hang on, mate. I'll get you out of there in just a moment. For Christ's sake don't lose your balance. Lean against the side.'

Millane realised at that moment that this was somebody else, not Arthur. It was a stranger who seemed concerned for his welfare.

A short while later a rope with a loop in it was lowered over the side of the boxing.

'Try to get that under your armpits, Millane, and I'll pull you out. Now I know you're an Irishman but try not to put it around your fucking neck. I've just killed a bloke to save you.'

Millane was too badly beaten and traumatised to even realise what the man had said, let alone see the funny side of it.

He tried hard to force a smile, but couldn't quite manage it. The strain of trying to get a rope loop under his armpits whilst he was up to his chest in concrete with his hands tied together was just about as much as he could manage. Eventually he achieved what seemed to him to be impossible and he felt the stranger above taking the strain, but at that moment the pain overcame him and he passed out.

★

It was all happening again. He was been drowned in concrete and it was pouring over him and he couldn't stop it. He was lying down and it was gradually covering him. Then he heard that voice again.

'Stay still, you dopey sod. How can I wash this bloody concrete off you if you won't stay still?'

He opened his eyes. The man was standing over him and was washing him down with water from a hosepipe. It was freezing cold but felt wonderful. After a few minutes the man turned the hose off and helped him to his feet. The moment he let go of him, however, the pain took hold and he collapsed.

'Bloody hell, they sure made a mess of you. You must have really got up Felix's nose.'

'You are going to have to explain some things to me, pal,' Millane said through badly split and swollen lips, 'but first I must thank you for saving my life.'

He said this with as much conviction as he could muster under the circumstances, realising that it must have sounded almost as weak as he was. He had been as near to death as anyone could ever be until just a few minutes before, and here he was, being hosed down with freezing water by a person he didn't even know, but who had just saved his life.

Before he could raise the energy to say anything else the man lifted him to his feet again and half carried him to a nearby shed. Once inside with the door closed the man sat him in a chair, then switched on a table lamp which barely illuminated the table top but was sufficiently bright for Millane to pick out the general features of his rescuer.

'Here, get those wet clothes off and put these on.' The man handed him a pair of jeans and a sweatshirt of some sort. 'I found them hanging behind the door. They're not much, but at least you'll be dry and warm. Oh, in case you are wondering what happened to the mate of the one I just shot, he's lying unconscious in that van you arrived in. Hopefully he can't go anywhere as I have locked him in and have taken his shoes and socks. They should swamp you, they are so big, but at least they will help you walk, with a bit of help.'

Just then his rescuer swayed on his feet and grabbed at the side of the table which together with the rickety old chair that Millane was sitting on was one of the few pieces of furniture in the shed.

Millane could see the man's face outlined by the eerie half-light of the table lamp, and he looked stressed out and on the verge of collapse.

'Jesus, what happened to you, are you all right?' was all he could think of saying. He was certainly in no fit shape to get up and help the man.

'I guess I'm all right. I've never killed anyone before. Until a few days ago I would have sworn on stacks of bibles that I just couldn't do it, let alone blow someone's fucking head off like I just did. I feel really sick. I suppose a bloke like you is used to this sort of thing. From what they told me you are some sort of hit man back in Northern Ireland.'

The revelation that this man, a complete stranger, knew of his Ulster connection shook Millane and brought him back to full awareness immediately. He forced himself to stand, and began to strip off his wet and filthy clothing. Then without bothering to dry himself, with great difficulty and considerable pain he slowly put on the clothes and shoes that his unknown benefactor had offered him. After he had dressed he sat down again and listened to the man as he tried to explain how he came to be at this very location at this most appropriate time.

\*

'My name is Phil Cartwright. Until a few weeks ago I was involved in something really nasty with an American guy named Felix.'

'This man wouldn't happen to be a little black man, would he?' Millane asked, anxious to piece together as many things as possible.

'Yes, that's him all right. I was one of his deliverymen in a drugs distribution system. I realised that there were others involved and some time ago I managed to suss out who another one of them was, a pilot named Grant. I really didn't feel safe with this guy Felix, and I guess I thought that by building up a dossier on the business, and in particular on my American mate, I was arranging an insurance policy of sorts that would keep him off my arse.

'Then I discovered that Felix had killed Grant, or at least he had him killed up in Queensland. It looked like he, and whoever he is working for, have decided to pack up shop and clean up any loose bits and pieces. There have been a lot of unexplained deaths in the Sydney area lately, and I'm pretty sure that Felix knows about most of them. I am also sure that I was to be one of the bits and pieces he wanted to clean up so I did a bolt for it and went into hiding.'

Millane remained silent. He was suffering quite considerable pain all over his body, but particularly in his head as the numbness caused by his beating had started to wear off. He was, however, relieved to find that his body was warming up and that the circulation was returning to his hands and feet which had been tied up for a long while. But even this positive factor had a negative side, in that the returning circulation was causing severe pains in those parts of his body also, even though they had not been subjected to the systematic beating that the rest of him had endured. All in all he felt very uncomfortable, to say the least.

'Well, luckily for you I have also done some deliveryman work for the bunch of Irishmen that you made contact with. The boss man is a guy named Kevin O'Reilly. He is a nasty bit of work but he pays well for services rendered. I gather he has already introduced himself to you in his own inimitable way. In fact, at the time that you was contacted by him I was already in hiding in one of his safe houses.

★

'That's only one of the things that we have in common, Mr Millane. Apart from Felix, who you obviously have pissed off very badly, I also met your boy, Sammy Marven, poor kid.'

He was startled by the sudden reference to Sammy, particularly coming out of the blue the way it did.

'How on earth did you know him? Hell, don't tell me he really was mixed up in your sordid drugs caper after all.' He felt sick at the thought of this being a possibility, but his mind was put at ease instantly.

'Shit no! That kid was never into drugs. I am convinced of that. I saw him laid out in the hospital, stripped to the waist. Not a mark on him other than that bloody great lump on his head and a bit of a black eye.

'No, the night before I went into hiding he tried to run my truck off the road over in Manly. He wasn't too smart, and he and his little VW came off worse and he got concussion. In the hospital he was delirious and was shouting out loud about a little black man. Well, there aren't too many of them around in Manly, or maybe there are, but I was real concerned about the one I knew so I came to the conclusion that in some way he knew about Felix. I even tried to warn him, but as you know that obviously failed.

'Our mutual Irish friend, Kevin, told me about your black man because I'd already told him about Felix and he thought there might be some connection.

'It was only when he told me about you that I found out that the boy had died. I knew that if you were asking after him and my old mate Felix was involved you would likely end up in deep shit also.

'Anyway, I persuaded Kevin to let me loose for the day so I could keep an eye on you. They didn't mind too much as they have a lot of funny business on their hands, and they aren't overly pleased to be looking after you. It seems that one of their group, the little athletic guy, doesn't trust you, and he's their mascot in this sort of thing. Their equivalent of a sniffer dog for suspect people. So, I am ordered to report my findings about you to them. Lucky for you I was quite near when that big bugger zapped you by their van. I then followed you to this place.

'Oh, Millane, or whatever your name is, I was told you had an Irish accent. What happened to that, I wonder?'

Millane was furious with himself for slipping up like that but how was he to know that his rescuer was in with the Irish mob?

'Don't worry about it, mate, I really don't give a stuff whether you're Irish or Martian. You are obviously after Felix so I want to help make sure that you get him. You are probably my only way of staying alive, my friend. The thought of that is beginning to make me feel less upset about killing that policeman.' He saw Millane's reaction to that comment and continued. 'Yes! He was the mate of that senior sergeant that you visited earlier today. I believe he has a double-barrelled name of some sort. Talking about that I think you had better help me get rid of that bastard up top. Perhaps we should dump him into the concrete shit that he was pouring on to you. The boxing is almost full. What do you think?'

Millane thought for a moment.

'I suppose that really depends on what we do to his friend the senior sergeant, doesn't it? There is probably no need to cement him in unless we are going to put his mate in with him.'

'Jesus Christ! You have got to be kidding me. One bleeding killing a day is more than I can handle, Millane. Please don't even suggest it. Why can't we just leave the bastard where he is? You can't just go around killing coppers as you like.'

'Not even bent ones? Killers?'

'He didn't try to kill me, Millane, only you. Anyway, the other copper didn't get a look at me, I promise. I just thumped him on the skull from behind with the gun that the Paddies gave me.'

Millane grabbed the table and gently raised himself to his feet.

'Here, give me a hand, Phil. And by the way, what and where the hell is this place?'

★

On the way to where the van was parked Cartwright explained that they were at the site of a freeway extension about fifty kilometres north of Sydney, and that the two policemen had been planning to set him in the concrete of one of the piers of an overpass. This amused Millane, as he thought of several similar sites in the UK which were alleged to be the burial grounds of well-known villains. The Hammersmith Flyover in London was alleged to contain the body of at least one criminal.

'They very nearly bloody succeeded, Phil. They nearly bloody did,' he said as they arrived at the rear of the large van.

It was obvious that Brickly-Davis was not very happy as he was shouting and swearing out loud to Arthur as he hammered on the metal walls of the van.

Before opening the door Millane took the gun from Phil, who protested loudly that he wanted no part of any further killing.

'There's no reason to kill this bastard,' Millane grimaced, 'providing he co-operates with me.'

As Cartwright pulled the door wide Brickly-Davis leapt out at him, apparently not even noticing Millane who was standing on the other side of the opening. He stopped in mid-air and crashed to the ground as the handle of the gun connected with his right ear. He was stunned but still conscious, and tried to get up. He would probably have succeeded had his legs not been kicked from under him at the same time as Millane touched his right temple with the gun.

'Jesus Christ! How did you get away from Arthur? Where the fuck is he?'

He stopped talking instantly when he heard the weapon cocked.

'Shut up, and don't you dare talk until I tell you to. Do you understand me?' Millane said with his voice full of menace, made even worse by the pain he was suffering from his swollen mouth.

The man nodded.

'Your unpleasant friend, Arthur, is dead. You will be joining him unless you do as you are told and tell me what I wish to know. Do you understand that also?'

'You won't get away with this, Millane. I promise you I will get you if—'

His voice broke into a whimper as Millane smashed the weapon into his mouth. He fell back to the ground, his hands trying to stem the flow of blood from his broken teeth and lacerated lips.

'Just a little bit of my own back. But that's just for starters, you bastard.'

At that moment Millane looked round and glared into the face of Phil Cartwright who looked as if he was about to protest. The words froze in Phil's mouth, and he backed off a few paces, obviously feeling it best to distance himself from whatever was about to happen.

'Three quick questions, copper. I want three quick answers or I'll shoot your right kneecap off. So make sure the answers are dead right.'

Brickly-Davis was terrified and began to cry.

'Cut the whimpering, arsehole. Who is Felix? Where can I find him? Who does he work for? Now, they are easy questions, aren't they?'

'I don't know who he is. I just get instructions on the phone,' the man replied through his tears.

'Wrong answer, my stupid friend.'

Millane shifted the gun just slightly and shot the man in the right kneecap. He screamed out in agony and grabbed his knee which was a terrible mess of blood and bones.

'Now didn't I promise you I'd do that? Answer me straight or I'll do the other knee, then the elbows, one by one.'

The policeman rolled over and vomited on the ground. At that very moment Cartwright was doing the same, out of sight on the other side of the van.

The obvious fear of more pain and imminent death was too much for the man. Suddenly the floodgates opened and he just couldn't stop talking. It appeared that, like Phil Cartwright, he was also in fear of his life from Felix, and had done some undercover investigating to discover as much as he could about the man just in case he later needed such leverage. He gave an address in the select harbourside suburb of Vaucluse, where the American lived alone in great luxury. Brickly-Davis also gave him the number of a white Holden car that Felix drove.

Millane felt sure that he knew more than he was telling, so he moved the gun slightly and cocked it once more. The man instantly fainted. At this Cartwright walked away out of sight, and Millane heard him vomiting again.

Brickly-Davis came to very quickly and started talking once more.

'I only know that he is not in charge of whatever it is he is up to. Arthur and I overheard him talking on his mobile to someone he referred to as boss. I think he also called him sir. It was long distance because he pressed too many buttons for a local call. Please don't kill me. I really had no choice with the boy. Felix told me to kill him and it would have been him or me. He didn't suffer, I promise you.'

His mouth opened and he was about to say something else, but he didn't succeed. The bullet passed through his skull just above and between his eyes.

★

With great difficulty due to the physical pain he was suffering Millane stooped down and removed the man's wallet from his pocket, placing it into the pocket of the jeans that Cartwright had given him. He then walked across to where Phil was standing, traumatised by shock at what had just happened.

'Don't get self-righteous with me, Phil. I owe you because you saved my life. But to do that you did exactly what I have just done. Neither of those bastards deserved to live. That one,' he pointed to the corpse by the van, 'just admitted to pumping junk into Sammy Marven until he was dead. He got his just desserts.

'Now, I'm going after Felix, and I'm going to kill him, as sure as God made little apples. It is not something to be squeamish about because if I don't get him then he is likely to get me, and without me to help you he will certainly get you, so are you with me or not?'

With that he turned on his heel and began to hobble painfully down the track with Cartwright walking several paces behind him. Neither man spoke a further word until they reached the car that Cartwright had parked off the roadway outside the construction site. It was well concealed so Millane decided that it was probably all right to use it, at least for the next stage of his plan.

## Chapter Twelve

They had driven in silence for nearly an hour when Phil Cartwright turned into a narrow cul-de-sac. It was the middle of the night and the only lights came from a few street lamps. Phil steered the car into a long driveway, at the top of which was a single storey building with what looked like a garage attached. As they approached the building Phil operated something under the dashboard and the garage doors automatically opened. He drove the car straight in and switched off its lights. At the same moment the garage doors closed shut behind them and the inside lights came on.

He led the way to an internal door which he opened with a key. Once inside he walked around closing curtains and switching on lights. They were in a spacious and obviously well-appointed house.

'For what it's worth I own this place, Millane, and a few others, under bogus names. I have occasionally used this one in the past as somewhere to bring friends, if you know what I mean. The bathroom is through there. There is a dressing gown in there that you can use. I'm afraid that I have no clothes that will fit you, I'll get some on Monday.'

'I can't wait until Monday, Cartwright. I have got to follow this through.'

'You may be a hard case, Mr Millane, but you've been done over badly, and at the moment I don't think you could fight your way out of a paper bag. You need a good rest before you start going after Felix. He's no slug, mate. In your present condition he'd eat you alive.'

The point was driven home hard by Cartwright, and Millane grudgingly accepted the inevitable, and the opportunity to have a bath and a good night's sleep. In the event he became quite feverish during Sunday and it took until Tuesday evening before he felt capable of doing anything at all strenuous.

★

The bodies were discovered at the construction site early on the Sunday morning by a security man doing his rounds. The television report indicated that a massive manhunt was under way for the perpetrators of the crime. Policemen had been killed. Crooked or not, the law would close ranks and claim them as something akin to heroes, at least for the time being. Late on Sunday evening, however, the force hedged its bets when a senior officer from Police Internal Affairs announced that both of the dead detectives had been the subject of investigations which would continue.

Cartwright had shopped on Monday and had bought a few full sets of clothes which fitted Millane perfectly. This made him feel much more comfortable, as he had felt very limited with only a dressing gown to wear.

★

So it was that they arrived in a tree-lined cul-de-sac near the address in Vaucluse that had been given to them by Brickly-Davis. After some discussion they agreed to leave Phil's car behind in case it could be identified and traced back to him, and had hired a small nondescript-looking car using a bogus driver's licence, one of several that Phil Cartwright had at his house.

The neighbourhood where Felix lived was one of the most exclusive in Sydney. The sort of place where two strangers to the district, on foot, would be noticed instantly. Accepting this possibility they had remained in the car and driven past the premises once to examine the exterior layout before making any decision to leave the vehicle. Their quarry lived in an apartment, the top of three, a penthouse in fact. There appeared to be no other way to get in other than through the front door. Having reconnoitred the area they sat quietly in the car whilst Millane considered the possibilities.

If he had been at his fittest there was an opportunity from the outside of the building where two large pipes extended from the ground to the roof. It was the sort of obstacle that all SAS raw recruits could handle.

However, the beating he had received at the hands, or rather the feet, of the police officer, Arthur, had left him very weak. He had sustained severe bruising to his legs and the lower back, and there was no way that he could attempt an outside entry, not yet anyway.

★

At that moment Felix was sitting at the bar in his apartment drinking his fourth straight bourbon. He was very worried. Sure, he knew that the two cops, Derek and Arthur, were not the best operators that he had ever employed, but they had done some good work for him in the past. He found it hard to believe that they were dead, killed by this man, Millane.

He was now convinced that the man was a special services operator of some sort, perhaps SAS. The way that he conducted himself put him streets ahead of the average private investigator, and he was beginning to consider the possibility that the man had been imported and put into the field by the Australian Federal Police. He had intended to raise this with the Senator when he spoke to him last, but had decided against it. After all, he had developed the reputation over the years, particularly with the Senator, that he was Mr Fixit, and that nothing was too much of a problem. So the less the Senator knew of his troubles, at least for the time being, the better.

He wondered whether he had gotten too old for this game, but consoled himself with the fact that the business was closing down. All he had left to do was to dispose of Cartwright and of course, this mystery man Millane. The *Palminto* situation would be resolved in seven days' time. Then he would just disappear and start to relax for the first time in many years.

But he could not get Millane out of his mind no matter what he did. He realised now how desperate he was to find this intruder, and to kill him, though this was a problem in itself. He had already disposed of all of the people who could possibly have helped him, and he was loath to get others involved. He had no choice but to do it himself.

Felix was not normally a drinker but this was a very difficult time for him, and he had felt that he really needed a drink or two, so he poured himself one more, and then another, until eventually he collapsed on the floor, too drunk to stand.

He slept a very restless sleep and dreamed very bad dreams, all about Millane. His dream took a bad turn at about three in the morning when Millane teamed up with Louis Leverdier, the ex-foreign legionnaire he had killed in that ambush so many years ago in Cambodia. Louis was as he last remembered him, shot to pieces, but there he was with this man with the limp, once again trying to kill him.

He woke up with a start, very badly hungover, but now determined to get Millane, if only to prevent him digging up the ghosts of his past.

He picked up the telephone and made the first of several calls.

# Chapter Thirteen

Saturday – 10 p.m.

After four days of complete inactivity Millane was frustrated and angry. He was also much fitter than he was on Tuesday evening. He had rested up and given his battered body a chance to recover sufficiently for him to complete a day of light limbering-up exercises. The bruising was still bad on his legs, and his kidneys and lower back ached like hell, but he could bend and manipulate his body to the point where he knew he could now get up into that apartment.

★

It seemed as if the entire population of Vaucluse was either in bed or out to dinner, as the whole neighbourhood was as quiet as the grave. Millane was dressed in black and wore light gloves that Phil had purchased for him in an army surplus store that afternoon in Parramatta, and he had a black canvas bag strapped over his shoulder. Leaving the car he walked the hundred metres or so to the apartment building, checking out the lie of the land as he walked. As soon as he reached the corner of the building he leapt into the shrubbery which bordered the roadway. Removing a tin of camouflage cream from his pocket he quickly touched up his face with a few casual strokes that would break up the general outline of his features and help him blend into the dark.

Just then he saw a car headlight brightly light up the whole street. The light flicked twice, then went back on full beam. This was Phil's signal that nobody was in the street. If the light turned off at any point Millane would know that he had to stop moving and try to blend in with his surroundings.

'What happens if you are halfway up that drainpipe at the time?' Phil had asked him just before he got out of the car.

'I guess I'll just have to act like a fucking drainpipe.' He now smiled grimly at that prospect.

There were no lights showing on the top floor, and whilst there were lights on the other two floors, those apartments had conveniently closed their blinds.

'Okay, Millane, get your bloody old body up that building,' he whispered to himself as he grabbed the bottom section of the pipe. He gave it a very hard pull, and was relieved to find that it was firm. The climb was easy, which surprised him as he had not yet fully recovered from his encounter with the late Arthur, just a week before.

Climbing over the balustrade of the balcony he lowered himself gently to the floor and waited for the signal.

Back in the car Phil had watched in amazement at the ease with which he had climbed to the top. Once he was sure that he was actually on the balcony he beeped his horn twice then checked his watch and started counting.

Having heard the signal, Millane knew that he had five minutes to get inside and prepare to open the door for Phil, who would now be counting the minutes.

First he checked the door frame to see if there was an alarm system. There didn't appear to be, but he had already decided not to open the door if he could help it. He checked the glass which appeared to be pretty standard in its thickness, and then withdrew a small glass cutter from his pocket. Quickly cutting two small round holes in the glass about thirty centimetres from the floor and about the same distance apart, he gently tapped these pieces of glass inside where they each fell on to the floor with a gentle tinkling sound.

He then took from the shoulder bag a spray can, to the nozzle of which he attached a long flexible plastic tube. Having shaken up the can he slipped the long tube through one of the holes and pressed the button at the top of the can. A whitish substance spewed out from the end of the tube, and as it touched the floor it expanded outwards and upwards. He directed the tube to another part of the floor and repeated the process. He then repeated the exercise through the second hole. Within a few moments there were several mounds of this foam-like substance spread over the apartment floor just inside the door.

He removed the tube from the can and replaced them in the bag. With the glass cutter he then cut a very large, flat oblong section out of the window and carefully pushed it inwards. It didn't hit the floor, but ended up propped on top of the foam mounds which were now beginning to harden. Leaning in through the large hole he was able to slide the entire section of glass out of the way and climb inside. The complete operation took three minutes, and not a sound could have been heard from outside the apartment.

He was delighted with the success of that part of the operation, and chuckled to himself at the thought of writing to the manufacturers of the revolutionary hole-filling product that he had seen advertised on the TV, thanking them for helping him with his burglary.

★

He reached the main door of the apartment and checked out the security device with which he could open the main entrance and lift doors for Phil. A few seconds later the door buzzer sounded. After ensuring that it was Phil he operated the button to permit his entry. The lift door slid open and Phil hurried into the room. He seemed very nervous about what they were doing and openly admitted that since Vietnam he had only broken into an aircraft hangar, and this really wasn't his usual Saturday night pastime.

'Don't be silly, Phil, this is far more exciting than sex. You can get your leg over any Saturday night.'

Phil Cartwright didn't appear to see the funny side of that comment.

Millane had already briefed him on what to do when conducting a search, and how to go about it to ensure that it was done in the most efficient manner. Having been quickly reminded he started in the bedroom while Millane tackled the living areas and the kitchen.

Thirty minutes later they had completed searching their areas and had found nothing. They were both disappointed but they had found sufficient evidence to satisfy themselves that they had the right place. The clothing in the wardrobes was small and flamboyant in appearance. Most of the items had US labels of some description.

'We had better get out of here, Phil, it appears that this idea of mine was a bummer. It looks like we will have to stake out this whole area and just physically watch what the man does and where he goes.'

'I thought the idea was just to dispose of him, not to form a liaison with him,' snapped Phil.

'Yes, Phil, so we bump him off. What if he's already set others on to us? A bloody lot that will achieve. No, we find him and tail him for a while to make sure we cover all the odds, and we can then dispose of him at will.'

Phil could not argue with the logic, but the way which Millane spoke so casually of death caused a cold chill to run through his body.

As previously agreed the men had taken any small valuable items that they came across during their search in order to give the impression that this was a simple burglary. So with the shoulder bag loaded with gold watches, cuff links, chains, rings and several other expensive-looking items they started to leave.

★

They were halfway out of the door when Millane stopped and quickly turned back into the room. He hurried to the telephone, and picking up the receiver he began to dial single and double digit numbers that one would use for speed dialling. He dialled the digits 01 and was lucky first time.

'You have reached the office of Senator Peter Filburton. Nobody is here to take your call at the moment, but if you would like to leave a message after the tone, the Senator's personal staff will address your enquiry at the earliest time.'

He replaced the receiver without waiting for the tone. He then dialled a range of other numbers. Two of them were answered by sleepy male voices, but no identification was given.

The last number that he rang was answered immediately. 'Duckton's. Can I help you?' He could hear the sound of noisy machinery in the background. 'Hello! Duckton's.'

He replaced the receiver.

Alongside the phone was a scribble pad. He tore the top two sheets off and stuffed them into his shoulder bag.

'Okay, Phil, I think we have got something.'

Later, back at Cartwright's place he took the sheets of paper and by scribbling lightly on them with a pencil was able to just make out a telephone number indented on one of the sheets. He wrote down the number on a pad and left it by the phone.

★

Felix was both angry and puzzled. Had his home been infiltrated by the man Millane? How could Millane have discovered where he lived? He couldn't have got it from either Derek or Arthur before he killed them, or could he? Is it possible that somehow they found out where he lived? After all, they were detectives, not that they appeared to be much good at it. In fact they must have been pretty useless to get themselves killed when they had the complete advantage over their intended victim.

If Millane didn't do it, then who did? It would have to have been a pretty clever burglar to have got up into his top-floor apartment without being seen, and that was a really smart way of getting in without making a noise. The neighbourhood was a wealthy one so there was every reason to believe that an enterprising thief would be targeting it at some stage. Whoever had done it had cleaned him out of nearly six thousand dollars worth of stuff. Not that he would be reporting it to the police or claiming on insurance or anything stupid like that. He would just have to accept it and write it off as bad luck.

He was confident that there was nothing in the place to even give an intruder the name of the occupant. There was certainly nothing that could have possibly led to anything to do with the drugs business. He was most thorough about that, and always had been. As far as he was concerned the place was as clean as a whistle and would foil any attempt to uncover incriminating information.

All of these thoughts were racing through his mind as he looked around his ransacked apartment. The more he thought about it, and the more bourbons he drank whilst thinking about it, the more sure he was that he had been the victim of a fit and enterprising cat burglar. It was with that final thought in his mind that he eventually lay down on his unmade bed and went to sleep.

## Chapter Fourteen

### Sunday Morning

Phil was angry with Millane. He had quizzed him all the way back to the house about what he had discovered on the telephone, but got no reply. Instead Millane asked a lot of seemingly unimportant questions about Vietnam.

He seemed most interested in where Phil had met Felix, and the circumstances under which they met. He wanted to know the names of places in Vietnam where he had served and at which he knew Felix had been. Then on arriving at the house he went to bed straight away, leaving Phil completely in the dark.

Over a cup of tea the following morning Millane asked, 'Who is Senator Peter Filburton?'

'He's a pollie in Canberra. Why do you ask?'

'Did he serve in Vietnam, Phil?'

'If he did I never heard of it. That's an interesting question actually, because in a television debate some years ago he went all hush-hush and strange when asked about Nam.'

'Why is that interesting? Surely some politicians have good reasons not to talk about that war, like for instance he might be governed by the Official Secrets Act.'

'That's true, but that wouldn't have applied to him because he didn't stand for parliament until several years after the war. In fact, nobody seems to know what he did while the war was on.'

Millane then went quiet once again and sat deep in thought. Suddenly he leapt up from his seat and asked if it was all right to use the telephone for an overseas call, promising that he would explain it all later. Having said that, and without waiting for a reply he walked into his bedroom. Phil heard the sound of the telephone buttons being punched, but decided he had better wait.

★

It was just after midnight at Hereford, and he was lucky with his timing. The Colonel was actually in his office preparing to leave the base for an emergency meeting with the Cabinet at Chequers, the official residence of the Prime Minister. He took Millane's call immediately and transferred it on to the scrambler.

'How can I help you, John? I know that you must be in some sort of bind, because you are too stubborn and bloody-minded to ask for help normally.'

Both men laughed at that comment. Millane did have the reputation of being a field agent who went undercover for real, and rarely, if ever, sought advice or assistance until the project was wound up or ready to be terminated.

'Well, sir, Douglas Marven was right. His son was murdered, but as yet I don't know why. I have dealt with the person who did the job, but am now up to my eyeballs with some really nasty buggers who are trying to stop me from getting to the head honcho who ordered it to be done.

'I have two names for you to check out for me. This may be difficult because I have little else but the names. One is Peter Filburton, a federal government senator in Canberra. The other is a man named Felix. I have no other names for him, but I can tell you that he is apparently American. He is a small man, and he is black. I've good reason to believe that both of these men are involved in an

638

international drugs racket. The man Felix is almost certainly ex-special services in Vietnam, but nobody seems to know what the senator did during the war. He could have been there as well.'

'You are asking me to delve into the life of a member of the government of a friendly nation, John. You had better be clear about what you are doing over there.'

'I don't know about that friendly nation bit, Colonel. It seems that a fair percentage of the population is trying to kill me at the moment.'

'Okay. Stay with me, John. I'll get on to this immediately, so don't go away.'

Millane waited in silence. He could hear the Colonel speaking to someone else, and guessed he was on the direct line to Special Branch at Scotland Yard or to one of his top secret associates in Whitehall. The Special Air Service was constantly working with these bodies, not only in the United Kingdom but in many parts of the world that the Government would not wish the British public to know about.

\*

Thirty minutes later Millane returned to the kitchen with a broad smile on his face.

'Put the kettle on, Phil, you and I have got a lot to talk about.'

I haven't got a bloody kettle, but I'll put the jug on,' Phil snarled at the thought that he was being treated like the hired help.

'Well, my old son, have I got a wonderful bedtime story for you,' Millane said in his best Ulster accent.

'Stop acting the Irish goat, Millane. What have you got to tell me?'

'Well, once upon a time there was this secret service agent, not really your plain and simple special forces man, but someone pretty close to the Government's department of nasty business. This guy went to Vietnam and came back a very rich man. While he was there he is alleged to have been involved in all sorts of jiggery-pokery that at times really got up the nose of the South Vietnamese Government. This guy's name was Peter Filburton. That was the name of the senator whose office I direct dialled from Felix's apartment last night. What a bloody coincidence.

'Anyway, prior to Vietnam this Peter Filburton ran a small team of mercenaries that did some pretty disgusting things in lots of places around the globe. At one stage they even got into the business of trying to recruit people from the top secret service agencies of the world, and if the people they approached refused to join they were bumped off. Naturally this really got up the nose of the top people in the CIA, KGB, MI5 and the like.

'It seems that in Vietnam our friend the senator, always worked under the code name 'Senator', now how's that for a strange coincidence? He led a team that concentrated on assassinations of top people who were allegedly getting in the way of the war effort.

'He was supposed to be concentrating his efforts on the enemy, but it seems that for the right type of reward he was not shy about bumping off allies, both South Vietnamese and American. Our people, who were there but weren't, if you know what I mean, tried to pass this information on to your people and the Yanks, but everyone they dealt with was either suspect themselves, or more often than not died suddenly. My friend in the UK believes that all records on this special unit, both before and during the Vietnam War have been destroyed, along with anyone who could possible have known about it. It appears that the senator is home and hosed, as you Aussies say.

'But now, Phil my old mate, listen to this little bit of nonsense. His number two at that time was an ex-Green Beret named Felix Josia Smith. His record shows him as being five feet two inches tall, and black.'

Phil nearly choked on his tea.

'Are you telling me that this senator, I mean, an Australian Government senator, is in business with, or the boss or partner of Felix, Smith, did you say his name was?'

'I don't know, Phil, but why not? It happens everywhere else in the world, why not here? All I am telling you for sure is what I have discovered from my sources back in Blighty. However, I might be stretching a long bow, but I think we may have a mix and match here.

'The question is, where do we go from here, and how do we manage to get these two unlikely compatriots in the same place at the same time, so if they are in this together we can nail them?'

'I don't suppose you are going to tell me who your sources are, John. It's been obvious since the word go that you are not Irish, and you are probably one of the dirty tricks mob that you talk so disparagingly about. Whoever your source is, they had better be good, or we are going to be in the shit way above our heads.'

'Isn't that where I always am anyway, Philip me darling.' Millane reverted to his Irish accent, and they both laughed out loud.

## Chapter Fifteen

Sunday – 10 p.m.
Wagga Wagga

Millane had let his fingers do the walking. He examined the Sydney telephone directories and the Yellow Pages, searching for a company by the name of Duckton's. He was sure that the number he had rung on the speed dial of Felix's phone had been a commercial premises of some sort because of the sound of machinery in the background. There was no such business in the Sydney region.

As Phil was more familiar with the regions and main centres of New South Wales and the eastern states generally he was delegated the task of checking with directory enquiries to discover the location of this company. Ten minutes later he had found what he was looking for. Duckton's Frozen Supplies was situated in Wagga Wagga in south-west New South Wales, about six hours' drive from Sydney.

What clinched it was that the number for Duckton's was the same number that Millane had lifted from the sheet of the telephone pad in Felix's apartment.

Millane immediately rang the number and listened for the background noise while the man who took the call was trying to discover who his caller was. The voice sounded the same as the one that had answered the call from Felix's phone, and the sound of machinery was identical.

'Bingo!' he called out as he put the receiver down. 'How do we get to Wagga Wagga, Phil?'

★

That was many hours before, and now they were sitting in a hired car in a lay-by about one kilometre north of RAAF Wagga Wagga, eating a snack and waiting for the right moment to make a surprise visit to Duckton's.

Phil had been elated when he discovered that the company dealt with frozen goods because it was this type of company that he had always made his deliveries to. He now felt sure that they were on the right track although he had no idea what Millane intended to do when he got there.

Phil's experience with the frozen food business was that these sorts of premises were manned around the clock, but that the night shift generally comprised just a few people.

On the basis of that advice Millane had decided that they would leave it until just after midnight before making their visit. When Phil tackled him regarding his plan of action, he merely said, 'I'm going to walk in the door and ask for Felix. If this place is important enough to be on Felix's speed dial I guess someone there will know who he is and probably what this is all about.'

'No killing though, John. I've had enough of that to last me a lifetime.'

'I've told you the ground rules, Phil. If anyone tries to get you or me, then they take their chances. I don't intend being a target any more.'

This seemed to be acceptable to Phil, who remained awake and silent for the next two hours while they waited to move off. It was obvious to him that his new-found associate was an old hand at this game for he slept like a baby for the whole period.

Suddenly Millane was awake and alert. Phil looked at his watch. It was exactly midnight.

'How the hell do you do that? If I don't have an alarm clock by my side I just cannot wake up on time, ever.'

'Years of practice, my old son. Years of practice and good honest living, of course.'

★

Duckton's was a small set-up in comparison with the freezer companies that Phil had always dealt with. It didn't even have a large yard which was considered to be essential for companies that dealt with frozen goods. The large trucks that transported such produce required lots of space to manoeuvre into the appropriate bays to load or unload their goods. This place had none of that.

'I think we have got the wrong place, John,' Phil whispered as they crawled on their hands and knees through the waist-high shrubs surrounding the perimeter fence of the company. 'This can't be a freezer company. It hasn't even got a loading bay.'

'You may be right, Phil, but we're here now, so let's go and have a look round. It certainly says Duckton's Frozen Supplies on that sign at the front gate, and there is a lot of machinery type noise coming from inside. I'll go in alone and see what's doing, but if I am not out within ten minutes you had better come looking for me just in case that noise we can hear is another concrete mixer.' He chuckled at his sick joke.

Cartwright did not see the funny side of the remark as it reminded him too vividly of the man he had killed on that previous occasion.

With that Millane stood up and strolled casually around the fence towards the main gate, then he walked across the yard towards what appeared to be a glass-fronted office area. On reaching the door he tried to open it, but it was locked. Alongside the door was a bell push. He looked back to where he knew that Phil was concealed and gave the thumbs up sign, then pressed the bell which sounded very loudly inside the building. He waited for a while but nothing happened.

Then he saw it. The camera was neatly concealed in the top left-hand corner of the foyer, hardly noticeable in the dim half-light of the entrance way. He was trained to see such things and cursed himself for not having spotted it before. He could see a small green strobe light flashing beneath the camera which was moving slowly from left to right. Whoever was in the building was taking no chances so they were checking to see if he was alone.

He hoped that they hadn't seen the signal he had just made to Phil. If these people were that well geared up with new technology, the chances were that they had some smart people on the other side of the door, but he decided to bluff it out.

'Hi!' he shouted out, positioning himself towards the semi-concealed camera. 'Come on guys, Felix told me you wouldn't fuck me about.'

To his surprise he was answered immediately. The voice sounded like the electronic voices that could be created by some of the more sophisticated computer programmes.

'Who are you and what do you want?'

'I'm Phil Cartwright. I understand Felix has been trying to get in touch with me. I have been told to come here.'

'Who told you to do that?'

Millane now knew that he was at the right place as there was no denial of the name Felix. He tensed himself for the possibility of immediate action of the worst sort, but it didn't happen.

'I got a message from my usual source in Manly. The usual police source.'

There was silence for several minutes, then suddenly the strange voice spoke again.

'Enter and place your hands on your head. Then wait for further instructions.'

The door swung open and he walked inside, placing his hands on his head. He stood still for a few moments then a door directly in front of him swung inwards. The strange voice directed him to walk on through. He did so and found himself in a large empty chamber. He was surprised, but shouldn't have been as Phil had told him that this wasn't the sort of place which would have been suitable for a frozen food operation. He immediately discovered where the engine noises were coming from. On the wall at the far end of the building was a generator of some sort that was operating noisily and didn't appear to serve any function other that to make a noise. It was obviously the cover sound for the bogus freezer operation and it was very effective in that regard.

To his left was a staircase leading up to what appeared to be offices built above the foyer of the building. These were brightly lit, but he could see nobody in them from where he stood.

'Stand perfectly still, Mr Cartwright.' The instruction came from behind him.

Then he felt something cold and metallic poking into his neck. 'This is a nasty little weapon, Mr Cartwright, and if I am obliged to pull the trigger it will remove your head. I trust that you are not going to do anything that is likely to precipitate that course of action.'

Millane felt himself being roughly searched, but the man doing it was not an expert. He checked the usual places, the armpits and between the legs, but failed to reach down to shoe level. If he had done so he would have discovered the police revolver that had been taken from the hapless detective, Arthur, at the construction site north of

Sydney. It was secured to his lower leg with sticking plaster. He was beginning to think that he may have to reach for it quickly and was not relishing the thought as his legs were so hairy that this would be a painful exercise.

The man prodded him quite violently in the back of the head.

'Up the stairs, Cartwright, and keep both of your hands on your head. Don't try anything stupid or I will have no choice but to shoot you. Do you understand me?'

Millane nodded and started up the stairs slowly. He felt sure that he could take this man easily, but wanted to find out if he had any accomplices waiting on the first floor before he tried anything. On top of which, even though the man was an obviously an amateur he did have a gun, or Millane had to assume he had a gun. But most importantly he had the advantage of being behind him.

As he reached the top of the stairs he realised that his caution had been most wise as there was another man standing inside the doorway. He was aged about fifty and was very thin and pale. He was obviously surprised and disturbed by Millane's presence. The man wore a long white coat, the sort that doctors wore, and was pointing a lethal-looking automatic at Millane's chest. The hand that held the weapon was shaking slightly. Millane decided that when the time came he would probably make him his first target.

This decision was confirmed when, for the first time, he saw the man who had searched him and followed him up the stairs. This man brought a completely different dimension to the situation.

Dimension is the operative word, Millane thought as he examined the man and weighed up the prospects of dealing with him. He decided that they were no longer as good as they had been.

The man was nearly two metres tall and built like a weight lifter or body builder. He was no older than thirty and had the look of a person who could handle himself.

Millane had seen many such men in his military career, and it was the look in their eyes that often made them more threatening than their physical size. This man was a giant, and a mean-looking bastard.

Then he saw the weapon that the man had placed at the back of his head so threateningly. The nasty little weapon that the man had referred to was an AK47 assault rifle.

No wonder he said it would remove my bleeding head. The thought sent a cold chill down his spine. He decided that this man was going to be one hell of an adversary if it came to a fight. However, he was still heartened by the very amateurish manner in which the big man had conducted the search.

Let's hope that you are not as smart as you are big, Goliath. He stared fixedly into his face as if trying to convey that challenge, but the man merely stared back.

'Sit there,' the older man ordered, pointing to a chair that he had placed in the centre of the office, 'and if you make one move my young friend here will shoot you without hesitation. I know of no person named Cartwright, and even assuming you are an associate of Felix there is no way known that he would have directed you to here. I think you are an intruder, Mr Cartwright, or whatever your name is, and I'm inclined to want to kill you right now. However, the way that the business is moving you just could be telling the truth. We'll find out, right now.'

The man walked to the desk and picked up the telephone. He pressed many buttons, too many for a local call, and waited. He had placed his automatic on the desk by the phone, but this was cold comfort to Millane because the man with the AK47 was standing two paces behind him with the gun pointing directly at his head. He could see his reflection in the glass wall that divided the office from the other part of the upper level.

★

Millane took this opportunity to quickly size up the situation in readiness for Phil Cartwright's almost certain intervention. The agreed ten minutes were now up and he felt sure that his accomplice would not be deterred by the locked front door. However, the thought of Phil barging in where angels feared to tread whilst he was confronted with two armed men frightened the hell out of him.

The top floor was divided into two rooms by a floor to ceiling glass wall. The room that they were in was comfortably appointed as an office, with phone, fax and computers. This room had the door that led out on to the small balcony which could also be reached by the stairs he had just climbed. The sole access to the second room was through a door situated behind the desk.

What he saw in there made his mind boggle. The room was long and sparsely furnished with two rows of narrow benches. The benches were piled high with small plastic bags filled with what looked like white powder. At the end of the bench nearest the door was a set of chemical scales, and by the scales was a large open-topped container alongside which was a stainless steel scoop.

Millane took an educated guess that in that box would be the glucose or other harmless material that would be mixed with the pure heroin or cocaine that Felix and his associates were peddling, to increase the amount of saleable material, whilst at the same time reducing the potency of the drug. This mixing, or cutting process, was the vital stage of any drug distribution operation. This was the point at which the street value of the product was increased by whatever percentage the principal dictated. It was also the stage where impure products were sometimes mixed with the drugs making them highly lethal. This operation, at first glance anyway, appeared to be quite clinical.

Alongside the container was a contraption that he recognised as a device for hermetically sealing the plastic bags once they had been filled with the correct measure of the cut drugs.

★

While he was taking in the drugs cutting operation in the next room he was also considering his escape options which he felt sure would become imperative within a short period of time. If the man in the white coat was trying to contact Felix and he got through, his story would soon be blown out of the water. The man behind him was placed in an ideal position. He was behind and too far away for Millane to attack him from the seated position before the man could pull the trigger of the weapon that he was pointing directly at him. The big man appeared to be most capable of using the weapon should he have to.

Where the hell is Cartwright? The ten minutes was up five minutes ago. Shit! I hope they haven't got him. If they have I'm dead, he thought as he pondered what his SAS colleagues would think of his abysmal track record so far. He'd been beaten up and captured twice within just a few days. He was beginning to wonder whether he might be just past his prime. Here he was looking down the barrel of death, and fast giving up hope of help from his inexperienced and less than enthusiastic associate, albeit one who had saved his life once already.

Unless something diverted the gunman behind him there was no way he could possibly reach the open doorway to the stairs some three metres away.

The man at the phone at last appeared to have got through to whoever he was calling. He briefly explained that he had a man who called himself Philip Cartwright sitting in his office and that the man stated he had been directed to come here.

'Is he Irish? I don't understand,' the man spoke out loud. A shock wave went through Millane. That surely must be Felix on the end of the line. He shuddered.

'No, he appears to be Australian, or maybe English. He certainly doesn't have an Irish accent. A limp? I never noticed.'

'Yes, he has got a limp. I saw it when I brought him through,' the man behind Millane interjected.

'Kill him? Sure.'

★

At that precise moment the entire building shook and the floor seemed to fall away from under him. The shock of whatever had happened threw Millane off the seat and on to his back. He was already feeling for the gun taped to his leg as his slid along the floor. The big man with the AK47 was also lying on the floor, which was now leaning at an ever-increasing angle away from Millane, and he was scrambling to get up.

His weapon was still in his hand but he was no longer in control of the situation. He had lost his opportunity and surprise and fear showed in his eyes at the moment he first saw the gun in Millane's hand. It was last thing he saw. Two bullets entered his head, one in the mouth and the second through the centre of his temple.

Just at the moment the floor collapsed completely and the man's body slid out of sight below.

The man with the white coat slid past Millane, a loud screaming curse coming from his fear-distorted mouth. His legs and lower trunk slid down into the space below the sloping floor. At that same moment the far end of the second room sagged and began to fall also. This served to lift the office floor back into place temporarily before the entire floor fell to the ground below. The man in the white coat screamed out loud as his body was crushed between the collapsing interior offices and the outside wall of the main building.

Millane also found himself beginning to slide down towards the gap when he saw a pair of large, ornate, brass coat hooks attached to the brick outside wall of the office. He saw his opportunity, and lifting himself to his feet he launched himself at the coat hooks. It was a huge leap from a very unsound footing but his right hand just caught the ornamental coat-hangers. He hung on for grim death for nearly a minute until the collapsing office building had finally all settled on to the ground floor amidst a cloud of white dust.

*

Only thirty seconds or so had elapsed since the moment that the building first shook and began to collapse. Two men were dead, and he was left hanging against the wall some six metres or more from the ground, but had no idea what had happened. He looked down and saw a fairly flat area with no dangerous protrusions, so pushing himself away from the wall he aimed for that spot. He landed in a crouch, choking loudly on the dust which he suddenly realised would almost certainly be heroin, or whatever it was that the men were working with just a few minutes before when he had so rudely intruded on their privacy.

It was then that he saw what had caused the offices to collapse in such a timely and spectacular fashion, and who had caused it to happen. Jutting out of the debris at the far end of what had been the long office where the drugs had been was the nose of a large prime mover truck, and climbing out of the open driver's window was a man covered from head to foot in the white powder. It was Phil Cartwright.

'How many times have I got to save your life?' he called out, clambering over the debris. 'Is this stuff what I think it is?'

'Yes, Phil. Pure bleeding heroin, although I've never been so close to this much of the stuff before.' He stumbled up to Phil and embraced him. 'One of these days I'll get round to repaying you. Isn't there an old Chinese proverb that says something about if you save someone's life, you are responsible for them for the rest of their life.'

'Shit! I hope not, John. I don't like the way death follows you around. I know that Felix is out to kill me, but it seems like every bastard wants to kill you. By the way, talking about death following you, it is likely to follow both of us unless we get out of here and stop inhaling this muck.'

With that both men headed towards the large gap where the glass foyer used to be until the truck had ploughed through it, smashing to smithereens the wooden uprights that held the first-floor offices in place.

★

Once outside they hurried towards the thick shrubbery where they had earlier concealed themselves. Millane kept watch while Phil stripped and shook out his clothing before re-dressing himself. Then he did the same.

'Sorry I was so late, John. I saw the guy with the gun and realised that I had to somehow get inside in a way that would kick up as much fuss as possible. I didn't want to wreck the hire car as we may need that in a hurry. Then I remembered seeing that truck parked up the road, quite a way off so I went to have a look see, and you know what happened from there on in.'

'You did cut it a bit fine. One of the two guys there had just received telephone instructions to kill me, from Felix I think. His mate, a big bugger with an AK47, was in the right position to do it to me. I did it to him though, thanks to you wrecking the building for me. Mind you, Phil, you could have easily killed me too, you mad sod.'

'Well, I'm sure you would rather be killed by a friend than by one of the bad blokes.' Phil chuckled and Millane joined in.

'What do we do about this mess? I mean, we can't just leave it alone, can we?' Phil asked.

'No, we can't just leave it. We'll make an anonymous call to the police, and to the *Sydney Morning Herald*, not necessarily in that order, telling them about the drugs. Meanwhile, I have got to find the body of the man with the white coat. I want to leave some clues for the police, or whoever gets here first.'

'Clues? Like what?'

'Like the names and addresses of Senator Peter Filburton and Felix Smith in his wallet. By the way, Phil, while I am doing this I want you to collect as many of the bags of drugs as you can find intact. At some stage I am going to leave some very incriminating evidence that will destroy Senator Filburton's reputation for ever. Not that he will worry about it as I don't intend for him to be alive when it happens.'

'You devious bastard,' Phil grunted as they made their way back into the building.

It only took Millane a short while to find the man he was looking for. A main floor joist of the office had virtually cut him in two. Phil hurriedly left the building when he saw the mess, and Millane could hear him being sick outside.

Luckily the man's wallet was in the jacket pocket under the white coat, so he didn't have to handle the body much. He found a business card in the wallet which appeared to identify the dead man as a chemist with a Canberra address. He removed the man's ballpoint pen from the pocket and carefully wrote both Filburton's and Felix Smith's details on the rear of the card. He was careful to identify Filburton as being Senator Filburton of Parliament House, Canberra. Replacing the wallet, he was about to leave when he noticed something very strange. The man was still clutching the telephone handset against his chest.

The thought immediately came to Millane that they would have to make their phone calls sooner rather than later. Felix, or whoever had been on the end of the phone at the time of Phil's dramatic entrance would almost certainly have heard the noise of the truck crashing through, and probably the gunshot reports. He, or his associates, might be on way at this very moment.

★

Felix was just thinking how fortunate he was that the cutting operation at Wagga Wagga was manned by such an efficient pair of operators. Having given the order to kill Millane, for that was who he was sure the intruder was, he was waiting to hear the gunshots that would indicate that his instructions had been carried out. Then, his eardrums were assaulted by the loud crashing noise, followed by screaming and two single gunshots before the line went dead. He had made several attempts to call back, but the line was not contactable.

He feared the worst. In fact he had a premonition that the man Millane had beaten him yet again, and he needed no confirmation of that fact. The man was just too good.

Picking up the phone once more he rang the Canberra number. The Senator was still in his office. Felix was relieved, because he hated to wake the boss up. To do so would have made matters only seem worse, he felt. Just how worse they could be whether Senator Filburton was awake or asleep, it would have been difficult to imagine.

'I don't believe this, Felix. Have you lost your grip man? One fuck-up after another. I guess we must accept the fact that he's terminated our two operators at Wagga Wagga. How many of our key people has he done for to date, Felix?

'A disaster is about to happen, if it hasn't already. Get us out of this or you are dead. I have too much to lose, and I'm not going to jail for any bastard, especially one I don't know and have never seen. He seems to have you by the short and curlies, Smith, so fix him. Do it now.'

The phone went dead in Felix's ears, for the second time in a short period of time.

He was disturbed by the way that the Senator had spoken to him. He had not called him by his surname for over twenty years. It was a bad omen. As if he didn't have a bad enough omen on his hands already, by the name of Millane, the Englishman, or Irishman, or whoever he was. Now to top it all he was obviously in league with Cartwright, or how else would he have even known the man's name? Millane and Cartwright together. How? How on earth could that have happened?

He made one further telephone call before pouring himself a very large bourbon. He arranged a meeting with a senior police officer whom he had not used for years, but who had been on a regular annual retainer of great proportions. He now had no choice but to bring his big guns to bear or everything would be lost.

# Chapter Sixteen

## Sydney – Monday Morning

Millane had made the first of his two phone calls within an hour of leaving Wagga Wagga. The first was to the night editor of the *Sydney Morning Herald*, the main Sydney daily. The man was very astute and didn't need telling twice. He said he would put someone on to it immediately. Millane advised him that he would have a head start on the police who would be notified within half an hour. Millane was sure that the paper would have someone based in the general region of Wagga Wagga who they would put on to the case right away.

Throughout the brief conversation, which he thought may be recorded, he spoke with his broadest Irish, Ulster accent. He had been trained well in this regard and was sure that even an experienced voice analyst would not have recognised it as being bogus.

Forty or so kilometres closer to Sydney he made the second call. This time it was to the police. He wanted to be as sure as possible that the matter would receive the highest level of investigation, so to achieve this he made his call to the Australian Federal Police headquarters in Canberra.

He had no idea what the relationship was between that force and the New South Wales Police, but guessed that by contacting the feds it would put an extra link into the investigation chain and lead to a better result. Again he played the Irishman in his conversation. This time he knew for certain that his voice would be on tape.

After the extraordinary activities of the night, and the long drive from Wagga Wagga, which both men shared, Phil had been totally exhausted. However, before going to bed he showered to remove the remaining traces of the heroin powder from his body and hair and threw his clothing into the rubbish bin. He was surprised that John Millane failed to follow his example, but instead went to his room immediately on reaching the house.

Don't these Poms ever wash? he asked himself as he dozed off to sleep.

★

Both men slept the day out, with Millane the first to wake. He decided to perform a kindness to the man who had saved his life twice, and having ransacked the cupboards and the refrigerator he prepared a fried meal of bacon and eggs. Phil was delighted with the gesture even though initially he had not been too pleased to be woken.

Having completed the meal Millane cleared away the dishes and made a pot of tea. As he sat down he instantly became serious and approached their situation as if he was discussing an ordinary business matter.

'Okay! We have really hurt Felix and the Senator. We have virtually busted up their distribution business or at least knocked a big hole in it, but we have to follow up on our successes and not let the bastards regroup. We mustn't lose sight of the fact that the dynamic duo are seriously in the business of saving their arses, and to do that they need to kill both you and me. We already know that they have some very unscrupulous and mean people working for them; people who in real life are supposed to be on the side of law and order. That puts us very much on the defensive, for the time being at least.'

Phil sat quietly, having nothing to say about what appeared to be a reasonable summary of the situation to date.

'Just one thing, John,' he asked when Millane had finished. 'How can you be so sure that Senator Filburton is the man? I mean, in his position he's a national identity.'

'Good question, Phil, but as far as I am concerned he is our man. I have a gut feeling about it and my gut feelings have never let me down before. If we are wrong, which I doubt, at least he won't be after killing us like Felix is, will he? I'd rather be sued than shot.'

Phil couldn't help but smile at the argument that his strange associate put forward.

'In fact, Phil, the evidence put forward by my people in the UK is really conclusive stuff, and they are almost always correct. Not to be can cost lives in our sort of business. I'm sure you've probably gathered by now that I am a full-time employee of sorts of Her Majesty's Government, and the things that you feel I do far too often are the things that I am trained to do. Does that make sense?'

This was the first time Millane had made any sort of reference to being a special forces type operative. Although Phil had made this assumption he felt reassured to hear it from Millane in this manner.

'Also, in case you are wondering, Phil, I don't normally screw up as often as I have done since my arrival in Australia. I'm on very strange ground and haven't got the back-up that people like me tend to have as a general rule. Or that was the case until you came along. Thanks again, my friend. I won't let you down, I promise.'

Phil felt flattered by this admission that a man like Millane needed someone like him to rely on. Until now he had considered that his interventions had been purely coincidental rather than deliberate acts of anything resembling bravery. Millane had really touched his weak spot. He enjoyed praise, but rarely in his life had he received any.

'We need some help, Phil. Some people on the ground. People who will not be too noticeable, but who are smart enough to get themselves out of the shit should the need arise. Now I don't know these Irishmen too well. You are better acquainted with them than me. Are they any good?'

'I think they may be, John, but they are up to so many things, I am not sure that we could rely on them being there as and when we really needed them. I have got some mates from Nam whom I trust implicitly. I have used them on numerous occasions in the past to assist me in my deliveryman business. The not-so-legitimate business, I mean.

'They're all bikies, and real hard cases, so I guess they may not meet your criteria of not being too noticeable. They will do just about anything for me though, and I am sure that they would be loyal to me regardless. However, I always pay them well, just to be sure.' He chuckled at his last comment.

\*

They left the house at about 9 p.m., and took a taxi to Sydney's Surry Hills. The taxi dropped them off outside a rough-looking pub with dozens of large motorcycles standing in rows outside. Most of them were Harley Davidsons of various models and ages. Millane decided that the value of the machines was probably twice that of the property they were parked outside.

They were both dressed casually, and Phil wore a very old and faded black leather jacket. He blended into the pub landscape instantly, for almost all of the men there wore leathers of some description. There were very few women present, and those that were looked as tough and able as the men. However, regardless of Phil's jacket he and Millane stuck out as being different immediately because neither had beards nor tattoos. Even the bikie women were heavily tattooed.

The anonymity of Millane's business made it very unwise to have any characteristics that could be used to identify him. As for Phil, he had reached the doorway of numerous tattoo parlours in Saigon but always changed his mind at the last moment. Basically he felt that it was stupid to brand oneself in such a permanent way.

It was instantly obvious that Phil was amongst friends, and being introduced as a good friend of his gave Millane immediate acceptance. He put some notes on the bar and told the barman to let him know when the money needed replenishing. Whilst his relationship with Phil was not explained, it was obviously accepted by the men and women present that he was involved in what they saw as Phil's fairly harmless criminal activities. This was the attitude that Millane and Phil played on during the next few hours.

★

Within an hour they had moved to a back room with a group of Phil's closest mates, those who he felt he could trust the most. They were given the story of an American black man who was muscling in on Phil's business, and they were told that they were to be part of a surveillance team keeping an eye on the movements of the black man in order that Phil could make plans to counter his intrusions on his territory. The story seemed to satisfy the men.

They didn't seem too surprised when they were told that the man was very dangerous, and would not hesitate to kill anyone who he felt was spying on him. The men were cautioned to take the greatest of care. A very generous level of remuneration was agreed, and each man was told that he would require a mobile phone for contacting Phil at a moment's notice, if the need arose. One of the men, an ex-infantryman named Willie, who had fought in two of Australia's bloodiest engagements in the Vietnam War, was obviously the accepted leader of the group. The others certainly appeared to defer to him at all times. This satisfied Millane.

Willie was given the role of arranging an around-the-clock surveillance schedule, an activity in which he appeared to have some previous experience. He was given as much information about Felix and his general description as Phil was able to give and it was agreed that the work should start at 6 a.m. the following morning.

Millane didn't know how they were planning to do the job but he hoped that they had taken on board the advice about Felix's violent tendencies.

He didn't share all of his thoughts in this regard with Phil as he was too friendly with the bikies. But then, he was not really too concerned for them. They were merely contractors. They had a job to do, and if they were stupid enough to get sussed, then be it on their own heads. They were being paid enough to be discreet. If they weren't, and they were caught out, then at the very least it might force Felix's hand and bring him into the open where he could be dealt with.

Primarily Millane wanted information, but confrontation would do just as well. Either result would satisfy him, as long as it enabled him to get within killing distance of Felix and the Senator.

# Chapter Seventeen

Wednesday Morning
Canberra – Australian Capital Territory

Phil had stayed in Sydney to co-ordinate the surveillance operation which he appeared to have more faith in than did his English associate.

'Believe it or not, John, even though they are bikies these guys have discipline. They are pretty smart operators, and I know because I've used them on several occasions in the past, and they have never let me down.'

'I hope that you are right, Phil, but there is a hell of a lot of difference between driving a truck load of stolen gear, and conducting a high-level surveillance against a man with the background that this Felix appears to have.'

The discussion arose from further information that Millane had obtained by phone the night before which listed the military records, both official and unofficial, of both Felix and the Senator.

'This guy will be highly trained in anti-surveillance procedures and he'll pick out your bikie mates as quick as a flash. Christ, they don't exactly blend into the surroundings, do they? In the yuppie area where Felix lives they will be reported to the police the moment they arrive.'

'They won't, John. Trust me. Leave it to Willie and the blokes.'

Unconvinced, and sure that it was all going to go wrong, he decided to shake the Senator up a bit on his home turf.

He reasoned that if it worked and Filburton was Felix's boss or his associate, he would call on Felix to help him out. Then he would have them together and would terminate them and their nasty racket.

Phil nearly choked when he was advised of this plan. He was still not sure that a man of Filburton's obvious standing could be the Filburton who was so graphically described in the information that John had received from England. He could see, however, that there was no way that he was going to persuade Millane to change his mind. So, thanking his lucky stars that he was not expected to be involved, he grudgingly agreed to the plan.

*

The Qantas flight was full, even in first class, which he had booked in order to gain access to the airline's lounge at Canberra. It appeared to Millane that Canberra must be a busy place, but having a cynical view about politicians and public servants he wondered just what it could be that they were so busy doing.

He had dressed himself in a smart, dark-grey business suit and really looked the part that he imagined was very Canberra. He rang the Senator's office from the airport and spoke to his private secretary. The man did not seem at all interested when he explained that he wished to speak to Filburton regarding information he had on an international drug smuggling ring here in Australia. However Millane impressed on him the need to advise the Senator, who he assured him would be interested. Leaving his real name and the number of the mobile phone that Phil Cartwright had supplied for him he settled down in the Qantas Club Lounge and waited.

The phone rang just thirty minutes later. He knew that it would be Filburton as he had instructed Phil that he was not to ring him under any circumstances.

'Good morning, Senator.' He felt good knowing that he had such an advantage over his opposition from the word go. 'I don't like being kept waiting although I guessed that you would have to consult with Felix before returning my call.'

The voice at the end of the phone was that of an educated and cultured man.

'I haven't the faintest idea what you are talking about, Mr Millane. Of course I had to return your call. Information on drugs is very important to us in the parliament.'

'How very commendable, Senator, but if you insist on sticking to the story that I have got it all wrong I suppose I had better go straight for the jugular. No point in fucking around, Filburton. There are a lot of people, not the least your parliamentary colleagues, especially those of the opposite political persuasion, who will be very interested in your military past.

'Shall I read out some of your exploits in Cambodia, Thailand, Tibet and Vietnam, Senator? I will of course notify some friends of mine in the CIA, MI5 and the French mob where they can get hold of you. They lost a few of their best people to you and your little black friend. Oh, and then there is Yuri Kesanoff, you'll remember him, Senator. You wasted his brother because he wouldn't leave the KGB to join you. Yuri will have you for breakfast.'

Millane was conscious of the heavy breathing on the end of the line.

'Speak to me, Senator. I want to hear your voice.'

'Where the fuck did you get all this information?' The cultured accent had disappeared. It was replaced with a hard, coarse voice. The voice of a man who had done things the hard way at some time in his life. 'You have gone too far, Millane, much too fucking far for your own good.

'Our little business down in Wagga was very important to me. I don't know how you got on to it or what you told the feds, but they have been all over me like a rash, and the media too. You have gone out of your way to make an enemy of me and nobody has ever done that and got away with it, I promise you.

'We are on to you, Millane. Felix is close to you right now. Mark my words, you are a dead man.' The line clicked as the Senator slammed down the receiver.

★

Within seconds he was speaking to Phil on the normal phone, informing him that things were happening fast. Whilst he was speaking to him he heard the ring of the mobile phone in the background. Phil excused himself and asked him to wait. He could hear muffled voices in the background, then suddenly Phil was back on the line.

'I don't know what you have done, John, but you are right on the button. Willie's man has just notified me that Felix came out of the underground car park where he lives like a bat out of hell. A team of them are after him now. I'll keep you posted.'

'For Christ's sake don't let him see them or it will stuff up everything down here.'

'Gotcha, John.'

'And by the way, Phil, for an extra bonus I want Willie to arrange for Felix's place to be made unliveable. You read me? Trashed! Destroyed! I want to push the little bastard right over the edge.'

He heard Phil chuckle. 'Sometimes I get the feeling that there is a mean streak in you, John Millane.'

'No, Phil. There is nothing mean or nasty about it, this is just the normal way I do business with people like him. If we seek and destroy everything in his wake he will have no alternative but to eventually lead us to the Senator, and who knows who else?

'Now, Phil, nobody else must be involved in the business at Felix's place. No civilian casualties. Get me?'

'Loud and clear, John. Loud and clear.'

# Chapter Eighteen

Thursday Evening
Sydney

'Felix is just cruising from restaurant to bar, and back to restaurant. This afternoon he called at three separate banks. I have the details of which ones they were but I'm afraid the boys couldn't follow him in. The mere sight of one of them and the bank alarms would be going mad.' Phil Cartwright was phoning in his hourly report to John Millane who was in a bar in The Rocks, almost underneath the Harbour Bridge.

'I wonder why?' Millane smiled to himself as he spoke. He was amazed that Felix hadn't picked up his tail, so noticeable were Phil's veteran friends. They just looked like criminals, or certainly would do so·to the general public. He could only imagine what the appearance of one of them in front of a teller in a bank would do to the individual behind the counter.

'As a matter of interest, Phil, just how do your friends do their own personal banking?'

'I guess they don't, John. Anyway, as I was saying, he has been moving about so much that I'm not completely sure that we haven't been tumbled. One of the boys who is on to him now has reported that he has seen the same car behind him a couple of times over the last hour or so. It is a blue Holden Berlina, 1995 model. He hasn't managed to get the number yet. There are two big guys in it. He thinks that there is a possibility that Felix is verifying that he is being followed before taking some action. If that is the case, then he has got some support that we aren't aware of.'

This surprise information was startling.

'When did he first notice this car?'

'Just after he made his first report an hour or so ago. He considered it to be routine as he wasn't sure if he was just imagining it.'

'Where is he now, Phil? I want him to call me direct, instantly.'

'You're the boss. I'll get on to him right away. Don't worry, John. He's a cool dude. He knows what he's doing.'

'Perhaps he does in a bar brawl, but we're dealing with people the likes of which I doubt he has ever even read about, let alone dealt with direct.'

The line went dead and it was obvious to Millane that his friend Phil Cartwright was less than pleased with the way he had responded to the information he had just been given. Phil thought he was overreacting, and maybe he was. However, he would rather overreact than not. There was too much at stake, especially for the man who was at this very moment following Felix whilst possibly under surveillance himself.

The mobile phone in his pocket rang with a shrill shriek. Even though he was expecting it his nerves were so taut that it startled him. He walked out into the yard at the rear of the bar and answered the call.

'He's not answering, John. His mobile is turned off. Something is very wrong.'

'Get over here fast, Phil, and call up Willie. I want him in on this right now.'

★

At the same time that Phil was contacting Millane with the news that the man following Felix had concerns about being followed, Felix was himself receiving a telephone call on his mobile.

'You're definitely being followed, boss, by some sort of bikie on a Harley. He's pretty good, but not good enough. So far he has been concentrating so hard on ensuring that you don't suss him that he has not even considered that we are on to him.'

The man speaking knew exactly what he was talking about. He had been in the surveillance business for almost ten of his twenty years' police service. His associate sitting in the driver's seat next to him was a younger man, but with the same level of experience. They were Felix's A Team. They knew that he only called them in when things had to be done that were not routine, and probably involved a high degree of danger.

Neither of them considered the bikie to be in their league, but they both knew that Felix did not make mistakes. There had to be a lot more involved than this semi-amateur on his big bike. The man stood out in a crowd with his outlandish clothes and his shining badge-bedecked machine, but in view of their experience with the little black American, and their knowledge of his method of operation they took no chances and treated this job in exactly the same professional manner in which they had treated all previous jobs for him. The motorcyclist was, therefore, treated with the utmost care even though he did not appear to deserve it.

'Is there anyone else with him?'

'No, boss, he is on his own. He's just pulled in and is calling someone on a mobile, or it might be a personal radio.'

'Get rid of him. Now!'

'Right you are, boss. First opportunity. It might help if you were to find a nice, quiet, narrow street or alley that you could drive into. Give us a bit of advance notice and as you drive out we'll go in and meet him head-on. It'll look like a failing to stop accident.'

'Right you are, my man. Pickles Place! Do you know it? I'll go in from the Bay Road end and come out into Cross Road. Get to the Cross Road end, right now.'

*

'What do you mean you don't know where he was when he last phoned in?' Willie was plainly angry with Phil.

'He was excited, Willie, and a bit confused, and he also wasn't sure if he was being tailed or not. The silly bugger had been seeing the same car for nearly an hour yet he chose not to tell me until it was time for his routine call in.'

'Okay! Cut that out.' John Millane's voice was loud and commanding.

They had returned to the pub where Phil had first introduced him to Willie and his bikie friends, and were now in the private room at the rear. It was clear that this was a less than happy occasion and that everybody feared the worst for David Bridges, the missing man.

Millane suddenly realised that this was the first time he had heard the man's name. Until now the only person he knew by name was Willie. They were all just bikies, mates of Phil, and he had begun to identify them by the tattoos that they wore rather than by a name.

He shrugged his shoulders. What sort of life do you lead, Millane? Don't you care about anything other than the operation? he thought as he tried to grapple with this sudden turnaround in his fortunes.

'It looks like our friend Felix has cottoned on to us, and it is possible that he has started to fight back.'

'What do we do if that is the case?' asked Willie.

'That depends on whether you and your friends are still in the game, Willie. I will understand if you want out.'

'Look, Millane, David is probably okay. He could have had a road accident, or his bike or his mobile could have broken down. He's probably trying to contact us right now.'

'If you really believe that I don't think I want you to continue, Willie. I come from the real world. It's a fucking wicked place, but in my world we don't kid ourselves. I warned you that Felix was dangerous. He has a reputation of killing people who get in his way and I am now sure that David is dead because he wasn't smart enough.'

Willie grimaced and clenched his fists, but Millane continued.

'He was being tailed but instead of getting back-up instantly as people in my world automatically do, he stuffed around living in hope that he was imagining things. Now, if you are still with me, from now on I call the tune and nobody moves without my say so.'

Willie mumbled under his breath, but nodded his head as Millane finished speaking.

'Okay! You're the boss, but from now on my mates will all be armed, and we don't want your money any more, Millane. We just want to get back at whoever killed our mate, assuming you are right and that is what has happened.'

Shit, that's all I need, a gang of vengeance seekers on my hands. They'll screw up everything. Then out loud, 'Good! Then let's get on with it. Now, we mustn't let Felix know that he has got us rattled. We have got to carry on as though it is business as usual. When have you scheduled Felix's apartment to be smashed, Phil?'

'The boys are going into his place tonight. Even now I can't see why you want this done, other than for sheer vindictiveness. The man is too cool to be fazed by this. If David is dead it means that he is taking the offensive. The blokes who do this will need to be very careful.'

'If they weren't intending to be careful they shouldn't be going near the apartment in the first place. Willie has already said that they will be armed from now on in, and as for it not fazing Felix, we'll just have to see about that. If you are right then at least me and David's friends will get some vindictive, to use your words, pleasure out of it.

'However, if they do their job properly he won't have anywhere to live. That in itself will probably force his hand and make him do something. I'm pretty sure I know my quarry, Phil. I've got him on the hook, and I think it may be getting near time to start reeling him in.'

I hope you know what you are talking about. Christ! All of a sudden you've become an authority on a bloke you've only known about for a few days, Phil thought to himself as he poured himself a cup of coffee.

★

The council of war over, Millane and Cartwright booked into a motel unit not far from the pub. The owner was a personal friend of Willie's, who assured them of his reliability.

## Chapter Nineteen

Friday Morning – 3 a.m.

Both men were sound asleep in their rooms when the phone rang. It seemed to wail like a banshee in the still of the night. Millane was instantly awake, but he had been sleeping so soundly that momentarily he was unaware of what the sound was and where it came from.

Instinct and years of training took effect to overcome this brief lapse in concentration, and he had his automatic in his hand the instant the noise commenced. At the same time he leapt from the bed and hit the floor in a characteristic defensive position, his weapon aimed unerringly in the direction of the intruding sound, before he realised what the sound was.

His concentration had only lapsed for a second or two but in a real-life attack situation it could have cost him his life. He felt quite stupid and unnerved by the incident, but also relieved that Phil was not around to see him skulking behind the bed. Leaping back on to the bed, he grasped at the telephone just as it ceased ringing.

'Shit!' he called out loud, then realised that he could hear Phil's voice speaking from the other bedroom.

He was halfway to the bedroom door when Phil burst into the room. He had a wide grin on his face.

'You were right again, John. It worked.'

'What in hell's name are you talking about? What worked?'

'I've just heard from Willie. The guys tore Felix's apartment to bits, and with a vengeance in view of what has apparently happened to David, who incidentally still has not been found.

'They were also quite entrepreneurial in what they did, in that they left little bits of cannabis and heroin about the grounds and in the hallway of the apartment block. Then Willie called a mate who works for a newspaper and let them know that a major drug dealer has just been done over by the opposition, and gave him the address.'

Millane winced at the thought of amateurs being entrepreneurial, but said nothing.

'It seems that Felix came home about twenty minutes ago and literally went off the planet. Apparently the blokes could hear him ranting and raving from down the street.

'He had hardly got in the door when the media turned up, followed closely by a police car with lights flashing and siren going. This must have really flipped Felix over the top, for Willie says he came out of the underground car park so fast that he clipped the edge of the brick wall with his rear fender and tore it off. The police car tried to give chase but gave up after a couple of blocks.'

'For Christ's sake! Don't tell me that we've lost him.'

'Oh ye of little faith, John. No! Don't worry. The boys followed him. Felix has just booked in at the Hilton. Willie has got it all under control and the boys will cover all entrances and exits and do it in shifts. And by the way, Willie asked me to advise you that they are no longer operating in bikie gear. They are wearing suits and are mostly in older model hire cars. A couple of the lads are using bikes, but they are using some borrowed ones, with ordinary motorcycle gear. I told you that they know what they are doing.'

'Great stuff, Phil. The Hilton, eh? An upmarket little prick is our Felix, there is no doubt about that.'

Both men laughed at the great success of the apartment-wrecking exercise, and the obvious anger that this had caused Felix Josia Smith.

'Well, Phil, his next move has got to be southwards to catch up with the Senator, unless of course the Senator is on his way to meet with him. By the time we've finished with them, pissed off is going to be one of their happier frames of mind, and I kid you not. Then you'll be safe, Phil. Safe to spend all that ill-gotten money you've been making as one of their deliverymen. Incidentally, my coffers are running dry and I need some financial assistance.'

'You've got it, John. From now on I am the banker for the operation. I've got the dough, and it will be money well spent.'

★

It was after six in the morning before they met up with Willie and took up their place as part of the surveillance team. Only from this moment Millane was firmly in charge.

# Chapter Twenty

Friday Morning
4 a.m.

It was still pitch black and the bridge crew were very nervous. This was especially so for the officer of the watch, Joseph Fernando. He was not used to having the Captain breathing down his neck at four in the morning, not out in the open ocean, and certainly not when there was absolutely no reason for him to be there anyway.

The weather is perfect and the ship is operating like clockwork, so why is the Captain up at this time of night. Is he checking up on me?' Fernando thought as he watched him out of the corner of his eye.

The ship was sailing northwards one hundred or so miles off the east coast of Australia. To the west lay the Great Barrier Reef, and further west Queensland's Cape Melville and the lush coastal region that lay inland from there.

Fernando generally got the night watches once the ship was safely into international waters, but he didn't mind the hours. He was aware that as the youngest officer on board he was expected to automatically pull the short straw with regard to the unsociable hours of the vessel's operation. Fernando actually liked working these hours as he found them to be the most pleasant time to have to work. The ship was always at its most silent, and somewhat serene at this time of night. The solitude that it provided gave him the time to plan for his future once this voyage was over.

Captain Brandon had told each crew member individually that at the end of this voyage they would be released from their contracts which involved them in the criminal extra-curricular activities of the *Palminto*, and would be permitted to retire how and where they wished.

He had accumulated a small fortune over the six years that he had worked for the Captain. In many ways he would miss the *Palminto* for she was a good ship which under Captain Brandon's command had changed the lives of every man on board, and had given each of them a respectability that they would never have had under other circumstances. He personally would never need to return to the life of crime that he had once lived. Well, not quite the same sort of crime as before.

If he not been selected to join the *Palminto*'s exclusive crew the Fraud Squad in Manila would most certainly have put him away long before now. He owed a lot to the little black American who had introduced himself as a sort of recruiting agent for the *Palminto*. Fernando had not been totally convinced initially, but the man had been true to his word.

The Captain of the *Palminto* needed a crew member with ocean-going officer qualifications, which he had. However, it soon became obvious that his criminal tendencies were as much part of the recruiting criteria as were his seamanship skills and experience.

He hadn't been on board long before the real reason became known to him. The drug smuggling enterprise was the reason why the Captain needed people with his sort of background, even though drugs weren't really his line of business. But who cares when the money is so unbelievably good? He smiled to himself at the thought.

He was going to open a bar in Manila. It would be a respectable place where he would gain status. It would also be the sort of place where gentlemen of substance could come to be pampered by top-class women. That part of the business would be against the law, but a few US dollars here and there in the palms of appropriate officials would ensure his security from the rank and file of the police force.

He knew that he had the money for such an enterprise, and Captain Brandon had promised to introduce him to a business agent who would put him on the right track and provide him with sound business advice. He felt very excited about the prospect and couldn't wait for this voyage to be over.

*

James Brandon had exactly the same feelings about the end of this, his last voyage. Only he knew that it would not turn out the way that young Fernando would have wished. There was not a lot of time left for him to complete his preparations.

Earlier in the evening he had given both the officers and crew members a virtual instruction to let their hair down and celebrate. He provided the officers' wardroom and the seamen's mess with crates of expensive alcohol. To cater for the crew members who did not drink, if in fact there were such crew members, he also provided a range of non-alcoholic beverages. The bottles had been delivered to the ship just before it left Melbourne, and Felix had assured Brandon that each bottle, although sealed, had been injected with a large dose of a sleep-inducing substance. He had just returned to the bridge having satisfied himself that all of the crew members who took part in the drinking session were soundly asleep.

Apart from the crew members on duty on the bridge, and the three men in the engine room, only two crew members had declined to join the parties that had been arranged.

Armed with an automatic pistol, it had taken Brandon fifteen minutes to track down both of the men. Whilst what he found disgusted him, it also did him a favour in that he only had to search in one place. The man who was to be his second victim was in the same bed as the officer whom Brandon had decided to track down first, and they were both asleep.

Probably exhausted by their disgusting activities, Brandon thought as he moved closer to the bed.

Ever since Vietnam when he had been accused by certain fellow officers of being homosexual he had retained a deep-seated anger against such people. What made it worse for him when he entered the officer's cabin was that the man in bed with him was an ordinary seaman. This greatly offended Brandon's officer-class attitude to life.

Neither man woke as he entered the cabin. Earlier when he had considered what he would do with crew members who failed to participate in the drinking sessions he had found it very difficult to come to grips with the thought of actually killing someone in cold blood. However, quite illogically the men's homosexuality made it very easy for him. He gave the matter no further thought and casually shot each man in the head.

The matter of the engine room personnel was proving to be slightly more difficult for him to come to a decision on. He knew that he needed the men on duty there to be able to respond to the bridge should the officer of the watch communicate with them.

Immediately after dispatching the two sleeping crew members he decided to go to the engine room to see whether there was a way in which he could perhaps leave the men alive, but locked in. As he entered, however, he realised that any decision that he may make would be purely academic. The three men were deeply asleep, and it was obvious from the bottles scattered nearby that they had decided to take advantage of the alcohol available based on the assumption that no emergencies would occur during the night.

As with the two men in bed together, Brandon could not think logically about the situation that he encountered. All he could think of was that the men were drinking on duty which was a serious offence whilst at sea.

*

He now only had three crew members left to take care of. Fernando, and the two seamen on the bridge. He had planned this last stage down to the smallest detail and decided to carry out the plan immediately. Returning to the bridge he summoned Fernando to his night cabin aft of the ship's control centre.

The man entered and closed the door. He turned and stood to attention.

'Yes, Captain. What can I do for you, sir?'

The bullet entered his forehead just as he finished speaking.

Returning to the bridge Brandon called to the seaman who was the senior of the two men present.

'Give me a hand. Mr Fernando has collapsed.'

The man needed no second telling. He immediately turned and ran into the sea cabin just ahead of Brandon. He bent down over the body of the officer and was thinking, Where did all this blood come from? when Brandon shot him in the back of the head.

Dispatching the final crew member was to be the easiest task. Brandon returned to the bridge and approached the man from the rear. He was concentrating hard on steering the ship and thought nothing of his Captain walking up behind him. Brandon struck him a very heavy blow on the skull with the pistol and the man collapsed unconscious at his feet.

The hardest task of all was dragging him to the gang rail. When he planned this final stage he had no idea who would be on duty. The roster was the responsibility of the ship's Number One, and he had just not considered the possibility that the man concerned would be so large and heavy. In fact, the man was so heavy that it took quite some time for Brandon just to get him to the side of the ship, by which time he had started to stir. He hit him a further hard blow on the head but the man continued to move, and appeared to be regaining consciousness regardless of his injuries.

In panic at the thought of his plans going wrong at this final, crucial stage, Brandon drew the automatic pistol and shot the man in the head. It then took him another five minutes to find the strength to lift the body over the rail and drop it into the sea. Had he been thinking rationally he would have realised that there was no need for him to dispose of the body in this manner.

Now was the time for him to prepare for his entry into the water. It took twenty minutes to get the life-raft on to the deck and to inflate it ready for his departure. He carefully checked that it was fully equipped with medical supplies, plenty of water, and of course the vital signal flares that would bring his rescuers to him. He then went to his cabin and brought up to the deck the two cases of food that he had specially prepared for this time.

At the moment that he sighted his rescuers he would put the remains of his substantial food supply over the side, where in the weighted bags that he had prepared they would sink to the bottom of the ocean. To all intents and purposes he would have been on the hastily inflated raft without any food and supplies for however long the rescue took to happen.

Weeks before he had spent some time carefully tearing the jacket and trousers of one of his uniforms and creating burn marks in the material. To look the part of a survivor he now donned this tattered uniform.

During the first few hours in the life-raft he would inflict some wounds to his body as near as possible in keeping with those one would expect on the survivor of a shipwreck. It was all planned to the final detail.

★

He felt bad about sinking *Palminto*, for she was a beautiful ship and he had grown to love her dearly. However, for him to commence his new life he had come to grips with the fact that she had to die. He spent nearly an hour walking around the ship, taking in every detail of her beauty and remembering the wonderful times that he had spent with her. Now was the time to leave her.

He slowly strolled to his cabin where he opened the door of his uniform wardrobe, and kneeling down he removed a small panel from the floor. Inside the exposed cavity was a small lever. This was the control for the detonation of the masses of explosives that Felix's experts had placed in strategic places throughout the ship.

All that Brandon would have to do now to finalise this chapter of his career was to pull the lever. He would then have thirty minutes exactly to abandon the ship and to row the life-raft well clear.

Had he known of the fate that the two men who had placed the explosives had met at Felix's hands he would have not felt so happy at pulling that lever, but he was blissfully unaware of what had happened to them.

Pulling hard on the lever he stood up and was just about to turn and make his way back on to the deck to prepare for his final departure when he heard the sound.

It was a deep rumbling noise that suddenly got louder. Then the ship trembled and shook for just one minute before it erupted in flames and was torn apart from end to end. The explosion was massive and it took only three minutes for the *Palminto* to disappear for ever, blown into a million pieces.

Captain James Brandon didn't even try to leave his cabin. He didn't even turn around. He never had the time to do so.

He did have time, however, to think to himself, just before his body evaporated, You bastard, Felix. You bastard!

# Chapter Twenty-One

Sydney
Friday morning – 6.30 a.m.

Felix obviously didn't enjoy a good night's sleep. At 6.30 a.m. precisely he walked out of the front door of the Hilton. John Millane and Phil Cartwright were the nearest surveillance unit at that time, having only just arrived and taken over when the man made his appearance.

Felix looked very irritated. He was marching up and down on the footpath, obviously waiting for someone to arrive. Just then a dark blue Holden Berlina drew into the forecourt of the hotel, and Felix walked towards the vehicle and hurriedly got into the rear seat.

Millane, sitting in the front passenger seat next to Cartwright was on the phone to Willie immediately, informing him that they were on the move. Willie's role was then to pass the message down the line to the other units. The plan was to have a minimum of five units interchanging during the pursuit. Allowing for the interference that would be caused by the other traffic on the road at any given time this was the maximum number of vehicles that he felt could be utilised if the surveillance and pursuit was to be effective.

It worked quite well, particularly when they were joined after half an hour by the two motorcyclists. Their arrival enabled the cars to pull well back out of sight and for each one to then take a turn in coming within visual range of the blue Holden.

Felix's vehicle was now on the Hume Highway heading south, which made the pursuit quite simple.

'How are we going to find out who owns that car, Phil?'

'I've got a mate who might be able to help me. I'll give it a go.'

He dialled a number and spoke for a short while, giving the Holden's registration number to whoever was on the end of the line.

'Let's hope a cop doesn't come along right at this moment, John. I'm not supposed to be using this while I am driving.' He broke into a wide smile. Suddenly the smile disappeared. 'Are you sure of that? Thanks mate, I owe you one.'

He turned to Millane.

'We are in the shit again, John. The blue car is a cop car. It belongs to a special unit. What do we do now?'

'What's new, Phil? Those bastards who tried to plant me in the flyover were coppers too. That didn't seem to faze you too much then so why all the fuss now? We already know that Felix has got the sort of money to be able to buy most people.'

'Yeh, I know that, but the special unit these guys belong to has got a ton of clout. A very special unit, John. I get the feeling it's the sort of outfit that you have worked with before. My mate says we shouldn't mess with them.'

'Thanks, Phil. At least we know whom we are up against. I will just have to be sure that we watch our arses from now on in.'

★

The rest of the journey went without a hitch, the cars and motorcycles driven by Willie and his associates working the pursuit wonderfully well. Millane merely rang Willie and ordered the necessary changes, then Willie rang the unit concerned. Considering they were operating with mobile phones and not radios Millane was most impressed with their overall performance, as moving in and out of a pursuit of this nature was not easy at the best of times.

As they approached the northern outskirts of Goulburn Millane instructed Willie to contact the cars and order them to pull in before the city, allowing only the motorcyclists to follow the Holden into town. He was sure that if Felix continued straight on through the city it would be easy enough to pick him up afterwards on the open road. What he didn't want was five cars and two motorcyclists falling over each other once they got into the city centre. If Felix then moved off the main road into side streets the pursuing vehicles would immediately become suspect.

Phil had advised him that there was a large truck stop takeaway on the left, so this was where he told Willie to bring his men. As well as wanting to clear the decks until the motorcyclists reported in, he also wanted to talk to them and give them a short briefing on how to conduct the observation if Felix ended up in one of the city's side streets.

He had some initial difficulty contacting Willie, and when he finally did get through to him he was conscious of a strangeness about the man's voice.

*

One by one the bikies entered the large, barn-like takeaway restaurant, and getting themselves food and drink they each sat down in the same general area. Willie was the last to enter, his face drawn and ashen in appearance. Millane instantly knew that something was wrong, but before he even got the chance to enquire the man sat down opposite him, a hard, unpleasant look on his face.

'You've got some evil fucking friends, John Millane. I have just been told by one of my mates back in Sydney,' he waved his mobile phone in front of Millane's face, 'that they've found David. He's dead. The bastards smashed him up good and proper. He was run down and left in an alley over in Redfern. Apparently, according to the doctor who examined him, he didn't die straight away. It took some hours, and he would have been in agony until the end.

'This is no longer just a surveillance job, John, I want blood. I am going to kill the bastards. Just give me a half a chance.'

'I'm sorry, Willie, but I must insist that you and your mates keep yourselves under control. You will get your chance, or if you don't I will get the chance for you. Someone will pay for David, that I do promise you.'

Just at that moment Willie's mobile phone rang loudly. Both men jumped.

'Yes? Okay, Ray, what's up?'

'They've pulled in, Willie. The cheeky bastards have pulled into the front of a warehouse. It's within spitting distance of the Police Academy. Jeez! They've got more front than Myer. What do we do now?'

'They've pulled in somewhere, John. Ray is there now and wants to know what to do.'

'Get the address and tell him to keep out of sight until we arrive. Whatever happens he mustn't be sussed. If they get suspicious, who knows what they will do?'

Millane waited while Willie snapped out his instructions, then he was back out into the parking lot and just about to get into the car when Willie's phone rang again.

Willie put the receiver to his ear and as he did so the blood drained from his face.

'I'll get you, you bastard,' the big man screamed.

★

Millane had taken the wheel because Willie didn't seem capable.

'He said he has taken care of Ray. He must have been calling on his mobile.'

'Who are you bloody talking about, Willie? How did he get your number?'

'For Christ's sake, Millane, I thought you were the fucking expert in this game. He didn't get my number. He's obviously done for Ray. He must have just pressed the send button and it would have automatically redialled the last number that Ray called. My fucking number!'

'Where is your other mate? John, isn't it?'

'I don't know. I tried calling his number but I got no reply. The message said that he was either switched off or out of range.'

God above! What a fucking mess. Switched off would be the right expression for these blokes. How did I ever get saddled with them? Millane thought as he changed gears at the bend in the highway where it bore left into Goulburn City.

The convoy of cars roared into a street on the right of the highway in close pursuit of Millane who was driving like a man possessed towards the place where Ray had called from just five minutes earlier. He had no idea where he was going, but Willie was directing him and seemed to know the area quite well.

★

The driver of the blue Berlina had first picked out the motorcyclist about twenty kilometres north of Goulburn.

He felt sure that he had seen him on several occasions during the trip from Sydney but that was nothing unusual. It was the main highway to Canberra and it was possible for two vehicles to be in constant contact throughout the entire trip on this road. In fact, there was nowhere else to go if both vehicles were heading to the same destination.

It was when he caught sight of the bike pulling off the highway into the exact same street that they had pulled into that he really became suspicious. After ten years on Special Branch he felt competent to pick up a tail at the best of times, but this bloke was a rank novice. Then he saw the other bike and realised that they were both following him. His suspicions were finally confirmed when the second bike overtook the first, taking the lead pursuit position.

It was so pathetically amateurish that he couldn't resist smiling to himself. He calmly advised his partner who carefully adjusted the electrically operated wing mirror on his side so that he could observe the men following them.

Felix had been asleep in the back seat for an hour but he woke instantly when the police officer touched him on the shoulder. He was immediately alert and extremely upset that he had not been woken earlier.

'There was no point, boss. I didn't suss the buggers until just now when we turned off the Hume Highway.'

'Let's get to the fucking warehouse. Then you two can do your firecracker business while I fix those two bastards. This is really pissing me off. Do what you have to do, and do it quick. I'll be ready to move out in about ten minutes.'

★

The car pulled into the forecourt of a desolate-looking building which had the appearance of not having been used very often. The paving of the forecourt was badly cracked with weeds growing out of the gaps.

The two men had worked for Felix in the past. Their speciality was explosives, and although they had engaged in the occasional act of violence for the American they were usually retained solely for their outstanding skills in the art of explosive sabotage.

They took some large bags out of the boot of the car and followed Felix to a door at the rear of the warehouse. He undid the large padlock and two other security locks, and having let them into the building immediately took off at a run around the rear of the premises into a nearby lane.

Felix was adept at moving stealthily. For many years it had been his speciality. He was aware of his lack of current field training but still felt sure that he could outsmart anybody who was stupid enough to announce their presence in the childish manner that the two motorcyclists had.

By going behind the other premises he was able to take full advantage of the fact that the two men he was going after had demonstrated that they were not skilled operators, certainly not at his level. He had already made up his mind that they must be working for the mystery man, Millane.

He skirted the rear of the building, the driveway of which the first of the motorcyclists had entered. All the time he was stalking this man he was endeavouring to locate the position of the second one who he was sure had disappeared into a gateway further down the street.

★

The motorcyclist, Ray, really was a novice at this game. He was a veteran of some very unpleasant military engagements in Vietnam but at best he was just a hard case who could hold his own in a punch-up.

He had not given a moment's thought to the possibility that he might become the hunted. If he had done so he might have been inspired to remove his crash helmet to give him a better field of vision. But Ray wasn't really that smart, and had kept his crash helmet on just in case he needed to resume the pursuit in a hurry.

Just before Felix first saw him, Ray had decided that he should let Willie know what was happening. In coming to this decision he also made two very grave mistakes. Firstly, his voice had carried further than he expected. Because his hearing was slightly hampered by the padding of the crash helmet, he thought that perhaps his phone was not operating very well. To counter this misconception he raised his voice slightly.

This enabled the little black man to instantly pinpoint his exact location and to plan for the most discreet approach. The second thing that Ray hadn't considered was that by wearing the crash helmet he had totally lost his peripheral vision.

However, his final stupidity was that he was so engrossed in advising Willie where the Holden was that he failed to remain alert and never even heard his attacker, let alone saw him. He had finished his call, and was busy tucking the mobile phone back into his jacket pocket when Felix thrust the fine point of his knife into the side of his throat just below the rim of the helmet. He felt the pain and tried to scream out, but no sound came from his mouth. As he slumped forward Ray was aware of a strange noise coming from over his right shoulder. What he didn't realise was that the noise was the sound of blood-filled air bubbles escaping from his own severed windpipe.

Felix took the weight of his body and lowered it gently to the ground. Not out of any sense of caring, but merely because he didn't want to make any unnecessary noise.

He felt into Ray's pocket and withdrew the mobile phone, quickly placing it into his inside pocket. Then, crouching down he continued towards the alley where he knew his second victim was waiting, unaware of the fate of his mate.

Felix smelt the tobacco smoke before he saw the man. He was sitting astride his machine, crouched forward and apparently looking through a hole in the nearby fence. Felix decided that the man was probably keeping the Holden in view. Like his associate he had his helmet firmly in place on his head.

Piece of cake, he thought as he crept up behind the man. If Millane is so damn smart, how come he is using such a bunch of dick wits?

He was able to get close to this man, so close that he could hear him humming a tune to himself.

It was all over in a few seconds. The bikie felt backwards on to the ground, a widening pool of blood and urine surrounding his body.

Felix quickly checked to ensure that he had not been seen, then he turned and left the alley at a fast pace. As he ran he was speaking into a mobile phone, a grim smile on his face. It was Ray's mobile phone.

*

The two Special Branch policemen were not pleased with the way things were panning out. They were both concerned that their cover might have been blown by the sudden appearance of the two motorcyclists. Unlike Felix, who always seemed prepared for the worst, they had expected to arrive, set up their nasty explosives, time them according to the specifications of the boss and then leave.

They had wired up the explosives. Now all they wanted to do now was to get the hell out of it and they were waiting less than patiently when Felix arrived back at the car with a broad grin on his face.

'All done, brother,' he said to the older man. 'Now set the goodies for five minutes and let's get the fuck out of here.'

The man needed no second telling. He ran into the building and was back out within a minute. He knew his business, and he knew that the explosives would go off exactly on time. He and his associate had set three separate explosive charges, and had also turned on the tap of a large chemical vat situated on the ground floor of the warehouse.

'All fixed, boss. This will go off like a mini Hiroshima. Where to now?'

'South for me. You guys will have to get back to Sydney, and quick. I want you to find out where this bastard Millane is working from and just who he is. I need that intel urgently. Got it?'

Both men nodded. They knew better than to question this man. They also knew that a large sum of money would arrive within the next day or so and that it would be clean and easy to handle. They never discussed a going rate with Felix, for whenever they had worked for him in the past the remuneration had always been beyond their expectations.

'I'll contact you tomorrow in the usual way, now get out of here.'

'What about you, boss? If we leave you'll have no transport. Those guys will be here in a minute or two.'

'I'll be okay. I'll take one of the motorbikes. These pricks have cost me a fortune. There is nearly ten million dollars worth of shit in this place. The bike will be part payment of the debt.' He laughed out loud, and turned to look at the warehouse building, shaking his head in dismay.

'I just wish I had the time to transfer the stuff somewhere else, but I haven't, and there may be something in there that could embarrass me. Best to get rid of it in one big bang. By the way, take care when dealing with this Millane guy. He is really something else. He's got to be either SAS, or the Company, but Christ knows what they are interested in me for. That's the bit that really gets up my nose. Anyway, take it easy. Keep cool.'

With that he turned and ran out of the forecourt of the warehouse and across the road towards where the first motorcycle was left standing alongside its newly dead rider.

*

Millane had just turned into the street when it happened.

A large building on the right-hand side of the street disappeared in a massive explosion. He saw the building literally lift from the ground a split second before he heard the violent explosions.

Jamming on the brakes he dived down low in the driver's seat, immediately realising that Willie had been quicker than he was and was in a safer position. He had slammed his seat back and was crouched low on the floor of the car on the passenger side, his head almost in the open glove compartment.

'Oh shit! He's beaten us to it, Willie. You had better get the boys to look for your two mates. I suspect that they are both dead. This man Felix is not one for compassion or half measures. Those words aren't in his dictionary.'

## Chapter Twenty-Two

Sydney – Friday Evening

What had happened since the time they discovered the bodies of Ray and John had even surprised Millane, who coming from his background and with his experience thought he was beyond ever being surprised again.

Willie and his associates had insisted that they were not leaving the bodies to be discovered, and for a police investigation to ensue. They carefully wrapped them in coats and loaded them into the boot of the largest of the cars. Then the group drove back to Sydney at such speed that Millane complained bitterly that should they get stopped by the police and the cars searched they could all end up on a double murder charge.

Phil said nothing, he just kept out of the debate and never spoke once during the long drive.

Willie took no notice of his protests and the convoy arrived in Liverpool on the south-western outskirts of Sydney just before 7 p.m.

Their first port of call was to a doctor's surgery where Willie hammered on the door until a dishevelled man with a look of thunder on his face opened it. The look faded instantly as he recognised Willie, who pushed past him into the building.

Ten minutes later Willie re-emerged and climbed into the front passenger seat of the car in the rear of which Phil and Millane sat. When they made their hurried getaway from the scene of the explosion Millane had insisted that they would not be occupying the same vehicle as the corpses.

'Would you mind telling me what the hell is going on, Willie? We have removed two bodies from the scene of a crime, a murder. We have broken every road rule in New South Wales, probably in Australia, and you have left us sitting in the car park of a doctor's surgery with two dead men in the boot of the car immediately behind us. I can't afford this kind of shit.'

'There wouldn't have been any shit but for you two. It's shit of your own making so don't give me a hard time. As for the scene of crime, crap, there was no crime, Millane. Our mates died of natural causes in two different locations and on two different days. Ray was an asthmatic, and he had a bad attack and died of heart failure. John had a coronary and died yesterday. I have just obtained two death certificates to prove it.

'We are not in the business of having our mates cut up in post-mortems, that's just not dignified. It didn't happen to them in Nam so it sure as hell is not going to happen here. Nor are we having the cops poke their noses into our affairs. That isn't good common sense.

'The boys were never in Goulburn, and they didn't get murdered. Do you get it? We don't expose ourselves to that sort of crap, and we protect our mates even if they are dead.'

'But what are you going to do with the bodies, Willie? It's all right getting some bent doctor to sign a death certificate, but you still have got to dispose of the evidence. You can't leave them in the boot of that bloody car.'

'Don't worry, John, they are going to be given the full rites, the proper treatment due to a vet.' He then gave some whispered instructions to the driver and the convoy of vehicles set off again.

During the journey Willie made a brief whispered phone call.

★

The next stop was at the gates of a public cemetery where they were greeted by a sombre-looking man in a black suit. He opened the gates and the vehicles drove in. The man locked the gates behind them and walked hurriedly to where they had come to a halt outside a grey stone building. The building was very near to the gates, but hidden from the road by a row of dense hedges behind which the cars parked.

The man in the black suit entered the building and came out a few moments later with a trolley on which both of the dead bodies were laid. Millane couldn't believe his eyes. What followed was a brief yet formal funeral ceremony, after which the bodies were wheeled away.

Back in the car he couldn't restrain himself any longer.

'What in hell's name was all that about, Willie?'

'Simple. We just gave our mates an honest funeral. Tomorrow we will get their ashes and the relevant documentation. I will then arrange to send the boys, or what's left of them, back home to their mums. It is all legal and above board. Well, legal enough to keep the cops off our arse, and it will save their rellies any unnecessary extra aggro.

'More to the point, it won't leave our calling card for your friend Felix and his crew. We need a bit of time to sort things out and to decide whether we want any more to do with you both.' He nodded his head towards Cartwright and Millane.

'You guys have brought us fuck all but grief so far.'

Millane was unable to answer that sort of logic. He felt washed out. Three men were dead. They were all the good guys whereas the objective had been to get the bad guys. Yet it had all gone wrong from the word go. He suddenly felt very old, and his leg wound had begun to ache badly. He knew that his limp would become even more pronounced than usual, which always happened when things went badly for him, or when he was under stress.

Phil had been very subdued ever since the discovery of the bodies of the bikies. He had been a friend of the men and was obviously taking their deaths as badly as Willie and the rest of the group.

What a bloody nuisance. I must dump these blokes. They are becoming a bloody liability.

Phil must have guessed what he was thinking for he suddenly leaned over and whispered in his ear, 'Don't you even dare think of leaving us out of this business, John. We now own a piece of this bastard Filburton and his mate Felix. We are going to cash them in, and as soon as you like.'

'I thought you weren't convinced about Filburton, Phil.'

'I'll take a chance on him being the right man. If I'm wrong who'll give a shit? He's a bloody politician so nobody will miss him or mourn him anyway.'

★

It was late when he and Phil arrived at the pub in Surry Hills. He didn't quite know what to expect. Two more men had been killed, yet within four hours they had been 'legally' certified dead by natural causes, and 'legally' cremated. Now he and Phil had been summoned to attend a sort of wake to be held for the men.

★

The pub was crowded, mostly with men, mostly bikies. The mood was sombre and the drinks flowed freely. He suddenly realised what it was to be. This was to be a send-off that was normally only given to military men by their peers, and these men still looked upon themselves as military men, even though in most instances their last encounter with the military was more than twenty years before.

The first thing that was confirmed at this event was that Willie was definitely the boss man. He was deferred to by all. Millane then noticed with great surprise the array of medals and military badges that each man wore. As a soldier he recognised the medal ribbons and most of the badges instantly and felt comfortable in these surroundings. He would merely be an interested guest and onlooker.

The music was all on guitar, played by a range of people and covering a wide range of styles and tempos. At a very late hour he was alerted to a special item on the programme by a sharp nudge from Phil Cartwright.

'This was Ray's song. He wrote it just after we came home from Nam. He used to sing it to his brother who was dying from some sort of cancer he got from fucking around with that Agent Orange stuff.'

The music was eerie and sad, and the words were the cry of pain of soldiers who had come home from a terrible war and had been ignored and badly treated by the Government and the Australian public.

Millane was aware of the historical facts of the events that had culminated in the Vietnam veterans being formally welcomed home over twenty years after the end of hostilities.

In his conversations with the bikies over the previous days he had come to the conclusion that none of them were too happy about the circumstances of their recognition after so long, nor did they believe that it made up for all that they had gone through over the years.

The bikie sang from his heart. His voice so beautiful and the words so sad that it brought a lump to Millane's throat.

> 'Twenty five years since I fired a rifle
> Since I lived through the blood and the gore
> Five hundred Aussies is really no trifle
> It was one hell of a cost
> But no battles we lost
> So who the bloody hell lost the war?
>
> 'Waltzing Matilda' we sang it so proudly
> They told us we were fighting to keep our land
>     free
> I came back from Vietnam a shattered young
>     man
> And Matilda would not dance with me.'

He looked around the dark, smoke-filled bar room in wonder. Men were crying, and many were linking hands with their comrades, and embracing each other as they mournfully joined in the chorus.

> 'We were spat on, abused and badly misused
> We were branded child killers and worse
> Our company unwelcome, friendship refused
> I wasn't a sinner
> Just a sad lottery winner
> I never dreamed winning could be such a curse
>
> 'Waltzing Matilda' we sang it so proudly
> Like Anzacs before us we fought our enemy
> I came back from Vietnam a bitter young man
> And Matilda would not dance with me

One in a hundred Aussies died in that war
But we stood our ground, never gave in
At Coral, Balmoral, Long Tan and more
We fought with honour and pride
Our mates by our side
And we stuck it through thick and through
    thin

'Waltzing Matilda' we sang it so proudly
Australians all, proud of our country
I came back from Vietnam only half of a man
And Matilda would not dance with me

It took twenty long years of heartaches and
    tears
Before they welcomed home us Vietnam Vets
You can't make amends with a band and free
    beers
With a smile and a fag
From folk ashamed of our flag
And politicians just hedging their bets

'Waltzing Matilda' we sang it so proudly
Proud Diggers all from the land of the free
Back from Vietnam, but no one gave a damn
And Matilda my darling
My sweetest of sweethearts
Matilda would not dance with me'

Phil and Millane were out in the street as the last words echoed into the night.

'Not a dry eye in the place, John. I just had to leave. I can't stand seeing grown men cry.'

'I don't mind them crying, Phil. I just hate to think how bloody hungover they are all going to be in the morning. They'll be stuff all use to us, that's for sure.'

Phil grunted in agreement as they both got into the car. Millane sat back and stretched, quite content for his companion to do the driving, and by the time they had reached the Harbour Bridge he was dozing off to sleep.

'For Christ's sake, John, I think we are being followed.'

Millane didn't even open his eyes.

'Do you mean the green BMW? It has been following us since we left the pub. I noticed it parked up the street when I went out earlier to stretch my legs. Two men in it. A pretty decent car. Too decent for that area. They gave themselves away from the word go. I wonder who Felix has put on to us now.'

Phil was both angry and amazed at the fact that Millane knew all along yet hadn't informed him they were under surveillance again, but decided to let the matter ride for the time being.

'So what now?'

'We find a place where we can ambush the bastards. Then we will have a little chat with them. Have you got your gun?'

'Oh shit!' Phil spat out as he settled down for a long drive under the guidance of John Millane.

★

After twenty minutes they pulled into the forecourt of a motel, parked the car and got out. They casually walked around the side of the nearest unit. Once out of sight both men ran across the garden bed to the wall bordering the roadway and climbed over on to the grass berm alongside the road. They were only twenty metres or so from the

BMW which had pulled into the kerbside and was sitting with its engine gently purring.

The man in the front passenger seat didn't know what hit him. He had been relaxing with his head resting against the window. Suddenly his support disappeared as Millane wrenched open the door. The man fell sideways and collapsed unconscious on the floor, not even feeling the chop to the temple that his assailant had administered.

At precisely the same moment Phil pulled the driver's door open, and jamming his gun into the throat of the man behind the wheel snatched the keys from the ignition. He leaned forward and whispered in his ear, 'One false move and I'll blow a fucking great hole in your head.'

He called out across the interior of the car. 'I hope you haven't killed that man, John. We need to get some information, but fast.'

'Nope! Just put him to sleep for a while whilst we talk nicely with his friend here. Mind you, if he doesn't play ball I'll kill the pair of them.'

During the following five minutes the men were searched, and the contents of their wallets were most enlightening. Both were detectives in the New South Wales Police Special Branch. The one who still had Phil's gun pressed closely to his head, was named Hippel. The unconscious one was named Barratt.

Hippel was questioned regarding the whereabouts of both Felix and the Senator. It was immediately obvious to Millane and Cartwright that he had no idea who the Senator was so the interrogation was confined to the black man, Felix. At first he denied all knowledge of anything to do with the man. To resolve this impasse Millane dragged his unconscious colleague around the car and pointed his gun at the man's temple. The driver of the car was apparently a person with some thought of honour.

'Please don't kill my mate, we are only doing a bit of moonlighting. Sure we know this Felix bloke, but we only work for him on the odd occasions.'

'What do you do for him on those odd occasions, kill people?'

'Christ no!' the man almost choked out the words. 'Charlie and me are good with explosives. We usually blow up things for Felix, I guess in order for him to put the frighteners on people who don't play ball. We never have anything to do with anything physical, if you know what I mean.'

'No, I don't know what you mean. Please explain.' Phil's demand was accompanied by a sharp jab of his gun into the man's head. Who killed those blokes down in Goulburn? We know you were with Felix down there, and from what you tell us, it was you pair who blew up that warehouse. What about the men who were killed?'

Hippel then made his second big mistake; the first one was allowing himself to be put in his present unenviable situation by Millane and Cartwright.

'Felix terminated them. They were only a couple of slags from Sydney. Felix said—'

He didn't finish the sentence. Phil was so enraged by the way he referred to his two dead friends that he smashed the man in the mouth with his gun. Blood and teeth were scattered over the dashboard of the car.

'They were my mates, you bastard.'

Then, before Millane could stop him Phil shot the policeman in the right side of the head, the blast throwing the man's body across into the passenger seat.

'Fucking marvellous, Phil. I was hoping to get a lot more from that guy. What the hell did you do that for?'

'I promised Willie that I would make sure that we got the bastards who did for Ray and John.'

'But you didn't, Phil. You didn't. All you have done is kill one of the men who blew up the building, you stupid arsehole. You killed that man for the sheer hell of it. I've had enough of working with you fucking idiots, Phil. From now on I am doing this on my own, and if Felix gets you then it's your hard luck.' With that he turned and ran back towards the wall of the motel which he cleared in one great leap.

Lights were coming on throughout the complex as he reached the car. At any moment now people would be venturing out to see what had caused the loud bang that had woken them from their sleep. He knew that his only hope lay in the fact that they would be sleepy and disoriented which would give him the opportunity to drive the car out of the motel without too much danger of it being identified.

He drove the car out at a normal speed with the headlights on full beam. Having just woken up, anyone who chanced to peep through the curtains would be less able to cope with such bright lights than at any other time. As it was he didn't see any curtains moving as he drove out on to the main road.

As he pulled away from the motel entrance he saw Phil running up from behind him, and slowed down sufficiently for him to drag the front passenger door open and leap in beside him.

'I reckon we have got ten minutes before the coppers start to close everything down, Phil. Give me directions to the nearest motorway or whatever it is you call them over here. I want to get as far away from this place as I can, in as short a time as possible.'

'Keep going, then take the first on the left,' Phil instructed.

★

Not another word was spoken for nearly twenty minutes, by which time they were on the Pacific Highway heading north out of Sydney at a very fast speed.

'If you don't slow down we will get ourselves pinched for speeding, John. Then we'll really be in the shit.'

Millane merely grunted, braking hard to reduce speed to the legal one hundred and ten kilometres an hour permitted on most of the state's major highways. Within an hour they were parked in a public car park on the coast at a place called The Entrance. Phil moved into the rear seat and both men prepared themselves for an uncomfortable sleep. Not a word had been spoken since Phil's reprimand about the excessive speed.

Just as Millane was beginning to nod off he heard Phil's sleepy voice from the rear of the car.

'I don't know how many cops there are in New South Wales, but at the rate you and I are going they'll have to have a major recruiting drive very soon.'

# Chapter Twenty-Three

Saturday – 2 a.m.

The police officer who Millane had knocked unconscious woke up amidst a sea of faces and bright lights. He was concussed and confused, but not too much so to realise that he was surrounded by uniformed police.

He knew he was in the shit but couldn't figure out what had happened. Albie Hippel, his mate, was nowhere to be seen, and he was lying on the pavement near the BMW. They hadn't expected any trouble so they had used Hippel's private car, and hadn't even discussed a cover story should anything go wrong. When they had started their night's work for Felix it had been inconceivable that anything would go wrong. After all, it was just a simple surveillance job to find out where the bikies and the Englishman Millane were to be found, and what they were up to.

The fact that they were all at that particular dive of a pub in Surry Hills didn't surprise Hippel or himself. They knew it was one of the places where this type of man hung out. He was firmly convinced that they were all layabouts, merely using Vietnam as an excuse for being into their sort of lifestyle.

Hippel had the view that if a check was done on the bikies, most of them would be found either to have never been in the military, or if they were, the nearest they would have got to Vietnam was through watching Rambo films.

During a recent drunken spree in King's Cross they had promised themselves that at the earliest opportunity they would lift a few of them and try out his theory. Had that eventuated both of the policemen would have been greatly surprised at the results of their enquiries. All of Willie's group were not only Vietnam veterans, but each had served with distinction in some of the worst military engagements of the war.

Barratt was beginning to focus upon what was going on around him. Amongst all of the police cars was an ambulance. Surely he wasn't injured enough for that to be for him. He tried moving his body and was convinced that he wasn't badly hurt, other than for the violent pain in the rear of his head that was making him feel quite sick.

Just then he saw it. Coming out from the other side of the BMW he saw two ambulance men wheeling a stretcher.

It's Albie. Thank God he is okay. He assumed that if his friend was on a stretcher he was probably being taken to the hospital for treatment. Probably bashed around a bit like himself. Then he noticed three things that caused him to panic.

Firstly, the ambulance men did not appear to be in a hurry. Secondly, unlike the police vehicles, the ambulance did not have its lights flashing. Lastly, and the most frightening thing of all, was that the stretcher was empty and someone in plain clothes appeared to be directing the men back to the ambulance.

He knew from bitter experience that if plain-clothes people were on the scene and giving orders something was really wrong.

'How are you feeling now, mate?' The enquiry came from a young police officer who was standing nearby. He had seen Barratt start to move and knelt down beside him.

'Where's Albie?'

'If you mean your mate, I'm afraid I have bad news for you. He's been shot. He's dead. Sorry.'

Barratt rolled over and was violently sick on the pavement.

Shit! Dead? Oh fuck, how am I going to tell Felix. Jesus! I am really in it now. If these guys don't get me then Felix will. His befuddled brain was working overtime as he considered his options, none of which looked good.

Such were his feelings of self-preservation that he never even thought of his late colleague's wife and two children, one of who was shortly to reach ten years of age and whose birthday party his entire family had been invited to attend.

All he could think of was how he was going to get out of his present difficult situation.

*

In fact, Felix was going to hear about it all very soon and from a most unlikely source.

One of the first things that Millane did when he woke up cold and cramped after about five hours of very uncomfortable and intermittent sleep was to go for a walk to stretch his legs. Whilst carrying out that essential rehabilitating exercise he searched for a public telephone. They were pretty thin on the ground in The Lakes area which resulted in his exercise taking longer than expected. He ended up walking more than five kilometres, not that he was able to measure the distance, before he came upon a phone that had not been vandalised. He made two telephone calls.

His first call was to the night editor of the *Sydney Morning Herald*. Luckily it was the same man whom he had spoken to after the Wagga Wagga incident. Once again he spoke in his Irish Ulster accent to ensure that he was recognised as being the same informant as before. The man was pleased to hear from him as the previous information had given him some excellent copy which ended up as a scoop for the paper.

After warning him not to attempt to trace the call, otherwise it would be the last he would receive, and then promising the man that he would shortly get the best story he had ever had, Millane told him of two incidents.

He explained that the Goulburn explosion, which the man was aware of but had not given any importance to at the time, was drug related and once again involved Senator Filburton and his American associate Felix Josia Smith. He asked the editor what the scuttlebutt had been on the explosion and was not surprised to hear that the incident was being played down.

'Get your best man down there straight away before they bulldoze the remains of the warehouse down. If you have any good contacts in the police I would involve them as well. You will discover that the building contained a large amount of illegal substances.'

'You mean drugs, don't you?' the newspaper man interjected.

'Yes, I mean a lot of fucking drugs. Now don't interrupt because I haven't got much time. A few hours ago two Special Branch coppers were done over north-west of Sydney. One of them was shot dead. Have the police released anything on it yet?'

'We had a report of a shooting which I have sent a man to, but there was no suggestion that it involved police. How do you know about this?'

'Never you mind. Now the two police officers are named Hippel and Barratt. Hippel was the one who was killed. They are both explosives experts and were responsible for blowing up the warehouse in Goulburn. If you can get enough experts on to it you should be able to put them in the frame for that one. They are in the employ of the Senator and the guy named Smith. Goulburn was another of their outlets. There is a rival group that is after them. That's all I can tell you at this stage.'

He finished by giving the man the details of Felix's luxury apartment and the fact that it had recently been trashed by the rival group.

'You play ball with me and give these bastards as much coverage as you can chuck at them and I'll make you famous. Now, you know my information is the real McCoy, so don't fuck me about. If you do the dirty on me I will come looking for you.'

He put the phone down, leaving the man protesting and asking a myriad of questions.

His next call was to the Australian Federal Police in Canberra, again using the number he had called after the Wagga Wagga incident. He knew for sure that his voice would be taped and that attempts would be made to trace the call so he made the message as brief as possible, giving the same information that he had supplied to the newspaper. As before he spoke using the Irish accent. He was not surprised to discover that nobody of importance was available this early on a Saturday morning. His experience was that most senior police officers worked the more sociable daylight shifts.

★

It was just becoming light when he arrived back at the car park only to find the car was missing. He was just about to make his way back into town when it returned with Phil at the wheel. Before he could say a word Phil announced that he had been to purchase breakfast.

He didn't even question where Millane had been, but merely said, 'I hope you didn't talk too long, they have very sophisticated tracing devices here in Australia. Bacon and egg sandwiches and coffee do you?'

★

The Senator heard about the call to the Australian Federal Police within the hour. Whilst not appreciative of being woken so early he expressed his extreme gratitude to the man on the other end of the line who he promised would receive an early Christmas present for his warning.

Filburton now knew that his informant's federal police colleagues would be on to him within an hour or so, which gave him the opportunity to tie up a few loose ends prior to their arrival. He was not due in the parliament until late morning, so having destroyed a few documents and cleared some information from his computer he decided to go back to bed. He felt sure it would look more natural for him to greet them at the door in his pyjamas, having obviously been woken up by their hammering on the door.

Just before going to bed he made one call. Felix was staggered with the information that his boss gave him.

'I don't know who is my biggest problem, you or that bastard Millane. Between the pair of you you've managed to bring the entire resources of the feds and New South Wales Police down on my head. This is the last time I warn you, Felix. Fix it, or else.'

★

Millane had guessed that a man with the obvious influence that Filburton had, both as a government Minister and from his criminal contacts, would have a person on the inside of the Australian Federal Police. This didn't bother him. The more sources that the Senator got his bad news from the better. At some stage in the not too distant future it was inevitable that he and Felix would be forced to meet. He wanted to be there when it happened. He would then avenge Sammy's death, and leave a trail of evidence that would blow the whole drugs empire, or what was left of it sky-high. The shit that would fly could have very serious political implications both in Australia and elsewhere, but that did not concern him. He would be on the first possible plane back home to England and to Colonel Marven's bedside.

He resolved that he would telephone the Colonel the following evening, late morning in England, and give him a progress report.

★

Two hours later they were back in Sydney and once again booked into the Surry Hills Motel owned by Willie's friend. The proprietor immediately recognised them and remembering Willie's assurances of their importance promised that the highest level of privacy and security would be afforded them.

# Chapter Twenty-Four

## Saturday Afternoon

Barratt was in real trouble, but things were already happening that could possibly go a long way to resolving his immediate and most important problem, his relationship with Felix Josia Smith.

Immediately after his return to Sydney from Goulburn in response to Felix's instructions his late friend and colleague, Detective Senior Constable Albie Hippel had instigated a search for Millane and his bikie associates. He and Barratt had circulated all of their informants with details of Millane and the information they had on the bikie group.

The reward being offered for information was so high that within an hour of their first contact over fifty very determined members of the criminal fraternity were putting every effort into earning it.

This was not a fifty or hundred dollar touch that was the norm for people of their level on the criminal social ladder. The thousands that were up for grabs was sufficient to merit their undivided attention and guarantee a result, if one was to be had at all.

Within a short period of time information had started to flow to the answerphone machine on the number given for responses.

★

Detective Constable Charlie Barratt had been subjected to a horrendous time at police headquarters. He had been questioned for six hours, and finally at 2 p.m. he had been suspended from duty; his badge and weapon taken from him.

It wasn't just the circumstances under which he and his dead colleague had been discovered, it was partly because in order to enable them to conduct the surveillance on Millane they had falsified records showing themselves as conducting an investigation elsewhere. It was also partly because they were using Hippel's private car, their police vehicle having been found parked in the driveway of his home. The senior officers investigating the death also considered it unlikely that a detective at his level could afford to drive such an expensive vehicle, not if he was an honest cop.

Their biggest concern, however, resulted from the fact that information received from the *Sydney Morning Herald*, which they claimed they had evidence to support, linked both Barratt and Hippel with the explosion at Goulbourn.

On top of all this the Internal Affairs Department had been investigating both men for some time as the result of information received, and since proved to be correct, that the detectives were big spenders in brothels in King's Cross and in the Casino at Darling Harbour.

As none of the venues in question were within the price range of any of the investigating officers, this had become very much a personal issue for some of them.

Barratt was panic-stricken. He felt sure that the game was up for him. His arrival home was not well received by his wife, who sensing something was very wrong decided to pack some bags and take the kids for a few days to her parent's home in the Blue Mountains.

As the result he was angry and full of self-pity when he decided to attack the grog cabinet, seeking some solace in alcohol.

He had barely got through his first drink when the telephone rang. He was about to abuse whoever was on the line, when he realised it was Felix.

'Is your line tapped, boy?'

'I doubt it, not this soon. Jesus, Felix.'

'Shut up and listen, you stupid bastard. Go to the place where the answering machine is and wait for my call there. If you are followed you're dead. Do you hear me?'

Barratt assured Felix that he understood. He was at a loss to know what to do. His friend and colleague Albie Hippel had always been the leader, the smarter of the two men, and he had grown to rely on him totally. Now that Albie was dead he really didn't know what to do, and he was scared of dealing with Felix alone. Charlie was intelligent enough to realise that to defy the man would surely mean his own demise, so it was with this clear belief that he set off to the location directed.

*

For over a year now the detectives had rented a small apartment on the north shore of Sydney Harbour. It was middle of the road in terms of Harbour dwellings but it still cost heaps.

He and Albie had shared the cost from their not inconsiderable extra earnings from Felix. The apartment was extremely convenient, and they used it to take the women whose sexual favours they purchased, or in many instances took for no payment under threat of arrest or worse.

It was a perfect set-up for that. Its telephone was also used as an answering service on various occasions, which was how they had arranged for information on the location and movements of Millane and his associates to be delivered by the people who were trying to earn the reward that had been posted.

Geographically it was only a short distance, some ten minutes or so by road, from Barratt's home. However, he knew that he would have to spend a considerable time getting there if he was to ensure that he wasn't being followed, which under his present circumstances was a distinct possibility.

Exactly one hour later, after leaving his car in a public car park, climbing a wall and using three separate cabs he arrived at the apartment. The first thing he did was to put the jug on and make himself a cup of tea. While he was doing this he noticed that there were four calls on the answerphone machine. He got a pen and paper and wrote down the messages, playing them each back twice to ensure that he had it right.

What came off the machine was very interesting information and could well save his bacon with Felix.

One informant, a man known as Dickie, advised that Millane and one other man were currently registered at the Blue Swan Motel, Paddington, in Room 205. Barratt was not to know that the information was false. He would have to check it out anyway.

The next two calls were probably of no use as they were so vague, but the final call was really interesting. Barratt felt sure that he had hit the jackpot.

'This is Reggie. About that reward. The leader of the bikies that is helping the Pommy bloke is a man named William Barry, known as Willie. He is an ex-Sergeant Major in the SAS. He served in Vietnam and is not a bloke you can stuff around with.

'Anyway, he owns a light aeroplane which he keeps at Bankstown Airport. He usually uses it on Saturdays or

Sundays for leisure purposes. His mechanic has just received a call telling him to get it ready for 9 a.m. tomorrow morning for a flight to Canberra with two passengers. Now guys, this is the real shit I'm giving you. It could get me killed so I expect that reward. You know where to get in touch with me.'

He had no sooner put the pen down when the phone rang. It startled him, particularly as he knew it could only be Felix. Deciding to take the initiative he immediately blurted out the news that he had received.

'That's good stuff, boy. Now you can save your own skin and at the same time earn yourself a big retirement fund, just in case those police pals of yours decide to do you over. What's with them guys anyway? Is there any way I can put them on the payroll?'

'I doubt it, Felix. I don't think that would work. They are all running around acting like the fucking Untouchables at the moment, all watching themselves with the new Commissioner.'

'Okay, my man. Listen in. This is what we will do.'

The detective spent the next ten minutes listening in silence while the little American gave him precise instructions. He was then made to repeat them twice just to assure Felix that he had them right.

Then Felix asked for the details of the two informants who had come up with positive leads. Barratt felt quite uncomfortable about giving such information away as informants were very personal. Not even his police bosses would ask for an informant's identity. It just wasn't done. It was widely considered that a detective is only as good as his informants, and these people had taken years to cultivate.

However, he knew that it was not wise to challenge Felix in any way so he grudgingly provided the detail that was demanded of him.

★

After fifteen frustrating minutes being given the run around and left hanging on the line Millane at last managed to reach somebody in authority at the hospital who could authorise that the Colonel be woken to receive the caller from Australia. Up until then he had been virtually beating his head against a wall. None of the nurses up to sister level would budge from their determination to refuse access to the Colonel who, according to everyone he spoke to, had had a very tiring morning of treatment.

It was only after raising his voice higher than they were able to that he was transferred to the senior administrator of the hospital.

He made his request very effectively, finishing with a glowing commendation for the nurses who had endeavoured to protect their patient from such untimely disturbance.

He had won, and after just a few moments he was through.

'Sorry to wake you, sir. I have news that I feel you should be privy to.'

'Thank you, my boy. How did you manage to get past the nurses here? If I was still fit and well I would be recommending them to the regiment as recruits. They're as tough as old boots, and very determined.'

The Colonel started to chuckle, but he was overcome by a bout of severe coughing. It sounded as if he was about to die there and then. Millane waited patiently until he recovered sufficiently, and when he had, insisted that he remain silent and listen, after which if he felt up to it he could ask questions. That was the normal army routine which seemed to satisfy the Colonel.

Millane assured him that he had terminated the man who had actually killed Sammy. He described the circumstances which had led the boy to his death, and filled the sick man in on what he had done to identify the man responsible for the drugs network into which Sammy had unwittingly intruded, and which had ultimately led to his death.

He concluded by telling the Colonel that he was about to confront the Senator in Canberra, and would be seeking to terminate him and his lieutenant, the black man named Felix, together with anyone else who got in the way.

Marven thanked him profusely and promised to make arrangements for any future calls that he made to be put through directly, or else. Millane smiled as he thought of the old man putting the entire hospital staff through their paces to ensure that his instructions were followed to the letter.

★

Immediately after phoning the Colonel he put a call through to the private residence of Senator Filburton. He had obtained the private and unlisted number through a friend of Willie, who was reported to have friends in high places.

'He is a poofter, and a lot of the high and mighty are screwing him so he has got them by the balls, in more ways than one. But he's a good bloke who owes me a few favours, of the non-homosexual variety,' he had hastened to add.

★

The call was greeted with a female voice on an answering service. Millane left the message that the Senator should call him immediately. He included the telephone number to call and advised that any attempt to trace the location of the call would meet with failure.

He then sat back and waited. Three Scotches later the phone rang.

'What do you want this time, shit heap? Oh, and by the way, I know where you are, and right at this very moment my people are closing in on you, so goodbye, sucker.' The voice on the end of the line was full of venom.

'Wrong again, Senator. You have no idea where we are. On the other hand I certainly know where you can be found and I'm coming for you. Meanwhile, my people are ready and waiting in case Felix tries to find us. Don't forget, arsehole, we may have lost a few troops but we have screwed your team at every turn so far.

'It gets better as well. The feds, the New South Wales Police and the National Crime Authority, plus a few of the more credible and respected newspapers are on to you, full bore.'

'What do you want, Millane? Just what the fuck do you want?'

'I want you, Filburton. You and that little black arse-licker of yours, Felix. I'm coming to Canberra to get you both. Say your prayers, Senator. You are dead.' With that Millane put the receiver down with a mighty bang.

Senator Filburton sat back in his high-backed leather chair and pondered his situation. For the first time in his life he felt unsure of himself. He also felt afraid. A cold chill ran through his body, and he had a strong premonition that he was shortly going to die.

★

'I don't think that is wise, boss. I reckon Millane is doing this on purpose to get us in the same place at the same time. Better I stay well away from you. I am sure I have fixed him

722

anyway.' Felix was trying his hardest to convince the Senator, but found it very difficult to achieve on the telephone.

'Don't argue with me, Felix. How long have you worked for me?'

'Thirty years, Senator, but that doesn't mean I can't have an opinion. I am convinced we should play the game according to our rules, not his. Trust me, I know what I am doing.'

'In thirty years you have never disobeyed me which is one of the reasons why we have been such a great team for so long, and I don't intend letting you challenge me now. I need you here in Canberra, soonest. He's already proved he is our match individually, but if we stick together he hasn't a show even if we are a pair of past-it old bastards. Get down here tonight. That is an order.'

'You're the boss. I hope you haven't got it wrong.' Felix's last words were wasted. The telephone receiver was already on its way down as he spoke.

Within the hour the American had booked a first-class ticket to Canberra. He felt it was no longer necessary to follow his usual security procedure of travelling economy. There no longer seemed any point in doing that. In the cab on the way to the airport he tried unsuccessfully to contact Barratt, and was concerned that the man was not available. He hoped that it was because he was carrying out the instructions he had been given earlier.

★

As Felix was trying to contact his associate, Millane was in earnest discussion with Phil and Willie. He was telling them that he had decided to go it alone from here on, and this had caused a great deal of anger.

'You owe us a chance to be in at the end, Millane. Three of our mates have died helping you, and for what? We have got fuck all to show for it yet. We need a break. My boys are full of anger and hate, and they need to take it out on whoever it was who did this to us.

'Now, Phil says it is the same guys who are trying to kill him, and you say they also killed your boss's son. Shit, we all have a bloody good reason for being in at the end. I know we are not as good at this as you would like us to be, but you do owe us.'

'Amen to that.' Phil was as angry as he had been in his life. 'I saved your miserable fucking life, twice. That gives me rights, whether you like it or not. I'm staying next to you if I have to superglue myself to you. And, Mr Smart-Arse, the boys are my mates so I am inviting them along also.'

'I don't believe this.' Millane threw his hands in the air in despair. 'Up until now we have been playing the third division team. When we get to Canberra we will be dealing with the first team, the super league. I will have my bloody work cut out watching my own arse without wet-nursing you lot. Phil, I'll take along, but not the rest of you. You are all likely to end up getting killed. Believe it or not, I have got quite attached to you, you dopey pack of bastards.'

The argument continued for hours into the night with Millane also expressing his concern about the plans for the following day, Sunday.

'This man Felix has got a network. He has been doing whatever it is he does for a bloody long time. He has got informants coming out of the woodwork, because he can afford to pay whatever it takes. Everything we are doing is dodgy. Also, I don't like making plans too far in advance the way we have. It's not good field practice. In fact it is down right bloody dangerous.

'While I'm on about good field practice, I need a weapon with a silencer. Phil nearly got us all arrested when he shot that bloody copper. The noise could have woken the dead, and I just can't afford to have any noise next time.'

The weapon was delivered to his room within the hour. It was an old gun, but he checked it out and it seemed to work all right.

★

The men had barely got to sleep when the alarm clocks went off all over the motel. It was a very bleary-eyed group of men who at 6 a.m. on Sunday morning eventually congregated in Millane's room.

The decision had been made. There were a lot of changes to the plan but it was finally agreed that all of the group would travel to Canberra after all. Willie's men would travel by motorbike and car and would meet up with the other three at a café in Dickson at 3 p.m.

After seeing them off Willie and Phil each made phone calls. Then after a light breakfast of tea and toast the three men set off to the airport to fly to Canberra. Their role was to get there early and make arrangements for accommodation for the main group, and to carry out some preliminary surveillance prior to their afternoon rendez-vous.

★

Willie's Beechcraft aeroplane was given clearance to take off at exactly 9.10 a.m. It taxied to the southern end of the main runway, and turned into the light breeze for take-off. The two passengers checked their seat belts, and the Beechcraft began rolling along the tarmac. It lifted off the ground about halfway along the runway and began to climb steeply whilst turning gently to the left.

Suddenly the aircraft appeared to leap backwards, its nose turning up vertically. At that moment flames engulfed the plane from front to rear, followed immediately by a massive explosion which tore the tiny aircraft into a thousand pieces which fell to the ground leaving a mass of burning debris across a wide area of the runway.

The emergency services were instantly on the scene and took just a few minutes to extinguish the burning wreckage. The main part of the cabin was found about one hundred metres from the rest of the wreckage. The three bodies were still strapped in their seats, and charred beyond recognition. The only item that was recognisable was the helmet worn by the body in the pilot's seat.

'That's an unusual type of headgear for a pilot,' one of the firefighters observed. 'Looks like a bikie helmet.'

'Does too,' his colleague replied. 'Is that a letter W carved in the front of it?'

'Probably. The control tower has identified the plane as belonging to a William Barry. Apparently he put in a flight plan to fly to Canberra with two passengers. Didn't get very far, did they?

'Too many bleeding amateurs flying too many bleeding unserviceable planes if you ask me. I wonder who the poor bastards are who bought it with him?'

# Chapter Twenty-Five

Monday Morning – 7.30 a.m.

The newscaster was on the footpath standing in front of a sign indicating that the premises behind him were the Abbey Park Motel. The car park of the motel was filled with police cars and the area was screened off with strips of blue and white chequered tape that one always saw when reports were made from scenes of crime. Dozens of police in uniform and several in plain clothes were moving around the car park.

The cameraman had perched himself on the roof of the outside broadcast van, and had homed in on the open door of one of the motel units which appeared to be the centre of the police activity.

The Coroner had been and gone, and the newscaster knew there was little point in trying to get any comment from that source.

A young man fussed around the newscaster trying his hardest to powder down a shiny spot on his nose which was causing the cameraman some concern.

'Okay, let's shoot it now,' said the newscaster, facing into the camera lens and putting on a deadpan face.

'I am Dudley Northern, speaking to you from the Abbey Park Motel in Fyshwick which has become the centre for one of the country's latest and most important criminal investigations.

'The Federal and New South Wales Police, in conjunction with the National Crime Authority are investigating the execution-style death of Senator Peter Filburton. He was found dead in unit three of this motel', the camera shot of the open door of the unit which had been taken minutes previously was slotted in for emphasis, 'this morning after an anonymous telephone tip-off to the *Sydney Morning Herald*.

'A police source has reported that the Senator was found bound and gagged, and had been shot several times. He had received bullet wounds to both kneecaps and below his lower abdomen, we are not sure what is meant by that.'

It was obvious from the look on the man's face that he had a pretty good idea what was meant. His half-smirk would have made it plain to most viewers that the newsman believed that the Senator had been shot in his private parts.

'He was also shot in the head. The body of a second man was found in the bathroom of the same unit. The man, whose name has not been disclosed, is believed to be an American citizen who served with the Senator during the Vietnam War. It is understood that he was killed in a similar manner to the Senator.

'A police spokesman who cannot be named believes that the wounds indicate a form of systematic torture, probably to try to obtain information. The spokesman also stated that the head wounds were the cause of death in each case and that both men were probably alive until that point.

'An anonymous source within the National Crime Authority has advised that a large amount of heroin was found in the motel unit and in two cars parked outside. One of the vehicles is believed to be Senator Filburton's official car.

'These brutal murders, together with information linking the two men to recent incidents at both Wagga Wagga and Goulburn where warehouses were destroyed and large consignments of drugs were found has caused a political furore. We have contacted the Prime Minister's office but he is not available, and his staff have declined to comment. It is expected that the leader of the opposition will raise the matter during Question Time later today.'

The news broadcast then transferred to Sydney where a smug-looking representative of the *Sydney Morning Herald* was declining to comment, other than to promise all its readers that the full and exclusive story would be revealed in full over the next few days.

The man had every right to feel good. It really was exclusive to his newspaper, and would increase circulation and revenue enormously.

★

The news then covered the story of an explosion in a light aircraft at Bankstown Airport which killed the pilot and two passengers. It reported that the identities of the deceased had yet to be confirmed, but it was believed that the aircraft was *en route* to Canberra when the explosion occurred.

'Investigators of the Civil Aviation Authority are on scene at the moment, and are examining the wreckage. A confidential source at the airport spoke of the explosion being caused by a leaking fuel pipe.'

This was certainly a day for anonymous and confidential informants. However, this second incident was given very little airtime in view of the major story regarding the death of the Senator.

Throughout the day all stations, both radio and television got into the act, and the story became very confused with all the speculation and differing views on how and why the Senator died. One station even called on the services of a well-known medium.

By nightfall on Monday the story had become an international scandal of immense proportions, confused even more by the fact that nobody could find information about, or would admit to knowing of the late Senator's service in the Vietnam War. Some commentators were even bold enough to suggest that he had never served in the military in any capacity. Others had already made him into a secret service operator.

One political colleague was claiming that Filburton was the innocent victim of a frame-up for reasons as yet unknown. Whilst not quite going as far as blaming it on the opposition, he certainly sowed the seed for that impression to be given.

\*

The following morning, Tuesday, all hell was let loose when the same news channel that was first on the scene at Fyshwick the previous day hit the airwaves with a further dramatic item. The newscaster was standing outside the block of apartments in which Barratt and Hippel had retained their *pied-à-terre* overlooking Sydney Harbour.

'Good morning, viewers. This is Dudley Northern speaking to you from the scene of the latest of a string of killings linked in some way to the alleged criminal affairs of the late Senator Filburton. The Senator was found murdered, together with another man, in a bizarre double execution yesterday morning at a motel in Fyshwick.'

The channel's lawyers had agonised over the wording of this news item for some time before releasing it for broadcast just minutes before it went to air.

'As a grim sequel to yesterday's double murders the New South Wales Police are now investigating the murder of a police detective, whose name has not been disclosed at this time. The man is believed to have been the partner of

Detective Albert Hippel who was also killed under strange circumstances just a few days ago.

'A *Sydney Morning Herald* source has reported that large amounts of money, drugs and explosives were found in the apartment in the building behind me, believed to be owned by the murdered detective. They also report that they have evidence to link this police officer and his late colleague with both Senator Filburton and the American who died with him.

As the result of further information supplied by the *Herald*, New South Wales Police are also investigating the possibility of a link between this dead detective and the explosion which destroyed a light aircraft at Bankstown Airport yesterday morning, killing the pilot and two passengers.

'The police have been invited to make a statement but have declined stating that it would be unwise for the public to speculate on the events which are in the very early stages of investigation. They have, however, denied that they are investigating links between the murders of the two detectives and the deaths of the Senator and the American.'

At that point the picture flashed across to the *Sydney Morning Herald* spokesperson, the same one as on the previous day.

'I can't understand why the police are denying that they are investigating the link between the dead detective and Senator Filburton and the American. We have given them all the proof. However, I don't believe they are covering anything up. It's probably just too soon in their investigations for them to make any statement.

'However,' he continued with a wide smile, 'our readers will be able to discover all of the details over the next few days.'

The newscast ended at that point.

At the very moment that the newspaper man was making his presentation the office of the Director of Public Prosecutions was on the telephone to both the TV channel and the newspaper warning of dire consequences if their reports in any way prejudiced the police investigations and any subsequent legal hearings.

These were to become lengthy legal and political issues which would outlive the newsworthiness of the events in question.

## Chapter Twenty-Six

Putney – England
Wednesday Morning

The nurse was reading a book as she kept watch over her patient. There was really nothing else she could do. She was performing what was known amongst the nurses as the death watch.

The shrivelled-up shadow of a man that lay in the bed beside where she sat had no right to still be alive, not medically speaking anyway.

The doctors had given him hours to live on numerous occasions over the past few weeks, yet it was if he just stubbornly refused to die. He was mostly in and out of fitful sleep and often delirious. He was certainly in the greatest of pain one could possibly imagine. However, regardless of his suffering he flatly refused to allow the doctors to provide him with the relief from pain that could so easily be given him.

'Relief from pain will merely amount to relief from brain,' he said constantly in response to the offers of help.

'If I lose my ability to think for myself; if I allow you to befuddle my brain I might as well be dead. I'll die in my own good time, thank you. I'll die when I know for certain that it's done.'

The doctors and nurses had no idea what he was talking about, and most assumed that his brain had already been affected by the immense pain that he was constantly suffering.

The nurse heard a light tapping on the door of the small private room. She looked up from her book and saw the staff nurse beckoning her through the window in the top of the door. She rose, placed her book on the seat, and started towards the door. Then instinctively she stopped and returned to the bedside of Colonel Marven and checked his pulse. It was very erratic and weak, but still there.

The man spoke, or rather croaked out a few words to her. 'Not gone yet, Nursie, my dear. Still waiting.'

'Don't you go away, Colonel my love. I shan't be a moment.' She gently squeezed his hand and smiled down at him.

★

The staff nurse was somewhat agitated. 'There's another phone call for him. Quite frankly I don't think we should let him be pestered. Some people have absolutely no consideration at all. However, after that nasty incident the other day I suppose we have no choice. Apparently his lawyer has also contacted the administration about ensuring that he is allowed to take calls. Is he awake?'

'He is, actually. The poor man just called me Nursie. He's very sweet. I can't understand how he is still with us, but I don't see how a phone call is going to make much difference at this time of his life. Oops! Sorry, Staff, I didn't mean to disagree with you.'

'No matter, Jane. I'll transfer the call. You go in and make sure he is able to manage it.'

The nurse returned to the bedside and picked up the nearby phone. She wheeled the trolley closer to the bed and then tenderly shook the sick man by the shoulder.

'Here you are, Colonel my love. Someone on the phone for you.' She handed the receiver to the man who pulled it down on to the pillow alongside his head.

'Marven. Yes?'

He lay silently listening for over five minutes. The nurse, not wishing to intrude had left the room and was watching through the window as her patient dealt with his call.

'All of them? They have all been punished for what they did to my boy? He must be buried with his mother and me. Promise me that will happen. Thank you, my friend, and God bless you.'

The nurse saw him push the telephone receiver away, so she walked quietly back into the room. As she approached the bed she noticed to her amazement that the Colonel was smiling contentedly. All of the pain had receded from his face. He looked so happy.

'Good news was it, Colonel?'

The man looked straight at her and continued to smile in a magnificently relaxed way. She was so happy for him. She had not seen him smile before now.

She picked up the telephone receiver and placed it back on its holder. She then lifted it up again and dialled three numbers.

'Doctor O'Dea? Colonel Marven has just died. 12.20 p.m. exactly. Yes, I was with him at the time. Right, I'll see you then.'

She leaned over the bed and gently closed the Colonel's eyes.

'Well, Colonel my love. That phone call was obviously what you were waiting for. I'm glad it made you so happy at the last.'

She picked up her book and sat down once more. The doctor would soon arrive to complete the formalities.

★

It was a cold day for June and cemeteries were not renowned for their warmth at any time of the year. It had been raining heavily for two days, but mercifully the rain had ceased just hours before. The grave had several inches of muddy water in it.

The row of SAS troopers stood rigidly to attention, their rifles at the high port. On the order they raised them to the firing position and fired three shots over the grave.

It was purely a military affair. There was no family. They were all in the grave with the Colonel. His wife in the coffin below his, and the ashes of his son, Samuel Frederick Thomas Alfred Peter Marven, in a small casket clenched in his hands.

His personal friend, the doctor who had treated his late wife through her brief terminal illness and had diagnosed his own cancer was there, and the kind nurse, Jane Little; not that the Colonel had ever learned her last name.

There were many officers, both junior and senior with whom Douglas Marven had served over the years, together with a wide range of other ranks; men who loved and respected him.

No sooner had the clergyman finished the traditional words over the grave when it started to rain once more. The funeral directors were quickly on hand with arms full of umbrellas which were handed out to the people around the grave.

On such sombre occasions rain had the effect of hastening the departure of people who as a rule would not wish to be seen to leave too soon in case it gave the wrong impression to relatives.

However, the Colonel had no living relatives, and every-one's shiny boots and shoes were becoming smattered with light brown mud. Under the circumstances it seemed most appropriate to leave as soon as the umbrellas were handed out, and everyone who had known Colonel Douglas Marven, SAS, retired, knew that he would not have minded in the least. In fact he would probably have applauded their most sensible decision and done likewise in a similar situation.

The cemetery soon emptied of people, and all that was left was the open grave. The torrential rain was causing rivulets of muddy water to pour steadily from under the artificial grass coverings of the duckboards surrounding the gaping hole, and on to the silent and sad oak cask lying below.

★

A short distance away two elderly gravediggers sheltered from the rain in a small tool shed. They looked forward with some misgivings to the two further interments that were to take place later that day.

'Filled in 1381 then, Josh?'

'No! Just about to do it when some geezer came up, ten minutes after everyone else had left, and just stands there looking into the hole getting bleeding soaked. Stupid sod will be getting pneumonia out there.'

'Never mind, good for business, pneumonia.'

Both men laughed out loud.

'Let's go and see if he is gone now, Josh. Then I'll give you a hand.'

The men trudged out into the rain and slowly made their way to grave number 1381 in which the Marven family had at last been joined together.

There was no one in sight. The area was deserted.

'Are you sure you weren't imagining it, Josh? Seen another of your ghosts, have you?'

'Don't be a smart-arse, Harry. Course I saw him. A big bloke with a bad limp.'

★

Four days later a traveller pulled on to the forecourt of the Sandhills Truck Stop, just south of Cairns, in Queensland. He filled up his car with fuel and checked the oil and water. Having completed that chore he strolled over to the cafeteria for a cup of tea and a sandwich.

'Where's Dolly, not here today?' he asked of the proprietor who was serving behind the counter, and obviously not handling the pressure too well.

'She shot through and I don't think she'll be back. Just up and left with some bloke. A bit older than her. Stupid cow has left me in the shit.'

'Who was the bloke?' asked the traveller, feeling quite sad at the prospect of not seeing Dolly again.

'Stuffed if I know. I'm bloody sure she could have done better for herself. She said something about him being a deliveryman.'